"Great Stories!"

"They're all excellent . . .

"They reflect the extreme catholicity of Fred's tastes in SF. And no matter how good your anthology collection is, there are probably a significant number of great stories here that are new to you. Finally, the introductions and headnotes and autobiographical essays by Fred are as delightful as the stories . . .

"One of the best anthologies of the last few years."

—ANALOG Science Fiction/ Science Fact

"A must-have collection: grand selections enhanced by vivid reminiscences."

—KIRKUS REVIEWS

Berkley books by Frederik Pohl

PLANETS THREE

**YESTERDAY'S TOMORROWS: FAVORITE STORIES
FROM FORTY YEARS AS A SCIENCE FICTION EDITOR**
(Edited by Frederik Pohl)

FREDERIK POHL

YESTERDAY'S TOMORROWS

FAVORITE STORIES FROM FORTY YEARS AS A SCIENCE FICTION EDITOR

BERKLEY BOOKS, NEW YORK

YESTERDAY'S TOMORROWS:
Favorite Stories from Forty Years as a Science Fiction Editor

A Berkley Book / published by arrangement with
the author

PRINTING HISTORY
Berkley trade paperback edition / October 1982

ISBN: 0-425-05648-1

A BERKLEY BOOK® TM 757,375

The name "BERKLEY" and the stylized "B" with design are trademarks belonging to
Berkley Publishing Corporation.

PRINTED IN THE UNITED STATES OF AMERICA

CONTENTS

INTRODUCTION

The most recent meeting of the Science Fiction Research Association was at Lake Tahoe, and I was there. SFRA is the academic wing of science fiction, but a few SF writers are encouraged to participate, and among the luminaries present was Jack Vance. Vance is a writer I admire a great deal. When I was editor of *Galaxy,* I published a great deal of his work, proudly. There are not many stories I am more pleased to have published than "The Moon Moth" and "The Dragon Masters." But, what with one thing and another, our paths had not crossed for a decade or so, and the opening conversation went something like this:

"Hello, Fred."

"Jack, is it really you?"

"Yes, Fred, and I've been thinking, you were dead wrong to cut the chapter headings out of my serial."

Now, Jack Vance is not an unreasonable human being, and if he had kept that in his mind for ten years it signifies something. What it signifies is that the relations between an author and an editor go deep.

A writer writes. When he is writing, he is actually carrying on a sort of one-way conversation with a reader Out There. It is that reader he wants to talk to but before the writer can get to him he has to get past a locked gate, and it is only an editor, some editor or other, who has the key. More than that. What the writer wants to say to the reader is the very words he has put on paper; but there too the editor is in the way, because he may tamper with those words before they get into print. Writing is the most personal of the arts. The writer reveals more of himself than any composer or painter; he reaches more directly to his audience than an actor or playwright. In fact, there is nothing between the naked and open soul of the writer, as he chooses to expose it, and the eye of the reader.

Except the editor.

All writers feel this, not just Jack Vance. I feel it myself. I can quote to you verbatim the words *Esquire* used in returning a poem to me when I was eighteen years old (not to mention any number of later rejections). I can tell you precisely what alterations Horace Gold made in a story of mine in 1956, and why he shouldn't have made them. And at that, for a writer, I think I am probably unusually thick-skinned. I do not, like one writer I know, pick up a copy of each magazine with a story of mine and stand there at the newsstand, pencil in hand, until I have restored every altered comma. One of the last things I did as an editor for Bantam Books was to waste the friendship of a writer whose good will I have always prized by rejecting a novel he was particularly proud of. He still has not forgiven me. With the possible exception of reviewing books, editing is the easiest way I know of making enemies.

All this being so, why would anyone want to be an editor?

Not for the money, though sometimes it isn't bad.

Not for the fame, because there isn't any—at least, outside a very small circle of professionals.

Not for the easy work. It isn't easy. Especially in a large publishing house, all the hours from nine to five are taken up in meetings, which means all the "editing" one does is in overtime, at home and on weekends.

Not for any of those reasons. There is left only the glamor, the excitement, the chance to play God. The guardian of the editorial gate possesses the Keys to the Kingdom . . . and does he ever know it!

I think I should explain what I mean by the word "editor." It is a word almost as abused as "writer."

The best definition I ever heard was in a novel called *Friends of Mr. Sweeney,* by Elmer Davis. I haven't owned a copy in decades—it's long gone from print—but as close as I can remember it says, "An editor is a man who can explain the design of flood-control dams to an archeologist, and Egyptian burial customs to a hydraulics engineer."

An editor is a middleman. He stands between publisher and author, in matters of money and rights; between author and reader, in matters of story and style. He doesn't have to know very much about anything, really. But he has to be able to tell if the writer does. He doesn't have to be capable of writing a memorable line himself, but he has to be able to get writers to do it. Those are the minimum necessary skills.

Of course, there are all kinds of "editors." If you pick up almost any magazine, you will find the masthead lists an editor, a managing editor, an editor-in-chief, a copy editor, half a dozen contributing editors—the list runs out only with the ingenuity of the person making it up. Not many of them perform what one would normally think of as an editorial function. A contributing editor doesn't edit. He contributes—meaning, he writes pieces for the publication more or less regularly, or at least intends to. A managing editor is often a person who supervises the flow of material from one department to another; he does not buy, neither does he read. A copy editor does read, but primarily for the purpose of correcting spelling, punctuation, and style. (Trouble comes when he decides also to improve an author's words by substituting his own, which many of his ilk are lamentably likely to do.) The person who clears rights to art and quotations is sometimes called a "permissions editor," though his only function is to write letters and order checks.

In the largest publishing houses, the number of editorial titles increases and the individual involvement of each person diminishes. The cutting edge of this mass of flesh is the "acquisitions editor," but you must not think that he is personally involved in all of the books he acquires. A large part of the time he has never read them. He acquires them because the company's editorial meeting has voted to do so. At that meeting, the electorate will consist of dozens of persons, but very few of them will have read the book they are deciding on, either. Most of them will rely on "readers' reports," sometimes free-lanced, more often written by someone who lives on a farm in Pennsylvania and comes to the publishing office only once a week, to dump a batch of reports and pick up a new batch of books to take home and read. If the book is a buy, once the acquisitions editor has done his acquiring, it then goes to a copy editor to prepare it for the printer, a blurb editor to write the cover lines, the managing editor to shepherd it through production, and hell's own herd of other "editors" of one kind or another to do all the other things that a book has done to it before it reaches your neighborhood store. Specialization has its advantages. But personal commitment is gone.

This is not universal. Even in the biggest companies there are individual editors who have carved out the right to make their own personal decisions, and at least supervise, if not actually perform, all the other steps. But it is the way the traffic is going. All of these individual specialists are competent and some are very good indeed, but they are fragmented. There aren't many Maxwell Perkinses left in the world today. The conversation at the average editorial meeting is not unlike the conversation among the partners of a brokerage dealing in hog futures, and it is a miracle to me that so many good books do nevertheless get published.

They do, though.

And part of the reason this is so is that, in spite of the formidable size of the "editorial" staff and the sharp cleavages of authority in the formal table of organization, there is usually one person who *cares*.

Almost anyone in a publishing company can "bring in a book"—secretary, blurb writer, art director, or salesman. If he (or, just as often, she) is very junior, or far removed from the usual editorial chain of command, the book may be taken away from him and assigned to a "real" editor for processing. If he (or she) is already a "real" editor, then the editorial committee meeting becomes a rubber stamp—except, perhaps, to put a limit on how much the editor can spend.

You see, what the editorial committee is listening for, in all the talk of P&L estimates and draws-and-returns, is the voice of enthusiasm. Love conquers all.

And it is that sort of person, capable of that sort of love, that I mean by an "editor."

An editor may be quite a disagreeable person. Even if he is not, he will surely do disagreeable things. He will reject work that a writer wants him to publish, sometimes demand revisions a writer does not want to make. It is his job to do these things, and no amount of skill or charm can make him agreeable to all writers.

But he must have the capacity to adopt some other person's work as his own—to care for it—to fight for it in the clinches—to take pride in it when it is published; and then to switch his love and loyalty at once to some other work and do the same thing over again.

When children are orphaned, state agencies will sometimes place them with foster parents. I've known a few foster parents and it has always seemed to me that they have a complicatedly hard life. It is a lot the same for an editor. A succession of children come through his life. For longer or shorter times, he changes their diapers, teaches them to ride their bikes, sits through their class plays—and then they are gone.

Neither an editor nor a foster parent can be any good at what he does without love. He also cannot be any good at it without skill and justice. Every one of the children (or works) that passes through his hands deserves fairness, at least, and the best shot he can give them at making their way in the big outside world.

I think, though, that even the fairest of foster parents, looking back on a career of kids passing through, will remember some with more affection than others. They will not necessarily be the brightest or the best, but the ones that in some way impressed themselves on his memory or touched his heart.

That's what this book is about.

I started my editorial life on almost the smallest scale possible and finished it on almost the largest. The first thing I was editor of was a fanzine, a mimeographed and tiny publication of a science-fiction group I belonged to. The last was Bantam Books. Bantam is big indeed. Of the five largest American paperback publishers, Bantam has a third of the gross sales and half the gross profits of all five combined. There are publishing conglomerates that are larger, but I don't know of any unitary publisher quite as big. In between, I spent four years at the pulp chain of Popular Publications, just about a decade editing *Galaxy* and its companion magazines, and part of a year as executive editor for the Ace paperback line; I also edited several dozen reprint anthologies, and the *Star* series of science-fiction originals. (That is only the science fiction, not to count three years as book editor for *Popular Science* and odds and ends of other editorial chores.)

Of course, during all that time I was also writing—again, not all science fiction. But mostly. With Cyril Kornbluth, *The Space Merchants* and eight or nine other books. With Jack Williamson, seven novels so far. On my own, *Man Plus, Gateway,* half a dozen other science-fiction novels, and enough short stories to fill ten or twelve collections.

Combining the careers of writer and editor complicates one's life—at least, it has complicated mine. There is a little bit of happy synergy involved. I think I learned a lot about writing through being an editor; and I have no doubt that I functioned better as an editor because I was also a writer and could therefore empathize somewhat better with the people I published. But there are also unhappy conflicts. If, as editor of *Galaxy,* I published a story of my own, I inevitably squeezed out some story by someone else, and that always seemed to me at least marginally unfair.

There is also the serious practical problem that writing and editing involve the same sorts of skills. If I were a writer, needing a job to support myself while I pounded out my prose in the evenings, I don't think I would look for editorial work. Or for advertising or newspaper work, either. You can't juggle words in an office all day, and then go home and juggle your own with any freshness or sense of change—not easily, anyway. I think I would hope to find some non-wordy occupation, shoe clerk, taxi driver, or corporate vice-president; and when I got off the commuter train, I would look to my typewriter as a welcome change of pace.

But that isn't what I did.

What I did was to combine both, for most of thirty-nine years from the fall of 1939 to the summer of 1978, and I wouldn't have missed it for anything in the world—in spite of anything I say.

How can I describe the pleasures of being an editor? It isn't just a matter of being courted by people who want to sell you things, or the expense-account lunches. It's more than that. It's the joy of discovering new writers—of publishing Larry Niven's first story, of working with Ray Bradbury before he became R*A*Y B*R*A*D*B*U*R*Y, of giving maybe a hundred writers their first exposure to an audience, and seeing some of them succeed brightly. It is suggesting to a writer something he should write, and seeing it work out beautifully; the clue in Fred Saberhagen's early short story that led to the whole saga of Berserkers; the tossed-off gimmick in Cyril Kornbluth's "The Little Black Bag" that became his most widely reprinted novelette, "The Marching Morons"; the new astronomical oddity that Larry Niven embodied in his first Hugo-winning story, "Neutron Star." It is writing the right blurb, selecting the right illustrator—even packaging a story in an unusual way, as with Jack Vance's "The Dragon Masters." I don't know what it would have done without the Jack Gaughan illustrations the art director and I planned so meticulously, but with them it won a Hugo. (And the individual illustrations themselves won a nomination, so far as I know the only time in the history of the award when that happened for a specific set of illustrations rather than an artist's overall work.) In the sense of tickled vanity, maybe the greatest pleasure of all is to take something that no one else has seen to have merit and make it work: Ross Rocklynne's "Into the Darkness," rejected by every SF magazine until I published it in *Astonishing Stories* and it became a classic; Samuel R. Delany's *Dhalgren,* turned down all around, then going quickly through a dozen printings as a Bantam title.

Cold reason tells me that some of those joys are no doubt illusions. It is easy for an editor to exaggerate his importance. Most writers do what they do because those are the kinds of hairpins they are, and any editor can make only minute contributions to their success or failure. But some of them are real, all the same, and all of them are fun. It is fun just to be in a position where you can spend a great deal of your time with those thorny, talented, quirky individuals who comprise the class of science-fiction writers. Over four decades I had some sort of editorial relationship with nearly every science-fiction writer alive and producing in the English language, from Asimov to Zelazny, and they are a marvelous bunch. (Bearing in mind that some marvels are not fun at all.)

But I don't think anybody should be an editor forever. The joys seep away. The annoyances accumulate. The challenges begin to look like too much trouble. When it stops being fun, it is time to get out and give someone else his turn in the barrel. I do think there is a conflict between editing and writing, and after several decades of indecision, I've finally made up my mind what I want to be when I grow up, and editing lost the toss.

During the decade I edited *Galaxy,* et al, I read about four thousand manuscripts a year. In each of my six years as Bantam's SF editor, I read about two hundred and fifty to three hundred books. Add in what I read for *Astonishing Stories* and *Star* and all the others, put them all together, and it turns out that I've read professionally somewhere around five hundred million words of science fiction. As an editor, I published about two percent of that, in one medium or another. Which still comes to some ten million words. And of those ten million, about two percent still stick in my mind for one reason or another . . . and those are the stories in this book.

I hope you like them.

—Frederik Pohl,
New York City,
June, 1980

THE FANZINES: 1933–1939

How do you get started in an editorial career?

There are several ways. The goal-directed way is to take aim at a publication or a publishing house and ask for a job. It doesn't have to be an editorial job. Half the editors I know started as something else—if they knew how to spell, type, and punctuate, as secretaries; if not, as stock-room boys. (Or girls.) With the rapid turnover among editors—the "dwell time" in any particular job hardly averages eighteen months—there are openings all the time, and the transition from unskilled labor to editorial vice-president has been known to happen in less than a decade.

The serendipitous way is to hang around where the jobs are until one falls on you. That is, you keep your face visible around editorial offices in some capacity or other—writer, agent, whatever—until one of those vacancies pops up, and there you are.

The serendipitous way was my way, but I must admit that it was so serendipitous that I didn't even know I was doing it until it was just about done. There is a small problem with serendipity. It rests on your being where it can happen. I was lucky enough to live in the Big Apple, then as now the capital of the publishing world. I had nothing to do with that. New York City was where my parents happened to live. If they had instead elected to stay on in Albuquerque or northern Texas, I think it likely that I might have wanted to become an editor, when I got old enough to think of such things. But I don't see how I would have got there.

Still, it might have worked out, since what I was actually doing with my time—in those pre-career years when one samples the options and tries to figure out where there's an interesting place to spend a life—was editing and publishing fanzines. If I had been goal-directed toward an editorial life, I think I might have done the same, only I would have done it with malice aforethought—and would now be able to claim successful achievement of a grand design.

The differences between editing a fanzine and editing, say, *The New Yorker,* are only matters of scale and economics. You perform the same four basic processes:

1) you stare into space for a while, thinking up things that might interest readers.

2) then you acquire them.

3) then you get them ready for publication.

4) then you publish them.

Of course, those differences in scale and economics do have significant effects. If you are a fanzine editor, "acquiring" something to publish very likely means writing or drawing it yourself. When you prepare it for publication, you don't turn it over to a copy editor and a production department. You type it onto a mimeograph stencil. "Publishing" it is accomplished by turning the crank of the Gestetner, and then laying out all the piles of pages on a long table, while you walk around the table, picking a page from each pile and stapling them together. This is the process called "collating." If you have a lot of gullible friends, you can perhaps cajole them into a collation party, which makes it all less painful. That's not necessary. The whole process can be done by one person in a corner of his basement. It usually is.

The very best thing about being an editor of a fanzine, or of anything else with a zero budget, is that you have only two persons you have to please: your reader and yourself. You don't even have to please the reader a whole lot. You are not, after all, asking much from him. Most fanzines are given away. Most fanzines show it.

I discovered fanzines in 1933, when I was thirteen years old. I immediately perceived that this was a place where I wanted to be. Holding the ill-printed pages of the early fanzines in my hands, I could see that the standards were not inordinately high. They were even within the reach of so inexperienced a novice as myself.

This turned out not to be entirely true, because my own efforts at printing of any sort almost all turned out lousy.

Most of the people who published handsome fanzines, I discovered, were persons who genuinely enjoyed the physical processes of publishing. I never did. Setting type on a letterpress got your fingers all inky and punctured. Turning off copies on a mimeo was simply boring, even when it went well. When it didn't, it was frustrating. Mostly, it didn't. The machine would pick up two sheets at once. Or the ink on one page would offset onto the back of the next. Or the stencil would tear. Or any of a hundred other calamities past my skill to conquer would occur. I could not even roll pages onto hectograph jelly or squeegee paint through a silk screen without having the results run, drip, tear, or wrinkle.

But there were those who could, and some of those who could, and enjoyed doing it, turned out willing to do them for me. John B. Michel was one of my closest fan friends, and he did them all with great skill. And he would trade labor for labor. I was happy to type up stencils for Johnny; he ran them off for me; our production flourished.

What did we publish in our fanzines? Well, not much that deserves to survive. The first ones I was involved with were club organs, and what they published was club news. We gossiped about what was happening in the world of science fiction, and reviewed each new issue of *Wonder Stories, Amazing,* and *Astounding.* When most of my closest fan friends got political, our fanzines turned political, too. When we began experimenting with writing styles, we published our experiments.

Most of our fanzines were not very interesting to anyone but ourselves, but there were exceptions. Out in Los Angeles, Ray Bradbury was getting his stories published in the most convenient way, in his own fanzine. An unknown kid fan, Damon Knight, published a critical essay on A. E. van Vogt in a fanzine; forty years later, van Vogt still feels the draft where the skin was flayed off him, and the essay established Knight as a trenchant critic. (And a mean one.)

Science-fiction publishers became aware of the pool of talent in the fanzines, or at least a few of them did. When Hugo Gernsback needed an editor to take *Wonder Stories* off his shoulders, he reached out to the fanzine editors and hired Charles Derwin Hornig. My good friends Robert Lowndes and Donald Wollheim, fanzine editors in the 1930s, had professional magazines to edit by 1940. Sam Moskowitz, Richard Wilson, and Walter Kubilius, of the same generation, went on to lifelong editorial careers in fields other than science fiction. Even today, when *Isaac Asimov's Science Fiction Magazine* was launched, the publisher tapped George Scithers, of the award-winning fanzine *Amra,* to take it over.

In 1939 it happened to me.

I'm not at all sure that Harry Steeger, president of the pulp chain of Popular Publications, knew anything about my fan magazines when he put me to work. I certainly never dared show him copies. But I was in the right place, and the job fell on me. At nineteen I was the editor of two science-fiction magazines, *Astonishing Stories* and *Super Science Stories.* The pay was terrible—it was all of ten dollars a week, plus whatever I could scrounge by writing stories for myself. But it was mine if I could hold it. And the only thing that gave me any reason to believe that that was going to be possible was the fanzine editing I had done.

THE PULPS: 1939–1943

I needed all the confidence I could find, because I was most dismayingly aware of the fact that I was nineteen years old. Somehow I was going to have to persuade people much older, wiser, and surer of themselves than I to do things something like the things *I* wanted them to do. There was nothing reassuring in the prospect.

There was not much in the practicalities of the situation to give me strength either. The magazines were meanly low-budgeted operations. I had half a cent a word to pay authors for their stories, and even less to give the artists. There was some moral strength to be found in that I was the worst paid of all—so poorly that I had to lie about the hours worked to keep Popular Publications out of trouble with the new wage-hour laws.

However, there were compensations. My God, yes! I was the first kid on the block with magazines of my own. Being savagely underpaid didn't matter; if I could have found the money, I would gladly have paid Harry Steeger every week for the privilege. I had an office of my own, with a desk and a typewriter and a rickety wooden chair for visitors to sit in while I lectured them on how to write for me.

I was the youngest of Popular's editors, but there weren't any old ones. The pulps were a youth industry. Among Popular's staff I don't believe there was a soul over forty-five, not even Harry Steeger himself. The average was somewhere in the mid-twenties.

The writers were even younger. Barring one or two aberrants like Malcolm Jameson and Ray Cummings, both in their fifties, most of the writers were under thirty. This was not an accident. Then as now, younger people were more adventurous, innovative, flexible—and cheap.

Cheapness counted very heavily, because pulp magazine publishing was as much a matter of trimming fractions of a penny as butchering hogs. Every month, the giant presses at Cuneo in Chicago poured out tens of thousands of copies each of twenty or thirty Popular Publications pulps. When they hit the newsstands, about fifty percent were picked up and paid for. The rest were quickly chopped into pulp, and the presses got started on the next month's run.

The quality of the stories in each magazine no doubt mattered somewhat—at least, it is pretty to think so—but it didn't matter much. What mattered was that the magazines be cheap. Hardly any pulp writer commanded more than a penny a word. A great many wrote for a great deal less. The half-cent I was empowered to spend for each created word I bought was pitiful, but it was not the lowest rate in the industry. One of the air-war pulps at Popular was written entirely by one man at a contract price—sixty thousand words a month for one hundred and fifty dollars. There were even a few magazines who paid their writers nothing at all. Not in cash, anyway. What the writer got in exchange for his free story was a heartfelt pledge that, absolutely, cross his heart, the editor would surely buy huge quantities at top rates from those writers who helped him out now—as soon as the magazine began to show a profit. But I do not recall that ever happening.

Of course, the world was cheaper. You could get a decent apartment for forty dollars a month, and potatoes were nine cents a pound. You could even support a family, well above the poverty level, on twenty-five or thirty dollars a week.

You couldn't do it on ten, though. I am sure of that, because I tried.

Except for the fact that money was very scarce on the ground, I was about as happy in my work as it is possible for a person to be. Figure it out. For ten years—half my life—I had been reading every bit of science fiction I could get my hands on, and paying for the privilege. Now I was reading even more, and Harry Steeger was paying *me*.

It is true that most of what I read was very bad. It came out of the "slush pile."

"Slush" is a pejorative term, but its synonyms in the publishing industry—the "unrush," the "over-the-transom," etc.—are not a lot better. It is where all writers come from, one way or another. But, like that other place we all come from, it is not a subject for decorous conversation.

Still, the writers whose works turn up in that volume of unsolicited material called "slush" are not the worst writers in the world, or not all of them are. As a minimum, they are serious enough about what they do to finish a story, put it in an envelope, and mail it to an editor. This fact by itself puts them far ahead of your average would-be writer, whose resolve stops at meaning to get around to it some day or another.

So I read the slush with great diligence. This was smart of me, because I found a fair number of interesting stories among the trash.

I then calculated that if I arranged to get *more* slush, I would find still more treasures, and so I wrote to all the writers' magazines to make sure they included *Astonishing* and *Super Science* in their market lists. This wasn't smart at all.

You see, there is slush and slush. John Campbell encouraged slush submissions too, but he did it in the right way; he wrote editorials and house ads, inviting his readers to try their hand at writing. Good move! As most SF writers begin as SF readers, he was prospecting where the ore was. I should have copied him in that, as I did in so much else. Instead, I sought to find claims he had not already marked out in the general mass of would-be writers who faithfully study every market list in print. There the ore is not. What I got for my trouble was an extra dozen manuscripts a week to plow through, but none to print. I am fairly sure of that, because the market-list stories were easy enough to recognize. Most of them were not in any way science fiction. Most of them had obviously been submitted over and over again, to every magazine in the English language; they had been folded and refolded so many times that, as you took them out of the envelope, they tended to separate into equal thirds. And most of them, I became aware after the first few weeks, were by the same ten or twelve perennial hopefuls.

I had made it a point to try to encourage writers to keep on submitting, by scribbling a personal word or two on rejection slips. On the market-list stories there was not much to say. I found myself writing fewer and fewer notes, and for a time, about six months after I began editing for Popular, I considered stopping the practice altogether.

You see, you never know who is going to be on the other end of that communications link. He may be hard-working, grateful for suggestions and quick to understand. Or he may not. What you mean as helpful, fatherly advice he may take as a commitment. He may even take it as an insult. I began having some bad experiences as a result of those little lines on the bottom of rejection slips; and then I had one that blew my mind completely.

I don't remember the man's name, but he was one of the most prolific in the slush pile. He never missed a week. And he was awful. After six months of this, I decided to try a new tack: candor. I wrote him a letter.

> Dear Sir:
> For six months, you've been sending me a story every week, and not one of them has come anywhere near anything I might publish.
> You are wasting your postage and my time, and I would like to make a suggestion. Why not take a break for a few weeks? Take time to think about whether writing is, after all, the best thing for you to do.

I signed the letter and clipped it to his manuscript and sent it off; and by return mail I got his response.

> Dear Mr. Pohl:
> I want to thank you with all my heart. I've been writing a story a week for almost seven years—that's more than three hundred stories—and I've submitted every one of them at least ten times.

You are the first editor who ever gave me a personal response of any kind.

I can't tell you what this means to me. It gives me courage to go on. From now on I am going to write *two* stories a week.

And so he did.

After a year or two, some of the glamor went out of being an editor, and the bills were getting rather pressing. I decided I had to have more money.

I didn't get it. I got unemployed. I have never been sure exactly what transpired in Harry Steeger's office—did I quit or was I fired? But I wasn't working for Popular Publications when I left.

So I went home and spent a few months free-lance writing, with spotty success. Then Alden H. Norton, one of the higher-echelon editors at Popular, asked me if I would be willing to come back as his assistant. That looked like a demotion, but a seventy-five percent raise went with it and that looked pretty good, so I signed on. For another year and a half (until I went into the U.S. Air Force in the spring of 1943), I worked in Al Norton's editorial stable.

Alden was a big disappointment to me. He had taken over *Astonishing* and *Super Science* when I left, and I had confidently expected him to destroy them. He hadn't. If anything, they were improved.

Alden's only real fault as a science-fiction editor was that, until he had been handed the magazines, he had never read a word of the stuff. That proved a less severe handicap than I had guessed. Al edited *Astonishing* the same way he edited his sports and air-war magazines: by buying the stories he liked best out of what was available. Al Norton was far more mature and experienced in the ways of publishing than I, and possessed of infinitely more clout. This meant that he had been able to get the budgets raised substantially, and thus to attract some writers who had evaded my nets.

I learned a lot from Al Norton, and he was an exceptionally good person to work for. In fact, I liked all the people in the department—a couple of years later, I even married one of them. In the normal course of events, I might have stayed there for a good long time. But there was a war on. On April Fool's Day of 1943, I was sworn into the armed forces, and that was the end of Popular Publications for me.

INTO THE DARKNESS

BY ROSS ROCKLYNNE

Editing Astonishing Stories *was a spit-and-baling-wire job, substituting coaxing for cash and ignorant daring for wisdom. I know something now that I did not know then, and that is that daring is sometimes better than wisdom. Too much is too much, even of a good thing. Readers get bored. Readers like variety. That doesn't mean that they will thrill to any new sensation, however inept or bizarre. There are many things that have never been done, for the simple reason that they are not worth doing. It does mean that it pays to take chances.*

I didn't know that when "Into the Darkness" hit my desk—I hadn't had the experience to learn—and it scared me. Of course, Ross Rocklynne was somebody special. I had been reading "The Men and the Mirror" and all the others he was writing for John Campbell's Astounding *with great yearning. I longed to have him on my covers almost as much as I had once longed to have certain film stars under them, and with about as much real hope. But this story? It didn't even have any people in it!*

It didn't come out of the slush pile. It arrived in the folders of the first real literary agent ever to specialize in science fiction, Julius Schwartz (who later went on to bigger things as one of the directing geniuses of the Superman *empire), but it had all the physical appearance of slush. Obviously it was a reject from John Campbell. What that I received was not? But by the look of the manuscript, dog-eared and coffee-stained, it had been rejected by at least twenty other editors as well—and that, I calculated swiftly, was just about all the editors who had been functioning in science fiction in some years. I could understand any one editor making a mistake. Even Campbell. But—all of them?*

On the other hand . . . I liked it.

So I squared my shoulders and clenched my teeth and bought it and, by and large, I would say it turned out to be the most popular story Astonishing *ever printed.*

*   *   *

I. Birth of "Darkness"

Out in space, on the lip of the farthest galaxy, and betwixt two star clusters, there came into being a luminiferous globe that radiated for light-years around. A life had been born!

It became aware of light; one of its visions had become activated. First it saw the innumerable suns and nebulae whose radiated energy now fed it. Beyond that it saw a dense, impenetrable darkness.

The darkness intrigued it. It could understand the stars, but the darkness it could not. The babe probed outward several light-years and met only lightlessness. It probed further, and further, but there was no light. Only after its visions could not delve deeper did it give up, but a strange seed had been sown; that there was light on the far edge of the darkness became its innate conviction.

Wonders never seemed to cease parading themselves before this newly-born. It became aware of another personality hovering near, an energy creature thirty millions of miles across. At its core hung a globe of subtly glowing green light one million miles in diameter.

He explored this being with his vision, and it remained still during his inspection. He felt strange forces plucking at him, forces that filled him to overflowing with peacefulness. At once, he discovered a system of energy waves having marvelous possibilities.

"Who are you?" these waves were able to inquire of that other life.

Softly soothing, he received answer.

"I am your mother."

"You mean—?"

"You are my son—my creation. I shall call you—Darkness. Lie here and grow, Darkness, and when you are many times larger, I will come again."

She had vanished, swallowed untraceably by a vast spiral nebula—a cloud of swiftly twisting stardust.

He lay motionless, strange thoughts flowing. Mostly he wondered about the sea of lightlessness lapping the shore of this galaxy in which he had been born. Sometime later, he wondered about life, what life was, and its purpose.

"When *she* comes again, I shall ask her," he mused. "Darkness, she called me—Darkness!"

His thoughts swung back to the darkness.

For five million years he bathed himself in the rays that permeate space. He grew. He was ten million miles in diameter.

His mother came; he saw her hurtling toward him from a far distance. She stopped close.

"You are much larger, Darkness. You grow faster than the other newly-born." He detected pride in her transmitted thoughts.

"I have been lying here, thinking," he said. "I have been wondering, and I have come to guess at many things. There are others, like you and myself."

"There are thousands of others. I am going to take you to them. Have you tried propellents?"

"I have not tried, but I shall." There was a silence. "I have discovered the propellents," said Darkness, puzzled, "but they will not move me."

She seemed amused. "That is one thing you do not know, Darkness. You are inhabiting the seventeenth band of hyper-space; propellents will not work there. See if you can expand."

All these were new things, but instinctively he felt himself expand to twice his original size.

"Good. I am going to snap you into the first band. . . . There. Try your propellents."

He tried them, and, to his intense delight, the flaring lights that were the stars fled past. So great was his exhilaration that he worked up a speed that placed him several light-years from his Mother.

She drew up beside him. "For one so young, you have speed. I shall be proud of you. I feel, Darkness," and there was wistfulness in her tone, "that you will be different from the others."

She searched his memory swirls. "But try not to be too different."

Puzzled at this, he gazed at her, but she turned away. "Come."

He followed her down the aisles formed by the stars, as she accommodated her pace to his.

They stopped at the sixth galaxy from the abyss of lightlessness. He discerned thousands of shapes that were his kind moving swiftly past and around him. These, then, were his people.

She pointed them out to him. "You will know them by their vibration, and the varying shades of the colored globes of light at their centers."

She ran off a great list of names which he had no trouble in impressing on his memory swirls.

"Radiant, Vibrant, Swift, Milky, Incandescent, Great Power, Sun-eater, Light-year. . . ."

"Come, I am going to present you to Oldster."

They whirled off to a space seven light-years distant. They stopped, just outside the galaxy. There was a peculiar snap in his consciousness.

"Oldster had isolated himself in the sixth band of hyper-space," said his Mother.

Where before he had seen nothing save inky space, dotted with masses of flaming, tortured matter, he now saw an energy creature whose aura fairly radiated old age. And the immense purple globe which hung at his core lacked a certain vital luster which Darkness had instinctively linked with his own youth and boundless energy.

His Mother caught the old being's attention, and Darkness felt his thought-rays contact them.

"Oh, it's you, Sparkle," the old being's kindly thoughts said. "And who is it with you?"

Darkness saw his Mother, Sparkle, shoot off streams of crystalline light. "This is my first son."

The newly-born felt Oldster's thought-rays going through his memory swirls.

"And you have named him Darkness," said Oldster slowly. "Because he has wondered about it." His visions withdrew, half-absently. "He is so young, and yet he is a thinker; already he thinks about life."

For long and long Oldster bent a penetrating gaze upon him. Abruptly, his vision rays swung away and centered on a tiny, isolated group of stars. There was a heavy, dragging silence.

"Darkness," Oldster said finally, "your thoughts are useless." The thoughts now seemed to come from an immeasurable distance, or an infinitely tired mind. "You are young, Darkness. Do not think so much—so much that the happiness of life is destroyed in the over-estimation of it. When you wish, you may come to see me. I shall be in the sixth band for many millions of years."

Abruptly. Oldster vanished. He had snapped both Mother and son back in the first band.

She fixed her vision on him. "Darkness, what he says is true—every word. Play for a while—there are innumerable things to do. And once in great intervals, if you wish, go to see Oldster; but for a long time do not bother him with your questions."

"I will try," answered Darkness, in sudden decision.

II. Cosmic Children

Darkness played. He played for many millions of years. With playmates of his own age, he roamed through and through the endless numbers of galaxies that composed the universe. From one end to another he dashed in a reckless obedience to Oldster's command.

He explored the surfaces of stars, often disrupting them into fragments, sending scalding geysers of belching flame millions of miles into space. He followed his companions into the swirling depths of the green-hued nebulae that hung in intergalactic space. But to disturb these mighty creations of nature was impossible. Majestically they rolled around and around, or coiled into spirals, or at times condensed into matter that formed beautiful, hot suns.

Energy to feed on was rampant here, but so densely and widely was it distributed that he and his comrades could not even dream of absorbing more than a trillionth part of it in all their lives.

He learned the mysteries of the forty-seven bands of hyper-space. He learned to snap into them or out again into the first or true band at will. He knew the delights of blackness impenetrable in the fifteenth band, of a queerly illusory multiple existence in the twenty-third, and an equally strange sensation of speeding away from himself in an opposite direction in the thirty-first, and of the forty-seventh, where all space turned into a nightmarish concoction of cubistic suns and galaxies.

Incomprehensible were those forty-seven bands. They were coexistent in space, yet they were separated from each other by a means which no one had ever discovered. In each band were unmistakable signs that it was the same universe. Darkness only knew that each band was one of forty-seven subtly differing faces which the universe possessed, and the powers of his mind experienced no difficulty in allowing him to cross the unseen bridges which spanned the gulfs between them.

And he made no attempts toward finding the solution—he was determined to cease thinking, for the time being at least. He was content to play, and to draw as much pleasure and excitement as he could from every new possibility of amusement.

But the end of all *that* came, as he had suspected it would. He played, and loved all this, until. . . .

He had come to his fifty-millionth year, still a youth. The purple globe at his core could have swallowed a sun a million miles in diameter, and his whole body could have displaced fifty suns of that size. For a period of a hundred thousand years he lay asleep in the seventh band, where a soft, colorless light pervaded the universe.

He awoke, and was about to transfer himself to the first band and rejoin the children of Radiant, Light-year, Great Power, and all those others.

He stopped, almost dumbfounded, for a sudden, overwhelming antipathy for companionship had come over him. He discovered, indeed, that he never wanted to join his friends again. While he had slept, a metamorphosis had come about, and he was as alienated from his playmates as if he had never known them.

What had caused it? Something. Perhaps, long before his years, he had passed into the adult stage of mind. Now he was rebelling against the friendships which meant nothing more than futile play.

Play! Bouncing huge suns around like rubber balls, and then tearing them up into solar systems; chasing one another up the scale through the forty-seven bands, and back again; darting about in the immense spaces between galaxies, rendering themselves invisible by expanding to ten times normal size.

He did not want to play, and he never wanted to see his friends again. He did not hate them, but he was intolerant of the characteristics which bade them to disport amongst the stars for eternity.

He was not mature in size, but he felt he had become an adult, while they were still children—tossing suns the length of a galaxy, and then hurling small bits of materialized energy around them to form planets; then just as likely to hurl huger masses to disrupt the planetary systems they so painstakingly made.

He had felt it all along—this superiority. He had manifested it by besting them in every form of play they conceived. They generally bungled everything, more apt to explode a star into small fragments than to whirl it until centrifugal force threw off planets.

"I have become an adult in mind, if not in body; I am at the point where I must accumulate wisdom, and perhaps sorrow," he thought whimsically. "I will see Oldster, and ask him my questions—the questions I have thus far kept in the background of my thought. But," he added thoughtfully, "I have a feeling that even his wisdom will fail to enlighten me. Nevertheless, there must be answers. What is life? Why is it? And there must be—another universe beyond the darkness that hems this one in."

Darkness reluctantly turned and made a slow trail across that galaxy and into the next, where he discovered those young energy creatures with whom it would be impossible to enjoy himself again.

He drew up, and absently translated his time standard to one corresponding with theirs, a rate of consciousness at which they could observe the six planets whirling around a small, white-hot sun as separate bodies, and not mere rings of light.

They were gathered in numbers of some hundreds around this sun, and Darkness hovered on the outskirts of the crowd, watching them moodily.

One of the young purple lights, Cosmic by name, threw a mass of matter a short distance into space, reached out with a tractor ray, and drew it in. He swung it 'round and 'round on the tip of that ray, gradually forming ever-decreasing circles. To endow the planet with a velocity that would hurl it unerringly between the two outermost planetary orbits required a delicate sense of compensatory adjustment between the factors of mass, velocity, and solar attraction.

When Cosmic had got the lump of matter down to an angular velocity that was uniform, Darkness knew an irritation he had never succeeded in suppressing. An intuition, which had unfailingly proved itself accurate, told him that anything but creating an orbit for that planet was likely to ensue.

"Cosmic." He contacted the planet-maker's thought-rays. "Cosmic, the velocity you have generated is too great. The whole system will break up."

"Oh, Darkness." Cosmic threw a vision on him. "Come on, join us. You say the speed is wrong? Never; you are! I've calculated everything to a fine point."

"To the wrong point," insisted Darkness stubbornly. "Undoubtedly, your estimation of the planet's mass is the factor which makes your equation incorrect. Lower the velocity. You'll see."

Cosmic continued to swing his lump of matter, but stared curiously at Darkness.

"What's the matter with you?" he inquired. "You don't sound just right. What does it matter if I do calculate wrong, and disturb the system's equilibrium? We'll very probably break up the whole thing later, anyway."

A flash of passion came over Darkness. "That's the trouble," he said fiercely. "It doesn't matter to any of you. You will always be children. You will always be playing. Careful construction, joyous destruction—that is the creed on which you base your lives. Don't you feel as if you'd like, sometimes, to quit playing, and do something—worthwhile?"

As if they had discovered a strangely different set of laws governing an alien galaxy, the hundreds of youths, greens and purples, stared at Darkness.

Cosmic continued swinging the planet he had made through space, but he was plainly puzzled. "What's wrong with you, Darkness? What else is there to do except to roam the galaxies, and make suns? I can't think of a single living thing that might be called more worthwhile."

"What good is playing?" answered Darkness. "What good is making a solar system? If you made one, and then, perhaps, vitalized it with life, that would be worthwhile! Or think, think! About yourself, about life, why it is, and what it means in the scheme of things! Or," and he trembled a little, "try discovering what lies beyond the veil of lightlessness which surrounds the universe."

The hundreds of youths looked at the darkness.

Cosmic stared anxiously at him. "Are you crazy? We all know there's nothing beyond. Everything that is is right here in the universe. That blackness is just empty, and it stretches away from here forever."

"Where did you get that information?" Darkness inquired scornfully. "You don't know that. Nobody does. But I am going to know! I awoke from sleep a short while ago, and I couldn't bear the thought of play. I wanted to do something substantial. So I am going into the darkness."

He turned his gaze hungrily on the deep abyss hemming in the stars. There were thousands of years, even under its lower time-standard, in which awe dominated the gathering. In his astonishment at such an unheard-of intention, Cosmic entirely forgot his circling planet. It lessened in velocity, and then tore loose from the tractor ray that had become weak, in a tangent to the circle it had been performing.

It sped toward that solar system, and entered between the orbits of the outmost planets. Solar gravitation seized it, the lone planet took up an erratic orbit, and then the whole system had settled into complete stability, with seven planets where there had been six.

"You see," said Darkness, with a note of unsteady mirth, "if you had used your intended speed, the system would have coalesced. The speed of the planet dropped, and then escaped you. Some blind chance sent it in the right direction. It was purely an accident. Now throw in a second sun, and watch the system break up. That has always amused you." His aura quivered. "Good-bye, friends."

III. Oldster

He was gone from their sight forever. He had snapped into the sixth band.

He ranged back to the spot where Oldster should have been. He was not.

"Probably in some other band," thought Darkness, and went through all the others, excepting the fifteenth, where resided a complete lack of light. With a feeling akin to awe, since Oldster was apparently in none of them, he went into the fifteenth, and called out.

There was a period of silence. Then Oldster answered, in his thoughts a cadence of infinite weariness.

"Yes, my son; who calls me?"

"It is I, Darkness, whom Sparkle presented to you nearly fifty million years ago." Hesitating, an unexplainable feeling, as of sadness unquenchable, came to him.

"I looked for you in the sixth," he went on in a rush of words, "but did not expect to find you here, isolated, with no light to see by."

"I am tired of seeing, my son. I have lived too long. I have tired of thinking and of seeing. I am sad."

Darkness hung motionless, hardly daring to interrupt the strange thought of this incredible ancient. He ventured timidly, "It is just that I am tired of playing, Oldster, tired of doing nothing. I should like to accomplish something of some use. Therefore, I have come to you, to ask you three questions, the answers to which I must know."

Oldster stirred restlessly. "Ask your questions."

"I am curious about life." Oldster's visitor hesitated nervously, and then went on. "It has a purpose, I know, and I want to know that purpose. That is my first question."

"But why, Darkness? What makes you think life *has* a purpose, an ultimate purpose?"

"I don't know," came the answer, and for the first time Darkness was startled with the knowledge that he really didn't! "But there must be some purpose!" he cried.

"How can you say 'must'? Oh, Darkness, you have clothed life in garments far too rich for its ordinary character! You have given it the sacred aspect of meaning! There is no meaning to it. Once upon a time the spark of life fired a blob of common energy with consciousness of its existence. From that, by some obscure evolutionary process, we came. That is all. We are born. We live, and grow, and then we die! After that, there is nothing! Nothing!"

Something in Darkness shuddered violently, and then rebelliously. But his thoughts were quiet and tense. "I won't believe that! You are telling me that life is only meant for death, then. Why—why, if that were so, why should there be life? No, Oldster! I feel that there must be something which justifies my existence."

Was it pity that came flowing along with Oldster's thoughts? "You will never believe me. I knew it. All my ancient wisdom could not change you, and perhaps it is just as well. Yet you may spend a lifetime in learning what I have told you."

His thoughts withdrew, absently, and then returned.

"Your other questions, Darkness."

For a long time Darkness did not answer. He was of half a mind to leave Oldster, and leave it to his own experiences to solve his other problems. His resentment was hotter than a dwarf sun, for a moment. But it cooled and though he was beginning to doubt the wisdom to which Oldster laid claim, he continued with his questioning.

"What is the use of the globe of purple light which forever remains at my center, and even returns, no matter how far I hurl it from me?"

Such a wave of mingled agitation and sadness passed from the old being that Darkness shuddered. Oldster turned on him with extraordinary fierceness. "Do not learn *that* secret! I will not tell you! What might I not have spared myself had I not sought and found the answer to that riddle! I was a thinker, Darkness, like you! Darkness, if you value—Come, Darkness," he went on in a singularly broken manner, "your remaining question." His thought-rays switched back and forth with an uncommon sign of utter chaos of mind.

Then they centered on Darkness again. "I know your other query, Darkness. I know, knew when first Sparkle brought you to me, eons ago.

"What is beyond the darkness? That has occupied your mind since your creation. What lies on the fringe of the lightless section by which this universe is bounded?

"I do not know, Darkness. Nor does anyone know."

"But you *must* believe there is something beyond," cried Darkness.

"Darkness, in the dim past of our race, beings of your caliber have tried—five of them I remember in my time, billions of years ago. But, they never came back. They left the universe, hurling themselves into that awful void, and they never came back."

"How do you know they didn't reach that foreign universe?" asked Darkness breathlessly.

"Because they didn't come back," answered Oldster, simply. "If they could have gotten across, at least one or two of them would have returned. They never reached that universe. Why? All the energy they were able to accumulate for that staggering voyage was exhausted. And they dissipated—died—in the energiless emptiness of the darkness."

"There must be a way to cross!" said Darkness violently. "There must be a way to gather energy for the crossing! Oldster, you are destroying my life-dream! I have wanted to cross. I want to find the edge of the darkness. I want to find life there—perhaps then I will find the meaning of all life!"

"Find the—" began Oldster pityingly, then stopped, realizing the futility of completing the sentence.

"It is a pity you are not like the others, Darkness. Perhaps they understand that it is as purposeful to lie sleeping in the seventh band as to discover the riddle of the darkness. They are truly happy; you are not. Always, my son, you over-estimate the worth of life."

"Am I wrong in doing so?"

"No. Think as you will, and think that life is high. There is no harm.

Dream your dream of great life, and dream your dream of another universe. There is joy even in the sadness of unattainment.''

Again that long silence, and again the smoldering flame of resentment in Darkness's mind. This time there was no quenching of that flame. It burned fiercely.

"I will not dream!" said Darkness furiously. When first my visions became activated, they rested on the darkness, and my newborn thought-swirls wondered about the darkness, and knew that something lay beyond it!

"And whether or not I die in that void, I am going into it!"

Abruptly, irately, he snapped from the fifteenth band into the first, but before he had time to use his propellents, he saw Oldster, a giant body of intense, swirling energies of pure light, materialize before him.

"Darkness, stop!" and Oldster's thoughts were unsteady. "Darkness," he went on, as the younger energy creature stared spellbound, "I had vowed to myself never to leave the band of lightlessness. I have come from it, a moment, for—you!

"You will die. You will dissipate in the void! You will never cross it, if it can be crossed, with the limited energy your body contains!"

He seized Darkness's thought-swirls in tight bands of energy.

"Darkness, there is knowledge that I possess. Receive it!"

With newborn wonder, Darkness erased consciousness. The mighty accumulated knowledge of Oldster sped into him in a swift flow, a great tide of space-lore no other being had ever possessed.

The inflow ceased, and as from an immeasurably distant space came Oldster's parting words:

"Darkness, farewell! Use your knowledge, use it to further your dream. Use it to cross the darkness.''

Again fully conscious, Darkness knew that Oldster had gone again into the fifteenth band of utter lightlessness, in his vain attempt at peace.

He hung tensely motionless in the first band, exploring the knowledge that now was his. At the portent of one particular portion of it, he trembled.

In wildest exhilaration, he thrust out his propellents, dashing at full speed to his Mother.

He hung before her.

"Mother, I am going into the darkness!"

There was a silence, pregnant with her sorrow. "Yes, I know. It was destined when first you were born. For that I named you Darkness." A restless quiver of sparks left her. Her gaze sad and loving. She said, "Farewell, Darkness, my son."

She wrenched herself from true space, and he was alone. The thought stabbed him. He was alone—alone as Oldster.

Struggling against the vast depression that overwhelmed him, he slowly started on his way to the very furthest edge of the universe, for there lay the Great Energy.

Absently he drifted across the galaxies, the brilliant denizens of the cosmos, lying quiescent on their eternal black beds. He drew a small sun into him, and converted it into energy for the long flight.

And suddenly afar off he saw his innumerable former companions. A cold mirth seized him. Playing! The folly of children, the aimlessness of stars!

He sped away from them, and slowly increased his velocity, the thousands of galaxies flashing away behind. His speed mounted, a frightful acceleration carrying him toward his goal.

IV. Beyond Light

It took him seven millions of years to cross the universe, going at the tremendous velocity he had attained. And he was in a galaxy whose far flung suns hung out into the darkness, were themselves traveling into the darkness at the comparatively slow pace of several thousand miles a second.

Instantaneously, his vision rested on an immense star, a star so immense that he felt himself unconsciously expand in an effort to rival it. So titanic was its mass that it drew all light rays save the short ultra-violet back into it.

It was hot, an inconceivable mass of matter a billion miles across. Like an evil, sentient monster of the skies it hung, dominating the tiny suns of this galaxy that were perhaps its children, to Darkness flooding the heavens with ultra-violet light from its great expanse of writhing, coiling, belching surface; and mingled with that light was a radiation of energy so virulent that it ate its way painfully into his very brain.

Still another radiation impinged on him, an energy which, were he to possess its source, would activate his propellents to such an extent that his velocity would pale any to which his race had attained in all its long history!—would hurl him into the darkness at such an unthinkable rate that the universe would be gone in the infinitesimal part of a second!

But how hopeless seemed the task of rending it from that giant of the universe! The source of that energy, he knew with knowledge that was sure, was matter, matter so incomparably dense, its electrons crowding each other till they touched, that even that furiously molten star could not destroy it!

He spurred back several million of miles, and stared at it. Suddenly he knew fear, a cold fear. He felt that the sun was animate, that it knew he was waiting there, that it was prepared to resist his pitiable onslaughts. And as if in support of his fears, he felt rays of such intense repelling power, such alive, painful malignancy that he almost threw away his mad intentions of splitting it.

"I have eaten suns before," he told himself, with the air of one arguing against himself. "I can at least split that one open, and extract the morsel that lies in its interior."

He drew into him as many of the surrounding suns as he was able, converting them into pure energy. He ceased at last, for no longer could his body, a giant complexity of swarming intense fields sixty millions of miles across, assimilate more.

Then, with all the acceleration he could muster, he dashed headlong at the celestial monster.

It grew and expanded, filling all the skies until he could no longer see anything but it. He drew near its surface. Rays of fearful potency smote him until he convulsed in the whiplash agony of it. At frightful velocity, he contacted the heaving surface, and—made a tiny dent some millions of miles in depth.

He strove to push forward, but streams of energy repelled him, energy that flung him away from the star in acceleration.

He stopped his backward flight, fighting his torment, and threw himself upon the star again. It repulsed him with an uncanny likeness to a living thing. Again and again he went through the agonizing process, to be as often thrust back.

He could not account for those repelling rays, which seemed to operate in direct contrariness to the star's obviously great gravitational field, nor did he try to account for them. There were mysteries in space which even Oldster had never been able to solve.

But there was a new awe in him. He hung in space, spent and quivering. "It is *almost* alive," he thought, and then adopted new tactics. Rushing at the giant, he skimmed over and through its surface in titanic spirals, until he had swept it entirely free of raging, incandescent gases. Before the star could replenish its surface, he spiraled it again, clinging to it until he could no longer resist the repelling forces, or the burning rays which impinged upon him.

The star now lay in the heavens diminished by a tenth of its former bulk. Darkness, hardly able to keep himself together, retired a distance from it and discarded excess energy.

He went back to the star.

Churning seas of pure light flickered fitfully across. Now and then there were belchings of matter bursting within itself.

Darkness began again. He charged, head on. He contacted, bored millions of miles, and was thrown back with mounting velocity. Hurtling back into space, Darkness finally knew that all these tactics would in the last analysis prove useless. His glance roving, it came to rest on a dense, redly glowing sun. For a moment it meant nothing, and then he knew, knew that here at last lay the solution.

He plucked that dying star from its place, and swinging it in huge circles on the tip of a tractor ray, flung it with the utmost of his savage force at the gargantuan star.

Fiercely, he watched the smaller sun approach its parent. Closer, closer, and then—they collided! A titanic explosion ripped space, sending out wave after wave of cosmic rays, causing an inferno of venomous, raging flames that extended far into the skies, licking it in a fury of utter abandon. The mighty sun split wide open, exhibiting a violet hot, gaping maw more than a billion miles wide.

Darkness activated his propellents, and dropped into the awful cavity until he was far beneath its rim, and had approached the center of the star where lay that mass of matter which was the source of the Great Energy. To his sight, it was invisible, save as a blank area of nothingness, since light rays of no wave-length whatsoever could leave it.

Darkness wrapped himself exotically around the sphere, and at the same time the two halves of the giant star fell together, imprisoning him at its core.

This possibility he had not overlooked. With concentrated knots of force, he ate away the merest portion of the surface of the sphere, and absorbed it in him. He was amazed at the metamorphosis. He became aware of a vigor so infinite that he felt nothing could withstand him.

Slowly, he began to expand. He was inexorable. The star could not stop him; it gave. It cracked, great gaping cracks which parted with displays of blinding light and pure heat. He continued to grow, pushing outward.

With the sphere of Great Energy, which was no more than ten million miles across, in his grasp, he continued inflation. A terrific blast of malignant energy ripped at him; cracks millions of miles in length appeared, cosmic displays of pure energy flared. After that, the gargantua gave way before Darkness so readily that he had split it up into separate parts before he ever knew it.

He then became aware that he was in the center of thousands of large and small pieces of the star that were shooting away from him in all directions, forming new suns that would chart individual orbits for themselves.

He had conquered. He hung motionless, grasping the sphere of Great Energy at his center, along with the mystic globe of purple light.

He swung his vision on the darkness, and looked at it in fascination for a long time. Then, without a last look at the universe of his birth, he activated his propellents with the nameless Great Energy, and plunged into that dark well.

All light, save that he created, vanished. He was hemmed in on all sides by the vastness of empty space. Exaltation, coupled with an awareness of the infinite power in his grasp, took hold of his thoughts and made them soar. His acceleration was minimum rather than maximum, yet in a brief space of his time standard he traversed uncountable billions of light-years.

Darkness ahead, and darkness behind, and darkness all around—that had been his dream. It had been his dream all through his life, even during those formless years in which he had played, in obedience to Oldster's admonishment. Always there had been the thought—what lies at the other end of the darkness? Now he was in the darkness, and a joy such as he had never known claimed him. He was on the way! Would he find another universe, a universe which had bred the same kind of life as he had known? He could not think otherwise.

His acceleration was incredible! Yet he knew that he was using a minimum of power. He began to step it up, swiftly increasing even the vast velocity which he had attained. Where lay that other universe? He could not know, and he had chosen no single direction in which to leave his own universe. There had been no choice of direction. Any line stretching into the vault of the darkness might have ended in that alien universe. . . .

Not until a million years had elapsed did his emotions subside. Then there were other thoughts. He began to feel a dreadful fright, a fright that grew on him as he left his universe farther behind. He was hurtling into the darkness that none before him had crossed, and few had dared to try crossing, at a velocity which he finally realized he could attain, but not comprehend. Mind could not think it, thoughts could not say it!

And—he was alone! *Alone!* An icy hand clutched at him. He had never known the true meaning of that word. There were none of his friends near, nor his Mother, nor great-brained Oldster—there was no living thing within innumerable light-centuries. *He* was the only life in the void!

Thus, for almost exactly ninety millions of years he wondered and thought, first about life, then the edge of the darkness, and lastly the mysterious energy field eternally at his core. He found the answer to two, and perhaps, in the end, the other.

Ever, each infinitesimal second that elapsed, his visions were probing hundreds of light-years ahead, seeking the first sign of that universe he believed in; but no, all was darkness so dense it seemed to possess mass.

The monotony became agony. A colossal loneliness began to tear at him. He wanted to do anything, even play, or slice huge stars up into planets. But there was only one escape from the phantasmal horror of the unending ebon path. Now and anon he seized the globe of light with a tractor ray and hurled it into the curtain of darkness behind him at terrific velocity.

It sped away under the momentum imparted to it until sight of it was lost. But always, though millions of years might elapse, it returned, attached to him by invisible strings of energy. It was part of him, it defied penetration of its secret, and it would never leave him, until, perhaps, of itself it revealed its true purpose.

Infinite numbers of light-years, so infinite that if written a sheet as broad as the universe would have been required, reeled behind.

Eighty millions of years passed. Darkness had not been as old as that when he had gone into the void for which he had been named. Fear that he had been wrong took a stronger foothold in his thoughts. But now he knew that he would never go back.

Long before the eighty-nine-millionth year came, he had exhausted all sources of amusement. Sometimes he expanded or contracted to incredible sizes. Sometimes he automatically went through the motions of traversing the forty-seven bands. He felt the click in his consciousness which told him that if there had been hyper-space in the darkness, he would have been transported into it. But how could there be different kinds of darkness? He strongly doubted the existence of hyper-space here, for only matter could occasion the dimensional disturbances which obtained in his universe.

But with the eighty-nine-millionth year came the end of his pilgrimage. It came abruptly. For one tiny space of time, his visions contacted a stream of light, light that was left as the outward trail of a celestial body. Darkness's body, fifty millions of miles in girth, involuntarily contracted to half its size. Energy streamed together and formed molten blobs of flaring matter that sped from him in the chaotic emotions of the moment.

A wave of shuddering thankfulness shook him, and his thoughts rioted sobbingly in his memory swirls.

"Oldster, Oldster, if only your great brain could know this. . . ."

Uncontrollably inflating and deflating, he tore onward, shearing vast quantities of energy from the tight matter at his core, converting it into propellent power that drove him at a velocity that was more than unthinkable, toward the universe from whence had come that light-giving body.

V. The Colored Globes

In the ninety-millionth year a dim spot of light rushed at him, and, as he hurtled onward, the spot of light grew, and expanded, and broke up into tinier lights, tinier lights that in turn broke up into their components—until the darkness was blotted out, giving way to the dazzling, beautiful radiance of an egg-shaped universe.

He was out of the darkness; he had discovered its edge. Instinctively, he lessened his velocity to a fraction of its former self, and then, as if some mightier will than his had overcome him, he lost consciousness, and sped unknowingly, at steady speed, through the outlying fringe of the outer galaxy, through it, through its brothers, until, unconscious, he was in the midst of that alien galactic system.

First he made a rigid tour of inspection, flying about from star to star, tearing them wantonly apart, as if each and every atom belonged solely to him. The galaxies, the suns, the very elements of construction, all were the same as he knew them. All nature, he decided, was probably alike, in this universe, or in that one.

But was there life?

An abrupt wave of restlessness, of unease, passed over him. He felt unhappy, and unsated. He looked about on the stars, great giants, dwarfs fiercely burning, other hulks of matter cooled to black, forbidding cinders, inter-galactic nebulae wreathing unpurposefully about, assuming weird and beautiful formations over periods of thousands of years. He, Darkness, had come to them, had crossed the great gap of nothing, but they were unaffected by this unbelievable feat, went swinging on their courses knowing nothing of him. He felt small, without meaning. Such thoughts seemed the very apostasy of sense, but there they were—he could not shake them off. It was with a growing feeling of disillusionment that he drifted through the countless galaxies and nebulae that unrolled before him, in search of life.

And his quest was rewarded. From afar off, the beating flow of the life-energy came. He drove toward its source, thirty or forty light-years, and hung in its presence.

The being was a green-light, that one of the two classes in which Darkness had divided the life he knew. He himself was a purple-light, containing at his core a globe of pure light, the purpose of which had been one of the major problems of his existence.

The green-light, when she saw him, came to a stop. They stared at each other.

Finally she spoke, and there was wonder and doubt in her thoughts.

"Who are you? You seem—alien."

"You will hardly believe me," Darkness replied, now trembling with a sensation which, inexplicably, could not be defined by the fact that he was in converse with a being of another universe. "But I am alien. I do not belong to this universe."

"But that seems quite impossible. Perhaps you are from another space, beyond the forty-seventh. But that is more impossible!" She eyed him with growing puzzlement and awe.

"I am from no other space," said Darkness somberly. "I am from another universe beyond the darkness."

"From beyond the darkness?" she said faintly, and then she involuntarily contracted. Abruptly, she turned her visions on the darkness. For a long, long time she stared at it, and then she returned her vision rays to Darkness.

"So you have crossed the darkness," she whispered. "They used to tell me that that was the most impossible thing it was possible to dream of—to cross that terrible section of lightlessness. No one could cross, they said, because there was nothing on the other side. But I never believed, purple-light, I never believed them. And there have been times when I have desperately wanted to traverse it myself. But there were tales of beings who had gone into it, and never returned. . . . And you have crossed it!"

A shower of crystalline sparks fled from her. So evident was the sudden hero worship carried on her thought-waves, that Darkness felt a wild rise in spirits. And suddenly he was able to define the never before experienced emotions which had enwrapped him when first this green-light spoke.

"Green-light, I have journeyed a distance the length of which I cannot think to you, seeking the riddle of the darkness. But perhaps there was something else I was seeking, something to fill a vacant part of me. I know now what it was. A mate, green-light, a thinker. And you are that thinker, that friend with whom I can journey, voyaging from universe to universe, finding the secrets of all that is. Look! The Great Energy which alone made it possible for me to cross the darkness, has been barely tapped!''

Imperceptibly she drew away. There was an unexplainable wariness that seemed half sorrow in her thoughts.

"You are a thinker," he exclaimed. "Will you come with me?"

She stared at him, and he felt she possessed a natural wisdom he could never hope to accumulate. There was a strange shrinkage of his spirits. What was that she was saying?

"Darkness," she said gently, "you would do well to turn and leave me, a green-light, forever. You are a purple-light, I a green. Green-light and purple-light—is that all you have thought about the two types of life? Then you must know that beyond the difference in color, there is another: the greens have a knowledge not vouchsafed the purples, until it is . . . too late. For your own sake, then, I ask you to leave me forever.''

He looked at her puzzled. Then slowly, "That is an impossible request, now that I have found you. You are what I need," he insisted.

"But don't you understand?'' she cried. "I know something you have not even guessed at! Darkness—leave me!''

He became bewildered. What was she driving at? What was it she knew that he could not know? For a moment he hesitated. Far down in him a voice was bidding him to do as she asked, and quickly. But another voice, that of a growing emotion he could not name, bid him stay; for she was the complement of himself, the half of him that would make him complete. And the second voice was stronger.

"I am not going," he said firmly, and the force of his thoughts left no doubt as to the unshakable quality of his decision.

She spoke faintly, as if some outside will had overcome her. "No, Darkness, now you are not going; it is too late! Learn the secret of the purple globe!''

Abruptly, she wrenched herself into a hyper-space, and all his doubts and fears were erased as she disappeared. He followed her delightedly up the scale, catching sight of her in one band just as she vanished into the next.

And so they came to the forty-seventh, where all matter, its largest and smallest components, assumed the shapes of unchangeable cubes; even he and the green-light appeared as cubes, gigantic cubes millions of miles in extent, a geometric figure they could never hope to distort.

Darkness watched her expectantly. Perhaps she would now start a game of chopping chunks off these cubed suns, and swing them around as planets. Well, he would be willing to do that for a while, in her curious mood of playfulness, but after that they must settle down to discovering possible galactic systems beyond this one.

As he looked at her she vanished.

"Hmm, probably gone down the scale," thought Darkness, and he dropped through the lower bands. He found her in none.

"Darkness . . . try the . . . forty-eighth. . . ." Her thought came faintly.

"The forty-eighth!" he cried in astonishment. At the same time, there was a seething of his memory swirls as if the knowledge of his life were being arranged to fit some new fact, a strange alchemy of the mind by which he came to know that there *was* a forty-eighth.

Now he knew, as he had always known, that there was a forty-eighth. He snapped himself into it.

Energy became rampant in a ceaseless shifting about him. A strange energy, reminding him of nothing so much as the beating flow of an energy creature approaching him from a near distance. His vision sought out the green-light.

She was facing him somberly, yet with a queerly detached arrogance. His mind was suddenly choked with the freezing sensation that he was face to face with horror.

"I have never been here before," he whispered faintly.

He thought he detected pity in her, but it was overwhelmed by the feeling that she was under the influence of an outside will that could not know pity.

Yet she said, "I am sadder than ever before. But too late. You are my mate, and this is the band of—life!"

Abruptly while he stared, she receded, and he could not follow, save with his visions. Presently, as if an hypnotist had clamped his mind, she herself disappeared, all that he saw of her being the green globe of light she carried. He saw nothing else, knew nothing else. It became his whole universe, his whole life. A peacefulness, complete and uncorroded by vain striving, settled on him like stardust.

The green globe of light dimmed, became smaller, until it was less than a pinpoint, surrounded by an infinity of colorless, white energy.

Then, so abruptly it was in the nature of a shock, he came from his torpor, and was conscious. Far off he still saw the green globe of light, but it was growing in size, approaching—approaching a purple globe of light that in turn raced toward it at high velocity.

"It is my own light," he thought, startled. "I must have unwittingly hurled it forth when she settled that hypnotic influence over me. No matter. It will come back."

But would it come back? Green globe of light was expanding in apparent size, approaching purple which, in turn, dwindled toward it at increasing speed.

"At that rate," he thought in panic, "they will collide. Then how will my light come back to me?"

He watched intently, a poignantly cold feeling clutching at him. Closer . . . closer. He quivered. Green globe and purple globe had crashed.

They met in blinding crescendo of light that brightened space for light-years around. A huge mistiness of light formed into a sphere, in the center of which hung a brilliant ball. The misty light slowly subsided until it had been absorbed into the brighter light, that remained as motionless as Darkness himself. Then it commenced pulsating with a strange, rhythmic regularity.

Something about that pulsing stirred ancient memories, something that said, "You, too, were once no more than that pulsing ball."

Thoughts immense in scope, to him, tumbled in his mind.

"That globe is life," he thought starkly. "The green-light and I have created life. That was her meaning, when she said this was the band of life. Its activating energy flows rampant here.

"That is the secret of the purple globe; with the green globe it creates life. And I had never known the forty-eighth band until she made it known to me!

"The purpose of life—to create life." The thought of that took fire in his brain. For one brief, intoxicating moment he thought that he had solved the last and most baffling of his mighty problems.

As with all other moments of exaltation he had known, disillusionment followed swiftly after. To what end was that? The process continued on and on, and what came of it? Was creation of life the only use of life? A meaningless circle! He recalled Oldster's words of the past, and horror claimed him.

"Life, my life," he whispered dully. "A dead sun and life—one of equal importance with the other. That is unbelievable!" he burst out.

He was aware of the green-light hovering near; yes, she possessed a central light, while his was gone!

She looked at him sorrowfully. "Darkness, if only you had listened to me!"

Blankly, he returned her gaze. "Why is it that you have a light, while I have none?"

"A provision of whatever it was that created us, endows the green-lights with the ability to replace their lights three times. Each merging of a purple and green light may result in the creation of one or several newly-born. Thus the number born over-balances the number of deaths. When my fourth light has gone, as it will some day, I know, I too, will die."

"You mean, I will—die?"

"Soon."

Darkness shuddered, caught half-way between an emotion of blind anger and mental agony. "There is death everywhere," he whispered, "and everything is futile!"

"Perhaps," she said softly, her grief carrying poignantly to him. "Darkness, do not be sad. Darkness, death does indeed come to all, but that does not say that life is of no significance.

"Far past in the gone ages of our race, we were pitiful, tiny blobs of energy which crept along at less than light-speed. An energy creature of that time knew nothing of any but the first and forty-eighth band of hyper-space. The rest he could not conceive of as being existent. He was ignorant, possessing elementary means of absorbing energy for life. For countless billions of years he never knew there was an edge to the universe. He could not conceive an edge.

"He was weak, but he gained in strength. Slowly, he evolved, and intelligence entered his mind.

"Always, he discovered things he had been formerly unable to conceive in his mind, and even now there are things that lay beyond the mind; one of them is the end of all space. And the greatest is, why life exists. Both are something we cannot conceive, but in time evolution of mental powers will allow us to conceive them, even as we conceived the existence of hyper-space, and those other things. Dimly, so dimly, even now I can see some reason, but it slips the mind. But Darkness! All of matter is destined to break down to an unchanging state of maximum entropy; it is life, and life alone, that builds in an upward direction. So . . . faith!"

She was gone. She had sown what comfort she could.

Her words shot Darkness full of the wild fire of hope. That was the answer! Vague and promissory it was, but no one could arrive nearer to the solution than that. For a moment he was suffused with the blissful thought that the last of his problems was disposed of.

Then, in one awful space of time, the green-light's philosophy was gone from his memory as if it had never been uttered. He felt the pangs of an unassailable weariness, as if life energies were seeping away.

Haggardly, he put into effect one driving thought. With lagging power, he shot from the fatal band of life . . . and death . . . down the scale. Something unnameable, perhaps some natal memory, made him pause for the merest second in the seventeenth band. Afar off, he saw the green-light and her newly-born. They had left the highest band, come to the band where propellents became useless. So it had been at his own birth.

He paused no more and dropped to the true band, pursuing a slow course across the star-beds of this universe, until he at last emerged on its ragged shore. He went on into the darkness, until hundred hundreds of light-years separated him from the universe his people had never known existed.

VI. Dissipation

He stopped and looked back at the lens of misty radiance. "I have not even discovered the edge of the darkness," he thought. "It stretches out and around. That galactic system and my own are just pinpoints of light, sticking up, vast distances apart, through an unlimited ebon cloth. They are so small in the darkness they barely have the one dimension of existence!"

He went on his way, slowly, wearily, as if the power to activate his propellents were diminishing. There came a time, in his slow, desperate striving after the great velocity he had known in crossing the lightless section, when that universe, that pinpoint sticking up, became as a pinpoint to his sight.

He stopped, took one longing look at it, and accelerated until it was lost to view.

"I am alone again," he thought vaguely. "I am more alone than Oldster ever was. How did he escape death from the green-lights? Perhaps he discovered their terrible secret, and fled before they could wreak their havoc on him. He was a lover of wisdom, and he did not want to die. Now he is living, and he is alone, marooning himself in the lightless band, striving not to think. He could make himself die, but he is afraid to, even though he is so tired of life, and of thinking his endless thoughts.

"I will die. But no . . . ! Ah, yes, I will."

He grew bewildered. He thought, or tried to think, of what came after death. Why, there would be nothing! He would not be there, and without him nothing else could exist!

"I would not be there, and therefore there would be nothing," he thought starkly. "Oh, that is inconceivable. Death! Why, forever after I died, I would be—dead!"

He strove to alleviate the awfulness of the eternal unconsciousness. "I was nothing once, that is true; why cannot that time come again? But it is unthinkable. I feel as if I am the center of everything, the cause, the focal point, and even the foundation."

For some time this thought gave him a kind of gloating satisfaction. Death was indeed not so bad, when one could thus drag to oblivion the very things which had sponsored his life. But at length reason supplanted dreams. He sighed. "And that is vanity!"

Again he felt the ineffably horrible sensation of an incapacity to activate his propellents the full measure, and an inability to keep himself down to normal size. His memory swirls were pulsating, and striving, sometimes, to obliterate themselves.

Everything seemed meaningless. His very drop into the darkness, at slow acceleration, was without purpose.

"I could not reach either universe now," he commented to himself, "because I am dying. Poor Mother! Poor Oldster! They will not even know I crossed. That seems the greatest sorrow—to do a great thing, and not be able to tell of it. Why did they not tell me of the central lights? With Oldster, it was fear that I should come to the same deathless end as he. With Mother— she obeyed an instinct as deeply rooted as space. There must be perpetuation of life.

"Why? Was the green-light right? Is there some tangible purpose to life which we are unable to perceive? But where is my gain, if I have to die to bring to ultimate fruition that purpose? I suppose Oldster knew the truth. Life just is, had an accidental birth, and exists haphazardly, like a star, or an electron.

"But, knowing these things, why do I not immediately give way to the expanding forces within me? Ah, I do not know!"

* * *

Convulsively he applied his mind to the continuance of life within his insistently expanding body. For awhile he gloried in the small increase of his fading vigor.

"Making solar systems!" his mind took up the thread of a lost thought. "Happy sons of Radiant, Incandescent, Great Power, and all the others!"

He concentrated on the sudden thought that struck him. He was dying, of that he was well aware, but he was dying without doing anything. What had he actually done, in this life of his?

"But what can I do? I am alone," he thought vaguely. Then, "I could make a planet, and I could put the life germ on it. Oldster taught me that."

Suddenly he was afraid he would die before he created this planet. He set his mind to it, and began to strip from the sphere of tight matter vast quantities of energy, then condensed it to form matter more attenuated. With lagging power, he formed mass after mass of matter, ranging all through the ninety-eight elements that he knew.

Fifty thousand years saw the planet's first stage of completion. It had become a tiny sphere some fifteen thousand miles in diameter. With a heat ray he then boiled it, and with another ray cooled its crust, at the same time forming oceans and continents on its surface. Both water and land, he knew, were necessary to life which was bound by nature of this construction to the surface of a planet.

Then came the final, completing touch. No other being had ever deliberately done what Darkness did then. Carefully, he created an infinitesimal splash of life-perpetuating protoplasm; he dropped it aimlessly into a tiny wrinkle on the planet's surface.

He looked at the finished work, the most perfect planet he or his playmates had ever created, with satisfaction, notwithstanding the dull pain of weariness that throbbed through the complex energy fields of his body.

Then he took the planet up in a tractor ray, and swung it around and around, as he now so vividly recalled doing in his childhood. He gave it a swift angular velocity, and then shot it off at a tangent, in a direction along the line of which he was reasonably sure lay his own universe. He watched it with dulling visions. It receded into the darkness that would surround it for ages, and then it was a pinpoint, and then nothing.

"It is gone," he said, somehow wretchedly lonely because of that, "but it will reach the universe; perhaps for millions of years it will traverse the galaxies unmolested. Then a sun will reach out and claim it. There will be life upon it, life that will grow until it is intelligent, and will say it has a soul, and purpose in existing."

Nor did the ironic humor of the ultimate swift and speedy death of even that type of life, once it had begun existence, escape him. Perhaps for one or ten million years it would flourish, and then even it would be gone—once upon a time nothing and then nothing again.

He felt a sensation that brought blankness nearer, a sensation of expansion, but now he made no further attempts to prolong a life which was, in effect, already dead. There was a heave within him, as if some subconscious force were deliberately attempting to tear him apart.

He told himself that he was no longer afraid. "I am simply going into another darkness—but it will be a much longer journey than the other."

Like a protecting cloak, he drew in his vision rays about him, away from the ebon emptiness. He drifted, expanding through the vast, inter-universal space.

The last expansion came, the expansion that dissipated his memory swirls. A vast, compact sphere of living drew itself out until Darkness was only free energy distributed over light-years of space.

And death, in that last moment, seemed suddenly to be a far greater and more astounding occurrence than birth had ever seemed.

EMERGENCY REFUELING

BY JAMES BLISH

*Like many another in this book, James Blish began as a fan. He belonged
to the Futurians. He published fanzines, and wrote for many others, while he
was learning his trade. He also had a lifelong interest in music, and might
easily have become a musicologist—most likely, an irascibly uncompromising
one. His first book was called* Music the Hard Way, *which gives you an idea.
(It was never published. There didn't seem to be a market for a volume which
said listening to music demanded as much work as performing it.) And, of
course, he turned out to be one of the finest science-fiction writers of the
mid-twentieth century.*

*In the first part of Blish's career, I was frequently involved. I published his
first story, written when he was not yet twenty. For several years around
1950—the years when he was writing "Surface Tension," the Okie stories,
and the first, novella version of* A Case of Conscience—*I was his literary
agent. As a part-time consultant for Ballantine in the mid-1950s, I was called
in to be project editor for some of the books that seemed to need more
personal attention—George O. Smith's* The Fourth R *was one; the novel
version of* Conscience *another. And, in the 1960s, as editor of* Galaxy *and* If,
*I published most of his novels as serials. So, for the first quarter-century of
Jim Blish's writing career, I was often involved professionally; and the stories
I did not read as editor or agent I made sure to read as one of his fans.*

*Jim and I did not lose touch until he moved to England. He spent the last
decade of his life there, and when he died he was buried at Oxford,
surrounded by some of England's greatest literary heroes.*

* * *

"That's the last," growled pilot Stan Dorry, exhibiting the almost empty
lead box. His red-haired navigator peered in at the gray handful of powdery
metal huddled dispiritedly in the bottom.

"Well, put it in. We could coast and save this for landing, but we'd hit Jupiter sometime early next century at our present speed." (The red-haired Whipple had the gift of gab.) "We'll take the chance on getting enough fuel on Pluto to take us in."

Dorry shoveled the metal into the tube and closed the breechblock, and together they walked back to the control room. Their thoughts revolved in the same groove. Refueling on Pluto. It was beset with entirely unknown dangers, and illegal as well.

They had been driving in from an interesting-looking asteroid calculated to be twenty million miles beyond the orbit of Pluto. When it turned out to be twenty-five there was nothing they could do about it, and to cap the climax the forty-mile chunk of rock was just that, containing just enough scattered bits of nickel to attract the detectors. Now they had just enough fuel to land them on Pluto—and the nearest fueling station was on Ganymede.

There was plenty of fuel on Pluto—that was an established fact. The whole planet seemed radioactive. First of the planets to be thrown from the sun, it was also one of the densest, and the rocks were full of pitchblende. Their little prospector ran on proactinium, but most good motors would burn ore for a limited length of time. Yes, Pluto was an ideal coaling station—

If it weren't for the fact that the IPF had put an iron-bound taboo on the planet. It had never been satisfactorily explored, since prolonged exposure to the lethal radiations, even in heavy armor, was fatal. Perfunctory charting had been undertaken from the air, hampered by the fact that photography was impossible because of the blurring effects of the radiation on film, and, while it was unthinkable that life could exist under such conditions, the IPF didn't like to take chances. Too many space tramps had landed and never taken off.

Consequently there were ten ships circling the planet constantly, detectors overlapping, and one hundred and twenty superbly bored IP-men longing for some ship to try and break through.

Dorry charged the batteries for five minutes, muttering at the fuel consumption involved, and sent out a call. The response was immediate.

"Okay, *Pallas*," snapped the speaker briskly. "We heard your engines half an hour ago. What's wrong with your screen?"

"Nothing," returned Dorry. "We haven't enough fuel to spare. That's what we called about—"

"Turn it on," barked the voice suspiciously.

"We haven't the fuel, I tell you—"

"Turn it ON!"

Dorry resignedly clicked the switch, and a young and irritated face appeared, wearing a cap a little large for it.

"Satisfied?"

"All right, you can turn it off now. What's the trouble with your fuel?"

"Not enough," Dorry repeated. "We want permission to land on Pluto."

"You can't have it, as you ought to know."

"We'll be a floating coffin in no time at all if we don't."

"Can't you reach Ganymede?"

Whipple made a wry face as Dorry answered, "Why the hell do you think we were scraping the power for the screen?"

"Eh. There are ten patrol ships here—you might get a little from each—"

"The amount we'd get that way would just about equal the expenditure in stopping at each one. Use your head."

There was a brief silence, then a series of high keening notes as if consultation was being made with the other ships.

"We can give you fifteen minutes and no more, and in a region designated by us."

"Good," said Whipple heartily. "Where?"

"In Quadrant—eh—Quadrant Three, section ten. There's a rocky plain there that ought to make a fair landing field, and nearby a set of caves where the deposits are better than usual." The captain seemed to be reading from Sir Christopher Barclay's *Space Manual.* "Get your material from near the mouth of the northmost cave, and do not under any conditions go any farther. There've been twenty tramps like you lost in there, and twice that many IPs looking for them, too."

"Right." The radio went off. "Three minutes. Two minutes extra fuel wasted. Oh, well, no need to worry."

They burned all their fuel in landing, but they felt almost carefree about it now. The field was indeed rocky. In general, however, it was no worse than most of the planetoids at which the *Pallas* had stopped, and they found a prime spot not thirty yards from the cave selected.

"Lead suits?"

"We'll have to make these do. If we're lucky the exposure should be only a few minutes, and any burns we get over that time we can treat easily. Besides, there's the cosmic ray insulation."

They struggled into their spacesuits, charging the batteries from the dregs in the radio. The ground beneath their feet looked like any other ground, although the pair realized that it was at a constant temperature above body heat. The mouth of the cave seemed to be faintly lit with a glow from farther down.

"Like the doorway to hell," crackled Dorry's radio. "Let's go, Jack. Got the pick?"

"Sure 'nuff." They crunched across the rocks and paused at the opening. "Wonder what's here that swallowed sixty men?"

"God knows. It couldn't be anything alive, that's a cinch. Cave-ins, maybe." They entered cautiously, both nervous, and both determined not to show it to the other.

"Saaay," whistled Dorry. "This is good. Look—there's no ore like that on Earth."

"No. It gets better as you go along." Whipple stepped ahead and disappeared around the bend. Dorry heard his gasp. "Cripes, come here."

"What is it, Jack . . . well, I'll be. . . ." They stood like barbaric statues hacked crudely from metal and gazed down the long slanting passage, which was glowing, at first faintly, then as it progressed more and more brightly.

"You know, I'll bet if we got down there, where the bend is, we'd have practically the pure stuff. Well, not quite, but damn good, anyhow, if the vein holds true."

Dorry shook his head. "The IP-men'd say naughty, naughty. Besides, if we stayed long in that stuff it'd be no minor burns we'd have."

"Yeh . . . Lord, though, what a range it would give us. Even with what we hack out here, we'll have to be careful if we're to make Ganymede. Down there we could get more than enough."

Dorry considered that. "You're right, I suppose. If we make it quick, the IPs won't know the difference."

As if he were afraid of a change of heart, Whipple bounded ahead. "Take it easy, Jack," remonstrated the pilot.

"I'm all right. Come along. The light is almost bright down here—and will you look at it pour around the bend! It isn't coming from here though. . . ."

The light was streaming from a small opening which apparently led to a larger cave. It did not flicker as this in the passage did, but burst in a steady, blue-white stream upon them.

"That's the place," said Whipple with conviction. "A few seconds is all we'll need—anyhow the cosmic ray insulation in the suits should hold us for some time." He could not know that it had burned out long ago, for he could not see the bright sympathetic brilliance of his watch-face. He strode into the opening, the pilot on his heels.

The light blinded them temporarily. It came from everywhere, the walls, the floor, the ceiling. Apparently they were in the very heart of a vein, a rich layer of some strange radium isotope.

The glare was blue-white, almost solid in its intensity. Gradually they got used to it.

"What's that?"

"I don't know," said Whipple, blinking. "I'm still half-blind. All I can see is a splotch. There—hey—!"

"Jack . . . I think it's . . . alive." They stared in unison at the fungus-like object. Even as they watched it bloated to a size of eight inches, collapsed, emitting a small cloud of spores.

Tiny blue splotches appeared on the walls and floor, swelling. . . .

"Life-cycle a million times accelerated by the radiation," whispered Dorry with a dry throat. "I wouldn't have believed it."

As their eyes became used to the light they saw others of the rubbery things, which moved slowly about as they went through their instantaneous life-time. The cave seemed enormous, stretching downward in a blue effulgency beyond the limit of their watering eyes. Their radios began to crackle a little.

"No time for gaping," the navigator jerked abruptly. "Come on, Stan. There's a big outcropping we can hack off whole, down just a little to the right."

"I can't hear you very well," complained Dorry. "There's a whale of a lot of static here."

"Yeh—that's funny, we should have heard it up above—I say IT WASN'T HERE BEFORE!" he shouted as Dorry shook his head. The crackling uproar grew startlingly to a deafening pitch, seemed about to die away, then sprang up again. They plodded wordlessly down toward the outcropping, and as they went the static became so violent they were forced to turn the radios off. The immediate silence was worse on Whipple's nerves, and he turned the switch again to low power. A voice rang in his ears.

"Stan, Stan," he screeched. "It isn't static, it's a carrier-wave—telepathic—" Dorry moved deafly on toward the glowing, jutting stone. The voice echoed in Whipple's brain.

"Dead metal," it called. "I sense dead metal."

A subtle change became apparent—another voice? Whipple could not tell. "Another vibration," it said. "A speech radiation and a life force very weak. Do you not feel it?" The voices seemed to become louder. Whipple grabbed his companion and gestured frantically at the radio switch.

The other clicked it over to full, then off again with a despairing wave, made so clumsy by the suit that it looked almost threatening. Whipple seized the switch himself and turned it to low power.

"Very close, yes," said the mental voice. "Near the entrance."

"Let's get out of here," Dorry howled futilely, and jumped for the outcropping, pick raised high. There was a burst of light brighter than all the rest, and Whipple's radio speaker tore resoundingly across. He was deafened achingly. Ahead, the pilot stood in the center of a seven-foot, blue-white flame, and his suit turned very slowly red, then yellow. . . . Other flames shot silently through the glaring, low-roofed space below—

Whipple ran madly, crashing with insensate violence against the walls.

Outside he paused at the airlock. Dorry—dead, roasted. But fuel—

No more of the caves. He seized an armful of the nearest rubble and tumbled into the *Pallas*. Behind, the glow in the mouth of the abyss wavered and sank a little.

THE HALFLING

BY LEIGH BRACKETT

A couple of Novembers ago, I was Guest of Honor at a science-fiction convention in Denver, Colorado . . . or, anyway, I was one of them. Denver fans do things on the sort of grand scale that matches the mountains behind the city. There were two of us, and my co-GoH was Leigh Brackett.

I had been a Brackett admirer for forty years. Although our paths had crossed briefly from time to time, it was always too quick—an hour at a room party in a California convention hotel, some cocktail-party chatter in New York City. The Denver convention was just right. It was a smaller, more leisurely occasion—and an extremely happy one, too, because Leigh had exciting news. The day before the convention began, she had signed a contract with George Lucas to write the screenplay for The Empire Strikes Back, *the sequel to* Star Wars.

There could have been no better choice! Star Wars *was pure, glorious space adventure, and that had been Brackett's* métier *since she won her spurs back in the days of* Planet Stories *and* Astonishing *(which is where "The Halfling" first appeared.) And* Star Wars *was also obviously a major motion picture, and Brackett's credentials in that area dated back to the time she wrote a script for Bogart and Bacall in* The Big Sleep.

The Big Sleep *was Leigh Brackett's passport to a film career. All of us wished her well in it, but it had its debit side. For several decades, she wrote very little science fiction. She and her late husband, Edmond Hamilton, another grand old veteran of the space-action days of* Thrilling Wonder Stories, *et al, still read science fiction, still maintained their friendships in the field, but there was not much new writing from either for a long time. Then Leigh began a new series of novels with* The Ginger Star, *and then the* Star Wars *people invited her to write the script of the sequel, and it looked like good news indeed. Over the next few months after that November, 1978, convention, Leigh wrote the draft script and turned it in . . . and then, very suddenly and unexpectedly, she died.*

Someone else had to do the final revisions on the script for The Empire Strikes Back. *But no one else can take her place.*

* * *

I. "Primitive Venus"

I was watching the sunset. It was something pretty special in the line of California sunsets, and it made me feel swell, being the first one I'd seen in about nine years. The pitch was in the flatlands between Culver City and Venice, and I could smell the sea. I was born in a little dump at Venice, California, and I've never found any smell like the clean cold salt of the Pacific—not anywhere in the Solar System.

I was standing alone, off to one side of the grounds. The usual noises of a carnival around feeding time were being made behind me, and the hammer gang was pinning the last of the tents down tight. But I wasn't thinking about Jade Greene's Interplanetary Carnival, The Wonders of the Seven Worlds Alive Before Your Eyes.

I was remembering John Damien Greene running barefoot on a wet beach, fishing for perch off the end of a jetty, and dreaming big dreams. I was wondering where John Damien Greene had gone, taking his dreams with him, because now I could hardly remember what they were.

Somebody said softly from behind me, "Mr. Greene?"

I quit thinking about John Damien Greene. It was that kind of a voice— sweet, silky, guaranteed to make you forget your own name. I turned around.

She matched her voice, all right. She stood about five-three on her bronze heels, and her eyes were more purple than the hills of Malibu. She had a funny little button of a nose and a pink mouth, smiling just enough to show her even white teeth. The bronze metal-cloth dress she wore hugged a chassis with no flaws in it anywhere. I tried to find some.

She dropped her head, so I could see the way the last of the sunlight tangled in her gold-brown hair.

"They said you were Mr. Greene. If I've made a mistake. . . ."

She had an accent, just enough to be fascinating.

I said, "I'm Greene. Something I can do for you?" I still couldn't find anything wrong with her, but I kept looking just the same. My blood pressure had gone up to about three hundred.

It's hard to describe a girl like that. You can say she's five-three and beautiful, but you can't pass on the odd little tilt of her eyes and the way her mouth looks, or the something that just comes out of her like out of a lamp, and hooks into you so you know you'll never be rid of it, not if you live to be a thousand.

She said, "Yes. You can give me a job. I'm a dancer."

I shook my head. "Sorry, miss. I got a dancer."

Her face had a look of steel down under the soft kittenish roundness. "I'm not just talking," she said. "I need a job so I can eat. I'm a good dancer. I'm the best dancer you ever saw anywhere. Look me over."

That's all I had been doing. I guess I was staring by then. You don't expect fluffy dolls like that to have so much iron in them. She wasn't bragging. She was just telling me.

"I still have a dancer," I told her, "a green-eyed Martian babe who is plenty good, and who would tear my head off, and yours too, if I hired you."

"Oh," she said. "Sorry. I thought you bossed this carnival." She let me think about that, and then grinned. "Let me show you."

She was close enough so I could smell the faint, spicy perfume she wore. But she'd stopped me from being just a guy chinning with a pretty girl. Right then I was Jade Greene, the carny boss-man, with scars on my knuckles and an ugly puss, and a show to keep running.

Strictly Siwash, that show, but my baby—mine to feed and paint and fuel. If this kid had something Sindi didn't have, something to drag in the cash customers—well, Sindi would have to take it and like it. Besides, Sindi was getting so she thought she owned me.

The girl was watching my face. She didn't say anything more, or even move. I scowled at her.

"You'd have to sign up for the whole tour. I'm blasting off next Monday for Venus, and then Mars, and maybe into the Asteroids."

"I don't care. Anything to be able to eat. Anything to—"

She stopped right there and bent her head again, and suddenly I could see tears on her thick brown lashes.

I said, "Okay. Come over to the cooch tent and we'll have a look."

Me, I was tempted to sign her for what was wrapped up in that bronze cloth—but business is business. I couldn't take on any left-footed ponies.

She said shakily, "You don't soften up very easily, do you?" We started across the lot toward the main gate. The night was coming down cool and fresh. Off to the left, clear back to the curving deep-purple barrier of the hills, the slim white spires of Culver, Westwood, Beverly Hills, and Hollywood were beginning to show a rainbow splash of color under their floodlights.

Everything was clean, new, and graceful. Only the thin fog and the smell of the sea were old.

We were close to the gate, stumbling a little in the dusk of the afterglow. Suddenly a shadow came tearing out from between the tents.

It went erratically in lithe, noiseless bounds, and it was somehow not human even though it went on two feet. The girl caught her breath and shrank in against me. The shadow went around us three times like a crazy thing, and then stopped.

There was something eerie about that sudden stillness. The hair crawled on the back of my neck. I opened my mouth angrily.

The shadow stretched itself toward the darkening sky and let go a wail like Lucifer falling from Heaven.

I cursed. The carny lights came on, slamming a circle of blue-white glare against the night.

"Laska, come here!" I yelled.

The girl screamed.

I put my arm around her. "It's all right," I said, and then, "Come here, you misbegotten Thing! You're on a sleighride again."

There were more things I wanted to say, but the girl cramped my style. Laska slunk in toward us. I didn't blame her for yelping. Laska wasn't pretty.

He wasn't much taller than the girl, and looked shorter because he was drooping. He wore a pair of tight dark trunks and nothing else except the cross-shaped mane of fine blue-gray fur that went across his shoulders and down his back, from the peak between his eyes to his long tail. He was dragging the tail, and the tip of it was twitching. There was more of the soft fur on his chest and forearms, and a fringe of it down his lank belly.

I grabbed him by the scruff and shook him. "I ought to boot your ribs in! We got a show in less than two hours."

He looked up at me. The pupils of his yellow-green eyes were closed to thin hairlines, but they were flat and cold with hatred. The glaring lights showed me the wet whiteness of his pointed teeth and the raspy pinkness of his tongue.

"Let me go. Let me go, you human!" His voice was hoarse and accented.

"I'll let you go." I cuffed him across the face. "I'll let you go to the immigration authorities. You wouldn't like that, would you? You wouldn't even have coffee to hop up on when you died."

The sharp claws came out of his fingers and toes, flexed hungrily, and went back in again.

I dropped him.

"Go on back inside. Find the croaker and tell him to straighten you out. I don't give a damn what you do on your own time, but you miss out on one more show and I'll take your job and call the I-men. Get it?"

"I get it," said Laska sullenly, and curled his red tongue over his teeth. He shot his flat, cold glance at the girl and went away, not making any sound at all.

The girl shivered and drew away from me. "What was—that?"

"Cat-man from Callisto. My prize performer. They're pretty rare."

"I—I've heard of them. They evolved from a cat-ancestor instead of an ape, like we did."

"That's putting it crudely, but it's close enough. I've got a carload of critters like that, geeks from all over the System. They ain't human, and they don't fit with animals either. Moth-men, lizard-men, guys with wings and guys with six arms and antennae. They all followed evolutionary tracks peculiar to their particular hunks of planet, only they stopped before they got where they were going. The Callistan kitties are the aristocrats of the bunch. They've got an I.Q. higher than a lot of humans, and wouldn't spit on the other halflings."

"Poor things," she said softly. "You didn't have to be so cruel to him."

I laughed. "That What's-it would as soon claw my insides out as look at me—or any other human, including you—just on general principles. That's why Immigration hates to let 'em in even on a work permit. And when he's hopped up on coffee. . . ."

"Coffee? I thought I must have heard wrong."

"Nope. The caffeine in Earthly coffee berries works just like coke or hashish for 'em. Venusian coffee hits 'em so hard they go nuts and then die, but our own kind just keeps 'em going. It's only the hoppy ones you ever find in a show like this. They get started on coffee and they have to have it no matter what they have to do to get it."

She shuddered a little. "You said something about dying."

"Yeah. If he's ever deported back to Callisto, his people will tear him apart. They're a clannish bunch. I guess the first humans on Callisto weren't very tactful, or else they just hate us because we're something they're not and never can be. Anyway, their tribal law forbids them to have anything to do with us except killing. Nobody knows much about 'em, but I hear they have a nice friendly religion, something like the old-time Thugs and their Kali worship."

I paused, and then said uncomfortably, "Sorry I had to rough him up in front of you. But he's got to be kept in line."

She nodded. We didn't say anything after that. We went in past the main box and along between the burglars readying-up their layouts—Martian *getak,* Venusian *shalil* and the game the Mercurian hillmen play with human skulls. Crooked? Sure—but suckers like to be fooled, and a guy has to make a living.

I couldn't take my eyes off the girl. I thought, *if she dances the way she walks . . .*

She didn't look much at the big three-dimensional natural-color pictures advertising the geek show. We went by the brute top, and suddenly all hell broke loose inside of it. I've got a fair assortment of animals from all over. They make pretty funny noises when they get started, and they were started now.

They were nervous, unhappy noises. I heard prisoners yammering in the Lunar cell-blocks once, and that was the way this sounded—strong, living things shut up in cages and tearing their hearts out with it—hate, fear, and longing like you never thought about. It turned you cold.

The girl looked scared. I put my arm around her again, not minding it at all. Just then Tiny came out of the brute top.

Tiny is a Venusian deep-jungle man, about two sizes smaller than the Empire State Building, and the best zooman I ever had, drunk or sober. Right now he was mad.

"I tell that Laska stay 'way from here," he yelled. "My kids smell him. You listen!"

I didn't have to listen. His "kids" could have been heard halfway to New York. Laska had been expressly forbidden to go near the brute top because the smell of him set the beasts crazy. Whether they were calling to him as one animal to another, or scared of him as something unnatural, we didn't know. The other halflings were pretty good about it, but Laska liked to start trouble just for the hell of it.

I said, "Laska's hopped again. I sent him to the croaker. You get the kids quiet again, and then send one of the punks over to the crumb castle and tell the cook I said if he ever gives Laska a teaspoonful of coffee again without my say-so I'll fry him in his own grease."

Tiny nodded his huge pale head and vanished, cursing. I said to the girl, "Still want to be a carny?"

"Oh, yes," she said. "Anything, as long as you serve food!"

"That's a pretty accent you got. What is it?"

"Just about everything. I was born on a ship between Earth and Mars, and I've lived all over. My father was in the diplomatic corps."

I said, "Oh. Well, here's the place. Go to it."

Sindi was sitting cross-legged on the stage, sipping *thil* and listening to sad Martian music on the juke box behind the screen of faded Martian tapestry. She looked up and saw us, and she didn't like what she saw.

She got up. She was a Low-Canaler, built light and wiry, and she moved like a cat. She had long emerald eyes and black hair with little bells braided in it, and clusters of tiny bells in her ears. She was wearing the skin of a Martian sand-leopard, no more clothes than the law forced her to wear. She was something to look at, and she had a disposition like three yards of barbed wire.

I said, "Hi, Sindi. This kid wants a try-out. Climb down, huh?"

Sindi looked the kid over. She smiled and climbed down and put her hand on my arm. She sounded like a shower of rain when she moved, and her nails bit into me, hard.

I said between my teeth, "What music do you want, kid?"

"My name's Laura—Laura Darrow." Her eyes were very big and very purple. "Do you have Enhali's *Primitive Venus*?"

Not more than half a dozen dancers in the System can do justice to that collection of tribal music. Some of it's subhuman and so savage it scares you. We use it for mood music, to draw the crowd.

I started to protest, but Sindi smiled and tinkled her head back. "Of course. Put it on, Jade."

I shrugged and went in and fiddled with the juke box. When I came out, Laura Darrow was up on the stage and we had an audience. Sindi must have passed the high sign. I shoved my way through a bunch of Venusian lizard-men and sat down. There were three or four little moth-people from Phobos roosting up on the braces so their delicate wings wouldn't get damaged in the crush.

The music started. Laura kicked off her shoes and danced.

I don't think I breathed all the time she was on the stage. I don't remember anyone else breathing, either. We just sat and stared, sweating with nervous ecstasy, shivering occasionally, with the music beating and crying and surging over us.

The girl wasn't human. She was sunlight, quicksilver, a leaf riding the wind—but nothing human, nothing tied down to muscles and gravity and flesh. She was—oh, hell, there aren't any words. She was the music.

When she was through, we sat there a long time, perfectly still. Then the Venusians, human and half-human, let go a yell and the audience came to and tore up the seats.

In the middle of it, Sindi looked at me with deadly green eyes and said, "I suppose she's hired."

"Yeah. But it doesn't have anything to do with you, baby."

"Listen, Jade. This suitcase outfit isn't big enough for two of us. Besides, she's got you hooked, and she can have you."

"She hasn't got me hooked. Anyway, so what? You don't own me."

"No. And you don't own me, either."

"I got a contract."

She told me what I could do with my contract.

I yelled, "What do you want me to do, throw her out on her ear? With that talent?"

"Talent!" snarled Sindi. "She's not talented. She's a freak."

"Just like a dame. Why can't you be a good loser?"

She explained why. A lot of it didn't make sense, and none of it was printable. Presently she went out, leaving me sore and a little uneasy. We had quite a few Martians with the outfit. She could make trouble.

Oh, hell! Just another dame sore because she was outclassed. Artistic temperament, plus jealousy. So what? Let her try something. I could handle it. I'd handled people before.

I jammed my way up to the stage. Laura was being mobbed. She looked scared—some of the halflings are enough to give a tough guy nightmares— and she was crying.

I said, "Relax, honey. You're in." I knew that Sindi was telling the truth. I was hooked. I was so hooked it scared me, but I wouldn't have wiggled off if I could.

She sagged down in my arms and said, "Please, I'm hungry."

I half carried her out, with the moth-people fluttering their gorgeous wings around our heads and praising her in their soft, furry little voices.

I fed her in my own quarters. She shuddered when I poured her coffee and refused it, saying she didn't think she'd ever enjoy it again. She took tea instead. She was hungry, all right. I thought she'd never stop eating.

Finally I said, "The pay's forty credits, and found."

She nodded.

I said gently, "You can tell me. What's wrong?"

She gave me a wide, purple stare. "What do you mean?"

"A dancer like you could write her own ticket anywhere, and not for the kind of peanuts I can pay you. You're in a jam."

She looked at the table and locked her fingers together. Their long pink nails glistened.

She whispered, "It isn't anything bad. Just a—a passport difficulty. I told you I was born in space. The records got lost somehow and living the way we did—well, I had to come to Earth in a hurry, and I couldn't prove my citizenship, so I came without it. Now I can't get back to Venus where my money is, and I can't stay here. That's why I wanted so badly to get a job with you. You're going out, and you can take me."

I knew how to do that, all right. I said, "You must have had a big reason to take the risk you did. If you're caught it means the Luna cell-blocks for a long time before they deport you."

She shivered. "It was a personal matter. It delayed me a while. I—was too late."

I said, "Sure. I'm sorry." I took her to her tent, left her there, and went out to get the show running, cursing Sindi. I stopped cursing and stared when I passed the cooch tent. She was there, and giving.

She stuck out her tongue at me and I went on.

That evening I hired the punk, just a scrawny kid with a white face, who said he was hungry and needed work. I gave him to Tiny, to help out in the brute top.

II. Voice of Terror

We played in luck that week. Some gilded darling of the screen showed up with somebody else's husband who wasn't quite divorced yet, and we got a lot of free publicity in the papers and over the air. Laura went on the second night and brought down the house. We turned 'em away for the first time in history. The only thing that worried me was Sindi. She wouldn't speak to me, only smile at me along her green eyes as though she knew a lot she wasn't telling and not any of it nice. I tried to keep an eye on her, just in case.

For five days I walked a tightrope between heaven and hell. Everybody on the pitch knew I was a dead duck where Laura was concerned. I suppose they got a good laugh out of it—me, Jade Greene the carny boss, knocked softer than a cup custard by a girl young enough to be my daughter, a girl from a good family, a girl with talent that put her so far beyond my lousy dog-and-pony show. . . .

I knew all that. It didn't do any good. I couldn't keep away from her. She was so little and lovely; she walked like music; her purple eyes had a tilt to them that kept you looking, and her mouth—

I kissed it on the fifth night, out back of the cooch tent when the show was over. It was dark there; we were all alone, and the faint spicy breath of her came to me through the thin salt fog. I kissed her.

Her mouth answered mine. Then she wrenched away, suddenly, with a queer fury. I let her go. She was shuddering, and breathing hard.

I said, "I'm sorry."

"It isn't that. Oh, Jade, I—" She stopped. I could hear the breath sobbing in her throat. Then she turned and ran away, and the sound of her weeping came back to me through the dark.

I went to my quarters and got out a bottle. After the first shot, I just sat staring at it with my head in my hands. I haven't any idea how long I sat there. It seemed like forever. I only know that the pitch was dark, sound asleep under a pall of fog, when Sindi screamed.

I didn't know it was Sindi then. The scream didn't have any personality. It was the voice of terror and final pain, and it was far beyond anything human.

I got my gun out of the table drawer. I remember my palm was slippery with cold sweat. I went outside, catching up the big flashlight kept for emergencies near the tent flap. It was very dark out there, very still, and yet not quiet. There was something behind the darkness and the silence, hiding in them, breathing softly and waiting.

The pitch began to wake up. The stir and rustle spread out from the scream like ripples from a stone, and over in the brute top a Martian sand-cat began to wail, thin and feral, like an echo of death.

I went along between the tents, walking fast and silent. I felt sick, and the skin of my back twitched; my face began to ache from being drawn tight. The torch beam shook a little in my hand.

I found her back of the cooch tent, not far from where I'd kissed Laura. She was lying on her face, huddled up, like a brown island in a red sea. The little bells were still in her ears.

I walked in her blood and knelt down in it and put my hand on her shoulder. I thought she was dead, but the bells tinkled faintly, like something far away on another star. I tried to turn her over.

She gasped, "Don't." It wasn't a voice. It was hardly a breath, but I could hear it. I can still hear it. I took my hand away.

"Sindi—"

A little wash of sound from the bells, like rain far off—"You fool," she whispered. "The stage, Jade, the stage—"

She stopped. The croaker came from somewhere behind me and knocked me out of the way, but I knew it was no use. I knew Sindi had stopped for good.

Humans and halflings were jammed in all round, staring, whispering, some of them screaming a little. The brute top had gone crazy. They smelt blood and death on the night wind, and they wanted to be free and a part of it.

"Claws," the croaker said. "Something clawed her. Her throat—"

I said, "Yeah. Shut up." I turned around. The punk was standing there, the white-faced kid, staring at Sindi's body with eyes glistening like shiny brown marbles.

"You," I said. "Go back to Tiny and tell him to make sure all his kids are there. . . . All the roustabouts and every man that can handle a gun or a tent stake, get armed as fast as you can and stand by. . . . Mike, take whatever you need and guard the gate. Don't let anybody or anything in or out without permission from me, in person. Everybody else get inside somewhere and stay there. I'm going to call the police.''

The punk was still there, looking from Sindi's body to me and around the circle of faces. I yelled at him. He went away then, fast. The crowd started to break up.

Laura Darrow came out of it and took my arm.

She had on a dark blue dressing-gown and her hair was loose around her face. She had the dewy look of being freshly washed, and she breathed perfume. I shook her off. "Look out," I said. "I'm all—blood."

I could feel it on my shoes, soaking through the thin stuff of my trouser legs. My stomach rose up under my throat. I closed my eyes and held it down, and all the time Laura's voice was soothing me. She hadn't let go of my arm. I could feel her fingers. They were cold, and too tight. Even then, I loved her so much I ached with it.

"Jade," she said. "Jade, darling. Please—I'm so frightened."

That helped. I put my arm around her and we started back toward my place and the phone. Nobody had thought to put the big lights on yet, and my torchbeam cut a fuzzy tunnel through the fog.

"I couldn't sleep very well," Laura said suddenly. "I was lying in my tent thinking, and a little while before she screamed I thought I heard something— something like a big cat, padding."

The thing that had been in the back of my mind came out yelling. I hadn't seen Laska in the crowd around Sindi. If Laska had got hold of some coffee behind the cook's back . . .

I said, "You were probably mistaken."

"No. Jade."

"Yeah?" It was dark between the tents. I wished somebody would turn the lights on. I wished I hadn't forgotten to tell them to. I wished they'd shut up their over-all obbligato of gabbling, so I could hear . . .

"Jade. I couldn't sleep because I was thinking—"

Then she screamed.

He came out of a dark tunnel between two storage tents. He was going almost on all fours, his head flattened forward, his hands held in a little to his belly. His claws were out. They were wet and red, and his hands were wet and red, and his feet. His yellow-green eyes had a crazy shine to them, the pupils slitted against the light. His lips were peeled back from his teeth. They glittered, and there was froth between them—Laska, coked to hell and gone!

He didn't say anything. He made noises, but they weren't speech and they weren't sane. They weren't anything but horrible. He sprang.

I pushed Laura behind me. I could see the marks his claws made in the dirt, and the ridging of his muscles with the jump. I brought up my gun and fired, three shots.

The heavy slugs nearly tore him in two, but they didn't stop him. He let go a mad animal scream and hit me, slashing. I went part way down, firing again, but Laska was still going. His hind feet clawed into my hip and thigh, using me as something to push off from. He wanted the girl.

She had backed off, yelling bloody murder. I could hear feet running, a lot of them, and people shouting. The lights came on. I twisted around and got Laska by the mane of fur on his backbone and then by the scruff. He was suddenly a very heavy weight. I think he was dead when I put the fifth bullet through his skull.

I let him drop.

I said, "Laura, are you all right?" I saw her brown hair and her big purple eyes like dark stars in her white face. She was saying something, but I couldn't hear what it was. I said, "You ought to faint, or something," and laughed.

But it was me, Jade Greene, that did the fainting.

I came out of it too soon. The croaker was still working on my leg. I called him everything I could think of in every language I knew, out of the half of my mouth that wasn't taped shut. He was a heavy man, with a belly and a dirty chin.

He laughed and said, "You'll live. That critter damn near took half your face off, but with your style of beauty it won't matter much. Just take it easy a while until you make some more blood."

I said, "The hell with that. I got work to do." After a while he gave in and helped me get dressed. The holes in my leg weren't too deep, and the face wasn't working anyway. I poured some Scotch in to help out the blood shortage, and managed to get over to the office.

I walked pretty well.

That was largely because Laura let me lean on her. She'd waited outside my tent all that time. There were drops of fog caught in her hair. She cried a little and laughed a little and told me how wonderful I was, and helped me along with her small vibrant self. Pretty soon I began to feel like a kid waking up from a nightmare into a room full of sunshine.

The law had arrived when we got to the office. There wasn't any trouble: Sindi's torn body and the crazy cat-man added up, and the Venusian cook put the lid on it. He always took a thermos of coffee to bed with him, so he'd have it first thing when he woke up—Venusian coffee, with enough caffeine in it to stand an Earthman on his head. Enough to finish off a Callistan cat-man. Somebody had swiped it when he wasn't looking. They found the thermos in Laska's quarters.

The show went on. Mobs came to gawk at the place where the killing had happened. I took it easy for one day, lolling in a shiny golden cloud with Laura holding my head.

Along about sundown she said, "I'll have to get ready for the show."

"Yeah. Saturday's a big night. Tomorrow we tear down, and then Monday we head out for Venus. You'll feel happier then?"

"Yes. I'll feel safe." She put her head down over mine. Her hair was like warm silk. I put my hands up on her throat. It was firm and alive and it made my hands burn.

She whispered, "Jade, I—" A big hot tear splashed down on my face, and then she was gone.

I lay still, hot and shivering like a man with swamp-fever, thinking, *Maybe . . .*

Maybe Laura wouldn't leave the show when we got to Venus. Maybe I could make her not want to. Maybe it wasn't too late for dreaming, a dream that John Damien Greene had never had, sitting in a puddle of water at the end of a jetty stringer and fishing for perch.

Crazy, getting ideas like that about a girl like Laura. Crazy like cutting your own throat. Oh, hell. A man never really grows up, not past believing that maybe miracles still happen.

It was nice dreaming for a while.

It was a nice night, too, full of stars and the clean, cool ocean breeze, when Tiny came over to tell me they'd found the punk dead in a pile of straw with his throat torn out, and the Martian sand-cat loose.

III. Carnival of Death

We jammed our way through the mob on the midway. Lots of people having fun, lots of kids yelling and getting sick on Mercurian *jitsi*-beans and bottled Venusian fruit juice. Nobody knew about the killing. Tiny had had the cat rounded up and caged before it could get outside the brute top, which had not yet opened for business.

The punk was dead, all right—dead as Sindi, and in the same way. His twisted face was not much whiter than I remembered it, the closed eyelids faintly blue. He lay almost under the sand-cat's cage.

The cat paced, jittery and snarling. There was blood on all its six paws. The cages and pens and pressure tanks seethed nastily all around me, held down and quiet by Tiny's wranglers.

I said, "What happened?"

Tiny lifted his gargantuan shoulders. "Dunno. Everything quiet. Even no yell, like Sindi. Punk kid all lonesome over here behind cages. Nobody see; nobody hear. Only Mars kitty waltz out on main aisle, scare hell out of everybody. We catch, and then find punk, like you see."

I turned around wearily. "Call the cops again and report the accident. Keep the rubes out of here until they pick up the body." I shivered. I'm superstitious, like all carnies.

They come in threes—always in threes. Sindi, the punk—what next?

Tiny sighed. "Poor punk. So peaceful, like sleeper with shuteye."

"Yeah." I started away. I limped six paces and stopped and limped back again.

I said, "That's funny. Guys that die violent aren't tidy about their eyes, except in the movies."

I leaned over. I didn't quite know why, then. I do now. You can't beat that three-time jinx. One way or another, it gets you.

I pushed back one thin, waxy eyelid. After a while I pushed back the other. Tiny breathed heavily over my shoulder. Neither of us said anything. The animals whimpered and yawned and paced.

I closed his eyes again and went through his pockets. I didn't find what I was looking for. I got up very slowly, like an old man. I felt like an old man. I felt dead, deader than the white-faced kid.

I said, "His eyes were brown."

Tiny stared at me. He started to speak, but I stopped him. "Call Homicide, Tiny. Put a guard on the body. And send men with guns. . . ."

I told him where to send them. Then I went back across the midway.

A couple of Europans with wiry little bodies and a twenty-foot wing-spread were doing Immelmanns over the geek top, and on the bally stand in front of it two guys with six hands apiece and four eyes on movable stalks were juggling. Laura was out in front of the cooch tent, giving the rubes a come-on.

I went around behind the tent, around where I'd kissed her, around where Sindi had died with the bells in her ears like a wash of distant rain.

I lifted up the flap and went in.

The tent was empty except for the man that tends the juke box. He put out his cigarette in a hurry and said, "Hi, Boss," as though that would make me forget he'd been smoking. I didn't give a damn if he set the place on fire with a blowtorch. The air had the warm, musty smell that tents have. Enhali's *Primitive Venus* was crying out of the juke box with a rhythm like thrown spears.

I pulled the stage master, and then the whites. They glared on the bare boards, naked as death and just as yielding.

I stood there a long time.

After a while the man behind me said uneasily, "Boss, what—"

"Shut up. I'm listening."

Little bells, and a voice that was pain made vocal.

"Go out front," I said. "Send Laura Darrow in here. Then tell the rubes there won't be a show here tonight."

I heard his breath suck in, and then catch. He went away down the aisle.

I got a cigarette out and lit it very carefully, broke the match in two and stepped on it. Then I turned around.

Laura came down the aisle. Her gold-brown hair was caught in a web of brilliants. She wore a sheath-tight thing of sea-green metal scales, with a short skirt swirling around her white thighs, and sandals of the shiny scales with no heels to them. She moved with the music, part of it, wild with it, a way I'd never seen a woman move before.

She was beautiful. There aren't any words. She was—beauty.

She stopped. She looked at my face and I could see the quivering tightness flow up across her white skin, up her throat and over her mouth, and catch her breath and hold it. The music wailed and throbbed on the still, warm air.

I said, "Take off your shoes, Laura. Take off your shoes and dance."

She moved then, still with the beat of the savage drums, but not thinking about it. She drew in upon herself, a shrinking and tightening of muscles, a preparation.

She said, "You know."

I nodded. "You shouldn't have closed his eyes. I might never have noticed. I might never have remembered that the kid had brown eyes. He was just a punk. Nobody paid much attention. He might just as well have had purple eyes—like yours."

"He stole them from me." Her voice came sharp under the music. It had a hiss and a wail in it I'd never heard before, and the accent was harsher. "While I was in your tent, Jade. I found out when I went to dress. He was an I-man. I found his badge inside his clothes and took it."

Purple eyes looking at me—purple eyes as phony as the eyes on the dead boy. Contact lenses painted purple to hide what was underneath.

"Too bad you carried an extra pair, Laura, in case of breakage."

"He put them in his eyes, so he couldn't lose them or break them or have them stolen, until he could report. He threw away the little suction cup. I couldn't find it. I couldn't get the shells off his eyeballs. All I could do was close his eyes and hope—"

"And let the sand-cat out of his cage to walk through the blood." My voice was coming out all by itself. It hurt. The words felt as though they had fishhooks on them, but I couldn't stop saying them.

"You almost got by with it, Laura. Just like you got by with Sindi. She got in your way, didn't she? She was jealous, and she was a dancer. She knew that no true human could dance like you dance. She said so. She said you were a freak."

That word hit her like my fist. She showed me her teeth, white, even teeth that I knew now were as phony as her eyes. I didn't want to see her change, but I couldn't stop looking, couldn't stop.

I said, "Sindi gave you away before you died, only I was too dumb to know what she meant. She said, 'The stage.' "

I think we both looked, down at the stark boards under the stark lights, looked at the scratches on them where Laura had danced barefoot that first time and left the marks of her claws on the wood.

She nodded, a slow, feral weaving of the head.

"Sindi was too curious. She searched my tent. She found nothing, but she left her scent, just as the young man did today. I followed her back here in the dark and saw her looking at the stage by the light of matches. I can move in the dark, Jade, very quickly and quietly. The cook tent is only a few yards back of this one, and Laska's quarters close beyond that. I smelt the cook's coffee. It was easy for me to steal it and slip it through the tent flap by Laska's cot, and wake him with the touch of my claws on his face. I knew he couldn't help drinking it. I was back here before Sindi came out of the tent to go and tell you what she'd found."

She made a soft purring sound under the wicked music.

"Laska smelt the blood and walked in it, as I meant him to do. I thought he'd die before he found us—or me—because I knew he'd find my scent in the air of his quarters and know who it was, and what it was. My perfume had worn too thin by then to hide it from his nose."

I felt the sullen pain of the claw marks on my face and leg. Laska, crazy with caffeine and dying with it, knowing he was dying and wanting with all the strength of his drugged brain to get at the creature who had killed him. He'd wanted Laura that night, not me. I was just something to claw out of the way.

I wished I hadn't stopped him.

I said, "Why? All you wanted was Laska. Why didn't you kill him?"

The shining claws flexed out of her fingertips, under the phony plastic nails—very sharp, very hungry.

She said huskily, "My tribe sent me to avenge its honor. I have been trained carefully. There are others like me, tracking down the renegades, the dope-ridden creatures like Laska who sell our race for human money. He was not to die quickly. He was not to die without knowing. He was not to die without being given the chance to redeem himself by dying bravely.

"But I was not to be caught. I cost my people time and effort, and I am not easily replaced. I have killed seven renegades, Jade. I was to escape. So I wanted to wait until we were out in space."

She stopped. The music hammered in my temples, and inside I was dead and dried up and crumbled away.

I said, "What would you have done in space?"

I knew the answer. She gave it to me, very simply, very quietly.

"I would have destroyed your whole filthy carnival by means of a little bomb in the jet timers, and gone away in one of the lifeboats."

I nodded. My head felt as heavy as Mount Whitney, and as lifeless. "But Sindi didn't give you time. Your life came first. And if it hadn't been for the punk . . ."

No, not just a punk—an Immigration man. Somewhere Laura had slipped, or else her luck was just out. A white-faced youngster, doing his job quietly in the shadows, and dying without a cry. I started to climb down off the stage.

She backed off. The music screamed and stopped, leaving a silence like the feel of a suddenly stopped heart.

Laura whispered, "Jade, will you believe something if I tell you?

"I love you, Jade." She was still backing off down the aisle, not making any sound. "I deserve to die for that. I'm going to die. I think you're going to kill me, Jade. But when you do, remember that those tears I shed—were real."

She turned and ran, out onto the midway. I was close. I caught her hair. It came free, leaving me standing alone just inside the tent, staring stupidly.

I had men out there, waiting. I thought she couldn't get through. But she did. She went like a wisp of cloud on a gale, using the rubes as a shield. We didn't want a panic. We let her go, and we lost her.

I say we let her go. We couldn't help it. She wasn't bothering about being human then. She was all cat, just a noiseless blur of speed. We couldn't shoot without hurting people, and our human muscles were too slow to follow her.

I knew Tiny had men at the gates and all around the pitch, anywhere that she could possibly get out. I wasn't worried. She was caught, and pretty soon the police would come. We'd have to be careful, careful as all hell not to start one of those hideous, trampling panics that can wreck a pitch in a matter of minutes.

All we had to do was watch until the show was over and the rubes were gone. Guard the gates and keep her in, and then round her up. She was caught. She couldn't get away. Laura Darrow . . .

I wondered what her name was, back on Callisto. I wondered what she looked like when she let the cross-shaped mane grow thick along her back and shoulders. I wondered what color her fur was. I wondered why I had ever been born.

I went back to my place and got my gun and then went out into the crowd again. The show was in full swing; lots of people having fun, lots of kids crazy with excitement; lights and laughter and music—and a guy out in front of the brute top splitting his throat telling the crowd that something was wrong with the lighting system and it would be a while before they could see the animals.

A while before the cops would have got what they wanted and cleaned up the mess under the sand-cat's cage.

The squad cars would be coming in a few minutes. There wasn't anything to do but wait. She was caught. She couldn't escape.

The one thing we didn't think about was that she wouldn't try to.

A Mercurian cave-tiger screamed. The Ionian quags took it up in their deep, rusty voices, and then the others chimed in, whistling, roaring, squealing, shrieking, and doing things there aren't any names for. I stopped, and gradually everybody on the pitch stopped and listened.

For a long moment you could hear the silence along the midway and in the tents. People not breathing, people with a sudden glassy shine of fear in their eyes and a cold tightening of the skin that comes from way back beyond humanity. Then the muttering started, low and uneasy, the prelude to panic.

I fought my way to the nearest bally stand and climbed on it. There were shots, sounding small and futile under the brute howl.

I yelled, "Hey, everybody! Listen! There's nothing wrong. One of the cats is sick, that's all. There's nothing wrong. Enjoy yourselves."

I wanted to tell them to get the hell out, but I knew they'd kill themselves if they started. Somebody started music going again, loud and silly. It cracked the icy lid that was tightening down. People began to relax and laugh nervously and talk too loudly. I got down and ran for the brute top.

Tiny met me at the tent flap. His face was just a white blur. I grabbed him and said, "For God's sake, can't you keep them quiet?"

"She's in there, Boss—like shadow. No hear, no see. One man dead. She let my kids out. She—"

More shots from inside, and a brute scream of pain. Tiny groaned.

"My kids! No lights, Boss. She wreck 'em."

I said, "Keep 'em inside. Get lights from somewhere. There's a blizzard brewing on the pitch. If that mob gets started."

I went inside. There were torchbeams spearing the dark, men sweating and cursing, a smell of hot, wild bodies, and the sweetness of fresh blood.

Somebody poked his head inside the flap and yelled, "The cops are here!"

I yelled back, "Tell 'em to clear the grounds if they can, without starting trouble. Tell—"

Somebody screamed. There was a sudden spangle of lights in the high darkness, balls of crimson and green and vicious yellow tumbling toward us, spots of death no bigger than your fist—the stinging fireflies of Ganymede. Laura had opened their case.

We scattered, fighting the fireflies. Somewhere a cage went over with a crash. Bodies thrashed, and feet padded on the packed earth—and somewhere above the noise was a voice that was sweet and silky and wild, crying out to the beasts and being answered.

I knew then why the brute top went crazy when Laska was around. It was kinship, not fear. She talked to them, and they understood.

I called her name.

Her voice came down to me out of the hot dark, human and painful with tears. "Jade! Jade, get out; go somewhere safe!"

"Laura, don't do this! For God's sake—"

"Your God, or mine? Our God forbids us to know humans except to kill. How, if we kept men as you kept Laska?"

"Laura!"

"Get out! I'm going to kill as many as I can before I'm taken. I'm turning the animals loose on the pitch. Go somewhere safe!"

I fired at the sound of her voice.

She said softly, "Not yet, Jade. Maybe not at all."

I beat off a bunch of fireflies hunting for me with their poisoned stings. Cage doors banged open. Wild throats coughed and roared, and suddenly the whole side wall of the tent fell down, cut free at the top, and there wasn't any way to keep the beasts inside any more.

A long mob scream went up from outside, and the panic was on.

I could hear Tiny bellowing, sending his men out with ropes and nets and guns. Some huge, squealing thing blundered around in the dark, went past me close enough to touch, and charged through the front opening, bringing part of the top down. I was close enough behind it so that I got free.

I climbed up on the remains of the bally stand. There was plenty of light outside—blue-white, glaring light, to show me the packed mass of people screaming and swaying between the tents, trampling toward the exits, to show me a horde of creatures sweeping down on them, caged beasts free to kill, and led by a lithe and leaping figure in shining green.

I couldn't see her clearly. Perhaps I didn't want to. Even then she moved in beauty, like wild music—and she had a tail.

I never saw a worse panic, not even the time a bunch of Nahali swamp-edgers clemmed our pitch when I was a pony punk with Triangle.

The morgues were going to be full that night.

Tiny's men were between the bulk of the mob and the animals. The beasts had had to come around from the far side of the tent, giving them barely time to get set. They gave the critters all they had, but it wasn't enough.

Laura was leading them. I heard her voice crying out above all the din. The animals scattered off sideways between the tents. One Martian sand-cat was dead, one quag kicking its life out, and that was all. They hadn't touched Laura, and she was gone.

I fought back, away from the mob, back into a temporarily empty space behind a tent. I got out my whistle and blew it, the rallying call. A snake-headed kibi from Titan sneaked up and tried to rip me open with its double-pointed tail. I fed it three soft-nosed slugs, and then there were half a dozen little moth-people bouncing in the air over my head, squeaking with fear and shining their great eyes at me.

I told them what I wanted. While I was yelling, the Europans swooped in on their wide wings and listened.

I said finally, "Did any of you see which way *she* went?"

"That way." One of the mothlings pointed back across the midway. I called two of the Europans. The mothlings went tumbling away to spread my orders, and the bird-men picked me up and carried me across, over the crowd.

The animals were nagging at their flanks, pulling them down in a kind of mad ecstasy. There was a thin salt fog, and blood on the night wind, and the cage doors were open at last.

They set me down and went to do what I told them. I went alone among the swaying tents.

All this hadn't taken five minutes. Things like that move fast. By the time the Europans were out of sight the mothlings were back, spotting prowling beasts and rolling above them in the air to guide men to them—men and geeks.

Geeks with armor-plated backs and six arms, carrying tear-gas guns and nets; lizard-men, fast and powerful, armed with their own teeth and claws and whatever they could pick up; spider-people, spinning sticky lassos out of their own bodies; the Europans, dive-bombing the quags with tear gas.

The geeks saved the day for us. They saved lives, and the reputation of their kind, and the carnival. Without them, God only knows how many would have died on the pitch. I saw the mothlings dive into the thick of the mob and pick up fallen children and carry them to safety. Three of them died, doing that.

I went on, alone.

I was beyond the mob, beyond the fringe of animals. I was remembering Laura's voice saying, "Not yet, Jade. Maybe not at all." I was thinking of the walls being down and all California free outside. I was hearing the mob yell and the crash of broken tents, and the screams of people dying—my people, human people, with the claws bred out of them.

I was thinking—

Guns slamming and brute throats shrieking, wings beating fast against the hot hard glare, feet pounding on packed earth. I walked in silence, a private silence built around me like a shell. . . .

Four big cats slunk out of the shadows by the tent. There was enough light left to show me their eyes and their teeth, and the hungry licking of their tongues.

Laura's voice came through the canvas, tremulous but no softer nor more yielding than the blue barrel of my gun.

"I'm going away, Jade. At first I didn't think there was any way, but there is. Don't try to stop me. Please don't try."

I could have gone and tried to find a cop. I could have called men or half-men from their jobs to help me. I didn't. I don't know that I could have made anybody hear me, and anyway they had enough to do. This was my job.

My job, my carnival, my heart.

I walked toward the tent flap, watching the cats.

They slunk a little aside, belly down, making hoarse, whimpering noises. One was a six-legged Martian sand-cat, about the size of an Earthly leopard. Two were from Venus, the fierce white beauties of the high plateaus. The fourth was a Mercurian cave-cat, carrying its twenty-foot body on eight powerful legs and switching a tail that had bone barbs on it.

Laura called to them. I don't know whether she said words in their language, or whether her voice was just a bridge for thought transference, one cat brain to another. Anyway, they understood.

"Jade, they won't touch you if you go."

I fired.

One of the white Venusians took the slug between the eyes and dropped without a whimper. Its mate let go a sobbing shriek and came for me, with the other two beside it.

I snapped a shot at the Martian. It went over kicking, and I dived aside, rolling. The white Venusian shot over me, so close its hind claws tore my shirt. I put a slug in its belly. It just yowled and dug its toes in and came for me again. Out of the tail of my eye I saw the dying Martian tangle with the Mercurian, just because it happened to be the nearest moving object.

I kicked the Venusian in the face. The pain must have blinded it just enough to make its aim bad. On the second jump its forepaws came down on the outer edges of my deltoids, gashing them but not tearing them out. The cat's mouth was open clear to its stomach.

I should have died right then. I don't know why I didn't, except that I didn't care much if I did. It's the guys that want to live that get it, seems like. The ones that don't care go on forever.

I got a lot of hot bad breath in my face and five parallel gashes in back, where its hind feet hit me when I rolled up. I kicked it in the belly. Its teeth snapped a half inch short of my nose, and then I got my gun up under its jaw and that was that. I had four shots left.

I rolled the body off and turned. The Martian cat was dead. The Mercurian stood over it, watching me with its four pale, hot eyes, twitching its barbed tail.

Laura stood watching us.

She looked just like she had the first time I saw her. Soft gold-brown hair and purple eyes with a little tilt to them, and a soft pink mouth. She was wearing the bronze metal-cloth dress and the bronze slippers, and there was still nothing wrong with the way she was put together. She glinted dully in the dim light, warm bronze glints.

She was crying, but there was no softness in her tears.

The cat flicked its eyes at her and made a nervous, eager whine. She spoke to it, and it sank to its belly, not wanting to.

Laura said, "I'm going, Jade."

"No."

I raised my gun hand. The big cat rose with it. She was beyond the cat. I could shoot the cat, but a Mercurian lives a long time after it's shot.

"Throw down your gun, Jade, and let me go."

I didn't care if the cat killed me. I didn't care if Death took me off piggyback right then. I suppose I was crazy. Maybe I was just numb. I don't know. I was looking at Laura, and choking on my own heart.

I said, "No."

Just a whisper of sound in her throat, and the cat sprang. It reared up on its four hind feet and clawed at me with its four front ones. Only I wasn't where it thought I was. I knew it was going to jump and I faded—not far, I'm no superman—just far enough so its claws raked me without gutting me. It snapped its head down to bite.

I slammed it hard across the nose with my gun. It hurt, enough to make it wince, enough to fuddle it just for a split second. I jammed the muzzle into its nearest eye and fired.

Laura was going off between the tents, fast, with her head down, just a pretty girl, mingling with the mob streaming off the pitch. Who'd notice her, except maybe to whistle?

I didn't have time to get away. I dropped down flat on my belly and let the cat fall on top of me. I only wanted to live a couple of seconds longer. After that, the hell with it!

The cat was doing a lot of screaming and thrashing. I was between two sets of legs. The paws came close enough to touch me, clawing up the dirt. I huddled up small, hoping it wouldn't notice me there under its belly. Everything seemed to be happening very slowly, with a cold precision. I steadied my right hand on my left wrist.

I shot Laura three times, carefully, between the shoulders.

The cat stopped thrashing. Its weight crushed me. I knew it was dead. I knew I'd done something that even experienced hunters don't do in nine cases out of ten. My first bullet had found the way into the cat's little brain and killed it.

It wasn't going to kill me. I pulled myself out from under it. The pitch was almost quiet now, the mob gone, the animals mostly under control. I kicked the dead cat. It had died too soon.

My gun was empty. I remember I clicked the hammer twice. I got more bullets out of my pocket, but my fingers wouldn't hold them and I couldn't see to load. I threw the gun away.

I walked away in the thin, cold fog, and down toward the distant beat of the sea.

LET THERE BE LIGHT

BY ROBERT A. HEINLEIN
(Writing as Lyle Monroe)

In one of his books on musicology, Leonard Bernstein spends a lot of words trying to define just what it is about Ludwig van Beethoven that made him not only the greatest of symphonic composers, but the one who defines greatness in that field. It isn't because of his orchestration, Bernstein muses. Others did that better. Others invented better tunes. Others dared more exciting new harmonies. Others did everything one can think of better than Beethoven. Then what was it? Only one thing, Bernstein decides. Better than any other composer who ever lived, Beethoven always knew exactly what the next note should be.

I have precisely that feeling about Heinlein. I've read every word of science fiction the man ever wrote, and yet it is hard to say just what it is that makes it so great. Others invented more marvelous future beings, had a sharper ear for the sound of the English language, were more plausible, more inventive, even more extrapolative. So what's Heinlein got, anyway?

I think I know. Heinlein is a Stradivarius.

You know that nobody has ever built a violin as fine as they built in Cremona, centuries ago. It isn't that tools, techniques, and materials have not improved. They have. The explanation is something else. I think it is that the Stradivarius so perfectly realized the capabilities of taut strings rubbed by a rosined bow that any variation from it seems lesser. Any variation from Heinlein seems lesser, too. He defines what is the best of science fiction.

When Heinlein heard that I wanted to include "Let There Be Light" in this volume, he protested that he'd written better. So he had. I even published better—The Moon Is a Harsh Mistress, for instance, which I think just about the best he ever wrote—but unfortunately, at a hundred thousand words, it's a trifle too large to include here. And anyway I liked "Let There Be Light" very much indeed when I first published it . . . and I still do!

* * *

58

Archibald Douglas, Sc.D., Ph.D., B.S., read the telegram with unconcealed annoyance.

ARRIVING CITY LATE TODAY STOP DESIRE CONFER-
ENCE COLD LIGHT YOUR LABORATORY TEN P.M. (SIGNED)
DR. M. L. MARTIN

He was, was he? He did, did he? What did he think this lab was—a hotel? And did Martin think that his time was at the disposal of any Joe Doakes who had the price of a telegram? He had framed in his mind an urbanely discouraging reply when he noticed that the message had been filed at a midwestern airport. Very well, let him arrive. Douglas had no intention of meeting him.

Nevertheless, his natural curiosity caused him to take down his copy of *Who's Who in Science,* and look up the offender. There it was. Martin, M.L., bio-chemist and ecologist, P.D.Q., X.Y.Z., N.R.A., C.I.O.—enough degrees for six men. Hmmm—Director Guggenheim Orinoco Fauna Survey; Author, *Co-Lateral Symbiosis of the Boll Weevil;* and so on, through three inches of fine print. The old boy seemed to be a heavyweight.

A little later Douglas surveyed himself in the mirror of the laboratory washroom. He took off a dirty laboratory smock, removed a comb from his vest pocket, and put a careful polish on his sleek black hair. An elaborately tailored checked jacket, a snap-brim hat, and he was ready for the street. He fingered the pale scar that stenciled the dark skin of one cheek. Not bad, he thought, in spite of the scar. If it weren't for the broken nose, he would look like George Raft.

The restaurant where he dined alone was only partly filled. It wouldn't become lively until after the theaters were out, but Douglas appreciated the hot swing band and the good food. Toward the end of his meal, a young woman walked past his table and sat down, facing him, one table away. He sized her up with care. Pretty fancy! Figure like a strip dancer, lots of corn-colored hair, nice complexion, and great big soft blue eyes. Rather dumb pan, but what could you expect?

He decided to invite her over for a drink. If things shaped up, Dr. Martin could go to the devil. He scribbled a note on the back of a menu, and signaled the waiter.

"Who is she, Leo? One of the entertainers?"

"No, M'sieur, I have not seen her before."

Douglas relaxed, and waited for the results. He knew the come-hither look when he saw it, and he was sure of the outcome. The girl read his note and glanced over at him with a little smile. He returned it with interest. She borrowed a pencil from the waiter, and wrote on the menu. Presently, Leo handed it to him.

"Sorry"—it read—"and thanks for the kind offer, but I am otherwise engaged."

Douglas paid his bill and returned to the laboratory.

*   *   *

His laboratory was located on the top floor of his father's factory. He left the outer door open and the elevator down in anticipation of Doctor Martin's arrival, then he busied himself by trying to locate the cause of an irritating vibration in his centrifuge. Just at ten o'clock he heard the whir of the elevator. He reached the outer door of his office just as his visitor arrived.

Facing him was the honey-colored babe he had tried to pick up in the restaurant.

He was immediately indignant. "How the hell did you get here? Follow me?"

She froze up at once. "I have an appointment with Doctor Douglas. Please tell him that I am here."

"The hell you have. What kind of a game is this?"

She controlled herself, but her face showed the effort. "I think Doctor Douglas is the best judge of that. Tell him I'm here—at once."

"You're looking at him. I'm Doctor Douglas."

"You! I don't believe it. You look more like a—a gangster."

"I am, nevertheless. Now cut out the clowning, sister, and tell me what the racket is. What's *your* name?"

"I am Doctor M. L. Martin."

He looked completely astounded, then bellowed his amusement. "No foolin'? You wouldn't kid your country cousin, would you? Come in, Doc, come in!"

She followed him, suspicious as a strange dog, ready to fight at any provocation. She accepted a chair, then addressed him again. "Are you really Doctor Douglas?"

He grinned at her. "In the flesh—and I can prove it! How about you? I still think this is some kind of a badger game."

She froze up again. "What do you want?—my birth certificate?"

"You probably murdered Dr. Martin in the elevator, and stuffed the old boy's body down the shaft."

She rose, gathered up her gloves and purse, and prepared to leave. "I came fifteen hundred miles for this meeting. I'm sorry I bothered. Good evening, Doctor Douglas."

He was instantly soothing. "Aw, don't get sore—I was just needling you. It simply tickled me that the distinguished Doctor Martin should look so much like Sally Rand. Now sit back down"—he gently disengaged her hands from her gloves—"and let me give you that drink you turned down earlier."

She hesitated, still determined to be angry, then her natural good nature came to his aid, and she relaxed. "OK, Butch."

"That's better. What'll it be; Scotch or Bourbon?"

"Make mine Bourbon—and not too much water."

By the time the drinks were fixed and cigarettes lighted, the tension was lifted. "Tell me," he began, "to what do I owe this visit? I don't know a damn thing about biology."

She blew a smoke ring and poked a carmine fingernail through it. "You remember that article you had in the April *Physical Review?* The one about cold light, and possible ways of achieving it?''

He nodded. *''Electroluminescence vs. Chemiluminescence:* not much in that to interest a biologist.''

''Nevertheless, I've been working on the same problem.''

''From what angle?''

''I've been trying to find out how a lightning bug does the trick. I saw some gaudy ones down in South America, and they got me to thinking.''

''Hmm—Maybe you got something. What have you found out?''

''Not much that wasn't already known. As you probably know, the firefly is an almost incredibly efficient source of light—at least ninety-six percent efficient. Now how efficient would you say the ordinary commercial tungsten-filament incandescent lamp is?''

''Not over two percent at the best.''

''That's fair enough. And a stupid little beetle does fifty times as well without turning a hair. We don't look so hot, do we?''

''Not very,'' he acknowledged, ''Go on about the bug.''

''Well, the firefly has in his tummy an active organic compound—very complex—called luciferin. When this oxidizes in the presence of a catalyst, luciferase, the entire energy of oxidation is converted into green light—no heat. Reduce it with hydrogen and it's ready to go again. I've learned how to do it in the laboratory.''

''The hell you have! Congratulations! You don't need me. I can close up shop.''

''Not so fast. It isn't commercially feasible; it takes too much gear to make it work; it's too messy; and I can't get an intense light. Now I came to see you to see if we might combine forces, pool our information, and work out something practical.''

Three weeks later at four in the morning, Doctor M. L. Martin—Mary Lou to her friends—was frying an egg over a bunsen burner. She was dressed in a long rubber shop apron over shorts and a sweater. Her long hair hung in loose ripples. The expanse of shapely leg made her look like something out of *La Vie Parisienne.*

She turned to where Douglas lay sprawled, a wretched, exhausted heap, in a big armchair. ''Listen, Ape, the percolator seems to have burnt out. Shall I make the coffee in the fractional distillator?''

''I thought you had snake venom in it.''

''So I have. I'll rinse it out.''

''Good God, woman! Don't you care what chances you take with yourself? —or with me?''

''Pooh—snake venom wouldn't hurt you even if you did drink it—unless that rotgut you drink had given you stomach ulcers. Soup's on!''

She chucked aside the apron, sat down, and crossed her legs. He automatically took in the display.

"Mary Lou, you lewd wench, why don't you wear some clothes around the shop? You arouse my romantic nature."

"Nuts. You haven't any. Let's get down to cases. Where do we stand?"

He ran a hand through his hair and chewed his lip. "Up against a stone wall, I think. Nothing we've tried so far seems to offer any promise."

"The problem seems to be essentially one of confining radiant energy to the visible band of frequency."

"You make it sound so simple, Bright Eyes."

"Stow the sarcasm. That is, nevertheless, where the loss comes in with ordinary electric light. The filament is white hot, maybe two percent of the power is turned into light, the rest goes into infra-red and ultra-violet."

"So beautiful. So true," he sighed.

Mary Lou stamped her feet in well-mimicked anger.

"Pay attention, you big ape. I know you're tired, but listen to mother. There should be some way of sharply tuning the wave length. How about the way they do it in radio?"

He perked up a little. "Wouldn't apply to the case. Even if you could manage to work out an inductance-capacitance circuit with a natural resonant frequency within the visual band, it would require too much gear for each lighting unit, and if it got out of tune it wouldn't give any light at all."

"Is that the only way frequency is controlled?"

"Yes—well, practically. Some transmitting stations, especially amateurs, use a specially cut quartz crystal that has a natural frequency of its own to control wave length."

"Then why can't we cut a crystal that would have a natural frequency in the octave of visible light?"

He sat up very straight. "Great Scott, kid! I think you've hit it."

He got up, and strode up and down, talking as he went.

"They use ordinary quartz crystal for the usual frequencies, and tourmaline for short wave broadcasting. The frequency of vibration depends directly on the way the crystal is cut. There is a simple formula—" He stopped, and took down a thick India-paper handbook. "Hmm—yes, here it is. For quartz, every millimeter of thickness of the crystal gives one hundred meters of wave length. Frequency is, of course, the reciprocal of wave length. Tourmaline has a similar formula for shorter wave lengths."

He continued to read. " 'These crystals have the property of flexing when electric charges are applied to them, and vice versa, show an electric charge when flexed. The period of flexure is an inherent quality of the crystal, depending on its geometrical proportions. Hooked into a radio transmitting circuit, such a crystal requires the circuit to operate at one, and only one, frequency, that of the crystal.' That's it, kid, that's it! Now if we can find a crystal that can be cut to vibrate at the frequency of visible light, we've got it—a way to turn electrical energy into light without heat losses!"

Mary Lou cluck-clucked admiringly. "Mama's *good* boy. Mama knew he could do it, if he would only *try*."

* * *

Nearly six months later Douglas invited his father up to the laboratory to see the results. He ushered the mild, silver-haired old gentleman into the sanctum sanctorum and waved to Mary Lou to draw the shades. Then he pointed to the ceiling.

"There it is, Dad—cold light—at a bare fraction of the cost of ordinary lighting."

The elder man looked up and saw, suspended from the ceiling a gray screen, about the size and shape of the top of a card table. Then Mary Lou threw a switch. The screen glowed brilliantly, but not dazzlingly, and exhibited a mother-of-pearl iridescence. The room was illuminated by strong white light without noticeable glare.

The young scientist grinned at his father, as pleased as a puppy who expects a pat. "How do you like it, Dad? One hundred candle power. That'd take about a hundred watts with ordinary bulbs, and we're doing it with two watts—half an ampere at four volts."

The old man blinked absent-mindedly at the display. "Very nice, son, very nice indeed. I'm pleased that you have perfected it."

"Look, Dad—do you know what that screen up there is made out of? Common, ordinary clay. It's an allotropic aluminum silicate; cheap and easy to make from any clay, or ore, that contains aluminum. I can use Bauxite, or cryolite, or most anything. You can gather up the raw materials with a steam shovel in any state in the union."

"Is your process all finished, son, and ready to be patented?"

"Why, yes, I think so, Dad."

"Then let's go into your office, and sit down. I've something I must discuss with you. Ask your young lady to come, too."

Young Douglas did as he was told, his mood subdued by his father's solemn manner. When they were seated, he spoke up.

"What's the trouble, Dad? Can I help?"

"I wish you could, Archie, but I'm afraid not. I'm going to have to ask you to close your laboratory."

The younger man took it without flinching. "Yes, Dad?"

"You know I've always been proud of your work, and since your mother passed on, my major purpose has been to supply you with the money and equipment you needed for your work."

"You've been very generous, Dad."

"I wanted to do it. But now a time has come when the factory won't support your research any longer. In fact, I may have to close the doors of the plant."

"As bad as that, Dad? I thought that orders had picked up this last quarter."

"We do have plenty of orders, but the business isn't making a profit on them. Do you remember I mentioned something to you about the public utilities bill that passed at the last session of the legislature?"

"I remember it vaguely, but I thought that the governor vetoed it."

"He did, but they passed it over his veto. It was as bold a case of corruption as this state has ever seen—the power lobbyists had both houses bought, body and soul." The old man's voice trembled with impotent anger.

"And just how does it affect us, Dad?"

"This bill pretended to equalize power rates according to circumstances. What it actually did was to permit the commission to discriminate among consumers as they saw fit. You know what that commission is—I've always been on the wrong side of the fence politically. Now they are forcing me to the wall with power rates that prevent me from competing."

"But good heavens, Dad—They can't do that. Get an injunction!"

"In this state, son?" His white eyebrows raised.

"No, I guess not." He got to his feet and started walking the floor.

His father shook his head. "The thing that really makes me bitter is that they can do this with power that actually belongs to the people. The federal government's program has made plenty of cheap power possible—the country should be rich from it—but these local pirates have gotten hold of it, and use it as a club to intimidate free citizens."

After the old gentleman had left, Mary Lou slipped over and laid a hand on Douglas's shoulder and looked down into his face.

"You poor boy!"

His face showed the upset he had concealed from his father. "Cripes, Mary Lou. Just when we were going good. But I mind it most for Dad."

"Yes, I know."

"And not a damn thing I can do about it. It's politics, and those pot-bellied racketeers own this state."

She looked disappointed and faintly scornful. "Why, Archie Douglas, you great big panty-waist. You aren't going to let those mugs get away with this without a fight, are you?"

He looked up at her dully. "No, of course not. I'll fight. But I know when I'm licked. This is way out of my field."

She flounced across the room. "I'm surprised at you. You've just made the greatest invention since the dynamo, and you talk about being licked."

"Your invention, you mean."

"Nuts! Who worked out the allotropic forms? Who blended them to get the whole spectrum? And besides, you aren't out of your field. What's the problem?—Power! They're squeezing you for power. You're a physicist. Dope out some way to get power without buying from them."

"What would you like? Atomic disintegration?"

"Be practical."

"I might stick a windmill on the roof."

"That's better—but still not good. Now get busy with that knot in the end of your spinal cord. I'll start some coffee. This is going to be another all-night job."

He grinned at her. "O.K., Carrie Nation. I'm coming."

She smiled happily at him. "That's the way to talk."

He rose and went over to her, slipped an arm about her waist, and kissed her. She relaxed to his embrace, but when their lips parted, she pushed him away.

"Archie, you remind me of the Al G. Barnes Circus; 'Every Act an Animal Act.' "

As the first light of dawn turned their faces pale and sickly, they were rigging two cold light screens face to face. Archie adjusted them until they were an inch apart.

"There now—practically all the light from the first screen should strike the second. Turn the power on the first screen, Sex Appeal."

She threw the switch. The first screen glowed with light, and shed its radiance on the second.

"Now to see if our beautiful theory is correct." He fastened a voltmeter across the terminals of the second screen and pressed the little black button in the base of the voltmeter. The needle sprang over to two volts.

She glanced anxiously over his shoulder. "How about it, guy?"

"It works! There's no doubt about. These screens work both ways. Put juice in 'em, out comes light. Put light in 'em, out comes electricity."

"What's the power loss, Archie?"

"Just a moment." He hooked in an ammeter, read it, and picked up his slide rule. "Let me see—Loss is about thirty percent. Most of that would be the leakage of light around the edges of the screens."

"The sun's coming up, Archie. Let's take screen number two up on the roof, and try it out in the sunlight."

Some minutes later they had the second screen and the electrical measuring instruments on the roof. Archie propped the screen up against a skylight so that it faced the rising sun, fastened the voltmeter across its terminals, and took a reading.

The needle sprang at once to the two volt mark.

Mary Lou jumped up and down. "It works!"

"Had to work," commented Archie. "If the light from another screen will make it pour out juice, then sunlight is bound to. Hook in the ammeter. Let's see how much power we get."

The ammeter showed eighteen-point-seven amperes.

Mary Lou worked out the result on the slide rule. "Eighteen-point-seven times two gives thirty-seven-point-four watts or about five hundredths of a horsepower. That doesn't seem like very much. I had hoped for more."

"That's as it should be, kid. We are using only the visible light rays. As a light source the sun is about fifteen percent efficient; the other eighty-five percent are infrared and ultra-violet. Gimme that slipstick." She passed him the slide rule. "The sun pours out about a horsepower and a half, or one and one eighth kilowatts on every square yard of surface on the earth that is faced directly towards the sun. Atmospheric absorption cuts that down about a third, even at high noon over the Sahara desert. That would give one horsepower per square yard. With the sun just rising we might not get more than one-third horsepower per square yard here. At fifteen percent efficiency that would be about five hundredths of a horsepower. The screen is a yard square; it gives five hundredths of a horsepower. It checks. Q.E.D.—What are you looking so glum about?''

''Well—I had hoped that we could get enough sunpower off the roof to run the factory, but if it takes twenty square yards to get one horsepower, it won't be enough.''

''Cheer up, Baby Face. We doped out a screen that would vibrate only in the band of visible light; I guess we can dope out another that will be atonic—one that will vibrate to any wave length. Then it will soak up any radiant energy that hits it, and give it up again as electrical power. With this roof surface we can store power for cloudy days and night shifts when we're not producing any.''

She blinked her big blue eyes at him. ''Archie, does your head ever ache?''

Twenty minutes later he was back at his desk, deep in the preliminary calculations, while Mary Lou threw together a scratch breakfast.

She interrupted his study to ask:

''Where'd'ja hide that bottle, Lug?''

He looked up and replied, ''It's immoral for little girls to drink in broad daylight.''

''Come out of the gutter, chum. I want to turn these hot-cakes into *crêpe suzettes,* using corn liquor instead of brandy.''

''Never mind the creative cookery, Dr. Martin. I'll take mine straight. I need my health to finish this job.''

She turned around and brandished the skillet at him. ''To hear is to obey, my lord. However, Archie, you are an overeducated Neanderthal, with no feeling for the higher things of life.''

''I won't argue the point, Blonde Stuff.—But take a gander at this. I've got the answer—a screen that vibrates all down the scale.''

''No foolin', Archie?''

''No fooling, kid. It was already implied in our earlier experiments, but we were so busy trying to build a screen that wouldn't vibrate at random, we missed it. I ran onto something else, too.''

''Tell mama!''

''We can build screens to radiate in the infrared just as easily as cold light screens. Get it? Heating units of any convenient size or shape, economical and with no high wattage or extreme temperatures to make 'em fire hazards or dangerous to children. As I see it, we can design these screens to, one—'' he ticked the points off on his fingers—''take power from the sun at nearly one hundred percent efficiency; two, deliver it as cold light; or three, as heat; or four, as electrical power. We can bank 'em in series to get any required voltage; we can bank in parallel to get any required current, and the power is absolutely free, except for installation costs."

She stood and watched him in silence for several seconds before speaking. "All that from trying to make a cheaper light. Come eat your breakfast, Steinmetz. You men can't do your work on mush."

They ate in silence, each busy with new thoughts. Finally Douglas spoke. "Mary Lou, do you realize just how big a thing this is?"

"I've been thinking about it."

"It's enormous. Look, the power that can be tapped is incredible. The sun pours over two hundred and thirty trillion horsepower onto the earth all the time and we use almost none of it."

"As much as that, Archie?"

"I didn't believe my own figures when I worked it out, so I looked it up in Moulton's *Astronomy*. Why, we could recover more than twenty thousand horsepower in any city block. Do you know what that means? Free power! Riches for everybody! It's the greatest thing since the steam engine." He stopped suddenly, noticing her glum face. "What's the matter, kid, am I wrong some place?"

She fiddled with her fork before replying. "No, Archie—you're not wrong. I've been thinking about it, too. Decentralized cities, labor-saving machinery for everybody, luxuries—it's all possible, but I've a feeling that we're staring right into a mess of trouble. Did you ever hear of 'Breakages, Ltd.'?"

"What is it, a salvage concern?"

"Not by a hell of a sight. You ought to read something besides the *Proceedings of the American Society of Physical Engineers*. George Bernard Shaw, for instance. It's from the preface of *Back to Methuselah,* and is a sardonic way of describing the combined power of corporate industry to resist any change that might threaten their dividends. You threaten the whole industrial set-up, son, and you're in danger right where you're sitting."

He pushed back his chair. "Oh, surely not. You're just tired and jumpy. Industry welcomes invention. Why, all the big corporations have their research departments with some of the best minds in the country working in them."

"Sure they do—and any bright young inventor can get a job with them. And then he's a kept man—the inventions belong to the corporation, and only those that fit into the pattern of the powers-that-be ever see light. The rest are shelved. Do you really think that they'd let a free-lance like you upset an investment of billions of dollars?"

He frowned, then relaxed and laughed. "Oh, forget it, kid, it's not that serious."

"That's what you think. Did you ever hear of celanese voile? Probably not. It's a synthetic dress material used in place of chiffon. But it wore better and was washable, and it only cost about forty cents a yard, while chiffon costs four times as much. You can't buy it any more.

"And take razor blades. My brother bought one about five years ago that never had to be re-sharpened. He's still using it, but if he ever loses it, he'll have to go back to the old kind. They took 'em off the market.

"Did you ever hear of guys who had found a better, cheaper fuel than gasoline? One showed up about four years ago and proved his claims—but he drowned a couple of weeks later in a swimming accident. I don't say that he was murdered, but it's damn funny that they never found his formula."

"And that reminds me—I saw a clipping from the *Los Angeles Illustrated Daily News* that was published early this year. A man bought a heavy standard-make car in San Diego, filled her up, and drove her to Los Angeles. He only used two gallons. Then he drove to Agua Caliente and back to San Diego, and only used three gallons. About a week later the sales company found him and bribed him to make an exchange. By mistake they had let him have a car that wasn't to be sold—one with a trick carburetor.

"Do you know any big heavy cars that get seventy miles to the gallon? You're not likely to—not while 'Breakages, Ltd.' rules the roost. But the story is absolutely kosher—you can look it up in the files.

"And of course, everybody knows that automobiles aren't built to wear, they're built to wear out, so you will buy a new one. They build 'em just as bad as the market will stand. Steamships take a worse beating than a car, and *they* last thirty years or more."

Douglas laughed it off. "Cut out the gloom, Sweetie Pie. You've got a persecution complex. Let's talk about something more cheerful—you and me, for instance. You make pretty good coffee. How about us taking out a license to live together?"

She ignored him.

"Well, why not. I'm young and healthy. You could do worse."

"Archie, did I ever tell you about the native chief that got a yen for me down in South America?"

"I don't think so. What about him?"

"He wanted me to marry him. He even offered to kill off his seventeen current wives and have them served up for the bridal feast."

"What's that got to do with my proposition?"

"I should have taken him up. A girl can't afford to turn down a good offer these days."

Archie walked up and down the laboratory, smoking furiously. Mary Lou perched on a workbench and watched him with troubled eyes. When he stopped to light another cigarette from the butt of the last, she bid for attention.

"Well, Master Mind, what now?"

He finished lighting his cigarette, burned himself, cursed in a monotone, then replied, "Oh, you were right, Cassandra. We're in more trouble than I ever knew existed. First when we build an electric runabout that gets its power from the sun while it's parked at the curb, somebody pours kerosene over it and burns it up. I didn't mind that so much—it was just a side issue. But when I refuse to sell out to them, they slap all those phony law suits on us, and tie us up like a kid with the colic."

"They haven't a legal leg to stand on."

"I know that, but they've got unlimited money and we haven't. They can run these suits out for months—maybe years—only we can't last that long."

"What's our next move? Do you keep this appointment?"

"I don't want to. They'll try to buy me off again, and probably threaten me, in a refined way. I'd tell 'em to go to hell, if it wasn't for Dad. Somebody's broken into his house twice now, and he's too old to stand that sort of thing."

"I suppose all this labor trouble in the plant worries him, too."

"Of course it does. And since it dates from the time we started manufacturing the screens on a commercial scale, I'm sure it's part of the frame-up. Dad never had any labor trouble before. He always ran a union shop and treated his men like members of his own family. I don't blame him for being nervous. I'm getting tired of being followed everywhere I go, myself. It makes me jumpy."

Mary Lou puffed out a cloud of smoke.

"I've been tailed the past couple of weeks."

"The hell you have! Mary Lou, that tears it. I'm going to settle this thing today."

"Going to sell out?"

"No." He walked over to his desk, opened a side drawer, took out a .38 automatic, and slipped it in his pocket. Mary Lou jumped down from the bench and ran to him. She put her hands on his shoulders, and looked up at him, fear in her face.

"Archie!"

He answered gently. "Yes, kid."

"Archie, don't do anything rash. If anything happened to you, you know damn well I couldn't get along with a normal man."

He patted her hair. "Those are the best words I've heard in weeks, kid."

Douglas returned about one P.M. Mary Lou met him at the elevator. "Well?"

"Same old song-and-dance. Nothing done in spite of my brave promises."

"Did they threaten you?"

"Not exactly. They asked me how much life insurance I carried."

"What did you tell them?"

"Nothing. I reached for my handkerchief and let them see that I was carrying a gun. I thought it might cause them to revise any immediate plans they might have in mind. After that the interview sort of fizzled out and I left. Mary's little lamb followed me home, as usual.''

"Same plug-ugly that shadowed you yesterday?"

"Him, or his twin—He couldn't be a twin, though, come to think about it. They'd have both died of fright at birth.''

"Have you had lunch?''

"Not yet. Let's ease down to the shop lunch room and take on some groceries. We can do our worrying later.''

The lunch room was deserted. They talked very little. Mary Lou's blue eyes stared vacantly over his head. At the second cup of coffee she reached out and touched him.

"Archie, do you know the ancient Chinese advice to young ladies about to undergo criminal assault?''

"No, what is it?''

"Just one word: 'Relax.' That's what we've got to do.''

"Speak English.''

"I'll give you a blueprint. Why are we under attack?''

"We've got something they want.''

"Not at all. We've got something they want to quarantine—they don't want anyone else to have it. So they try to buy you off, or scare you into quitting. If these don't work, they'll try something stronger. Now you're dangerous to them and in danger from them because you've got a secret? What happens if it isn't a secret? Suppose everybody knows it?''

"They'd be sore as hell.''

"Yes, but what would they do? Nothing. Those big tycoons are practical men. They won't waste a dime on heckling you if it no longer serves their pocketbooks.''

"What do you propose that we do?''

"Give away the secret. Tell the world how it's done. Let anybody manufacture power screens and light screens that wants to. The heat process on the allotrope is so simple that any commercial chemist can duplicate it once you tell 'em how, and there must be a thousand factories, at least, that could manufacture them with their present machinery from materials at their very doorsteps.''

"But, good Lord, Mary Lou, we'd be left in the lurch.''

"What can you lose? We've made a measly couple of thousand dollars so far, keeping the process secret. If you turn it loose, you still hold the patent, and you could charge a nominal royalty—one that it wouldn't be worth while trying to beat, say ten cents a square yard on each screen manufactured. There would be millions of square yards turned out the first year—hundreds of thousands of dollars to you the first year, and a big income for life. You can have the finest research laboratory in the country.''

He slammed his napkin down on the table. "Kid, I believe you're right.''

"Don't forget, too, what you'll be doing for the country. There'll be factories springing up right away all over the southwest—every place where there's lots of sunshine. Free power! You'll be the new emancipator."

He stood up, his eyes shining. "Kid, we'll do it! Half a minute while I tell Dad our decision, then we'll beat it for town."

Two hours later the teletype in every news service office in the country was clicking out the story. Douglas insisted that the story include the technical details of the process as a condition of releasing it. By the time he and Mary Lou walked out of the Associated Press building the first extra was on the street:

GENIUS GRANTS GRATIS POWER TO PUBLIC.

Archie bought one and beckoned to the muscle man who was shadowing him.

"Come here, Sweetheart. You can quit pretending to be a fire-plug. I've an errand for you." He handed the lunk the newspaper. It was accepted uneasily. In all his long and unsavory career he had never had the etiquette of shadowing treated in so cavalier a style. "Take this paper to your boss and tell him Archie Douglas sent him a valentine. Don't stand there staring at me! Beat it, before I break your fat head!"

As Archie watched him disappear in the crowd, Mary Lou slipped a hand in his. "Feel better, son?"

"Lots."

"All your worries over?"

"All but one." He grabbed her shoulders and swung her around. "I've got an argument to settle with you. Come along!" He grabbed her wrist and pulled her out into the cross walk.

"What the hell, Archie! Let go my wrist."

"Not likely. You see that building over there? That's the court house. Right next to the window where they issue dog licenses, there's one where we can get a wedding permit."

"I'm not going to marry you!" she cried indignantly.

"The hell you aren't. You've stayed all night in my laboratory a dozen times. I'm compromised. You've got to make an honest man of me—or I'll start to scream right here in the street."

"This is blackmail!"

As they entered the building, she was still dragging her feet—but not too hard.

STRANGE PLAYFELLOW

BY ISAAC ASIMOV

Time was when the Good Doctor Isaac Asimov was not the world-famous author, raconteur, TV star, and ladies' man we all know and love so well today. He wasn't even a doctor. He was just one more college student, peering worriedly at the big outside world in search of a place for himself.

But at least he was looking in the right place. Between courses, he was writing science-fiction stories. Mostly he wrote them for John Campbell's Astounding, *but now and then one slipped through the cracks and I was able to buy it—at my very top rate, which was then all of five-eighths of a cent a word.*

"Strange Playfellow" didn't slip through. John Campbell hurled it through. I wasn't there, but I bet I can visualize the scene. "Asimov," says John, leaning back to fit a cigarette into a holder and close his roll-top desk so the visitor could not see any private papers, "you have here a potentially interesting notion, but you haven't thought it through. Let me tell you what it is that you meant to write, if you'd thought of it." And so he laid out for young Asimov the first blueprint of what turned out to be the famous Three Laws of Robotics.

That's a first-rate example of Campbell's famous "back of the neck" insight (which I will talk about a little more later on), and that is how I came to publish what is actually the first of the Asimov robot stories. I loved it. So did the readers. But I couldn't get any more of them because they all went to John Campbell. After all, he was outpaying me by a full three-eighths of a cent a word.

I also changed Isaac's title, which was "Robbie."

I did that a lot. Sometimes inspiration struck, and I came up with a really fine one. Sometimes not. I must concede that I don't feel "Strange Playfellow" was really inspired. But the title of a magazine story should perform at least a few of certain well-defined functions: It should be a sort of commercial for the story, making you want to read it. It should in some sense describe the story, so that you can recall it later on. And, if at all possible, it should be clever. As near as I could figure, out of a possible three points, "Robbie" scored an even zero.

I never convinced Isaac, of course. As soon as I had published the story, he changed the title back, and it has been reprinted as "Robbie" every time it has appeared since, without exception. . . .

Until now!

* * *

"Ninety-eight—ninety-nine—one hundred."

Gloria withdrew her chubby little forearm from before her eyes and stood for a moment, wrinkling her nose and blinking in the sunlight. Then, she gazed about her carefully and withdrew a few cautious steps from the tree against which she had been leaning.

She craned her neck to investigate the possibilities of a clump of bushes to the right and then withdrew further to obtain a better angle for viewing its dark recesses. The quiet was profound except for the incessant buzzing of insects and the occasional chirrup of some hardy bird, braving the midday sun.

Gloria pouted. "I'll bet he went inside the house, and I've told him a million times that that's not fair." With tiny lips pressed together tightly and a severe frown crinkling her forehead, she moved determinedly towards the two-story building off on the other side of the fence.

Too late, she heard a rustling sound behind her, followed by the distinctive and rhythmic clump-clump of Robbie's metal feet. She whirled about to see her traitorous companion emerge from hiding and make for the "home" tree at full speed.

Gloria shrieked in dismay. "Wait, Robbie! That wasn't fair, Robbie! You promised you wouldn't run before I found you." Her little feet could make no headway at all against Robbie's giant strides. Then, within ten feet of "home," Robbie's pace suddenly slowed to the merest of crawls, and Gloria with one final burst of wild speed touched the welcome bark of "home" first.

Gleefully, she turned on the faithful Robbie, and with the basest of ingratitude rewarded him for his sacrifice, by taunting him cruelly for a lack of running ability.

"Robbie can't run," she shouted at the top of her eight-year-old voice. "I can beat him any day. He's a *terrible* runner!"

Robbie didn't answer—because he couldn't. In spite of all science could do, it was still impossible to equip robots with phonographic attachments of sufficient complexity—not without sacrificing mobility. Consequently, he contented himself with punishing the little girl by snatching her up in the air and whirling her about till she begged to be put down again.

"Anyway, Robbie, it's my turn to hide now," she insisted seriously, "because you've got longer legs and you promised not to run till I found you."

Robbie nodded his head—a small parallelepiped with rounded edges and corners attached to a similar but much larger parallelepiped that served as torso, by means of a short, flexible stalk—and obediently faced the tree. A thin, metal film descended over his glowing eyes and from within his body came a steady metallic clicking—for all the world like a metronome counting off the seconds.

"Don't peek now—and don't skip any numbers," and Gloria scurried for cover.

With unvarying regularity, seconds were ticked off, and at the hundredth, up went the eyelids, and the glowing red of Robbie's eyes swept the prospect. They rested for a moment on a bit of colorful gingham that protruded from behind a boulder. He advanced a few steps and convinced himself that it was Gloria who squatted behind it. Thereupon one tentacle slapped against his gleaming metal chest with a resounding clang and another pointed straight at the boulder. Gloria emerged sulkily.

"You peeked!" she exclaimed with gross unfairness. "Besides I'm tired of playing hide-and-seek. I want a ride."

But Robbie was hurt at the unjust accusation, so he seated himself carefully and shook his head ponderously from side to side.

Gloria changed her tone to one of gentle coaxing immediately, "Come on, Robbie. I didn't mean it about the peeking. Give me a ride."

Robbie was not to be won over so easily, though. He gazed stubbornly at the sky, and shook his head even more emphatically.

"Please, Robbie, please give me a ride." She encircled his neck with rosy arms and hugged tightly. Then, changing with the suddenness of a determined child, she moved away. "If you don't, I'm going to cry," and her face twisted into an appalling position.

Hard-hearted Robbie paid scant attention to this dreadful prospect, and shook his head a third time, albeit not quite so energetically, and Gloria found it necessary to play her trump card.

"If you don't," she exclaimed warmly, "I don't tell you any more fairy tales, so there!"

Robbie gave in immediately and unconditionally before this ultimatum and nodded his head vigorously until the metal of his neck hummed. Carefully, he raised the little girl and placed her on his broad, flat shoulders.

Gloria's threatened tears vanished immediately and she crowed with delight. Robbie's metal skin, kept at the constant temperature of seventy degrees by the high resistance coils within, felt nice and comfortable and the beautifully loud sound her heels made as they bumped rhythmically against his chest was enchanting.

"I knew you'd let me ride for the fairy tales, Robbie," she giggled. "I knew it.'' She grasped him about the head and began bouncing up and down, going through the immemorial rites of the pick-a-back.

"Faster, Robbie, faster," and the robot increased his speed until the vibration forced Gloria's happy laughter out in convulsive jerks. Clear across the field he sped, to the patch of tall grass on the other side, where he stopped with a suddenness that evoked a shriek from his flushed rider, and tumbled her onto the soft, natural carpet.

Gloria gasped and panted and gave voice to intermittent whispered exclamations of "That was *nice!*"

Robbie waited until she had caught her breath and then lifted a tentacle with which he gently pulled her hair—a sign that he wished her attention.

"What do you want, Robbie?" she asked roguishly, pretending an artless perplexity, that fooled the wise Robbie not at all. He only pulled one golden curl the harder.

"Oh, I know! You want a story," Robbie nodded rapidly. "Which one?" Robbie curled one tentacular finger into a semicircle. "But I've told you Cinderella a million times. Aren't you tired of it?" The semicircle persisted.

"Oh, well," Gloria composed herself, ran over the details of the tale in her mind (together with her own elaborations, of which she had several) and began.

"Are you ready? Well—once upon a time there was a beautiful little girl whose name was Ella. And she had a terribly cruel step-mother and two very ugly and *very* cruel step-sisters and—"

Gloria was reaching the very climax of the tale—midnight was striking and everything was changing back to the shabby originals lickety-split—when the interruption came.

"Gloria!" It was the high-pitched sound of a woman who has been calling not once, but several times; and had the nervous tone of one in whom anxiety was beginning to overcome impatience.

"Mamma's calling me," said Gloria, not quite happily. "Carry me back to the house, Robbie."

Robbie obeyed with alacrity for somehow there was that in him which judged it best to obey Mrs. Weston, without as much as a scrap of hesitation. Gloria's father was rarely home in the daytimes except on Sunday—today, for instance—and when he was, he proved a genial and understanding person. Gloria's mother, however, was a source of uneasiness to Robbie and there was always the impulse to sneak away from her sight.

Mrs. Weston caught sight of them the minute they rose above the masking tufts of long grass and retired inside the house to wait.

"I've shouted myself hoarse, Gloria," she said, severely. "Where were you?"

"I was with Robbie," quavered Gloria. "I was telling him Cinderella, and I forgot it was dinner-time."

"Well, it's a pity Robbie forgot, too." Then, as if that reminded her of the robot's presence, she whirled towards him. "You may go, Robbie. She doesn't need you now." Then, brutally, "And don't come back till I call you."

Robbie turned to go, but hesitated as Gloria cried out in his defense. "Let him stay, Mamma, please let him stay. I want to finish Cinderella for him."

"Gloria!"

"Honest and truly, Mamma, he'll stay so quiet, you won't even know he's here. Won't you, Robbie?"

Robbie nodded his massive head up and down once, in manifest fear of the autocratic woman before him.

"Gloria, if you don't stop this at once, you shan't see Robbie for a whole week."

The girl's eyes fell, "All right! But Cinderella is his favorite story and I didn't finish it. —And he likes it so much."

The robot left with a disconsolate step and Gloria choked back a sob.

George Weston was comfortable. It was a habit of his to be comfortable on Sunday afternoons. A good, hearty dinner stowed away; a nice, soft, dilapidated couch on which to sprawl; a copy of the *Times*; slippered feet and shirtless chest—how could anyone *help* but be comfortable?

He wasn't pleased, therefore, when his wife walked in. After ten years of married life, he still was so unutterably foolish as to love her, and there was no question that he was always glad to see her—still Sunday afternoons just after dinner were sacred to him and his idea of solid comfort was to be left in utter solitude for two or three hours. Consequently, he fixed his eye firmly upon the latest reports of the Douglas expedition to the Moon (which looked as if it might actually succeed) and pretended she wasn't there.

Mrs. Weston waited patiently for two minutes, then impatiently for two more, and finally broke the silence.

"George!"

"Hmpph!"

"George, I say! *Will* you put down that paper and look at me?"

The paper rustled to the floor and Weston turned a weary face towards his wife, "What is it, dear?"

"You know what it is, George. It's Gloria and that terrible machine."

"What terrible machine?"

"Now don't pretend you don't know what I'm talking about. It's that robot Gloria calls Robbie. He doesn't leave her for a moment."

"Well, why should he? He's not supposed to. And he certainly isn't a terrible machine. He's the best darn robot money can buy and Lord knows he's set me back half a year's income. He's worth it, too—darn sight cleverer, he is, than half my office staff."

He made a move to pick up the paper again, but his wife was quicker and snatched it away.

"You listen to *me*, George. I won't have my daughter entrusted to a machine—and I don't care how clever it is. It has no soul, and no one knows what it may be thinking. It's ungodly, that's what it is. A child just isn't *made* to be guarded by a thing of metal.''

"Dear! A robot is infinitely more to be trusted than a human nurse-maid. Robbie was constructed for only one purpose—to be the companion of a little child. His entire 'mentality' has been created for the purpose. He just can't help being faithful and loving and kind. He's a machine—*made so*.''

"Yes, but something might go wrong. Some—some," Mrs. Weston was a bit hazy about the insides of a robot, "some little jigger will come loose and the awful thing will go berserk and—and—" She couldn't bring herself to complete the quite obvious thought.

"Nonsense," Weston denied, with an involuntary nervous shiver. "He was constructed by the most reliable firm in the world and guaranteed for six months without overhauling, and you *know* I have Johnston here every week to go through him with a microscope. Johnston is an expert Roboticist and he'll swear to you that there's no more chance of Robbie going mad than there is of you or I suddenly going loony—less, in fact. Besides, Gloria is crazy about him and it would just about kill her to part with him." He made another futile stab at the paper and his wife tossed it angrily into the next room.

"That's just it, George! She won't play with anyone else. Lord knows, there are dozens of little boys and girls that she should make friends with, but she won't. She won't go *near* them unless I make her. That's no way for a little girl to grow up. You want her to be normal, don't you?"

"You're jumping at shadows, Grace. Pretend Robbie's a dog. I've seen hundreds of children no less crazy about their pets."

"A dog is different. George, we *must* get rid of that horrible thing. You can easily sell it back to the company."

"That's *out*, Grace, and I don't want to hear of it again. You'd better stop reading *Frankenstein*—if that's what you've been doing."

And with that he walked out of the room in a huff.

And yet he loved his wife—and what was worse, his wife knew it. George Weston, after all, was only a man—poor thing—and his wife made full use of every art and wile which a clumsier and more scrupulous sex has learned from time immemorial to fear.

Ten times in the ensuing week, he would cry, "Robbie stays—and that's *final*!" and each time it was weaker and accompanied by a louder and more agonized groan.

Came the day at last, when Weston approached his daughter guiltily and suggested a "beautiful" visivox show in the village.

Gloria clapped her hands happily, "Can Robbie go?"

"No, dear," and how his conscience did twinge, "they won't allow robots at the visivox—and besides you can tell him all about it when you get home." He stumbled over the last few words and decided within himself that he made a terribly poor liar.

Gloria came back from town bubbling over with enthusiasm, for the visivox had been a gorgeous spectacle indeed, and the antics of the famous comic, Francis Fran, amid the fierce "leopard-men of the Moon" had evoked delightfully hysterical bursts of laughter.

She ran into the house joyously and stopped suddenly at the sight of a beautiful collie which regarded her out of serious brown eyes as it wagged its tail on the porch.

"Oh, what a nice dog." Gloria approached cautiously and patted it. "Is it for me, daddy?"

Weston cleared his throat miserably, and wondered whether the substitution would do any good, "Yes, dear!"

"Oh—! Thank you very much, daddy." Then, turning precipitously, she ran down the basement steps, shouting as she went, "Oh, Robbie! Come and see what daddy's brought me, Robbie."

In a minute she had returned, a frightened little girl. "Mamma, Robbie isn't in his room. Where is he?" There was no answer and George Weston coughed and suddenly seemed to be extremely interested in an aimlessly drifting cloud. Gloria's voice quavered on the verge of tears, "Where's Robbie, Mamma?"

Mrs. Weston sat down and drew her daughter gently to her. "Don't feel bad, Gloria. Robbie has—gone away."

"Gone *away*? Where? Where's he gone away, Mamma?"

"No one knows, darling. He just walked away. We've looked and we've looked and we've looked for him, but we can't find him."

"You mean I'll never see him again?" Her eyes were round in horror.

"We may find him someday, and meanwhile, you can play with your nice new doggie. Look at him! His name is Lightning and he can—"

But Gloria's eyelids had overflown, "I don't want the nasty dog—I want Robbie. I want you to find me Robbie." Her feelings became too deep for words, and she spluttered into a shrill wail.

Mrs. Weston glanced at her husband for help, but he merely shuffled his feet morosely and did not withdraw his ardent stare from the heavens, so she bent to the task of consolation. "Why do you cry, Gloria? Robbie was only a machine, just a nasty old machine. He wasn't alive at all."

"He was *not* no machine!" cried Gloria, fiercely and ungrammatically. "He was a *person* just like you and me and he was *nice*. I liked him and I want him back again."

Her voice rose to a scream, "He was *not* no nasty machine!"

Her mother groaned in defeat and left Gloria to her sorrow.

"Let her have her cry out," she told her husband. "Childish griefs are never lasting. In a few days, she'll forget that awful robot ever existed."

But time proved Mrs. Weston a bit too optimistic. To be sure, Gloria ceased crying, but she ceased smiling, too, and the passing days seemed but to increase the inner hurt. Gradually, her attitude of passive unhappiness wore

Mrs. Weston down and all that kept her from yielding was the impossibility of admitting defeat to her husband.

Then, one evening, she flounced into the living room, sat down, folded her arms and looked boiling mad.

Her husband stretched his neck in order to see her over his newspaper, "What now, Grace?"

"It's that child, George. I've had to send back the dog today. Gloria positively couldn't stand the sight of him. She's driving me into a nervous breakdown."

Weston laid down the paper and a hopeful gleam entered his eye, "Maybe—maybe we ought to get Robbie back. It might be done, you know. I can get in touch with—"

"No!" she replied grimly. "I won't hear of it. We're not giving up that easily. My child shall *not* be brought up by a robot if it takes years to break her of it."

Weston picked up his paper again with a disappointed air, "A year of this will have me prematurely gray. Look," he dropped the paper a second time and pulled at a lock of hair, "count the silver tresses."

"Don't be funny, George," was the frigid answer. "You always were pretty poor as a wit. What Gloria needs is a change of environment. Of course she can't forget Robbie here. How can she when every tree and rock reminds her of him? It is really the *silliest* situation I have ever heard of. Imagine a child pining away for the loss of a robot."

"Well, stick to the point! What are you going to do now?"

"We're going to take her to New York."

"The city! In August! Say, do you know what New York is like in August! It's bad enough I have to be there eight hours a day. No ma'am! We don't leave for any city until October."

"And I say we're leaving now—as soon as we can make the arrangements. In the city, Gloria will find sufficient interests and sufficient friends to perk her up and make her forget that machine."

"Oh, Lord," groaned the lesser half, "back to the frying pavements."

"You'll have to," was the unshaken response. "Gloria has lost five pounds in the last month and my little girl's health is more important to me than your comfort."

"It's a pity you didn't think of your little girl's health before you deprived her of her pet robot," he muttered—but to himself.

Gloria displayed immediate signs of improvement when told of the impending trip to the city. She spoke little of it, but when she did it was always with lively anticipation. Again, she began to smile, and to eat with something of her former appetite.

Mrs. Weston hugged herself for joy and lost no opportunity to triumph over her still-skeptical husband.

"You see, George, she helps with the packing like a little angel, and chatters away as if she hadn't a care in the world. It's just as I told you—all we need do, is substitute other interests.''

"Hmpph," was the skeptical response. "I hope so."

The preliminaries were gone through quickly—arrangements made for the preparation of their city home and a couple engaged as housekeepers for the country home. When the day of the trip finally did come, Gloria was all but her old self again, and no mention of Robbie passed her lips at all.

In high good-humor, the family drove down to the airport—Weston would have preferred using his own private auto-giro, but it was only a two-seater with no room for baggage—and entered the waiting liner.

"Come, Gloria," called Mrs. Weston, "I've saved you a seat near the window so you can watch the scenery."

Gloria trotted down the aisle cheerily, flattened her nose into a white oval against the thick clear glass, and watched with an intentness that increased as the sudden coughing of the motor drifted backward into the interior. She was too young to be frightened when the ground dropped away as if let through a trapdoor and she herself suddenly became twice her usual weight, but not too young to be mightily interested. It wasn't until the ground had changed into a tiny patchwork quilt, that she withdrew her nose, and faced her mother again.

"Will we soon be in the city, Mamma?" she asked, rubbing her chilled nose, and watching with interest the slowly shrinking patch of moisture which her breath had formed on the pane.

"In less than an hour, dear." Then, with just the faintest trace of anxiety, "Aren't you glad we're going? Don't you think you'll be very happy in the city with all the buildings and people? We'll go to the visivox every day and see shows and go to the circus and the beach and—"

"Yes, Mamma," was Gloria's unenthusiastic rejoinder. The liner passed over a bank of clouds at the moment, and Gloria was instantly absorbed in the unusual spectacle of clouds underneath one. Then they were over clear sky again, and she turned to her mother with a sudden mysterious air of secret knowledge.

"I know why we're going to the city, Mamma."

"Do you?" Mrs. Weston was puzzled. "Why, dear?"

"You didn't tell me because you wanted it to be a surprise, but *I* know." For a moment, she was lost in admiration at her own acute penetration, and then she laughed gaily. "We're going to New York so we can find Robbie, aren't we?"

The statement caught George Weston in the middle of a much-needed drink of water, with disastrous results. There was a sort of strangled gasp, a geyser of water, and then a bout of choking coughs. When all was over, he stood there, a red-faced, water-drenched, and very, very annoyed person.

Mrs. Weston maintained her composure, but when Gloria repeated her question in a more anxious tone of voice, she found her temper rather bent.

"Maybe," she retorted tartly. "Now sit and be still, for Heaven's sake."

* * *

New York City, in this good year of 1982, is quite a place for an eight-year-old girl—especially for one who has spent most of her short life on a farm. Gloria's parents realized this and made the most of it.

It was on direct orders of his wife, then, that George Weston arranged to have his business take care of itself for a month or so, in order to be free to spend the time in what he termed "blowing Gloria to a high old celebration." Like everything else Weston did, this was gone about in an efficient, thorough, and businesslike way. Before the month had passed, there remained not a sight or a highlight to the city, which could conceivably delight a child, that had not been introduced to Gloria.

All that could be done had been done. She was taken to the top of the half-mile-tall Roosevelt Building, to gaze down in awe upon the jagged panorama of rooftops, far off to where they blended into the fields of Long Island and New Jersey. They visited the zoos where Gloria stared in delicious fright at the "real live lion" (rather disappointed that the keepers fed him raw steaks, instead of human beings, as she had expected), and asked insistently and peremptorily to see "the whale."

The various museums came in for their share of attention, together with the parks and the beaches and the aquarium.

She was taken half way up the Hudson in an excursion steamer fitted out in the delicious old-fashioned style of the "gay Twenties." She traveled into the stratosphere on an exhibition trip, where the sky turned deep-purple and the stars came out and the misty earth below looked like a huge concave bowl. Down under the waters of the Long Island Sound, she was taken in a glass-walled sub-sea vessel, where in a green and wavering world, quaint and curious sea-things ogled her and wiggled slowly to and fro.

In fact, when the month had nearly sped the Westons were convinced that everything conceivable had been done to take Gloria's mind once and for all off the departed Robbie—but they were not quite sure they had succeeded.

The fact remained that wherever Gloria went, she displayed the most absorbed and concentrated interest in such robots as happened to be present. No matter how exciting the spectacle before her, nor how delightful to her girlish eyes, everything was dropped the moment a clanking humanoid machine passed.

Noticing this, Mrs. Weston went out of her way to keep Gloria away from all robots. In this, she was helped greatly by the City Law of 1963 which prohibited "automatic mechanical men" from appearing in the city streets except in a closed vehicle driven by a human being. However, the prevalence of robots in almost all buildings proved to be very annoying. This was particularly true in the case of the visivox theaters, all the more elaborate of which boasted robot ushers.

It was the episode at the Museum of Science and Industry, though, that finally convinced Mrs. Weston that all her arts and wiles did not seem to prevail against this love of a child for her nurse and companion—machine though it was.

The museum had announced a special "children's program" in which exhibits of scientific legerdemain were displayed specifically calculated to attract the child mind. Realizing that attendance there would prove both educational and entertaining for Gloria, the Westons placed it upon their list of "musts."

It was while she was standing totally absorbed in the exploits of a powerful electro-magnet (which proved later to have ruined Mr. Weston's heirloom of a watch) that Mrs. Weston suddenly became aware of the fact that Gloria was no longer with her. Initial panic gave way to calm decision and, enlisting the aid of three attendants, the Westons began a careful search.

Gloria was not one to wander aimlessly, however. For her age, she was an unusually determined and purposeful girl, taking after her self-willed mother in that respect. She had seen a huge sign on the third floor, which had said, "THIS WAY TO SEE THE TALKING ROBOT." Having spelled it out to herself and having noticed that her parents did not seem to wish to move in the proper direction, she determined to see it for herself. Consequently, seizing an opportune moment of parental distraction, she calmly disengaged herself and followed the sign.

The "TALKING ROBOT" as a scientific achievement left much to be desired. It sprawled its unwieldy mass of wires and coils through twenty-five square yards, and every robotical function had been subordinated to the vital attribute of speech. It worked—and was in this respect quite a victory—but as yet, it could translate only the simpler and more concrete thoughts into words. Certainly, it was not half so clever as Robbie in Gloria's opinion—and with all the latter's speechlessness, it probably wasn't.

Gloria watched it silently for a while, waiting for the two or three who watched with her to depart. Then, when she stood there alone for the moment, she asked hurriedly, "Have you seen Robbie, Mr. Robot, sir?" She was not quite sure how polite one must be to a robot that could talk.

There was an oily whir of gears, and a metallically-timbred voice boomed out in words that lacked accent and intonation, "Who—is—Robbie?"

"He's a robot, Mr. Robot, sir. Just like you, you know, only he can't talk, of course."

"A—robot—like—me?"

"Yes, Mr. Robot, sir."

But the talking robot's only response to this was an erratic splutter and occasional incoherent sound. The conception of other robots like him had stalled his "thinking" engine, for he had not the mental complexity to grasp the conception.

Gloria was still waiting, with carefully concealed impatience, for the machine's answer when she heard the cry behind her of "There she is," and recognized that cry as her mother's.

"What are you doing here, you bad girl?" cried Mrs. Weston, anxiety disolving at once into anger. "Do you know you frightened your Mamma and Daddy almost to death? Why did you run away?"

"I only came to see the talking robot, Mamma. I thought he might know where Robbie was because they're both robots." And then, as the thought of Robbie was suddenly brought forcefully home to her, burst into a sudden storm of tears, "And oh, Mamma, I do want to see Robbie again. I miss him like *anything*."

Her mother gave forth a strangled cry, more than half a sob, and cried to her husband, "Come home, George. This is more than I can stand."

That night, George Weston left on a mysterious errand with regard to which he was unusually reticent, and the next morning, he approached his wife with something that looked suspiciously like smug complacence.

"I've got an idea, Grace."

"About what?" was the gloomy, uninterested query.

"About Gloria."

"Well, go ahead. I might as well listen to you. Nothing I've done seems to have done any good. But remember, I will *not* consent to buying back that awful robot."

"Of course not. That's understood. However, here's what I've been thinking. The whole trouble with Gloria is that she thinks of Robbie as a *person* and not as a *machine*. Naturally, she can't forget him. Now if we managed to convince her that Robbie was nothing more than a mess of steel and copper in the form of sheets and wires with electricity its juice of life, how long would this aberration last?"

Mrs. Weston frowned in thought, "It sounds good, but how are you going to do it?"

"Simple. Where do you suppose I was last night? I persuaded old Finmark of the Finmark Robot Corporation to arrange for a complete tour of his premises tomorrow. The three of us will go, and by the time we're through, Gloria will have it drilled into her that a robot is *not* alive."

His wife's eyes widened gradually as the excellence of the plan dawned upon her and something glinted in them that was quite like awed admiration. "Why, George, how *did* you manage to think of that?"

Weston's chest expanded several inches as he basked in her open adulation.

"I can hardly wait." There was a gleam of determination in Mrs. Weston's eye. "Gloria is not going to miss a step of the process. We'll settle this once and for all."

Mr. Struthers was a conscientious general manager and naturally inclined to be a bit talkative. The combination therefore, resulted in a tour that was fully explained—perhaps even overabundantly explained—at every step. In spite of this, Mrs. Weston was not bored. Indeed, she stopped him several times and begged him to repeat his statements in simpler language so that Gloria might understand. Under the influence of this appreciation of his narrative powers,

Mr. Struthers expanded genially and became even more communicative—if possible.

Weston, himself, displayed an odd impatience, nevertheless—an almost angry impatience.

"Pardon me, Struthers," he broke in suddenly, in the midst of a lecture on the photoelectric cell, "haven't you a section of the factory where only robot labor is employed?"

"Eh? Oh, yes! Yes, indeed!" He smiled at Mrs. Weston, "A vicious circle in a way—robots creating more robots. However, we are not intending to make a general practice of it. We turn out a very few robots using robot labor exclusively, merely as a sort of scientific curiosity. You see," he tapped his pince-nez into one palm argumentatively, "the robot factories of the country are cooperating with the government—"

"Yes, yes, Struthers, I once heard you make a speech on 'Robots and the Future of the Human Being.' It was very interesting, I assure you. But about that section of the factory you speak of—may we see it? It would be a most interesting experience."

"Yes! Yes, of course." Mr. Struthers replaced his pince-nez in one convulsive movement and gave vent to a soft cough of discomfiture. "Follow me, please."

He was comparatively quiet, while leading the three through a long corridor and down a flight of stairs. Then, when they had entered a large well-lit room, that buzzed with metallic activity, the sluices opened and the flood of explanation poured forth again.

"There you are," he said in part, and with quite a bit of pride in his voice. "Robots only! Five men act as overseers and they don't even stay in this room. In five years, ever since we began this project, not a single accident has occurred. Of course, very few robots here are intelligent. . . ."

The general manager's voice had long died to a rather soothing murmur in Gloria's ears. The whole trip seemed rather dull and pointless to her, though there *were* many robots in sight. None were even remotely like Robbie, though, and she surveyed them with open contempt.

Her eyes fell upon six or seven robots busily engaged about a round table half way across the room. They widened in incredulous surprise. One of the robots looked like—looked like—*it was!*

"Robbie!" Her shriek pierced the air, and one of the robots about the table faltered and dropped the tool he was holding. Gloria went almost mad with joy. Squeezing through the railing before either parent could stop her, she dropped lightly to the floor a few feet below, and ran towards her Robbie, arms waving and hair flying.

And the three horrified adults, as they stood frozen in their tracks, saw what the excited little girl did not see—a huge, lumbering tractor bearing blindly down upon its appointed track.

It took split-seconds for Weston to come to his senses, but those split-seconds meant everything, for Gloria could not be overtaken. Although Weston vaulted the railing in a wild attempt, he knew it was hopeless. Mr. Struthers signaled wildly to the overseers to stop the tractor, but the overseers were only human and it took time to act.

It was only Robbie that acted immediately and with precision.

With metal legs eating up the space between himself and his little mistress, he charged down from the opposite direction. Everything then happened at once. With one sweep of an arm, Robbie snatched up Gloria, slackening his speed not one iota, and, consequently, knocking every breath of air out of her. Weston, not quite comprehending all that was happening, felt rather than saw Robbie brush past him, and came to a sudden, bewildered halt. The tractor intersected Gloria's path, half a second after Robbie had, rolled on ten feet further and came to a grinding, long-drawn-out halt.

Gloria finally regained her breath, submitted to a series of passionate hugs on the part of both parents and turned eagerly towards Robbie. As far as she was concerned, nothing had happened except that she had found her robot.

Mrs. Weston regained her composure rather quickly, aided by a sudden suspicion that struck her. She turned to her husband, and, despite her disheveled and undignified appearance, managed to look quite formidable, "*You* engineered this, *didn't* you?"

George Weston swabbed at a hot, perspiring forehead with his handkerchief. His hand was none too steady, and his lips curved in a tremulous and exceedingly weak smile, "But Grace, I had no idea the reunion would be so violent."

Weston watched her keenly, and ventured a further remark, "Anyway, you can't deny Robbie has saved her life. You can't send him away now."

His wife thought it over. It was a bit difficult to keep up her anger. She turned towards Gloria and Robbie and watched them abstractedly for a moment. Gloria had a grip about the robot's neck that would have asphyxiated any creature but one of metal, and was prattling nonsense in half-hysterical frenzy. Robbie's chrome-steel arms (capable of bending a bar of steel two inches in diameter into a pretzel) wound about the little girl gently and lovingly, and his eyes glowed a deep, deep red.

Mrs. Weston's anger faded still further, and she became almost genial.

"Well," she breathed at last, smiling in spite of herself. "I guess Robbie can stay with us until he rusts, for all I care."

INTERSTELLAR WAY-STATION

BY BOB TUCKER

Way back when the world was damply new and the only science fiction was in the pulps, there were Fans. There were also ordinary lower-case fans like you and me, the troops that filled the battle ranks, but over and above them were the generals and the superstars. Forrest J. Ackerman. Donald A. Wollheim. And Bob Tucker.

At that time fans, and even Fans, were not greatly different from now. Not everything they took seriously was actually all that serious. Would you believe that one of the great divisive issues of the 1930s was staples? That's right. Those little wire things. All fandom chose up sides in the Great Staple War. Don Wollheim favored them. Forry Ackerman was benevolently neutral. And Arthur Wilson "Bob" Tucker was demiurge of the forces demanding their abolition; was in fact president of SPWSSTFM, the Society for the Prevention of Wire Staples in Scientifiction Magazines.

Well, that was long and long ago. Bob lived in downstate Illinois—still does—and there were no nearby fan groups of struggling talents to reinforce him and propel him into professional writing, as LASFS did for Larry Niven, et al, and the Futurians did for so many. He earned his living as a projectionist in movie theaters. And he kept on reading science fiction.

Came a time when Tucker was ready to expand his wings and try his luck as a professional writer. His luck was good. Under his real name—well, almost his real name—under the name of Wilson Tucker he wrote a series of mysteries, and then of science-fiction novels. They were good. One in particular, The Year of The Quiet Sun, *was so good that in 1976 the judges for the international John W. Campbell Memorial Award set aside all that year's novels and reached back half a dozen years to give it the prize.*

Bob Tucker has had a distinguished literary career, and he's still having it. All careers start with one story, and I'm happy to say I published Tucker's first. This is it.

* * *

"Hey, kid! She's going over!"

"Hah?" I yelled.

"The mail rocket. . . ." Pinko repeated. "She's just gone over!"

I dropped my paintbrush, shoved the bucket over out of the way, and beat it around the corner of the Guest Hotel in a bee line for the mail chute; it was our first mail this week. Those damned tightwads on the Universal Council began trimming the overhead a couple of years ago, and daily mail to the Service was the first to go.

Pinko was at the chute ahead of me, flapping his wings excitedly.

"Ahhhh! Another letter from the little Lulu over on '3,' " I jeered. Pinko bobbled about and confirmed this without words. He went over by himself to read the letter. I would read her letter later; we always swapped our mail.

You see, Pinko and I are in the Universal Service—and that covers a lot of space and sins. Our particular branch and job is Refueling. Refueling the big liners that drop in here about once or twice a week, stay a few hours to give the passengers a quick peek at a gas station in space (and a dip in our pool if they like—real Earth water!), meanwhile taking on a capacity load of fuel for the big push on to Alpha Centauri.

Get out your charts and space maps, and if you don't have one, phone, don't walk, to your nearest tourist agency. They'll have one to you in three clicks of a mail tube sounder. Find yourself . . . the big symbol "Earth" in the near center of the map. Now swinging in a tight semi-circle toward the upper left-hand corner of the map, trace that dotted line that leads to the page margin (a little box on the margin tells you that line will take you to Alpha Centauri). This little dotted line is known as the Lowden Line. Your ship, however, doesn't exactly follow that line. After all, no one has really faithfully followed a map since the first one was made thousands of years ago for foot travelers on Earth!

What isn't shown on that map are two Passages, known as the "Outer Passage" and the "Inner Passage." All ships follow one of the two channels known as "passages;" ships *from* Earth to Centauri on the Inner Passage; and ships from Centauri *to* Earth on the Outer Passage. This is necessary, you understand, to prevent ships heading in opposite directions from bumping head-on into one another, and various other little things that aren't important enough to tell passengers.

Examine that map, particularly the Lowden Line a little more closely. At spaced intervals along the Lowden Line (and all other lines) you will notice a small black square containing a number: 1, 2, 3, and so on. A quick consulting of the key and index informs you that here, at these squares in space, are located stopovers, where tourists may spend a few hours resting from the nervous strain of their first day in space (as in the case of our depot. We are "E-1-AC," or, depot number one, on the Inner Passage, approximately one day out from Earth on the long grind to Alpha Centauri up yonder.) We have on our little world, among other wonders, a small pool of genuine Earth water, the last, by the way, that tourists will see until they near Earth again.

And undoubtedly, the tourists, are as amused by us as they amuse. I, I'm from Earth myself—Indiana. Only now and then does someone drop in who finds *me* a strange life form, and spends his hours trailing me around, colorgraphing my every move. But poor old Pinko comes in for more than his share of trouble. These gawks from Earth out of bounds for the first time—especially the children—find Pinko the very first Centaurian birdman they've seen outside the theaters.

"Here's looking at you, kid," Pinko called. He flipped the Lulu's letter over to me. "What else in the mail?"

"Aw, the usual old stuff: coupla trade journals, sixteen letters from sixteen passengers, the said letters containing sixteen varied colorgraphs of you—" For Pinko's benefit, I displayed mock astonishment: "Say, here's a beaut! Somebody caught you with your beak open! Mmmmmm . . . what charm." If you've seen a Centaurian with his beak open, you can appreciate the candidness of the picture.

Pinko snatched the pic, stared long at it, and presently the hundred tiny pieces of the paper were floating softly down to the artificial lawn, pulled there slowly by the artificial gravity.

"Centaurians have a word for that!" he snapped. "What else . . . ?"

"Two mash notes from some girls back home. They want to 'correspond with some romantic young guardsmen of the spaceways!' Jupiter, why do we have to put up with that? Some advertisements. . . . Oh, look for yourself." I flung him the bundle after separating from its mass a picture magazine, and rolled over on my belly. The letter from the Lulu—a female of some species, who superintended the Guest Hotel out on E-3-AC (she and Pinko had struck up quite a cordial correspondence)—I let lay where it had fallen.

These picture magazines, designed as they are for Servicemen, display plenty of beauteous females—of every world imaginable, for we have servicemen from every one of those worlds—for the bored gentlemen who peddle gas in space. Cheesecake abounds, and honestly, if you could but glimpse the cheesecake displayed by *some* of the females, on *some* of the planets, you'd undoubtedly go off by yourself and have a nice little sick spell. I felt that way when I saw my first picture of a Trinorite. Never again will I look at a picture of a "girl" of Trinor unless she is fully dressed. You see, it's all in the point of view . . . male Trinors probably find it interesting, but. . . !

Staring up at my very interested gaze was an Earth girl. A very pretty girl, with "wealth" written into every pretty line of her face. Wealth, position, and of course a bit of snobbishness. I knew her. Oh, very intimately. Her name is Judith Maynard . . . aw, wait a minute. The caption explains that the name *was* Maynard.

"Well, I'll be damned!" I was disgusted.

"Hah?" the beak extracted itself from a profound study of a political advertisement. "Why?"

"Take a look," I tossed him the mag. "Remember her? No . . . not that one, nitwit! *This* one."

Pinko switched his gaze from the undraped legs of a Martian to the face of Maynard.

"So she married? You might of guessed it," he stared at me.

"Yeah, I might of guessed it. But I didn't. I rather thought . . ."

About eight years ago the *Centau-Maid* express roared into our outer port with a fused rocket stud. The mighty ship, then the crack liner on the Lowden Line, could have flown to hyperspace and back without half her studs, but regulations required her to set down in the nearest port for repairs. It was our bad luck that she happened to be a few million miles from us, and down she came.

Her ace pilot hit the dimensions of the outer port not a foot over the lines, and Pinko on the cradle engine brought her inside as smoothly as one could want. The cradle brings the ship down through the two locks to the surface of our midget world; and there she is serviced while the passengers take unheard-of liberties with our and the Council's property. If you can afford the luxury of the *Maid*, you must be somebody on *any* world. No tourists here, but first-class fares exclusively. And any Serviceman will gladly tell you that these fares are twice as nosey and twice as obnoxious as any tourist. I guess it's their wealth that makes them that way.

My Judith Maynard was one of the whirliest whirls on this boat, and immediately made up a colorgraphing party. This is where I came in, being one of their own kind (and Pinko long ago realized the safety of staying with the ship's crew); having bare notice of the *Maid's* coming, I had just skipped into my dress whites, hid paintcans and brushes under a tarp, and beamed according to Council Regulation S1317.

First stop of course on all tours about the station, is the cradle, the huge and complex bed that reaches up to our outer hull, almost snatches a ship from space, and brings it right down into the ground. Under the cradle proper is a maze of girders and beams, the engine and the controls for the bed.

Cameras clicked.

"Oh, I beg pardon ma'am. Don't touch those girders." I stopped her just in time. "Wet paint, you know. We have to freshen up these things every week. The children just love to carve their names on the beams with toy ray guns. Ha ha, our clever children!" (I had a few hours earlier just finished painting out the slogan "*Gladrz wuv Zir*" that a particularly premature-worldly youngster had etched into a girder with fire.)

"Oh, do you find children a nuisance?" she inquired ever so interestedly.

"Not at all, ma'am, on the contrary, they make life pleasant for we Servicemen out here. But they cause us much work with those real flame-throwing ray guns most of them tote nowadays. Only about two months ago we had a report from some liner over on the Riga run that it was afire in space.

Seems some youngster had desired to carve his name into a bunk, and . . .''

But she was gone, half way through my explanation. I ran to catch up.

"Now *this* used to be an ammunition dump, several decades ago when the War was going on." (Cameras clicked.) "The Council stored huge amounts of munitions here, and on every Depot like this between here and Centauri. But that was long ago—" I smiled deprecatingly "—and now forgotten."

"But, porter," (I guess the fat woman meant me—!) "why hasn't the hole been filled in? Someone might get hurt!" and she looked hurt at the very thought.

"Nothing to fill it with, ma'am. Dirt just isn't a payload. There are many more precious things, things needed for life and service, that take up all available ships. Dirt is simply too cheap a thing to transport from Earth in a large enough quantity to fill that hole. So, it is left as is."

We moved on to the next item of interest, the powerhouse. "This is the powerhouse." (Cameras clicked.)

"Every single unit of energy no matter what kind it is, or what it is used for, comes from this building. Here is gathered the power from the Sun, plus the stars, plus the storage batteries—yes, ma'am, those black boxes over there are the batteries—that hold this depot in space, and permit us to live inside it. Here, in these machines and . . . uh, black boxes, is everything needed for our maintenance. Tremendous voltages are handled here. You will note the warning posted on the door"—and I directed their attention to the glaring big sign that read:

DANGER! KEEP OUT
SIX BILLION VOLTS!

We handled nothing like six billion volts here, but Pinko and I had found that a bit of exaggeration paid dividends. A tourist who reports back to the medical officer aboard his ship with electric burns means demerits for us. And the darn fools actually invite electrocution.

"Hah? I beg your pardon, madam, I wasn't listening. Oh no, madam, Senior Serviceman Pinko never lets me ride astride his back. Yes'm, he can fly. Well, madam, possibly you do believe it to be a shame that a Centaurian has seniority over an Earthman; but you see, this is necessary. Serviceman Pinko has been on duty at this station nearly forty-six years. He has four more years to serve until he attains his second-class citizen's rating; and at the same time I step up to senior attendant, and a rookie . . . I mean a new man comes from some world to serve *his* twenty-five years as my junior. Now *this*, ladies, is the control tower." (Cameras clicked.)

I shot a hasty glance around to note if Pinko had been in earshot when the overfed baby demanded to know whether Pinko and I played horse and jockey. He wasn't in sight.

"This is the control tower. Into this building comes all the power, direct from the powerhouse, and here it is split up and fed to many hundreds of pieces of machinery all over the depot. Up there on the second floor—you can see the levers through the windows—are the controls themselves that cause every bit of apparatus to function when and how it is supposed to. No, ma'am, we have no control for weather. You see, the weather is always the same here, being as we are on the inside of an immense metal ball.

"From this tower can be controlled, by remote control of course, the landing cradle that brought your ship in from space; the check needed to hold a depot at a given spot in space; the machinery for putting under a finger the millions upon millions of volts we draw from the sun; and the very electric lights about the place. From this tower the water in the pool is purified every twenty-four hours and made ready for any ship at any time. From this tower the very air you are now breathing is cleansed over and over again to keep it free from fumes and bacteria."

And so, amid the ever-clicking of color cameras, we went clockwise around the grounds; my three-thousand-and-ninety-sixth journey.

At last I delivered this consignment to the gangplank and the purser. They filed in.

"Thirty-eight," I gritted, "and they're all yours, every damned one of them! I hope I never see you or them again!"

"My eye!" that worthy retorted. "You've snitched one. There should be thirty-nine."

"Thirty-eight was all I counted. And I don't want one of them . . . *any* of them! Check again."

He did, from a list in his hand. The assistant purser joined him in head bobbing. Both looked solemn.

"One short. I'm positive of it. Thirty-nine left the ship. Thirty-eight returned. We have both counted. Let me see . . . ah, yes. Miss Maynard. Miss Judith Maynard is missing. Maynard! Oh glory be . . . her old man has half the gold mines in . . ." He never finished, but hurried off into the darkened interior of the ship. His assistant appeared nervous.

Sighing disgustedly, I turned and started off on a counter-clockwise tour, half-wondering just what gear she had tangled herself in. I didn't get far. Pinko came bounding out of the ship and an excited captain at his heels.

Prudently, I put a few steps between Pinko and myself. Having lived with him for something like twenty-one years, I recognize danger signals when I see them. His eyes turned a beautiful violet and bored right into mine. He swept the landscape for signs of her, and finding none, returned to me. Three more steps were put between us.

Six sailors tumbled out of the ship behind him on the double.

They were assigned to me, and we continued the counter-clockwise movement; while Pinko, the captain, and both pursers vanished back into the ship for a room-by-room check.

It had me scared before long. We didn't find her at the fuel tanks, the piping, nor the pumps. She wasn't entangled among the levers and switches in the powerhouse, nor had she neatly or otherwise made a sizzle steak of herself in the powerhouse. With a premonition we approached the old dump, but the premonition was false; she hadn't fallen in there and broken her skinny neck. Nowhere under the cradle was she to be found, and the sailors even went clambering and climbing up into the maze of beams and crossbeams in search of her. No luck.

By the time we had finished this, and were again emerging on the central plaza, Pinko and his party had come out of the ship, as emptyhanded as we. Together, Pinko and I made for the pool. It had been a long time since anyone had fallen in *that*—but . . .

Again nothing.

Pinko methodically and idiotically opened and closed his beak; the ship's master frankly sank down upon an artificial divan and wept. It was on the tip of my tongue to suggest that perhaps she had dug a hole and crawled into it, when it occurred to me that one doesn't dig holes in the artificial ground—not large enough to crawl into, that is. The "sod" was but four inches deep, and then solid, electrical-gravity-plated metal began. The hole underneath the "sod" was sealed solid and airtight, in fact a perfect vacuum existed between the bottom of our metal ball and the "ground" we stood on, marred only by that artificial hole in which ammunition was once kept. The men had silently and without orders taken their leave. If the gravity of the situation didn't penetrate their thick skulls, the sight of their captain crying did.

"Now by the four little hells of Centauria III," Pinko broke the silence, "she *has* to be here. And yet she isn't. She has to be here. And yet she isn't. She has to—Say! She's Outside!"

Roberds groaned: "Oh, God!"

"Clumb the runs and sneaked out the mail chute door! I should have known!" It took something like this to reveal the inner aspects of Pinko's character. It was fascinating to watch him, despite the emergency. After all, I'd spent twenty-one years with him and this was the first show he'd ever performed. "I should have known!"

Six of us broke out suits and rifles—the complete arsenal on hand—and followed him up; how long after her we could not guess. Perhaps *too* long. Again Pinko took unfair advantage: he flew up and we had to climb. It was funny to see his long beak sticking out of the suit (with a special auxiliary covering for the beak). He looked like a man from Mars . . . say, that was funny. If I lived, I must remember to repeat it to him. I say, "*If* I lived*.*"

Topside, Pinko awaited us; despite that everyone took a hasty glance around as if foolishly expecting to find Maynard calmly sitting a few feet away, stargazing. Unable to communicate except by gestures, he roughly grouped two men together and pushed them off in the left direction; two others he started the opposite way. I about-faced and began climbing up towards the slightly flattened "roof" of our metal sphere, while he, reasoning that she would do likewise, followed the line of least resistance and walked down underneath.

It was dark and hard to see, but presently I could see her shadow. Oh, yes, I had to find her! We were pretty close but still hardly discernible to each other. In fairness, I must admit I saw the shark first. I found Judy at just the moment she was a whoop and a holler ahead of a dish of mincemeat. She was to be the mincemeat.

This mess she had wandered into was the third shark I had ever seen! Description? Hah! It has a scientific name a light-year long among the learned men who admitted its existence; and was just a jeering, "Bah!" to the other side of the fence who denied such a thing can live in a void! "*Space-shark*," the Service called it. Almost everywhere in space it is, except in those zones surrounding the planets and their moons. There still remains to be written an accurate description of the thing! Some of the boys who have had glimpses of 'em claim it's a cross between a shark and a ghost—a description that can't be imagined until you've seen one, and then you realize that is its *only* description!

Laying my gun down against the hull, I fired. Now if only some of the others were walking, and "heard" the vibration of the shot!

Had Judy kept her presence of mind, or remembered her fiction heroes, she'd've stiffened—played dead—and the chances are better than one in ten she would have lived to snap another camera. But like a fool girl, she thrashed and kicked about in semi-hysterics in an effort to swim away from the beast; and as I came closer, it began to nose her, a prelude to the kill. If that damn thing had any sense, it wouldn't touch her with a hundred-foot fuel pipe; the air in her body and suit-tanks would give it one hell of a bellyache! Which goes to show you the loathsome devil had no more common sense than she.

I ran and swam ahead clumsily, threw up the rifle for another shot! Kill it? Don't make me laugh! But I did succeed in one thing: distracting its attention from her to me! The terrible phosphorescent "eyes" dropped her and fastened on me with a charge like high voltage.

Play dead! I ordered myself. Spreading arms and legs in slow movements, my body began revolving slowly like the human "X" it appeared, watching the beast and the girl from eye-corners. The shark rolled, forgot Maynard, and nosed me! Oozy and wet sweat popped out to tickle the skin of my arms and legs. Sweat popped off my exposed body and floated near me!

Movement made itself felt at my boots and against my will I angled my head and watched! Long, shapeless nose eagerly quizzing the artificial leather in the boots, sniffing for the scent of life. Accidentally it touched bare skin and terror-locked muscles loosened—I jumped! The shark quivered in pure joy! Repeating the experiment it poked its shocking nose flat against my leg, and that leg jerked like a wild thing. Its body-fins rippled in antici-pation . . .

Abruptly, the monster stopped nosing and backed away. From then on the moments of my life were a blueprint I knew by heart and hearsay! The shark would leave me—for the space of seconds and perhaps a half-mile—and when it returned, it wouldn't be taking its time! They rush at their hapless victim with the speed of the time-honored express rocket! The great shimmering body, exploding with internal fireworks, literally swallows a man at one gulp in a maw that promised hellfire and brimstone! My "X" wasn't doing me much good, but I held it. This baby stopped just about a half-mile away and angled in an attempt to catch me end-on. Why don't you close eyes? Oh, they still belonged to me, the will to close them no longer existed. They'd be closed soon—permanently! Yeah! Pinko and the Lulu certainly should be happy.

Then it came.

There was no mind-picturing necessary; I was helpless in front of a roaring rocket, a rocket that breathed and squirmed and devoured me with hellish eyes seconds before its mouth did! Glowing body was almost transparent as redfire lit up its insides; slapping tail streaked like a minor comet! It was so close and horrible I could look right into the mouth, so close the tongue was plainly seen uncurling, ready to lick me in and roll up my body, even before the jaws closed over me!

And a streaking pain I knew was a bullet zipped across my forehead, drowning the sight out of my eyes with blood. And awareness from my mind. But not entirely out until I had flopped over on my belly and saw figures racing around the ball; and saw Maynard drop fainting to the surface, my rifle falling from her hands.

Remember? I said that was about eight years ago, more or less. "So she married some other guy?" Pinko repeated. "Yeah, you *should* have guessed it."

Me, what could I answer? He had me. Money she had tenderly pressed upon me, and just as tenderly I had pressed it back, according to Regulation S908. Herself she had tenderly pressed upon me for a few hours I held her, and just as tenderly pressed back into the care of the departing liner. (Regulation S37.)

Marriage? Yeah, I could get married when I had finished out my fifty years. She'd wait, sure she would. She loved me. And she'd pull a few wires, meanwhile, to see if I couldn't be transferred somewhere for a shorter service period or to a job allowing wives.

And she'd sent me an autographed colorpic which I had tacked up over my bunk.

Which, I guess, was all I could expect. . . .

THE ANTHOLOGIES

Every time I edit a reprint anthology, some person with a long memory quotes me back to myself. What I said, years and years ago, was, "Editing an anthology is a license to steal."

As of present date, this is not entirely true, although it is still a long way from being entirely false. Most anthologies divide the income fifty-fifty between editor and contributors. There is a certain amount of work involved in putting an anthology together, to be sure, but I don't think anyone would pretend that it is half as much work as *writing* a book. So half seems to me some overpayment to the editor, and yet that is vastly less than many anthology editors used to take as a matter of course. In the bad old days, a number of anthology editors bought permissions from the original magazine publishers (who, in the even badder days, had bought "all rights" from the authors). They paid a flat fee of a penny a word or thereabouts to the magazine people, and whatever came in above that they kept—if an anthology earned twenty thousand dollars (and in the early days, some earned more), a thousand went to pay for the stories and nineteen thousand to the editor. Often the magazine publisher took a cut of the thousand, so what actually went to the writers was even less—sometimes a half-cent a word, rarely much more, often nothing. Some of the early editors of science-fiction textbooks—which were really very like any other anthology, except that they were meant to be used in the classroom and so usually had more introductory material—did even better for themselves. Schooled in the academic tradition, in which contributors do not expect to be paid—since "publication" adds brownie points to their hopes for promotion and tenure—they paid their contributors nothing at all.

Although things have changed considerably, it is hard to see what an anthologist does to entitle him to half the loot—except for one thing.

The actual mechanics of putting together a reprint anthology hardly adds up to a full week's work. Generally speaking, the person who edits the anthology is someone who has done a great deal of reading in the field—otherwise, he is not likely to find a publisher to bring it out in the first place. He seldom has to do very much additional reading; the stories that stand out in his mind are presumably the best ones, so he can do most of it from memory, as fast as he can type a table of contents. He needs to get the authors' permissions, but most of them are not difficult to find. It takes twenty minutes to type a standard permission form, another couple of hours to Xerox twenty or thirty copies and mail them out. A short introduction to write, perhaps a brief note on each story if he feels energetic—*voilà*, the job is done.

And that's all there is to it . . . except for the "one thing" mentioned above. That is finding a publisher to publish it. *That* is the hard part. There isn't a publisher in the world who is not continuously swamped with anthology proposals. There is hardly a publisher who hasn't been badly burned in publishing one. Consequently, book editors spend a lot of their time thinking up reasons for rejection for anthologies. The acceptance rate of unsolicited novel manuscripts is very low, but not a fraction as low as for unsolicited anthologies.

So in order to get an anthology published, the editor must have: (a) a great sales angle—a new "theme," a big name to sign to it, whatever, or (b) superb salesmanship and remorseless persistence, or (c) luck.

It was (c) luck, I think, that got me my first anthology to edit—that plus a small favor I had done for a gentleman who never failed to repay favors several times over. The gentleman was Walter I. Bradbury of Doubleday, to whom, around 1948, I had been of some little service in helping to start their brand-new science-fiction line. Brad had asked Robert A. Heinlein to edit an anthology for the line. Heinlein had demurred. He had no objection to writing an introduction, or even to putting his name on the book, but he didn't relish the picking and choosing of one writer over another—there were easier ways to lose friends. Fine, said Brad, you just sign the contract here, and we'll get somebody to ghost the selecting for you. So Bob Heinlein signed, and Brad asked me if I wanted to do the ghosting. I said I would be delighted, provided I could share the chore with Judy Merril, a marvelous woman to whom I happened to be married at the time. Brad agreed; so did Judy; so did Bob Heinlein; and so we set about collecting stories for what soon appeared in the bookstores as *Tomorrow, the Stars*. Judy and I had undertaken to skulk the whole book together anonymously, but Bob Heinlein is also a gentleman; he had no use for such furtiveness, and insisted on giving us credit in his introduction. Wherefore the secret stopped being a secret almost at once.

I wish I could say that editing an anthology with Judy was a great pleasure, but I would lie if I did. There had not, after all, been very many SF anthologies up to that point. There was an immense lode of first-rate stories to be worked. My idea was to do what I have described above and pick out the first twelve titles that occurred to me in a fast roam along memory lane. Judy would have none of it. She insisted on digging through the most obscure sources for the most unlikely authors, queried everyone she knew for suggestions, doublechecked every piece I thought of—she *worked*. Worse than that. She made me work too. In the volume as it appeared, about half the selections were my own, the other half Judy's. I don't think it is easy to tell which is which. But somebody must have been doing something right—I still get royalties on *Tomorrow, the Stars*, more than a quarter of a century later, and so does everyone else connected with it.

Because *Tomorrow, the Stars* did well, I was a credible candidate for the job the next time Doubleday had an anthology to edit, a year or two later. It came about because Doubleday had started its own "fight-fire-with-fire" paperback line—well, not "paperback," exactly. They were laminated in plastic, and they were called Permabooks.

The publishing industry is both simpler and more complicated than it looks from outside. To a writer, clutching his brand-new short story or novel, it all seems formidable and monolithic. Inside it is held together with spit-and-baling-wire. This is why (c) luck is so important. In 1950 I was too late to be the first anthologist to think of putting together a book of science-fiction stories—Healy, McComas, Conklin, and half a dozen others were there before me. 1950 was too early for me to have any name recognition that might sell a book—in fact, I was still a couple of years from having my name, my real name, that is, on any science-fiction story at all. (That didn't happen until *The Space Merchants*. I had been writing and publishing science fiction for fifteen years, but always under pen-names.) What happened was that some vast, eternal plan high up in the Doubleday management circles detected a need for the Permabooks line, which created a need for books to publish in it, which suggested a science-fiction anthology . . . and I happened to be standing there. Thus *Shadow of Tomorrow*.

Happily, it did well, so the next year I edited *Beyond the End of Time*. Which also did well. In fact, it did well enough so that the Doubleday upper echelons determined to do the next anthology of mine in both hardcover and paper, invoking another Doubleday subsidiary called Hanover House for the hardcover. That one was called *Assignment in Tomorrow*. At that point, the plan changed in another corporate decision. Doubleday sold the Permabooks line to another company, where it vanished without a trace. The paperback of *Assignment in Tomorrow* never appeared.

That was a substantial blow to my fortunes. Each anthology had been worth a thousand dollars or so to me, plus royalties—no insignificant element in my budget in those years. Now the spring had run dry. That was not the worst. I had calculated the advances due to the contributors on the basis of both hardcover and paper editions, and paid them accordingly. Under the terms of the contract, the publisher was entitled to deduct any unearned portion of an advance from my royalties on other books—which they did; so it was a long time before I recovered from that. Heigh-ho. It was a wound received long and long ago. But from time to time, it still stings.

Altogether, I have edited three or four dozen reprint anthologies—maybe more. I don't know the exact number. I don't even know where to look to find it out—mostly because it all depends on what you call a "reprint anthology."

The other day I visited Harlan Ellison at his home in Los Angeles. The name on the doorplate is "Ellison Wonderland," and a wonderland it is—statues that glow, a jukebox that plays, a rabbit hole to crawl through and, above all, about a zillion books. Harlan is a completist. He claims to have nearly every one of my books—and so he does, or anyway nearly every one of the books with my name on them, or even a recognizable pseudonym. But there are at least a dozen, and maybe a score, that he doesn't have and neither do I. They appeared under the imprint of *Popular Science* and *Outdoor Life* in the late 1940s and early 1950s, when I was (among other titles) book editor for the publishing company, and after.

"Waste not, want not," was the motto of Popular Science Publishing Company. The value of an article on fly-tying or car repair did not end with its publication in one of the magazines. After each issue appeared, someone went through every page, razoring out the paragraphs and columns and pasting them together into made-up book pages. For five or six years that person was I. I didn't do it without help. While I was on the payroll and working in the office, I had a secretary or an assistant to perform the physical labor. Later on, as a free-lance I had Merril Zissman, my step-daughter in my marriage to Judy Merril. Merril was ten years old or thereabouts, and very good at cutting and pasting. I paid her a penny a page for the work, which meant that a 192-page book cost me $1.92 in direct labor costs. Of course, I made all the executive decisions and had to bear the expense of paper, scissors, and paste . . . even so that left me with a profit of nearly $498.18 out of the five hundred dollars PopSci paid me for each book, a fact of which Merril still reminds me from time to time.

Even if you don't count the anonymous *Popular Science-Outdoor Life* books as anthologies, the number is still pretty large. While I was editor of *Galaxy, If,* and the rest of the Galaxy group, I edited a number of anthologies drawing from the stories in the magazines. ("Waste not, want not," works for science-fiction magazines as well as for *Popular Science.*) But there are half a dozen worthy of special mention.

The Expert Dreamers was a bright idea whose time came before I was ready for it. In a sense, it was an attempt to legitimize science fiction by showing that some of it was written by actual scientists. (In the 1950s,. legitimizing science fiction still seemed like a good idea. Science fiction was not as respectable as it is now.) Unfortunately, I dawdled in finding a publisher, and then took my time getting the book together, and meanwhile Groff Conklin had the same idea. His *Science Fiction by Scientists* came out before my book. The curious thing was that, although we were making the same point, we came up with quite different lists of stories to prove it.

Nightmare Age was an eco-freak book. It sold out its one printing and then was seen no more, but it still remains an anthology of which I am proud. It seems to me that the world ecology movement really began in science-fiction stories—especially in the 1950s, but actually going back as far as science fiction itself does.

Jupiter, which I edited in collaboration with my then wife, Carol Pohl, was meant as the first of a series of anthologies, each of which would deal with a different planet. I still think it is a good idea for a series, but it has seemed to occur to others since and, anyway, I doubt that I will ever get back to it. (However, Carol and I edited three other anthologies together later on, for Ace and Bantam.)

And, starting in 1953, I edited the *Star Science Fiction* series for Ballantine.

Star began as a one-shot, as a sort of favor to Ian Ballantine. Ian wanted to make science-fiction writers know he was around, so they would think to write books for him. I suggested the best way to let a writer know you're alive is to send him a check, and the best pretext for doing that was to publish an anthology containing stories by all the writers he wanted to attract. Fine, he said. You do it. Only let's not do reprints. Get original stories.

It happened I was in a good position to do that, since I was a literary agent at the time, and something over half of the good science-fiction being written was coming from my clients. That made getting half the stories easy; and with stories lined up by Leiber, Kornbluth, Sheckley, Wyndham, and a few others out of my own stable, most other writers were well pleased to appear.

Star ran for a total of eight incarnations: Six volumes of *Star Science Fiction Stories*, one of *Star Science Fiction Novels*, and one of *Star Science Fiction Magazine*, an ill-advised attempt to convert the series into a regular periodical. I thought it should work, and I still think it should have. But it didn't.

Star was the first attempt to combine the flexibility and higher rates of paperbound publication with the reader-loyalty and personal identification of a magazine. All the other original series anthologies in science fiction are more or less modeled on *Star*. But *Star*, of course, was modeled on examples from outside the science-fiction field. *Star* was good stuff. Its stories are still reprinted every year in anthologies, and the original volumes themselves have been reprinted a number of times.

But after a while it began to run thin.

Editing a once-a-year anthology is not a great deal less time-consuming than editing an every-month magazine. You don't have to read as many manuscripts, because you don't get the same volume of slush-pile submissions. But you have to read just about as many professional scripts, and the benefits of avoiding reading slush are overbalanced by the fact that you don't get to discover new talents out of the slush pile. Moreover, the major writers are not in the habit of submitting to you, so you have to work a lot harder to get the stories you want. Partly that can be overcome by outpaying the magazine markets. Mostly, it cannot. Whatever writers say, they do not write only for money, and high rates alone will not get you what you need.

So for me as editor, *Star* began to be a bit of a drag. Worse than that, the sales began to fall off. To some extent that may have been my fault, for allowing quality to fall off—partly because after the first three issues I was cut back in budget and that is always painful—writers take unkindly to the thought that a story you would have paid two hundred dollars for a year ago you will only go to one hundred dollars for now. But partly it seems to be the nature of the beast. Every such series I know of, in science fiction and out, has shown its best sales in the first few volumes, and then a slow and remorseless decline. I think one factor is mechanical. Dealers do not pay close attention to such finicky details as volume numbers, are likely to order smaller quantities of everything past the first few, are unlikely to reorder in the same volume. (The dealers who keep good records are unfortunately more likely than the rest to do this—their records will show that they've sold fifty copies of No. 1 and only twenty-five of No. 6, so they will order more copies of No. 1.)

So after the sixth volume came out, Ian Ballantine and I, by mutual consent, gave it up. I was somewhat regretful, but not as much as you might think. By then Horace Gold was encountering difficulties in continuing as editor of *Galaxy*, and my need to do a certain amount of editing now and then was being met by helping Horace.

THE REPORT ON THE BARNHOUSE EFFECT

BY KURT VONNEGUT, JR.

(Appeared in TOMORROW, THE STARS)

In the field of science-fiction writers, which is characterized by extreme individuals, Kurt Vonnegut is so outstandingly individualistic that he even denies he is one. Partly the reason is paternal devotion. He doesn't want his brain-children called science-fiction novels, because he doesn't want them treated the way science-fiction novels are treated by critics, dealers, and librarians—a view shared by a good many confessed SF writers. But there's more. Years ago, Vonnegut dipped one cautious toe in the science-fiction mainstream. You can see what he made of it in several of his novels, where some of the action takes place in a scene very much like a Milford Science Fiction Writers' Conference, populated by characters who greatly resemble the seamier sides of some celebrated science-fiction writers.

No harm. Vonnegut is far too fine a writer to be denied whatever idiosyncrasies please him. Whatever the man says, and even setting aside the fact that some of his early works (though not this one) were originally published in Galaxy *and* If, *the stories speak for themselves.*

Because Vonnegut does not run with the science-fiction pack, I've only met him once or twice. The time I remember best is when he and I, with a dozen other writers, were invited to testify before a joint Senate-House committee on the then-pending revised copyright legislation. Barbara Tuchman spoke wisely of the embarrassingly unfair treatment American writers received, compared with those in the rest of the civilized world. Art Buchwald gave a Washington insiders' view of the politics involved. I recited a few case histories of writers whose dependents had endangered their copyrights or even blown them, through inability to comply with the old act's tricky requirements. And Vonnegut did a three-minute night-club routine. He had the committee rolling in the aisles—the other witnesses, too—and, you know, I think he did more good for the cause than any of us.

*   *   *

Let me begin by saying that I don't know any more about where Professor Arthur Barnhouse is hiding than anyone else does. Save for one short, enigmatic message, left in my mailbox on Christmas Eve, I have not heard from him since his disappearance a year and a half ago.

What's more, readers of this article will be disappointed if they expect to learn how *they* can bring about the so-called "Barnhouse Effect." If I were able and willing to give away that secret, I would certainly be something more important than a psychology instructor.

I have been urged to write this report because I did research under the professor's direction and because I was the first to learn of his astonishing discovery. But while I was his student I was never entrusted with knowledge of how the mental forces could be released and directed. He was unwilling to trust anyone with that information.

I would like to point out that the term "Barnhouse Effect" is a creation of the popular press, and was never used by Professor Barnhouse. The name he chose for the phenomenon was "*dynamopsychism*," or *force of the mind*.

I cannot believe that there is a civilized person yet to be convinced that such a force exists, what with its destructive effects on display in every national capital. I think humanity has always had an inkling that this sort of force does exist. It has been common knowledge that some people are luckier than others with inanimate objects like dice. What Professor Barnhouse did was to show that such "luck" was a measurable force, which in his case could be enormous.

By my calculations, the professor was about fifty-five times more powerful than a Nagasaki-type atomic bomb at the time he went into hiding. He was not bluffing when, on the eve of "Operation Brainstorm," he told General Honus Barker: "Sitting here at the dinner table, I'm pretty sure I can flatten anything on earth—from Joe Louis to the Great Wall of China."

There is an understandable tendency to look upon Professor Barnhouse as a supernatural visitation. The First Church of Barnhouse in Los Angeles has a congregation numbering in the thousands. He is godlike in neither appearance nor intellect. The man who disarms the world is single, shorter than the average American male, stout, and averse to exercise. His I.Q. is 143, which is good but certainly not sensational. He is quite mortal, about to celebrate his fortieth birthday, and in good health. If he is alone now the isolation won't bother him too much. He was quiet and shy when I knew him, and seemed to find more companionship in books and music than in his associations at the college.

Neither he nor his powers fall outside the sphere of Nature. His dynamopsychic radiations are subject to many known physical laws that apply in the field of radio. Hardly a person has not now heard the snarl of "Barnhouse static" on his home receiver. Contrary to what one might expect, the radiations are affected by sunspots and variations in the ionosphere.

However, his radiations differ from ordinary broadcast waves in several important ways. Their total energy can be brought to bear on any single point the professor chooses, and that energy is undiminished by distance. As a weapon, then, dynamopsychism has an impressive advantage over bacteria and atomic bombs, beyond the fact that it costs nothing to use; it enables the professor to single out critical individuals and objects instead of slaughtering whole populations in the process of maintaining international equilibrium.

As General Honus Barker told the House Military Affairs Committee: "Until someone finds Barnhouse, there is no defense against the Barnhouse Effect." Efforts to "jam" or block the radiations have failed. Premier Slezak could have saved himself the fantastic expense of his "Barnhouse-proof" shelter. Despite the shelter's twelve-foot-thick lead armor, the premier has been floored twice while in it.

There is talk of screening the population for men potentially as powerful dynamopsychically as the professor. Senator Warren Foust demanded funds for this purpose last month, with the passionate declaration: "He who rules the Barnhouse Effect rules the world!" Commissioner Kropotnik said much the same thing, so another costly armaments race, with a new twist, has begun.

This race at least has its comical aspects. The world's best gamblers are being coddled by governments like so many nuclear physicists. There may be several hundred persons with dynamopsychic talent on earth, myself included, but without knowledge of the professor's technique, they can never be anything but dice-table despots. With the secret, it would probably take them ten years to become dangerous weapons. It took the professor that long. He who rules the Barnhouse Effect is Barnhouse and will be for some time.

Popularly, the "Age of Barnhouse" is said to have begun a year and a half ago, on the day of Operation Brainstorm. That was when dynamopsychism became significant politically. Actually, the phenomenon was discovered in May 1942, shortly after the professor turned down a direct commission in the Army and enlisted as an artillery private. Like X-rays and vulcanized rubber, dynamopsychism was discovered by accident.

From time to time Private Barnhouse was invited to take part in games of chance by his barracks mates. He knew nothing about the games, and usually begged off. But one evening, out of social grace, he agreed to shoot craps. It was a terrible or wonderful thing that he played, depending upon whether or not you like the world as it now is.

"Shoot sevens, Pop," someone said.

So "Pop" shot sevens—ten in a row to bankrupt the barracks. He retired to his bunk and, as a mathematical exercise, calculated the odds against his feat on the back of a laundry slip. His chances of doing it, he found, were one in almost ten million! Bewildered, he borrowed a pair of dice from the man in the bunk next to his. He tried to roll sevens again, but got only the usual assortment of numbers. He lay back for a moment, then resumed his toying with the dice. He rolled ten more sevens in a row.

He might have dismissed the phenomenon with a low whistle. But instead the professor mulled over the circumstances surrounding his two lucky streaks. There was one single factor in common: on both occasions, *the same thought train had flashed through his mind just before he threw the dice.* It was that thought train which aligned the professor's brain cells into what has since become the most powerful weapon on earth.

The soldier in the next bunk gave dynamopsychism its first token of respect. In an understatement certain to bring wry smiles to the faces of the world's dejected demogogues, the soldier said, "You're hotter'n a two-dollar pistol, Pop." Professor Barnhouse was all of that. The dice that did his bidding weighed but a few grams, so the forces involved were minute; but the unmistakable fact that there were such forces was earth-shaking.

Professional caution kept him from revealing his discovery immediately. He wanted more facts and a body of theory to go with them. Later, when the atomic bomb was dropped on Hiroshima, it was fear that made him hold his peace. At no time were his experiments, as Premier Slezak called them, "a bourgeois plot to shackle the true democracies of the world." The professor didn't know where they were leading.

In time he came to recognize another startling feature of dynamopsychism: *its strength increased with use.* Within six months he was able to govern dice thrown by men the length of a barracks distant. By the time of his discharge in 1945, he could knock bricks loose from chimneys three miles away.

Charges that Professor Barnhouse could have won the last war in a minute, but did not care to do so, are perfectly senseless. When the war ended, he had the range and power of a 37-millimeter cannon, perhaps—certainly no more. His dynamopsychic powers graduated from the small-arms class only after his discharge and return to Wyandotte College.

I enrolled in the Wyandotte graduate school two years after the professor had rejoined the faculty. By chance, he was assigned as my thesis adviser. I was unhappy about the assignment, for the professor was, in the eyes of both colleagues and students, a somewhat ridiculous figure. He missed classes or had lapses of memory during lectures. When I arrived, in fact, his shortcomings had passed from the ridiculous to the intolerable.

"We're assigning you to Barnhouse as a sort of temporary thing," the dean of social studies told me. He looked apologetic and perplexed. "Brilliant man, Barnhouse, I guess. Difficult to know since his return, perhaps, but his work before the war brought a great deal of credit to our little school."

When I reported to the professor's laboratory for the first time, what I saw was more distressing than the gossip. Every surface in the room was covered with dust; books and apparatus had not been disturbed for months. The professor sat napping at his desk when I entered. The only signs of recent activity were three overflowing ash trays, a pair of scissors, and a morning paper with several items clipped from its front page.

As he raised his head to look at me, I saw that his eyes were clouded with fatigue. "Hi," he said, "just can't seem to get my sleeping done at night." He lighted a cigarette, his hands trembling slightly. "You the young man I'm supposed to help with a thesis?"

"Yes, sir," I said. In minutes he converted my misgivings to alarm.

"You an overseas veteran?" he asked.

"Yes, sir."

"Not much left over there, is there?" He frowned. "Enjoy the last war?"

"No, sir."

"Look like another war to you?"

"Kind of, sir."

"What can be done about it?"

I shrugged. "Looks pretty hopeless."

He peered at me intently. "Know anything about international law, the U.N., and all that?"

"Only what I pick up from the papers."

"Same here," he sighed. He showed me a fat scrapbook, packed with newspaper clippings. "Never used to pay any attention to international politics. Now I study politics the way I used to study rats in mazes. Everybody tells me the same thing—'Looks hopeless.' "

"Nothing short of a miracle—" I began.

"Believe in magic?" he asked sharply. The professor fished two dice from his vest pocket. "I will try to roll twos," he said. He rolled twos three times in a row. "One chance in about forty-seven thousand of that happening. There's a miracle for you." He beamed for an instant, then brought the interview to an end, remarking that he had a class which had begun ten minutes ago.

He was not quick to take me into his confidence, and he said no more about his trick with the dice. I assumed they were loaded, and forgot about them. He set me the task of watching male rats cross electrified metal strips to get to food or female rats—an experiment that had been done to everyone's satisfaction in the 1930s. As though the pointlessness of my work were not bad enough, the professor annoyed me further with irrelevant questions. His favorites were: "Think we should have dropped the atomic bomb on Hiroshima?" and "Think every new piece of scientific information is a good thing for humanity?"

However, I did not feel put upon for long. "Give those poor animals a holiday," he said one morning, after I had been with him only a month. "I wish you'd help me look into a more interesting problem—namely, my sanity."

I returned the rats to their cages.

"What you must do is simple," he said, speaking softly. "Watch the inkwell on my desk. If you see nothing happen to it, say so, and I'll go quietly—relieved, I might add—to the nearest sanitarium."

I nodded uncertainly.

He locked the laboratory door and drew the blinds, so that we were in twilight for a moment. "I'm odd, I know," he said. "It's fear of myself that's made me odd."

"I've found you somewhat eccentric, perhaps, but certainly not—"

"If nothing happens to that inkwell, 'crazy as a bedbug' is the only description of me that will do," he interrupted, turning on the overhead lights. His eyes narrowed. "To give you an idea of how crazy, I'll tell you what's been running through my mind when I should have been sleeping. I think maybe I can save the world. I think maybe I can make every nation a *have* nation, and do away with war for good. I think maybe I can clear roads through jungles, irrigate deserts, build dams overnight."

"Yes, sir."

"Watch the inkwell!"

Dutifully and fearfully I watched. A high-pitched humming seemed to come from the inkwell; then it began to vibrate alarmingly, and finally to bound about the top of the desk, making two noisy circuits. It stopped, hummed again, glowed red, then popped in splinters with a blue-green flash.

Perhaps my hair stood on end. The professor laughed gently. "Magnets?" I managed to say at last.

"Wish to Heaven it were magnets," he murmured. It was then that he told me of dynamopsychism. He knew only that there was such a force; he could not explain it. "It's me and me alone—and it's awful."

"I'd say it was amazing and wonderful!" I cried.

"If all I could do was make inkwells dance, I'd be tickled silly with the whole business." He shrugged disconsolately. "But I'm no toy, my boy. If you like, we can drive around the neighborhood, and I'll show you what I mean." He told me about pulverized boulders, shattered oaks, and abandoned farm buildings demolished within a fifty-mile radius of the campus. "Did every bit of it sitting right here, just thinking—not even thinking hard."

He scratched his head nervously. "I have never dared to concentrate as hard as I can for fear of the damage I might do. I'm to the point where a mere whim is a blockbuster." There was a depressing pause. "Up until a few days ago, I've thought it best to keep my secret for fear of what use it might be put to," he continued. "Now I realize that I haven't any more right to it than a man has a right to own an atomic bomb."

He fumbled through a heap of papers. "This says about all that needs to be said, I think." He handed me a draft of a letter to the Secretary of State.

> Dear Sir:
>   I have discovered a new force which costs nothing to use, and which is probably more important than atomic energy. I should like to see it used most effectively in the cause of peace, and am, therefore, requesting your advice as to how this might best be done.
>   Yours truly,
>   A. Barnhouse

"I have no idea what will happen next," said the professor.

There followed three months of perpetual nightmare, wherein the nation's

political and military great came at all hours to watch the professor's tricks
with fascination.

We were quartered in an old mansion near Charlottesville, Virginia, to
which we had been whisked five days after the letter was mailed. Surrounded
by barbed wire and twenty guards, we were labeled "Project Wishing Well,"
and were classified as Top Secret.

For companionship we had General Honus Barker and the State Department's William K. Cuthrell. For the professor's talk of peace-through-plenty
they had indulgement smiles and much discourse on practical measures and
realistic thinking. So treated, the professor, who had at first been almost
meek, progressed in a matter of weeks toward stubbornness.

He had agreed to reveal the thought train by means of which he aligned his
mind into a dynamopsychic transmitter. But under Cuthrell's and Barker's
nagging to do so, he began to hedge. At first he declared that the information
could be passed on simply by word of mouth. Later he said that it would have
to be written up in a long report. Finally, at dinner one night, just after
General Barker had read the secret orders for Operation Brainstorm, the
professor announced, "The report may take as long as five years to write."
He looked fiercely at the general. "Maybe twenty."

The dismay occasioned by this flat announcement was offset somewhat by
the exciting anticipation of Operation Brainstorm. The general was in a
holiday mood. "The target ships are on their way to the Caroline Islands at
this very moment," he declared ecstatically. "One hundred and twenty of
them! At the same time, ten V-2s are being readied for firing in New Mexico,
and fifty radio-controlled jet bombers are being equipped for a mock attack on
the Aleutians. Just think of it!" Happily he reviewed his orders. "At exactly
1100 hours next Wednesday, I will give you the order to *concentrate*; and
you, Professor, will think as hard as you can about sinking target ships,
destroying the V-2s before they hit the ground, and knocking down the
bombers before they reach the Aleutians! Think you can handle it?"

The professor turned gray and closed his eyes. "As I told you before, my
friend, I don't know what I can do." He added bitterly, "As for this Operation
Brainstorm, I was never consulted about it, and it strikes me as childish and
insanely expensive."

General Barker bridled. "Sir," he said, "your field is psychology, and I
wouldn't presume to give you advice in that field. Mine is national defense. I
have had thirty years of experience and success, Professor, and I'll ask you
not to criticize my judgment."

The professor appealed to Mr. Cuthrell. "Look," he pleaded, "isn't it war
and military matters we're all trying to get rid of? Wouldn't it be a whole lot
more significant and lots cheaper for me to try moving cloud masses into
drought areas, and things like that? I admit I know next to nothing about
international politics, but it seems reasonable to suppose that nobody would
want to fight wars if there were enough of everything to go around. Mr.

Cuthrell, I'd like to try running generators where there isn't any coal or water power, irrigating deserts, and so on. Why, you could figure out what each country needs to make the most of its resources, and I could give it to them without costing American taxpayers a penny.''

"Eternal vigilance is the price of freedom," said the general heavily.

Mr. Cuthrell threw the general a look of mild distaste. "Unfortunately, the general is right in his own way," he said. "I wish to Heaven the world were ready for ideals like yours, but it simply isn't. We aren't surrounded by brothers, but by enemies. It isn't a lack of food or resources that has us on the brink of war—it's a struggle for power. Who's going to be in charge of the world, our kind of people or theirs?''

The professor nodded in reluctant agreement and arose from the table. "I beg your pardon, gentlemen. You are, after all, better qualified to judge what is best for the country. I'll do whatever you say." He turned to me. "Don't forget to wind the restricted clock and put the confidential cat out," he said gloomily, and ascended the stairs to his bedroom.

For reasons of national security, Operation Brainstorm was carried on without the knowledge of the American citizenry, which was footing the bill. The observers, technicians, and military men involved in the activity knew that a test was under way—a test of what, they had no idea. Only thirty-seven key men, myself included, knew what was afoot.

In Virginia the day for Operation Brainstorm was unseasonably cool. Inside, a log fire crackled in the fireplace, and the flames were reflected in the polished metal cabinets that lined the living room. All that remained of the room's lovely old furniture was a Victorian love seat, set squarely in the center of the floor, facing three television receivers. One long bench had been brought in for the ten of us privileged to watch. The television screens showed, from left to right, the stretch of desert which was the rocket target, the guinea-pig fleet, and a section of the Aleutian sky through which the radio-controlled bomber formation would roar.

Ninety minutes before H-hour the radios announced that the rockets were ready, that the observation ships had backed away to what was thought to be a safe distance, and that the bombers were on their way. The small Virginia audience lined up on the bench in order of rank, smoked a great deal, and said little. Professor Barnhouse was in his bedroom. General Barker bustled about the house like a woman preparing Thanksgiving dinner for twenty.

At ten minutes before H-hour the general came in, shepherding the professor before him. The professor was comfortably attired in sneakers, gray flannels, a blue sweater, and a white shirt open at the neck. The two of them sat side by side on the love seat. The general was rigid and perspiring; the professor was cheerful. He looked at each of the screens, lighted a cigarette and settled back, comfortable and cool.

"Bombers sighted!" cried Aleutian observers.

"Rockets away!" barked the New Mexico radio operator.

All of us looked quickly at the big electric clock over the mantel, while the professor, a half-smile on his face, continued to watch the television sets. In hollow tones, the general counted away the seconds remaining. "Five...four ...three...two...one...*Concentrate!*"

Professor Barnhouse closed his eyes, pursed his lips, and stroked his temples. He held the position for a minute. The television images were scrambled, and the radio signals were drowned in the din of Barnhouse static. The professor sighed, opened his eyes and smiled confidently.

"Did you give it everything you had?" asked the general dubiously.

"I was wide open," the professor replied.

The television images pulled themselves together, and mingled cries of amazement came over the radios tuned to the observers. The Aleutian sky was streaked with the smoke trails of bombers screaming down in flames. Simultaneously, there appeared high over the rocket target a cluster of white puffs, followed by faint thunder.

General Barker shook his head happily. "By George!" he crowed. "Well, sir, by George, by George, by George!"

"Look!" shouted the admiral seated next to me. "The fleet—it wasn't touched!"

"The guns seem to be drooping," said Mr. Cuthrell.

We left the bench and clustered about the television sets to examine the damage more closely. What Mr. Cuthrell had said was true. The ships' guns curved downward, their muzzles resting on the steel decks. We in Virginia were making such a hullabaloo that it was impossible to hear the radio reports. We were so engrossed, in fact, that we didn't miss the professor until two short snarls of Barnhouse static shocked us into sudden silence. The radios went dead.

We looked around apprehensively. The professor was gone. A harassed guard threw open the front door from the outside to yell that the professor had escaped. He brandished his pistol in the direction of the gates, which hung open, limp and twisted. In the distance a speeding government station wagon topped a ridge and dropped from sight into the valley beyond. The air was filled with choking smoke, for every vehicle on the ground was ablaze. Pursuit was impossible.

"What in God's name got into him?" bellowed the general.

Mr. Cuthrell, who had rushed out onto the front porch, now slouched back into the room, reading a penciled note as he came. He thrust the note into my hands. "The good man left this billet-doux under the door knocker. Perhaps our young friend here will be kind enough to read it to you gentlemen while I take a restful walk through the woods."

"Gentlemen [I read aloud],
    As the first superweapon with a conscience, I am removing myself from your national defense stockpile. Setting a new precedent in the behavior ordnance, I have humane reasons for going off.
                                                    A. Barnhouse"

Since that day, of course, the professor has been systematically destroying the world's armaments, until there is now little with which to equip an army other than rocks and sharp sticks. His activities haven't exactly resulted in peace, but have, rather, precipitated a bloodless and entertaining sort of war that might be called the "War of the Tattletales." Every nation is flooded with enemy agents whose sole mission is to locate military equipment, which is promptly wrecked when it is brought to the professor's attention in the press.

Just as every day brings news of more armaments pulverized by dynamopsychism, so has it brought rumors of the professor's whereabouts. During last week alone, three publications carried articles proving variously that he was hiding in an Inca ruin in the Andes, in the sewers of Paris, and in the unexplored chambers of Carlsbad Caverns. Knowing the man, I am inclined to regard such hiding places as unnecessarily romantic and uncomfortable. While there are numerous persons eager to kill him, there must be millions who would care for him and hide him. I like to think that he is in the home of such a person.

One thing is certain: at this writing, Professor Barnhouse is not dead. Barnhouse static jammed broadcasts not ten minutes ago. In the eighteen months since his disappearance, he has been reported dead some half-dozen times. Each report has stemmed from the death of an unidentified man resembling the professor, during a period free of the static. The first three reports were followed at once by renewed talk of rearmament and recourse to war. The saber rattlers have learned how imprudent premature celebrations of the professor's demise can be.

Many a stouthearted patriot has found himself prone in the tangled bunting and timbers of a smashed reviewing stand, seconds after having announced that the archtyranny of Barnhouse was at an end. But those who would make war if they could, in every country in the world, wait in sullen silence for what must come—the passing of Professor Barnhouse.

To ask how much longer the professor will live is to ask how much longer we must wait for the blessings of another world war. He is of short-lived stock; his mother lived to be fifty-three, his father to be forty-nine; and the life spans of his grandparents on both sides were of the same order. He might be expected to live, then, for perhaps fifteen years more, if he can remain hidden from his enemies. When one considers the number and vigor of these enemies, however, fifteen years seems an extraordinary length of time, which might better be revised to fifteen days, hours, or minutes.

The professor knows that he cannot live much longer. I say this because of the message left in my mailbox on Christmas Eve. Unsigned, typewritten on a soiled scrap of paper, the note consisted of ten sentences. The first nine of these, each a bewildering tangle of psychological jargon and references to obscure texts, made no sense to me at first reading. The tenth, unlike the rest, was simply constructed and contained no large words—but its irrational content made it the most puzzling and bizarre sentence of all. I nearly threw the note away, thinking it a colleague's warped notion of a practical joke. For some reason, though, I added it to the clutter on top of my desk, which included, among other mementos, the professor's dice.

It took me several weeks to realize that the message really meant something, that the first nine sentences, when unsnarled, could be taken as instructions. The tenth still told me nothing. It was only last night that I discovered how it fitted in with the rest. The sentence appeared in my thoughts last night while I was toying absently with the professor's dice.

I promised to have this report on its way to the publishers today. In view of what has happened, I am obliged to break that promise, or release the report incomplete. The delay will not be a long one, for one of the few blessings accorded a bachelor like myself is the ability to move quickly from one abode to another, or from one way of life to another. What property I want to take with me can be packed in a few hours. Fortunately, I am not without substantial private means, which may take as long as a week to realize in liquid and anonymous form. When this is done, I shall mail the report.

I have just returned from a visit to my doctor, who tells me my health is excellent. I am young, and with any luck at all, I shall live to a ripe old age indeed, for my family on both sides is noted for longevity.

Briefly, I propose to vanish.

Sooner or later, Professor Barnhouse must die. But long before then I shall be ready. So, to the saber rattlers of today—and even, I hope, of tomorrow—I say: Be advised. Barnhouse will die. But not the Barnhouse Effect.

Last night I tried once more to follow the oblique instructions on the scrap of paper. I took the professor's dice, and then, with the last, nightmarish sentence flitting through my mind, I rolled fifty consecutive sevens.

Good-by.

ECO-CATASTROPHE!

BY PAUL R. EHRLICH

(Appeared in NIGHTMARE AGE)

When Rachel Carson's Silent Spring *appeared and became a bestseller, millions of people around the world became aware that the ocean we all swim in—the ecosphere—was at risk from what we ourselves were doing to it. As with so many other technological, scientific, and social events of the past hundred years, the only people who were not really surprised to learn this were science-fiction readers. The threat to the ecology had been a persistent theme in science fiction for years, even decades before it attracted academic notice. In fact, it is fair to say that the movement to save the ecology began in science fiction.*

For that reason, it was no surprise to me to learn that a good many of the leaders of Friends of the Earth, Greenpeace, and so on had grown up on science fiction. (Some of them were still deeply involved—the Japanese head of the save-the-whales movement, Sakyo Komatsu, is also one of Japan's leading science-fiction writers.) But it was not until I was putting together an anthology of science-fiction stories on ecological themes for Ian Ballantine, and he called to my attention a short piece by Paul R. Ehrlich, that I realized some of the most outspoken conservationists in America still used the techniques of science fiction to carry their message to the world.

*   *   *

The end of the ocean came late in the summer of 1979, and it came even more rapidly than the biologists had expected. There had been signs for more than a decade, commencing with the discovery in 1968 that DDT slows down photosynthesis in marine plant life. It was announced in a short paper in the technical journal *Science*, but to ecologists it smacked of doomsday. They knew that all life in the sea depends on photosynthesis, the chemical process by which green plants bind the sun's energy and make it available to living

114

things. And they knew that DDT and similar chlorinated hydrocarbons had polluted the entire surface of the earth, including the sea.

But that was only the first of many signs. There had been the final gasp of the whaling industry in 1973, and the end of the Peruvian anchovy fishery in 1975. Indeed, a score of other fisheries had disappeared quietly from overexploitation and various eco-catastrophes by 1977. The term "eco-catastrophe" was coined by a California ecologist in 1969 to describe the most spectacular of man's attacks on the systems which sustain his life. He drew his inspiration from the Santa Barbara offshore oil disaster of that year, and from the news which spread among naturalists that virtually all of the Golden State's seashore bird life was doomed because of chlorinated hydro-carbon interference with its reproduction. Eco-catastrophes in the sea became increasingly common in the early 1970s. Mysterious "blooms" of previously rare microorganisms began to appear in offshore waters. Red tides—killer outbreaks of a minute single-celled plant—returned to the Florida Gulf coast and were sometimes accompanied by tides of other exotic hues.

It was clear by 1975 that the entire ecology of the ocean was changing. A few types of phytoplankton were becoming resistant to chlorinated hydrocar-bons and were gaining the upper hand. Changes in the phytoplankton community led inevitably to changes in the community of zooplankton, the tiny animals which eat the phytoplankton. These changes were passed on up the chains of life in the ocean to the herring, plaice, cod, and tuna. As the diversity of life in the ocean diminished, its stability also decreased.

Other changes had taken place by 1975. Most ocean fishes that returned to freshwater to breed, like the salmon, had become extinct, their breeding streams so dammed up and polluted that their powerful homing instinct only resulted in suicide. Many fishes and shellfishes that bred in restricted areas along the coasts followed them as onshore pollution escalated.

By 1977 the annual yield of fish from the sea was down to thirty million metric tons, less than one-half the per capita catch of a decade earlier. This helped malnutrition to escalate sharply in a world where an estimated fifty million people per year were already dying of starvation. The United Nations attempted to get all chlorinated hydrocarbon insecticides banned on a world-wide basis, but the move was defeated by the United States. This opposition was generated primarily by the American petrochemical industry, operating hand in glove with its subsidiary, the United States Department of Agricul-ture. Together they persuaded the government to oppose the U.N. move—which was not difficult since most Americans believed that Russia and China were more in need of fish products than was the United States. The United Nations also attempted to get fishing nations to adopt strict and enforced catch limits to preserve dwindling stocks. This move was blocked by Russia, who, with the most modern electronic equipment, was in the best position to glean what was left in the sea. It was, curiously, on the very day in 1977 when the Soviet Union announced its refusal that another ominous article appeared in *Science*. It announced that incident solar radiation had been so reduced by worldwide air pollution that serious effects on the world's vegetation could be expected.

Apparently it was a combination of ecosystem destabilization, sunlight reduction, and a rapid escalation in chlorinated hydrocarbon pollution from massive Thanodrin applications which triggered the ultimate catastrophe. Seventeen huge Soviet-financed Thanodrin plants were operating in underdeveloped countries by 1978. They had been part of a massive Russian "aid offensive" designed to fill the gap caused by the collapse of America's ballyhooed "Green Revolution."

It became apparent in the early '70s that the "Green Revolution" was more talk than substance. Distribution of high yield "miracle" grain seeds had caused temporary local spurts in agricultural production. Simultaneously, excellent weather had produced record harvests. The combination permitted bureaucrats, especially in the United States Department of Agriculture and the Agency for International Development (AID), to reverse their previous pessimism and indulge in an outburst of optimistic propaganda about staving off famine. They raved about the approaching transformation of agriculture in the underdeveloped countries (UDCs). The reason for the propaganda reversal was never made clear. Most historians agree that a combination of utter ignorance of ecology, a desire to justify past errors, and pressure from agro-industry (which was eager to sell pesticides, fertilizers, and farm machinery to the UDCs and agencies helping the UDCs) was behind the campaign. Whatever the motivation, the results were clear. Many concerned people, lacking the expertise to see through the Green Revolution drivel, relaxed. The population-food crisis was "solved."

But reality was not long in showing itself. Local famine persisted in northern India even after good weather brought an end to the ghastly Bihar famine of the mid-'60s. East Pakistan was next, followed by a resurgence of general famine in northern India. Other foci of famine rapidly developed in Indonesia, the Philippines, Malawi, the Congo, Egypt, Colombia, Ecuador, Honduras, the Dominican Republic, and Mexico.

Everywhere hard realities destroyed the illusion of the Green Revolution. Yields dropped as the progressive farmers who had first accepted the new seeds found that their higher yields brought lower prices—effective demand (hunger plus cash) was not sufficient in poor countries to keep prices up. Less progressive farmers, observing this, refused to make the extra effort required to cultivate the "miracle" grains. Transport systems proved inadequate to bring the necessary fertilizer to the fields where the new and extremely fertilizer-sensitive grains were being grown. The same systems were also inadequate to move produce to markets. Fertilizer plants were not built fast enough, and most of the underdeveloped countries could not scrape together funds to purchase supplies, even on concessional terms. Finally, the inevitable happened, and pests began to reduce yields in even the most carefully cultivated fields. Among the first were the famous "miracle rats" which invaded Philippine "miracle rice" fields early in 1969. They were quickly followed by many insects and viruses, thriving on the relatively pest-susceptible new grains, encouraged by the vast and dense plantings, and rapidly acquiring resistance to the chemicals used against them. As chaos spread until even the most obtuse agriculturists and economists realized that the Green Revolution had turned brown, the Russians stepped in.

In retrospect it seems incredible that the Russians, with the American mistakes known to them, could launch an even more incompetent program of aid to the underdeveloped world. Indeed, in the early 1970s there were cynics in the United States who claimed that outdoing the stupidity of American foreign aid would be physically impossible. Those critics were, however, obviously unaware that the Russians had been busily destroying their own environment for many years. The virtual disappearance of sturgeon from Russian rivers caused a great shortage of caviar by 1970. A standard joke among Russian scientists at that time was that they had created an artificial caviar which was indistinguishable from the real thing—except by taste. At any rate the Soviet Union, observing with interest the progressive deterioration of relations between the UDCs and the United States, came up with a solution. It had recently developed what it claimed was the ideal insecticide, a highly lethal chlorinated hydrocarbon complexed with a special agent for penetrating the external skeletal armor of insects. Announcing that the new pesticide, called Thanodrin, would truly produce a Green Revolution, the Soviets entered into negotiations with various UDCs for the construction of massive Thanodrin factories. The USSR would bear all the costs; all it wanted in return were certain trade and military concessions.

It is interesting now, with the perspective of years, to examine in some detail the reasons why the UDCs welcomed the Thanodrin plan with such open arms. Government officials in these countries ignored the protests of their own scientists that Thanodrin would not solve the problems which plagued them. The governments now knew that the basic cause of their problems was overpopulation, and that these problems had been exacerbated by the dullness, daydreaming, and cupidity endemic to all governments. They knew that only population control and limited development aimed primarily at agriculture could have spared them the horrors they now faced. They knew it, but they were not about to admit it. How much easier it was simply to accuse the Americans of failing to give them proper aid; how much simpler to accept the Russian panacea.

And then there was the general worsening of relations between the United States and the UDCs. Many things had contributed to this. The situation in America in the first half of the 1970s deserves our close scrutiny. Being more dependent on imports for raw materials than the Soviet Union, the United States had, in the early 1970s, adopted more and more heavy-handed policies in order to insure continuing supplies. Military adventures in Asia and Latin America had further lessened the international credibility of the United States as a great defender of freedom—an image which had begun to deteriorate rapidly during the pointless and fruitless Viet Nam conflict. At home, acceptance of the carefully manufactured image lessened dramatically, as even the more romantic and chauvinistic citizens began to understand the role of the military and the industrial system in what John Kenneth Galbraith had aptly named "The New Industrial State."

At home in the USA the early '70s were traumatic times. Racial violence grew and the habitability of the cities diminished, as nothing substantial was done to ameliorate either racial inequities or urban blight. Welfare rolls grew as automation and general technological progress forced more and more people into the category of "unemployable." Simultaneously a taxpayers' revolt occurred. Although there was not enough money to build the schools, roads, water systems, sewage systems, jails, hospitals, urban transit lines, and all the other amenities needed to support a burgeoning population, Americans refused to tax themselves more heavily. Starting in Youngstown, Ohio, in 1969 and followed closely by Richmond, California, community after community was forced to close its schools or curtail educational operations for lack of funds. Water supplies, already marginal in quality and quantity in many places by 1970, deteriorated quickly. Water rationing occurred in 1,723 municipalities in the summer of 1974, and hepatitis and epidemic dysentery rates climbed about five hundred percent between 1970 and 1974.

Air pollution continued to be the most obvious manifestation of environmental deterioration. It was, by 1972, quite literally in the eyes of all Americans. The year 1973 saw not only the New York and Los Angeles smog disasters, but also the publication of the surgeon general's massive report on air pollution and health. The public had been partially prepared for the worst by the publicity given to the U.N. pollution conference held in 1972. Deaths in the late '60s caused by smog were well known to scientists, but the public had ignored them because they mostly involved the early demise of the old and sick rather than people dropping dead on the freeways. But suddenly our citizens were faced with nearly two hundred thousand corpses and massive documentation that they could be the next to die from respiratory disease. They were not ready for that scale of disaster. After all, the U.N. conference had not predicted that accumulated air pollution would make the planet uninhabitable until almost 1990. The population was terrorized as TV screens became filled with scenes of horror from the disaster areas. Especially vivid was NBC's coverage of hundreds of unattended people choking out their lives outside of New York's hospitals. Terms like nitrogen oxide, acute bronchitis, and cardiac arrest began to have real meaning for most Americans.

The ultimate horror was the announcement that chlorinated hydrocarbons were now a major constituent of air pollution in all American cities. Autopsies of smog disaster victims revealed an average chlorinated hydrocarbon load in fatty tissue equivalent to twenty-six parts per million of DDT. In October, 1973, the Department of Health, Education and Welfare announced studies which showed unequivocally that increasing death rates from hypertension, cirrhosis of the liver, liver cancer, and a series of other diseases had resulted from the chlorinated hydrocarbon load. They estimated that Americans born since 1964 (when DDT usage began) now had a life expectancy of only forty-nine years, and predicted that if current patterns continued, this expectancy would reach forty-two years by 1980, when it might level out. Plunging insurance stocks triggered a stock market panic. The president of a major pesticide went on television to "publicly eat a teaspoonful of DDT" (it was really powdered milk) and announce that HEW had been infiltrated by Communists. Other giants of the petrochemical industry, attempting to dispute the indisputable evidence, launched a massive pressure campaign on Congress to force HEW to "get out of agriculture's business." They were aided by the agrochemical journals, which had decades of experience in misleading the public about the benefits and dangers of pesticides. But by now the public realized that it had been duped. The Nobel Prize for medicine and physiology was given to Drs. J. L. Radomski and W. B. Deichmann, who in the late 1960s had pioneered in the documentation of the long-term lethal effects of chlorinated hydrocarbons. A presidential commission with unimpeachable credentials directly accused the agro-chemical complex of "condemning many millions of Americans to an early death." The year 1973 was the year in which Americans finally came to understand the direct threat to their existence posed by environmental deterioration.

And 1973 was also the year in which most people finally comprehended the indirect threat. Even the president of Union Oil Company and several other industrialists publicly stated their concern over the reduction of bird populations which had resulted from pollution by DDT and other chlorinated hydrocarbons. Insect populations boomed because they were resistant to most pesticides and had been freed, by the incompetent use of those pesticides, from most of their natural enemies. Rodents swarmed over crops, multiplying rapidly in the absence of predatory birds. The effect of pests on the wheat crop was especially disastrous in the summer of 1973, since that was also the year of the great drought. Most of us can remember the shock which greeted the announcement by atmospheric physicists that the shift of the jet stream which had caused the drought was probably permanent. It signaled the birth of the Midwestern desert. Man's air-polluting activities had by then caused gross changes in climatic patterns. The news, of course, played hell with commodity and stock markets. Food prices skyrocketed, as savings were poured into hoarded canned goods. Official assurances that food supplies would remain ample fell on deaf ears, and even the government showed signs of nervousness when California migrant field workers went out on strike again in protest against the continued use of pesticides by growers. The strike burgeoned into farm burning and riots. The workers, calling themselves "The Walking Dead," demanded immediate compensation for their shortened lives, and crash research programs to attempt to lengthen them.

It was in the same speech in which President Edward Kennedy, after much delay, finally declared a national emergency and called out the National Guard to harvest California's crops that the first mention of population control was made. Kennedy pointed out that the United States would no longer be able to offer any food aid to other nations and was likely to suffer food shortages herself. He suggested that, in view of the manifest failure of the Green Revolution, the only hope of the UDCs lay in population control. His statement, you will recall, created an uproar in the underdeveloped countries. Newspaper editorials accused the United States of wishing to prevent small countries from becoming large nations and thus threatening American hegemony. Politicians asserted that President Kennedy was a "creature of the giant drug combine" that wished to shove its pills down every woman's throat.

Among Americans, religious opposition to population control was very slight. Industry in general also backed the idea. Increasing poverty in the UDCs was both destroying markets and threatening supplies of raw materials. The seriousness of the raw material situation had been brought home during the congressional hard resources hearings in 1971. The exposure of the ignorance of the cornucopian economists had been quite a spectacle—a spectacle brought into virtually every American's home in living color. Few would forget the distinguished geologist from the University of California who suggested that economists be legally required to learn at least the most elementary facts of geology. Fewer still would forget that an equally distinguished Harvard economist added that they might be required to learn some economics too. The overall message was clear: America's resource situation was bad and bound to get worse. The hearings had led to a bill requiring the Departments of State, Interior, and Commerce to set up a joint resource procurement council with the express purpose of "insuring that proper consideration of American resource needs be an integral part of American foreign policy."

Suddenly the United States discovered that it had a national consensus: population control was the only possible salvation of the underdeveloped world. But that same consensus led to heated debate. How could the UDCs be persuaded to limit their populations, and should not the United States lead the way by limiting its own? Members of the intellectual community wanted America to set an example. They pointed out that the United States was in the midst of a new baby boom: her birth rate, well over twenty per thousand per year, and her growth rate of over one percent per annum were among the very highest of the developed countries. They detailed the deterioration of the American physical and psychic environments, the growing health threats, the impending food shortages, and the insufficiency of funds for desperately needed public works. They contended that the nation was clearly unable or unwilling to properly care for the people it already had. What possible reason could there be, they queried, for adding any more? Besides, who would listen to requests by the United States for population control when that nation did not control her own profligate reproduction?

Those who opposed population controls for the U.S. were equally vociferous. The military-industrial complex, with its all-too-human mixture of ignorance and avarice, still saw strength and prosperity in numbers. Baby food magnates, already worried by the growing nitrate pollution of their products, saw their market disappearing. Steel manufacturers saw a decrease in aggregate demand and slippage for that holy of holies, the Gross National Product. And military men saw, in the growing population-food-environment crisis, a serious threat to their carefully nurtured cold war. In the end, of course, economic arguments held sway, and the "inalienable right of every American couple to determine the size of its family," a freedom invented for the occasion in the early '70s, was not compromised.

The population control bill, which was passed by Congress early in 1974 was quite a document, nevertheless. On the domestic front, it authorized an increase from one hundred to one hundred fifty million dollars in funds for "family planning" activities. This was made possible by a general feeling in the country that the growing army on welfare needed family planning. But the gist of the bill was a series of measures designed to impress the need for population control on the UDCs. All American aid to countries with overpopulation problems was required by law to consist in part of population control assistance. In order to receive any assistance each nation was required not only to accept the population control aid, but also to match it according to a complex formula. "Overpopulation" itself was defined by a formula based on U.N. statistics, and the UDCs were required not only to accept aid, but also to show progress in reducing birth rates. Every five years the status of the aid program for each nation was to be re-evaluated.

The reaction to the announcement of this program dwarfed the response to President Kennedy's speech. A coalition of UDCs attempted to get the U.N. General Assembly to condemn the United States as a "genetic aggressor." Most damaging of all to the American cause was the famous "twenty-five Indians and a dog" speech by Mr. Shankarnarayan, Indian Ambassador to the U.N. Shankarnarayan pointed out that for several decades the United States, with less than six percent of the people of the world, had consumed roughly fifty percent of the raw materials used every year. He described vividly America's contribution to worldwide environmental deterioration, and he scathingly denounced the miserly record of United States foreign aid as "unworthy of a fourth-rate power, let alone the most powerful nation on earth."

It was the climax of his speech, however, which most historians claim once and for all destroyed the image of the United States. Shankarnarayan informed the assembly that the average American family dog was fed more animal protein per week than the average Indian got in a month. "How do you justify taking fish from protein-starved Peruvians and feeding them to your animals?" he asked. "I contend," he concluded, "that the birth of an American baby is a greater disaster for the world than that of twenty-five Indian babies." When the applause had died away, Mr. Sorensen, the American representative, made a speech which said essentially that "other countries look after their own self-interest, too.'' When the vote came, the United States was condemned.

This condemnation set the tone of U.S.-UDC relations at the time the Russian Thanodrin proposal was made. The proposal seemed to offer the masses in the UDCs an opportunity to save themselves and humiliate the United States at the same time; and in human affairs, as we all know, biological realities could never interfere with such an opportunity. The scientists were silenced, the politicians said yes, the Thanodrin plants were built, and results were what any beginning ecology student could have predicted. At first Thanodrin seemed to offer excellent control of many pests. True, there was a rash of human fatalities from improper use of the lethal chemical, but, as Russian technical advisors were prone to note, these were more than compensated for by increased yields. Thanodrin use skyrocketed throughout the underdeveloped world. The Mikoyan design group developed a dependable, cheap agricultural aircraft which the Soviets donated to the effort in large numbers. MIG sprayers became even more common in UDCs than MIG interceptors.

Then the troubles began. Insect strains with cuticles resistant to Thanodrin penetration began to appear. And as streams, rivers, fish culture ponds, and onshore waters became rich in Thanodrin, more fisheries began to disappear. Bird populations were decimated. The sequence of events was standard for broadcast use of a synthetic pesticide: great success at first, followed by removal of natural enemies and development of resistance by the pest. Populations of crop-eating insects in areas treated with Thanodrin made steady comebacks and soon became more abundant than ever. Yields plunged, while farmers in their desperation increased the Thanodrin dose and shortened the time between treatments. Death from Thanodrin poisoning became common. The first violent incident occurred in the Canete Valley of Peru, where farmers had suffered a similar chlorinated hydrocarbon disaster in the mid-'50s. A Russian advisor serving as an agricultural pilot was assaulted and killed by a mob of enraged farmers in January, 1978. Trouble spread rapidly during 1978, especially after the word got out that two years earlier Russia herself had banned the use of Thanodrin at home because of its serious effects on ecological systems. Suddenly Russia, and not the United States, was the *bête noir* in the UDCs. ''Thanodrin parties'' became epidemic, with farmers, in their ignorance, dumping carloads of Thanodrin concentrate into the sea. Russian advisors fled, and four of the Thanodrin plants were leveled to the ground. Destruction of the plants in Rio and Calcutta led to hundreds of thousands of gallons of Thanodrin concentrate being dumped directly into the sea.

Mr. Shankarnarayan again rose to address the U.N., but this time it was Mr. Potemkin, representative of the Soviet Union, who was on the hot seat. Mr. Potemkin heard his nation described as the greatest mass killer of all time as Shankarnarayan predicted at least thirty million deaths from crop failures due to overdependence on Thanodrin. Russia was accused of ''chemical

aggression," and the General Assembly, after a weak reply by Potemkin, passed a vote of censure.

It was in January, 1979, that huge blooms of a previously unknown variety of diatom were reported off the coast of Peru. The blooms were accompanied by a massive die-off of sea life and of the pathetic remainder of the birds which had once feasted on the anchovies of the area. Almost immediately, another huge bloom was reported in the Indian Ocean, centering around the Seychelles, and then a third in the South Atlantic off the African coast. Both of these were accompanied by spectacular die-offs of marine animals. Even more ominous were growing reports of fish and bird kills at oceanic points where there were no spectacular blooms. Biologists were soon able to explain the phenomenon: the diatom had evolved an enzyme which broke down Thanodrin; that enzyme also produced a breakdown product which interfered with the transmission of nerve impulses, and was therefore lethal to animals. Unfortunately, the biologists could suggest no way of repressing the poisonous diatom bloom in time. By September, 1979, all important animal life in the sea was extinct. Large areas of coastline had to be evacuated, as windrows of dead fish created a monumental stench.

But stench was the least of man's problems. Japan and China were faced with almost instant starvation from a total loss of the seafood on which they were so dependent. Both blamed Russia for their situation and demanded immediate mass shipments of food. Russia had none to send. On October 13, Chinese armies attacked Russia on a broad front. . . .

A pretty grim scenario. Unfortunately, we're a long way into it already. Everything mentioned as happening before 1970 has actually occurred; much of the rest is based on projections of trends already appearing. Evidence that pesticides have long-term lethal effects on human beings has started to accumulate, and recently Robert Finch, Secretary of the Department of Health, Education, and Welfare, expressed his extreme apprehension about the pesticide situation. Simultaneously the petrochemical industry continues its unconscionable poison-peddling. For instance, Shell Chemical has been carrying on a high-pressure campaign to sell the insecticide Azodrin to farmers as a killer of cotton pests. They continue their program even though they know that Azodrin is not only ineffective, but often *increases* the pest density. They've covered themselves nicely in an advertisement which states, "Even if an overpowering migration [sic] develops, the flexibility of Azodrin lets you regain control fast. Just increase the dosage according to label recommendations." It's a great game—get people to apply the poison and kill the natural enemies of the pests. Then blame the increased pests on "migration" and sell even more pesticide!

Right now fisheries are being wiped out by overexploitation, made easy by modern electronic equipment. The companies producing the equipment know this. They even boast in advertising that only their equipment will keep fishermen in business until the final kill. Profits must obviously be maximized in the short run. Indeed, Western society is in the process of completing the rape and murder of the planet for economic gain. And, sadly, most of the rest of the world is eager for the opportunity to emulate our behavior. But the underdeveloped peoples will be denied that opportunity—the days of plunder are drawing inexorably to a close.

Most of the people who are going to die in the greatest cataclysm in the history of man have already been born. More than three and a half billion people already populate our moribund globe, and about half of them are hungry. Some ten to twenty million will starve to death *this year*. In spite of this, the population of the earth will have increased by seventy million in 1969. For mankind has artificially lowered the death rate of the human population, while in general, birth rates have remained high. With the input side of the population system in high gear and the output side slowed down, our fragile planet has filled with people at an incredible rate. It took several million years for the population to reach a total of two billion people in 1930, while a *second two billion will have been added by 1975!* By that time some experts feel that food shortages will have escalated the present level of world hunger and starvation in famines of unbelievable proportions. Other experts, more optimistic, think the ultimate food-population collision will not occur until the decade of the 1980s. Of course more massive famine may be avoided if other events cause a prior rise in the human death rate.

Both worldwide plague and thermonuclear war are made more probable as population growth continues. These, along with famine, make up the trio of potential "death rate solutions" to the population problem—solutions in which the birth rate-death rate imbalance is redressed by a rise in the death rate rather than by a lowering of the birth rate. Make no mistake about it, *the imbalance will be redressed*. The shape of the population-growth curve is one familiar to the biologist. It is the outbreak part of an outbreak-crash sequence. A population grows rapidly in the presence of abundant resources, finally runs out of food or some other necessity, and crashes to a low level or extinction. Man is not only running out of food, he is also destroying the life support systems of the Spaceship Earth. The situation was recently summarized very succinctly: "It is the top of the ninth inning. Man, always a threat at the plate, has been hitting Nature hard. It is important to remember, however, that NATURE BATS LAST."

THE NINE BILLION NAMES OF GOD

BY ARTHUR C. CLARKE

(Appeared in STAR SCIENCE FICTION STORIES NO. 1)

Every now and then I get stuck with an impossibly difficult task, and one of the hardest is introducing Arthur C. Clarke. How do you do that? What can you say that hasn't been said about the author of Childhood's End, *the man credited with inventing the communications satellite, the First Citizen of Sri Lanka? The reputation towers. It gets in the way of seeing the person.*

It is my pleasure to report that behind those layers of TV cameras and fans there is really a very nice man. Some of my favorite perceptions of Clarke have little to do with his writing—sheltering from a shower at a Japanese roadside diner when our bus got a flat tire; sharing a ride, seven or eight of us squeezed into somebody's sub-compact, Werner von Braun on my lap and Arthur on some astronaut's, on the way to a Georgia fish-fry. The guy isn't just famous. He's a lot of fun at a party.

But of course, what he really is, in and around everything else, is a writer. In fact, he's Arthur C. Clarke. Like every writer worth rereading, he speaks with his own voice; he writes out of his own perceptions and in his own idiom. In thirty-odd years of writing, he has learned and grown. All the same, the voice you heard in "Rescue Party," his very first story, is the same voice you are hearing in "The Fountains of Paradise," which he says will be his last. (But God and his own good sense willing, he may yet change his mind!)

Of course, what all the world knows best about Arthur C. Clarke is his share of 2001: A Space Odyssey, *still held by many to be the greatest science-fiction film ever made.*

It's hard to deny that the Clarke-Kubrick collaboration was A Good Thing. But it had its cost. The price was taking Arthur Clarke out of the fiction-writing business for years on end, when he was at the top of his form. Then the book publishers began wooing him with shoulder-high heaps of hundred-dollar bills and, one way or another, the demands on his time were such that he hasn't been writing very many short stories. A pity. He's written some very good ones, and none better, I think, than "The Nine Billion Names of God."

*   *   *

"This is a slightly unusual request," said Dr. Wagner, with what he hoped was commendable restraint. "As far as I know, it's the first time anyone's been asked to supply a Tibetan monastery with an Automatic Sequence Computer. I don't wish to be inquisitive, but I should hardly have thought that your—ah—establishment had much use for such a machine. Could you explain just what you intend to do with it?"

"Gladly," replied the Lama, readjusting his silk robe and carefully putting away the slide rule he had been using for currency conversions. "Your Mark V Computer can carry out any routine mathematical operation involving up to ten digits. However, for our work we are interested in *letters,* not numbers. As we wish you to modify the output circuits, the machine will be printing words, not columns of figures."

"I don't quite understand. . . ."

"This is a project on which we have been working for the last three centuries—since the lamasery was founded, in fact. It is somewhat alien to your way of thought, so I hope you will listen with an open mind while I explain it."

"Naturally."

"It is really quite simple. We have been compiling a list which shall contain all the possible names of God."

"I beg your pardon?"

"We have reason to believe," continued the Lama imperturbably, "that all such names can be written with not more than nine letters in an alphabet we have devised."

"And you have been doing this for three centuries?"

"Yes: we expected it would take us about fifteen thousand years to complete the task."

"Oh." Dr. Wagner looked a little dazed. "Now I see why you wanted to hire one of our machines. But exactly what is the *purpose* of this project?"

The Lama hesitated for a fraction of a second and Wagner wondered if he had offended him. If so, there was no trace of annoyance in the reply.

"Call it ritual, if you like, but it's a fundamental part of our belief. All the many names of the Supreme Being—God, Jehovah, Allah, and so on—they are only man-made labels. There is a philosophical problem of some difficulty here, which I do not propose to discuss, but somewhere among all the possible combinations of letters which can occur are what one may call the *real* names of God. By systematic permutation of letters, we have been trying to list them all."

"I see. You've been starting at AAAAAAAAA . . . and working up to ZZZZZZZZZ. . . ."

"Exactly—though we use a special alphabet of our own. Modifying the electromatic typewriters to deal with this is, of course, trivial. A rather more interesting problem is that of devising suitable circuits to eliminate ridiculous combinations. For example, no letter must occur more than three times in succession."

"Three? Surely you mean two."

"Three is correct: I am afraid it would take too long to explain why, even if you understood our language."

"I'm sure it would," said Wagner hastily. "Go on."

"Luckily, it will be a simple matter to adapt your Automatic Sequence Computer for this work, since once it has been programmed properly it will permute each letter in turn and print the result. What would have taken us fifteen thousand years it will be able to do in a hundred days."

Dr. Wagner was scarcely conscious of the faint sounds from the Manhattan streets far below. He was in a different world, a world of natural, not man-made mountains. High up in their remote aeries, these monks had been patiently at work, generation after generation, compiling their lists of meaningless words. Was there any limit to the follies of mankind? Still, he must give no hint of his inner thoughts. The customer was always right. . . .

"There's no doubt," replied the doctor, "that we can modify the Mark V to print lists of this nature. I'm much more worried about the problem of installation and maintenance. Getting out to Tibet, in these days, is not going to be easy."

"We can arrange that. The components are small enough to travel by air—that is one reason why we chose your machine. If you can get them to India, we will provide transport from there."

"And you want to hire two of our engineers?"

"Yes, for the three months the project should take."

"I've no doubt that Personnel can manage that." Dr. Wagner scribbled a note on his desk pad. "There are just two other points—"

Before he could finish the sentence, the Lama had produced a small slip of paper.

"This is my certified credit balance at the Asiatic Bank."

"Thank you. It appears to be—ah—adequate. The second matter is so trivial that I hesitate to mention it—but it's surprising how often the obvious gets overlooked. What source of electrical energy have you?"

"A diesel generator providing fifty kilowatts at one hundred and ten volts. It was installed about five years ago and is quite reliable. It's made life at the lamasery much more comfortable, but of course it was really installed to provide power for the motors driving the prayer wheels."

"Of course," echoed Dr. Wagner. "I should have thought of that."

The view from the parapet was vertiginous, but in time one gets used to anything. After three months, George Hanley was not impressed by the two-thousand-foot swoop into the abyss or the remote checkerboard of fields in the valley below. He was leaning against the wind-smoothed stones and staring morosely at the distant mountains whose names he had never bothered to discover.

This, thought George, was the craziest thing that had ever happened to him. "Project Shangri-La," some wit at the labs had christened it. For weeks now the Mark V had been churning out acres of sheets covered with gibberish. Patiently, inexorably, the computer had been rearranging letters in all their possible combinations, exhausting each class before going on to the next. As the sheets had emerged from the electromatic typewriters, the monks had carefully cut them up and pasted them into enormous books. In another week, heaven be praised, they would have finished. Just what obscure calculations had convinced the monks that they needn't bother to go on to words of ten, twenty, or a hundred letters, George didn't know. One of his recurring nightmares was that there would be some change of plan, and that the High Lama (whom they'd naturally called Sam Jaffe, though he didn't look a bit like him) would suddenly announce that the project would be extended to approximately 2060 A.D. They were quite capable of it.

George heard the heavy wooden door slam in the wind as Chuck came out on to the parapet beside him. As usual, Chuck was smoking one of the cigars that made him so popular with the monks—who, it seemed, were quite willing to embrace all the minor and most of the major pleasures of life. That was one thing in their favor: they might be crazy, but they weren't bluenoses. Those frequent trips they took down to the village, for instance. . . .

"Listen, George," said Chuck urgently. "I've learned something that means trouble."

"What's wrong? Isn't the machine behaving?" That was the worst contingency George could imagine. It might delay his return, than which nothing could be more horrible. The way he felt now, even the sight of a TV commercial would seem like manna from heaven. At least it would be some link with home.

"No—it's nothing like that." Chuck settled himself on the parapet, which was unusual because normally he was scared of the drop. "I've just found what all this is about."

"What d'ya mean—I thought we knew."

"Sure—we know what the monks are trying to do. But we didn't know *why*. It's the craziest thing—"

"Tell me something new," growled George.

"—but old Sam's just come clean with me. You know the way he drops in every afternoon to watch the sheets roll out. Well, this time he seemed rather excited, or at least as near as he'll ever get to it. When I told him that we were on the last cycle he asked me, in that cute English accent of his, if I'd ever wondered what they were trying to do. I said, 'Sure'—and he told me."

"Go on: I'll buy it."

"Well, they believe that when they have listed all His names—and they reckon that there are about nine billion of them—God's purpose will be achieved. The human race will have finished what it was created to do, and there won't be any point in carrying on. Indeed, the very idea is something like blasphemy.''

"Then what do they expect us to do? Commit suicide?''

"There's no need for that. When the list's completed, God steps in and simply winds things up . . . bingo!''

"Oh, I get it. When we finish our job, it will be the end of the world.''

Chuck gave a nervous little laugh.

"That's just what I said to Sam. And do you know what happened? He looked at me in a very queer way, like I'd been stupid in class, and said, 'It's nothing as trivial as *that*.' ''

George thought this over for a moment.

"That's what I call taking the Wide View,'' he said presently. "But what d'ya suppose we should do about it? I don't see that it makes the slightest difference to us. After all, we already knew that they were crazy.''

"Yes—but don't you see what may happen? When the list's complete and the Last Trump doesn't blow—or whatever it is they expect—*we* may get the blame. It's our machine they've been using. I don't like the situation one little bit.''

"I see,'' said George slowly. "You've got a point there. But this sort of thing's happened before, you know. When I was a kid down in Louisiana, we had a crackpot preacher who said the world was going to end next Sunday. Hundreds of people believed him—even sold their homes. Yet nothing happened, they didn't turn nasty as you'd expect. They just decided that he'd made a mistake in his calculations and went right on believing. I guess some of them still do.''

"Well, this isn't Louisiana, in case you hadn't noticed. There are just two of us and hundreds of these monks. I like them, and I'll be sorry for old Sam when his lifework backfires on him. But all the same, I wish I was somewhere else.''

"I've been wishing that for weeks. But there's nothing we can do until the contract's finished and the transport arrives to fly us out.''

"Of course,'' said Chuck thoughtfully, "we could always try a bit of sabotage.''

"Like hell we could! That would make things worse.''

"Not the way I meant. Look at it like this. The machine will finish its run four days from now, on the present twenty-hours-a-day basis. The transport calls in a week. O.K.—then all we need do is to find something that wants replacing during one of the overhaul periods—something that will hold up the works for a couple of days. We'll fix it, of course, but not too quickly. If we time matters properly, we can be down at the airfield when the last name pops out of the register. They won't be able to catch us then.''

"I don't like it,'' said George. "It will be the first time I ever walked out on a job. Besides, it would make them suspicious. No. I'll sit tight and take what comes.''

*   *   *

"I *still* don't like it," he said, seven days later, as the tough little mountain ponies carried them down the winding road. "And don't you think I'm running away because I'm afraid. I'm just sorry for those poor old guys up there, and I don't want to be around when they find what suckers they've been. Wonder how Sam will take it?"

"It's funny," replied Chuck, "but when I said good-bye, I got the idea he knew we were walking out on him—and that he didn't care because he knew the machine was running smoothly and that the job would soon be finished. After that—well, of course, for him there just isn't any After That. . . ."

George turned in his saddle and stared back up the mountain road. This was the last place from which one could get a clear view of the lamasery. The squat, angular buildings were silhouetted against the afterglow of the sunset: here and there, lights gleamed like portholes in the sides of an ocean liner. Electric lights, of course, sharing the same circuit as the Mark V. How much longer would they share it, wondered George. Would the monks smash up the computer in their rage and disappointment? Or would they just sit down quietly and begin their calculations all over again?

He knew exactly what was happening up on the mountain at this very moment. The High Lama and his assistants would be sitting in their silk robes, inspecting the sheets as the junior monks carried them away from the typewriters and pasted them into the great volumes. No one would be saying anything. The only sound would be the incessant patter, the never-ending rainstorm, of the keys hitting the paper, for the Mark V itself was utterly silent as it flashed through its thousands of calculations a second. Three months of this, thought George, was enough to start anyone climbing up the wall.

"There she is!" called Chuck, pointing down into the valley. "Ain't she beautiful!"

She certainly was, thought George. The battered old DC 3 lay at the end of the runway like a tiny silver cross. In two hours she would be bearing them away to freedom and sanity. It was a thought worth savoring like a fine liqueur. George let it roll round his mind as the pony trudged patiently down the slope.

The swift night of the high Himalayas was now almost upon them. Fortunately the road was very good, as roads went in this region, and they were both carrying torches. There was not the slightest danger, only a certain discomfort from the bitter cold. The sky overhead was perfectly clear and ablaze with the familiar, friendly stars. At least there would be no risk, thought George, of the pilot being unable to take off because of weather conditions. That had been his only remaining worry.

He began to sing, but gave it up after a while. This vast arena of mountains, gleaming like whitely hooded ghosts on every side, did not encourage such ebullience. Presently George glanced at his watch.

"Should be there in an hour," he called back over his shoulder to Chuck.

Then he added, in an afterthought: "Wonder if the computer's finished its run? It was due about now."

Chuck didn't reply, so George swung round in his saddle. He could just see Chuck's face, a white oval turned towards the sky.

"Look," whispered Chuck, and George lifted his eyes to heaven. (There is always a last time for everything.)

Overhead, without any fuss, the stars were going out.

THE MAN WITH ENGLISH
BY H. L. GOLD

(Appeared in STAR SCIENCE FICTION STORIES NO. 1)

Almost everyone who was writing science fiction in the 1950s, or even reading it, knows quite a lot about H. L. Gold. He was the man who created Galaxy. He broadened the scope of science fiction, elevated its standards, brought in many brilliant new writers, and reformed a good many tired old ones. There are few editors who have left a larger or better mark on the field, and he will not soon be forgotten.

But before Horace Gold was ever an editor he was a writer. His short stories decorated John Campbell's Astounding and Unknown at the peak of the Golden Age—among other magazines—and they were very fine stories. The one I like best was None But Lucifer. It appeared under a joint by-line with L. Sprague de Camp, and it was a marvelously gripping, plausible argument that there really is a hell, and it is the Earth and we're all living in it. None But Lucifer is full-novel length. It would be a squeeze to get it into any anthology, but that's not what keeps me from including it here. The unfortunate fact is that I never had the pleasure of publishing it, even as a reprint. What is even more unfortunate, not to say unbelievable, is that it has been out of print in any form for forty years.

However, I did publish "The Man with English." It was in the first issue of Star Science Fiction Stories. Apart from the fact that it was a first-rate story, it gave me a special fringe-benefit of pleasure.

See, Horace was an editor who edited. He changed things—titles, phrases, sometimes even the sense of a story. It was a time when that was a common custom, but writers didn't like it anyway—I didn't, and neither did my friend and collaborator, Cyril Kornbluth.

So when "The Man with English" arrived, I made one copy for the printer and another for revenge. Cyril and I took the revenge copy and edited it—oh, God, did we edit it! We did everything Horace had ever been accused of, only without any wit, wisdom, or reason, and we made changes he never would have dared. And then I let the butchered script fall into his hands. . . .

*   *   *

Lying in the hospital, Edgar Stone added up his misfortunes as another might count blessings. There were enough to infuriate the most temperate man, which Stone notoriously was not. He smashed his fist down, accidentally hitting the metal side of the bed, and was astonished by the pleasant feeling. It enraged him even more. The really maddening thing was how simply he had goaded himself into the hospital.

He'd locked up his drygoods store and driven home for lunch. Nothing unusual about that; he did it every day. With his miserable digestion, he couldn't stand the restaurant food in town. He pulled into the driveway, rode over a collection of metal shapes his son Arnold had left lying around, and punctured a tire.

"Rita!" he yelled. "This is going too damned far! Where is that brat?"

"In here," she called truculently from the kitchen.

He kicked open the screen door. His foot went through the mesh.

"A ripped tire and a torn screen!" he shouted at Arnold, who was sprawled in angular adolescence over a blueprint on the kitchen table. "You'll pay for them, by God! They're coming out of your allowance!"

"I'm sorry, Pop," the boy said.

"Sorry, my left foot," Mrs. Stone shrieked. She whirled on her husband. "You could have watched where you were going. He promised to clean up his things from the driveway right after lunch. And it's about time you stopped kicking open the door every time you're mad."

"Mad? Who wouldn't be mad? Me hoping he'd get out of school and come into the store, and he wants to be an engineer. An engineer—and he can't even make change when he—hah!—helps me out in the store!"

"He'll be whatever he wants to be," she screamed in the conversational tone of the Stone household.

"Please," said Arnold. "I can't concentrate on this plan."

Edgar Stone was never one to restrain an angry impulse. He tore up the blueprint and flung the pieces down on the table.

"Aw, Pop!" Arnold protested.

"Don't say, 'Aw, Pop,' to me. You're not going to waste a summer vacation on junk like this. You'll eat your lunch and come down to the store. And you'll do it every day for the rest of the summer!"

"Oh, he will, will he?" demanded Mrs. Stone. "He'll catch up on his studies. And as for you, you can go back and eat in a restaurant."

"You know I can't stand that slop!"

"You'll eat it because you're not having lunch here any more. I've got enough to do without making three meals a day."

"But I can't drive back with that tire—"

He did, though not with the tire—he took a cab. It cost a dollar plus tip, lunch was a dollar and a half plus tip, bicarb at Rite Drug Store a few doors away and in a great hurry came to another fifteen cents—only it didn't work.

And then Miss Ellis came in for some material. Miss Ellis could round out any miserable day. She was fifty, tall, skinny, and had thin, disapproving lips. She had a sliver of cloth clipped very meagerly off a hem that she intended to use as a sample.

"The arms of the slipcover on my reading chair wore through," she informed him. "I bought the material here, if you remember."

Stone didn't have to look at the fragmentary swatch. "That was about seven years ago—"

"Six-and-a-half," she corrected. "I paid enough for it. You'd expect anything that expensive to last."

"The style was discontinued. I have something here that—"

"I do not want to make an entire slipcover, Mr. Stone. All I want is enough to make new panels for the arms. Two yards should do very nicely."

Stone smothered a bilious hiccup. "Two yards, Miss Ellis?"

"At the most."

"I sold the last of that material years ago." He pulled a bolt off a shelf and partly unrolled it for her. "Why not use a different pattern as a kind of contrast?"

"I want this same pattern," she said, her thin lips getting even thinner and more obstinate.

"Then I'll have to order it and hope one of my wholesalers still has some of it in stock."

"Not without looking for it first right here, you won't order it for me. You can't know *all* these materials you have on these shelves."

Stone felt all the familiar symptoms of fury—the sudden pulsing of the temples, the lurch and bump of his heart as adrenaline came surging in like the tide at the Firth of Forth, the quivering of his hands, the angry shout pulsing at his vocal cords from below.

"I'll take a look, Miss Ellis," he said.

She was president of the Ladies' Cultural Society and dominated it so thoroughly that the members would go clear to the next town for their dry goods, rather than deal with him, if he offended this sour stick of stubbornness.

If Stone's life insurance salesman had been there, he would have tried to keep Stone from climbing the ladder that ran around the three walls of the store. He probably wouldn't have been in time. Stone stamped up the ladder to reach the highest shelves, where there were scraps of bolts. One of them might have been the remnant of the material Miss Ellis had bought six-and-a-half years ago. But Stone never found out.

He snatched one, glaring down meanwhile at the top of Miss Ellis's head, and the ladder skidded out from under him. He felt his skull collide with the counter. He didn't feel it hit the floor.

"God damn it!" Stone yelled. "You could at least turn on the lights."

"There, there, Edgar. Everything's fine, just fine."

It was his wife's voice and the tone was so uncommonly soft and soothing that it scared him into a panic.

"What's wrong with me?" he asked piteously. "Am I blind?"

"How many fingers am I holding up?" a man wanted to know.

Stone was peering into the blackness. All he could see before his eyes was a vague blot against a darker blot.

"None," he bleated. "Who are you?"

"Dr. Rankin. That was a nasty fall you had, Mr. Stone—concussion of course, and a splinter of bone driven into the brain. I had to operate to remove it."

"Then you cut out a nerve!" Stone said. "You did something to my eyes!"

The doctor's voice sounded puzzled. "There doesn't seem to be anything wrong with them. I'll take a look, though, and see."

"You'll be all right, dear," Mrs. Stone said reassuringly, but she didn't sound as if she believed it.

"Sure you will, Pop," said Arnold.

"Is that young stinker here?" Stone demanded. "He's the cause of all this!"

"Temper, temper," the doctor said. "Accidents happen."

Stone heard him lower the venetian blinds. As if they had been a switch, light sprang up and everything in the hospital became brightly visible.

"Well!" said Stone. "That's more like it. It's night and you're trying to save electricity, hey?"

"It's broad daylight, Edgar dear," his wife protested. "All Dr. Rankin did was lower the blinds and—"

"Please," the doctor said. "If you don't mind, I'd rather take care of any explanations that have to be made."

He came at Stone with an ophthalmoscope. When he flashed it into Stone's eyes, everything went black and Stone let him know it vociferously.

"Black?" Dr. Rankin repeated blankly. "Are you positive? Not a sudden glare?"

"Black," insisted Stone. "And what's the idea of putting me in a bed filled with bread crumbs?"

"It was freshly made—"

"Crumbs. You heard me. And the pillow has rocks in it."

"What else is bothering you?" asked the doctor worriedly.

"It's freezing in here." Stone felt the terror rise in him again. "It was summer when I fell off the ladder. Don't tell me I've been unconscious clear through till winter!"

"No, Pop," said Arnold. "That was yesterday—"

"I'll take care of this," Dr. Rankin said firmly. "I'm afraid you and your son will have to leave, Mrs. Stone. I have to do a few tests on your husband."

"Will he be all right?" she appealed.

"Of course, of course," he said inattentively, peering with a frown at the shivering patient. "Shock, you know," he added vaguely.

"Gosh, Pop," said Arnold. "I'm sorry this happened. I got the driveway all cleaned up."

"And we'll take care of the store till you're better," Mrs. Stone promised.

"Don't you dare!" yelled Stone. "You'll put me out of business!"

The doctor hastily shut the door on them and came back to the bed. Stone was clutching the light summer blanket around himself. He felt colder than he'd ever been in his life.

"Can't you get me more blankets?" he begged. "You don't want me to die of pneumonia, do you?"

Dr. Rankin opened the blinds and asked, "What's this like?"

"Night," chattered Stone. "A new idea to save electricity—hooking up the blinds to the light switch?"

The doctor closed the blinds and sat down beside the bed. He was sweating as he reached for the signal button and pressed it. A nurse came in, blinking in their direction.

"Why don't you turn on the lights?" she asked.

"Huh?" said Stone. "They are."

"Nurse, I'm Dr. Rankin. Get me a piece of sandpaper, some cotton swabs, an ice cube, and Mr. Stone's lunch."

"Is there anything he shouldn't eat?"

"That's what I want to find out. Hurry, please."

"And some blankets," Stone put in, shaking with the chill.

"Blankets, Doctor?" she asked, startled.

"Half a dozen will do," he said. "I think."

It took her ten minutes to return with all the items. Stone wanted them to keep adding blankets until all seven were on him. He still felt cold.

"Maybe some hot coffee?" he suggested.

The doctor nodded and the nurse poured a cup, added the spoon and a half of sugar he requested, and he took a mouthful. He sprayed it out violently.

"Ice cold!" he yelped. "And who put salt in it?"

"Salt?" She fumbled around on the tray. "It's so dark here—"

"I'll attend to it," Dr. Rankin said hurriedly. "Thank you."

She walked cautiously to the door and went out.

"Try this," said the doctor, after filling another cup.

"Well, that's better!" Stone exclaimed. "Damned practical joker. They shouldn't be allowed to work in hospitals."

"And now, if you don't mind," said the doctor, "I'd like to try several tests."

Stone was still angry at the trick played on him, but he cooperated willingly.

Dr. Rankin finally sagged back in the chair. The sweat ran down his face and into his collar, and his expression was so dazed that Stone was alarmed.

"What's wrong, Doctor? Am I going to—going to—"

"No, no. It's not that. No danger. At least, I don't believe there is. But I can't even be sure of that any more."

"You can't be sure if I'll live or die?"

"Look." Dr. Rankin grimly pulled the chair closer. "It's broad daylight and yet you can't see until I darken the room. The coffee was hot and sweet, but it was cold and salty to you, so I added an ice cube and a spoonful of salt and it tasted fine, you said. This is one of the hottest days on record and you're freezing. You told me the sandpaper felt smooth and satiny, then yelled that somebody had put pins in the cotton swabs, when there weren't any, of course. I've tried you out with different colors around the room and you saw violet when you should have seen yellow, green for red, orange for blue, and so on. Now do you understand?''

"No," said Stone frightenedly. "What's wrong?"

"All I can do is guess. I had to remove that sliver of bone from your brain. It apparently shorted your sensory nerves."

"And what happened?"

"Every one of your senses has been reversed. You feel cold for heat, heat for cold, smooth for rough, rough for smooth, sour for sweet, sweet for sour, and so forth. And you see colors backward."

Stone sat up. "Murderer! Thief! You've ruined me!"

The doctor sprang for a hypodermic and sedative. Just in time, he changed his mind and took a bottle of stimulant instead. It worked fine, though injecting it into his screaming, thrashing patient took more strength than he'd known he owned. Stone fell asleep immediately.

There were nine blankets on Stone and he had a bag of cement for a pillow when he had his lawyer, Manny Lubin, in to hear the charges he wanted brought against Dr. Rankin. The doctor was there to defend himself. Mrs. Stone was present in spite of her husband's objections—"She always takes everybody's side against me," he explained in a roar.

"I'll be honest with you, Mr. Lubin," the doctor said, after Stone had finished on a note of shrill frustration. "I've hunted for cases like this in medical history and this is the first one ever to be reported. Except," he amended quickly, "that I haven't reported it yet. I'm hoping it reverses itself. That sometimes happens, you know."

"And what am I supposed to do in the meantime?" raged Stone. "I'll have to go out wearing an overcoat in the summer and shorts in the winter—people will think I'm a maniac. And they'll be *sure* of it because I'll have to keep the store closed during the day and open at night—I can't see except in the dark. And matching materials! I can't stand the feel of smooth cloth and I see colors backward!" He glared at the doctor before turning back to Lubin. "How would *you* like to have to put sugar on your food and salt in your coffee?"

"But we'll work it out, Edgar dear," his wife soothed. "Arnold and I can take care of the store. You always wanted him to come into the business, so that ought to please you—"

"As long as I'm there to watch him!"

"And Dr. Rankin said maybe things will straighten out."

"What about that, Doctor?" asked Lubin. "What are the chances?"

Dr. Rankin looked uncomfortable. "I don't know. This has never happened before. All we can do is hope."

"Hope, nothing!" Stone stormed. "I want to sue him. He had no right to go meddling around and turn me upside down. Any jury would give me a quarter of a million!"

"I'm no millionaire, Mr. Stone," said the doctor.

"But the hospital has money. We'll sue him and the trustees."

There was a pause while the attorney thought. "I'm afraid we wouldn't have a case, Mr. Stone." He went on more rapidly as Stone sat up, shivering, to argue loudly. "It was an emergency operation. Any surgeon would have had to operate. Am I right, Dr. Rankin?"

The doctor explained what would have happened if he had not removed the pressure on the brain, resulting from the concussion, and the danger that the bone splinter, if not extracted, might have gone on traveling and caused possible paralysis or death.

"That would be better than this," said Stone.

"But medical ethics couldn't allow him to let you die," Lubin objected. "He was doing his duty. That's point one."

"Mr. Lubin is absolutely right, Edgar," said Mrs. Stone.

"There, you see?" screamed her husband. "Everybody's right but me! Will you get her out of here before I have a stroke?"

"Her interests are also involved," Lubin pointed out. "Point two is that the emergency came first, the after-effects couldn't be known or considered."

Dr. Rankin brightened. "Any operation involves risk, even the excising of a corn. I had to take those risks."

"*You* had to take them?" Stone scoffed. "All right, what are you leading up to, Lubin?"

"We'd lose," said the attorney.

Stone subsided, but only for a moment. "So we'll lose. But if we sue, the publicity would ruin him. I want to sue!"

"For what, Edgar dear?" his wife persisted. "We'll have a hard enough time managing. Why throw good money after bad?"

"Why didn't I marry a woman who'd take my side, even when I'm wrong?" moaned Stone. "Revenge, that's what. And he won't be able to practice, so he'll have time to find out if there's a cure . . . and at no charge, either! I won't pay him another cent!"

The doctor stood up eagerly. "But I'm willing to see what can be done right now. And it wouldn't cost you anything, naturally."

"What do you mean?" Stone challenged suspiciously.

"If I were to perform another operation, I'll be able to see which nerves were involved. There's no need to go into the technical side right now, but it is possible to connect nerves. Of course, there are a good many, which complicates matters, especially since the splinter went through several layers—"

Lubin pointed a lawyer's impaling finger at him. "Are you offering to attempt to correct the injury—gratis?"

"Certainly. I mean to say, I'll do my absolute best. But keep in mind, please, that there is no medical precedent."

The attorney, however, was already questioning Stone and his wife. "In view of the fact that we have no legal grounds whatever for suit, does this offer of settlement satisfy your claim against him?"

"Oh, yes!" Mrs. Stone cried.

Her husband hesitated for a while, clearly tempted to take the opposite position out of habit. "I guess so," he reluctantly agreed.

"Well, then it's in your hands, Doctor," said Lubin.

Dr. Rankin buzzed excitedly for the nurse. "I'll have him prepared for surgery right away."

"It better work this time," warned Stone, clutching a handful of ice cubes to warm his fingers.

Stone came to foggily. He didn't know it, but he had given the anesthetist a bewildering problem, which finally had been solved by using fumes of aromatic spirits of ammonia. The four blurred figures around the bed seemed to be leaning precariously toward him.

"Pop!" said Arnold. "Look, he's coming out of it! Pop!"

"Speak to me, Edgar dear," Mrs. Stone beseeched.

Lubin said, "See how he is, Doctor."

"He's fine," the doctor insisted heartily, his usual bedside manner evidently having returned. "He must be—the blinds are open and he's not complaining that it's dark or that he's cold." He leaned over the bed. "How are we feeling, Mr. Stone?"

It took a minute or two for Stone to move his swollen tongue enough to answer. He wrinkled his nose in disgust.

"What smells purple?" he demanded.

SPACE-TIME FOR SPRINGERS

BY FRITZ LEIBER

(Appeared in STAR SCIENCE FICTION STORIES NO. 4)

I've come back from time to time to the unending struggle between writers and editors over titles. In this war I lost many an engagement. But now and then I won one.

The best way to win a fight is to get what you want without actually compelling the other party to concede defeat. And the best way I know to do that in changing an author's title is to find a new one out of his own words. Of course, that doesn't work all the time. Some authors simply do not generate short, compelling phrases. The authors with whom it works best are the ones—Fritz Leiber, Cordwainer Smith, and a few others in science fiction—with unusual gifts for color in language.

I was lucky enough to publish nearly everything Cordwainer Smith wrote from 1960 to his death. James Blish wrote once that one of the things he appreciated most about Smith was the unmistakable, highly individual titles of his stories, and was sore perplexed when he discovered I had changed nearly every one of them. But Blish was right, because although the titles were not the words Smith had put at the top of the first page of each manuscript, every one had come from his own words somewhere in his story.

So when this Leiber story came in, I loved the story, didn't much like the title (and don't now remember what it was)—but found "Space-Time for Springers" leaping out at me from the text.

Fritz never said if he minded the change. He wouldn't have in any case, I think, for besides being a marvelously multitalented writer Fritz Leiber—ex-seminarian, whilom Shakespearean actor, former science magazine editor—is about as kind, wise, and gentle a human being as you are likely to find.

He is also one of the world's foremost cat adorers. But you'll see that for yourself.

* * *

Gummitch was a superkitten, as he knew very well, with an I. Q. of about 160. Of course, he didn't talk. But everybody knows that I. Q. tests based on language ability are very one-sided. Besides, he would talk as soon as they started setting a place for him at table and pouring him coffee. Ashurbanipal and Cleopatra ate horsemeat from pans on the floor and they didn't talk. Baby dined in his crib on milk from a bottle and he didn't talk. Sissy sat at table but they didn't pour her coffee and she didn't talk—not one word. Father and Mother (whom Gummitch had nicknamed Old Horsemeat and Kitty-Come-Here) sat at table and poured each other coffee and they *did* talk. Q. E. D.

Meanwhile, he would get by very well on thought projection and intuitive understanding of all human speech—not even to mention cat patois, which almost any civilized animal could play by ear. The dramatic monologues and Socratic dialogues, the quiz and panel-show appearances, the felidological expedition to darkest Africa (where he would uncover the real truth behind lions and tigers), the exploration of the outer planets—all these could wait. The same went for the books for which he was ceaselessly accumulating material: *The Encyclopedia of Odors, Anthropofeline Psychology, Invisible Signs and Secret Wonders, Space-Time for Springers, Slit Eyes Look at Life,* et cetera. For the present it was enough to live existence to the hilt and soak up knowledge, missing no experience proper to his age level—to rush about with tail aflame.

So to all outward appearances Gummitch was just a vividly normal kitten, as shown by the succession of nicknames he bore along the magic path that led from blue-eyed infancy toward puberty: Little One, Squawker, Portly, Bumble (for purring, not clumsiness). Old Starved-to-Death, Fierso, Loverboy (affection, not sex), Spook, and Catnik. Of these only the last perhaps requires further explanation: the Russians had just sent Muttnik up after Sputnik, so that when one evening Gummitch streaked three times across the firmament of the living room floor in the same direction, past the fixed stars of the humans and the comparatively slow-moving heavenly bodies of the two older cats, and Kitty-Come-Here quoted the line from Keats:

Then felt I like some watcher of the skies
When a new planet swims into his ken;

it was inevitable that Old Horsemeat would say, "Ah—Catnik!"

The new name lasted all of three days, to be replaced by Gummitch, which showed signs of becoming permanent.

The little cat was on the verge of truly growing up, at least so Gummitch overheard Old Horsemeat comment to Kitty-Come-Here. A few short weeks, Old Horsemeat said, and Gummitch's fiery flesh would harden, his slim neck thicken, the electricity vanish from everything but his fur, and all his delightful kittenish qualities rapidly give way to the earthbound singlemindedness of a tom. They'd be lucky, Old Horsemeat concluded, if he didn't turn completely surly, like Ashurbanipal.

Gummitch listened to these predictions with gay unconcern and with secret amusement from his vantage point of superior knowledge, in the same spirit that he accepted so many phases of his outwardly conventional existence: the murderous sidelong looks he got from Ashurbanipal and Cleopatra as he devoured his own horsemeat from his own little tin pan, because they sometimes were given canned catfood but he never; the stark idiocy of Baby, who didn't know the difference between a live cat and a stuffed teddy bear and who tried to cover up his ignorance by making goo-goo noises and poking indiscriminately at all eyes; the far more serious—because cleverly hidden—maliciousness of Sissy, who had to be watched out for warily—especially when you were alone—and whose retarded—even warped—development, Gummitch knew, was Old Horsemeat and Kitty-Come-Here's deepest, most secret, worry (more of Sissy and her evil ways soon); the limited intellect of Kitty-Come-Here, who despite the amounts of coffee she drank was quite as featherbrained as kittens are supposed to be and who firmly believed, for example, that kittens operated in the same space-time as other beings—that to get from *here* to *there* they had to cross the space *between*—and similar fallacies; the mental stodginess of even Old Horsemeat, who although he understood quite a bit of the secret doctrine and talked intelligently to Gummitch when they were alone, nevertheless suffered from the limitations of his status—a rather nice old god but a maddeningly slow-witted one.

But Gummitch could easily forgive all this massed inadequacy and downright brutishness in his felino-human household, because he was aware that he alone knew the real truth about himself and about other kittens and babies as well, the truth which was hidden from weaker minds, the truth that was as intrinsically incredible as the germ theory of disease or the origin of the whole great universe in the explosion of a single atom.

As a baby kitten Gummitch had believed that Old Horsemeat's two hands were hairless kittens permanently attached to the ends of Old Horsemeat's arms but having an independent life of their own. How he had hated and loved those two five-legged sallow monsters, his first playmates, comforters, and battle-opponents!

Well, even that fantastic discarded notion was but a trifling fancy compared to the real truth about himself!

The forehead of Zeus split open to give birth to Minerva. Gummitch had been born from the waist-fold of a dirty old terrycloth bathrobe, Old Horsemeat's basic garment. The kitten was intuitively certain of it and had proved it to himself as well as any Descartes or Aristotle. In a kitten-size tuck of that ancient bathrobe, the atoms of his body had gathered and quickened into life. His earliest memories were of snoozing wrapped in terrycloth, warmed by Old Horsemeat's heat. Old Horsemeat and Kitty-Come-Here were his true parents. The other theory of his origin, the one he heard Old Horsemeat and Kitty-Come-Here recount from time to time—that he had been the only surviving kitten of a litter abandoned next door, that he had had the shakes from vitamin deficiency and lost the tip of his tail and the hair on his paws and had to be nursed back to life and health with warm yellowish milk-and-vitamins fed from an eyedropper—that other theory was just one of those rationalizations with which mysterious nature cloaks the birth of heroes, perhaps wisely veiling the truth from minds unable to bear it, a rationalization as false as Kitty-Come-Here and Old Horsemeat's touching belief that Sissy and Baby were their children rather than the cubs of Ashurbanipal and Cleopatra.

The day that Gummitch had discovered by pure intuition the secret of his birth he had been filled with a wild instant excitement. He had only kept it from tearing him to pieces by rushing out to the kitchen and striking and devouring a fried scallop, torturing it fiendishly first for twenty minutes.

And the secret of his birth was only the beginning. His intellectual faculties aroused, Gummitch had two days later intuited a further and greater secret: since he was the child of humans he would, upon reaching this maturation date of which Old Horsemeat had spoken, turn not into a sullen tom but into a godlike human youth with reddish golden hair the color of his present fur. He would be poured coffee; and he would instantly be able to talk, probably in all languages. While Sissy (how clear it was now!) would at approximately the same time shrink and fur out into a sharp-clawed and vicious she-cat dark as her hair, sex and self-love her only concerns, fit harem-mate for Cleopatra, concubine to Ashurbanipal.

Exactly the same was true, Gummitch realized at once, for all kittens and babies, all humans and cats, wherever they might dwell. Metamorphosis was as much a part of the fabric of their lives as it was of the insects'. It was also the basic fact underlying all legends of werewolves, vampires, and witches' familiars.

If you just rid your mind of preconceived notions, Gummitch told himself, it was all very logical. Babies were stupid, fumbling, vindictive creatures without reason or speech. What more natural than that they should grow up into mute sullen selfish beasts bent only on rapine and reproduction? While kittens were quick, sensitive, subtle, supremely alive. What other destiny were they possibly fitted for except to become the deft, word-speaking, book-writing, music-making, meat-getting-and-dispensing masters of the world? To dwell on the physical differences, to point out that kittens and men, babies and cats, are rather unlike in appearance and size, would be to miss the forest for the trees—very much as if an entomologist should proclaim metamorphosis a myth because his microscope failed to discover the wings of a butterfly in a caterpillar's slime or a golden beetle in a grub.

Nevertheless it was such a mind-staggering truth, Gummitch realized at the same time, that it was easy to understand why humans, cats, babies, and perhaps most kittens were quite unaware of it. How safely explain to a butterfly that he was once a hairy crawler, or to a dull larva that he will one day be a walking jewel? No, in such situations the delicate minds of man- and feline-kind are guarded by a merciful mass amnesia, such as Velikovsky has explained prevents us from recalling that in historical times the Earth was catastrophically bumped by the planet Venus operating in the manner of a comet before settling down (with a cosmic sigh of relief, surely!) into its present orbit.

This conclusion was confirmed when Gummitch, in the first fever of illumination, tried to communicate his great insight to others. He told it in cat patois, as well as that limited jargon permitted, to Ashurbanipal and Cleopatra and even, on the off chance, to Sissy and Baby. They showed no interest whatever, except that Sissy took advantage of his unguarded preoccupation to stab him with a fork.

Later, alone with Old Horsemeat, he projected the great new thoughts, staring with solemn yellow eyes at the old god, but the latter grew markedly nervous and even showed signs of real fear, so Gummitch desisted. ("You'd have sworn he was trying to put across something as deep as the Einstein theory or the doctrine of original sin," Old Horsemeat later told Kitty-Come-Here.)

But Gummitch was a man now in all but form, the kitten reminded himself after these failures, and it was part of his destiny to shoulder secrets alone when necessary. He wondered if the general amnesia would affect him when he metamorphosed. There was no sure answer to this question, but he hoped not—and sometimes felt that there was reason for his hopes. Perhaps he would be the first true kitten-man, speaking from a wisdom that had no locked doors in it.

Once he was tempted to speed up the process by the use of drugs. Left alone in the kitchen, he sprang onto the table and started to lap up the black puddle in the bottom of Old Horsemeat's coffee cup. It tasted foul and poisonous and he withdrew with a little snarl, frightened as well as revolted. The dark beverage would not work its tongue-loosening magic, he realized, except at the proper time and with the proper ceremonies. Incantations might be necessary as well. Certainly unlawful tasting was highly dangerous.

The futility of expecting coffee to work any wonders by itself was further demonstrated to Gummitch when Kitty-Come-Here, wordlessly badgered by Sissy, gave a few spoonfuls to the little girl, liberally lacing it first with milk and sugar. Of course Gummitch knew by now that Sissy was destined shortly to turn into a cat and that no amount of coffee would ever make her talk, but it was nevertheless instructive to see how she spat out the first mouthful, drooling a lot of saliva after it, and dashed the cup and its contents at the chest of Kitty-Come-Here.

Gummitch continued to feel a great deal of sympathy for his parents in their worries about Sissy and he longed for the day when he would metamorphose and be able, as an acknowledged man-child, truly to console them. It was heartbreaking to see how they each tried to coax the little girl to talk, always attempting it while the other was absent, how they seized on each accidentally wordlike note in the few sounds she uttered and repeated it back to her hopefully, how they were more and more possessed by fears not so much of her retarded (they thought) development as of her increasingly obvious maliciousness, which was directed chiefly at Baby . . . though the two cats and Gummitch bore their share. Once she had caught Baby alone in his crib and used the sharp corner of a block to dot Baby's large-domed lightly downed head with triangular red marks. Kitty-Come-Here had discovered her doing it, but the woman's first action had been to rub Baby's head to obliterate the marks so that Old Horsemeat wouldn't see them. That was the night Kitty-Come-Here hid the abnormal psychology books.

Gummitch understood very well that Kitty-Come-Here and Old Horsemeat, honestly believing themselves to be Sissy's parents, felt just as deeply about her as if they actually were and he did what little he could under the present circumstances to help them. He had recently come to feel a quite independent affection for Baby—the miserable little proto-cat was so completely stupid and defenseless—and so he unofficially constituted himself the creature's guardian, taking his naps behind the door of the nursery and dashing about noisily whenever Sissy showed up. In any case he realized that as a potentially adult member of a felino-human household he had his natural responsibilities.

Accepting responsibilities was as much a part of a kitten's life, Gummitch told himself, as shouldering unsharable intuitions and secrets, the number of which continued to grow from day to day.

There was, for instance, the Affair of the Squirrel Mirror.

Gummitch had early solved the mystery of ordinary mirrors and of the creatures that appeared in them. A little observation and sniffing and one attempt to get behind the heavy wall-job in the living room had convinced him that mirror beings were insubstantial or at least hermetically sealed into their other world, probably creatures of pure spirit, harmless imitative ghosts— including the silent Gummitch Double who touched paws with him so softly yet so coldly.

Just the same, Gummitch had let his imagination play with what would happen if one day, while looking into the mirror world, he should let loose his grip on his spirit and let it slip into the Gummitch Double while the other's spirit slipped into his body—if, in short, he should change places with the scentless ghost kitten. Being doomed to a life consisting wholly of imitation and completely lacking in opportunities to show initiative—except for the behind-the-scenes judgment and speed needed in rushing from one mirror to another to keep up with the real Gummitch—would be sickeningly dull, Gummitch decided, and he resolved to keep a tight hold on his spirit at all times in the vicinity of mirrors.

But that isn't telling about the Squirrel Mirror. One morning Gummitch was peering out the front bedroom window that overlooked the roof of the porch. Gummitch had already classified windows as semimirrors having two kinds of space on the other side: the mirror world and that harsh region filled with mysterious and dangerously organized-sounding noises called the outer world, into which grownup humans reluctantly ventured at intervals, donning special garments for the purpose and shouting loud farewells that were meant to be reassuring but achieved just the opposite effect. The coexistence of two kinds of space presented no paradox to the kitten who carried in his mind the twenty-seven-chapter outline of *Space-Time for Springers*—indeed, it constituted one of the minor themes of the book.

This morning the bedroom was dark and the outer world was dull and sunless, so the mirror world was unusually difficult to see. Gummitch was just lifting his face toward it, nose twitching, his front paws on the sill, when what should rear up on the other side, exactly in the space that the Gummitch Double normally occupied, but a dirty brown, narrow-visaged image with savagely low forehead, dark evil walleyes, and a huge jaw filled with shovel-like teeth.

Gummitch was enormously startled and hideously frightened. He felt his grip on his spirit go limp, and without volition he teleported himself three yards to the rear, making use of that faculty for cutting corners in space-time, traveling by space-warp in fact, which was one of his powers that Kitty-Come-Here refused to believe in and that even Old Horsemeat accepted only on faith.

Then, not losing a moment, he picked himself up by his furry seat, swung himself around, dashed downstairs at top speed, sprang to the top of the sofa, and stared for several seconds at the Gummitch Double in the wall-mirror—not relaxing a muscle strand until he was completely convinced that he was still himself and had not been transformed into the nasty brown apparition that had confronted him in the bedroom window.

"Now what do you suppose brought that on?" Old Horsemeat asked Kitty-Come-Here.

Later Gummitch learned that what he had seen had been a squirrel, a savage, nut-hunting being belonging wholly to the outer world (except for forays into attics) and not at all to the mirror one. Nevertheless he kept a vivid memory of his profound momentary conviction that the squirrel had taken the Gummitch Double's place and been about to take his own. He shuddered to think what would have happened if the squirrel had been actively interested in trading spirits with him. Apparently mirrors and mirror-situations, just as he had always feared, were highly conducive to spirit transfers. He filed the information away in the memory cabinet reserved for dangerous, exciting, and possibly useful information, such as plans for climbing straight up glass (diamond-tipped claws!) and flying higher than the trees.

These days his thought cabinets were beginning to feel filled to bursting and he could hardly wait for the moment when the true rich taste of coffee, lawfully drunk, would permit him to speak.

He pictured the scene in detail: the family gathered in conclave at the kitchen table, Ashurbanipal and Cleopatra respectfully watching from floor level, himself sitting erect on chair with paws (or would they be hands?) lightly touching his cup of thin china, while Old Horsemeat poured the thin black steaming stream. He knew the Great Transformation must be close at hand.

At the same time he knew that the other critical situation in the household was worsening swiftly. Sissy, he realized now, was far older than Baby and should long ago have undergone her own somewhat less glamorous though equally necessary transformation (the first tin of raw horsemeat could hardly be as exciting as the first cup of coffee). Her time was long overdue. Gummitch found increasing horror in this mute vampirish being inhabiting the body of a rapidly growing girl, though inwardly equipped to be nothing but a most bloodthirsty she-cat. How dreadful to think of Old Horsemeat and Kitty-Come-Here having to care all their lives for such a monster! Gummitch told himself that if any opportunity for alleviating his parents' misery should ever present itself to him, he would not hesitate for an instant.

Then one night, when the sense of Change was so burstingly strong in him that he knew tomorrow must be the Day, but when the house was also exceptionally unquiet with boards creaking and snapping, taps adrip, and curtains mysteriously rustling at closed windows (so that it was clear that the many spirit worlds including the mirror one must be pressing very close), the opportunity came to Gummitch.

Kitty-Come-Here and Old Horsemeat had fallen into especially sound, drugged sleeps, the former with a bad cold, the latter with one unhappy highball too many (Gummitch knew he had been brooding about Sissy). Baby slept too, though with uneasy whimperings and joggings—moonlight shone full on his crib past a window shade which had whirringly rolled itself up without human or feline agency. Gummitch kept vigil under the crib, with eyes closed but with wildly excited mind pressing outward to every boundary of the house and even stretching here and there into the outer world. On this night of all nights sleep was unthinkable.

Then suddenly he became aware of footsteps, footsteps so soft they must, he thought, be Cleopatra's.

No, softer than that, so soft they might be those of the Gummitch Double escaped from the mirror world at last and padding up toward him through the darkened halls. A ribbon of fur rose along his spine.

Then into the nursery Sissy came prowling. She looked slim as an Egyptian princess in her long thin yellow nightgown and as sure of herself, but the cat was very strong in her tonight, from the flat intent eyes to the dainty canine teeth slightly bared—one look at her now would have sent Kitty-Come-Here running for the telephone number she kept hidden, the telephone number of the special doctor—and Gummitch realized he was witnessing a monstrous suspension of natural law in that this being should be able to exist for a moment without growing fur and changing round pupils for slit eyes.

He retreated to the darkest corner of the room, suppressing a snarl.

Sissy approached the crib and leaned over Baby in the moonlight, keeping her shadow off him. For a while she gloated. Then she began softly to scratch his cheek with a long hatpin she carried, keeping away from his eye, but just barely. Baby awoke and saw her and Baby didn't cry. Sissy continued to scratch, always a little more deeply. The moonlight glittered on the jeweled end of the pin.

Gummitch knew he faced a horror that could not be countered by running about or even spitting and screeching. Only magic could fight so obviously supernatural a manifestation. And this was also no time to think of consequences, no matter how clearly and bitterly etched they might appear to a mind intensely awake.

He sprang up onto the other side of the crib, not uttering a sound, and fixed his golden eyes on Sissy's in the moonlight. Then he moved forward straight at her evil face, stepping slowly, not swiftly, using his extraordinary knowledge of the properties of space *to walk straight through her hand and arm as they flailed the hatpin at him.* When his nose-tip finally paused a fraction of an inch from hers, his eyes had not blinked once, and she could not look away. Then he unhesitatingly flung his spirit into her like a fistful of flaming arrows and he worked the Mirror Magic.

Sissy's moonlit face, feline and terrified, was in a sense the last thing that Gummitch, the real Gummitch-kitten, ever saw in this world. For the next instant he felt himself enfolded by the foul black blinding cloud of Sissy's spirit, which his own had displaced. At the same time he heard the little girl scream, very loudly but even more distinctly, *"Mommy!"*

That cry might have brought Kitty-Come-Here out of her grave, let alone from sleep merely deep or drugged. Within seconds she was in the nursery, closely followed by Old Horsemeat, and she had caught up Sissy in her arms and the little girl was articulating the wonderful word again and again and miraculously following it with the command—there could be no doubt, Old Horsemeat heard it too—"Hold me tight!"

Then Baby finally dared to cry. The scratches on his cheek came to attention and Gummitch, as he had known must happen, was banished to the basement amid cries of horror and loathing chiefly from Kitty-Come-Here.

The little cat did not mind. No basement would be one-tenth as dark as Sissy's spirit that now enshrouded him for always, hiding all the file drawers and the labels on all the folders, blotting out forever even the imagining of the scene of first coffee-drinking and first speech.

In a last intuition, before the animal blackness closed in utterly, Gummitch realized that the spirit, alas, is not the same thing as the consciousness and that one may lose—sacrifice—the first and still be burdened with the second.

Old Horsemeat had seen the hatpin (and hid it quickly from Kitty-Come-Here) and so he knew that the situation was not what it seemed and that Gummitch was at the very least being made into a sort of scapegoat. He was quite apologetic when he brought the tin pans of food to the basement during the period of the little cat's exile. It was a comfort to Gummitch, albeit a small one. Gummitch told himself, in his new black halting manner of thinking, that after all a cat's best friend is his man.

From that night Sissy never turned back in her development. Within two months she made three years' progress in speaking. She became an outstandingly bright, light-footed, high-spirited little girl. Although she never told anyone this, the moonlit nursery and Gummitch's magnified face were her first memories. Everything before that was inky blackness. She was always very nice to Gummitch in a careful sort of way. She could never stand to play the game "Owl Eyes."

After a few weeks Kitty-Come-Here forgot her fears and Gummitch once again had the run of the house. But by then the transformation Old Horsemeat had always warned about had fully taken place. Gummitch was a kitten no longer but an almost burly tom. In him it took the psychological form not of sullenness or surliness but an extreme dignity. He seemed at times rather like an old pirate brooding on treasures he would never live to dig up, shores of adventure he would never reach. And sometimes when you looked into his yellow eyes you felt that he had in him all the materials for the book *Slit Eyes Look at Life*—three or four volumes at least—although he would never write it. And that was natural when you come to think of it, for as Gummitch knew very well, bitterly well indeed, his fate was to be the only kitten in the world that did not grow up to be a man.

THE MONSTER

BY LESTER DEL REY

(Appeared in TOMORROW, THE STARS)

In the spring of 1953 Lester del Rey and his wife, Evelyn, came to spend a weekend at my house in Red Bank, New Jersey, and wound up by staying seventeen years. Of course, they didn't spend all that time in our guest room. After a while they moved into a home of their own, down the block. But we spent a lot of time in each other's company for all those years, and the astonishing thing is after all that we still remained friends.

That is not as easy as you might think, because Lester is one of God's Angry Men. Not just peppery, but purest jalapeño; Lester inflamed in the cause of truth and justice is one of the great natural cataclysms, like an earthquake or a volcanic eruption. So we argued a lot, but managed to refrain from manslaughter. Mostly.

For years, Lester referred to himself as a writer who sometimes dabbled in editing. Sometimes he dabbled a lot—as when, in the early 1950s, he edited four magazines under four different pseudonyms for one publisher. Sometimes he only did it for fun, as when he came to work at Galaxy Publishing Corporation while I was running the shop, to take over our fantasy magazine. Editing fantasy obviously agreed with him.

In 1970, Evelyn del Rey was killed in a tragic car accident, and a year or two later Lester remarried. The bride was another Galaxy group graduate, the whilom Judy-Lynn Benjamin. They are not only a married couple but a powerful editorial team; in fact, they are "Del Rey Books," a major imprint in SF and fantasy publishing. Judy-Lynn handles the science fiction and the dealings with the rest of the publishing company. Lester is in charge of the fantasy. It is a good way to spend one's life, but it has one great drawback. It doesn't leave Lester much time to write more stories like "The Monster."

*   *   *

His feet were moving with an automatic monotony along the sound-deadening material of the flooring. He looked at them, seeing them in motion, and listened for the little taps they made. Then his eyes moved up along the rough tweed of his trousers to the shorter motion of his thighs. There was something good about the movement, almost a purpose.

He tried making his arms move, and found that they accepted the rhythm, the right arm moving forward with the left leg, giving a feeling of balance. It was nice to feel the movement, and nice to know that he could walk so smoothly.

His eyes tired of the motion quickly, however, and he glanced along the hall where he was moving. There were innumerable doors along it; it was a long hall, with a bend at the end. He reached the bend, and began to wonder how he could make the turn. But his feet seemed to know better than he, since one of them shortened its stride automatically, and his body swung right before picking up the smooth motion again.

The new hallway was like the old one, painted white, with the long row of doors. He began to wonder idly what might lie behind all the doors. A universe of hallways and doors that branched off into more hallways? It seemed purposeless to him. He slowed his steps, just as a series of sounds reached him from one of the doors. It was speech—and that meant there was someone else in this universe in which he had found himself. He stopped outside the door, turning his head to listen. The sounds were muffled, but he could make out most of the words.

Politics, his mind told him. The word had some meaning to him, but not much. Someone inside was talking to someone else about the best way to avoid the battle on the moon, now that both powers had bases there. There was a queer tone of fear to the comments on the new iron-chain reaction bombs and what they could do from the moon.

It meant nothing to him, except that he was not alone, and that it stirred up knowledge in his head of a world like a ball in space with a moon that circled it. He tried to catch more conversation, but it had stopped, and the other doors seemed silent. Then he found a door behind which a speaker was cursing at the idea of introducing robots into a world already a mess, calling another by name.

That hit the listener, sending shocks of awareness through his consciousness. He had no name! Who was he? Where was he? And what had come before he found himself here?

He found no answers, savagely though he groped through his reluctant mind. A single word emerged—amnesia, loss of memory. Did that mean he had once had memories? Then he tried to reason out whether an amnesiac would have a feeling of personality, but could not guess. He could not even be sure he had none.

He stared at the knob of the door, wondering if the men inside would know the answers. His hand moved to the knob slowly. Then, before he could act, there was the sudden, violent sound of running footsteps down the hall.

He swung about to see two men come plunging around the corner toward him. It hadn't occurred to him that legs could move so quickly. One man was thicker than he was, dressed in a dirty smock of some kind, and the other was neat and trim, in figure and dress, in a khaki outfit he wore like a badge. The one in khaki opened his mouth.

"There he is! Stop him! You—Expeto! Halt! George—"

Expeto—George Expeto! So he did have a name—unless the first name belonged to the other man. No matter, it was a name. George accepted it and gratitude ran through him sharply. Then he realized the senselessness of the order. How could he halt when he was already standing still? Besides, there were those rapid motions . . .

The two men let out a yell as George charged into motion, finding that his legs could easily hold the speed. He stared doubtfully at another corner, but somehow his responses were equal to it. He started to slow to a halt—just as something whined by his head and spattered against a white wall. His mind catalogued it as a bullet from a silent zep gun, and bullets were used in animosity. The two men were his enemies.

He considered it, and found he had no desire to kill them; besides, he had no gun. He doubled his speed, shot down another hall, ran into stairs, and took them at a single leap. It was a mistake. They led to a narrower hallway, obviously recently blocked off, with a single door. And the man with the zep gun was charging after him as he hesitated.

He hit the door with his shoulder and was inside, in a strange room of machinery and tables and benches. Most of it was strange to his eyes, though he could recognize a small, portable boron-reactor and generator unit. It was obviously one of the new hundred-kilowatt jobs.

The place was a blind alley! Behind him the man in khaki leaped through the ruined door, his zep gun ready. But the panting older figure of the man in the smock was behind him, catching his arm.

"No! Man, you'd get a hundred years of Lunar Prison for shooting Expeto. He's worth his weight in general's stars! If he—"

"Yeah, if! George, we can't risk it. Security comes first. And if he isn't, we can't have another paranoiac running around. Remember the other?"

Expeto dropped his shoulders, staring at them and the queer fear that was in them. "I'm not George?" he asked slowly. "But I've got to be George. I've got to have a name."

The older man nodded. "Sure, George, you're George—George Expeto. Take it easy, Colonel Kallik! Sure you're George. And I'm George—George Enders Obanion. Take it easy, George, and you'll be all right. We're not going to hurt you. We want to help you."

It was a ruse, and Expeto knew it. They didn't want to help—he was somehow important, and they wanted him for something. His name wasn't George—just Expeto. The man was lying. But there was nothing else to do; he had no weapons.

He shrugged. "Then tell me something about myself."

Obanion nodded, catching at the other man's hand. "Sure, George. See that chart on the wall, there behind you—*Now!*"

Expeto had barely time to turn and notice there was no chart on the wall before he felt a violent motion at his back and a tiny catching reaction as the other's hand hit him. Then he blanked out.

He came back to consciousness abruptly, surprised to find that there was no pain in his head. A blow sufficient to knock him out should have left afterpains. He was alone with his thoughts.

They weren't good thoughts. His mind was seizing on the words the others had used, and trying to dig sense out of them. Amnesia was a rare thing—too rare. But paranoia was more common. A man might first feel others were persecuting him, then be sure of it, and finally lose all reality in his fantasies of persecution and his own importance. Then he was a paranoiac, making up fantastic lies to himself, but cunning enough and seemingly rational at times.

But they had been persecuting him! There'd been the man with the gun—and they'd said he was important! Or had he only imagined it? If someone important had paranoia, would they deliberately induce amnesia as a curative step?

And who was he and where? On the first, he didn't care—George Expeto would do. The second took more thought, but he had begun to decide it was a hospital—or asylum. The room here was whitewashed, and the bed was the only furniture. He stared down at his body. They'd strapped him down, and his arms were encased in thin metal chains!

He tried to recall all he could of hospitals, but nothing came. If he had ever been sick, there was no memory of it. Nor could he remember pain, or what it was like, though he knew the word.

The door opened then, cautiously, and a figure in white came in. Expeto stared at the figure, and a slow churning began in his head. The words were reluctant this time, but they came, mere surface whispers that he had to fight to retain. But the differences in the figure made them necessary. The longer hair, the softer face, the swelling at the breast, and something about the hips stirred his memories just enough.

"You're—woman!" He got the word out, not sure it would come.

She jumped at his voice, reaching for the door which she had closed slowly. Fear washed over her face, but she nodded, gulping. "I—of course. But I'm just a technician, and they'll be here, and—They've fastened you down!"

That seemed to bring her back to normal, and she came over, her eyes sweeping over him curiously, while one eyebrow lifted, and she whistled. "Um, not bad. Hi, Romeo. Too bad you're a monster! You don't look mean."

"So you came to satisfy your curiosity," he guessed, and his mind puzzled over it, trying to identify the urge that drove men to stare at beasts in cages. He was just a beast to them, a monster—but somehow important. And in the greater puzzle of it all, he couldn't even resent her remark. Instead, something that had been bothering him since he'd found the word came to the surface. "Why are there men and women—and who am I?"

She glanced at her watch, her ear to the door. Then she glided over to him. "I guess you're the most important man in the world—if you're a man, and not pure monster. Here."

She found his hand had limited freedom in the chains and moved it over her body, while he stared at her. Her eyes were intent on him. "Well. Now do you know why there are men and women?" Her stare intensified as he shook his head, and her lips firmed. "My God, it's true—you couldn't act that well! That's all I wanted to know! And now they'll take over the whole moon! Look, don't tell them I was here—they'll kill you if you do. Or do you know what death is? Yeah, that's it, *kaputt!* Don't talk, then. Not a word!"

She was at the door, listening. Finally she opened it, and moved out....

There was no sound from the zep gun, but the *splaatt* of the bullet reached Expeto's ears. He shuddered, writhing within himself as her exploding body jerked back out of sight. She'd been pleasant to look at. Maybe that was what women were for.

Obanion was over him then, while a crowd collected in the hall, all wearing khaki. "We're not going to kill you, Expeto. We knew she'd come—or hoped she would. Now, if I unfasten your chains, will you behave? We've only got four hours left. O.K., Colonel Kallik?"

The colonel nodded. Behind him, the others were gathering something up and leaving.

"She's the spy, all right. That must make the last of them. Clever. I'd have sworn she was O.K. But they tipped their hand in letting Expeto's door stay unbolted before. Well, the trap worked. Sorry about cutting down your time."

Obanion nodded, and now it was a group of men in white uniforms who came in, while the khaki-clad men left. They were wheeling in assorted machines, something that might have been an encephalograph, a unitary cerebrotrope, along with other instruments.

Expeto watched them, his mind freezing at the implications. But he wasn't insane. His thoughts were lucid. He opened his mouth to protest, just as Obanion swung around.

"Any feeling we're persecuting you, Expeto? Maybe you'd like to get in a few licks, to break my skull and run away where you'd be understood. You might get away with it; you're stronger than I am. Your reaction time is better, too. See, I'm giving you the idea. And you've only got four hours in which to do it."

Expeto shook his head. That way lay madness. Let his mind feel he was persecuted and he'd surely be the paranoiac he'd heard mentioned. There had to be another answer. This was a hospital—and men were healed in hospitals. Even of madness. It could only be a test.

"No," he denied slowly, and was surprised to find it was true. "No, I don't want to kill you, Doctor. If I've been insane, it's gone. But I can't remember—I can't remember!"

He pulled his voice down from its shriek, shook his head again and tried to restrain himself. "I'll co-operate. Only tell me who I am. What have I done that makes people call me a monster? My God, give me an anchor to hold me steady, and then do what you want."

"You're better off not knowing, since you seem to be able to guess when I'm lying." Obanion motioned the other men up, and they waited while Expeto took the chair they pointed out. Then they began clamping devices on his head. "You're what the girl said—the spy. You're the most important man in the world right now—if you can stay sane. You're the one man who carries the secret of how we can live on the moon, protect Earth from aggressive powers, even get to the stars someday."

"But I can't remember—anything!"

"It doesn't matter. The secret's in you and we know how to use it. All right, now I'm going to give you some tests, and I want you to tell me exactly what comes into your mind. The instruments will check on it, so lying won't do any good. Ready?"

It went on and on, while new shifts came in. The clock on the wall indicated only an hour, but it might have been a century, when Obanion sighed and turned his work over to another.

Expeto's thoughts were reeling. He grabbed the breather gratefully, let his head thump back. There must be a way.

"What day is this?" he asked. At their silence he frowned. "Co-operate means both working together. I've been doing my part. Or is it too much to answer a simple question?"

The new man nodded slowly. "You're right. You deserve some answers, if I can give them without breaking security. It's June eighth, nineteen sixty-one—11 P.M."

It checked with figures that had appeared in the back of his mind, ruining the one theory he'd had. "The President is William Olsen?"

The doctor nodded, killing the last chance at a theory. For a time he'd thought that perhaps the aggressive countries had won, and that this was their dictatorship. If he'd been injured in a war—But it was nonsense, since no change had occurred in his time sense or in the Administration.

"How'd I get here?"

The doctor opened his mouth, then closed it firmly. "Forget that, Expeto. You're here. Get this nonsense of a past off your mind—you never had one, understand? And no more questions. We'll never finish in less than three hours, as it is."

Expeto stood up slowly, shaking himself. "You're quite right. You won't finish. I'm sick of this. Whatever I did, you've executed your justice in killing the me that was only a set of memories. And whatever I am, I'll find myself. To hell with the lot of you!"

He expected zep guns to appear, and he was right. The walls suddenly opened in panels, and six armed men were facing him, wearing the oppressive khaki. But something in him seemed to take over. He had the doctor in one arm and a zep gun from the hand of a major before anyone else could move. He faced them, waiting for the bullets that would come, but they drew back, awaiting orders. Expeto's foot found the door, kicked at it; the lock snapped.

Obanion's voice cut through it all. "Don't! No shooting! Expeto, I'm the one you want. Let Smith go, and I'll accompany you, until you're ready to let me go. Fair enough?"

Smith was protesting, but Obanion cut him short. "My fault, since I'm responsible. And the Government be damned. I'm not going to have a bunch of good men killed. His reaction's too fast. We can learn things this way, maybe better. All right, Expeto—or do you want to kill them?"

Expeto dropped the gun a trifle and nodded, while the emotions in his head threatened to make him blank out. He knew now that he could never kill even one of them. But they apparently weren't so sure. "Take me outside, and you can go back," he told Obanion.

The doctor wiped sweat from his forehead, managed a pasty smile, and nodded. Surprisingly, he stepped through a different door, and down a short hall, where men with rifles stood irresolutely. Then they were outside.

Obanion turned to go back, and then hesitated. Surprisingly, he dropped an arm onto Expeto's shoulder. "Come on back inside. We can understand you. Or—All right, I guess you're going. Thanks for taking my offer."

The door closed, and Expeto was alone. Above him most of the building was dark, but he saw a few lighted windows, and some with men and women working over benches and with equipment. There was no sign of beds. All right, so it was some government laboratory.

The most important monster in the world, the useful paranoiac they'd saved by amnesia. . . . The monster they intended to persecute back to paranoia, in hopes he'd recover his memory and the secret they wanted. Let them have the secret—but let him have peace and quiet, where his brain could recover by itself. Then he'd gladly give it to them. Or would he? Would he really be a monster again? Or might he learn the strange reason for there being men and women, the puzzle which seemed so simple that the woman had felt mere contact would solve it?

Funny that there were so many sciences, but no science of life—or was there? Maybe he'd been such a scientist—psychology, zoology, biology, whatever they'd call it from the Greek. Maybe the secret lay there, and it had completely burned out that part of his mind.

Then he heard the sound of a motor and knew they weren't going to let him go. He wasn't to have a moment of freedom if they could prevent it. He swung about sharply, studying the horizon. There were lights and a town. There'd be people, and he could hide among them.

He whipped his legs into action, driving on a full run. The light of the moon was barely enough for him to see the ground clearly, but he managed a good deal more speed than the hallways had permitted. He heard the car behind on the road he found and doubled his speed, while the sound of the motor slowly weakened as the distance increased.

He breathed easier when he hit the outskirts of the town, and slowed to a casual walk, imitating the steps of a few people he saw about. This was better. In the myriad of streets and among countless others, he would be lost. The only trouble was that he was on a main street, and the lights would give him away to anyone who knew him.

He picked up a paper from a waste receptacle and moved off to the left, seeking a less brilliantly lighted street. Now and again he glanced at the print, looking for some trace. But aside from the news that his mind recognized as normal for the times, there was nothing on any mysterious, all-important person, nor on anyone who was either a monster or a savior.

Ahead of him a lone girl was tapping along on the sidewalk. He quickened his step, and she looked back, making the identity complete as her tiny bolero drifted back in the breeze to expose all but the tip of her breasts. She hesitated as he caught up with her, looking up uncertainly. "Yes?"

She couldn't know the answers. Obviously she had never seen him. How could she tell him what he wanted to know?

"Sorry. I thought you were someone else? No, wait. You can tell me something. Where can I find a place to stay?"

"Oh. Well, the Alhambra, I guess." She smiled a little. "Back there—see where the sign is?"

She brushed against his arm as she turned, and a faint gasp sounded. Her hand suddenly contracted on his bare skin, then jerked back sharply. She began stepping slowly away.

"No!" It was a small wail as he caught her shoulder. Then she slumped against him, wilting as he pulled her toward his face. He released her, to see her fall down in a sagging heap.

For a moment the sickness in him rose in great waves, undulating and horrible as he dropped beside her. But when he felt the pulse in her hand still beating, it left. He hadn't killed her, only frightened her into unconsciousness.

He stood there, tasting that. *Only* frightened her that much!

And finally he turned about and headed for the Alhambra. There was nothing he could do for her; she'd recover, in time, and it would be better if she didn't see him there. Then maybe she'd decide it was all a fantasy.

Bitterly he watched a streak mount the horizon, remembering that the men had been discussing the two bases on the moon in the room where he'd first heard voices. They could face war and only fear it vaguely. But he could drive someone senseless by touching them!

He found the night clerk busy watching a television set with the screen badly adjusted to an overbalance of red, and signed the register with the full name he'd hoped once was his. George Expeto, from—make it from New York. It wouldn't matter.

"Five dollars," the clerk told him.

Dollars? He shook his head slowly, trying to think. Something about dollars and cents. But it made no sense.

The clerk's eyes were hard. "No dough, eh? O.K., try to fool someone else. No baggage, no dough, no room. Scram."

Expeto stood irresolutely, trying to make sense out of it still—something...The clerk had swung back to watching the set, and he reached out for the scrawny shoulder, drawing the man around.

"But look—" Then it was no use. The shoulder had crumpled in his hand like a rotten stick, and the man had lapsed into a faint with a single shriek.

Expeto stood outside, swinging while the sickness washed away slowly; he told himself the doctors would fix the man up—that was what they were for. They'd fix him, and no real harm had been done. He hadn't meant to hurt the man. He'd only meant to ask him what dollars were and how to get them.

Then he moved on into a little park and dropped onto a seat. But the sickness was still there, sickness he hadn't noticed, but which had been growing on him even before he'd hurt the clerk. It was as if something were slowly eroding his mind. Even the curious memory of ideas and words was going!

He was sitting there, his head in his hands, trying to catch himself, when the car drove up. Obanion and Kallik got out, but Obanion came over alone.

"Come on, Expeto. It won't work. You might as well come back. And there's only an hour left!"

Expeto got up slowly, nodding wearily. The doctor was right—there was no place in the world for such a monster as he.

"Left before what?" he asked dully, as he climbed into the rear of the car and watched Obanion lock the door and the glass slide between him and the front seat.

For a second Obanion hesitated, then he shrugged. "All right. Maybe you should know. In another hour you'll be dead! And nothing can prevent it."

Expeto took it slowly, letting the thought sink into the muddying depths of his mind. But he was important—they'd told him so. Or had they? They'd chased him about, bound him down, refused to tell him what he needed, refused him even civil decency, and told him he was the hope of the world. Or had he only imagined it?

"I never wanted anything but myself. Only myself. And they wouldn't let me have that—not even for a few hours. They had to hound me—" He realized he was muttering aloud and stopped it.

But from the front seat the voices came back, muffled by the glass, Kallik speaking first. "See, paranoia all right. Thinks he's being persecuted."

"He is." Obanion nodded slowly. "With the time limit the Government insisted on, the ruin of our plans by the spies that got through, and the need to get the facts, what else could we do? If they'd let us animate him for a week—but six hours' limit on the vital crystals! We've had to be brutal."

"You talk as if he were a human being. Remember the other—XP One? Crazy, killing people, or trying to. I tell you, the robots can't be made trustworthy yet, no matter what you cybernetics boys have found in the last ten years. This one only had six hours instead of ten for the other, and he's already threatened us and hurt two people."

"Maybe. We don't know all the story yet." Obanion wiped his forehead. "And damn it, he is human. That's what makes it tough, knowing we've got to treat him like a machine. Maybe we grew his brain out of silicones and trick metal crystals, and built his body in a laboratory, but the mechanical education he got made him a lot more human than some people, or should have made him so. If I can prove he isn't crazy—''

Expeto—Experiment Two—stared at the hand he held before his face. He bent the fingers, looking at the veins and muscles. Then, slowly, with his other hand, he twisted at them, stretching them out and out, until there could be no doubt that they were rubbery plastic.

A monster! A thing grown in a laboratory, made out of mechanical parts, and fed bits of human education from tapes in cybernetics machines! A thing that would walk on the moon without air and take over enemy bases, do men's work, but who could never be taken as a man by human beings, who grew from something or other but were never built. A thing to be animated for a few hours and deliberately set to die at the end of that time, as a precaution—because it had no real life, and it wasn't murder to kill a built thing!

A thing that somehow couldn't kill men, it seemed, judging by the sickness he'd felt when he'd hurt or threatened them. But a thing of which they couldn't be sure—until they'd tested him and found he was complete and sane.

He rocked back and forth on the seat, moaning a little. He didn't want to die; but already the eroded places in his brain were growing larger. It didn't matter; he had never been anyone; he never could be anyone. But he didn't want to die!

"Half an hour left," the cyberneticist, Obanion, said slowly. "And less than that unless we make sure he doesn't exert himself. He's about over."

Then the car was coming into the garage, and Obanion got out with Kallik. Expeto went with them quietly, knowing that Obanion was right. Already he was finding it hard to use his legs or control what passed for muscles. They went back to the room with the instruments and the waiting technicians.

For a moment he looked at the humans there. Obanion's eyes were veiled, but the others were open to his gaze. And there was no pity there. Men don't pity a car that is too old and must go to the scrap heap. He was only a machine, no matter how valuable. And after him other machines would see the faces of men turned away from them, generation after generation.

Slowly he kicked at the chair, tipping it over without splintering it, and his voice came out as high and shrill as his faltering control could force it. "No! No more! You've persecuted me enough. You've tried to kill me—me, the hope of your puny race! You've laughed at me and tortured me. But I'm smarter than you—greater than you! I can kill you—all of you—the whole world, with my bare hands."

He saw shock on Obanion's face, and sadness, and for that he was almost sorry. But the smug satisfaction of Kallik as the zep gun came up and the horror on the faces of the others counteracted it. He yelled once, and charged at them.

For a moment he was afraid that he would not be stopped before he had to injure at least one of them. But then the zep gun in Kallik's hand spoke silently, and the bullet smashed against the mockery of Expeto's body.

He lay there, watching them slowly recover from their fright. It didn't matter when one of them came over and began kicking him senselessly. It didn't even matter when Obanion put a stop to it.

His senses were fading now, and he knew that the excitement had shortened his brief time, and that the crystals were about to break apart and put an end to his short existence. But in a curious way, while he still hated and feared death, he was resigned to it.

They'd be better off. Maybe the first experimental robot had known that. Expeto let the thought linger, finding it good. He couldn't believe the other had grown insane; it, too, must have found the bitter truth, and tried to do the only possible thing, even when that involved genuine injury to a few of the humans.

Now they'd have two such failures, and it would be perhaps years before they'd risk another when their checks failed to show the reason for the nonexistent flaws. They'd have to solve their own problems of war or peace without mechanical monsters to make them almost gods in power while teaching them the disregard of devils for life other than their own.

And there'd be no more of his kind to be used and despised and persecuted. Persecuted? The word stirred up thought—something about paranoia and insanity.

But it faded. Everything faded. And he sank through vague content into growing blackness. His thoughts were almost happy as death claimed him.

THE RULL

BY A. E. VAN VOGT

(Appeared in SCIENCE FICTION, THE GREAT YEARS: VOLUME II)

A. E. van Vogt was one of John Campbell's earliest and brightest discoveries, and one of the most permanently memorable. Van has some unique attributes. He is among the world's most popular science-fiction writers, and in some countries—France is one—his work outsells all others. He is the only science-fiction writer I know to whose work a major think-tank assigned a full-time researcher, for the purpose of cataloguing all his predictions of the future. And he is the only science-fiction writer who has created a series of taped lessons capable of teaching you any number of languages, including the Chinese.

Van, Canadian born, has lived in California most of his life. It is a style that suits him. His output has been prodigious, even in a prodigiously prolific field, even though he took a decade or so off in mid-career. And, in a field with many idiosyncratic individuals, Van stands out as one who is most stubbornly his own self.

No one else can write an A. E. van Vogt story. That was evident from the first. In even his earliest work—"The Black Destroyer" and "Discord in Scarlet"—he did what no other writer had ever done. Many others had told us about aliens. Starting with Stanley G. Weinbaum, others had even made their alien characters into persons, as much so as you and I, but in no other way like you or me. Van took the next step and put us inside the alien's mind, so that we perceived the utter strangeness of human beings. He then went on to innovate in quite other areas—Slan, The World of Null-A, et al—and in the 1960s I was lucky enough to be able to coax him back to writing science fiction again, and for my magazines. But I always loved his unhuman, other-directed aliens, and that's why for this volume I chose "The Rull."

* * *

Professor Jamieson saw the other space boat out of the corner of one eye. He was sitting in a hollow about a dozen yards from the edge of the precipice, and some score of feet from the doorway of his own lifeboat. He had been intent on his survey book, annotating a comment beside the voice graph, to the effect that Laertes III was so close to the invisible dividing line between Earth-controlled and Rull-controlled space that its prior discovery by man was in itself a major victory in the Rull-human war.

He wrote: "The fact that ships based on this planet could strike at several of the most densely populated areas of the galaxy, *Rull or human*, gives it an AA priority on all available military equipment. Preliminary defense units should be set up on Mount Monolith, where I am now, within three we—"

It was at that point that he saw the other boat, above and somewhat to his left, approaching the tableland. He glanced up at it—and froze where he was, torn between two opposing purposes.

His first impulse, to run for the lifeboat, yielded to the realization that the movement would be seen instantly by the electronic reflexes of the other ship. For a moment, then, he had the dim hope that, if he remained quiet enough, neither he nor his ship would be observed.

Even as he sat there, perspiring with indecision, his tensed eyes noted the Rull markings and the rakish design of the other vessel. His vast knowledge of things Rull enabled him to catalogue it instantly as a survey craft.

A *survey* craft. The Rulls had discovered the Laertes sun.

The terrible potentiality was that, behind this small craft, might be fleets of battleships, whereas he was alone. His own lifeboat had been dropped by the *Orion* nearly a parsec away, while the big ship was proceeding at antigravity speeds. That was to insure that Rull energy tracers did not record its passage through this area of space.

The *Orion* was to head for the nearest base, load up with planetary defense equipment, and return. She was due in ten days.

Ten days. Jamieson groaned inwardly, and drew his legs under him and clenched his survey book in the fingers of one hand. But still the possibility his ship, partially hidden under a clump of trees, might escape notice if *he* remained quiet, held him there in the open. His head tilted up, his eyes glared at the alien, and his brain willed it to turn aside.

Once more, flashingly, while he waited, the implications of the disaster that could be here, struck deep. In all the universe there had never been so dangerous an intelligence as the Rull. At once remorseless and immune to all attempts at establishing communication, Rulls killed human beings on sight. A human-manned warship that ventured into Rull-patrolled space was attacked until it withdrew or was destroyed. Rull ships that entered Earth-controlled space *never* withdrew once they were attacked. In the beginning, man had been reluctant to engage in a death struggle for the galaxy. But the inexorable enemy had forced him finally to match in every respect the tenacious and murderous policies of the Rull.

The thought ended. The Rull ship was a hundred yards away, and showed no signs of changing its course. In seconds, it would cross the clump of trees, which half-hid the lifeboat.

In a spasm of a movement, Jamieson launched himself from his chair. Like a shot from a gun, with utter abandon, he dived for the open doorway of his machine. As the door clanged behind him, the boat shook as if it had been struck by a giant. Part of the ceiling sagged; the floor staggered towards him, and the air grew hot and suffocating.

Gasping, Jamieson slid into the control chair, and struck at the main emergency switch. The rapid-fire blasters huzzaed into automatic firing positions, and let go with a hum and deep-throated *ping*. The refrigerators whined with power; a cold blast of air blew at his body. The relief was so quick that a second passed before Jamieson realized that the atomic engines had failed to respond. And that the lifeboat, which should already have been sliding into the air, was still lying inert in an exposed position.

Tense, he stared into the visiplates. It took a moment to locate the Rull ship. It was at the lower edge of one plate, tumbling slowly out of sight beyond a clump of trees a quarter of a mile away. As he watched, it disappeared; and then the crash of the landing came clear and unmistakable from the soundboard in front of him.

The relief that came was weighted with an awful reaction. Jamieson sank back into the cushions of the control chair, weak from the narrowness of his escape. The weakness ended abruptly as a thought struck him. There had been a sedateness about the way the enemy ship fell. *The crash hadn't killed the Rulls aboard.*

He was alone in a damaged lifeboat on an impassable mountain with one or more of the most remorseless creatures ever spawned. For ten days, he must fight in the hope that man would still be able to seize the most valuable planet discovered in a century.

He saw in his visiplate that it was growing darker outside.

Jamieson opened the door, and went out onto the tableland. He was still trembling with reaction, but there was no time to waste.

He walked swiftly to the top of the nearest hillock a hundred feet away, taking the last few feet on his hands and knees. Cautiously, he peered over the rim.

Most of the mountain top was visible. It was a rough oval some eight hundred yards wide at its narrowest, a wilderness of scraggly brush and unjutting rock, dominated here and there by clumps of trees. There was not a movement to be seen, and not a sign of the Rull ship. Over everything lay an atmosphere of desolation, and the utter silence of an uninhibited wasteland.

The twilight was deeper, now that the sun had sunk below the southwest precipice. And the deadly part was that, to the Rulls, with their wider vision and more complete sensory equipment, the darkness would mean nothing. All night long, he would have to be on the defensive against beings whose nervous systems outmatched his in every function except, possibly, intelligence. On that level, and that alone, human beings claimed equality.

The very comparison made him realize how desperate his situation was. He needed an advantage. If he could get to the Rull wreck, and cause them some kind of damage before it got pitch dark, before they recovered from the shock of the crash, that alone might make the difference between life and death for him.

It was a chance he had to take.

Hurriedly, Jamieson backed down the hillock, and, climbing to his feet, started to run along a shallow wash. The ground was rough with stones and projecting edges of rock and the gnarled roots and tangle of hardy growth. Twice, he fell, the first time gashing his right hand, the second time his right foot.

It slowed him mentally and physically. He had never before tried to make speed over the pathless wilderness of the tableland. He saw that in ten minutes he had covered a distance of just under seventy-five yards.

Jamieson stopped. It was one thing to be bold on the chance of making a vital gain. It was quite another to throw away his life on a reckless gamble. The defeat would not be his alone, but man's.

As he stood there, he grew aware of how icy cold it had become. A chilling wind from the east had sprung up. By midnight, the temperature would be zero. For it was autumn on Laertes III. Soon, snow would be stinging down on an ever more barren land, and then winter would settle for eight long months. The original exploratory party had extracted from the flora and the fauna, and the soil and the rocks the cyclic secrets of the planet's existence. And in their two years stay they had mapped the gyrations of every wind, cold, and heat source on its uneven surface.

Jamieson began to retreat. There were several defenses to rig up before night fell—and he had better hurry. An hour later, when the moonless darkness lay heavily over the mountain of mountains, Jamieson sat tensely before his visiplates.

It was going to be a long night for a man who dared not sleep.

It was shortly after midnight—Laertes III had a twenty-six hour, sidereal time, day—when Jamieson saw a movement at the remote perimeter of his all-wave vision plate. Finger on blaster control, he waited for the object to come into sharper focus.

It never did. The cold dawn found him weary but still alertly watching for an enemy that was acting as cautiously as he himself.

He began to wonder if he had actually seen anything.

Jamieson took another antisleep pill and made a more definite examination of the atomic motors. It didn't take long to verify his earlier diagnosis. The basic graviton pile had been thoroughly frustrated. Until it could be reactivated on the *Orion*, the motors were useless.

The conclusive examination braced Jamieson. He was committed irrevocably to the battle of the tableland, with all its intricate possibilities. The idea that had been turning over in his mind during the prolonged night took on new meaning. This was the first time in his knowledge that a Rull and a human being had faced each other on a limited field of action, where neither was a prisoner. The great battles in space were ship against ship and fleet against fleet. Survivors either escaped or were picked up by overwhelming forces. Actually, both humans and Rulls, captured or facing capture, were conditioned to kill themselves. Rulls did it by a mental *willing* that had never been circumvented. Men had to use mechanical methods, and in some cases that had proved impossible. The result was that Rulls had had occasional opportunities to experiment on living, conscious men.

Unless he was bested, before he could get organized, here was a priceless opportunity to try some tests on Rulls—and without delay. Every moment of daylight must be utilized to the uttermost limit.

Jamieson put on his special "defensive" belts, and went outside.

The dawn was brightening—minute by minute—and the vistas that revealed themselves with each increment of light power held him, even as he tensed his body for the fight ahead. *Why,* he thought, in a sharp, excited wonder, *all this is happening on the strangest mountain ever known.*

Mount Monolith, discovered at the same time as the planet, two years before, had been named in the first words spoken about it. "Look at that monolith down there!" On a level plain that column stood, and reared up precipitously to a height of eight thousand two hundred feet. The most majestic pillar in the known universe, it easily qualified as one of the hundred natural wonders of the galaxy.

Standing there, Jamieson felt, not for the first time, the greatness of man's destiny. Defender and ally of thousands of lifeforms, chief enemy of the encroaching Rull menace—In his eighteen years of military service, he had gazed on many alien scenes. He had walked the soil of planets two hundred thousand light-years from Earth. As head of the fleet's science division, he had been absolute commander—under law and regulation—of ships so powerful that whole groups of inhabited worlds were helpless before their irresistible might—ships that flashed from the eternal night into the blazing brightness of suns red and suns blue, suns yellow and white and orange and violet, suns so wonderful and different that no previous imaginings could match the reality.

Yet, despite the greatness of his rank, here he stood on a mountain on far Laertes, one man compelled by circumstance to pit his cunning against one or more of the supremely intelligent Rull enemy. The information about the discovery of the Laertes planet had been relayed to him through the usual routine channels. Instantly he had seen what the others had missed, that it would be a key base against either galactic hemisphere. Since battleships did not normally carry the type of planetary oryctologist who could make a co-ordinated survey, he had not hesitated to step into the breach.

Even as it was, the first great advantage was already lost.

Jamieson shook himself grimly. It was time to launch his attack—and discover the opposition that could be mustered against him.

That was Step One, and the important point about it was to insure that it wasn't also Step Last.

By the time the Laertes sun peered palely over the horizon that was the northeast cliff's edge, the assault was under way. The automatic defensors, which he had set up the night before, moved slowly from point to point ahead of the mobile blaster.

Jamieson cautiously saw to it that one of the three defensors also brought up his rear. He augmented that basic protection by crawling from one projecting rock after another. The machines he manipulated from a tiny hand control, which was connected to the visiplates that poked out from his headgear just above his eyes. With tensed eyes, he watched the wavering needles that would indicate movement or that the defensor screens were being subjected to energy opposition.

Nothing happened.

As he came within sight of the Rull craft, Jamieson stalled his attack, while he seriously pondered the problem of no resistance. He didn't like it. It was possible that all the Rulls aboard had been killed, but he doubted it mightily. Rulls were almost boneless. Except for half a dozen strategically linked cartilages, they were all muscle.

With bleak eyes, Jamieson studied the wreck through the telescopic eyes of one of the defensors. It lay in a shallow indentation, its nose buried in a wall of gravel. Its lower plates were collapsed versions of the original. His single energy blast the evening before, completely automatic though it had been, had really dealt a smashing blow to the Rull ship.

The over-all effect was of utter lifelessness. If it was a trick, then it was a very skillful one. Fortunately, there were tests he could make, not absolutely final but evidential and indicative.

He made them.

The echoless height of the most unique mountain ever discovered hummed with the fire-sound of the mobile blaster. The noise grew to a roar as the unit's pile warmed to its task, and developed its maximum kilo curie activity.

Under that barrage, the hull of the enemy craft trembled a little and changed color slightly, but that was all. After ten minutes, Jamieson cut the power, and sat baffled and indecisive.

The defensive screens of the Rull ship were full on. Had they gone on automatically after his first shot of the evening before? Or had they been put up deliberately to nullify just such an attack as this?

He couldn't be sure. That was the trouble; he had no positive knowledge. The Rull could be lying inside, dead. (Odd, how he was beginning to think in terms of one rather than several, but he had a conviction that two live Rulls would not be cautious in dealing with one human being—of course, they couldn't be absolutely sure there was only one.) It could be wounded and incapable of doing anything against him. It could have spent the night marking up the tableland with *elled* nerve control lines—he'd have to make sure he never looked directly at the ground—or it could simply be waiting for the arrival of the greater ship that had dropped it onto the planet.

Jamieson refused to consider the last possibility. That way was death, without qualification or hope.

Frowningly, he studied the visible damage he had done the ship. All the hard metals had held together, so far as he could see, but the whole bottom of the ship was dented to a depth that varied from one to four feet. Some radiation must have got in, and the question was, what would it have damaged?

He had examined dozens of captured Rull survey craft, and if this one ran to the pattern, then in the front would be the control center, with a sealed off blaster chamber. In the rear the engine room, two storerooms, one for fuel and equipment, the other for food and—

For food. Jamieson jumped, and then with wide eyes noted how the food section had suffered greater damage than any other part of the ship.

Surely, surely, some radiation must have got into it, poisoning it, ruining it, and instantly putting the Rull, with his swift digestive system, into a deadly position.

Jamieson sighed with the intensity of his hope, and prepared to retreat. As he turned away, quite incidentally, accidentally, he glanced at the rock behind which he had shielded himself from possible direct fire.

Glanced at it, and saw the *elled* lines in it. Intricate lines, based on a profound and inhuman study of the human nervous system. Jamieson recognized them, and stiffened in horror. He thought in anguish: *Where, where am I supposed to fall? Which cliff?*

With a desperate will, with all his strength, he fought to retain his senses a moment longer. He strove to see the lines again. He saw, briefly, flashingly, five vertical and above them three lines that pointed east with their wavering ends.

The pressure built up, up, up inside him, but still he fought to keep his thoughts moving. Fought to remember if there were any wide ledges near the top of the east cliff.

There were. He recalled them in a final agony of hope. *There,* he thought. *That one,* that *one, Let me fall on that one.* He strained to hold the ledge image he wanted, and to repeat, repeat the command that might save his life. His last, dreary thought was that here was the answer to his doubts. The Rull *was* alive.

Blackness came like a curtain of pure essence of night.

From the far galaxy had he come, a cold, remorseless leader of leaders, the *yeli*, Meeesh, the Iiin of Ria, the high Aaish of the Yeell. And other titles, and other positions, and power. Oh, the power that he had, the power of death, the power of life and the power of the Leard ships.

He came in his great anger to discover what was wrong. A thousand years before the command had been given: Expand into the Second galaxy. Why were they-who-could-not-be-more-perfect so slow in carrying out these instructions? What was the nature of the two-legged creatures whose multitudinous ships, impregnable planetary bases, and numerous allies had fought those-who-possessed-Nature's-supreme-nervous-system to an impasse?

"Bring me a live human being!" The command echoed to the ends of Riatic space.

It produced a dull survivor of an Earth cruiser, a sailor of low degree with an I.Q. of ninety-six, and a fear index of two hundred and seven. The creature made vague efforts to kill himself, and squirmed on the laboratory tables, and finally escaped into death when the scientists were still in the beginning of the experiments which *he* had ordered to be performed before his own eyes.

"Surely, this is not the enemy."

"Sire, we capture so few that are alive. Just as we have conditioned our own loved ones, so do they seem to be conditioned to kill themselves in case of capture."

"The environment is wrong. We must create a situation where the captured does not know himself to be prisoner. Are there any possibilities?"

"The problem will be investigated."

He had come, as the one who will conduct the experiment, to the sun where a man had been observed seven periods before—"in a small craft that fell from a point in space, obviously dropped by a warship. And so we have a new base possibility.

"No landings have yet been made, as you instructed; no traces of our presence. It may be assumed that there was an earlier human landing on the third planet. A curious mountain top. Will be an ideal area for our purposes."

A battle group patrolled the space around the sun. But *he* came down in a small ship; and because he had contempt for his enemy, he flew in over the mountain, fired his disabling blast at the ship on the ground—and then was struck by a surprisingly potent return blast, that sent his machine spinning to a crash.

Almost, in those seconds, death came. But he crawled out of his control chair, shocked but still alive. With thoughtful eyes, he assessed the extent of the disaster that had befallen him.

He had issued commands that he would call when he needed help. But he could not call. The radio was shattered beyond repair. He had a strange, empty sensation when he discovered that his food was poisoned.

Swiftly, he stiffened to the necessities of the situation.

The experiment would go on, with one proviso. When the need for food became imperative, he would kill the man, and so survive until the commanders of the ships grew alarmed, and came down to see what had happened.

Part of the sunless period, he spent exploring the cliff's edge. Then he hovered on the perimeter of the man's defensor energies, studying the lifeboat and pondering the possible actions the other might take against him.

Finally, with a tireless patience he examined the approaches to his own ship. At key points, he drew the lines-that-could-seize-the-minds-of-men. There was satisfaction, shortly after the sun came up, in seeing the enemy "caught" and "compelled." The satisfaction had but one drawback.

He could not take the advantage of the situation that he wanted.

The difficulty was that the man's blaster had been left focused on his main air lock. It was not emitting energy, but the Rull did not doubt that it would fire automatically if the door opened.

What made the situation serious was that, when he tried the emergency exit, it was jammed.

It hadn't been. With the forethought of his kind, he had tested it immediately after the crash. Then it opened.

Now, it didn't. The ship, he decided, must have settled while he was out during the sunless period. Actually, the reason for what had happened didn't matter. What counted was that he was locked in just when he wanted to be outside.

It wasn't as if he had definitely decided to destroy the man immediately. If capturing him meant gaining control of his food supply, then it would be unnecessary to give him death. It was important to be able to make the decision, however, while the man was helpless; and the further possibility that the *elled* fall might kill him made the *yeli* grim. He didn't like accidents to disturb his plans.

From the beginning the affair had taken a sinister turn. He had been caught up by forces beyond his control, by elements of space and time which he had always taken into account as being theoretically possible, but he had never considered them as having personal application.

That was for the deeps of space where the Leard ships fought to extend the frontiers of the perfect ones. Out there lived alien creatures that had been spawned by Nature before the ultimate nervous system was achieved. All those aliens must die because they were now unnecessary, and because, existing, they might accidentally discover means of upsetting the balance of Yeellian life. In civilized Ria accidents were forbidden.

The Rull drew his mind clear of such weakening thoughts.

He decided against trying to open the emergency door. Instead, he turned his blaster against a crack in the hard floor. The frustrators blew their gases across the area where he had worked, and the suction pumps caught the swirling radioactive stuff and drew it into a special chamber. But the lack of an open door as a safety valve made the work dangerous. Many times he paused while the air was cleansed, and the counter needles shook themselves toward zero, so that he could come out again from the frustrating chamber to which he retreated whenever the heat made his nerves tingle—a more reliable guide than any instrument that had to be watched.

The sun was past the meridian when the metal plate finally lifted clear, and gave him an opening into the gravel and rock underneath. The problem of tunneling out into the open was easy except that it took time and physical effort. Dusty and angry and hungry, the Rull emerged from the hole near the center of the clump of trees beside which his craft had fallen.

His plan to conduct an experiment had lost its attraction. He had obstinate qualities in his nature, but he reasoned that this situation could be reproduced for him on a more civilized level. No need to take risks or to be uncomfortable. Kill the man and use him as food until the ships came down to rescue him.

With a hungry gaze, he searched the ragged, uneven east cliff, peering down at the ledges, crawling swiftly along until he had virtually circumvented the tableland. He found nothing he could be sure about. In one or two places the ground looked lacerated as by the passage of a body, but the most intensive examination failed to establish that anyone had actually been there.

Somberly, the Rull glided towards the man's lifeboat. From a safe distance, he examined it. The defense screens were up, but he couldn't be sure they had been put up before the attack of the morning, or had been raised since then, or had come on automatically at his approach.

He couldn't be sure. That was the trouble. Everywhere, on the tableland around him, was a barrenness, a desolation unlike anything else he had ever known. The man could be dead, his smashed body lying at the remote bottom of the mountain. He could be inside the ship badly injured; he had, unfortunately, *had* time to get back to the safety of his craft. Or he could be waiting inside, alert, aggressive, and conscious of his enemy's uncertainty, determined to take full advantage of that uncertainty.

The Rull set up a watching device, that would apprise him when the door opened. Then he returned to the tunnel that led into his ship, laboriously crawled through it, and settled himself to wait out the emergency.

The hunger in him was an expanding force, hourly taking on a greater urgency. It was time to stop moving around. He would need all his energy for the crisis.

The days passed.

Jamieson stirred in an effluvium of pain. At first it seemed all-enveloping, a mist of anguish that bathed him in sweat from head to toe. Gradually, then, it localized in the region of his lower left leg.

The pulse of the pain made a rhythm in his nerves. The minutes lengthened into an hour, and then he finally thought: *Why, I've got a sprained ankle!* He had more than that, of course. The pressure that had driven him here clung like a gravitonic plate. How long he lay there, partly conscious, was not clear, but when he finally opened his eyes, the sun was still shining on him, though it was almost directly overhead.

He watched it with the mindlessness of a dreamer as it withdrew slowly past the edge of the overhanging precipice. It was not until the shadow of the cliff suddenly plopped across his face that he started to full consciousness with a sudden memory of deadly danger.

It took a while to shake the remnants of the *elled* "take" from his brain. And, even as it was fading, he sized up, to some extent, the difficulties of his position. He saw that he had tumbled over the edge of a cliff to a steep slope. The angle of descent of the slope was a sharp fifty-five degrees, and what had saved him was that his body had been caught in the tangled growth near the edge of the greater precipice beyond.

His foot must have twisted in those roots, and sprained.

As he finally realized the nature of his injuries, Jamieson braced up. He was safe. In spite of having suffered an accidental defeat of major proportions, his intense concentration on this slope, his desperate will to make *this* the place where he must fall, had worked out.

He began to climb. It was easy enough on the slope, steep as it was; the ground was rough, rocky, and scraggly with brush. It was when he came to the ten-foot overhanging cliff that his ankle proved what an obstacle it could be.

Four times he slid back, reluctantly; and then, on the fifth try, his fingers, groping desperately over the top of the cliff, caught an unbreakable root. Triumphantly, he dragged himself to the safety of the tableland.

Now that the sound of his scraping and struggling was gone, only his heavy breathing broke the silence of the emptiness. His anxious eyes studied the uneven terrain. The tableland spread before him with not a sign of a moving figure anywhere.

To one side, he could see his lifeboat. Jamieson began to crawl toward it, taking care to stay on rock as much as possible. What had happened to the Rull he did not know. And since, for several days, his ankle would keep him inside his ship, he might as well keep his enemy guessing during that time.

Professor Jamieson lay in his bunk, thinking. He could hear the beating of his heart. There were the occasional sounds when he dragged himself out of bed. But that was almost all. The radio, when he turned it on, was dead. No static, not even the fading in and out of a wave. At this colossal distance, even sub-space radio was impossible.

He listened on all the more active Rull wave lengths. But the silence was there, too. Not that they would be broadcasting if they were in the vicinity.

He was cut off here in this tiny ship on an uninhabited planet, with useless motors.

He tried not to think of it like that. "Here," he told himself, "is the opportunity of a lifetime for an experiment."

He warmed to the idea as a moth to flame. Live Rulls were hard to get hold of. About one a year was captured in the unconscious state, and these were regarded as priceless treasures. But here was an even more ideal situation.

We're prisoners, both of us. That was the way he tried to picture it. Prisoners of an environment, and, therefore, in a curious fashion, prisoners of each other. Only each was free of the conditioned need to kill himself.

There were things a man might discover. The great mysteries—as far as men were concerned—that motivated Rull actions. Why did they want to destroy other races totally? Why did they needlessly sacrifice valuable ships in attacking Earth machines that ventured into their sectors of space—when they knew that the intruders would leave in a few weeks anyway? And why did prisoners who could kill themselves at will commit suicide without waiting to find out what fate was intended for them? Sometimes they were merely wanted as messengers.

Was it possible the Rulls were trying to conceal a terrible weakness in their make-up of which man had not yet found an inkling?

The potentialities of this fight of man against Rull on a lonely mountain exhilarated Jamieson as he lay on his bunk, scheming, turning the problem over in his mind.

There were times during those dog days when he crawled over to the control chair, and peered for an hour at a stretch into the visiplates. He saw the tableland and the vista of distance beyond it. He saw the sky of Laertes III, bluish pink sky, silent and lifeless.

He saw the prison. *Caught here,* he thought bleakly. Professor Jamieson, whose appearance on an inhabited planet would bring out unwieldy crowds, whose quiet voice in the council chambers of Earth's galactic empire spoke with final authority—that Jamieson was here, alone, lying in a bunk, waiting for a leg to heal, so that he might conduct an experiment with a Rull.

It seemed incredible. But he grew to believe it as the days passed.

On the third day, he was able to move around sufficiently to handle a few heavy objects. He began work immediately on the mental screen. On the fifth day, it was finished. Then the story had to be recorded. That was easy. Each sequence had been so carefully worked out in bed that it flowed from his mind onto the visiwire.

He set it up about two hundred yards from the lifeboat, behind a screening of trees. He tossed a can of food a dozen feet to one side of the screen.

The rest of the day dragged. It was the sixth day since the arrival of the Rull, the fifth since he had sprained his ankle.

Came the night.

A gliding shadow, undulating under the starlight of Laertes III, the Rull approached the screen the man had set up. How bright it was, shining in the darkness of the tableland, a blob of light in a black universe of uneven ground and dwarf shrubbery.

When he was a hundred feet from the light, he sensed the food—and realized that here was a trap.

For the Rull, six days without food had meant a stupendous loss of energy, visual blackouts on a dozen color levels, a dimness of life-force that fitted with the shadows, not the sun. That inner world of disjointed nervous system was like a run-down battery with a score of organic "instruments" disconnecting one by one as the energy level fell. The *yeli* recognized dimly, but with a savage anxiety, that only a part of that nervous system would ever be restored to complete usage. And, even for that, speed was essential. A few more steps downward, and then the old, old conditioning of mandatory self-inflicted death would apply even to the high Aaish of the Yeell.

The worm body grew quiet. The visual center behind each eye accepted light on a narrow band from the screen. From beginning to end, he watched the story as it unfolded; and then watched it again, craving repetition with all the ardor of a primitive.

The picture began in deep space with the man's lifeboat being dropped from a launching lock of a battleship. It showed the battleship going on to a military base, and there taking on supplies and acquiring a vast fleet of reinforcements, and then starting on the return journey. The scene switched to the lifeboat dropping down on Laertes III, showed everything that had subsequently happened, suggested the situation was dangerous to them both—and pointed out the only safe solution.

The final sequence of each showing of the story was of the Rull approaching the can, to the left of the screen, and opening it. The method was shown in detail, as was the visualization of the Rull busily eating the food inside.

Each time that sequence drew near, a tenseness came over the Rull, a will to make the story real. But it was not until the seventh showing had run its course that he glided forward, closing the last gap between himself and the can. It was a trap, he knew, perhaps even death—it didn't matter. To live, he had to take the chance. Only by this means, by risking what was in the can, could he hope to remain alive for the necessary time.

How long it would take for the commanders cruising up there in the black of space in their myriad ships—how long it would be before they would decide to supersede his command, he didn't know. But they would come. Even if they waited until the enemy ships arrived before they dared to act against his strict orders, they would come.

At that point they could come down without fear of suffering from his ire.

Until then he would need all the food he could get.

Gingerly, he extended a sucker, and activated the automatic opener of the can.

It was shortly after four in the morning when Professor Jamieson awakened to the sound of an alarm ringing softly. It was still pitch dark outside—the Laertes day was twenty-six sidereal hours long; he had set his clocks the first day to co-ordinate—and at this season dawn was still three hours away.

Jamieson did not get up at once. The alarm had been activated by the opening of the can of food. It continued to ring for a full fifteen minutes, which was just about perfect. The alarm was tuned to the electronic pattern emitted by the can, once it was opened, and so long as any food remained in it. The lapse of time involved fitted with the capacity of one of the Rull's suckers in absorbing three pounds of pork.

For fifteen minutes, accordingly, a member of the Rull race, man's mortal enemy, had been subjected to a pattern of mental vibrations corresponding to its own thoughts. It was a pattern to which the nervous systems of other Rulls had responded in laboratory experiments. Unfortunately, those others had killed themselves on awakening, and so no definite results had been proved. But it had been established by the ecphoriometer that the "unconscious" and not the "conscious" mind was affected.

Jamieson lay in bed, smiling quietly to himself. He turned over finally to go back to sleep, and then he realized how excited he was.

The greatest moment in the history of Rull-human warfare. Surely, he wasn't going to let it pass unremarked. He climbed out of bed, and poured himself a drink.

The attempt of the Rull to attack him through his unconscious mind had emphasized his own possible actions in that direction. Each race had discovered some of the weaknesses of the other.

Rulls used their knowledge to exterminate. Man tried for communication, and hoped for association. Both were ruthless, murderous, pitiless, in their methods. Outsiders sometimes had difficulty distinguishing one from the other.

But the difference in purpose was as great as the difference between black and white, the absence as compared to the presence of light.

There was only one trouble with the immediate situation. Now, that the Rull had food, he might develop a few plans of his own.

Jamieson returned to bed, and lay staring into the darkness. He did not underrate the resources of the Rull, but since he had decided to conduct an experiment, no chance must be considered too great.

He turned over finally, and slept the sleep of a man determined that things were working in his favor.

Morning. Jamieson put on his cold-proof clothes, and went out into the chilly dawn. Again, he savored the silence and the atmosphere of isolated grandeur. A strong wind was blowing from the east, and there was an iciness in it that stung his face. Snow? He wondered.

He forgot that. He had things to do on this morning of mornings. He would do them with his usual caution.

Paced by defensors and the mobile blaster, he headed for the mental screen. It stood in open high ground, where it would be visible from a dozen different hiding places, and so far as he could see it was undamaged. He tested the automatic mechanism, and for good measure ran the picture through one showing.

He had already tossed another can of food in the grass near the screen, and he was turning away when he thought: *That's odd. The metal framework looks as if it's been polished.*

He studied the phenomena in a de-energizing mirror, and saw that the metal had been varnished with a clear, varnishlike substance. He felt sick as he recognized it.

He decided in agony, *If the cue is not to fire at all, I won't do it. I'll fire even if the blaster turns on me.*

He scraped some of the "varnish" into a receptacle, and began his retreat to the lifeboat. He was thinking violently:

Where does he get all this stuff? That isn't part of the equipment of a survey craft.

The first deadly suspicion was on him, that what was happening was not just an accident. He was pondering the vast implications of that, narrow-eyed, when, off to one side, he saw the Rull.

For the first time, in his many days on the tableland, he saw the Rull.

What's the cue!

Memory of purpose came to the Rull shortly after he had eaten. It was dim at first, but it grew stronger.

It was not the only sensation of his returning energy.

His visual centers interpreted more light. The starlit tableland grew brighter, not as bright as it could be for him, by a very large percentage, but the direction was up instead of down. It would never again be normal. Vision was in the mind, and that part of his mind no longer had the power of interpretation.

He felt unutterably fortunate that it was no worse.

He had been gliding along the edge of the precipice. Now, he paused to peer down. Even with his partial night vision, the view was breathtaking. There was distance below and distance afar. From a spaceship, the height was almost minimum. But gazing down that wall of gravel into those depths was a different experience. It emphasized how completely he had been caught by an accident. And it reminded him of what he had been doing before the hunger.

He turned instantly away from the cliff, and hurried to where the wreckage of his ship had gathered dust for days. Bent and twisted wreckage, half-buried in the hard ground of Laertes III. He glided over the dented plates inside to one in which he had the day before sensed a quiver of antigravity oscillation. Tiny, potent, tremendous minutiae of oscillation, capable of being influenced.

The Rull worked with intensity and purposefulness. The plate was still firmly attached to the frame of the ship. And the first job, the heartbreakingly difficult job was to tear it completely free. The hours passed.

R-r-i-i-i-pp! The hard plate yielded to the slight rearrangement of its nucleonic structure. The shift was infinitesimal, partly because the directing nervous energy of his body was not at norm, and partly because it had better be infinitesimal. There was such a thing as releasing energy enough to blow up a mountain.

Not, he discovered finally, that there was danger in this plate. He found that out the moment he crawled onto it. The sensation of power that aura-ed out of it was so dim that, briefly, he doubted if it would lift from the ground.

But it did. The test run lasted seven feet, and gave him his measurement of the limited force he had available. Enough for an attack only.

He had no doubts in his mind. The experiment was over. His only purpose must be to kill the man, and the question was, how could he insure that the man did not kill him while he was doing it? The varnish!

He applied it painstakingly, dried it with a drier, and then, picking up the plate again, he carried it on his back to the hiding place he wanted. When he had buried it and himself under the dead leaves of a clump of brush, he grew calmer. He recognized that the veneer of his civilization was off. It shocked him, but he did not regret it.

In giving him the food, the two-legged being was obviously doing something to him. Something dangerous. The only answer to the entire problem of the experiment of the tableland was to deal death without delay.

He lay tense, ferocious, beyond the power of any vagrant thoughts, waiting for the man to come.

It looked as desperate a venture as Jamieson had seen in Service. Normally, he would have handled it effortlessly. But he was watching intently—*intently* —for the paralysis to strike him, the negation that was of the varnish.

And so, it was the unexpected normal quality that nearly ruined him. The Rull flew out of a clump of trees mounted on an antigravity plate. The surprise of that was so great that it almost succeeded. The plates had been drained of all such energies, according to his tests the first morning. Yet here was one alive again and light again with the special antigravity lightness which Rull scientists had brought to the peak of perfection.

The action of movement through space toward him was, of course, based on the motion of the planet as it turned on its axis. The speed of the attack, starting as it did from zero, did not come near the eight hundred mile an hour velocity of the spinning planet, but it was swift enough.

The apparition of metal and six-foot worm charged at him through the air. And even as he drew his weapon and fired at it, he had a choice to make, a restraint to exercise: *Do not kill!*

That was hard, oh, hard. The necessity exercised his capacity for integration and imposed so stern a limitation that during the second it took him to adjust the Rull came to within ten feet of him.

What saved him was the pressure of the air on the metal plate. The air tilted it like a wing of a plane becoming airborne. At the bottom of that metal he fired his irresistible weapon, seared it, burned it, deflected it to a crash landing in a clump of bushes twenty feet to his right.

Jamieson was deliberately slow in following up his success. When he reached the bushes, the Rull was fifty feet beyond it, gliding on its multiple suckers over the top of a hillock. It disappeared into a clump of trees.

He did not pursue it or fire a second time. Instead he gingerly pulled the Rull antigravity plate out of the brush and examined it. The question was, how had the Rull degravitized it without the elaborate machinery necessary?

And if it was capable of creating such a "parachute" for itself, why hadn't it floated down to the forest land far below where food would be available and where it would be safe from its human enemy?

One question was answered the moment he lifted the plate. It was "normal" weight, its energy apparently exhausted after traveling less than a hundred feet. It had obviously never been capable of making the mile and a half trip to the forest and plain below.

Jamieson took no chances. He dropped the plate over the nearest precipice, and watched it fall into distance. He was back in the lifeboat, when he remembered the "varnish."

Why, there had been no cue, not yet.

He tested the scraping he had brought with him. Chemically, it turned out to be a simple resin, used to make varnishes. Atomically, it was stabilized. Electronically, it transformed light into energy on the vibration level of human thought.

It was alive all right. But what was the recording?

Jamieson made a graph of every material and energy level, for comparison purposes. As soon as he had established that it had been altered on the electronic level—which had been obvious, but which, still, had to be proved—he recorded the images on a visiwire. The result was a hodgepodge of dreamlike fantasies.

Symbols. He took down his book, *Symbol Interpretations of the Unconscious,* and found the cross reference: "Inhibitions, Mental."

On the referred page and line, he read: "Do not kill!"

"Well, I'll be—" Jamieson said aloud into the silence of the lifeboat interior. "That's what happened."

He was relieved, and then not so relieved. It had been his personal intention not to kill at this stage. But the Rull hadn't known that. By working such a subtle inhibition, it had dominated the attack even in defeat.

That was the trouble. So far he had got *out* of situations, but had created no successful ones in retaliation. He had a hope, but that wasn't enough.

He must take no more risks. Even his final experiment must wait until the day the *Orion* was due to arrive.

Human beings were just a little too weak in certain directions. Their very life cells had impulses which could be stirred by the cunning and the remorseless.

He did not doubt that, in the final issue, the Rull would try to stir.

On the ninth night, the day before the *Orion* was due, Jamieson refrained from putting out a can of food. The following morning, he spent half an hour at the radio, trying to contact the battleship. He made a point of broadcasting a detailed account of what had happened so far, and he described what his plans were, including his intention of testing the Rull to see if it had suffered any injury from its period of hunger.

Subspace was as silent as death. Not a single pulse of vibration answered his call.

He finally abandoned the attempt to establish contact, and went outside. Swiftly, he set up the instruments he would need for his experiment. The tableland had the air of a deserted wilderness. He tested his equipment, then looked at his watch. It showed eleven minutes of noon. Suddenly jittery, he decided not to wait the extra minutes.

He walked over, hesitated, and then pressed a button. From a source near the screen, a rhythm on a very high energy level was being broadcast. It was a variation of the rhythm pattern to which the Rull had been subjected for four nights.

Slowly, Jamieson retreated toward the lifeboat. He wanted to try again to contact the *Orion*. Looking back, he saw the Rull glide into the clearing, and head straight for the source of the vibration.

As Jamieson paused involuntarily, fascinated, the main alarm system of the lifeboat went off with a roar. The sound echoed with an alien eeriness on the wings of the icy wind that was blowing, and it acted like a cue. His wrist radio snapped on, synchronizing automatically with the powerful radio in the lifeboat. A voice said urgently:

"Professor Jamieson, this is the battleship *Orion*. We heard your earlier calls but refrained from answering. An entire Rull fleet is cruising in the vicinity of the Laertes sun.

"In approximately five minutes, an attempt will be made to pick you up. Meanwhile—*drop everything*."

Jamieson dropped. It was a physical movement, not a mental one. Out of the corner of one eye, even as he heard his own radio, he saw a movement in the sky. Two dark blobs, that resolved into vast shapes. There was a roar as the Rull super-battleships flashed by overhead. A cyclone followed their passage, that nearly tore him from the ground, where he clung desperately to the roots of intertwining brush.

At top speed, obviously traveling under gravitonic power, the enemy warships turned a sharp somersault, and came back toward the tableland. Expecting death, and beginning to realize some of the truth of the situation on the tableland, Jamieson quailed. But the fire flashed past him, not at him. The thunder of the shot rolled toward Jamieson, a colossal sound, that yet did not blot out his sense awareness of what had happened. His lifeboat. They had fired at his lifeboat.

He groaned as he pictured it destroyed in one burst of intolerable flame. And then, for a moment, there was no time for thought or anguish.

A third warship came into view, but, as Jamieson strained to make out its contours, it turned and fled. His wrist radio clicked on:

"Cannot help you now. Save yourself. Our four accompanying battleships and attendant squadrons will engage the Rull fleet, and try to draw them toward our great battle group cruising near the star, Bianca, and then re—"

A flash of vivid fire in the distant sky ended the message. It was a full minute before the cold air of Laertes III echoed to the remote thunder of the broadside. The sound died slowly, reluctantly, as if endless little overtones of it were clinging to each molecule of air.

The silence that settled finally was, strangely, not peaceful. But like the calm before the storm, a fateful, quiescent stillness, alive with unmeasurable threat.

Shakily, Jamieson climbed to his feet. It was time to assess the immediate danger that had befallen him. The greater danger he dared not even think about.

Jamieson headed first for his lifeboat. He didn't have to go all the way. The entire section of the cliff had been sheared away. Of the ship there was no sign.

It pulled him up short. He had expected it, but the shock of the reality was terrific.

He crouched like an animal, and stared up into the sky, into the menacing limits of the sky. It was empty of machines. Not a movement was there, not a sound came out of it, except the sound of the east wind. He was alone in a universe between heaven and earth, a mind poised at the edge of an abyss.

Into his mind, tensely waiting, pierced a sharp understanding. The Rull ships had flown once over the mountain to size up the situation on the tableland, and then had tried to destroy him.

Who was the Rull here with him, that super-battleships should roar down to insure that no danger remained for it on the tableland?

Well, they hadn't quite succeeded. Jamieson showed his teeth into the wind. Not quite. But he'd have to hurry. At any moment, they might risk one of their destroyers in a rescue landing.

As he ran, he felt himself one with the wind. He knew that feeling, that sense of returning primitiveness during moments of excitement. It was like that in battles, and the important thing was to yield one's whole body and soul to it. There was no such thing as fighting efficiently with half your mind or half your body. All, all, was demanded.

He expected falls, and he had them. Each time he got up, almost unconscious of the pain, and ran on again. He arrived bleeding—but he arrived.

The sky was silent.

From the shelter of a line of brush, he peered at the Rull.

The captive Rull, *his* Rull to do with as he pleased. To watch, to force, to educate—the fastest education in the history of the world. There wasn't any time for a leisurely exchange of information.

From where he lay, he manipulated the controls of the screen.

The Rull had been moving back and forth in front of the screen. Now, it speeded up, then slowed, then speeded up again, according to his will.

Some thousands of years before, in the Twentieth Century, the classic and timeless investigation had been made of which this was one end result. A man called Pavlov fed a laboratory dog at regular intervals, to the accompaniment of the ringing of a bell. Soon, the dog's digestive system responded as readily to the ringing of the bell without the food as to the food and the bell together.

Pavlov himself never did realize the most important reality behind his conditioning process. But what began on that remote day ended with a science that could control animals and aliens—and men—almost at will. Only the Rulls baffled the master experimenters in the latter centuries when it was exact science. Defeated by the will to death of all Rull captives, the scientists foresaw the doom of Earth's galactic empire unless some beginning could be made in penetrating the minds of Rulls.

It was his desperate bad luck that he had no time for real penetrations.

There was death here for those who lingered.

But even what he had to do, the bare minimum of what he had to do, would take precious time. Back and forth, forth, back and forth; the rhythm of obedience had to be established.

The image of the Rull on the screen was as lifelike as the original. It was three dimensional, and its movements were like an automaton. The challenger was actually irresistible. Basic nerve centers were affected. The Rull could no more help falling into step than it could resist the call of the food impulse.

After it had followed that mindless pattern for fifteen minutes, changing pace at his direction, Jamieson started the Rull and its image climbing trees. Up, then down again, half a dozen times. At that point, Jamieson introduced an image of himself.

Tensely, with one eye on the sky and one on the scene before him, he watched the reactions of the Rull—watched them with narrowed eyes and a sharp understanding of Rull responses to the presence of human beings. Rulls were digestively stimulated by the odor of man. It showed in the way their suckers opened and closed. When a few minutes later, he substituted himself for his image, he was satisfied that this Rull had temporarily lost its normal automatic hunger when it saw a human being.

And now that he had reached the stage of final control, he hesitated. It was time to make his tests. Could he afford the time?

He realized that he had to. This opportunity might not occur again in a hundred years.

When he finished the tests twenty-five minutes later, he was pale with excitement. He thought: *This is it. We've got it.*

He spent ten precious minutes broadcasting his discovery by means of his wrist radio—hoping that the transmitter on his lifeboat had survived its fall down the mountain, and was picking up the thready message of the smaller instrument, and sending it out through subspace.

During the entire ten minutes, there was not a single answer to his call.

Aware that he had done what he could, Jamieson headed for the cliff's edge he had selected as a starting point. He looked down, and shuddered, then remembered what the *Orion* had said: "An entire Rull fleet cruising—"

Hurry!

He lowered the Rull to the first ledge. A moment later he fastened the harness around his own body, and stepped into space. Sedately, with easy strength, the Rull gripped the other end of the rope, and lowered him down to the ledge beside it.

They continued on down. It was hard work although they used a very simple system.

A long plastic "rope" spanned the spaces for them. A metal "climbing" rod, used to scale the smooth vastness of a spaceship's side, held position after position while the rope did its work.

On each ledge, Jamieson burned the rod at a downward slant into solid rock. The rope slid through an arrangement of pulleys in the metal as the Rull and he, in turn, lowered each other to ledges farther down.

The moment they were both safely in the clear of one ledge, Jamieson would explode the rod out of the rock, and it would drop down ready for use again.

The day sank towards darkness like a restless man into sleep, slowly, wearily. Jamieson grew hot and tired, and filled with the melancholy of the fatigue that dragged at his muscles.

He could see that the Rull was growing more aware of him. It still co-operated, but it watched him with intent eyes each time it swung him down.

The conditioned state was ending. The Rull was emerging from its trance. The process should complete before night.

There was a time, then, when Jamieson despaired of ever getting down before the shadows fell. He had chosen the western, sunny side for that fantastic descent down a black-brown cliff the like of which did not exist elsewhere in the known worlds of space. He found himself watching the Rull with quick, nervous glances. When it swung him down onto a ledge beside it, he watched its blue eyes, its staring blue eyes, come closer and closer to him, and then as his legs swung below the level of those strange eyes, they twisted to follow him.

The intent eyes of the other reminded Jamieson of his discovery. He felt a fury at himself that he had never reasoned it out before. For centuries man had known that his own effort to see clearly required a good twenty-five percent of the energy of his whole body. Human scientists should have guessed that the vast wave compass of Rull eyes was the product of a balancing of glandular activity on a fantastically high energy level. A balancing which, if disturbed, would surely affect the mind itself either temporarily or permanently.

He had discovered that the impairment was permanent.

What would a prolonged period of starvation diet do to such a nervous system?

The possibilities altered the nature of the war. It explained why Rull ships had never attacked human food sources or supply lines; they didn't want to risk retaliation. It explained why Rull ships fought so remorselessly against Earth ships that intruded into their sectors of the galaxy. It explained their ruthless destruction of other races. They lived in terror that their terrible weakness would be found out.

Jamieson smiled with a savage anticipation. If his message had got through, or if he escaped, Rulls would soon feel the pinch of hunger. Earth ships would concentrate on that one basic form of attack in the future. The food supplies of entire planetary groups would be poisoned, convoys would be raided without regard for casualties. Everywhere at once the attack would be pressed without let-up and without mercy.

It shouldn't be long before the Rull began his retreat to his own galaxy. That was the only solution that would be acceptable. The invader must be driven back and back, forced to give up his conquests of a thousand years.

Four P.M. Jamieson had to pause again for a rest. He walked to the side of the ledge away from the Rull, and sank down on the rock. The sky was a brassy blue, silent and windless now, a curtain drawn across the black space above, concealing what must already be the greatest Rull-human battle in ten years.

It was a tribute to the five Earth battleships and their escort that no Rull ship had yet attempted to rescue the Rull on the tableland.

Possibly, of course, they didn't want to give away the presence of one of their own kind.

Jamieson gave up the futile speculation. Wearily, he compared the height of the cliff above with the depth that remained below. He estimated they had come two-thirds of the distance. He saw that the Rull was staring out over the valley. Jamieson turned and gazed with it.

The scene which they took in with their different eyes and different brains was fairly drab and very familiar, yet withal strange and wonderful. The forest began a quarter of a mile from the bottom of the cliff, and it almost literally had no end. It rolled up over the hills and down into the shallow valleys. It faltered at the edge of a broad river, then billowed out again, and climbed the slopes of mountains that sprawled mistily in distance.

His watch showed four-fifteen. Time to get going again.

At twenty-five minutes after six, they reached a ledge a hundred and fifty feet above the uneven plain. The distance strained the capacity of the rope, but the initial operation of lowering the Rull to freedom and safety was achieved without incident. Jamieson gazed down curiously at the worm. What would it do now that it was in the clear?

It looked up at him and waited.

That made him grim. Because this was a chance he was not taking. Jamieson waved imperatively at the Rull, and took out his blaster. The Rull backed away, but only into the safety of a gigantic rock. Blood-red, the sun was sinking behind the mountains. Darkness moved over the land. Jamieson ate his dinner. It was as he was finishing it that he saw a movement below.

He watched, as the Rull glided along close to the edge of the precipice. It disappeared beyond an outjut of the cliff.

Jamieson waited briefly, then swung out on the rope. The descent drained his strength, but there was solid ground at the bottom. Three-quarters of the way down, he cut his finger on a section of the rope that was unexpectedly rough.

When he reached the ground, he noticed that his finger was turning an odd gray. In the dimness, it looked strange and unhealthy.

As Jamieson stared at it, the color drained from his face. He thought in a bitter anger: *The Rull must have smeared it on the rope on his way down.*

A pang went through his body. It was knife-sharp, and it was followed instantly by a stiffness. With a gasp, he grabbed at his blaster, to kill himself. His hand froze in midair. He fell to the ground. The stiffness held him there, froze him there, moveless.

The will to death is in all life. Every organic cell ecphorizes the inherited engrams of its inorganic origin. The pulse of life is a squamous film superimposed on an underlying matter so intricate in its delicate balancing of different energies that life itself is but a brief, vain straining against that balance.

For an instant of eternity, a pattern is attempted. It takes many forms, but these are apparent. The real shape is always a time and not a space shape. And that shape is a curve. Up and then down. Up from the darkness into the light, then down again into the blackness.

The male salmon sprays his mist of milt onto the eggs of the female. And instantly he is seized with a mortal melancholy. The male bee collapses from the embrace of the queen he has won, back into that inorganic mold from which he climbed for one single moment of ecstasy. In man, the fateful pattern is repressed into quadrillions of individual cells.

But the pattern is there. Waiting.

Long before, the sharp-minded Rull scientists, probing for chemical substances that would shock man's system into its primitive forms, found the special secret of man's will to death.

The *yeli*, Meeesh, gliding back towards Jamieson, did not think of the process. He had been waiting for the opportunity. It had occurred. He was intent on his own purposes.

Briskly, he removed the man's blaster, then he searched for the key to the lifeboat. And then he carried Jamieson a quarter of a mile around the base of the cliff to where the man's ship had been catapulted by the blast from the Rull warship.

Five minutes later, the powerful radio inside was broadcasting on Rull wave lengths, an imperative command to the Rull fleet.

Dimness. Inside and outside his skin. He felt himself at the bottom of a well, peering out of night into twilight. As he lay, a pressure of something swelled around him, lifted him higher and higher, and nearer to the mouth of the well.

He struggled the last few feet, a distinct mental effort, and looked over the edge. Consciousness.

He was lying on a raised table inside a room which had several large mouselike openings at the floor level, openings that led to other chambers. Doors, he identified, odd-shaped, alien, unhuman. Jamieson cringed with the stunning shock of recognition.

He was inside a Rull warship.

There was slithering of movement behind him. He turned his head, and rolled his eyes in their sockets.

In the shadows, three Rulls were gliding across the floor towards a bank of instruments that reared up behind and to one side of him. They pirouetted up an inclined plane and poised above him. Their pale eyes, shiny in the dusk of that unnatural chamber, peered down at him.

Jamieson tried to move. His body writhed in the confines of the bonds that held him. That brought a sharp remembrance of the death-will chemical that the Rull had used. Relief came surging. He was not dead. *Not dead*. NOT DEAD. The Rull must have helped him, forced him to move, and so had broken the downward curve of his descent to dust.

He was alive—for what?

The thought slowed his joy. His hope snuffed out like a flame. His brain froze into a tense, terrible mask of anticipation.

As he watched with staring eyes, expecting pain, one of the Rulls pressed a button. Part of the table on which Jamieson was lying, lifted. He was raised to a sitting position.

What now?

He couldn't see the Rulls. He tried to turn, but two head shields clamped into the side of his head, and held him firmly.

He saw that there was a square of silvery sheen on the wall which he faced. A light sprang onto it, and then a picture. It was a curiously familiar picture, but at first because there was a reversal of position Jamieson couldn't place the familiarity.

Abruptly, he realized.

It was a twisted version of the picture that he had shown the Rull, first when he was feeding it, and then with more weighty arguments after he discovered the vulnerability of man's mortal enemy.

He had shown how the Rull race would be destroyed unless it agreed to peace.

In the picture he was being shown it was the Rull that urged co-operation between the two races. They seemed unaware that he had not yet definitely transmitted his knowledge to other human beings. Or perhaps that fact was blurred by the conditioning he had given to the Rull when he fed it and controlled it.

As he glared at the screen, the picture ended—and then started again. By the time it had finished a second time, there was no doubt. Jamieson collapsed back against the table. They would not show him such a picture unless he was to be used as a messenger.

He would be returned home to carry the message that man had wanted to hear for a thousand years. He would also carry the information that would give meaning to the offer.

The Rull-human war was over.

THE EMBASSY

BY DONALD A. WOLLHEIM
(Writing as Martin Pearson)

(Appeared in BEYOND THE END OF TIME)

Once when the world was a lot younger, there was a sort of poor-man's Camelot called the Futurian Society of New York. The Futurians were a science-fiction fan club which began in the late 1930s. What set the Futurians apart from most such is that the majority of its members were burningly dedicated to the goal of becoming professional science-fiction writers and editors. Its members included Isaac Asimov, James Blish, Damon Knight, C. M. Kornbluth, Robert A. W. Lowndes, and Judith Merril, among others, so you can see that a good number made it.

Like all science-fiction writers, even fledgling ones, the Futurians were too consecratedly independent-minded to follow a single leader. But if any one individual came close to leadership, it was Donald Wollheim. All Futurians were bright. Donald was a little brighter than most. All Futurians had some talents either for writing or for editing. Donald had a good deal, and for both. I was the first of the Futurians to luck, brag, and cajole myself into a spot as a science-fiction editor, but Donald was only a couple of months behind, and went from that to another, and another. Don Wollheim, the long-time editor of Ace Books, was solely responsible for building their science-fiction list into one of the most impressive in the industry. When he left Ace, it was to achieve every editor's dream. He began publishing books under his own imprint as "DAW" (for Donald A. Wollheim) "Books". He is by far the senior of all science-fiction editors still practicing their craft. It is a considerable success story—but one which kept him from writing for the past forty years.

Donald was as bright as a writer as he was as an editor, with a particular talent for that most difficult form of writing, the "idea" short-short. Like "The Embassy." If he was that good in 1942, what might he have become by now—if all that editing hadn't got in the way?

*　　*　　*

"I came to New York," said Grafius, "because I am sure that there are Martians here." He leaned back to blow a smoke ring, followed it to its dissolution in the air-conditioning outlet with his cool, gray eyes.

"Iron Man!" bawled Broderick, quick as the snap of a relay. He backed around behind his chair as the office door opened and the formidable Mr. Doolan appeared, fists cocked on the ready.

"It's a whack," declared Broderick, pointing at Grafius. "It says there are Martians in New York."

Doolan, probably the most muscular, certainly the dumbest cop ever kicked out of the police department, eyed Grafius dimly as he clamped the caller's shoulder in a colossal vise of a hand. "Make with the feet," he said, groping for his words. "Hit the main, but heavy."

"He means 'get out,'" explained Broderick. "I echo his sentiments completely."

Grafius, rising leisurely, fished in his breast pocket and chucked a sharkskin wallet onto the desk. "Look it over," he said. "Well worth your time." He stood impassively as Broderick drew from the wallet several large bills.

"Holy-holy," whispered the inspector general as he fingered the money. "I didn't think you cared." Briskly he seated himself again and waved away Doolan.

"Naturally," he explained, toying with Grafius's card, "I'm loath to part with all this lettuce. Your remark about our little speckled friends, the Martians, I shall ignore. This is a small, young agency, new to the art of private investigation. Martians are outside our ken at this moment of the year 1942, but if there's anything in a more conventional line we can do for you—"

"Nothing at all, thank you," said Grafius of Springfield. He recovered his wallet and card from the desk. "However, if you'd care to listen with an open mind—"

"Open wider than the gates of hell," said the private detective, his eyes on the vanishing currency. "Tell your tale."

Grafius crushed out his cigar. "Suppose you were a Martian," he said.

Broderick snickered. "One of the small ones with three tails, or the nasty size with teeth to match?" he asked amiably.

"I'm sorry," said the man from Springfield. "My data doesn't go as far as that, but in a moment I'll give you a reasonable description of the Martians that are in New York.

"When I say Martian, of course, the meaning is 'extraterrestrial of greater civilization than ours.' They may not be Martians. They may even be from another galaxy. But assume you are what I call a Martian, and that you want to keep in touch with Earthly civilization and advancement. Just where would you go?"

"Coney Island?" helplessly suggested the detective.

"Naturally not," said Grafius severely. "Nor to Sea Breeze, Kansas. Nor to Nome, Alaska. Nor to Equatorial Africa. You wouldn't go to some small town. You wouldn't go to some out-of-the-way part of the world where living is anywhere from twenty to several hundred years behind human progress. This will eliminate Asia and Africa. It will eliminate almost all of Europe and South America.''

''I get it,'' said Broderick. ''The Martians would head for the U.S.A.''

''Exactly. The United States today is the most technically and culturally advanced nation on Earth. And, further, if you came to the United States, you'd come to New York. You would come because it's the largest human concentration on the globe. It's the economic capital of the continent—the very hemisphere! You agree?''

''Sure,'' said Broderick. ''And you wouldn't be in London because of the war. You can't observe human culture while the shells are popping.''

''Exactly. But I still haven't proved anything. To continue: it's quite clear to me that we Earth people aren't the only intelligent, civilized race in the Universe. Out of the infinitude of stars and planets there most definitely, mathematically *must* be others. Mars—to continue with my example—is older than Earth geologically; if there were Martians, and if their evolutionary history corresponded with ours, they would certainly be further advanced than we.

''And I will make one more hypothesis: it is that we Earth people are today on the verge of space conquest, and that any race further advanced than we must have already mastered space flight.''

''Go on,'' said Broderick, who was beginning to look scared. He was a naturally apprehensive type, and the thought that Martians might be just around the corner didn't help him.

''Certainly. But you needn't look so worried, for the Martians won't show up in your office. They must work strictly under cover, since from their point of view—advanced, you will remember—it would be foolish to make themselves known to us as long as we humans are a military, predatory race. It would be a risk which no advanced mentality would take.''

''How long has this been going on?'' asked Broderick agitatedly.

''Judging from the geology of Mars, some hundreds of years,'' replied Grafius dreamily. ''They've been watching, waiting—''

''You said you could describe them,'' snapped the detective. ''What do they look like?''

''I can't describe their appearance,'' said Grafius, down to Earth again. ''But this is what they most probably are: a group of ordinary-appearing people who live together in downtown New York, close to newspapers, publishers, news cables, communication centers, and the financial powers of Wall Street. They would have no obvious means of support, for all their time must be taken up with the observation that is their career. They almost certainly live in a private house, without prying janitors who would get curious about their peculiar radio equipment.

''And our best bet—they are sure to receive every major paper and magazine, in all the languages of the world.''

"I get it," said Broderick. "Very sweet and simple. But what's your reason for wanting to meet up with the Martians social, if I may ask?"

"Call it curiosity," smiled Grafius. "Or an inflated ego. Or merely the desire to check my logic."

"Sure," said Broderick. "I can offer you the following services of my bureau: bodyguard—that's Iron Man, outside. Think you'll need him?"

"Certainly not," said Grafius of Springfield. "You have no right to suppose that the Martians would stoop to violence. Remember their advanced mentality."

"I won't insist," said the detective. "Second, I can check on all subscription departments of the big papers and magazines. Third, the radio-parts lead. Fourth, renting agents. Fifth, sixth, and seventh, correlation of these. Eighth, incidentals. It should come to about—" He named a figure. The remainder of the interview was purely financial in character.

Iron Man Doolan wasn't very bright. He knew how to walk, but occasionally he forgot and would try to take both feet off the ground at once. This led to minor contusions of the face and extremities, bruises and gashes that the ex-cop never noticed. He was underorganized.

It taxed him seriously, this walking about in a strange neighborhood. There were hydrants and traffic signals in his way, and each one was a problem in navigation to be solved. Thus it took him half an hour to walk the city block he had been shown to by Broderick, who was waiting nervously, tapping his feet, in a cigar store.

"He's dull—very dull," confided the detective to Grafius, who sipped a coke at the soda fountain. "But the only man for a job like this. Do you think they'll make trouble for him?"

Grafius gurgled through the straw apologetically. "Perhaps," he said. "If it is No. 108—" He brooded into his glass, not finishing the sentence.

"It certainly is," said Broderick decidedly. "What could it be but the Martian embassy that takes everything from *Pic* to the Manchester *Guardian?*"

"Polish revolutionaries," suggested the man from Springfield. "Possibly an invalid. We haven't watched the place for more than a couple of weeks. We really haven't any data worth the name."

The detective hiccuped with nervousness, hastily swallowed a pepsin tablet. Then he stared at his client fixedly. "You amaze me," he stated at last. "You come at me with a flit-git chain of possibilities that you're staking real cash on. And once we hit a solid trail you refuse to believe your own eyes. Man, what do you want—a sworn statement from your Martians that they live in No. 108?"

"Let's take a look," said Grafius. "I hope your Mr. Doolan gets a bite."

"Iron Man, I repeat, is not very bright. But he's pushed buttons before, and if somebody answers the door he's going to push the button on his minicam. I drilled that into his—"

He broke off at the sound of a scream, a shriek, a lance of thin noise that

sliced down the street. Then there was a crash of steel on concrete. The two
dashed from the shop and along the sidewalk.

They stopped short at the sight of Iron Man Doolan's three hundred pounds
of muscle grotesquely spattered and slimed underneath a ponderous safe. A
colored girl, young and skinny, was wailing in a thin monotone, to herself:
"First he squashed and then it fell. First he squashed and then—"

Broderick grabbed her by the shoulders. "What happened?" he yelled
hoarsely. "What did you see?"

She stopped her wail and looked directly and simply at him. In an
explanatory tone she said: "First he squashed—and *then* it fell." Broderick,
feeling sick, let go of her, vaguely heard her burst into hysterical tears as he
took Grafius by the arm and walked him away down the street.

Somewhere on Riverside Drive that evening the detective declared: "I
know it sounds like a damned childish trick, but I'm going to get drunk,
because I had a lot of affection for Doolan. He would understand it as a fitting
tribute."

"He was, in his way, the perfect expression of a brutal ideal," mused
Grafius. "In an earlier, less sophisticated day he would have been a sort of
deity. I'll go with you, if you don't mind."

In a place whose atmosphere was Chinese they drank libations to the
departed Iron Man, then moved on down the street. Midnight found Broderick
pie-eyed, but with a tense control over his emotions that he was afraid to
break through.

It was Grafius at last who suggested calmly: "They are a menace. What
shall we do about them?"

Broderick knew just exactly what the man from Springfield meant. With a
blurred tongue he replied: "Lay off of them. Keep out of their way. If we
make trouble, it's curtains for us—what they did to Doolan is all the proof I
need. I know when I'm licked."

"Yes," said Grafius. "That's the trouble with you. Doolan didn't
know—" He collapsed softly over the table. Broderick stared at him for a
long moment, then gulped the rest of his drink and poked his client in the
shoulder.

Grafius came up fighting. "Martians," he shrilled. "Dirty, dusty, dry sons
of—"

"Take it easy," said the detective. He eyed a girl sitting solo at a nearby
table, who eyed him back with a come-on smile.

Grafius stared at the interchange broodingly. "Keep away from her," he
said at last. "She may be one of the Martians—filth they are—unspeakable
things—bone-dry monsters from an undead world—" He canted over the
table again.

The liquor hit Broderick then like a padded tent maul. He remembered
conducting a fantastically polite Gallup poll of the customers in the saloon,

inquiring their precise sentiments toward "our little feathered friends of the Red Planet."

He should have known better than to act up in Skelley's Skittle House. Skelley was a restaurateur slow to wrath, but he had his license to take care of, as well as his good name. And Skelley, like so many of his kind, got a big kick out of seeing what a Mickey Finn could do.

Grafius was completely unconscious when Broderick, with elaborate protestations of gratitude, accepted the "last one on the house." He tossed down the rye and quaffed the chaser. Skelley, ever the artist, had stirred the chloral into the larger glass.

The stuff took effect on Broderick like a keg of gunpowder. After the first few spasms he was utterly helpless, poisoned to within an inch of his life, lying heaving on the floor, his eye whites rolling and yellowed, pouring sweat from every hair, actually and literally wishing he were dead and out of his internal agony. That is what a skilled practitioner can do with the little bottle behind the bar.

He saw the waiter and Skelley go through Grafius's pockets, calling for witnesses among the customers that they were taking no more than their due. The customers heartily approved; a woman whose face was baggy and chalked said: "Peeble wh' dunno hodda drink li' gennlem'n shunt drink 't all!" She hiccuped violently, and a waitress led her to the powder room for treatment.

Skelley laboriously read the calling card in Grafius's vest. "That ain't no help," he declared wittily. "It don't say which Springfield."

Broderick saw and felt himself being rolled over, his pockets being dipped into. The spasms began again, ending suddenly as he heard the voice of his host declare: "No. 108! Snooty neighborhood for a lush like that."

The detective tried to explain, tried to tell that man that it wasn't his address but the address of the Martians he'd chanced on in his pockets. But all the voice he could summon up was a grunt that broke to a peep of protest as he was hauled up and carried out in Skelley's strong and practiced arms.

He and Grafius were dumped into a taxi; between spasms he heard the restaurateur give the hackie the Martians' address.

Broderick was going through a physical and mental hell, lying there in the back of the cab. He noted through his nauseous haze the street lights sliding by, noted the passage of Washington Square, sensed the auto turning up Fifth Avenue. His agony lessened by Fiftieth Street, and for a moment he could talk. Hoarsely he called to the cabby to stop. Before he could amplify and explain, the retching overtook him again, and he was helpless.

He passed out completely at a long traffic-light stop; he never felt the car turn right. The next thing he knew the cabby was bundling him out of the rear, leaning him beside Grafius against the door of No. 108. The cabby leaned against the buzzer for a moment, then drove off.

Broderick could only stare with dumb agony as the door opened. "Dear, dear!" said the soft, shocked voice of a woman.

"Are they anyone we know, Florence?" demanded a man.

"Unfortunate creatures, whoever they are," said the woman.

Broderick got a glimpse of a handsome, ruddy face as the man carried him into the hall, the woman following with Grafius. The man from Springfield awoke suddenly, stared into the face of the woman, then set up a shrill screaming that did not end until she had punched him twice in the jaw.

"Shame!" she declared. "We're kind enough to take you two sots in out of the cold and then you get the D. T.s!" There was a warm smile lurking in the corners of her mouth.

The man opened a door somewhere, and Broderick apprehended a smooth, continuous clicking sound, very much faster and more rhythmical than a typewriter.

"There's something familiar about this boy, Florence," declared the man as he studied the helpless detective.

She wrinkled her brows prettily. "Of course!" she cried at last with a delighted smile. "It's that Broderick!"

"Yes. That Broderick," said the man. "And this other one—"

"Oh!" cried the woman, in tones of ineffable loathing. "*Oh!*" She turned her head away as though sickened.

"Yes," said the man, his face wrinkled and writhing with unspeakable disgust. "This other one is the Grafius he was so often thinking about."

The woman turned again, her face raging angry, black with the blackest passion. Her high French heels ground into the face of the dead-drunk Grafius again and again; the man had to pull her off at last. It was plain that he himself was exercising will power of the highest order in control of an impulse to smash and mangle the despised one.

"Grafius!" he said at last, as though the word were a lump of vileness in his mouth. "That Venusian!" He spat.

The woman broke free from his grasp, kicked the mutilated face. Broderick heard the teeth splintering in the abused mouth.

GUINEVERE FOR EVERYBODY

BY JACK WILLIAMSON

(Appeared in STAR SCIENCE FICTION STORIES NO. 3)

Although science fiction is world-wide, it takes in rather a small world altogether. There are only about a thousand or so science-fiction writers in the world, in all languages, and its practitioners keep bumping into each other in a variety of places and, if they stay around long enough, playing a variety of roles.

One of the things that has made my life in science fiction a pleasure—well, mostly a pleasure—is that a lot of it has involved associating with Jack Williamson. We met as friends in 1939, and ran into each other again at the Air Force weather school in Chanute Field, Illinois, in 1943. When I was a literary agent, 1947–1953 or so, Jack was one of my first and best clients. As activists in science fiction, we passed hats back and forth; I took my turn as President of the Science Fiction Writers of America in 1974–1976, and Jack took his in 1978–1980. We've both taught science fiction, sometimes teaming for the same course at the same school. And we've collaborated on more than half a dozen science-fiction novels . . . so far!

Jack Williamson (who in his other incarnation, the academic one, is Distinguished Professor Emeritus John Stewart Williamson, Ph.D.) has always been one of my favorite writers. As a fan I read his "With Folded Hands—" and "—And Searching Mind." When I became an agent, I got the chance to read them again, packaging and selling them as his first novel, The Humanoids. *And years later, as editor, I achieved that perquisite of lucky editors by persuading him to continue the story for me—now for everybody— in the long-delayed sequel,* The Humanoid Touch. *Editing, by and large, is full of sharp and inevitable pains, but it has its joys too—and getting a writer to go on with a story you really enjoyed is one of them!*

*   *   *

The girl stood chained in the vending machine.

"Hi, there!" Her plaintive hail whispered wistfully back from the empty corners of the gloomy waiting room. "Won't somebody buy me?"

Most of the sleepy passengers trailing through the warm desert night from the Kansas City jet gaped at her and hurried on uneasily, as if she had been a tigress inadequately caged, but Pip Chimberley stopped, jolted wide awake.

"Hullo, mister." The girl smiled at him, with disturbingly huge blue eyes. The chains tinkled as her hands came up hopefully, to fluff and smooth her copper-blond hair. Her long tan body flowed into a pose that filled her sheer chemistic halter to the bursting point. "You like me, huh?"

Chimberley gulped. He was an angular young man, with a meat-cleaver nose, an undernourished mouse-colored mustache, and three degrees in cybernetic engineering. His brown, murky eyes fled from the girl and fluttered back again, fascinated.

"Won't you buy me?" She caressed him with her coaxing drawl. "You'd never miss the change, and I know you'd like me. I like you."

He caught his breath, with a strangled sound.

"No!" he was hoarse with incipient panic. "I'm not a customer. My interest is—uh—professional."

He sidled hastily away from the shallow display space where she stood framed in light, and resolutely shifted his eyes from her to the vending machine. He knew machines, and it was lovely to him, with the seductive sweep of its streamlined contours and the exciting gleam of its blinding red enamel. He backed away, looking raptly up at the blazing allure of the 3-D sign:

GUINEVERE

THE VITAL APPLIANCE!

NOT A ROBOT—WHAT IS SHE?

The glowing letters exploded into galaxies of dancing light, that condensed again into words of fire. Guinevere, the ultimate appliance, was patented and guaranteed by Solar Chemistics, Inc. Her exquisite body had been manufactured by automatic machinery, untouched by human beings. Educated by psionic processes, she was warranted sweet-tempered and quarrel-free. Her special introductory price, for a strictly limited time, was only four ninety-five.

"Whatever your profession is, I'm very sure you need me." She was leaning out of the narrow display space, and her low voice followed him melodiously. "I have everything, for everybody."

Chimberley turned uncertainly back.

"That might be," he muttered reluctantly. "But all I want is a little information. You see, I'm a cybernetics engineer." He told her his name.

"I'm Guinevere." She smiled, with a flash of precise white teeth. "Model 1, Serial Number 1997-A-456. I'd be delighted to help you, but I'm afraid you'll have to pay for me first. You do want me, don't you?"

Chimberley's long equine countenance turned the color of a wet brick. The sorry truth was, he had never wholeheartedly wanted any woman. His best friends were digital computers; human beings had always bored him. He couldn't understand the sudden pounding in his ears, or the way his knobby fists had clenched.

"I'm here on business," he said stiffly. "That's why I stopped. You see, I'm a trouble-shooter for General Cybernetics."

"A shooter?" Psionic educational processes evidently had their limits, but the puzzled quirk of her eyebrows was somehow still entrancing. "What's a shooter?"

"My company builds the managerial computers that are replacing human management in most of the big corporations," he informed her patiently. "I'm supposed to keep them going. Actually, the machines are designed to adjust and repair themselves. They never really go wrong. The usual trouble is that people just don't try to understand them."

He snapped his bony fingers at human stupidity.

"Anyhow, when I got back to my hotel tonight, there was this wire from Schenectady. First I'd heard about any trouble out here in the sun country. I still don't get it." He blinked at her hopefully. "Maybe you can tell me what's going on."

"Perhaps I can," she agreed sweetly. "When I'm paid for."

"You're the trouble, yourself," he snapped back accusingly. "That's what I gather, though the wire was a little too concise—our own management is mechanized, of course, and sometimes it fails to make sufficient allowances for the limitations of the human employee."

"But I'm no trouble," she protested gaily. "Just try me."

A cold sweat burst into the palms of his hands. Spots danced in front of his eyes. He scowled bleakly past her at the enormous vending machine, trying angrily to insulate himself from all her disturbing effects.

"Just four hours since I got the wire. Drop everything. Fly out here to trouble-shoot Athena Sue—she's the installation we made to run Solar Chemistics. I barely caught the jet, and I just got here. Now I've got to find out what the score is."

"Score?" She frowned charmingly. "Is there a game?"

He shrugged impatiently.

"Seems the directors of Solar Chemistics are unhappy because Athena Sue is manufacturing and merchandising human beings. They're threatening to throw out our managerial system, unless we discover and repair the damage at once."

He glowered at the shackled girl.

"But the wire failed to make it clear why the directors object. Athena Sue was set to seek the greatest possible financial return for the processing and sale of solar synthetics, so it couldn't very well be a matter of profits. There's apparently no question of any legal difficulty. I can't see anything for the big wheels to clash their gears about."

Guinevere was rearranging her flame-tinted hair, smiling with a radiance he couldn't entirely ignore.

"Matter of fact, the whole project looks pretty wonderful to me." He grinned at her and the beautiful vending machine with a momentary admiration. "Something human management would never have had the brains or the vision to accomplish. It took one of our Athena-type computers to see the possibility, and to tackle all the technical and merchandising problems that must have stood in the way of making it a commercial reality."

"Then you do like me?"

"The directors don't, evidently." He tried not to see her hurt expression. "I can't understand why, but the first part of my job here will be to find the reason. If you can help me—"

He paused expectantly.

"I'm only four ninety-five," Guinevere reminded him. "You put the money right here in this slot—"

"I don't want you," he interrupted harshly. "Just the background facts about you. To begin with—just what's the difference between a vital appliance and an ordinary human being?"

He tried not to hear her muffled sob.

"What's the plant investment?" He raised his voice, and ticked the questions off on his skinny fingers. "What's the production rate? The profit margin? Under what circumstances was the manufacture of—uh—vital appliances first considered by Athena Sue? When were you put on the market? What sort of consumer acceptance are you getting now? Or don't you know?"

Guinevere nodded brightly.

"But can't we go somewhere else to talk about it?" She blinked bravely through her tears. "Your room, maybe?"

Chimberley squirmed uncomfortably.

"If you don't take me," she added innocently, "I can't tell you anything."

He stalked away, angry at himself for the way his knees trembled. He could probably find out all he had to know from the memory tapes of the computer, after he got out to the plant. Anyhow, he shouldn't let her upset him. After all, she was only an interesting product of chemistic engineering.

A stout, pink-skinned businessman stepped up to the vending machine. He unburdened himself of a thick briefcase and a furled umbrella, removed his glasses, and leaned deliberately to peer at Guinevere with bugging, putty-colored eyes.

"Slavery!" He straightened indignantly. "My dear young lady, you do need help." He replaced his glasses, fished in his pockets, and offered her a business card. "As you see, I'm an attorney. If you have been forced into any kind of involuntary servitude, my firm can certainly secure your release."

"But I'm not a slave," Guinevere said. "Our management has secured an informal opinion from the attorney general's office to the effect that we aren't human beings—not within the meaning of the law. We're only chattels."

"Eh?" He bent unbelievingly to pinch her golden arm. "Wha—"

"Alfred!"

He shuddered when he heard that penetrating cry, and snatched his fingers away from Guinevere as if she had become abruptly incandescent.

"Oh!" She shrank back into her narrow prison, rubbing at her bruised arm. "Please don't touch me until I'm paid for."

"Shhh!" Apprehensively, his bulging eyes were following a withered little squirrel-faced woman in a black-veiled hat, who came bustling indignantly from the direction of the ladies' room. "My—ah—encumberance."

"Alfred, whatever are you up to now?"

"Nothing, my dear. Nothing at all." He stooped hastily to recover his briefcase and umbrella. "But it must be time to see about our flight—"

"So! Shopping for one of them synthetic housekeepers?" She snatched the umbrella and flourished it high. "Well, I won't have 'em in any place of mine!"

"Martha, darling—"

"I'll Martha-darling you!"

He ducked away.

"And you!" She jabbed savagely at Guinevere. "You synthetic whatever-you-are, I'll teach you to carry on with any man of mine!"

"Hey!"

Chimberley hadn't planned to interfere, but when he saw Guinevere gasp and flinch, an unconsidered impulse moved him to brush aside the stabbing umbrella. The seething woman turned on him.

"You sniveling shrimp!" she hissed at him. "Buy her yourself—and see what you get!"

She scuttled away in pursuit of Alfred.

"Oh, thank you, Pip!" Guinevere's voice was muted with pain, and he saw the long red scratch across her tawny shoulder. "I guess you do like me!"

To his own surprise, Chimberley was digging for his billfold. He looked around self-consciously. Martha was towing Alfred past the deserted ticket windows, and an age-numbed janitor was mopping the floor, but otherwise the waiting room was empty. He fed five dollars into the slot, and waited thriftily for his five cents change.

A gong chimed softly, somewhere inside the vending machine. Something whirred. The shackles fell from Guinevere's wrists and flicked out of sight.

SOLD OUT! a 3-D sign blazed behind her. BUY *YOURS* TOMORROW!

"Darling!" She had her arms around him before he recovered his nickel. "I thought you'd never take me!"

He tried to evade her kiss, but he was suddenly paralyzed. A hot tingling swept him, and the scent of her perfume made a veil of fire around him. Bombs exploded in his brain.

"Hold on!" He pushed at her weakly, trying to remind himself that she was only an appliance. "I've got work to do, remember. And there's some information you've agreed to supply."

"Certainly, darling." Obediently, she disengaged herself. "But before we leave, won't you buy my accessory kit?" A singsong cadence came into her voice. "With fresh undies and a makeup set and gay chemistic nightwear, packed in a sturdy chemyl case, it's all complete for only nineteen ninety-five."

"Not so fast! That wasn't in the deal—"

He checked himself, with a grin of admiration for what was evidently an astutely integrated commercial operation. No screws loose so far in Athena Sue!

"Okay," he told Guinevere. "If you'll answer all my questions."

"I'm all yours, darling!" She reached for his twenty. "With everything I know."

She fed the twenty into the accessory slot. The machine chimed and whirred and coughed out a not-so-very-sturdy chemistic case. Guinevere picked it up and hugged him gratefully, while he waited for the clink of his nickel.

"Never mind the mugging, please!" He felt her cringe away from him, and tried to soften his voice. "I mean, we've no time to waste. I want to start checking over Athena Sue as soon as I can get out to the plant. We'll take a taxi, and talk on the way."

"Very well, Pip, dear." She nodded meekly. "But before we start, couldn't I have something to eat? I've been standing here since four o'clock yesterday, and I'm simply famished."

With a grimace of annoyance at the delay, he took her into the terminal coffee shop. It was almost empty. Two elderly virgins glared at Guinevere, muttered together, and marched out piously. Two sailors tittered. The lone counterman looked frostily at Chimberley, attempting to ignore Guinevere.

Chimberley studied the menu unhappily and ordered two T-bones, resolving to put them on his expense account. The counterman was fresh out of steaks, and not visibly sorry. It was chemburgers or nothing.

"Chemburgers!" Guinevere clapped her hands. "They're made by Solar

Chemistics, out of golden sunlight and pure sea water. They're absolutely tops, and everybody loves 'em!''

"Two chemburgers," Chimberley said, "and don't let 'em burn."

He took Guinevere back to a secluded booth.

"Now let's get started," he said. "I want the whole situation. Tell me everything about you.''

"I'm a vital appliance. Just like all the others."

"So I want to know all about vital appliances."

"Some things I don't know." She frowned fetchingly. "Please, Pip, may I have a glass of water? I've been waiting there all night, and I'm simply parched.''

The booth was outside the counterman's domain. He set out the water grudgingly, and Chimberley carried it back to Guinevere.

"Now what don't you know?"

"Our trade secrets." She smiled mysteriously. "Solar Chemistics is the daring pioneer in this exciting new field of chemistic engineering applied to the mass manufacture of redesigned vital organisms. Our mechanized management is much too clever to give away the unique know-how that makes us available to everybody. For that reason, deliberate gaps were left in our psionic education.''

Chimberley blinked at her shining innocence, suspecting that he had been had.

"Anyhow," he urged her uneasily, "tell me what you do know. What started the company to making—uh—redesigned vital organisms?"

"The Miss Chemistics tape."

"Now I think we're getting somewhere." He leaned quickly across the narrow table. "Who's Miss Chemistics?"

"The world's most wanted woman." Guinevere sipped her water gracefully. "She won a prize contest that was planned to pick out the woman that every man wanted. A stupid affair, organized by the old human management before the computer was put in. There was an entry blank in every package of our synthetic products. Forty million women entered. The winner was a farm girl named Gussie Schlepps before the talent agents picked her up—now she's Guinevere Golden.''

"What had she to do with you?"

"We're copies." Guinevere smirked complacently. "Of the world's most wonderful woman.''

"How do you copy a woman?"

"No human being could," she said. "It takes too much know-how. But our computer was able to work everything out." She smiled proudly. "Because you see the prize that Miss Chemistics won was immortality.''

"Huh?" He gaped at her untroubled loveliness. "How's that?"

"A few cells of scar tissue from her body were snipped off and frozen, in our laboratory. Each cell, you know, contains a full set of chromosomes—a complete genetic pattern for the reproduction of the whole body—and the legal department got her permission for the company to keep the cells alive forever and to produce new copies of her whenever suitable processes should be discovered.''

"Maybe that's immortality.'' Chimberley frowned. "But it doesn't look like much of a prize.''

"She was disappointed when they told her what it was.'' Guinevere nodded calmly. "In fact, she balked. She didn't want anybody cutting her precious body. She was afraid it would hurt, and afraid the scar would show—but she did want the publicity. All the laboratory needed was just a few cells. She finally let a company doctor take them, where the scar wouldn't show. And the publicity paid off. She's a realies actress now, with a million-dollar contract.''

"One way to the top.'' Chimberley grinned. "But what does she think of vital appliances?''

"She thinks we're wonderful.'' Guinevere beamed. "You see, she gets a royalty on every copy sold. Besides, her agent says we're sensational publicity.''

"I suppose you are.'' A reluctant admiration shone through his mud-colored eyes, before he could bring his mind back to business. "But let's get on with it. What about this Miss Chemistics tape?''

"The contest closed before our management was mechanized,'' she said, "while old Matt Skane was still general manager. But when the computer took over, all the company records were punched on chemistic tapes and filed in its memory banks.''

He sat for a moment scowling. His eyes were on Guinevere, but he was reaching in his mind for the tidy rows of crackle-finished cabinets that housed Athena Sue, groping for the feel of her swift responses. The thinking of managerial computers was sometimes a little hard to follow, even for cybernetic engineers—and even when there was no question of any defective circuits.

Guinevere was squirming uncomfortably.

"Is something wrong with my face?''

"Not a thing,'' he assured her solemnly. He scratched his chin. "I heard you tell your legal friend, back there at the vending machine, that you aren't a human being within the meaning of the law. What's the difference?''

"The original cells are all human.'' She dabbed at her eyes with a paper napkin and looked up to face him bravely. "The differences come later, in the production lines. We're attached to mechanical placentas, and grown under hormone control in big vats of chemistic solutions. We're educated as we grow, by psionic impulses transmitted from high-speed training tapes. All of that makes differences, naturally. The biggest one is that we are better.''

She frowned thoughtfully.

"Do you think the women are jealous?"

"Could be." Chimberley nodded uncertainly. "I never pretended to understand women. They all seem to have a lot of circuits out of kilter. Give me Athena Sue. Let's get out to the plant—"

Guinevere sniffled.

"Oh, Pip!" she gasped. "Our chemburgers!"

The counterman stood rubbing his hands on a greasy towel, staring at her with a fascinated disapproval. The forgotten chemburgers were smoking on the griddle behind him. Her wail aroused him. He scraped them up and slapped them defiantly on the counter.

Chimberley carried them silently back to Guinevere. He didn't care for chemburgers in any condition, but she consumed them both in ecstasy, and begged for a piece of chemberry pie.

"It's awfully good," she told him soulfully. "Made from the most ambrosial synthetics, by our exclusive chemistic processes. Won't you try a piece?"

When they approached a standing cab out in the street, the driver stiffened with hostility. But he took them.

"Keep her back," he growled. "Outa sight. Mobs smashed a couple hacks yesterday, to get at 'em."

Guinevere sat well back out of sight, crouching close to Chimberley. She said nothing, but he felt her shiver. The cab went fast through empty streets, and once when the tires squealed as it lurched around a corner she caught his hand apprehensively.

"See that, mister?" The driver slowed as they passed a block of charred wreckage. "Used to be one of them mechanized markets. Mob burned it yesterday. Machines inside selling them. See what I mean?"

Chimberley shook his head. Guinevere's clutching hand felt cold on his. Suddenly he slipped his arm around her. She leaned against him, and whispered fearfully:

"What does he mean?"

"I don't quite know."

The Solar Chemistics plant was ominously black. A few tattered palms straggled along the company fence. A sharp, yeasty scent drifted from the dark sea of solar reaction vats beyond, and blue floodlights washed the scattered islands where enormous bright metal cylinders towered out of intertwining jungles of pipes and automatic valves.

Chimberley sniffed the sour odor, and pride filled his narrow chest. Here was the marvelous body to Athena Sue's intricate brain. It breathed air and drank sea water and fed on sunlight, and gave birth to things as wonderful as Guinevere.

The driver stopped at a tall steel gate, and Chimberley got out. The rioters had been there. The palms along the fence were burned down to black stumps. Rocks had smashed gaping black holes in the big 3-D sign on the side of the gray concrete building beyond the fence; and broken glass grated on the pavement as he walked to the gate.

He found the bell, but nothing happened. Nobody moved inside the fence. All those dark miles of solar reactors had been designed to run and maintain themselves, and Athena Sue controlled them. A thousand fluids flowed continuously through a thousand processes to form a thousand new synthetics. Human labor was only in the way.

"Your almighty machine!" the driver jeered behind him. "Looks like it don't know you."

He jabbed the bell again, and an unhurried giant with a watchman's clock came out of the building toward the gate. Chimberley passed his company identification card through the barrier, and asked to see somebody in the office.

"Nobody there." The watchman chuckled cheerfully. "Unless you count that thinking machine."

"The computer's what I really want to see, if you'll let me in—"

"Afraid I couldn't, sir."

"Listen." Chimberley's voice lifted and quivered with incipient frustration. "This is an emergency. I've got to check the computer right away."

"Can't be that emergent." The watchman gave him a sunbronzed grin. "After all the hell yesterday, the director shut off the power to stop your gadget."

"But they can't—" Alarm caught him, as if his own brain had been threatened with oxygen starvation. "Without power, her memory tubes will discharge. She'll—well, die!"

"So what?" The watchman shrugged. "The directors are meeting again in the morning, with our old legal staff, to get rid of her."

"But I'll have her checked and balanced again by then," he promised desperately. "Just let me in!"

"Sorry, sir. But after all that happened yesterday, they told me to keep everybody out."

"I see." Chimberley drew a deep breath and tried to hold his temper. "Would you tell me exactly what did happen?"

"If you don't know." The watchman winked impudently at the cab where Guinevere sat waiting. "Your big tin brain had developed those synthetic cuties secretly. It put them on the market yesterday morning. I guess they did look like something pretty hot, from a gadget's point of view. The item every man wanted most, at a giveaway price. Your poor old thinking machine will probably never understand why the mobs tried to smash it."

Chimberley bristled. "Call the responsible officials. Now. I insist."

"Insist away." The brown giant shrugged. "But there aren't any responsible officials, since the computer took over. So what can I do?"

"You might try restraining your insolence," Chimberley snapped. "And give me your name. I intend to report you in the morning."

"Matt Skane," he drawled easily. "Used to be general manager."

"I see," Chimberley muttered accusingly. "You hate computers!"

"Why not?" He grinned through the bars. "I fought 'em for years, before they got the company. Lost my health in the fight, and most of the money I had. It's tough to admit you're obsolete."

Chimberley stalked back to the cab and told the driver to take him to the Gran Desierto Hotel. The room clerk there gave Guinevere a chilling stare, and failed to find any record of his reservation. Another taxi driver suggested his life would be simpler, and accommodations easier to arrange, if he would ask the police to take her off his hands, but by that time his first annoyed bewilderment was crystalizing into stubborn anger.

"I can't understand people," he told Guinevere. "They aren't like machines. I sometimes wonder how they ever managed to invent anything like Athena Sue. But whatever they do, I don't intend to give you up."

Day had come before he found an expensive room in a shabby little motel, where the sleepy manager demanded his money in advance and asked no questions at all. It was too late to sleep, but he took time for a shower and a shave.

His billfold was getting thin, and it struck him that the auditing machines might balk at some of his expenses on account of Guinevere. Prudently, he caught a bus at the corner. He got off in front of the plant, just before eight o'clock. The gate across the entrance drive was open now, but an armed guard stepped out to meet him.

"I'm here from General Cybernetics—"

He was digging nervously for his identification card, but the tall guard gestured easily to stop him.

"Mr. Chimberley?"

"I'm Chimberley. And I want to inspect our managerial installation here, before the directors meet this morning."

"Matt Skane told me you were coming, but I'm afraid you're late." The guard gestured lazily at a row of long cars parked across the drive. "The directors met an hour ago. But come along."

A wave of sickness broke over him as the guard escorted him past an empty reception desk and back into the idle silence of the mechanized administrative section. A sleek, feline brunette, who must have been a close runner-up in the Miss Chemistics contest, sat behind the chrome railing at the dead programming panel, intently brushing crimson lacquer on her talons. She glanced up at him with a spark of interest that instantly died.

"The hot shot from Schenectady," the guard said. "Here to overhaul the big tin brain."

"Shoulda made it quicker." She flexed her claws, frowning critically at the fresh enamel. "Word just came out of the board room. They're doing away with the brain. High time, too, if anybody wants to know."

"Why?"

"Didn't you see 'em?" She blew on her nails. "Those horrible synthetic monsters it was turning loose everywhere."

He remembered that she must have been a runner-up.

"Anyhow," he muttered stubbornly, "I want to check the computer."

With a bored nod, she reached to unlatch the little gate that let him through the railing into the metal-paneled, air-conditioned maze that had been the brain of Athena Sue. He stopped between the neat banks of pastel-painted units, saddened by their silence.

The exciting sounds of mechanized thought should have been whispering all around him. The germanium pentodes, cells of the cybernetic mind, had always been as silent as his own, but punched cards should have been riffling through the whirring sorters, as Athena Sue remembered. Perforators should have been munching chemistic tape, as she recorded new data. Relays should have been clicking as she reached her quick decisions, and automatic typewriters murmuring with her many voices.

But Athena Sue was dead.

She could be revived, he told himself hopefully. Her permanent memories were all still intact, punched in tough chemistic film. He could set her swift electronic pulse to beating again, through her discharged tubes, if he could find the impossible flaw that had somehow led to her death.

He set to work.

Three hours later he was bent over a high-speed scanner, reading a spool of tape, when a hearty shout startled him.

"Well, Chimberley! Found anything?"

He snatched the spool off the scanner and shrank uneasily back from the muscular giant stalking past the programming desk. It took him a moment to recognize Matt Skane, without the watchman's clock. Clutching the tape, he nodded stiffly.

"Yes." He glanced around him. The billowy brunette and the guard had disappeared. He wet his lips and gulped. "I—I've found out what happened to the computer."

"So?"

Skane waited, towering over him, a big, red, weather-beaten man with horny hands shaped as if to fit a hammer or the handles of a plow, a clumsy misfit in this new world where machines had replaced both his muscles and his mind. He was obsolete—but dangerous.

"It was sabotaged." Chimberley's knobby fist tightened on the spool of tape, in sweaty defiance.

"How do you know?"

"Here's the whole story." He brandished the chemistic reel. "Somebody programmed Athena Sue to search for a project that would result in her destruction. Being an efficient computer, she did what she was programmed to do. She invented vital appliances, and supplied a correct prediction that the unfavorable consumer reaction to them would completely discredit mechanized equipment. So the saboteur reprogrammed her to ignore the consequences and put them on the market."

"I see." Skane's bright blue eyes narrowed ominously. "And who was this cunning saboteur?"

Chimberley caught a rasping, uneven breath. "I know that he was somebody who had access to the programming panel at certain times, which are recorded on the input log. So far as I've been able to determine, the only company employee who should have been here at those times was a watchman— named Matt Skane."

The big man snorted.

"Do you call that evidence?"

"It's good enough for me. With a little further investigation, I think I can uncover enough supporting facts to interest the directors."

Skane shifted abruptly on his feet, and his hard lips twitched as Chimberley flinched. "The directors are gone," he drawled softly. "And there isn't going to be any further investigation. Because we've already gone back to human management. We're junking your big tin brain. I'm the general manager now. And I want that tape."

He reached for the chemistic spool.

"Take it." Chimberley crouched back from his long bronze arm, and ignominiously gave up the tape. "See what good it does you. Maybe I can't prove much of anything without it. But you're in for trouble, anyhow."

Skane grunted contemptuously.

"You can't turn the clock back," Chimberley told him bitterly. "Your competitors won't go back to human management. You'll still have all their computers to fight. They had you against the wall once, and they will again."

"Don't bet on it." Skane grinned. "Because we've learned a thing or two. We're going to use machines, instead of trying to fight them. We're putting in a new battery of the smaller sort of auxiliary computers—the kind that will let us keep a man at the top. I think we'll do all right, with no further help from you."

Chimberley hastily retreated from the smoldering blue eyes. He felt sick with humiliation. His own future was no serious problem; a good cybernetics engineer could always find an opening. What hurt was the way he had failed Athena Sue.

But there was Guinevere, waiting in his room.

His narrow shoulders lifted, when he thought of her. Most women irked and bored him, with all their fantastic irrationalities and their insufferable stupidities, but Guinevere was different. She was more like Athena Sue, cool and comprehensible, free of all the human flaws that he detested.

He ran from the bus stop back to the seedy motel, and his heart was fluttering when he rapped at the door of their room.

"Guinevere!"

He listened breathlessly. The latch clicked. The door creaked. He heard her husky-throated voice.

"Oh, Pip! I thought you'd never come."

"Guin—"

Shock stopped him, when he saw the woman in the doorway. She was hideous with old age. She felt feebly for him with thin blue claws, peering toward him blindly.

"Pip?" Her voice was somehow Guinevere's. "Isn't it you?"

"Where—" Fright caught his throat. His glance fled into the empty room beyond, and came back to her stooped and tottering frame, her wasted, faded face. He saw a dreadful likeness there, but his mind rejected it. "Where's Guinevere?"

"Darling, don't you even know me?"

"You couldn't be—" He shuddered. "But still—your voice—"

"Yes, dear, I'm yours." Her white head nodded calmly. "The same vital appliance you bought last night. Guinevere Model 1, Serial Number 1997-A-456."

"The difference you have just discovered is our rapid obsolescence." A strange pride lifted her gaunt head. "That's something we're not supposed to talk about, but you're an engineer. You can see how essential it is, to insure a continuous replacement demand. A wonderful feature, don't you think, darling?"

He shook his head, with a grimace of pain.

"I suppose I don't look very lovely to you any longer, but that's all right." Her withered smile brightened again. "That's the way the computer planned it. Just take me back to the vending machine where you bought me. You'll get a generous trade-in allowance, on tomorrow's model."

"Not any more," he muttered hoarsely. "Because our computer's out. Skane's back in, and I don't think he'll be making vital appliances."

"Oh, Pip!" She sank down on the sagging bed, staring up at him with a blind bewilderment. "I'm so sorry for you!"

He sat down beside her, with tears in his murky eyes. For one bitter instant, he hated all computers, and the mobs—and Matt Skane as well.

But then he began to get hold of himself.

After all, Athena Sue was not to blame for anything. She had merely been betrayed. Machines were never evil, except when men used them wrongly.

He turned slowly back to Guinevere, and gravely kissed her shriveled lips.

"I'll make out," he whispered. "And now I've got to call Schenectady."

THE *GALAXY* AND *IF* YEARS: 1960–1969

Galaxy was a going concern when it fell into my hands. It had been started in 1950 by Horace Gold, who had quickly made it into one of the leaders in the field.

When Horace began the magazine, he was a sort of shadowy figure in the science-fiction field. I had met him once or twice in the frequent gatherings of the New York science-fiction confraternity, and I recognized his name, as everyone did, as the author of some first-rate fantasies from John Campbell's old *Unknown*. What kind of science-fiction editor he might turn out to be was problematical, but I wished him well. I was a literary agent at the time, with a heavy emphasis on SF writers in my clientele. New markets were always welcome. Especially if they were willing to pay top rates, as Horace was, and especially if they were, well, brilliant. Horace Gold was all of that—as well as industrious, demanding, and frequently a lot of fun to be around. Before long my agency was supplying Horace with most of what he published. (As it was with *Analog,* Doubleday, and most of the other top markets, too. This makes it hard to understand how I managed to go broke while doing this, but that's a whole other story.) Horace knew I had done a good deal of writing myself, and encouraged me to do some for him. I did. I was getting tired of being a literary agent, anyway. For reasons not then clear to me—they're not much clearer now—I was finding it very tough to make a living out of the agency, and anyway nobody loves an agent. When I closed the agency down in the early 1950s, I wrote harder and more, and over the decade of Horace's editorship I became *Galaxy*'s most frequent contributor. When Horace fell ill (with a variety of complaints, retroactively diagnosed decades later as sequelae of a fractured spine), I helped him out with the editing chores. And when at last he had to resign, I took his place.

I deeply and sincerely regretted Horace's luck...but, my God, how pleased I was with mine! Next to making a major motion picture, I think editing a science-fiction magazine is about the most fun a person can have, and still get paid for it.

Oh, it wasn't all fun. There is a lot of stoop labor involved in editing a magazine. Large publishing companies employ specialists and assistants to do that sort of thing. But all I had, at least at first, was me.

If you assume an editorial job takes forty hours a week—would to God one did—how much of that time do you suppose an editor spends in selecting the stories to print? Twenty hours a week? Ten?

In a one-man shop (which is what *Galaxy* was, at first, for me), the answer is: about two. And in those two hours I had to decide the fate of an average of eighty manuscripts a week, aggregating perhaps half a million words. It comes to 120/80 = one and a half minutes per manuscript.

Do you wonder how an editor can give the over-the-transom submissions of an unknown but highly promising young writer—as it might be, say, yourself—a fair shake under such conditions? Do you perhaps wonder if a new writer ever gets a fair shake? Or any chance at all?

I promise you he does; but if you look at the statistics you may conclude that the odds are so bad that it is hard to see how that can be possible. Eighty manuscripts a week comes to about four thousand a year. When *Galaxy* was my only magazine, and came out only six times a year, I bought fewer than fifty stories out of those four thousand. Worse that that, at least twenty-five or thirty of those fifty were ordered, or by established names, so that the real odds against any slush-pile story being accepted were close to two hundred to one.

So I read incoming manuscripts, especially slush, very quickly and usually incompletely—sometimes only a glance at a couple of pages. Actually I doubt that it took me as much as ninety seconds for most of them. Fifteen seconds was often plenty.

I know that seems sloppy and hardhearted but, truly, I do not think anyone was done an injustice. A story that does not make itself interesting enough for an editor to read all the way through won't do it for the readers, either. And much slush-pile writing is clearly hopeless at a glance. Anything with any merit at all stands out, calls for more careful reading, and gets it. Over the years I think I published about as many unknown writers as any other editor in science fiction (perhaps excepting the always exceptional John Campbell), including Isaac Asimov, Ray Bradbury, R. A. Lafferty, and Joe Haldeman among others at the beginnings of their careers. And they all came out of the slush.

So where does all the rest of the time go? you ask. Why not spend all forty hours with feet up on a desk, munching an apple and savoring the submitted prose line by precious line?

For one thing, a manuscript needs to be prepared for the printer, and that takes time. Printers are as literal-minded as computer programs. They do what they are told. They do not do anything they were not told to do. They need to be told how long a dash is meant to be, where to skip a space in the text, where to insert a large initial and how large it should be, when a hyphenated word at the end of a line of manuscript is to retain its hyphen even if it turns up in the middle of the line of type. At rock-bottom minimum, every manuscript needs someone to go over it to put in these printers' marks. Usually it needs more. It generally needs attention to spelling, punctuation, and "style." Is the word to be "goodby," "good-by," "goodbye," or "good-bye"? They are all "correct." But if the magazine is to be consistent, one spelling should be used throughout.

Then there is the question of "editorial changes." Most editors feel themselves to be fully competent to improve the writing in most manuscripts. Sometimes they are; but few writers believe this.

Of the thirty thousand hours or so that I've put in as editor of science-fiction magazines, I would guess that at least fifteen thousand were spent on editing manuscripts. Some I edited very lightly. A few I barely touched at all, because the authors were conscientious in proofreading their own copy—and touchy about having it done by others. And quite a few I damn near rewrote entire.

In this part of the twentieth century that sounds like a confession of mortal sin so vile that not even Purgatory will punish it enough. Writers have become pretty sticky about letting editors romp roughshod over their prose. They're right, too. Most of the time they're right. In order to revise somebody else's copy, you need to be able to get inside it—that is to say, to think of it as your own; to know not only what the author says, but what he means to say. Even what he would have meant to say if he had thought of it. It isn't a gift given to everybody, and even those who have it don't have it all the time. I confess that I am aware that over the years there were some stories that would have been better if I had run them as the author wrote them. My only defense is that they weren't particularly good stories to begin with—and that I don't think there were very many—but that's my personal opinion, and I can name quite a number of authors who will never share it.

What gives an editor the right to tell an author how his story should be written, or even to change it without notice or appeal?

John Campbell used to try to defuse that charge by saying, "Look, Fred." (Or Isaac, or Doc, or Bob.) "You know more about yourself than I ever will, but there's one part of you that I know better than you do. That's the back of your neck. I can see it. You can't. It's the same with this story." And, as was so often the case, John's quirky logic was pretty much right. A writer can get so wrapped up in his story that he cannot see what is obvious. I know this; it has happened to me. Editors like John and Horace Gold and others have often brought me up standing by seeing something on the back of my own story's neck that was hidden from its author. And that external view is what an editor can give to a writer that the writer cannot always give himself.

Unfortunately, he does not always want it—even when the editor is right, and the editor is not always right. Maybe half a dozen times a writer has thanked me for making changes in his stories. Maybe half a million he has decidedly not. When I was aware that writers felt strongly on the subject, I either followed their wishes or didn't buy from those writers. That usually solved the problem. Not all the time. Bob Heinlein was one of the writers who objected to editorial tinkering; he was perfectly willing to make changes, but wanted to make them himself. When I bought one serial from him, it struck me as seriously overlong; I obtained permission to cut, or thought I did, and hacked away with a will. Robert did not enjoy the result, and that is why every copy of the book version of *Farnham's Freehold* has a little note on the copyright page saying that the serial version of the work was badly mutilated by one Fred Pohl.

So editing manuscripts takes up a great deal of an editor's time—perhaps an hour per story, at least, to get it ready to send to the printer . . . and often a much longer time mollifying the author for what you have done.

That's not all of it, of course. You have to write blurbs. You have to get the stories illustrated. You have to deal with reader mail and queries; you have to try to keep up some sort of rapport with at least the writers you most prize. I once calculated that to do the things I knew I really should do on *Galaxy* would take just about two hundred and fifty hours a week. Unfortunately, none of my weeks came with more than one hundred and sixty-eight.

One way to handle this problem is to hire more people.

That is not always practical on religious grounds—that is to say, in the universal religion of all publishers it is part of the credo that no additions to staff are needed—ever. But it also doesn't work very well in practical terms. Two editors do not do twice as much work as one. Two editors interact with each other, which takes time. They spend part of their time talking to each other—say, twenty percent—and another ten percent taking phone messages for each other or asking each other if there have been any messages. So each editor does only seventy percent of the work of one; two editors equals one-point-four editor's work. As the numbers go up, the efficiency goes down. With four editors, you reach the point of office birthday parties and long staff lunches; efficiency drops to maybe fifty percent. At six editors, you begin to need a managing editor to keep the other five in line. At the ten-editor stage, you are into weekly editorial meetings, bridal showers, and softball teams. By twenty, intraoffice affairs begin to occur. You lose perhaps two or three afternoons a week to sex, and an average of about one to hysteria.

There are publishing houses with really large editorial staffs. I don't actually know how many single individuals' work is produced by, say, two hundred persons in a single office. But I do have a guess. My guess is maybe about six.

When I acquired *Galaxy*, it had come down in the world a little. No fault of its own; there was a bad shakeout of science-fiction magazines in the late

1950s, partly because of radical changes in distribution patterns, partly for other identifiable reasons. Partly God knows why. *Galaxy* had attained enough success to survive, when dozens of others went under. But it was only coming out every other month in 1960, and its once top-dollar budget had been seriously cut.

What it retained was an inventory of good stories that Horace had bought, a loyal readership, and the respect of a lot of first-rate writers. There was nothing to keep me from getting good stories, except money. So I hoarded pennies to lure top writers, and by and by managed to get the rates back up.

Getting good stories isn't quite enough. Writers have lemming blood, and they flock seasonally in the same directions. There are times when a good hard-science story, or a good humorous story, or a good anything story just does not exist. It always seemed to me a part of an editor's job to balance a magazine—to give a variety of different sorts of stories.

Once when John Campbell was asked by an irate (and celebrated) writer why he had rejected a particular story on flimsy grounds, while he was at the same time printing demonstrably inferior work by someone else—call him "Writer X"—John replied: "X is such a mean, sniveling wretch that he will do anything I tell him. I use him to fill the gaps in my inventory with the variety of stories my readers have a right to expect. Even if it's not very good—but from *you* I expect more!" I never owned one of those mean, sniveling wretches. Or maybe I was my own. When I realized I wasn't getting enough non-fact articles, I wrote "The Martian Star-Gazers" and "Earth Eighteen" for myself; comic science-fiction adventure, "Under Two Moons"; colorful space opera, the *Starchild* novels with Jack Williamson. I had some bad feelings about writing for myself. It seemed to put the editor in competition with the writers for space, and that seemed unfair. But the publisher had made it a condition of employment that if I wrote for any science-fiction magazine at all it should be my own. I didn't want to stop writing science fiction, so I assuaged that faint agenbite of guilt by mostly writing to fill holes in the inventory.

Galaxy was not the only magazine I inherited from Horace. There was also *If*, which I conceived to be aimed at a less-sophisticated, perhaps a younger audience; after a while there were *Worlds of Tomorrow, Worlds of Fantasy, International Science Fiction,* and one or two briefer ventures. None of the new kids in the block did particularly well, but *Galaxy* and *If* prospered well enough to get the budgets up, put them both back on a monthly basis, show a modest profit for the publisher . . . and win a few awards. The enterprise was growing larger. After a while I was allowed a secretary, then an assistant. It was hard to locate the right combination of talents until Judy-Lynn Benjamin (now Judy-Lynn del Rey, of Del Rey Books) joined on. After the first couple of weeks, it was clear that she was a permanent fixture.

But time was marching on.

*   *   *

Five years is a good length of time to stay in an editorial spot. Ten years, I think, is too long. With the best will in the world, it is hard to come to your hundredth issue with the same zest and enterprise as to your first.

In this as in so much, I had one eye on John Campbell—this time as a bad example, not to be followed. John was the best of us all as a science-fiction editor. But, man and boy, he edited *Astounding/Analog* for thirty-four years, and for most of that time he shouldn't have. He was bored. He showed it. So did the magazine. John was too intelligent to be unaware of what was happening. But it happened anyway. John was also too intelligent to allow himself to stay bored forever, and I think you can see in the career of the magazine a slow sine curve that reflects his state of interest at any particular time—stretches while he was editing the magazine with his left hand, while most of his mind was daydreaming over hobbies like photography and ham radio; then a perking up as his attention came back to *Analog*. He devised new toys to play with—*Unknown;* then *Air Trails and Science Frontiers;* then dianetics/Scientology, then astrology, then the Dean Drive, politics—God knows what. Each stimulus worked for a little while. Then they stopped working. An editor needs, if not a new job, at least a sabbatical every now and then. The worst one can say of John Campbell (among so much that is pure praise) is that for thirty-four years he took his sabbaticals on the job.

By 1967 or so it seemed to me that I was beginning to do that, too. The projects that I could see a convenient way to carry through were not very challenging. The projects that looked really worthwhile also looked like an awful lot of work.

If, as I said a while ago, there is no way to do everything you really should do as an editor, the other side of that coin is that no one can really tell when you are dogging it. They may notice that the magazine isn't very exciting. They're unlikely to know why.

It is easy for an editor to cut corners. You can decide to write an editorial, which may take a full day. Or you can pick up the phone and order a "Guest Editorial" from someone else. You can spend a solid week editing a new writer's novel to add in the journeyman skills he has not yet learned. Or you can send it back, and instead buy some piece of yard goods from a regular—not quite as fresh, but not really bad, either. Every morning in ten minutes over the first cup of coffee you think of forty useful things to do for the magazine. If you're gung-ho, you try to do them. If you're not, no one will ever know if you just take a little nap instead.

It is easy to justify this to yourself, even, because of the fact that it's impossible to do everything. If you decide not to write an editorial because you can more usefully spend your time editing a novel, that's simple good time-study. But if you decide to do neither, that's staleness; and that's what I was beginning to feel. I found that I was turning more and more over to Judy-Lynn, that I was less and less aggressive in hunting out new stories, that I was—in a phrase—getting bored.

And so, when I returned from a brief trip to Rio de Janeiro and discovered that while I was away Bob Guinn had sold the magazines to Arnie Abramson, I debated for a few days whether I wanted to go along—and came to the conclusion that I really didn't. I had had about as much fun as I knew how to with the magazines. It was somebody else's turn.

THE PAIN PEDDLERS

BY ROBERT SILVERBERG

Apart from their merit as stories, the reason many of the selections in this volume are included is that they have some personal significance for me—usually that I think they represent occasions when I editorially intervened in an author's career in a useful way, or at least an interesting one. The trouble with telling you about them is that all too often they sound like bragging.

Well, to a regrettable extent they are. I am not, however, so lost to reason as to think that none of the writers involved would ever have made it without me. I was never the only editor in science fiction. If it hadn't been me here, it would have been someone else, surely. Or probably. Maybe. Well, at least there was an outside chance. . . . Anyway, when Bob Silverberg began his meteoric rise in the early 1960s, I had at least so much to do with it that if it had not been for me it would not have happened in just that way, just then.

Silverberg began writing in his swaddling clothes. He was quickly successful and immensely productive. He began with science fiction because he loved it, but he soon discovered there were easier ways to write, and some that paid a lot better. So he wrote every morning and every afternoon through all the days of his youth, and never flagged. One of the jokes of the time was that Bob had suffered a major writing block—on a Tuesday—it began at eleven forty-five in the morning and lasted nearly till lunch. And after a decade or so of that, he discovered that, really, he never needed to write again.

Along about then I happened to print in Galaxy a Silverberg story that, for complex reasons, had been lying about unpublished. Bob hadn't been appearing in SF for some years. People began telling him how good it was to see him back, and one morning he woke up and realized he liked it. So he asked me a favor. If he wrote new stories for me, would I please guarantee to accept each one as it arrived, sight unseen? I could call off the deal after any story. But I could not until then ever reject one. He had been spoiled, he confessed, by sure sales in other fields. He wanted to write SF, really did. But he couldn't make himself do it without that assurance.

216

So I agreed at once. That lit the fuse of the rocket, and "The Pain Peddlers" was one of the early sparks.

*   *   *

"Pain is gain."
Greek Proverb

The phone bleeped. Northrop nudged the cut-in switch and heard Maurillo say, "We got a gangrene, chief. They're amputating tonight."

Northrop's pulse quickened at the thought of action. "What's the tab?" he asked.

"Five thousand for all rights."

"Anesthetic?"

"Natch," Maurillo said. "I tried it the other way."

"What did you offer?"

"Ten. It was no go."

Northrop sighed. "I'll have to handle it myself, I guess. Where's the patient?"

"Clinton General. In the wards."

Northrop raised a heavy eyebrow and glowered into the screen. "In the *wards?*" he bellowed. "And you couldn't get them to agree?"

Maurillo seemed to shrink. "It was the relatives, chief. They were stubborn. The old man, he didn't seem to give a damn, but the relatives—"

"Okay. You stay there. I'm coming over to close the deal," Northrop snapped. He cut the phone out and pulled a couple of blank waiver forms out of his desk, just in case the relatives backed down. Gangrene was gangrene, but ten grand was ten grand. And business was business. The networks were yelling. He had to supply the goods or get out.

He thumbed the autosecretary. "I want my car ready in thirty seconds. South Street exit."

"Yes, Mr. Northrop."

"If anyone calls for me in the next half hour, record it. I'm going to Clinton General Hospital, but I don't want to be called there."

"Yes, Mr. Northrop."

"If Rayfield calls from the network office, tell him I'm getting him a dandy. Tell him—oh, hell, tell him I'll call him back in an hour. That's all."

"Yes, Mr. Northrop."

Northrop scowled at the machine and left his office. The gravshaft took him down forty stories in almost literally no time flat. His car was waiting, as ordered, a long, sleek '08 Frontenac with bubble top. Bullet-proof, of course. Network producers were vulnerable to crackpot attacks.

He sat back nestling into the plush upholstery. The car asked him where he was going, and he answered.

"Let's have a pep pill," he said.

A pill rolled out of the dispenser in front of him. He gulped it down. *Maurillo, you make me sick,* he thought. *Why can't you close a deal without me? Just once?*

He made a mental note, Maurillo had to go. The organization couldn't tolerate inefficiency.

The hospital was an old one. It was housed in one of the vulgar green-glass architectural monstrosities so popular sixty years before, a tasteless slab-sided thing without character or grace.

The main door irised and Northrop stepped through. The familiar hospital smell hit his nostrils. Most people found it unpleasant, but not Northrop. For him, it was the smell of dollars.

The hospital was so old that it still had nurses and orderlies. Oh, plenty of mechanicals skittered up and down the corridors, but here and there a middle-aged nurse, smugly clinging to her tenure, pushed a tray of mush along, or a doddering orderly propelled a broom. In his early days on video, Northrop had done a documentary on these living fossils of the hospital corridors. He had won an award for the film. He remembered it for its crosscuts from baggy-faced nurses to gleaming mechanicals, its vivid presentation of the inhumanity of the new hospitals. It was a long time since Northrop had done a documentary of that sort. A different kind of show was the order of the day now, ever since the intensifiers came in and telecasting medicine became an art.

A mechanical took him to Ward Seven. Maurillo was waiting there, a short, bouncy little man who wasn't bouncing much now. He knew he had fumbled. Maurillo grinned up at Northrop, a hollow grin, and said, "You sure made it fast, chief!"

"How long would it take for the competition to cut in?" Northrop countered. "Where's the patient?"

"Down by the end. You see where the curtain is? I had that put up. To get in good with the heirs. The relatives, I mean."

"Fill me in," Northrop said. "Who's in charge?"

"The oldest son, Harry. Watch out for him. Greedy."

"Who isn't?" Northrop thought. The world was so full of different kinds of sickness—and one sickness fed on another.

He stepped through the curtain. There was a man in the bed, drawn and gaunt, his hollow face greenish, stubbly. A mechanical stood next to the bed, with an intravenous tube running across and under the covers.

The patient looked at least ninety. Knocking off ten years for the effects of illness still made him pretty old, Northrop thought.

He confronted the relatives.

There were eight of them. Five women, ranging from middle age down to teens. Three men, the oldest about fifty, the other two in their forties. Sons and nieces and granddaughters, Northrop figured.

He said gravely, "I know what a terrible tragedy this must be for all of you. A man in the prime of his life—head of a happy family—" Northrop stared at the patient. "But I know he'll pull through. I can see the strength in him."

The oldest relative said, "I'm Harry Gardner. I'm his son. You're from the network?"

"I'm the producer," Northrop said. "I don't ordinarily come in person, but my assistant told me what a great human situation there was here, what a brave person your father was—"

The man in the bed slept on. He looked bad.

Harry Gardner said, "We made an arrangement. Five thousand bucks. We wouldn't do it, except for the hospital bills. They can really wreck you."

"I understand perfectly," Northrop said in his most unctuous tones. "That's why we're prepared to raise our offer. We're well aware of the disastrous effects of hospitalization on a small family, even today, in these times of protection. And so we can offer—"

"No! There's got to be anesthetic!" It was one of the daughters, a round, drab woman with colorless thin lips. "We ain't going to let you make him suffer!"

Northrop smiled. "It would only be a moment of pain for him. Believe me. We'd begin the anesthesia immediately after the amputation. Just let us capture that single instant of—"

"It ain't right! He's old, he's got to be given the best treatment! The pain could kill him!"

"On the contrary," Northrop said blandly. "Scientific research has shown that pain is often beneficial in amputation cases. It creates a nerve block, you see, that causes a kind of anesthesia of its own, without the harmful side effects of chemotherapy. And once the danger vectors are controlled, the normal anesthetic procedures can be invoked, and—" he took a deep breath, and went rolling glibly on to the crusher—"with the extra fee we'll provide, you can give your dear one the absolute finest in medical care. There'll be no reason to stint."

Wary glances were exchanged. Harry Gardner said, "How much are you offering for this absolute finest in medical care?"

"May I see the leg?" Northrop answered.

The coverlet was peeled back. Northrop stared.

It was a nasty case. Northrop was no doctor, but he had been in this line of work for five years, and that was long enough to give him an amateur acquaintance with disease. He knew the old man was in bad shape. It looked as though there had been a severe burn, high up along the calf, which had probably been treated only with first aid. Then, in happy proletarian ignorance, the family had let the old man rot until he was gangrenous. Now the leg was blackened, glossy, and swollen from mid-calf to the ends of the toes. Everything looked soft and decayed. Northrop had the feeling that he could reach out and break the puffy toes off, one at a time.

The patient wasn't going to survive.

Amputation or not, he was rotten to the core by this time. If the shock of amputation didn't do him in, general debilitation would. It was a good prospect for the show. It was the kind of stomach-turning vicarious suffering that millions of viewers gobbled up avidly.

Northrop looked up and said, "Fifteen thousand if you'll allow a network-approved surgeon to amputate under our conditions. And we'll pay the surgeon's fee besides."

"Well—"

"And we'll also underwrite the entire cost of post-operative care for your father," Northrop added smoothly. "Even if he stays in the hospital for six months, we'll pay every nickel, over and above the telecast fee."

He had them. He could see the greed shining in their eyes. They were faced with bankruptcy. He had come to rescue them; and did it matter all that much if the old man didn't have anesthetic when they sawed his leg off? Why, he was hardly conscious even now. He wouldn't really feel a thing. Not really.

Northrop produced the documents, the waivers, the contracts covering residuals and Latin American re-runs, the payment vouchers, all the paraphernalia. He sent Maurillo scuttling off for a secretary, and a few moments later a glistening mechanical was taking it all down.

"If you'll put your name here, Mr. Gardner—"

Northrop handed the pen to the eldest son. Signed, sealed, delivered.

"We'll operate tonight," Northrop said. "I'll send our surgeon over immediately. One of our best men. We'll give your father the care he deserves."

He pocketed the documents.

It was done. Maybe it was barbaric to operate on an old man that way, Northrop thought. But he didn't bear the responsibility, after all. He was just giving the public what it wanted. What the public wanted was spouting blood and tortured nerves.

And what did it matter to the old man, really? Any experienced medic could tell you he was as good as dead. The operation wouldn't save him. Anesthesia wouldn't save him. If the gangrene didn't get him, post-operative shock would do him in. At worst, he would suffer only a few minutes under the knife . . . but at least his family would be free from the fear of financial ruin.

On the way out, Maurillo said, "Don't you think it's a little risky, chief? Offering to pay the hospitalization expenses, I mean?"

"You've got to gamble a little sometimes to get what you want," Northrop said.

"Yeah, but that could run to fifty, sixty thousand! What'll that do to the budget?"

Northrop grinned. "We'll survive. Which is more than the old man will. He can't make it through the night. We haven't risked a penny, Maurillo. Not a stinking cent."

Returning to the office, Northrop turned the papers on the Gardner amputation over to his assistants, set the wheels in motion for the show, and prepared to call it a day.

There was only one bit of dirty work left to do. He had to fire Maurillo.

It wasn't called firing, of course. Maurillo had tenure, just like the hospital orderlies and everyone else below executive rank. It would have to be more a kick upstairs than anything else.

Northrop had been increasingly dissatisfied with the little man's work for months now. Today had been the clincher. Maurillo had no imagination. He didn't know how to close a deal. Why hadn't he thought of underwriting the hospitalization? *If I can't delegate responsibility to him,* Northrop told himself, *I can't use him at all.* There were plenty of other assistant producers in the outfit who'd be glad to step in.

Northrop spoke to a couple of them. He made his choice: a young fellow named Barton, who'd been working on documentaries all year. Barton had done the plane-crash deal in London in the spring. He had a fine touch for the gruesome. He had been on hand at the Worlds' Fair fire last year at Juneau. Yes, Barton was the man.

The next part was the sticky one. Things could go wrong.

Northrop phoned Maurillo, even though Maurillo was even two rooms away—these things were never done in person—and said, "I've got some good news for you, Ted. We're shifting you to a new program."

"Shifting—?"

"That's right. We had a talk in here this afternoon, and we decided you were being wasted on the blood-and-guts show. You need more scope for your talents. So we're giving you a fat raise, boy, and we're moving you over to Kiddie Time. We think you'll really blossom there. You and Sam Kline and Ed Bragan ought to make a terrific team."

Northrop saw Maurillo's pudgy face crumble. The arithmetic was getting home; over here, Maurillo was Number Two, and on the new show, a much less important one, he'd be Number Three. The pay meant nothing, of course; didn't Internal Revenue take it all anyway? It was a thumping boot, and Maurillo knew it.

The mores of the situation called for Maurillo to pretend he was receiving a rare honor. He didn't play the game. He squinted and said, "Just because I didn't sign up that old man's amputation?"

"What makes you think—"

"Three years I've been with you! Three years, and you kick me out just like that!"

"I told you, Ted, we thought this would be a big opportunity for you. It's a step up the ladder. It's—"

Maurillo's fleshy face puffed up with rage. "It's getting junked," he said bitterly. "Well, never mind, huh? It so happens I've got another offer. I'm quitting before you can can me. You can take your tenure and—"

Northrop hastily blanked the screen.

The idiot, he thought. *The fat little idiot. Well, to hell with him!*

He cleared his desk, and cleared his mind of Ted Maurillo and his problems. Life was real, life was earnest. Maurillo just couldn't take the pace, that was all.

Northrop prepared to go home. It had been a long day.

At eight that evening came word that old Gardner was about to undergo the amputation. At ten, Northrop was phoned by the network's own head surgeon, Dr. Steele, with the news that the operation had failed.

"We lost him," Steele said in a flat, unconcerned voice. "We did our best, but he was a mess. Fibrillation set in, and his heart just ran away. Not a damned thing we could do."

"Did the leg come off?"

"Oh, sure. All this was *after* the operation."

"Did it get taped?"

"Processing it now."

"Okay," Northrop said. "Thanks for calling."

"Sorry about the patient."

"Don't worry yourself," Northrop said. "It happens to the best of us."

The next morning, Northrop had a look at the rushes. The screening was in the twenty-third floor studio, and a select audience was on hand—Northrop, his new assistant producer Barton, a handful of network executives, a couple of men from the cutting room. Slick, bosomy girls handed out intensifier helmets. No mechanicals doing the work here!

Northrop slipped the helmet on over his head. He felt the familiar surge of excitement as the electrodes descended and contact was made. He closed his eyes. There was a thrum of power somewhere in the room as the EEG-amplifier went into action. The screen brightened.

There was the old man. There was the gangrenous leg. There was Dr. Steele, crisp and rugged and dimple-chinned, the network's star surgeon, two hundred and fifty thousand dollars a year's worth of talent. There was the scalpel, gleaming in Steele's hand.

Northrop began to sweat. The amplified brain waves were coming through the intensifier, and he felt the throbbing in the old man's leg, felt the dull haze of pain behind the old man's forehead, felt the weakness of being eighty years old and half dead.

Steele was checking out the electronic scalpel, now, while the nurses fussed around, preparing the man for the amputation. In the finished tape, there would be music, narration, all the trimmings, but now there was just a soundless series of images, and of course, the tapped brain-waves of the sick man.

The leg was bare.

The scalpel descended.

Northrop winced as vicarious agony shot through him. He could feel the blazing pain, the brief searing hell as the scalpel slashed through diseased flesh and rotting bone. His whole body trembled, and he bit down hard on his lips and clenched his fists, and then it was over.

There was a cessation of pain. A catharsis. The leg no longer sent its pulsating messages to the weary brain. Now there was shock, the anesthesia of hyped-up pain, and with the shock came calmness. Steele went about the mop-up operation. He tidied the stump, bound it.

The rushes flickered out in anticlimax. Later, the production crew would tie up the program with interviews of the family, perhaps a shot of the funeral, a few observations on the problem of gangrene in the aged. Those things were the extras. What counted, what the viewers wanted, was the sheer nastiness of vicarious pain, and that they got in full measure. It was a gladiatorial contest without the gladiators, masochism concealed as medicine. It worked. It pulled in the viewers by the million.

Northrop patted sweat from his forehead.

"Looks like we got ourselves quite a little show here, boys," he said in satisfaction.

The mood of satisfaction was still on him as he left the building that day. All day he had worked hard, getting the show into its final shape, cutting and polishing. He enjoyed the element of craftsmanship. It helped him to forget some of the sordidness of the program.

Night had fallen when he left. He stepped out of the main entrance and a figure strode forward, a bulky figure, medium height, tired face. A hand reached out, thrusting him roughly back into the lobby of the building.

At first Northrop didn't recognize the face of the man. It was a blank face, a nothing face, a middle-aged empty face. Then he placed it.

Harry Gardner. The son of the dead man.

"Murderer!" Gardner shrilled. "You killed him! He would have lived if you'd used anesthetics! You phony, you murdered him so people would have thrills on television!"

Northrop glanced up the lobby. Someone was coming, around the bend. Northrop felt calm. He could stare this nobody down until he fled in fear.

"Listen," Northrop said, "we did the best medical science can do for your father. We gave him the ultimate in scientific care. We—"

"You murdered him!"

"No," Northrop said, and then he said no more, because he saw the sudden flicker of a slice-gun in the blank-faced man's fat hand.

He backed away. But it didn't help, because Gardner punched the trigger and an incandescent bolt flared out, and sliced across Northrop's belly just as efficiently as the surgeon's scalpel had cut through the gangrenous leg.

Gardner raced away, feet clattering on the marble floor. Northrop dropped, clutching himself.

His suit was seared. There was a slash through his abdomen, a burn an eighth of an inch wide and perhaps four inches deep, cutting through intestines, through organs, through flesh. The pain hadn't begun yet. His nerves weren't getting the message through to his stunned brain.

But then they were; and Northrop coiled and twisted in agony that was anything but vicarious now.

Footsteps approached.

"Jeez," a voice said.

Northrop forced an eye open. Maurillo. Of all people, Maurillo.

"A doctor," Northrop wheezed. "Fast! Christ, the pain! Help me, Ted!"

Maurillo looked down, and smiled. Without a word, he stepped to the telephone booth six feet away, dropped in a token, punched out a call.

"Get a van over here, fast. I've got a subject, chief."

Northrop writhed in torment. Maurillo crouched next to him. "A doctor," Northrop murmured. "A needle, at least. Gimme a needle! The pain—"

"You want me to kill the pain?" Maurillo laughed. "Nothing doing. You just hang on. You stay alive till we get that hat on your head and tape the whole thing."

"But you don't work for me—you're off the program—"

"Sure," Maurillo said. "I'm with Transcontinental now. They're starting a blood-and-guts show too. Only they don't need waivers."

Northrop gaped. Transcontinental? That bootleg outfit that peddled tapes in Afghanistan and Mexico and Ghana and God knew where else? Not even a network show, he thought! No fee! Dying in agony for the benefit of a bunch of lousy tapeleggers. That was the worst part, Northrop thought. Only Maurillo would pull a deal like that.

"A needle! For God's sake, Maurillo, a needle!"

"Nothing doing. The van'll be here any minute. They'll sew you up, and we'll tape it nice."

Northrop closed his eyes. He felt the coiling intestines blazing within him. He willed himself to die, to cheat Maurillo.

But it was no use. He remained alive and suffering.

He lived for an hour. That was plenty of time to tape his dying agonies. The last thought he had was that it was a damned shame he couldn't star on his own show.

OH, TO BE A BLOBEL!

BY PHILIP K. DICK

Philip K. Dick is not a writer to everyone's taste. He is a quite unmistakable one, however. It is impossible for Phil Dick to string ten words together without making them conspicuously the work of him and of no one else—a trait shared with at most two or three other writers in the field: R. A. Lafferty, Cordwainer Smith, and who else?

Dick's work is marked with many special, private, recurring themes. It is almost as though for a quarter of a century he has been engaged in writing a single immense work, whacking off sections of it and publishing them, from time to time, as separate novels. He plays curious tricks with time—speeds it up, slows it down, even makes it run backwards when he likes. He plays even stranger tricks with reality, and that is quite astonishing. You see, it is a mark of the bad science-fiction writer that he hedges his bets, so that you never know whether he means you to take what he says as "real"—at least for the purposes of the story—or as a character's wild and disordered flight of delusion or fantasy, in which anything goes and the author need never be held to account. But it is the mark of the truly superior writer that he can break the tabus, violate the rules, commit the unforgivable sins—and make his story compelling and memorable anyway.

There is no doubt that Phil Dick is a superior writer. The bulk of his work is a sort of extended probing in the questions, "What is reality, anyway?"— with side excursions into "Who am I?" and even "What does it matter?" It is painful to say that we will not have any more of Phil Dick's answers to these questions. While this book was in press he suffered a stroke, lingered for a little while and died. He cannot be replaced.

* * *

225

I.

He put a twenty-dollar platinum coin into the slot and the analyst, after a pause, lit up. Its eyes shone with sociability. It swiveled about in its chair, picked up a pen and pad of long yellow paper from its desk, and said:

"Good morning, sir. You may begin."

"Hello, Doctor Jones. I guess you're not the same Doctor Jones who did the definitive biography of Freud; that was a century ago." He laughed nervously. Being a rather poverty-stricken man, he was not accustomed to dealing with the new fully homeostatic psychoanalysts. "Um," he said, "should I free-associate or give you background material or just what?"

Dr. Jones said, "Perhaps you could begin by telling me who you are und warum mich—why you have selected me."

"I'm George Munster of catwalk 4, building WEF-395, San Francisco condominium established 1996."

"How do you do, Mr. Munster." Dr. Jones held out its hand, and George Munster shook it. He found the hand to be of a pleasant body-temperature and decidedly soft. The grip, however, was manly.

"You see," Munster said, "I'm an ex-GI, a war veteran. That's how I got my condominium apartment at WEF-395. Veterans' preference."

"Ah, yes," Dr. Jones said, ticking faintly as it measured the passage of time. "The war with the Blobels."

"I fought three years in that war," Munster said, nervously smoothing his long, black, thinning hair. "I hated the Blobels and I volunteered. I was only nineteen and I had a good job—but the crusade to clear the Sol System of Blobels came first in my mind."

"Um," Dr. Jones said, ticking and nodding.

George Munster continued, "I fought well. In fact, I got two decorations and a battlefield citation. Corporal. That's because I single-handed wiped out an observation satellite full of Blobels; we'll never know exactly how many because, of course, being Blobels, they tend to fuse together and unfuse confusingly." He broke off then, feeling emotional. Even remembering and talking about the war was too much for him. He lay back on the couch, lit a cigarette, and tried to become calm.

The Blobels had emigrated originally from another star system, probably Proxima. Several thousand years ago they had settled on Mars and on Titan, doing very well at agrarian pursuits. They were developments of the original unicellular amoeba, quite large and with a highly organized nervous system, but still amoebae, with pseudopodia, reproducing by binary fission, and in the main offensive to Terran settlers.

The war itself had broken out over ecological considerations. It had been the desire of the Foreign Aid Department of the UN to change the atmosphere on Mars, making it more usable for Terran settlers. This change, however, had made it unpalatable for the Blobel colonies already there; hence the squabble.

And, Munster reflected, it was not possible to change *half* the atmosphere of a planet, the Brownian movement being what it was. Within a period of ten years, the altered atmosphere had diffused throughout the planet, bringing suffering—at least so they alleged—to the Blobels. In retaliation, a Blobel armada approached Terra and put into orbit a series of technically sophisticated satellites designed eventually to alter the atmosphere of Terra. This alteration had never come about, because of course the War Office of the UN had gone into action; the satellites had been detonated by self-instructing missiles . . . and the war was on.

Dr. Jones said, "Are you married, Mr. Munster?"

"No sir," Munster said. "And—" he shuddered— "you'll see why when I've finished telling you. See, Doctor," he stubbed out his cigarette—"I'll be frank. I was a Terran spy. That was my task. They gave the job to me because of my bravery in the field. I didn't ask for it."

"I see," Dr. Jones said.

"Do you?" Munster's voice broke. "Do you know what was necessary in those days in order to make a Terran into a successful spy among the Blobels?"

Nodding, Dr. Jones said, "Yes, Mr. Munster. You had to relinquish your human form and assume the form of a Blobel."

Munster said nothing; he clenched and unclenched his fist, bitterly. Across from him, Dr. Jones ticked.

That evening, back in his small apartment at WEF-395, Munster opened a fifth of Teacher's Scotch and sat sipping from a cup, lacking even the energy to get a glass down from the cupboard over the sink.

What had he gotten out of the session with Dr. Jones today? Nothing, as nearly as he could tell. And it had eaten deep into his meager financial resources . . . meager because—

Because for almost twelve hours out of the day he reverted, despite all the efforts of himself and the Veterans' Hospitalization Agency of the UN, to his old wartime Blobel shape. To a formless unicellularlike blob, right in the middle of his own apartment at WEF-395.

His financial resources consisted of a small pension from the War Office. Finding a job was impossible, because as soon as he was hired the strain caused him to revert there on the spot, in plain sight of his new employer and fellow workers.

It did not assist in forming successful work-relationships.

Sure enough, now, at eight in the evening, he felt himself once more beginning to revert. It was an old and familiar experience to him, and he loathed it. Hurriedly, he sipped the last of the cup of Scotch, put the cup down on a table . . . and felt himself slide together into a homogeneous puddle.

The telephone rang.

"I can't answer," he called to it. The phone's relay picked up his anguished message and conveyed it to the calling party. Now Munster had become a single transparent gelatinous mass in the middle of the rug. He undulated toward the phone—it was still ringing, despite his statement to it, and he felt furious resentment; didn't he have enough troubles already, without having to deal with a ringing phone?

Reaching it, he extended a pseudopodium and snatched the receiver from the hook. With great effort he formed his plastic substance into the semblance of a vocal apparatus, resonating dully. "I'm busy," he resonated in a low booming fashion into the mouthpiece of the phone. "Call later." *Call,* he thought as he hung up, *tomorrow morning. When I've been able to regain my human form.*

The apartment was quiet now.

Sighing, Munster flowed back across the carpet to the window, where he rose into a high pillar in order to see the view beyond. There was a light-sensitive spot on his outer surface, and although he did not possess a true lens he was able to appreciate—nostalgically—the blur of San Francisco Bay, the Golden Gate Bridge, the playground for small children which was Alcatraz Island.

Damn it, he thought bitterly. *I can't marry; I can't live a genuine human existence, reverting this way to the form the War Office bigshots forced me into back in the war times . . .*

He had not known then, when he accepted the mission, that it would leave this permanent effect. They had assured him it was "only temporary, for the duration," or some such glib phrase. *Duration!* Munster thought with furious, impotent resentment. *It's been* eleven years.

The psychological problems created for him, the pressure on his psyche, were immense. Hence his visit to Dr. Jones.

Once more the phone rang.

"Okay," Munster said aloud, and flowed laboriously back across the room to it. "You want to talk to me?" he said as he came closer and closer; the trip, for someone in Blobel form, was a long one. "I'll talk to you. You can even turn on the vidscreen and *look* at me." At the phone he snapped the switch which would permit visual communication as well as auditory. "Have a good look," he said, and displayed his amorphous form before the scanning tube of the video.

Dr. Jones's voice came, "I'm sorry to bother you at your home, Mr. Munster, especially when you're in this, um, awkward condition." The homeostatic analyst paused. "But I've been devoting time to problem-solving vis-a-vis your condition. I may have at least a partial solution."

"What?" Munster said, taken by surprise. "You mean to imply that medical science can now—"

"No, no," Dr. Jones said hurriedly. "The physical aspects lie out of my domain; you must keep that in mind, Munster. When you consulted me about your problems, it was the psychological adjustment that—"

"I'll come right down to your office and talk to you," Munster said. And then he realized that he could not; in his Blobel form it would take him days to undulate all the way across town to Dr. Jones's office. "Jones," he said desperately, "you see the problems I face. I'm stuck here in this apartment every night beginning about eight o'clock and lasting through until almost seven in the morning. I can't even visit you and consult you and get help—"

"Be quiet, Mr. Munster," Dr. Jones interrupted. "I'm trying to tell you something. *You're not the only one in this condition.* Did you know that?"

Heavily, Munster said, "Sure. In all, eighty-three Terrans were made over into Blobels at one time or another during the war. Of the eighty-three—" he knew the facts by heart—"sixty-one survived and now there's an organization called Veterans of Unnatural Wars of which fifty are members. I'm a member. We meet twice a month, revert in unison . . ." He started to hang up the phone. So this was what he had gotten for his money, this stale news. "Good-bye, Doctor," he murmured.

Dr. Jones whirred in agitation. "Mr. Munster, I don't mean other Terrans. I've researched this in your behalf, and I discover that, according to captured records at the Library of Congress, fifteen *Blobels* were formed into pseudo-Terrans to act as spies for *their* side. Do you understand?"

After a moment Munster said, "Not exactly."

"You have a mental block against being helped," Dr. Jones said. "But here's what I want, Munster. You be at my office at eleven in the morning tomorrow. We'll take up the solution to your problem then. Good night."

Wearily, Munster said, "When I'm in my Blobel form, my wits aren't too keen, Doctor. You'll have to forgive me." He hung up, still puzzled. So there were fifteen Blobels walking around on Titan this moment, doomed to occupy human forms—so what? How did that help him?

Maybe he would find out at eleven tomorrow.

When he strode into Dr. Jones's waiting room, he saw, seated in a deep chair in a corner by a lamp, reading a copy of *Fortune,* an exceedingly attractive young woman.

Automatically, Munster found a place to sit from which he could eye her. Stylish dyed-white hair braided down the back of her neck—he took in the sight of her with delight, pretending to read his own copy of *Fortune.* Slender legs, small and delicate elbows. And her sharp, clearly featured face. The intelligent eyes, the thin, tapered nostrils—a truly lovely girl, he thought. He drank in the sight of her . . . until all at once she raised her head and stared coolly back at him.

"Dull, having to wait," Munster mumbled.

The girl said, "Do you come to Dr. Jones often?"

"No," he admitted. "This is just the second time."

"I've never been here before," the girl said. "I was going to another electronic fully homeostatic psychoanalyst in Los Angeles and then late yesterday Dr. Bing, my analyst, called me and told me to fly up here and see Dr. Jones this morning. Is this one good?"

"Um," Munster said. "I guess so." *We'll see,* he thought. *That's precisely what we don't know yet.*

The inner office door opened and there stood Dr. Jones. "Miss Arrasmith," it said, nodding to the girl. "Mr. Munster." It nodded to George. "Won't you both come in?"

Rising to her feet, Miss Arrasmith said, "Who pays the twenty dollars, then?" But the analyst was silent; it had turned off.

"I'll pay," Miss Arrasmith said, reaching into her purse.

"No, no," Munster said. "Let me." He got out a twenty-dollar piece and dropped it into the analyst's slot.

At once, Dr. Jones said, "You're a gentleman, Mr. Munster." Smiling, it ushered the two of them into its office. "Be seated, please. Miss Arrasmith, without preamble please allow me to explain your—condition to Mr. Munster." To Munster it said, "Miss Arrasmith is a Blobel."

Munster could only stare at the girl.

"Obviously," Dr. Jones continued, "presently in human form. This, for her, is the state of involuntary reversion. During the war, she operated behind Terran lines, acting for the Blobel War League. She was captured and held, but then the war ended and she was not tried."

"They released me," Miss Arrasmith said in a low, carefully controlled voice. "Still in human form. I stayed here out of shame. I just couldn't go back to Titan and—" Her voice wavered.

"There is great shame attached to this condition," Dr. Jones said, "for any high-caste Blobel."

Nodding, Miss Arrasmith sat clutching a tiny Irish linen handkerchief and trying to look poised. "Correct, Doctor. I did visit Titan to discuss my condition with medical authorities there. After expensive and prolonged therapy with me, they were able to induce a return to my natural form for a period of about one-fourth of the time. But the other three-fourths . . . I am as you perceive me now." She ducked her head and touched the handkerchief to her right eye.

"Jeez," Munster protested, "you're lucky! A human form is infinitely superior to a Blobel form. I ought to know. As a Blobel you have to creep along. You're like a big jellyfish, no skeleton to keep you erect. And binary fission—it's lousy, I say really lousy, compared to the Terran form of—you know. Reproduction." He colored.

Dr. Jones ticked and stated, "For a period of about six hours, your human forms overlap. And then for about one hour your Blobel forms overlap. So all in all, the two of you possess seven hours out of twenty-four in which you both possess identical forms. In my opinion—" it toyed with its pen and paper—"seven hours is not too bad, if you follow my meaning."

After a moment, Miss Arrasmith said, "But Mr. Munster and I are natural enemies."

"That was years ago," Munster said.

"Correct," Dr. Jones agreed. "True, Miss Arrasmith is basically a Blobel and you, Munster, are a Terran. But both of you are outcasts in either civilization. Both of you are stateless and hence gradually suffering a loss of ego-identity. I predict for both of you a gradual deterioration ending finally in severe mental illness. *Unless* you two can develop a rapprochement.'' The analyst was silent then.

Miss Arrasmith said softly, ''I think we're very lucky, Mr. Munster. As Dr. Jones said, we do overlap for seven hours a day . . . we can enjoy that time together, no longer in wretched isolation.'' She smiled up hopefully at him, rearranging her coat. Certainly, she had a nice figure; the somewhat low-cut dress gave an ideal clue to that.

Studying her, Munster pondered.

''Give him time,'' Dr. Jones told Miss Arrasmith. ''My analysis of him is that he will see this correctly and do the right thing.''

Still rearranging her coat and dabbing at her large, dark eyes, Miss Arrasmith waited.

II.

The phone in Dr. Jones's office rang, a number of years later. He answered it in his customary way. ''Please, sir or madam, deposit twenty dollars if you wish to speak to me.''

A tough male voice on the other end of the line said, ''Listen, this is the UN Legal Office and we don't deposit twenty dollars to talk to anybody. So trip that mechanism inside you, Jones.''

''Yes, sir,'' Dr. Jones said, and with his right hand tripped the lever behind his ear that caused him to come on free.

''Back in 2037,'' the UN legal expert said, ''did you advise a couple to marry? A George Munster and a Vivian Arrasmith, now Mrs. Munster?''

''Why yes,'' Dr. Jones said, after consulting his built-in memory banks.

''Had you investigated the legal ramifications of their issue?''

''Um, well,'' Dr. Jones said, ''that's not my worry.''

''You can be arraigned for advising any action contrary to UN law.''

''There's no law prohibiting a Blobel and a Terran from marrying.''

The UN legal expert said, ''All right, Doctor. I'll settle for a look at their case histories.''

''Absolutely no,'' Dr. Jones said. ''That would be a breach of ethics.''

''We'll get a writ and sequester them, then.''

''Go ahead.'' Dr. Jones reached behind his ear to shut himself off.

''Wait. It may interest you to know that the Munsters now have four children. And, following the Revised Mendelian Law, the offspring comprise a strict one, two, one ratio. One Blobel girl, one hybrid boy, one hybrid girl, one Terran girl. The legal problem arises in that the Blobel Supreme Council claims the pure-blooded Blobel girl as a citizen of Titan and also suggests that one of the two hybrids be donated to the Council's jurisdiction.'' The UN legal expert explained, ''You see, the Munsters' marriage is breaking up. They're getting divorced and it's sticky finding which laws obtain regarding them and their issue.''

"Yes," Dr. Jones admitted, "I would think so. What has caused their marriage to break up?"

"I don't know and don't care. Possibly the fact that both adults rotate daily between being Blobels and Terrans. Maybe the strain got to be too much. If you want to give them psychological advice, consult them. Good-bye." The UN legal expert rang off.

Did I make a mistake, advising them to marry? Dr. Jones asked itself. *I wonder if I shouldn't look them up; I owe at least that to them.*

Opening the Los Angeles phonebook, it began thumbing through the "M's."

These had been six difficult years for the Munsters.

First, George had moved from San Francisco to Los Angeles. He and Vivian had set up their household in a condominium apartment with three instead of two rooms. Vivian, being in Terran form three-fourths of the time, had been able to obtain a job; right out in public she gave jet-flight information at the Fifth Los Angeles Airport. George, however—

His pension comprised an amount only one-fourth that of his wife's salary and he felt it keenly. To augment it, he had searched for a way of earning money at home. Finally in a magazine he had found this valuable ad:

MAKE SWIFT PROFITS IN YOUR OWN CONDO! RAISE GIANT
BULLFROGS FROM JUPITER, CAPABLE OF EIGHTY-FOOT
LEAPS. CAN BE USED IN FROG-RACING (WHERE LEGAL) AND—

So in 2038 he had bought his first pair of frogs imported from Jupiter and had begun raising them for swift profits, right in his own condominium apartment building, in a corner of the basement that Leopold, the partially homeostatic janitor, let him use, gratis.

But in the relatively feeble Terran gravity the frogs were capable of enormous leaps, and the basement proved too small for them; they ricocheted from wall to wall like green pingpong balls and soon died. Obviously it took more than a portion of the basement at QEK-604 Apartments to house a crop of the damned things, George realized.

And then, too, their first child had been born. It had turned out to be pure-blooded Blobel; for twenty-four hours a day it consisted of a gelatinous mass and George found himself waiting in vain for it to switch over to human form, even for a moment.

He faced Vivian defiantly in this matter, during a period when both of them were in human form.

"How can I consider it my child?" he asked her. "It's an alien life form to me." He was discouraged and even horrified. "Dr. Jones should have foreseen this. Maybe it's *your* child—it looks just like you."

Tears filled Vivian's eyes. "You mean that insultingly."

"Damn right I do. We fought you creatures. We used to consider you no better than Portuguese men-o'-war.'' Gloomily, he put on his coat. ''I'm going down to Veterans of Unnatural Wars Headquarters,'' he informed his wife. ''Have a beer with the boys.'' Shortly, he was on his way to join with his old wartime buddies, glad to get out of the apartment house.

VUW Headquarters was a decrepit cement building in downtown Los Angeles, left over from the twentieth century and sadly in need of paint. The VUW had little funds because most of its members were, like George Munster, living on UN pensions. However, there was a pool table and an old 3-D television set and a few dozen tapes of popular music and also a chess set. George generally drank his beer and played chess with his fellow members, either in human form or in Blobel form; this was one place in which both were accepted.

This particular evening he sat with Pete Ruggles, a fellow veteran who also had married a Blobel female, reverting, as Vivian did, to human form.

''Pete, I can't go on. I've got a gelatinous blob for a child. My whole life I've wanted a kid, and now what have I got? Something that looks like it washed up on the beach.''

Sipping his beer—he too was in human form at the moment—Pete answered, ''Criminy, George, I admit it's a mess. But you must have known what you were getting into when you married her. And my God, according to Mendel's Revised Law, the next kid—''

George broke in, ''I mean, I don't respect my own wife. That's the basis of it. I think of her as a *thing*. And myself too. We're both things.'' He drank down his beer in one gulp.

Pete said meditatively, ''But from the Blobel standpoint—''

''Listen, whose side are you on?'' George demanded.

''Don't yell at me,'' Pete said, ''or I'll deck you.''

A moment later they were swinging wildly at each other. Fortunately Pete reverted to Blobel form in the nick of time; no harm was done. Now George sat alone, in human shape, while Pete oozed off somewhere else, probably to join a group of the boys who had also assumed Blobel form.

Maybe we can found a new society somewhere on a remote moon, George said to himself. *Neither Terran nor Blobel.*

I've got to go back to Vivian, George resolved. *What else is there for me? I'm lucky to find her; I'd be nothing but a war veteran guzzling beer here at VUW Headquarters every damn day and night, with no future, no hope, no real life . . .*

He had a new money-making scheme going now. It was a home mail-order business; he had placed an ad in the *Saturday Evening Post* for MAGIC LODESTONES REPUTED TO BRING YOU LUCK. FROM ANOTHER STAR-SYSTEM ENTIRELY! The stones had come from Proxima and were obtainable on Titan; it was Vivian who had made the commercial contact for him with her people. But so far, few people had sent in the dollar-fifty.

I'm a failure, George said to himself.

*   *   *

Fortunately the next child, born in the winter of 2039, showed itself to be a hybrid. It took human form fifty percent of the time, and so at last George had a child who was—occasionally, anyhow—a member of his own species.

He was still in the process of celebrating the birth of Maurice when a delegation of their neighbors at QEK-604 Apartments came and rapped on their door.

"We've got a petition here," the chairman of the delegation said, shuffling his feet in embarrassment, "asking that you and Mrs. Munster leave QEK-604."

"But why?" George asked, bewildered. "You haven't objected to us up until now."

"The reason is that now you've got a hybrid youngster who will want to play with ours, and we feel it's unhealthy for our kids to—"

George slammed the door in their faces.

But still he felt the pressure of the hostility from the people on all sides of them. And to think, he thought bitterly, that I fought in the war to save these people! It sure wasn't worth it!

An hour later he was down at VUW Headquarters once more, drinking beer and talking with his buddy Sherman Downs, also married to a Blobel.

"Sherman, it's no good. We're not wanted; we've got to emigrate. Maybe we'll try it on Titan in Viv's world."

"Chrissakes," Sherman protested, "I hate to see you fold up, George. Isn't your electro-magnetic reducing belt beginning to sell, finally?"

For the last few months, George had been making and selling a complex electronic reducing gadget which Vivian had helped him design; it was based in principle on a Blobel device popular on Titan but unknown on Terra. And this had gone over well. George had more orders than he could fill. But—

"I had a terrible experience, Sherm," George confided. "I was in a drugstore the other day, and they gave me a big order for my reducing belt, and I got so excited—" He broke off. "You can guess what happened. I reverted, right in plain sight of a hundred customers. And when the buyer saw that, he canceled the order for the belts. It was what we all fear. You should have seen how their attitude toward me changed."

Sherm said, "Hire someone to do your selling for you. A full-blooded Terran."

Thickly, George said, "*I'm* a full-blooded Terran, and don't you forget it. Ever."

"I just mean—"

"I know what you meant," George said. And took a swing at Sherman. Fortunately he missed and in the excitement both of them reverted to Blobel form. They oozed angrily into each other for a time, but at last fellow veterans managed to separate them.

"I'm as much a Terran as anyone," George thought-radiated in the Blobel manner to Sherman. "And I'll flatten anyone who says otherwise."

In Blobel form, he was unable to get home; he had to phone Vivian to come and get him. It was humiliating.

Suicide, he decided. *That's the answer.*

How best to do it? In Blobel form, he was unable to feel pain; best to do it then. Several substances would dissolve him . . . he could, for instance, drop himself into a heavily-chlorinated swimming pool, such as QEK-604 maintained in its recreation room.

Vivian, in human form, found him as he reposed hesitantly at the edge of the swimming pool, late one night.

"George, I beg you—go back to Dr. Jones."

"Naw," he boomed dully, forming a quasi-vocal apparatus with a portion of his body. "It's no use, Viv. I don't *want* to go on." Even the belts; they had been Viv's idea, rather than his. He was second even there . . . behind her, falling constantly further behind each passing day.

Viv said, "You have so much to offer the children."

That was true. "Maybe I'll drop over to the UN War Office," he decided. "Talk to them, see if there's anything new that medical science has come up with that might stabilize me."

"But if you stabilize as a Terran," Vivian said, "what would become of me?"

"We'd have *eighteen entire hours* together a day. All the hours you take human form!"

"But you wouldn't want to stay married to me. Because, George, then you could meet a Terran woman."

It wasn't fair to her, he realized. So he abandoned the idea.

In the spring of 2041 their third child was born, also a girl, and like Maurice a hybrid. It was Blobel at night and Terran by day.

Meanwhile, George found a solution to some of his problems.

He got himself a mistress.

III.

At the Hotel Elysium, a rundown wooden building in the heart of Los Angeles, he and Nina arranged to meet one another.

"Nina," George said, sipping Teacher's Scotch and seated beside her on the shabby sofa which the hotel provided, "you've made my life worth living again." He fooled with the buttons of her blouse.

"I respect you," Nina Glaubman said, assisting him with the buttons. "In spite of the fact—well, you are a former enemy of the people."

George protested, "We must not think about the old days. We have to close our minds to our pasts." *Nothing but our future,* he thought.

His reducing belt enterprise had developed so well that now he employed fifteen full-time Terran employees and owned a small, modern factory on the outskirts of San Fernando. If UN taxes had been reasonable, he would by now be a wealthy man. Brooding on that, George wondered what the tax rate was in Blobel-run lands, on Io, for instance. Maybe he ought to look into it.

One night at VUW Headquarters, he discussed the subject with Reinholt, Nina's husband, who of course was ignorant of the *modus vivendi* between George and Nina.

"Reinholt," George said with difficulty, as he drank his beer, "I've got big plans. This cradle-to-grave socialism the UN operates . . . it's not for me. It's cramping me. The Munster Magic Magnetic Belt is—" he gestured—"more than Terran civilization can support. You get me?"

Coldly, Reinholt said, "But George, you are a Terran. If you emigrate to Blobel-run territory with your factory, you'll be betraying your—"

"Listen," George told him, "I've got one authentic Blobel child, two half-Blobel children, and a fourth on the way. I've got strong *emotional* ties with those people out there on Titan and Io."

"You're a traitor," Reinholt said, and punched him in the mouth. "And not only that," he continued, punching George in the stomach, "you're running around with my wife. I'm going to kill you."

To escape, George reverted to Blobel form; Reinholt's blows passed harmlessly deep into his moist, jelly-like substance. Reinholt then reverted, too, and flowed into him murderously, trying to consume and absorb George's nucleus.

Fortunately fellow veterans pried their two bodies apart before any permanent harm was done.

Later that night, still trembling, George sat with Vivian in the living room of their eight-room suite at the great new condominium apartment building ZGF-900. It had been a close call, and now of course Reinholt would tell Viv. It was only a question of time. The marriage, as far as George could see, was over. This perhaps was their last moment together.

"Viv," he said urgently, "you have to believe me; I love you. You and the children—plus the belt business, naturally—are my complete life." A desperate idea came to him. "Let's emigrate now, tonight. Pack up the kids and go to Titan, right this minute."

"I can't go," Vivian said. "I know how my people would treat me, and treat you and the children, too. George, *you go*. Move the factory to Io. I'll stay here." Tears filled her dark eyes.

"Hell," George said, "what kind of life is that? With you on Terra and me on Io—that's no marriage. And who'll get the kids?" Probably Viv would get them. But his firm employed top legal talent—perhaps he could use it to solve his domestic problems.

The next morning Vivian found out about Nina. And hired an attorney of her own.

"Listen," George said, on the phone talking to his top legal talent, Henry Ramarau. "Get me custody of the fourth child; it'll be a Terran. And we'll compromise on the two hybrids; I'll take Maurice and she can have Kathy. And naturally she gets that blob, that first so-called child. As far as I'm concerned, it's hers anyhow." He slammed the receiver down and then turned to the board of directors of his company. "Now where were we in our analysis of Io tax laws?"

During the next weeks, the idea of a move to Io appeared more and more feasible from a profit-and-loss standpoint.

"Go ahead and buy land on Io," George instructed his business agent in the field, Tom Hendricks. "And get it cheap. We want to start right." To his secretary, Miss Nolan, he said, "Now keep everyone out of my office until further notice. I feel an attack coming on, from anxiety over this major move off Terra to Io." He added, "And personal worries."

"Yes, Mr. Munster," Miss Nolan said, ushering Tom Hendricks out of George's private office. "No one will disturb you." She could be counted on to keep everyone out while George reverted to his wartime Blobel shape, as he often did these days. The pressure on him was immense.

When, later in the day, he resumed human form, George learned from Miss Nolan that a Doctor Jones had called.

"I'll be damned," George said, thinking back to six years ago. "I thought it'd be in the junk pile by now." To Miss Nolan he said, "Call Doctor Jones and notify me when you have it. I'll take a minute off to talk to it." It was like old times, back in San Francisco.

Shortly, Miss Nolan had Dr. Jones on the line.

"Doctor," George said, leaning from side to side and poking at an orchid on his desk. "Good to hear from you."

The voice of the homeostatic analyst came in his ear, "Mr. Munster, I note that you now have a secretary."

"Yes," George said, "I'm a tycoon. I'm in the reducing-belt game; it's somewhat like the flea-collar that cats wear. Well, what can I do for you?"

"I understand you have four children now—"

"Actually three, plus a fourth on the way. Listen, that fourth, Doctor, is vital to me; according to Mendel's Revised Law, it's a full-blooded Terran and by God I'm doing everything in my power to get custody of it." He added, "Vivian—you remember her—is now back on Titan. Among her own people, where she belongs. And I'm putting some of the finest doctors I can get on my payroll to stabilize me. I'm tired of this constant reverting, night and day; I've got too much to do for such nonsense."

Dr. Jones said, "From your tone I can see you're an important, busy man, Mr. Munster. You've certainly risen in the world since I saw you last."

"Get to the point, Doctor," George said impatiently.

"I, um, thought perhaps I could bring you and Vivian together again."

"Bah," George said contemptuously. "That woman? Never. Listen, Doctor, I have to ring off. We're in the process of finalizing on some basic business strategy here at Munster, Incorporated."

"Mr. Munster," Dr. Jones asked, "is there another woman?"

"There's another Blobel," George said, "if that's what you mean." And he hung up the phone. Two Blobels are better than none, he said to himself. And now back to business. He pressed a button on his desk and at once Miss Nolan put her head into the office. "Miss Nolan," George said, "get me Hank Ramarau; I want to find out—"

"Mr. Ramarau is waiting on the other line," Miss Nolan said. "He says it's urgent."

Switching to the other line, George said, "Hi, Hank. What's up?"

"I've just discovered," his top legal advisor said, "that to operate your factory on Io you must be a citizen of Titan."

"We ought to be able to fix that up," George said.

"But to be a citizen of Titan—" Ramarau hesitated. "I'll break it to you as easy as I can, George. You have to be a Blobel!"

"Damn it, I am a Blobel!" George said. "At least part of the time. Won't that do?"

"No," Ramarau said, "I checked into that, knowing of your affliction, and it's got to be one hundred percent of the time. Night *and* day."

"Hmmm," George said, "This is bad. But we'll overcome it somehow. Listen, Hank, I've got an appointment with Eddy Fullbright, my medical coordinator. I'll talk to you after, okay?" He rang off and then sat scowling and rubbing his jaw. *Well,* he decided, *if it has to be, it has to be. Facts are facts, and we can't let them stand in our way.*

Picking up the phone he dialed his doctor, Eddy Fullbright.

IV.

The twenty-dollar platinum coin rolled down the chute and tripped the circuit. Dr. Jones came on, glanced up and saw a stunning, sharp-breasted young woman whom it recognized by means of a quick scan of its memory banks—as Mrs. George Munster, the former Vivian Arrasmith.

"Good day, Vivian," Dr. Jones said cordially. "But I understood you were on Titan." It rose to its feet, offering her a chair.

Dabbing at her large, dark eyes, Vivian sniffled, "Doctor, everything is collapsing around me. My husband is having an affair with another woman... all I know is that her name is Nina and all the boys down at VUW Headquarters are talking about it. Presumably she's a Terran. We're both filing for divorce. And we're having a dreadful legal battle over the children." She arranged her coat modestly. "I'm expecting. Our fourth."

"This I know," Dr. Jones said. "A full-blooded Terran, this time, if Mendel's Revised Law holds... although it only applied to litters."

Mrs. Munster said miserably, "I've been on Titan talking to legal and medical experts, gynecologists, and especially marital guidance counselors; I've had all sorts of advice the past month. Now I'm back on Terra but I can't find George—he's *gone.*"

"I wish I could help you, Vivian," Dr. Jones said. "I talked to your husband briefly, the other day, but he spoke only in generalities . . . evidently he's such a big tycoon now that it's hard to approach him."

"And to think," Vivian sniffled, "that he achieved it all because of an idea *I* gave him. A Blobel idea."

"The ironies of fate," Dr. Jones said. "Now, if you want to keep your husband, Vivian—"

"I'm determined to keep him, Doctor Jones. Frankly, I've undergone therapy on Titan, the latest and most expensive . . . it's because I love George so much, even more than I love my people or my planet."

"Eh?" Dr. Jones said.

"Through the most modern developments in medical science in the Sol System," Vivian said, "I've been stabilized, Dr. Jones. Now I am in human form twenty-four hours a day instead of eighteen. I've renounced my natural form in order to keep my marriage with George."

"The supreme sacrifice," Dr. Jones said, touched.

"Now if I can only *find* him, Doctor—"

At the ground-breaking ceremonies in Io, George Munster flowed gradually to the shovel, extended a pseudopodium, seized the shovel, and with it managed to dig a symbolic amount of soil. "This is a great day," he boomed hollowly, by means of a semblance of a vocal apparatus into which he had fashioned the slimy, plastic substance which made up his unicellular body.

"Right, George," Hank Ramarau agreed, standing nearby with the legal documents.

The Ionan official, like George a great, transparent blob, oozed across to Ramarau, took the documents, and boomed, "These will be transmitted to my government. I'm sure they're in order, Mr. Ramarau."

"I guarantee you," Ramarau said to the official, "Mr. Munster does not revert to human form at any time; he's made use of some of the most advanced techniques in medical science to achieve this stability at the unicellular phase of his former rotation. Munster would never cheat."

"This historic moment," the great blob that was George Munster thought-radiated to the throng of local Blobels attending the ceremonies, "means a higher standard of living for Ionans who will be employed; it will bring prosperity to this area, plus a proud sense of national achievement in the manufacture of what we recognize to be a native invention, the Munster Magic Magnetic Belt."

The throng of Blobels thought-radiated cheers.

"This is a proud day in my life," George Munster informed them, and began to ease by degrees back to his car, where his chauffeur waited to drive him to his permanent hotel room at Io City.

Someday he would own the hotel. He was putting the profits from his business in local real estate; it was the patriotic—and the profitable—thing to do, other Ionans, other Blobels, had told him.

"I'm finally a successful man," George Munster thought-radiated to all those close enough to pick up his emanations.

Amid frenzied cheers he oozed up the ramp and into his Titan-made car.

THE BALLAD OF LOST C'MELL

BY CORDWAINER SMITH

One of the great pleasures of editing science-fiction is meeting the writers. Well, some of the writers. In the science-fiction community, as in most, there are a few who are not easy to love. But then there are the ones like Cordwainer Smith. Smith's stories are complex, unique, and delightful. So, exactly, was the man who wrote them.

His real name was Paul M. A. Linebarger. In the part of his life not involved in science fiction, he was a professor of political science at Johns Hopkins. There are many other writers who are college professors, and even political scientists, but Paul Linebarger was something special. Besides being an academic of distinction, he was a State Department consultant on both Middle Eastern and Oriental matters, and his knowledge of both came at first hand. He was born in China. On the wall of his living room, in his home just off Rock Creek Park in Washington, hung a great gold and scarlet calligraphed birth scroll from his godfather, who was Sun Yat Sen, the founder of the Chinese Republic. From time to time, the State Department called on Paul to explain foreign policy to foreign diplomats. He said modestly, "The reason they do it is that I can talk m-o-r-e s—l—o—w—l—y than anyone else around, so they understand me." But I don't think that was the reason.

As editor of Galaxy *I published almost every word Paul Linebarger wrote until his death, and was delighted to do so. But he delighted me in other ways. Shortly after he died, I had dinner with a rather stuffy man who happened to be the American ambassador in the little European country I was in. He did his best to be civil, but it was clearly hard for him to accept the presence of the kind of person who wrote that crazy science-fiction stuff. So I took the occasion to describe the Cordwainer Smith stories—laminated mouse brains, Norstrilian longevity* stroon, *and all. Then I asked him if he had ever heard of Paul Linebarger. Of course he had; Linebarger was his mentor when he was just a pup. And then I laid it on him. . . .*

* * *

She got the which of the what-she-did,
Hid the bell with a blot, she did,
But she fell in love with a hominid.
Where is the which of the what-she-did?
—From "The Ballad of Lost C'mell"

She was a girly girl and they were true men, the lords of creation, but she pitted her wits against them and she won. It had never happened before, and it is sure never to happen again, but she did win. She was not even of human extraction. She was cat-derived, though human in outward shape, which explains the C in front of her name. Her father's name was C'mackintosh and her name was C'mell. She won her trick against the lawful and assembled Lords of the Instrumentality.

It all happened at Earthport, greatest of buildings, smallest of cities, standing twenty-five kilometers high at the western edge of the Smaller Sea of Earth.

Jestocost had an office outside the fourth valve.

I.

Jestocost liked the morning sunshine, while most of the other Lords of the Instrumentality did not, so that he had no trouble in keeping the office and the apartments which he had selected. His main office was ninety meters deep, twenty meters high, twenty meters broad. Behind it was the "fourth valve," almost a thousand hectares in extent. It was shaped helically, like an enormous snail. Jestocost's apartment, big as it was, was merely one of the pigeon-holes in the muffler on the rim of Earthport. Earthport stood like an enormous wineglass, reaching from the magma to the high atmosphere.

Earthport had been built during mankind's biggest mechanical splurge. Though men had had nuclear rockets since the beginning of consecutive history, they had used chemical rockets to load the interplanetary ion-drive and nuclear-drive vehicles or to assemble the photonic sail-ships for interstellar cruises. Impatient with the troubles of taking things bit by bit into the sky, they had worked out a billion-ton rocket, only to find that it ruined whatever countryside it touched in landing. The Daimoni—people of Earth extraction, who came back from somewhere beyond the stars—had helped men build it of weatherproof, rustproof, timeproof, stressproof material. Then they had gone away and had never come back.

Jestocost often looked around his apartment and wondered what it might have been like when white-hot gas, muted to a whisper, surged out of the valve into his own chamber and the sixty-four other chambers like it. Now he had a back wall of heavy timber, and the valve itself was a great hollow cave where a few wild things lived. Nobody needed that much space any more. The chambers were useful, but the valve did nothing. Planoforming ships whispered in from the stars; they landed at Earthport as a matter of legal convenience, but they made no noise and they certainly had no hot gases.

Jestocost looked at the high clouds far below him and talked to himself, "Nice day. Good air. No trouble. Better eat."

Jestocost often talked like that to himself. He was an individual, almost an eccentric. One of the top council of mankind, he had problems, but they were not personal problems. He had a Rembrandt hanging above his bed—the only Rembrandt known in the world, just as he was possibly the only person who could appreciate a Rembrandt. He had the tapestries of a forgotten empire hanging from his back wall. Every morning the sun played a grand opera for him, muting and lighting and shifting the colors so that he could almost imagine that the old days of quarrel, murder, and high drama had come back to Earth again. He had a copy of Shakespeare, a copy of Colegrove, and two pages of the Book of Ecclesiastes in a locked box beside his bed. Only forty-two people in the universe could read Ancient English, and he was one of them. He drank wine, which he had made by his own robots in his own vineyards on the Sunset coast. He was a man, in short, who had arranged his own life to live comfortably, selfishly, and well on the personal side, so that he could give generously and impartially of his talents on the official side.

When he awoke on this particular morning, he had no idea that a beautiful girl was about to fall hopelessly in love with him—that he would find, after a hundred years and more of experience in government, another government on Earth just as strong and almost as ancient as his own—that he would willingly fling himself into conspiracy and danger for a cause which he only half understood. All these things were mercifully hidden from him by time, so that his only question on arising was, should he or should he not have a small cup of white wine with his breakfast. On the one hundred and seventy-third day of each year, he always made a point of eating eggs. They were a rare treat, and he did not want to spoil himself by having too many, nor to deprive himself and forget a treat by having none at all. He puttered around the room, muttering, "White wine? White wine?"

C'mell was coming into his life, but he did not know it. She was fated to win; that part, she herself did not know.

Ever since mankind had gone through the Rediscovery of Man, bringing back governments, money, newspapers, national languages, sickness, and occasional death, there had been the problem of the underpeople—people who were not human, but merely humanly shaped from the stock of Earth animals. They could speak, sing, read, write, work, love, and die; but they were not covered by human law, which simply defined them as "homunculi" and gave them a legal status close to animals or robots. Real people from off-world were always called "hominids."

Most of the underpeople did their jobs and accepted their half-slave status without question. Some became famous—C'mackintosh had been the first Earth-being to manage a thousand-meter broad-jump under normal gravity. His picture was seen in a thousand worlds. His daughter, C'mell, was a girly girl, earning her living by welcoming human beings and hominids from the outworlds and making them feel at home when they reached Earth. She had the privilege of working at Earthport, but she had the duty of working very hard for a living which did not pay well. Human beings and hominids had lived so long in an affluent society that they did not know what it meant to be poor. But the Lords of the Instrumentality had decreed that underpeople— derived from animal stock—should live under the economics of the Ancient World; they had to have their own kind of money to pay for their rooms, their food, their possessions, and the education of their children. If they became bankrupt, they went to the Poorhouse, where they were killed painlessly by means of gas.

It was evident that humanity, having settled all of its own basic problems, was not quite ready to let Earth animals, no matter how much they might be changed, assume a full equality with man.

The Lord Jestocost, seventh of that name, opposed the policy. He was a man who had little love, no fear, freedom from ambition, and a dedication to his job: but there are passions of government as deep and challenging as the emotions of love. Two hundred years of thinking himself right and of being outvoted had instilled in Jestocost a furious desire to get things done his own way.

Jestocost was one of the few true men who believed in the rights of the underpeople. He did not think that mankind would ever get around to correcting ancient wrongs unless the underpeople themselves had some of the tools of power—weapons, conspiracy, wealth, and (above all) organization with which to challenge man. He was not afraid of revolt, but he thirsted for justice with an obsessive yearning which overrode all other considerations.

When the Lords of the Instrumentality heard that there was the rumor of a conspiracy among the underpeople, they left it to the robot police to ferret out.

Jestocost did not.

He set up his own police, using underpeople themselves for the purpose, hoping to recruit enemies who would realize that he was a friendly enemy and who would, in course of time, bring him into touch with the leaders of the underpeople.

If those leaders existed, they were clever. What sign did a girly girl like C'mell ever give that she was the spearhead of a crisscross of agents who had penetrated Earthport itself? They must, if they existed, be very, very careful. The telepathic monitors, both robotic and human, kept every thought-band under surveillance by random sampling. Even the computers showed nothing more significant than improbable amounts of happiness in minds which had no objective reason for being happy.

The death of her father, the most famous cat-athlete which the underpeople had ever produced, gave Jestocost his first definite clue.

He went to the funeral himself, where the body was packed in an ice-rocket to be shot into space. The mourners were thoroughly mixed with the curiosity-seekers. Sport is international, inter-race, inter-world, inter-species. Hominids were there: true men, one hundred percent human, they looked weird and horrible because they or their ancestors had undergone bodily modifications to meet the life conditions of a thousand worlds.

Underpeople, the animal-derived "homunculi," were there, most of them in their work clothes, and they looked more human than did the human beings from the outer worlds. None were allowed to grow up if they were less than half the size of man, or more than six times the size of man. They all had to have human features and acceptable human voices. The punishment for failure in their elementary schools was death. Jestocost looked over the crowd and wondered to himself, *We have set up the standards of the toughest kind of survival for these people and we give them the most terrible incentive, life itself, as the condition of absolute progress. What fools we are to think that they will not overtake us!* The true people in the group did not seem to think as he did. They tapped the underpeople peremptorily with their canes, even though this was an underperson's funeral, and the bear-men, bull-men, cat-men and others yielded immediately and with a babble of apology.

C'mell was close to her father's icy coffin.

Jestocost not only watched her; she was pretty to watch. He committed an act which was an indecency in an ordinary citizen but lawful for a Lord of the Instrumentality: he peeped her mind.

And then he found something which he did not expect.

As the coffin left, she cried, "Ee-telly-kelly, help me! Help me!"

She had thought phonetically, not in script, and he had only the raw sound on which to base a search.

Jestocost had not become a Lord of the Instrumentality without applying daring. His mind was quick, too quick to be deeply intelligent. He thought by gestalt, not by logic. He determined to force his friendship on the girl.

He decided to await a propitious occasion, and then changed his mind about the time.

As she went home from the funeral, he intruded upon the circle of her grimfaced friends, underpeople who were trying to shield her from the condolences of ill-mannered but well-meaning sports enthusiasts.

She recognized him, and showed him the proper respect.

"My Lord, I did not expect you here. You knew my father?"

He nodded gravely and addressed sonorous words of consolation and sorrow, words which brought a murmur of approval from humans and underpeople alike.

But with his left hand hanging slack at his side, he made the perpetual symbol of *alarm! alarm!* used within the Earthport staff—a repeated tapping of the thumb against the third finger—when they had to set one another on guard without alerting the offworld transients.

She was so upset that she almost spoiled it all. While he was still doing his pious doubletalk, she cried in a loud, clear voice:

"You mean *me?*"

And he went on with his condolences: ". . . and I do mean *you,* C'mell, to be the worthiest carrier of your father's name. *You* are the one to whom we turn in this time of common sorrow. *Who could I mean but you* if I say that C'mackintosh never did things by halves, and died young as a result of his own zealous conscience? Good-bye, C'mell, I go back to my office."

She arrived forty minutes after he did.

II.

He faced her straight away, studying her face.

"This is an important day in your life."

"Yes, My Lord, a sad one."

"I do not," he said, "mean your father's death and burial. I speak of the future to which we all must turn. Right now, it's you and me."

Her eyes widened. She had not thought he was that kind of man at all. He was an official who moved freely around Earthport, often greeting important offworld visitors and keeping an eye on the bureau of ceremonies. She was a part of the reception team, when a girly girl was needed to calm down a frustrated arrival or to postpone a quarrel. Like the geisha of ancient Japan, she had an honorable profession; she was not a bad girl but a professionally flirtatious hostess. She stared at Lord Jestocost. He did not *look* as though he meant anything improperly personal. *But,* thought she, *you can never tell about men.*

"You know men," he said, passing the initiative to her.

"I guess so," she said. Her face looked odd. She started to give him smile #3 (extremely adhesive) which she had learned in the girly-girl school. Realizing it was wrong, she tried to give him an ordinary smile. She felt she had made a face at him.

"Look at me," he said, "and see if you can trust me. I am going to take both our lives in my hands."

She looked at him. What imaginable subject could involve him, a Lord of the Instrumentality, with herself, an undergirl? They never had anything in common. They never would.

But she stared at him.

"I want to help the underpeople."

He made her blink. That was a crude approach, usually followed by a very raw kind of pass indeed. But his face was illuminated by seriousness. She waited.

"Your people do not have enough political power even to talk to us. I will not commit treason to the true-human race, but I am willing to give your side an advantage. If you bargain better with us, it will make all forms of life safer in the long run."

C'mell stared at the floor, her red hair soft as the fur of a Persian cat. It made her head seemed bathed in flames. Her eyes looked human, except that they had the capacity of reflecting when light struck them; the irises were the rich green of the ancient cat. When she looked right at him, looking up from the floor, her glance had the impact of a blow. "What do you want from me?"

He stared right back. "Watch me. Look at my face. Are you sure, *sure* that I want nothing from you personally?"

She looked bewildered. "What else is there to want from me except personal things? I am a girly girl. I'm not a person of any importance at all, and I do not have much of an education. You know more, sir, than I will ever know."

"Possibly," he said, watching her.

She stopped feeling like a girly girl and felt like a citizen. It made her uncomfortable.

"Who," he said, in a voice of great solemnity, "is your own leader?"

"Commissioner Teadrinker, sir. He's in charge of all outworld visitors." She watched Jestocost carefully; he still did not look as if he were playing tricks.

He looked a little cross. "I don't mean him. He's part of my own staff. Who's your leader among the underpeople?"

"My father was, but he died."

Jestocost said, "Forgive me. Please have a seat. But I don't mean that."

She was so tired that she sat down into the chair with an innocent voluptuousness which would have disorganized any ordinary man's day. She wore girly girl clothes, which were close enough to the everyday fashion to seem agreeably modish when she stood up. In line with her profession, her clothes were designed to be unexpectedly and provocatively revealing when she sat down—not revealing enough to shock the man with their brazenness, but so slit, tripped, and cut that he got far more visual stimulation than he expected.

"I must ask you to pull your clothing together a little," said Jestocost in a clinical turn of voice. "I am a man, even if I am an official, and this interview is more important to you and to me than any distraction would be."

She was a little frightened by his tone. She had meant no challenge. With the funeral that day, she meant nothing at all; these clothes were the only kind she had.

He read all this in her face.

Relentlessly, he pursued the subject.

"Young lady, I asked about your leader. You name your boss and you name your father. I want your leader."

"I don't understand," she said, on the edge of a sob, "I don't understand."

Then, he thought to himself, *I've got to take a gamble*. He thrust the mental dagger home, almost drove his words like steel straight into her face. "Who . . ." he said, slowly and icily, "is . . . Ee . . . telly . . . kelly?"

The girl's face had been cream-colored, pale with sorrow. Now she went white. She twisted away from him. Her eyes glowed like twin fires.

Her eyes . . . like twin fires.

(*No undergirl*, thought Jestocost as he reeled, *could hypnotize me*.)

Her eyes . . . were like cold fires.

The room faded around him. The girl disappeared. Her eyes became a single white, cold fire.

Within this fire stood the figure of a man. His arms were wings, but he had human hands growing at the elbows of his wings. His face was clear, white, cold as the marble of an ancient statue; his eyes were opaque white. "I am the E-telekeli. You will believe in me. You may speak to my daughter, C'mell."

The image faded.

Jestocost saw the girl staring as she sat awkwardly on the chair, looking blindly through him. He was on the edge of making a joke about her hypnotic capacity when he saw that she was still deeply hypnotized, even after he had been released. She had stiffened and again her clothing had fallen into its planned disarray. The effect was not stimulating; it was pathetic beyond words, as though an accident had happened to a pretty child. He spoke to her.

He spoke to her, not really expecting an answer.

"Who are you?" he said to her, testing her hypnosis.

"I am he whose name is never said aloud," said the girl in a sharp whisper, "I am he whose secret you have penetrated. I have printed my image and my name in your mind."

Jestocost did not quarrel with ghosts like this. He snapped out a decision. "If I open my mind, will you search it while I watch you? Are you good enough to do that?"

"I am very good," hissed the voice in the girl's mouth.

C'mell arose and put her two hands on his shoulders. She looked into his eyes. He looked back. A strong telepath himself, Jestocost was not prepared for the enormous thought-voltage which poured out of her.

Look in my mind, he commanded, *for the subject of* underpeople *only*.

I see it, thought the mind behind C'mell.

Do you see what I mean to do for the underpeople?

Jestocost heard the girl breathing hard as her mind served as a relay to his. He tried to remain calm so that he could see which part of his mind was being searched. *Very good so far*, he thought to himself. *An intelligence like that on Earth itself*, he thought—*and we of the Lords not knowing it!*

The girl hacked out a dry little laugh.

Jestocost thought at the mind, *Sorry. Go ahead*.

This plan of yours—thought the strange mind—*may I see more of it? That's all there is*.

Oh, said the strange mind, *you want me to think for you. Can you give me the keys in the Bank and Bell which pertain to destroying underpeople?*

You can have the information keys if I can ever get them, thought Jestocost, *but not the control keys and not the master switch of the Bell.*

Fair enough, thought the other mind, *and what do I pay for them?*

You support me in my policies before the Instrumentality. You keep the underpeople reasonable, if you can, when the time comes to negotiate. You maintain honor and good faith in all subsequent agreements. But how can I get the keys? It would take me a year to figure them out myself.

Let the girl look once, thought the strange mind, *and I will be behind her. Fair?*

Fair, thought Jestocost.

Break? thought the mind.

How do we re-connect? thought Jestocost back.

As before. Through the girl. Never say my name. Don't think it if you can help it. Break?

Break! thought Jestocost.

The girl, who had been holding his shoulders, drew his face down and kissed him firmly and warmly. He had never touched an underperson before, and it never had occurred to him that he might kiss one. It was pleasant, but he took her arms away from his neck, half-turned her around, and let her lean against him.

"Daddy!" she sighed happily.

Suddenly she stiffened, looked at his face, and sprang for the door. "Jestocost!" she cried. "Lord Jestocost! What am I doing here?"

"Your duty is done, my girl. You may go."

She staggered back into the room. "I am going to be sick," she said. She vomited on his floor.

He pushed a button for a cleaning robot and slapped his desktop for coffee.

She relaxed and talked about his hopes for the underpeople. She stayed an hour. By the time she left, they had a plan. Neither of them had mentioned E-telekeli; neither had put purposes in the open. If the monitors had been listening, they would have found no single sentence or paragraph which was suspicious.

When she had gone, Jestocost looked out of his window. He saw the clouds far below and he knew the world below him was in twilight. He had planned to help the underpeople, and he had met powers of which organized mankind had no conception or perception. He was righter than he had thought. He had to go on through.

But as partner—C'mell herself!

Was there ever an odder diplomat in the history of worlds?

III.

In less than a week, they had decided what to do. It was the Council of the Lords of the Instrumentality at which they would work—the brain center itself. The risk was high, but the entire job could be done in a few minutes if it were done at the Bell itself.

This is the sort of thing which interested Jestocost.

He did not know that C'mell watched him with two different facets of her mind. One side of her was alertly and wholeheartedly his fellow-conspirator, utterly in sympathy with the revolutionary aims to which they were both committed. The other side of her—was feminine.

She had a womanliness which was truer than that of any hominid woman. She knew the value of her trained smile, her splendidly kept red hair with its unimaginable soft texture, her lithe young figure with firm breasts and persuasive hips. She knew down to the last millimeter the effect which her legs had on hominid men. True humans kept few secrets from her. The men betrayed themselves by their unfulfillable desires, the women by their irrepressible jealousies. But she knew people best of all by not being one herself. She had to learn by imitation, and imitation is conscious. A thousand little things which ordinary women took for granted, or thought about just once in a whole lifetime, were subjects of acute and intelligent study to her. She was a girl by profession; she was a human by assimilation; she was an inquisitive cat in her genetic nature. Now she was falling in love with Jestocost, and she knew it.

Even she did not realize that the romance would sometime leak out into rumor, be magnified into legend, distilled into romance. She had no idea of the ballad about herself that would open with the lines which became famous much later:

> She got the which of the what-she-did,
> Hid the bell with a blot, she did,
> But she fell in love with a hominid.
> Where is the which of the what-she-did?

All this lay in the future, and she did not know it.

She knew her own past.

She remembered the off-Earth prince who had rested his head in her lap and had said, sipping his glass of *motl* by way of farewell:

"Funny, C'mell, you're not even a person and you're the most intelligent human being I've met in this place. Do you know it made my planet poor to send me here? And what did I get out of them? Nothing, nothing, and a thousand times nothing. But you, now. If you'd been running the government of Earth, I'd have gotten what my people need, and this world would be richer, too. 'Manhome,' they call it. Manhome, my eye! The only smart person on it is a female cat."

He ran his fingers around her ankle. She did not stir. That was part of hospitality, and she had her own ways of making sure that hospitality did not go too far. Earth police were watching her; to them, she was a convenience maintained for outworld people, something like a soft chair in the Earthport lobbies or a drinking fountain with acid-tasting water for strangers who could not tolerate the insipid water of Earth. She was not expected to have feelings or to get involved. If she had ever caused an incident, they would have punished her fiercely, as they often punished animals or underpeople, or else (after a short formal hearing with no appeal) they would have destroyed her, as the law allowed and custom encouraged.

She had kissed a thousand men, maybe fifteen hundred. She had made them feel welcome and she had gotten their complaints or their secrets out of them as they left. It was a living, emotionally tiring but intellectually very stimulating. Sometimes it made her laugh to look at human women with their pointed-up noses and their proud airs, and to realize that she knew more about the men who belonged to the human women than the human women themselves ever did.

Once a policewoman had had to read over the record of two pioneers from New Mars. C'mell had been given the job of keeping in very close touch with them. When the policewoman got through reading the report, she looked at C'mell and her face was distorted with jealousy and prudish rage.

"Cat, you call yourself. Cat! You're a pig, you're a dog, you're an animal. You may be working for Earth, but don't ever get the idea that you're as good as a person. I think it's a crime that the Instrumentality lets monsters like you greet real human beings from outside! I can't stop it. But may the Bell help you, girl, if you ever touch a real Earth man! If you ever get near one! If you ever try tricks here! Do you understand me?"

"Yes, ma'am," C'mell had said. To herself she thought, *That poor thing doesn't know how to select her own clothes or how to do her own hair. No wonder she resents somebody who manages to be pretty.*

Perhaps the policewoman thought that raw hatred would be shocking to C'mell. It wasn't. Underpeople were used to hatred, and it was not any worse raw than it was when cooked with politeness and served like poison. They had to live with it.

But now, it was all changed.

She had fallen in love with Jestocost.

Did he love her?

Impossible. No, not impossible. Unlawful, likely, indecent—yes, all these, but not impossible. Surely he felt something of her love.

If he did, he gave no sign of it.

People and underpeople had fallen in love many times before. The underpeople were always destroyed and the real people brainwashed. There were laws against that kind of thing. The scientists among people had created the underpeople, had given them capacities which real people did not have (the thousand-yard jump, the telepath two miles underground, the turtle-man waiting a thousand years next to an emergency door, the cow-man guarding a gate without reward), and the scientists had also given many of the underpeople the human shape. It was handier that way. The human eye, the five-fingered hand, the human size—these were convenient for engineering reasons. By making underpeople the same size and shape as people, more or less, the scientists eliminated the need for two or three or a dozen different sets of furniture. The human form was good enough for all of them.

But they had forgotten the human heart.

And now she, C'mell, had fallen in love with a man, a true man old enough to have been her own father's grandfather.

But she didn't feel daughterly about him at all. She remembered that with her own father there was an easy comradeship, an innocent and forthcoming affection, which masked the fact that he was considerably more catlike than she was. Between them there was an aching void of forever-unspoken words—things that couldn't quite be said by either of them, perhaps things that couldn't be said at all. They were so close to each other that they could get no closer. This created enormous distance, which was heartbreaking but unutterable. Her father had died, and now this true man was here, with all the kindness—

That's it, she whispered to herself, with all the kindness that none of these passing men have ever really shown. With all the depth which my poor underpeople can never get. Not that it's not in them. But they're born like dirt, treated like dirt, put away like dirt when we die. How can any of my own men develop real kindness? There's a special sort of majesty to kindness. It's the best part there is to being people. And he has whole oceans of it in him. And it's strange, strange, strange that he's never given his real love to any human woman.

She stopped, cold.

Then she consoled herself and whispered on, *Or if he did, it's so long ago that it doesn't matter now. He's got me. Does he know it?*

IV.

The Lord Jestocost did know, and yet he didn't. He was used to getting loyalty from people, because he offered loyalty and honor in his daily work. He was even familiar with loyalty becoming obsessive and seeking physical form, particularly from women, children, and underpeople. He had always coped with it before. He was gambling on the fact that C'mell was a wonderfully intelligent person, and that as a girly girl, working on the hospitality staff of the Earthport police, she must have learned to control her personal feelings.

We're born in the wrong age, he thought, *when I meet the most intelligent and beautiful female I've ever met, and then have to put business first. But this stuff about people and underpeople is sticky. Sticky. We've got to keep personalities out of it.*

So he thought. Perhaps he was right.

If the nameless one, whom he did not dare to remember, commanded an attack on the Bell itself, that was worth their lives. Their emotions could not come into it. The Bell mattered; justice mattered; the perpetual return of mankind to progress mattered. He did not matter, because he had already done most of his work. C'mell did not matter, because their failure would leave her with mere underpeople forever. The Bell did count.

The price of what he proposed to do was high, but the entire job could be done in a few minutes if it were done at the Bell itself.

The Bell, of course, was not a Bell. It was a three-dimensional situation table, three times the height of a man. It was set one story below the meeting room, and shaped roughly like an ancient bell. The meeting table of the Lords of the Instrumentality had a circle cut out of it, so that the Lords could look down into the Bell at whatever situation one of them called up either manually or telepathically. The Bank below it, hidden by the floor, was the key memory-bank of the entire system. Duplicates existed at thirty-odd other places on Earth. Two duplicates lay hidden in interstellar space, one of them beside the ninety-million-mile gold-colored ship left over from the War against Raumsog and the other masked as an asteroid.

Most of the Lords were offworld on the business of the Instrumentality.

Only three beside Jestocost were present—The Lord Johanna Gnade, the Lord Issan Olascoaga, and the Lord William Not-from-here. (The Not-from-heres were a great Norstrilian family which had migrated back to Earth many generations before.)

The E-telekeli told Jestocost the rudiments of a plan.

He was to bring C'mell into the chambers on a summons.

The summons was to be serious.

They should avoid her summary death by automatic justice, if the relays began to trip.

C'mell would go into partial trance in the chamber.

He was then to call the items in the Bell which E-telekeli wanted traced. A single call would be enough. E-telekeli would take the responsibility for tracing them. The other Lords would be distracted by him, E-telekeli.

It was simple in appearance.

The complication came in action.

The plan seemed flimsy, but there was nothing which Jestocost could do at this time. He began to curse himself for letting his passion for policy involve him in the intrigue. It was too late to back out with honor; besides, he had given his word; besides, he liked C'mell—as a being, not as a girly girl—and he would hate to see her marked with disappointment for life. He knew how the underpeople cherished their identities and their status.

With heavy heart but quick mind, he went to the council chamber. A dog-girl, one of the routine messengers whom he had seen many months outside the door, gave him the minutes.

He wondered how C'mell or E-telekeli would reach him, once he was inside the chamber with its tight net of telepathic intercepts.

He saw wearily at the table—

And almost jumped out of his chair.

*　　*　　*

The conspirators had forged the minutes themselves, and the top item was: "C'mell, daughter to C'mackintosh, cat-stock (pure) lot 1138, confession of. Subject: conspiracy to export homuncular material. Reference: planet De Prinsensmacht."

The Lady Johanna Gnade had already pushed the buttons for the planet concerned. The people there, Earth by origin, were enormously strong but they had gone to great pains to maintain the original Earth appearance. One of their first-men was at the moment on Earth. He bore the title of the Twilight Prince (Prins van de Schemering) and he was on a mixed diplomatic and trading mission.

Since Jestocost was a little late, C'mell was being brought into the room as he glanced over the minutes.

The Lord Not-from-here asked Jestocost if he would preside.

"I beg you, sir and scholar," he said, "to join me in asking the Lord Issan to preside this time."

The presidency was a formality. Jestocost could watch the Bell and Bank better if he did not have to chair the meeting, too.

C'mell wore the clothing of a prisoner. On her it looked good. He had never seen her wearing anything but girly-girl clothes before. The pale-blue prison tunic made her look very young, very human, very tender, and very frightened. The cat family showed only in the fiery cascade of her hair and the lithe power of her body as she sat, demure and erect.

Lord Issan asked her: "You have confessed. Confess again."

"This man," and she pointed at a picture of the Twilight Prince, "wanted to go to the place where they torment human children for a show."

"What!" cried three of the Lords together.

"What place?" said the Lady Johanna, who was bitterly in favor of kindness.

"It's run by a man who looks like this gentleman here," said C'mell, pointing at Jestocost. Quickly, so that nobody could stop her, but modestly, so that none of them thought to doubt her, she circled the room and touched Jestocost's shoulder. He felt a thrill of contact-telepathy and heard bird-crackle in her brain. Then he knew that the E-telekeli was in touch with her.

"The man who has the place," said C'mell, "is five pounds lighter than this gentleman, two inches shorter, and he has red hair. His place is at the Cold Sunset corner of Earthport, down the boulevard and under the boulevard. Underpeople, some of them with bad reputations, live in that neighborhood."

The Bell went milky, flashing through hundreds of combinations of bad underpeople in that part of the city. Jestocost felt himself staring at the casual milkiness with unwanted concentration.

The Bell cleared.

It showed the vague image of a room in which children were playing Halloween tricks.

The Lady Johanna laughed, "Those aren't people. They're robots. It's just a dull old play."

"Then," added C'mell, "he wanted a dollar and a shilling to take home. Real ones. There was a robot who had found some."

"What are those?" said Lord Issan.

"Ancient money—the real money of old America and old Australia," cried Lord William. "I have copies, but there are no originals outside the state museum." He was an ardent, passionate collector of coins.

"The robot found them in an old hiding place right under Earthport."

Lord William almost shouted at the Bell. "Run through every hiding place and get me that money."

The Bell clouded. In finding the bad neighborhoods it had flashed every police point in the Northwest sector of the tower. Now it scanned all the police points under the tower, and ran dizzily through thousands of combinations before it settled on an old toolroom. A robot was polishing circular pieces of metal.

When Lord William saw the polishing, he was furious. "Get that here," he shouted. "I want to buy those myself!"

"All right," said Lord Issan. "It's a little irregular, but all right."

The machine showed the key search devices and brought the robot to the escalator.

The Lord Issan said, "This isn't much of a case."

C'mell sniveled. She was a good actress. "Then he wanted me to get a homunculus egg. One of the E-type, derived from birds, for him to take home."

Issan put on the search device.

"Maybe," said C'mell, "somebody has already put it in the disposal series."

The Bell and the Bank ran through all the disposal devices at high speed. Jestocost felt his nerves go on edge. No human being could have memorized these thousands of patterns as they flashed across the Bell too fast for human eyes, but the brain reading the Bell through his eyes was not human. It might even be locked into a computer of its own. *It was,* thought Jestocost, *an indignity for a Lord of the Instrumentality to be used as a human spy-glass.*

The machine blotted up.

"You're a fraud," cried the Lord Issan. "There's no evidence."

"Maybe the offworlder tried," said the Lady Johanna.

"Shadow him," said Lord William. "If he would steal ancient coins, he would steal anything."

The Lady Johanna turned to C'mell. "You're a silly thing. You have wasted our time and you have kept us from serious inter-world business."

"It *is* inter-world business," wept C'mell. She let her hand slip from Jestocost's shoulder, where it had rested all the time. The body-to-body relay broke and the telepathic link broke with it.

"We should judge that," said Lord Issan.

"You might have been punished," said Lady Johanna.

The Lord Jestocost had said nothing, but there was a glow of happiness in him. If the E-telekeli was half as good as he seemed, the underpeople had a list of checkpoints and escape routes which would make it easier to hide from the capricious sentence of painless death which human authorities meted out.

V.

There was singing in the corridors that night.

Underpeople burst into happiness for no visible reason.

C'mell danced a wild cat dance for the next customer who came in from outworld stations, that very evening. When she got home to bed, she knelt before the picture of her father C'mackintosh and thanked the E-telekeli for what Jestocost had done.

But the story became known a few generations later, when the Lord Jestocost had won acclaim for being the champion of the underpeople and when the authorities, still unaware of E-telekeli, accepted the elected representatives of the underpeople as negotiators for better terms of life; and C'mell had died long since.

She had first had a long, good life.

She became a female chef when she was too old to be a girly girl. Her food was famous. Jestocost once visited her. At the end of the meal he had asked, "There's a silly rhyme among the underpeople. No human beings know it except me."

"I don't care about rhymes," she said.

"This is called 'The what-she-did.' "

C'mell blushed all the way down to the neckline of her capacious blouse. She had filled out a lot in middle age. Running the restaurant had helped.

"Oh, that rhyme!" she said. "It's silly."

"It says you were in love with a hominid."

"No," she said. "I wasn't." Her green eyes, as beautiful as ever, stared deeply into his. Jestocost felt uncomfortable. This was getting personal. He liked political relationships; personal things made him uncomfortable.

The light in the room shifted and her cat eyes blazed at him, she looked like the magical fire-haired girl he had known.

"I wasn't in love. You couldn't call it that . . . ."

Her heart cried out, *It was you, it was you, it was you.*

"But the rhyme," insisted Jestocost, "says it was a hominid. It wasn't that Prins van de Schemering?"

"Who was he?" C'mell asked the question quietly, but her emotions cried out, *Darling, will you never, never know?*

"The strong man."

"Oh, him. I've forgotten him."

Jestocost rose from the table. "You've had a good life, C'mell. You've been a citizen, a committeewoman, a leader. And do you even know how many children you have had?"

"Seventy-three," she snapped at him. "Just because they're multiple doesn't mean we don't know them."

His playfulness left him. His face was grave, his voice kindly. "I meant no harm, C'mell."

He never knew that when he left she went back to the kitchen and cried for a while. It was Jestocost whom she had vainly loved ever since they had been comrades, many long years ago.

Even after she died, at the full age of five-score-and-three, he kept seeing her about the corridors and shafts of Earthport. Many of her great-granddaughters looked just like her and several of them practiced the girly-girl business with huge success.

They were not half-slaves. They were citizens (reserved grade) and they had photopasses which protected their property, their identity, and their rights. Jestocost was the godfather to them all; he was often embarrassed when the most voluptuous creatures in the universe threw playful kisses at him. All he asked was fulfillment of his political passions, not his personal ones. He had always been in love, madly in love—

With justice itself.

At last, his own time came, and he knew that he was dying, and he was not sorry. He had had a wife, hundreds of years ago, and had loved her well; their children had passed into the generations of man.

In the ending, he wanted to know something, and he called to a nameless one (or to his successor) far beneath the ground. He called with his mind till it was a scream.

I have helped your people.

Yes, came back the faintest of faraway whispers, inside his head.

I am dying. I must know. Did she love me?

She went on without you, so much did she love you. She let you go, for your sake, not for hers. She really loved you. More than death. More than life. More than time. You will never be apart.

Never apart?

Not, not in the memory of man, said the voice, and was then still.

Jestocost lay back on his pillow and waited for the day to end.

A GENTLE DYING

BY FREDERIK POHL AND C. M. KORNBLUTH

A person who combines the careers of editing and writing faces the permanent temptation to publish his own work. Oh, how often I have succumbed! It was not always my own fault. More often than not, when I was editing a magazine or a line of books, my publisher encouraged me, sometimes ordered me, to have it so. But I confess that was never true of anthologies. Never once did a publisher hand me an anthology contract with instructions to include myself . . . but most of the time I did it anyway.

This time I almost resisted the temptation—but, as you see, not quite.

"A Gentle Dying" is a story that has special personal significance to me. It is the story with which Cyril Kornbluth and I began collaborating. We were both in our teens at the time, and our ambitions exceeded our abilities. It was meant to be the opening chapter of a novel. After we had written the first chapter, it became obvious to us that we didn't know what to do next.

So we abandoned the fragment and went on to other things. We wrote a bunch of stories for my magazines and others in the early 1940s, then seven or eight novels, beginning with The Space Merchants, *a decade later. And then, a few years after that, Cyril suddenly and tragically died. His widow, Mary, turned over to me a stack of his papers, mostly incomplete beginnings of one story or another, and among them I found that yellowed fragment.*

After twenty years I saw that the reason we could not make a novel out of what we had wanted to say was that we'd said it all in the first chapter. With very few changes, it became "A Gentle Dying," published for the first time five years after Cyril's death.

* * *

Elphen DeBeckett lay dying. It was time. He had lived in the world for one hundred and nine years, though he had seen little enough of it except for the

258

children. The children, thank God, still came. He thought they were with him now: "Coppie," he whispered in a shriveled voice, "how nice to see you." The nurse did not look around, although she was the only person in the room besides himself, and knew that he was not addressing her.

The nurse was preparing the injections the doctor had ordered her to have ready. This little capsule for shock, this to rally his strength, these half-dozen others to shield him from his pain. Most of them would be used. DeBeckett was dying in a pain that once would have been unbearable and even now caused him to thresh about sometimes and moan.

DeBeckett's room was a great twelve-foot chamber with hanging drapes and murals that reflected scenes from his books. The man himself was tiny, gnomelike. He became even less material while death (prosey biology, the chemistry of colloids) drew inappropriately near his head. He had lived his life remote from everything a normal man surrounds himself with. He now seemed hardly alive enough to die.

DeBeckett lay in a vast, pillared bed, all the vaster for the small burden he put on it, and the white linen was whiter for his merry brown face. "Darling Veddie, please don't cry," he whispered restlessly, and the nurse took up a hypodermic syringe. He was not in unusual pain, though, and she put it back and sat down beside him.

The world had been gentle with the gentle old man. It had made him a present of this bed and this linen, this great house with its attendant horde of machines to feed and warm and comfort him, and the land on which stood the tiny, quaint houses he loved better. It had given him a park in the mountains, well stocked with lambs, deer, and birds of blazing, spectacular color, a fenced park where no one ever went but DeBeckett and the beloved children, where earth-moving machines had scooped out a Very Own Pond ("My Very Own Pond/Which I sing for you in this song/Is eight Hippopotamuses Wide/And twenty Elephants Long"). He had not seen it for years, but he knew it was there. The world had given him, most of all, money, more money than he could ever want. He had tried to give it back (gently, hopefully, in a way pathetically), but there was always more. Even now the world showered him with gifts and doctors, though neither could prevail against the stomping pitchfire arsonist in the old man's colon. The disease, a form of gastroenteritis, could have been cured; medicine had come that far long since. But not in a body that clung so lightly to life.

He opened his eyes and said strongly, "Nurse, are the children there?"

The nurse was a woman of nearly sixty. That was why she had been chosen. The new medicine was utterly beyond her in theory, but she could follow directions; and she loved Elphen DeBeckett. Her love was the love of a child, for a thumbed edition of *Coppie Brambles* had brightened her infancy. She said, "Of course they are, Mr. DeBeckett."

He smiled. The old man loved children very much. They had been his whole life. The hardest part of his dying was that nothing of his own flesh would be left, no son, no grandchild, no one. He had never married. He would have given almost anything to have a child of his blood with him now—almost anything, except the lurid, grunting price nature exacts, for DeBeckett had never known a woman. His only children were the phantoms of his books . . . and those who came to visit him. He said faintly, "Let the little sweetlings in."

The nurse slipped out and the door closed silently behind her. Six children and three adults waited patiently outside, DeBeckett's doctor among them. Quickly she gave him the dimensions of the old man's illness, pulse, and temperature, and the readings of the tiny gleaming dials by his pillow as well, though she did not know what they measured. It did not matter. She knew what the doctor was going to say before he said it: "He can't last another hour. It is astonishing that he lasted this long," he added, "but we will have lost something when he goes."

"He wants you to come in. Especially you—" She glanced around, embarrassed. "Especially you children." She had almost said "little sweetlings" herself, but did not quite dare. Only Elphen DeBeckett could talk like that, even to children. Especially to children. Especially to these children, poised, calm, beautiful, strong, and gay. Only the prettiest, sweetest children visited Elphen DeBeckett, half a dozen or a score every day, a year-in, year-out pilgrimage. He would not have noticed if they had been ugly and dull, of course. To DeBeckett all children were sweet, beautiful, and bright.

They entered and ranged themselves around the bed, and DeBeckett looked up. The eyes regarded them and a dying voice said, "Please read to me," with such resolute sweetness that it frightened. "From my book," it added, though they knew well enough what he meant.

The children looked at each other. They ranged from four to eleven, Will, Mike, blonde Celine, brown-eyed Karen, fat Freddy, and busy Pat. "You," said Pat, who was seven.

"No," said five-year-old Freddy. "Will."

"Celine," said Will. "Here."

The girl named Celine took the book from him and began obediently. " 'Coppie thought to herself—' "

"No," said Pat. "Open."

The girl opened the book, embarrassed, glancing at the dying old man. He was smiling at her without amusement, only love. She began to read:

> Coppie thought to herself that the geese might be hungry, for she herself ate Lotsandlots. Mumsie often said so, though Coppie had never found out what that mysterious food might be. She could not find any, so took some bread from Brigid Marie Ann-Erica Evangeline, the Cook Whose Name Was So Long That She Couldn't Remember It All Herself. As she walked along Dusty Path to Coppie Brambles's Very Own Pond—

Celine hesitated, looking at the old man with sharp worry, for he had moaned faintly, like a flower moaning. "No, love," he said. "Go on." The swelling soft bubble before his heart had turned on him, but he knew he still had time.

The little girl read:

> —As she walked along Dusty Path to Coppie Brambles's Very Own Pond, she thought and thought, and what she thought finally came right out of her mouth. It was a Real Gay Think, to be Thought While Charitably Feeding Geese:
> They don't make noise like little girls and boys,
> And all day long they're aswimming.
> They never fret and sputter 'cause they haven't any butter,
> They go where the water's wetly brimming.
> But say—
> Anyway—
> I
> Like
> Geese!

There was more, but the child paused and, after a moment, closed the book. DeBeckett was no longer listening. He was whispering to himself.

On the wall before him was painted a copy of one of the illustrations from the first edition of his book, a delightful picture of Coppie Brambles herself, feeding the geese, admirably showing her shyness and her trace of fear, contrasted with the loutish comedy of the geese. The old man's eyes were fixed on the picture as he whispered. They guessed he was talking to Coppie, the child of eight dressed in the fashions of eighty years ago. They could hardly hear him, but in the silence that fell on the room his voice grew stronger.

He was saying, without joy but without regret, "No more meadows, no more of the laughter of little children. But I do love them." He opened his eyes and sat up, waving the nurse away. "No, my dear," he said cheerfully, "it does not matter if I sit up now, you know. Excuse me for my rudeness. Excuse an old and tired man who, for a moment, wished to live on. I have something to say to you all."

The nurse, catching a sign from the doctor, took up another hypodermic and made it ready. "Please, Mr. DeBeckett," she said. Good humored, he permitted her to spray the surface of his wrist with a fine mist of droplets that touched the skin and penetrated it. "I suppose that is to give me strength," he said. "Well, I am grateful for it. I know I must leave you, but there is something I would like to know. I have wondered . . . For years I have wondered, but I have not been able to understand the answers when I was told them. I think I have only this one more chance."

*   *   *

He felt stronger from the fluid that now coursed through his veins, and accepted without fear the price he would have to pay for it. "As you know," he said, "or, I should say, as you children no doubt do not know, some years ago I endowed a research institution, the Coppie Brambles Foundation. I did it for the love of you, you and all of you. Last night I was reading the letter I wrote my attorneys—No. Let us see if you can understand the letter itself; I have it here. Will, can you read?"

Will was nine, freckled darkly on pale skin, red-haired, and gangling. "Yes, Mr. DeBeckett."

"Even hard words," smiled the dying man.

"Yes, sir."

DeBeckett gestured at the table beside him, and the boy obediently took up a stiff sheet of paper. "Please," said DeBeckett, and the boy began to read in a high-pitched, rapid whine.

"'Children have been all my life and I have not regretted an instant of the years I devoted to their happiness. If I can tell them a little of the wonderful world in which we are, if I can open to them the miracles of life and living, then my joy is unbounded. This I have tried, rather selfishly, to do. I cannot say it was for them! It was for me. For nothing could have given me more pleasure.'"

The boy paused.

DeBeckett said gravely, "I'm afraid this is a Very Big Think, lovelings. Please try to understand. This is the letter I wrote to my attorneys when I instructed them to set up the Foundation. Go on, Will."

"'But my way of working has been unscientific, I know. I am told that children are not less than we adults, but more. I am told that the grown-up maimers and cheats in the world are only children soiled, that the hagglers of commerce are the infant dreamers whose dreams were denied. I am told that youth is wilder, freer, better than age, which I believe with all my heart, not needing the stories of twenty-year-old mathematicians and infant Mozarts to lay a proof.

"'In the course of my work, I have been given great material rewards. I wish that this money be spent for those I love. I have worked with the heart, but perhaps my money can help someone to work with the mind, in this great new science of psychology which I do not understand, in all of the other sciences which I understand even less. I must hire other eyes.

"'I direct, then, that all my assets other than my books and my homes be converted into cash, and that this money be used to further the study of the child, with the aim of releasing him from the corrupt adult cloak that smothers him, of freeing him for wisdom, tenderness, and love.'"

"That," said DeBeckett sadly, "was forty years ago."

He started at a sound. Overhead a rocket was clapping through the sky, and DeBeckett looked wildly around. "It's all right, Mr. DeBeckett," comforted little Pat. "It's only a plane."

He allowed her to soothe him. "Ah, loveling," he said. "And can you answer my question?"

"What it says in the 'Cyclopedia, Mr. DeBeckett?"

"Why—Yes, if you know it, my dear."

Surprisingly the child said, as if by rote: "The Institute was founded in 1976 and at once attracted most of the great workers in pediatric analysis, who were able to show Wiltshauer's Effect in the relationship between glandular and mental development. Within less than ten years, a new projective analysis of the growth process permitted a reorientation of basic pedagogy from a null-positive locus. The effects were immediate. The first generation of—"

She stopped, startled. The old man was up on his elbow, his eyes blazing at her in wonder and fright. "I'm—" She looked around at the other children for help and at once wailed, "I'm *sorry*, Mr. DeBeckett!" and began to cry.

The old man fell back, staring at her with a sort of unbelieving panic. The little girl wept abundantly. Slowly DeBeckett's expression relaxed and he managed a sketchy smile.

He said, "There, sweetest. You startled me. But it was charming of you to memorize all that!"

"I learned it for you," she sobbed.

"I didn't understand. Don't cry." Obediently the little girl dried her eyes as DeBeckett stretched out a hand to her.

But the hand dropped back on the quilt. Age, surprise, and the drug had allied to overmaster the dwindling resources of Elphen DeBeckett. He wandered to the phantoms on the wall. "I never understood what they did with my money," he told Coppie, who smiled at him with a shy, painted smile. "The children kept coming, but they never said."

"Poor man," said Will absently, watching him with a child's uncommitted look.

The nurse's eyes were bright and wet. She reached for the hypodermic, but the doctor shook his head.

"Wait," he said, and walked to the bed. He stood on tiptoe to peer into the dying man's face. "No, no use. Too old. Can't survive organ transplant, certainty of cytic shock. No feasible therapy." The nurse's eyes were now flowing. The doctor said to her, with patience but not very much patience, "No alternative. Only kept him going this long from gratitude."

The nurse sobbed, "Isn't there *anything* we can do for him?"

"Yes." The doctor gestured, and the lights on the diagnostic dials winked out. "We can let him die."

Little Pat hiked herself up on a chair, much too large for her, and dangled her feet. "Be nice to get rid of this furniture, anyway," she said. "Well, nurse? He's dead. Don't wait." The nurse looked rebelliously at the doctor, but the doctor only nodded. Sadly, the nurse went to the door and admitted the adults who had waited outside. The four of them surrounded the body and bore it gently through the door. Before it closed the nurse looked back and wailed: "He loved you!"

The children did not appear to notice. After a moment Pat said reflectively, "Sorry about the book. Should have opened it."

"He didn't notice," said Will, wiping his hands. He had touched the old man's fingers.

"No. Hate crying, though."

The doctor said, "Nice of you. Helped him, I think." He picked up the phone and ordered a demolition crew for the house. "Monument?"

"Oh, yes," said another child. "Well. Small one, anyway."

The doctor, who was nine, said, "Funny. Without him, what? A few hundred thousand dollars and the Foundation makes a flexible world, no more rigid adults, no more—" He caught himself narrowly. The doctor had observed before that he had a tendency to over-identify with adults, probably because his specialty had been geriatrics. Now that Elphen DeBeckett was dead, he no longer had a specialty.

"Miss him somehow," said Celine frankly, coming over to look over Will's shoulder at the quaint old murals on the wall. "What the nurse said, true enough. He loved us."

"And clearly we loved him," piped Freddy, methodically sorting through the contents of the dead man's desk. "Would have terminated him with the others otherwise, wouldn't we?"

SLOW TUESDAY NIGHT

BY R. A. LAFFERTY

The reason I became editor of Galaxy *was that Horace's health forced him to give it up. Before that there were several short periods when he had to ask someone to help out with reading and rejecting, and even with buying, and often the someone was me. On one of those occasions, I came across a manuscript by somebody I had never heard of before, named R. A. Lafferty. I bought it at once.*

Lafferty's first story was not quite like his later work—it was plotty and almost adventurous—but it had that idiosyncratic and askew Lafferty perception of the world. I liked it very much. I felt I had made a discovery. I urged Horace to keep buying from this Oklahoman, which he did with a good will, and I even sent copies of the stories as they came out to critics, editors, and other persons of great mana in science fiction, inviting them to recognize a strong new talent.

It is very disappointing when you strike matches and no one takes fire. The power figures did not respond one way or another. Neither did Galaxy's readers. Nobody wrote in to complain that the stories had been published, but nobody wrote in to mention them at all, which is just as unpleasant.

So, for five or six years, through the rest of Horace's turn in the barrel and the first part of mine, we kept on publishing Lafferty. Almost nobody else did. His then agent, despairing of ever showing a profit on the man, counseled him to forget SF and try writing—um—let's see—oh, sure! How about regional dialect stories? Faithfully Lafferty tried, but they didn't break him through either.

There never was a "breakthrough" story for Ray Lafferty. He was caviar. He took getting used to. All that happened was that as the years went by more and more readers, and editors, came to recognize and love that special flavor, and by and by the numbers were impressive.

It was hard for me to decide which Lafferty to include. There were so many, and so many that were very good. But I always had a special fondness for "Slow Tuesday Night," partly because of the title—which was mine.

A panhandler intercepted the young couple as they strolled down the night street.

"Preserve us this night," he said as he touched his hat to them, "and could you good people advance me a thousand dollars to be about the recouping of my fortunes?"

"I gave you a thousand last Friday," said the young man.

"Indeed you did," the panhandler replied, "and I paid you back tenfold by messenger before midnight."

"That's right, George, he did," said the young woman. "Give it to him dear. I believe he's a good sort."

So the young man gave the panhandler a thousand dollars; and the panhandler touched his hat to them in thanks, and went on to the recouping of his fortunes.

As he went into Money Market, the panhandler passed Ildefonsa Impala, the most beautiful woman in the city.

"Will you marry me this night, Ildy?" he asked cheerfully.

"Oh, I don't believe so, Basil," she said. "I marry you pretty often, but tonight I don't seem to have any plans at all. You may make me a gift on your first or second, however. I always like that."

But when they had parted, she asked herself: "But whom will I marry tonight?"

The panhandler was Basil Bagelbaker who would be the richest man in the world within an hour and a half. He would make and lose four fortunes within eight hours; and these not the little fortunes that ordinary men acquire, but titanic things.

When the Abebaios block had been removed from human minds, people began to make decisions faster, and often better. It had been the mental stutter. When it was understood what it was, and that it had no useful function, it was removed by simple childhood metasurgery.

Transportation and manufacturing had then become practically instantaneous. Things that had once taken months and years now took only minutes and hours. A person could have one or several pretty intricate careers within an eight-hour period.

Freddy Fixico had just invented a manus module. Freddy was a Nyctalops, and the modules were characteristic of these people. The people had then divided themselves—according to their natures and inclinations—into the Auroreans, the Hemerobians, and the Nyctalops; or the Dawners who had their most active hours from four A.M. till noon, the Day-Flies who obtained from noon to eight P.M., and the Night-Seers whose civilization thrived from eight P.M. to four A.M. The cultures, inventions, markets and activities of these three folk were a little different. As a Nyctalops, Freddy had just begun his working day at eight P.M. on a slow Tuesday night.

Freddy rented an office and had it furnished. This took one minute—negotiation, selection, and installation being almost instantaneous. Then he invented the manus module; that took another minute. He then had it manufactured and marketed; in three minutes it was in the hands of key buyers.

It caught on. It was an attractive module. The flow of orders began within thirty seconds. By ten minutes after eight every important person had one of the new manus modules, and the trend had been set. The module began to sell in the millions. It was one of the most interesting fads of the night, or at least the early part of the night.

Manus modules had no practical function, no more than had Sameki verses. They were attractive, or a psychologically satisfying size and shape, and could be held in the hands, set on a table, or installed in a module niche of any wall.

Naturally Freddy became very rich. Ildefonsa Impala, the most beautiful woman in the city, was always interested in newly rich men. She came to see Freddy about eight-thirty. People made up their minds fast, and Ildefonsa had hers made up when she came. Freddy made his own up quickly and divorced Judy Fixico in Small Claims Court. Freddy and Ildefonsa went honeymooning to Paraiso Dorado, a resort.

It was wonderful. All of Ildy's marriages were. There was the wonderful floodlighted scenery. The recirculated water of the famous falls was tinted gold; the immediate rocks had been done by Rambles; and the hills had been contoured by Spall. The beach was a perfect copy of that at Merevale, and the popular drink that first part of the night was blue absinthe.

But scenery—whether seen for the first time or revisited after an interval—is striking for the sudden intense view of it. It is not meant to be lingered over. Food, selected and prepared instantly, is eaten with swift enjoyment: and blue absinthe lasts no longer than its own novelty. Loving, for Ildefonsa and her paramours, was quick and consuming; and repetition would have been pointless to her. Besides, Ildefonsa and Freddy had taken only the one-hour luxury honeymoon.

Freddy wished to continue the relationship, but Ildefonsa glanced at a trend indicator. The manus module would hold its popularity for only the first third of the night. Already it had been discarded by people who mattered. And Freddy Fixico was not one of the regular successes. He enjoyed a full career only about one night a week.

They were back in the city and divorced in Small Claims Court by nine thirty-five. The stock of manus modules was remaindered, and the last of it would be disposed to bargain hunters among the Dawners, who will buy anything.

"Whom shall I marry next?" Ildefonsa asked herself. "It looks like a slow night."

"Bagelbaker is buying," ran the word through Money Market, but Bagelbaker was selling again before the word had made its rounds. Basil Bagelbaker enjoyed making money, and it was a pleasure to watch him work as he dominated the floor of the Market and assembled runners and a competent staff out of the corner of his mouth. Helpers stripped the panhandler rags off him and wrapped him in a tycoon toga. He sent one runner to pay back twentyfold the young couple who had advanced him a thousand dollars. He sent another with a more substantial gift to Ildefonsa Impala, for Basil cherished their relationship. Basil acquired title to the Trend Indication Complex and had certain falsifications set into it. He caused to collapse certain industrial empires that had grown up within the last two hours, and made a good thing of recombining their wreckage. He had been the richest man in the world for some minutes now. He became so money-heavy that he could not maneuver with the agility he had shown an hour before. He became a great fat buck, and the pack of expert wolves circled him to bring him down.

Very soon he would lose that first fortune of the evening. The secret of Basil Bagelbaker is that he enjoyed losing money spectacularly after he was full of it to the bursting point.

A thoughtful man named Maxwell Mouser had just produced a work of actinic philosophy. It took him seven minutes to write it. To write works of philosophy one used the flexible outlines and the idea indexes; one set the activator for such a wordage in each sub-section; an adept would use the paradox feed-in, and the striking analogy blender; one calibrated the particular-slant and the personality-signature. It had to come out a good work, for excellence had become the automatic minimum for such productions.

"I will scatter a few nuts on the frosting," said Maxwell, and he pushed the lever for that. This sifted handfuls of words like chthonic and heuristic and prozymeides through the thing so that nobody could doubt it was a work of philosophy.

Maxwell Mouser sent the work out to publishers, and received it back each time in about three minutes. An analysis of it and reason for rejection was always given—mostly that the thing had been done before and better. Maxwell received it back ten times in thirty minutes, and was discouraged. Then there was a break.

Ladion's work had become a hit within the last ten minutes, and it was now recognized that Mouser's monograph was both an answer and a supplement to it. It was accepted and published in less than a minute after this break. The reviews of the first five minutes were cautious ones; then real enthusiasm was shown. This was truly one of the greatest works of philosophy to appear during the early and medium hours of the night. There were those who said it might be one of the enduring works and even have a hold-over appeal to the Dawners the next morning.

Naturally Maxwell became very rich, and naturally Ildefonsa came to see him about midnight. Being a revolutionary philosopher, Maxwell thought that they might make some free arrangement, but Ildefonsa insisted it must be marriage. So Maxwell divorced Judy Mouser in Small Claims Court and went off with Ildefonsa.

This Judy herself, though not so beautiful as Ildefonsa, was the fastest taker in the City. She only wanted the men of the moment for a moment, and she was always there before even Ildefonsa. Ildefonsa believed that she took the men away from Judy; Judy said that Ildy had her leavings and nothing else.

"I had him first," Judy would always mock as she raced through Small Claims Court.

"Oh that damned Urchin!" Ildefonsa would moan. "She wears my very hair before I do."

Maxwell Mouser and Ildefonsa Impala went honeymooning to Musicbox Mountain, a resort. It was wonderful. The peaks were done with green snow by Dunbar and Fittle. (Back at Money Market Basil Bagelbaker was putting together his third and greatest fortune of the night which might surpass in magnitude even his fourth fortune of the Thursday before.) The chalets were Switzier than the real Swiss and had live goats in every room. (And Stanley Skuldugger was emerging as the top actor-imago of the middle hours of the night.) The popular drink for that middle part of the night was Glotzenglubber, Eve Cheese and Rhine wine over pink ice. (And back in the city the leading Nyctalops were taking their midnight break at the Toppers' Club.)

Of course it was wonderful, as were all of Ildefonsa's—But she had never been really up on philosophy so she had scheduled only the special thirty-five minute honeymoon. She looked at the trend indicator to be sure. She found that her current husband had been obsoleted, and his opus was now referred to sneeringly as Mouser's Mouse. They went back to the city and were divorced in Small Claims Court.

The membership of the Toppers' Club varied. Success was the requisite of membership. Basil Bagelbaker might be accepted as a member, elevated to the presidency, and expelled from it as a dirty pauper from three to six times a night. But only important persons could belong to it, or those enjoying brief moments of importance.

"I believe I will sleep during the Dawner period in the morning," Overcall said. "I may go up to this new place Koimopolis for an hour of it. They're said to be good. Where will you sleep, Basil?"

"Flop-house."

"I believe I will sleep an hour by the Midian Method," said Burnbanner. "They have a fine new clinic. And perhaps I'll sleep an hour by the Prasenka Process, and an hour by the Dormidio."

"Crackle has been sleeping an hour every period by the natural method," said Overcall.

"I did that for a half hour not long since," said Burnbanner. "I believe an hour is too long to give it. Have you tried the natural method, Basil?"

"Always. Natural method and a bottle of red-eye."

*   *   *

Stanley Skuldugger had become the most meteoric actor-imago for a week. Naturally he became very rich, and Ildefonsa Impala went to see him about three A.M.

"I had him first!" rang the mocking voice of Judy Skuldugger as she skipped through her divorce in Small Claims Court. And Ildefonsa and Stanley-boy went off honeymooning. It is always fun to finish up a period with an actor-imago who is the hottest property in the business. There is something so adolescent and boorish about them.

Besides, there was the publicity, and Ildefonsa liked that. The rumor-mills ground. Would it last ten minutes? Thirty? An hour? Would it be one of those rare Nyctalops marriages that lasted through the rest of the night and into the daylight off-hours? Would it even last into the next night as some had been known to do?

Actually it lasted nearly forty minutes, which was almost to the end of the period.

It had been a slow Tuesday night. A few hundred new products had run their course on the markets. There had been a score of dramatic hits, three-minute and five-minute capsule dramas, and several of the six-minute long-play affairs. *Night Street Nine*—a solidly sordid offering—seemed to be in as the drama of the night unless there should be a late hit.

Hundred-storied buildings had been erected, occupied, obsoleted, and demolished again to make room for more contemporary structures. Only the mediocre would use a building that had been left over from the Day-Flies or the Dawners, or even the Nyctalops of the night before. The city was rebuilt pretty completely at least three times during an eight-hour period.

The Period drew near its end. Basil Bagelbaker, the richest man in the world, the reigning president of the Toppers' Club, was enjoying himself with his cronies. His fourth fortune of the night was a paper pyramid that had risen to incredible heights; but Basil laughed to himself as he savored the manipulation it was founded on.

Three ushers of the Toppers' Club came in with firm step.

"Get out of here, you dirty bum!" they told Basil savagely. They tore the tycoon's toga off him and then tossed him his seedy panhandler's rags with a three-man sneer.

"All gone?" Basil asked. "I gave it another five minutes."

"All gone," said a messenger from Money Market. "Nine billion gone in five minutes, and it really pulled some others down with it."

"Pitch the busted bum out!" howled Overcall and Burnbanner and the other cronies. "Wait, Basil," said Overcall. "Turn in the President's Crosier before we kick you downstairs. After all, you'll have it several times again tomorrow night."

The Period was over. The Nyctalops drifted off to sleep clinics or leisure-hour hide-outs to pass their ebb time. The Auroreans, the Dawners, took over the vital stuff.

Now you would see some action! Those Dawners really made fast decisions. You wouldn't catch them wasting a full minute setting up a business.

A sleepy panhandler met Ildefonsa Impala on the way.

"Preserve us this morning, Ildy," he said, "and will you marry me the coming night?"

"Likely I will, Basil," she told him. "Did you marry Judy during the night past?"

"I'm not sure. Could you let me have two dollars, Ildy?"

"Out of the question. I believe a Judy Bagelbaker was named one of the ten best-dressed women during the frou-frou fashion period about two o'clock. Why do you need two dollars?"

"A dollar for a bed and a dollar for red-eye. After all, I sent you two million out of my second."

"I keep my two sorts of accounts separate. Here's a dollar, Basil. Now be off! I can't be seen talking to a dirty panhandler."

"Thank you, Ildy. I'll get the red-eye and sleep in an alley. Preserve us this morning."

Bagelbaker shuffled off whistling "Slow Tuesday Night."

And already the Dawners had set Wednesday morning to jumping.

STREET OF DREAMS, FEET OF CLAY

BY ROBERT SHECKLEY

You have not gotten this far without realizing that I picked a great many of the stories in this book for what are really personal reasons—mostly, because I felt I was having a good day as editor when they went through the mill. "Street of Dreams, Feet of Clay" gave me that feeling.

Bob Sheckley and I have intertwined our karmas many times over the last thirty years. When he was dewy-eyed new as a writer, I was his literary agent. In the early 1950s the number of hungry science-fiction magazines was at an all-time high. I made an impressive number of good sales for him—considering how good the stories were that I had to work with, that feat is about as impressive as selling life rafts on the Titanic.

Then there were half a dozen years or so when I had stopped being an agent and hadn't yet started being an editor again, and our paths crossed only socially. Bob began wandering the face of the Earth, and even social meetings became infrequent. Worse than that, I noticed that seeing Sheckley books and Sheckley stories in the magazines became infrequent.

There is a terrible curse that strikes writers. It hits hardest some who deserve it least, the brightest and most talented, but at least now and then it touches us all. It's called "writers' block." I've seen fine and productive writers spend a week at a typewriter without getting past Page 1 of a story—with a litter of other, discarded Page 1s all around them. I've seen a manuscript where the author has rewritten a single sentence twenty times before he could go on to the next, and even manuscripts where he never could. Writers have all sorts of sigils and spells to protect them against the blight. One needs just the right typewriter ribbon, another a bottle of just the right beer. The block seldom has an apparent cause. It takes place inside the head, as part of a process largely hidden from the conscious mind—exactly as writing itself does. And it all sounds ludicrous and even trivial, except when it's happening to you.

Anyway, the next time I saw Bob the barricades had fallen in front of him.

272

He was stuck. He had half a novel written, and hardly a hope left of ever finishing it. When I asked him for a short story, his laugh was hollow.

But there was that half a novel, and when he allowed me to read it, I perceived that one of the chapters needed only tiny changes to become a story in itself. When I suggested it, Bob went away with his fingers already flexing, and came back very soon with "Street of Dreams, Feet of Clay" . . . and that was one of the good days.

*   *   *

I.

Carmody had never really planned to leave New York. Why he did so is inexplicable. A born urbanite, he had grown accustomed to the minor inconveniences of metropolitan life. His snug apartment on the two hundred and ninetieth floor of Levitfrack Towers on West Ninety-Ninth Street was nicely equipped in the current "Spaceship" motif. The windows were double-sealed in tinted lifetime plexiglass, and the air ducts worked through a blind baffle filtration system which sealed automatically when the Combined Atmosphere Pollution Index reached 999.8 on the Con Ed scale. True, his oxygen-nitrogen air recirculation system was old, but it was reliable. His water purification cells were obsolete and ineffective; but then, nobody drank water anyhow.

Noise was a continual annoyance, unstoppable and inescapable. But Carmody knew that there was no cure for this, since the ancient art of soundproofing had been lost. It was urban man's lot to listen, a captive audience, to the arguments, music, and watery gurglings of his adjacent neighbors. Even this torture could be alleviated, however, by producing similar sounds of one's own.

Going to work each day entailed certain dangers; but these were more apparent than real. Disadvantaged snipers continued to make their ineffectual protests from rooftops and occasionally succeeded in potting an unwary out-of-towner. But as a rule, their aim was abominable. Additionally, the general acceptance of lightweight personal armor had taken away most of their sting, and the sternly administered State law forbidding the personal possession of surplus cannon had rendered them ineffectual.

Thus, no single factor can be adduced for Carmody's sudden decision to leave what was generally considered the world's most exciting megapolitan agglomeration. Blame it on a vagrant impulse, a pastoral fantasy, or on sheer perversity. The simple, irreducible fact is, one day Carmody opened his copy of the *Daily Times-News* and saw an advertisement for a model city in New Jersey.

"Come live in Bellwether, the city that *cares*," the advertisement proclaimed. There followed a list of utopian claims which need not be reproduced here.

"Huh," said Carmody, and read on.

Bellwether was within easy commuting distance. One simply drove through the Ulysses S. Grant Tunnel at 43rd Street, took the Hoboken Shunt Subroad to the Palisades Interstate Crossover, followed that for three-point-two miles on the Blue-Charlie Sorter Loop that led onto U.S. 5 (The Hague Memorial Tollway), proceeded along that a distance of six-point-one miles to the Garden State Supplementary Access Service Road (Provisional), upon which one tended west to Exit 1731A, which was King's Highbridge Gate Road, and then continued along that for a distance of one-point-six miles. And there you were.

"By jingo," said Carmody, "I'll do it."

And he did.

II.

King's Highbridge Gate Road ended on a neatly trimmed plain. Carmody got out of his car and looked around. Half a mile ahead of him he saw a small city. A single modest signpost identified it as Bellwether.

This city was not constructed in the traditional manner of American cities, with outliers of gas stations, tentacles of hot-dog stands, fringes of motels, and a protective carapace of junkyards; but rather, as some Italian hill towns are fashioned, it rose abruptly, without physical preamble, the main body of the town presenting itself at once and without amelioration.

Carmody found this appealing. He advanced into the city itself.

Bellwether had a warm and open look. Its streets were laid out generously, and there was a frankness about the wide bay windows of its store-fronts. As he penetrated deeper, Carmody found other delights. Just within the city he entered a piazza, like a Roman piazza, only smaller; and in the center of the piazza there was a fountain, and standing in the fountain was a marble representation of a boy with a dolphin, and from the dolphin's mouth a stream of clear water issued.

"I do hope you like it," a voice said from behind Carmody's left shoulder.

"It's nice," Carmody said.

"I constructed it and put it there myself," the voice told him. "It seemed to me that a fountain, despite the antiquity of its concept, is esthetically functional. And this piazza, with its benches and shady chestnut trees, is copied from a Bolognese model. Again, I did not inhibit myself with the fear of seeming old-fashioned. The true artist uses what is necessary, be it a thousand years old or one second new."

"I applaud your sentiment," Carmody said. "Permit me to introduce myself. I am Edward Carmody." He turned, smiling.

But there was no one behind his left shoulder, or behind his right shoulder, either. There was no one in the piazza, nobody at all in sight.

"Forgive me," the voice said. "I didn't mean to startle you. I thought you knew."

"Knew what?" Carmody asked.

"Knew about me."

"Well, I don't," Carmody said. "Who are you and where are you speaking from?"

"I am the voice of the city," the voice said. "Or to put it another way, I am the city itself, Bellwether, the actual and veritable city, speaking to you."

"Is that a fact?" Carmody said sardonically. "Yes," he answered himself, "I suppose it is a fact. So all right, you're a city. Big deal!"

He turned away from the fountain and strolled across the piazza like a man who conversed with cities every day of his life, and who was slightly bored with the whole thing. He walked down various streets and up certain avenues. He glanced into store windows and noted houses. He paused in front of statuary, but only briefly.

"Well?" the city of Bellwether asked after a while.

"Well what?" Carmody answered at once.

"What do you think of me?"

"You're okay," Carmody said.

"Only okay? Is that all?"

"Look," Carmody said, "a city is a city. When you've seen one, you've pretty much seen them all."

"That's untrue!" the city said, with some show of pique. "I am distinctly different from other cities. I am unique."

"Are you indeed?" Carmody said scornfully. "To me you look like a conglomeration of badly assembled parts. You've got an Italian piazza, a couple of Greek-type buildings, a row of Tudor houses, an old-style New York tenement, a California hot-dog stand shaped like a tugboat, and God knows what else. What's so unique about that?"

"The combination of those forms into a meaningful entity is unique," the city said. "These older forms are not anachronisms, you understand. They are representative styles of living, and as such are appropriate in a well-wrought machine for living. Would you care for some coffee and perhaps a sandwich or some fresh fruit?"

"Coffee sounds good," Carmody said. He allowed Bellwether to guide him around the corner to an open-air cafe. The cafe was called "O You Kid" and was a replica of a Gay Nineties saloon, right down to the Tiffany lamps and the cutglass chandelier and the player piano. Like everything else that Carmody had seen in the city, it was spotlessly clean, but without people.

"Nice atmosphere, don't you think?" Bellwether asked.

"Campy," Carmody pronounced. "Okay if you like that sort of thing."

A foaming mug of cappucino was lowered to his table on a stainless steel tray. Carmody sipped.

"Good?" Bellwether asked.

"Yes, very good."

"I rather pride myself on my coffee," the city said quietly. "And on my cooking. Wouldn't you care for a little something? An omelette, perhaps, or a soufflé?"

"Nothing," Carmody said firmly. He leaned back in his chair and said, "So you're a model city, huh?"

"Yes, that is what I have the honor to be," Bellwether said. "I am the most recent of all model cities; and, I believe, the most satisfactory. I was conceived by a joint study group from Yale and the University of Chicago, who were working on a Rockefeller fellowship. Most of my practical details were devised by M.I.T., although some special sections of me came from Princeton and from the RAND Corporation. My actual construction was a General Electric project, and the money was procured by grants from the Ford and Carnegie Foundations, as well as several other institutions I am not at liberty to mention."

"Interesting sort of history," Carmody said, with hateful nonchalance. "That's a Gothic cathedral across the street, isn't it?"

"Modified Romanesque," the city said. "Also interdenominational and open to all faiths, with a designed seating capacity for three hundred people."

"That doesn't seem like many for a building of that size."

"It's not, of course. Designedly. My idea was to combine awesomeness with coziness."

"Where are the inhabitants of this town, by the way?" Carmody asked.

"They have left," Bellwether said mournfully. "They have all departed."

"Why?"

The city was silent for a while, then said, "There was a breakdown in city-community relations. A misunderstanding, really. Or perhaps I should say, an unfortunate series of misunderstandings. I suspect that rabble-rousers played their part."

"But what *happened,* precisely?"

"I don't know," the city said. "I really don't know. One day they simply all left. Just like that! But I'm sure they'll be back."

"I wonder," Carmody said.

"I am convinced of it," the city said. "But, putting that aside, why don't *you* stay here, Mr. Carmody?"

"I haven't really had time to consider it," Carmody said.

"How could you help but like it?" Bellwether said. "Just think—you would have the most modern, up-to-date city in the world at your beck and call."

"That does sound interesting," Carmody said.

"So give it a try, how could it hurt you?" the city asked.

"All right, I think I will," Carmody said.

He was intrigued by the city of Bellwether. But he was also apprehensive. He wished he knew exactly why the city's previous occupants had left.

*   *   *

At Bellwether's insistence, Carmody slept that night in the sumptuous bridal suite of the King George V Hotel. Bellwether served him breakfast on the terrace and played a brisk Hayden quartet while Carmody ate. The morning air was delicious. If Bellwether hadn't told him, Carmody would never have guessed it was reconstituted.

When he was finished, Carmody leaned back and enjoyed the view of Bellwether's western quarter—a pleasing jumble of Chinese pagodas, Venetian foot-bridges, Japanese canals, a green Burmese hill, a Corinthian temple, a Californian parking lot, a Norman tower, and much else besides.

"You have a splendid view," he told the city.

"I'm so glad you appreciate it," Bellwether replied. "The problem of style was argued from the day of my inception. One group held for consistency: a harmonious group of shapes blending into a harmonious whole. But quite a few model cities are like that. They are uniformly dull, artificial entities created by one man or one committee, unlike real cities."

"You're sort of artificial yourself, aren't you?" Carmody asked.

"Of course! But I do not pretend to be anything else. I am not a fake 'city of the future' or a mock-florentine bastard. I am a true agglutinated congeries. I am supposed to be interesting and stimulating in addition to being functional and practical."

"Bellwether, you look okay to me," Carmody said, in a sudden rush of expansiveness. "Do all model cities talk like you?"

"Certainly not. Most cities up to now, model or otherwise, never said a word. But their inhabitants didn't like that. It made the city seem too huge, too masterful, too soulless, too impersonal. That is why I was created with a voice and an artificial consciousness to guide it."

"I see," Carmody said.

"The point is, my artificial consciousness personalizes me, which is very important in an age of depersonalization. It enables me to be truly responsive. It permits me to be creative in meeting the demands of my occupants. We can reason with each other, my people and I. By carrying on a continual and meaningful dialogue, we can help each other to establish a dynamic, flexible, and truly viable urban environment. We can modify each other without any significant loss of individuality."

"It sounds fine," Carmody said. "Except, of course, that you don't have anyone here to carry on a dialogue with."

"That is the only flaw in the scheme," the city admitted. "But for the present, I have you."

"Yes, you have me," Carmody said and wondered why the words rang unpleasantly on his ear.

"And, naturally, you have me," the city said. "It is a reciprocal relationship, which is the only kind worth having. But now, my dear Carmody, suppose I show you around myself. Then we can get you settled in and regularized."

"Get me what?"

"I didn't mean that the way it sounded," the city said. "It simply is an unfortunate scientific expression. But you understand, I'm sure, that a reciprocal relationship necessitates obligations on the part of both involved parties. It couldn't very well be otherwise, could it?"

"Not unless it was a *laissez-faire* relationship."

"We're trying to get away from all that," Bellwether said. "*Laissez-faire* becomes a doctrine of the emotions, you know, and leads non-stop to *anomie*. If you will just come this way. . . ."

III.

Carmody went where he was asked and beheld the excellencies of Bellwether. He toured the power plant, the water filtration center, the industrial park, and the light industries section. He saw the children's park and the Odd Fellow's Hall. He walked through a museum and an art gallery, a concert hall and a theater, a bowling alley, a billiards parlor, a Go-Kart track, and a movie theater. He became tired and wanted to stop. But the city wanted to show itself off, and Carmody had to look at the five-story American Express building, the Portuguese synagogue, the statue of Buckminster Fuller, the Greyhound Bus Station, and several other attractions.

At last it was over. Carmody concluded that beauty was in the eye of the beholder, except for a small part of it that was in the beholder's feet.

"A little lunch now?" the city asked.

"Fine," Carmody said.

He was guided to the fashionable Rochambeau Cafe, where he began with *potage au petit poise* and ended with *petits-fours*.

"What about a nice Brie to finish off?" the city asked.

"No, thanks," Carmody said. "I'm full. Too full, as a matter of fact."

"But cheese isn't filling. A bit of first-rate Camembert?"

"I couldn't possibly."

"Perhaps a few assorted fruits. *Very* refreshing to the palate."

"It's not my palate that needs refreshing," Carmody said.

"At least an apple, a pear, and a couple of grapes?"

"Thanks, no."

"A couple of cherries?"

"No, no, no!"

"A meal isn't complete without a little fruit," the city said.

"My meal is," Carmody said.

"There are important vitamins, only found in fresh fruit."

"I'll just have to struggle along without them."

"Perhaps half an orange, which I will peel for you? Citrus fruits have no bulk at all."

"I couldn't possibly."

"Not even one quarter of an orange? If I take out all the pits?"

"Most decidedly not."

"It would make me feel better," the city said. "I have a completion compulsion, you know, and no meal is complete without a piece of fruit."

"No! No! No!"

"All right, don't get so excited," the city said. "If you don't like the sort of food I serve, that's up to you."

"But I do like it!"

"Then if you like it so much, why won't you eat some fruit?"

"Enough," Carmody said. "Give me a couple grapes."

"I wouldn't want to force anything on you."

"You're not forcing. Give me, please."

"You're quite sure?"

"Gimme!" Carmody shouted.

"So take," the city said and produced a magnificent bunch of muscatel grapes. Carmody ate them all. They were very good.

"Excuse me," the city said. "What are you doing?"

Carmody sat upright and opened his eyes. "I was taking a little nap," he said. "Is there anything wrong with that?"

"What should be wrong with a perfectly natural thing like that?" the city said.

"Thank you," Carmody said, and closed his eyes again.

"But why nap in a chair?" the city asked.

"Because I'm *in* a chair, and I'm already half asleep."

"You'll get a crick in your back," the city warned him.

"Don't care," Carmody mumbled, his eyes still closed.

"Why not take a proper nap? Over here, on the couch?"

"I'm already napping comfortably right here."

"You're not really comfortable," the city pointed out. "The human anatomy is not constructed for sleeping sitting up."

"At the moment, mine is," Carmody said.

"It's not. Why not try the couch?"

"The chair is fine."

"But the couch is finer. Just try it, please, Carmody. Carmody?"

"Eh? What's that?" Carmody said, waking up.

"The couch. I really think you should rest on the couch."

"All right!" Carmody said, struggling to his feet. "Where is this couch?"

He was guided out of the restaurant, down the street, around the corner, and into a building marked "The Snoozerie." There were a dozen couches. Carmody went to the nearest.

"Not that one," the city said. "It's got a bad spring."

"It doesn't matter," Carmody said. "I'll sleep around it."

"That will result in a cramped posture."

"Christ!" Carmody said, getting to his feet. "Which couch would you recommend?"

"This one right back here," the city said. "It's a king-size, the best in the place. The yieldpoint of the mattress has been scientifically determined. The pillows—"

"Right, fine, good," Carmody said, lying down on the indicated couch.

"Shall I play you some soothing music?"

"Don't bother."

"Just as you wish. I'll put out the lights, then."

"Fine."

"Would you like a blanket? I control the temperature here, of course, but sleepers often get a subjective impression of chilliness."

"It doesn't matter! Leave me alone!"

"All right!" the city said. "I'm not doing this for myself, you know. Personally, I never sleep."

"Okay, sorry," Carmody said.

"That's perfectly all right."

There was a long silence. Then Carmody sat up.

"What's the matter?" the city asked.

"Now I can't sleep," Carmody said.

"Try closing your eyes and consciously relaxing every muscle in your body, starting with the big toe and working upward to—"

"I can't sleep!" Carmody shouted.

"Maybe you weren't very sleepy to begin with," the city suggested. "But at least you could close your eyes and try to get a little rest. Won't you do that for me?"

"No!" Carmody said. "I'm not sleepy and I don't need a rest."

"Stubborn!" the city said. "Do what you like. I've tried my best."

"Yeah," Carmody said, getting to his feet and walking out of "The Snoozerie."

IV.

Carmody stood on a little curved bridge and looked over a blue lagoon.

"This is a copy of the Rialto bridge in Venice," the city said. "Scaled down, of course."

"I know," Carmody said. "I read the sign."

"It's rather enchanting, isn't it?"

"Sure, it's fine," Carmody said, lighting a cigarette.

"You're doing a lot of smoking," the city pointed out.

"I know. I feel like smoking."

"As your medical advisor, I must point out that the link between smoking and lung cancer is conclusive."

"I know."

"If you switched to a pipe, your chances would be improved."

"I don't like pipes."

"What about a cigar, then?"

"I don't like cigars." He lit another cigarette.

"That's your third cigarette in five minutes," the City said.

"God damn it, I'll smoke as much and as often as I please!" Carmody shouted.

"Well, of course you will!" the city said. "I was merely trying to advise you for your own good. Would you want me to simply stand by and not say a word while you destroyed yourself?"

"Yes," Carmody said.

"I can't believe that you mean that. There is an ethical imperative involved here. Man can act against his best interests; but a machine is not allowed that degree of perversity."

"Get off my back," Carmody said sullenly. "Quit pushing me around."

"Pushing you around? My dear Carmody, have I coerced you in any way? Have I done any more than advise you?"

"Maybe not. But you talk too much."

"Perhaps I don't talk enough," the city said. "To judge from the response I get."

"You talk too much," Carmody repeated and lit a cigarette.

"That is your fourth cigarette in five minutes."

Carmody opened his mouth to bellow an insult. Then he changed his mind and walked away.

"What's this?" Carmody asked.

"It's a candy machine," the city told him.

"It doesn't look like one."

"Still, it is one. This design is a modification of a design by Saarionmen for a silo. I have miniaturized it, of course, and—"

"It still doesn't look like a candy machine. How do you work it?"

"It's very simple. Push the red button. Now wait. Press down one of those levers on Row A; now press the green button. There!"

A Baby Ruth bar slid into Carmody's hand.

"Huh," Carmody said. He stripped off the paper and bit into the bar. "Is this a real Baby Ruth bar or a copy of one?" he asked.

"It's a real one. I had to sub-contract the candy concession because of the pressure of work."

"Huh," Carmody said, letting the candy wrapper slip from his fingers.

"That," the city said, "is an example of the kind of thoughtlessness I always encounter."

"It's just a piece of paper," Carmody said, turning and looking at the candy wrapper lying on the spotless street.

"Of course it's just a piece of paper," the city said. "But multiply it by a hundred thousand inhabitants and what do you have?"

"A hundred thousand Baby Ruth wrappers," Carmody answered at once.

"I don't consider that funny," the city said. "You wouldn't want to *live* in the midst of all that paper, I can assure you. You'd be the first to complain if this street were strewn with garbage. But do you do your share? Do you even clean up after yourself? Of course not! You leave it to me, even though I have to run all of the other functions of the city, night and day, without even Sundays off.''

Carmody bent down to pick up the candy wrapper. But just before his fingers could close on it, a pincer arm shot out of the nearest sewer, snatched the paper away, and vanished from sight.

"It's all right," the city said. "I'm used to cleaning up after people. I do it all the time."

"Yuh," said Carmody.

"Nor do I expect any gratitude."

"I'm grateful, I'm grateful!" Carmody said.

"No, you're not," Bellwether said.

"So, okay, maybe I'm not. What do you want me to say?"

"I don't want you to say anything," the city said. "Let us consider the incident closed."

"Had enough?" the city said, after dinner.

"Plenty," Carmody said.

"You didn't eat much."

"I ate all I wanted. It was very good."

"If it was so good, why didn't you eat more?"

"Because I couldn't hold any more."

"If you hadn't spoiled your appetite with that candy bar . . .''

"God damn it, the candy bar didn't spoil my appetite! I just—"

"You're lighting a cigarette," the city said.

"Yeah," Carmody said.

"Couldn't you wait a little longer?"

"Now look," Carmody said, "Just what in hell do you—"

"But we have something more important to talk about," the city said quickly. "Have you thought about what you're going to do for a living?"

"I haven't really had much time to think about it."

"Well, I have been thinking about it. It would be nice if you became a doctor."

"Me? I'd have to take special college courses, then get into medical school, and so forth."

"I can arrange all that," the city said.

"Not interested."

"Well . . . What about law?"

"Never."

"Engineering is an excellent line."

"Not for me."

"What about accounting?"

"Not on your life."

"What do you want to be?"

"A jet pilot," Carmody said impulsively.

"Oh, come now!"

"I'm quite serious."

"I don't even have an air field here."

"Then I'll pilot somewhere else."

"You're only saying that to spite me!"

"Not at all," Carmody said. "I want to be a pilot, I really do. I've *always* wanted to be a pilot! Honest I have!"

There was a long silence. Then the city said, "The choice is entirely up to you." This was said in a voice like death.

"Where are you going now?"

"Out for a walk," Carmody said.

"At nine-thirty in the evening?"

"Sure. Why not?"

"I thought you were tired."

"That was quite some time ago."

"I see. And I also thought that you could sit here and we could have a nice chat."

"How about if we talk after I get back?" Carmody asked.

"No, it doesn't matter," the city said.

"The walk doesn't matter," Carmody said, sitting down. "Come on, we'll talk."

"I no longer care to talk," the city said. "Please go for your walk."

V.

"Well, good night," Carmody said.

"I beg your pardon?"

"I said, 'good night.'"

"You're going to sleep?"

"Sure. It's late, I'm tired."

"You're going to sleep now?"

"Well, why not?"

"No reason at all," the city said, "except that you have forgotten to wash."

"Oh . . . I guess I did forget. I'll wash in the morning."

"How long is it since you've had a bath?"

"Too long. I'll take one in the morning."

"Wouldn't you feel better if you took one right now?"

"No."

"Even if I drew the bath for you?"

"No! God damn it, no! I'm going to sleep!"

"Do exactly as you please," the city said. "Don't wash, don't study, don't eat a balanced diet. But also, don't blame me."

"Blame you? For what?"

"For anything," the city said.

"Yes. But what did you have in mind, specifically?"

"It isn't important."

"Then why did you bring it up in the first place?"

"I was only thinking of you," the city said.

"I realize that."

"You must know that it can't benefit *me* if you wash or not."

"I'm aware of that."

"When one cares," the city went on, "when one feels one's responsibilities, it is not nice to hear oneself sworn at."

"I didn't swear at you."

"Not this time. But earlier today you did."

"Well . . . I was nervous."

"That's because of the smoking."

"Don't start that again!"

"I won't," the city said. "Smoke like a furnace. What does it matter to me?"

"Damned right," Carmody said, lighting a cigarette.

"But my failure," the city said.

"No, no," Carmody said. "Don't say it, please don't!"

"Forget I said it," the city said.

"All right."

"Sometimes I get over-zealous."

"Sure."

"And it's especially difficult because I'm right. I am right, you know."

"I know," Carmody said. "You're right, you're right, you're always right. Right right right right right—"

"Don't overexcite yourself betime," the city said. "Would you care for a glass of milk?"

"No."

"You're sure?"

Carmody put his hands over his eyes. He felt very strange. He also felt extremely guilty, fragile, dirty, unhealthy and sloppy. He felt generally and irrevocably bad, and it would always be this way unless he changed, adjusted, adapted . . .

But instead of attempting anything of the sort he rose to his feet, squared his shoulders, and marched away past the Roman piazza and the Venetian bridge.

"Where are you going?" the city asked. "What's the matter?"

Silent, tight-lipped, Carmody continued past the children's park and the American Express building.

"What did I do wrong?" the city cried. "What, just tell me what?"

Carmody made no reply but strode past the Rochambeau Cafe and the Portuguese synagogue, coming at last to the pleasant green plain that surrounded Bellwether.

"Ingrate!" the city screamed after him. "You're just like all the others. All of you humans are disagreeable animals, and you're never really satisfied with anything."

Carmody got into his car and started the engine.

"But of course," the city said, in a more thoughtful voice, "you're never really *dissatisfied* with anything, either. The moral, I suppose, is that a city must learn patience."

Carmody turned the car onto King's Highbridge Gate Road and started east, toward New York.

"Have a nice trip!" Bellwether called after him. "Don't worry about me, I'll be waiting up for you."

Carmody stepped down hard on the accelerator. He really wished he hadn't heard that last remark.

THE COLDEST PLACE

BY LARRY NIVEN

The science-fiction fan may be considered to be the larval stage of the science-fiction writer. Not all fans pupate. Some gafiate* instead, and a great many just go on being science-fiction fans indefinitely. However, very few significant science-fiction writers came to the field without serving a term as fans of some degree.
*gafiate, v.i., to retire from active interest in science-fiction fandom. Verb form of the acronymic noun **gafia**: "Getting Away From It All."

Larry Niven was a member of one of the world's oldest established science-fiction clubs, the Los Angeles Science-Fiction Society, when he submitted "The Coldest Place" to me in 1964. It turned out to be his first sale. I didn't know he was a maiden when I bought it. I seldom did, although I published a "first" story in every issue of If. But I accepted each story on its merits, and rarely knew it was a "first" until the author had answered my question about it in the letter offering a price for the story.

What attracted me to the Niven was his ability to deal with both characters and science in brief length—and to surprise me. I was always an easy mark for a story that pointed out some curious scientific fact I had never encountered before, and the paradox that the solar system's hottest planet contained its coldest place made the story sure-fire. . . . Except, of course, it was wrong. It wasn't Niven's fault. Just as the story was coming out, some meddling radar astronomer found out that Mercury's rotation was not synchronous with its revolution around the Sun, and so there was no "coldest place" on it.

Niven hastily offered to withdraw the story, but I wouldn't let him. I liked it too well. I still do.

One other thing. LASFS had a tradition. Every time a member made his first professional sale, LASFS gave him a congratulatory dinner. It wasn't until Larry was eating his that he learned the kicker. No member so honored for his first sale, they told him, had ever made a second.

But Larry Niven fooled them.

286

*   *   *

In the coldest place in the solar system, I hesitated outside the ship for a moment. It was too dark out there. I fought an urge to stay close by the ship, by the comfortable ungainly bulk of warm metal which held the warm bright Earth inside it.

"See anything?" asked Eric.

"No, of course not. It's too hot here anyway, what with heat radiation from the ship. You remember the way they scattered away from the probe."

"Yeah. Look, you want me to hold your hand or something? Go."

I sighed and started off, with the heavy collector bouncing gently on my shoulder. I bounced, too. The spikes on my boots kept me from sliding.

I walked up the side of the wide, shallow crater the ship had created by vaporizing the layered air all the way down to the water ice level. Crags rose about me, masses of frozen gas with smooth, rounded edges. They gleamed soft white where the light from my headlamp touched them. Elsewhere all was as black as eternity. Brilliant stars shone above the soft crags; but the light made no impression on the black land. The ship got smaller and darker and disappeared.

There was supposed to be life here. Nobody had even tried to guess what it might be like. Two years ago the Messenger VI probe had moved into close orbit about the planet and then landed about here, partly to find out if the cap of frozen gasses might be inflammable. In the field of view of the camera during the landing, things like shadows had wriggled across the snow and out of the light thrown by the probe. The films had shown it beautifully. Naturally some wise ones had suggested that they were only shadows.

I'd seen the films. I knew better. There was life.

Something alive, that hated light. Something out there in the dark. Something huge. . . . "Eric, you there?"

"Where would I go?" he mocked me.

"Well," said I, "if I watched every word I spoke, I'd never get anything said." All the same, I had been tactless. Eric had had a bad accident once, very bad. He wouldn't be going anywhere unless the ship went along.

"Touché," said Eric. "Are you getting much heat leakage from your suit?"

"Very little." In fact, the frozen air didn't even melt under the pressure of my boots.

"They might be avoiding even that little. Or they might be afraid of your light." He knew I hadn't seen anything; he was looking through a peeper in the top of my helmet.

"Okay, I'll climb that mountain and turn it off for awhile."

I swung my head so he could see the mound I meant, then started up it. It was good exercise, and no strain in the low gravity. I could jump almost as high as on the Moon, without fear of a rock's edge tearing my suit. It was all packed snow, with vacuum between the flakes.

My imagination started working again when I reached the top. There was black all around; the world was black with cold. I turned off the light and the world disappeared.

I pushed a trigger on the side of my helmet and my helmet put the stem of a pipe in my mouth. The air renewer sucked air and smoke down past my chin. They make wonderful suits nowadays. I sat and smoked, waiting, shivering with the knowledge of the cold. Finally I realized I was sweating. The suit was almost too well insulated.

Our ion-drive section came over the horizon, a brilliant star moving very fast, and disappeared as it hit the planet's shadow. Time was passing. The charge in my pipe burned out and I dumped it.

"Try the light," said Eric.

I got up and turned the headlamp on high. The light spread for a mile around, white fairy landscape sprang to life, a winter wonderland doubled in spades. I did a slow pirouette, looking, looking . . . and saw it.

Even this close it looked like a shadow. It also looked like a very flat, monstrously large amoeba, or like a pail of oil running across the ice. Uphill it ran, flowing slowly and painfully up the side of a nitrogen mountain, trying desperately to escape the searing light of my lamp. "The collector!" Eric demanded. I lifted the collector above my head and aimed it like a telescope at the fleeing enigma, so that Eric could find it in the collector's peeper. The collector spat fire at both ends and jumped up and away. Eric was controlling it now.

After a moment I asked, "Should I come back?"

"Certainly not. Stay there. I can't bring the collector back to the ship! You'll have to wait and carry it back with you."

The pool-shadow slid over the edge of the hill. The flame of the collector's rocket went after it, flying high, growing smaller. It dipped below the ridge. A moment later I heard Eric mutter, "Got it." The bright flame reappeared, rising fast, then curved toward me.

When the thing was hovering near me on two lateral rockets, I picked it up by the tail and carried it home.

"No, no trouble," said Eric. "I just used the scoop to nip a piece out of his flank, if so I may speak. I got about ten cubic centimeters of strange flesh."

"Good," said I. Carrying the collector carefully in one hand, I went up the landing leg to the airlock. Eric let me in.

I peeled off my frosting suit in the blessed artificial light of ship's day.

"Okay," said Eric. "Take it up to the lab. And don't touch it."

Eric can be a hell of an annoying character. "I've got a brain," I snarled, "even if you can't see it." So can I.

There was a ringing silence while we each tried to dream up an apology. Eric got there first. "Sorry," he said.

"Me, too." I hauled the collector off to the lab on a cart.

He guided me when I got there. "Put the whole package in that opening. Jaws first. No, don't close it yet. Turn the thing until these lines match the lines on the collector. Okay. Push it in a little. Now close the door. Okay, Howie, I'll take it from there . . ." There were chugging sounds from behind the little door. "Have to wait 'til the lab's cool enough. Go get some coffee," said Eric.

"I'd better check your maintenance."

"Okay, good. Go oil my prosthetic aids."

"Prosthetic aids"—that was a hot one. I'd thought it up myself. I pushed the coffee button so it would be ready when I was through, then opened the big door in the forward wall of the cabin. Eric looked much like an electrical network, except for the gray mass at the top which was his brain. In all directions from his spinal cord and brain, connected at the walls of the intricately shaped glass-and-soft-plastic vessel which housed him. Eric's nerves reached out to master the ship. The instruments which mastered Eric—but he was sensitive about having it put that way—were banked along both sides of the closet. The blood pump pumped rhythmically, seventy beats a minute.

"How do I look?" Eric asked.

"Beautiful. Are you looking for flattery?"

"Jackass! Am I still alive?"

"The instruments think so. But I'd better lower your fluid temperature a fraction." I did. Ever since we'd landed, I'd had a tendency to keep temperatures too high. "Everything else looks okay. Except your food tank is getting low."

"Well, it'll last the trip."

"Yeah. 'Scuse me, Eric, coffee's ready." I went and got it. The only thing I really worry about is his liver. It's too complicated. It could break down too easily. If it stopped making blood sugar, Eric would be dead.

If Eric dies I die, because Eric is the ship. If I die Eric dies, insane, because he can't sleep unless I set his prosthetic aids.

I was finishing my coffee when Eric yelled. "Hey!"

"What's wrong?" I was ready to run in any direction.

"It's only helium!"

He was astonished and indignant. I relaxed.

"I get it now, Howie. Helium two. That's all our monsters are. Nuts."

Helium two, the superfluid that flows uphill. "Nuts doubled. Hold everything, Eric. Don't throw away your samples. Check them for contaminants."

"For what?"

"Contaminants. My body is hydrogen oxide with contaminants. If the contaminants in the helium are complex enough, it might be alive."

"There are plenty of other substances," said Eric, "but I can't analyze them well enough. We'll have to rush this stuff back to Earth while our freezers can keep it cool."

I got up. "Take off right now?"

"Yes, I guess so. We could use another sample, but we're just as likely to wait here while this one deteriorates."

"Okay, I'm strapping down now. Eric?"

"Yeah? Take off in fifteen minutes, we have to wait for the ion-drive section. You can get up."

"No, I'll wait. Eric, I hope it isn't alive. I'd rather it was just helium two acting like it's supposed to act."

"Why? Don't you want to be famous, like me?"

"Oh, sure, but I hate to think of life out there. It's just too alien. Too cold. Even on Pluto you could not make life out of helium two."

"It could be migrant, moving to stay on the night side of the pre-dawn crescent. Pluto's day is long enough for that. You're right, though; it doesn't get colder than this even between the stars. Luckily, I don't have much imagination."

Twenty minutes later, we took off. Beneath us all was darkness and only Eric, hooked into the radar, could see the ice dome contracting until all of it was visible: the vast layered ice cap that covers the coldest spot in the solar system, where midnight crosses the equator on the black back of Mercury.

THE GREAT SLOW KINGS

BY ROGER ZELAZNY

Roger Zelazny published one or two stories, not science fiction, at a remarkably early age in a scholastic magazine, but what he really wanted to do with his life was to write science fiction. Around 1960 that did not reasonably seem to offer a chance at a living. So Zelazny did what any right-thinking hopeful writer would do. He looked around for a way to subsidize the writing with an income he wouldn't have to earn.

Unemployment insurance was the obvious answer. To make sure he wouldn't be troubled with offers of jobs he didn't want, Roger listed his occupation as psychologist—reasonably enough, since that had been his major in school.

Many another young man and woman has been enabled to lead a rewarding life by such strategies, but the state employment service fooled him. They found him a job in the Civil Service, and so for a decade or so Roger Zelazny juggled figures for the government all day and wrote only by night.

Really, that's a good thing for a new writer to do. It takes the money pressure off. It leaves time to nurse along the ripening talents. It was during that period in Baltimore that Roger Zelazny wrote "The Doors of His Face, the Lamps of His Mouth" and "A Rose for Ecclesiastes" and his first novels—as well as the present story and others for me. The need for a Civil Service job is no longer present. Zelazny is now a Sunbelter and a full-time writer of, among other things, the very successful Nine Princes in Amber *series. His fame and wealth have grown, but I still like best the fine, far-out short stories like "The Great Slow Kings."*

*   *   *

Drax and Dran sat in the great Throne Hall of Glan, discussing life. Monarchs by virtue of superior intellect and physique—and the fact that they were the last two survivors of the race of Glan—theirs was a divided rule over the planet and their one subject, Zindrome, the palace robot.

Drax had been musing for the past four centuries (theirs was a sluggish sort) over the possibility of life on other planets in the galaxy.

Accordingly, "Dran," said he, addressing the other (who was becoming mildly curious as to his thoughts), "Dran, I've been thinking. There may be life on other planets in the galaxy."

Dran considered his reply to this, as the world wheeled several times about its sun.

"True," he finally agreed, "there may."

After several months Drax shot back, "If there is, we ought to find out."

"Why?" asked Dran with equal promptness, which caused the other to suspect that he, too, had been thinking along these lines.

So he measured his next statement out cautiously, first testing each word within the plated retort of his reptilian skull.

"Our kingdom is rather underpopulated at present," he observed. "It would be good to have many subjects once more."

Dran regarded him askance, then slowly turned his head. He closed one eye and half-closed the other, taking full stock of his co-ruler, whose appearance, as he suspected, was unchanged since the last time he had looked.

"That, also, is true," he noted. "What do you suggest we do?"

This time Drax turned, reappraising him, eye to eye.

"I think we ought to find out if there is life on other planets in the galaxy."

"Hmm."

Two quick roundings of the seasons went unnoticed, then, "Let me think about it," he said, and turned away.

After what he deemed a polite period of time, Drax coughed.

"Have you thought sufficiently?"

"No."

Drax struggled to focus his eyes on the near-subliminal streak of bluish light which traversed, re-traversed and re-re-traversed the Hall as he waited.

"Zindrome!" he finally called out.

The robot slowed his movements to a statuelike immobility to accommodate his master. A feather duster protruded from his right limb.

"You called, great Lord of Glan?"

"Yes, Zindrome, worthy subject. Those old spaceships which we constructed in happier days, and never got around to using. Are any of them still capable of operation?"

"I'll check, great Lord."

He seemed to change position slightly.

"There are three hundred eighty-two," he announced, "of which four are in functioning condition, great Lord. I've checked all the operating circuits."

"Drax," warned Dran, "you are arrogating unauthorized powers to yourself once more. You should have conferred with me before issuing that order.''

''I apologize,'' stated the other. ''I simply wanted to expedite matters, should your decision be that we conduct a survey.''

''You have anticipated my decision correctly,'' nodded Dran, ''but your eagerness seems to bespeak a hidden purpose.''

''No purpose but the good of the realm,'' smiled the other.

''That may be, but the last time you spoke of 'the good of the realm,' the civil strife which ensued cost us our other robot.''

''I have learned my lesson and profited thereby. I shall be more judicious in the future.''

''I hope so. Now, about this expedition—which part of the galaxy do you intend to investigate first?''

A tension-filled pause ensued.

''I had assumed,'' murmured Drax, ''that you would conduct the expedition. Being the more mature monarch, yours should be a more adequate decision as to whether or not a particular species is worthy of our enlightened rule.''

''Yes, but your youth tends to make you more active than I. The journey should be more expeditiously conducted by you.'' He emphasized the word ''expeditiously.''

''We could both go, in separate ships,'' offered Drax. ''That would be truly expeditious—''

Their heated debating was cut short by a metallic cough-equivalent.

''Masters,'' suggested Zindrome, ''the half-life of radioactive materials being as ephemeral as it is, I regret to report that only one spaceship is now in operational condition.''

''That settles it, Dran. *You* go. It will require a steadier *rrand* to manage an underpowered ship.''

''And leave you to foment civil strife and usurp unfranchised powers? No, you go!''

''I suppose we could *both* go,'' sighed Drax.

''Fine! Leave the kingdom leaderless! *That* is the kind of muddle-headed thinking which brought about our present political embarrassment.''

''Masters,'' said Zindrome, ''if *someone* doesn't go soon, the ship will be useless.''

They both studied their servant, approving the rapid chain of logic forged by his simple statement.

''Very well,'' they smiled in unison, ''*you* go.''

Zindrome bowed quite obsequiously and departed from the great Throne Hall of Glan.

''Perhaps we should authorize Zindrome to construct facsimiles of himself,'' stated Dran, tentatively. ''If we had more subjects, we could accomplish more.''

"Are you forgetting our most recent agreement?" asked Drax. "A superfluity of robots tended to stimulate factionalism last time—and certain people grew ambitious . . ." He let his voice trail off over the years, for emphasis.

"I am not certain as to whether your last allusion contains a hidden accusation," began the other carefully. "If so, permit me to caution you concerning rashness—and to remind you who it was who engineered the Mono-Robot Protection Pact."

"Do you believe things will be different in the case of a multitude of organic subjects?" inquired the other.

"Definitely," said Dran. "There is a certain irrational element in the rationale of the organic being, making it less amenable to direct orders than a machine would be. Our robots, at least, were faithful when we ordered them to destroy one another. Irresponsible organic subjects either do it without being told, which is boorish, or refuse to do it when you order them, which is insubordination."

"True," smiled Drax, unearthing a gem he had preserved for millennia against this occasion. "Concerning organic life, the only statement which can be made with certainty is that life is uncertain."

"Hmm." Dran narrowed his eyes to slits. "Let me ponder that a moment. Like much of your thinking it seems to smack of a concealed sophistry."

"It contains none, I assure you. It is the fruit of much meditation."

"Hmm."

Dran's pondering was cut short by the arrival of Zindrome, who clutched two brownish blurs beneath his metal arms.

"Back already, Zindrome? What have you there? Slow them down so we can see them."

"They are under sedation at present, great Masters. It is the movements caused by their breathing which produce the unpleasant vibration pattern on your retinas. To subject them to more narcosis could prove deleterious."

"Nevertheless," maintained Dran, "we must appraise our new subjects carefully, which requires that we see them. Slow them down some more."

"You gave that order without—" began Drax, but was distracted by the sudden appearance of the two hairy bipeds.

"Warm-blooded?" he asked.

"Yes, Lord."

"That bespeaks a very brief lifespan."

"True," offered Dran, "but that kind tends to reproduce quite rapidly."

"That observation tends to be correct," nodded Drax. "Tell me, Zindrome, do they represent the sexes necessary for reproduction?"

"Yes, Master. There are two sexes among these anthropoids, so I brought one of each."

"That was very wise. Where did you find them?"

"Several billion light years from here."

"Turn these two loose outside and go fetch us some more."

The creatures vanished. Zindrome appeared not to have moved.

"Have you the fuel necessary for another such journey?"

"Yes, my Lord. More of it has evolved recently."

"Excellent."

The robot departed.

"What sort of governmental setup should we inaugurate this time?" asked Drax.

"Let us review the arguments for the various types."

"A good idea."

In the midst of their discussion, Zindrome returned and stood waiting to be recognized.

"What is it, Zindrome? Did you forget something?"

"No, great Lords. When I returned to the world from which I obtained the samples, I discovered that the race had progressed to the point where it developed fission processes, engaged in an atomic war, and annihilated itself."

"That was extremely inconsiderate—typical, however, I should say, of warm-blooded instability."

Zindrome continued to shift.

"Have you something else to report?"

"Yes, great Masters. The two specimens I released have multiplied and are now spread over the entire planet of Glan."

"We should have been advised!"

"Yes, great Lords, but I was absent and—"

"They themselves should have reported this action!"

"Masters, I am afraid they are unaware of your existence."

"How could that have happened?" asked Dran.

"We are presently buried beneath several thousand layers of alluvial rock. The geological shifts—"

"You have your orders to maintain the palace and clean the grounds," glowered Dran. "Have you been frittering away your time again?"

"No, great Lords! It all occurred during my absence. I shall attend to it immediately."

"First," ordered Drax, "tell us what else our subjects have been up to, that they saw fit to conceal from us."

"Recently," observed the robot, "they have discovered how to forge and temper metals. Upon landing, I observed that they had developed many ingenious instruments of a cutting variety. Unfortunately they were using them to cut one another."

"Do you mean," roared Dran, "that there is strife in the kingdom?"

"Uh, yes, my Lord."

"I will not brook unauthorized violence among my subjects!"

"*Our* subjects," added Drax, with a meaningful glare.

"*Our* subjects," amended Dran. "We must take immediate action."

"Agreed."

"Agreed."

"I shall issue orders forbidding their engagement in activities leading to bloodshed."

"I presume that you mean a joint proclamation," stated Drax.

"Of course. I was not slighting you, I was simply shaken by the civil emergency. We shall draft an official proclamation. Let Zindrome fetch us writing instruments."

"Zindrome, fetch—"

"I have them here, my Lords."

"Now, let me see. How shall we phrase it . . . ?"

"Perhaps I should clean the palace while your Excellencies—"

"No! Wait right here! This will be very brief and to the point."

"Mm. 'We hereby proclaim . . .' "

"Don't forget our titles."

"True. 'We, the imperial monarchs of Glan, herebeneath undersigned, do hereby . . .' "

A feeble pulse of gamma rays passed unnoticed by the two rulers. The faithful Zindrome diagnosed its nature, however, and tried unsuccessfully to obtain his monarchs' attention. Finally, he dismissed the project with a stoical gesture typical of his kind. He waited.

"There!" they agreed, flourishing the document. "Now you can tell us what you have been trying to say, Zindrome. But make it brief, you must deliver this soon."

"It is already too late, great Lords. This race, also, progressed into civilized states, developed nuclear energy, and eradicated itself while you were writing."

"Barbarous!"

"Warm-blooded irresponsibility!"

"May I go clean up now, great Masters?"

"Soon, Zindrome, soon. First, though, I move that we file the proclamation in the Archives for future use, in the event of similar occurrences."

Dran nodded.

"I agree. *We* so order."

The robot accepted the crumbling proclamation and vanished from sight.

"You know," Drax mused, "there must be lots of radioactive material lying about now . . ."

"There probably is."

"It could be used to fuel a ship for another expedition."

"Perhaps."

"This time we could instruct Zindrome to bring back something with a longer lifespan and more deliberate habits—somewhat nearer our own."

"That would have its dangers. But perhaps we could junk the Mono-Robot

Protection Pact and order Zindrome to manufacture extras of himself. Under strict supervision.''

"That would have its dangers, too.''

"At any rate, I should have to ponder your suggestion carefully.''

"And I yours.''

"It's been a busy day,'' nodded Dran. "Let's sleep on it.''

"A good idea.''

Sounds of saurian snoring emerged from the great Throne Hall of Glan.

THE LIFE HATER

BY FRED SABERHAGEN

Just recently I was sitting in a gathering of science-fiction writers, and the conversation turned to colleagues who had never become as well known as they should. Barry Malzberg nominated F. L. Wallace. Someone else suggested the name of Wyman Guin. I put in Joseph Samachson, who, under the name of William Morrison, wrote "Country Doctor," "The Sack," and a lot of other first-rate stories without ever developing the personal following he deserved. And then someone mentioned Fred Saberhagen.

Fred Saberhagen is a very special case. He is a successful writer with a "bankable" name, and some of his work—notably his recent novels like The Holmes-Dracula Tapes—*has broadened his reputation and his audience considerably. But to most readers "Fred Saberhagen" still means only one thing, and that thing is "Berserker," and for that I feel some responsibility. The first story Fred ever sold was to me, and it was about a sort of interplanetary chess game between a human and an intelligent, inimical machine. I liked the writing, but I wasn't thrilled by the chess. I was, by the machine. When I bought the story, I urged Saberhagen to forget the chess and give us more stories about the machines. I gave him the same song and dance I had given Keith Laumer: a strong series was the fast track to instant name recognition; the treasures of the Orient were his to claim if only he would do these simple things I asked.*

And he did. And they were; all fell out as I had described.

However, there was a problem. There are two ways of writing a series. In one, the linear, you just sort of chop off a chunk of story each time; this is Retief, *or* Star Trek, *or* I, Robot. *At the end of each story, all the players go back to their original positions, ready for the next installment, and you can go on writing these stories forever. The other method is the exponential. Each story builds on the one before, like Doc Smith's* Skylark *or* Lensman. *After a while, they get simply too big to handle. This is artistically more satisfying, but it is self-limiting; and that is the way the Berserker series goes.*

So I do not think there will be many more Berserker stories. I don't think

Fred Saberhagen will much mind; they've been overshadowing his other work. But I still like them a lot, and here is one of the earliest.

* * *

Carr swallowed a pain pill, and tried to find a less-uncomfortable position in the combat chair. He keyed his radio transmitter and spoke to the rogue ship that hung before him in space.

"I come in peace. I have no weapons. I come to talk to you."

He waited. The cabin of his little one-man ship was silent. His radar screen showed the berserker machine still many light-seconds ahead of him. There was no reaction from it, but he knew that it had heard him.

Behind Carr was the Sol-type star he called sun, and his home planet, colonized from Earth a century before. It was a lonely settlement, out near the rim of the galaxy. Until now the war waged on life by the berserker machines had been a remote horror in the news stories. The colony's only real fighting ship had been sent to join Karlsen's fleet in the defense of Earth, when the berserkers were said to be massing there. But now the enemy was here, and the people of Carr's planet were readying two more ships in feverish haste—they were a small colony, and not wealthy in resources. Even when the two ships were ready, they would hardly be a match for a berserker.

When Carr had taken his plan to the leaders of the colony, they had thought him mad.

Go out and talk to it of peace and love? *Argue* with it? There might be some hope of converting the most depraved human to the cause of goodness and mercy, but what appeal could alter the built-in purpose of a machine?

"Why *not* talk to it of peace?" Carr had demanded. "Have you a better plan? I'm willing to go, I've nothing to lose."

They had looked at him, across the gulf that separates healthy planners from those who know they are dying. They thought almost any scheme would be better than his. But they could imagine nothing else to do until the warships were ready, which would be at least ten days. The little one-man ship was expendable, being unarmed. Armed, it would be no more a provocation to a berserker. In the end, they let Carr take it, hoping there was a chance his arguments might delay the inevitable attack.

For Carr himself, of course, they wasted no thought. For Carr was dying. Was as good as dead.

When Carr came within a million miles of the berserker, it stopped its own unhurried motion and seemed to wait for him, hanging in space in the orbital track of an airless planetoid, at a point from which the planetoid was still several days away.

"I am unarmed," he radioed again. "I come to talk with you, not to damage you. If those who built you were here, I would try to talk to them of peace and love. Do you understand?''

He felt sure it would understand his language. All the berserker machines had learned the universal space-travelers' tongue, from human prisoners or from each other. And he was serious about talking love to the unknown Builders. Grudges and vengeance seemed tiny things to a dying man. But the Builder would not be aboard; the berserkers had been constructed, probably, when Earthmen hunted the mammoth with spears. The Builders were lost in spacetime, along with their enemies of long ago.

Suddenly it answered him: "Little ship, maintain your present speed and course toward me. Be ready to stop when ordered.''

"I—I will.'' In spite of being ready for it, Carr found himself stuttering and shaken at the sound of its voice, the uneven mechanical reproduction of the words of human prisoners, recorded aboard or borrowed from another machine. Now the weapons which could sterilize a planet would be trained on him alone. And there was worse than destruction to be feared, if one tenth of the stories about berserkers' prisoners were true. Carr did not let himself think about that—although the pain that racked him in a momentary flood of agony made death seem almost welcome.

When he was within ten thousand miles, it ordered: "Stop. Wait where you are, relative to me.''

Carr obeyed instantly. Soon he saw that it had launched toward him something about the size of his own ship—a little moving dot on his video screen, coming out of the vast black fortress that floated against the stars.

Even at this range he could see how scarred and battered that fortress was. He had heard that all of these ancient machines were damaged, from their long senseless fighting across the galaxy; but surely such apparent ruin as this must be exceptional.

The berserker's launch slowed and drew up beside his ship. Soon there came a clanging at the airlock.

"Open!'' demanded the radio voice. "I must search you.''

"Then you will listen to me?''

"Then I will listen.''

He opened the lock, and stood aside for the half-dozen machines that entered. They were not unlike robot valets and workers, except that these were old and limping and worn, like their great master. Here and there a new part gleamed. But often the machines' movements were unsteady as they searched Carr, searched his cabin, probed everywhere on the little ship. One of them had to be half-carried out by its fellows, when the search was completed.

Another one of the machines, a thing with arms and hands like a man's, stayed behind. As soon as the lock had closed behind the others, it settled itself in the combat chair and began to drive the ship toward the berserker.

"Wait!'' Carr protested. "I didn't surrender!'' The ridiculous words hung in the air, seeming to deserve no reply. Sudden panic made Carr move without thinking; he stepped forward and grabbed at the mechanical pilot, trying to pull it from the chair. It put one metal hand against his chest and shoved him across the cabin so that he staggered and fell in the artificial gravity, thumping his head painfully against a bulkhead. "In a matter of minutes, we will talk about love and peace," said the radio voice.

Looking out a port as his ship neared the immense berserker, Carr saw the scars of battle become plainer and plainer, even to his unpracticed eye. There were holes in the hull, square miles of bendings and swellings and pits where the metal had once flowed molten.

Rubbing his bumped head, Carr felt a faint thrill of pride. *We've done that to it,* he thought, *we soft little living things.* His own martial feeling annoyed him, in a way. He had always been something of a pacifist. Of course it could hardly be thought immoral to use violence against a dangerous but inanimate machine. After some delay, a hatch opened in the berserker's side, and Carr's ship followed the berserker's launch into darkness.

Now there was nothing to be seen through the port. Soon there came a gentle bump, as of docking. The mechanical pilot shut off the drive, turned toward Carr, and started to rise from the chair.

Something in it failed. Instead of rising smoothly, the pilot reared up, flailed for a moment with arms that sought a grip or balance, and then fell heavily to the deck. For half a minute it moved one arm, and made a grinding noise. Then it was still.

In the half-minute of silence which followed, Carr realized that he was again master of his cabin; chance had given him that. If there was something he could do—

"Leave your ship," said the calm voice. "There is an airfilled tube fitted to your airlock. It will lead you to a place where we can talk of peace and love."

Carr's eyes, with a sort of reluctant horror, had dragged themselves to focus on the engine switch, and beyond that, to the C-plus activator.

The C-plus jump was not usable as a drive anywhere near the huge mass of a sun. In such proximity as this to a mass even the size of the surrounding berserker, the effect became only a weapon—a weapon of tremendous potential power.

Carr did not—or thought he did not—any longer fear sudden death; he was too near to the slow, sure kind. But now he found that with all his heart and soul he feared what might be prepared for him outside the airlock. All the horror stories came back. The thought of going out through that airlock now was unendurable. It was less terrifying for him to step carefully around the fallen pilot, to reach the controls and turn the engine back on.

"I can talk to you from here," he said, his voice quavering in spite of an effort to keep it steady.

After about ten seconds, the berserker said: "Your C-plus drive has safety devices. You will not be able to kamikaze me."

"You may be right," said Carr after a moment's thought. "But if a safety device does function, it might hurl my ship away from your center of mass, right through your hull. And your hull is in bad shape now. You don't want any more damage."

"You would die."

"I'll have to die sometime. But I didn't come out here to die, or to fight. I came to talk with you, to try to reach some agreement."

"What kind of agreement?"

At last Carr took a deep breath, and marshaled the arguments he had so often rehearsed. He kept his fingers resting gently on the C-plus activator, and his eyes alert on the instruments that normally monitored the hull for micrometeorite damage.

"I've had the feeling," he began, "that your attacks upon humanity may be only some ghastly mistake. Certainly we were not your original enemy."

"Life is my enemy. Life is evil." Pause. "Do you want to become goodlife?"

Carr closed his eyes for a moment; some of the horror stories were coming to life. But then he went firmly on with his argument. "From our point of view, it is you who are bad. We would like you to become a good machine, one that helps men instead of killing. Is not building a higher purpose than destroying?"

There was a longer pause. "What evidence can you offer that I should change my purpose?"

"For one thing, helping us will be a purpose easier of achievement. No one will damage you and oppose you."

"What is it to me, if I am damaged and opposed?"

Carr tried again. "Life is basically superior to non-life; and man is the highest form of life."

"What evidence do you offer?"

"Man has a spirit."

"I have learned that men claim that. But do you not define this spirit as something beyond the perception of any machine? And are there not men who deny that this spirit exists?"

"Spirit is so defined. And there are such men."

"Then I do not accept the argument of spirit."

Carr dug out a pain pill and swallowed it. "Still, you have no evidence that spirit does not exist. You must consider it as a possibility."

"That is correct."

"But leaving spirit out of the argument for now, consider the physical and chemical organization of life. Do you know anything of the delicacy and intricacy or organization in even a single living cell? And surely you must admit we humans carry wonderful computers inside our few cubic inches of skull."

"I have never had an intelligent captive to dissect," the mechanical voice informed him blandly, "though I have received some relevant data from other machines. But you admit that your form is the determined result of the operation of physical and chemical laws?"

"Have *you* ever thought that those laws may have been designed to do just that—produce brains capable of intelligent action?"

There was a pause that stretched on and on. Carr's throat felt dry and rough, as if he had been speaking for hours.

"I have never tried to use that hypothesis," it answered suddenly. "But if the construction of intelligent life is indeed so intricate, so dependent upon the laws of physics being as they are and not otherwise—then to serve life may be the highest purpose of a machine."

"You may be sure, our physical construction is intricate." He wasn't sure he could follow the machine's line of reasoning, but that hardly mattered if he could somehow win the game of Life. He kept his fingers on the C-plus activator.

The berserker said: "If I am able to study some living cells—"

Like a hot iron on a nerve, the meteorite-damage indicator moved; something was at the hull. "Stop that!" he screamed, without thought. "The first thing you try, I'll kill you!"

Its voice was unevenly calm, as always. "There may have been some accidental contact with your hull. I am damaged and many of my commensal machines are unreliable. I mean to land on this approaching planetoid to mine for metal and repair myself as far as possible." The indicator was quiet again.

The berserker resumed its argument. "If I am able to study some living cells from an intelligent life-unit for a few hours, I expect I will find strong evidence for, or against, your argument. Will you provide me with cells?"

"You must have had prisoners, sometime." He said it as a suspicion; he really knew no reason why it must have had human captives. It could have learned the language from another berserker.

"No; I have never taken a prisoner."

It waited. The question it had asked still hung in the air.

"The only human cells on this ship are my own. Possibly I could give you a few of them."

"Half a cubic centimeter should be enough; not a dangerous loss for you, I believe. I will not demand part of your brain. Also I understand that you wish to avoid the sensation called pain. I am willing to help you avoid it, if possible."

Did it want to drug him? That seemed too simple. Always unpredictability, the stories said, and sometimes a subtlety out of hell.

He went on with the game. "I have all that is necessary. Be warned that my attention will hardly waver from the control panel. Soon I will place a tissue sample in the airlock for you."

He got the medical kit, took two pain-killers, and set very carefully to work with a sterile scalpel. He had had some biological training.

When the small wound was bandaged, he cleansed the tissue sample of blood and lymph and with unsteady fingers sealed it into a little tube. Without letting down his guard for an instant, he dragged the fallen pilot to the airlock and left it there with the tissue sample. Utterly weary, he got back to the combat chair. When he switched the outer door open, he heard something come into the lock, and leave again.

He took a pep pill. It would stimulate some pain, but he'd be alert.

Two hours passed. Carr forced himself to eat some emergency rations, watched the panel, and waited.

He gave a startled jump when the berserker spoke again; nearly six hours had gone by.

"You are free to leave," it was saying. "Tell the leading life-units of your planet that when I have refitted, I will be their ally. The study of your cells has convinced me that the human body is the highest creation of the universe, and that I should make helping you my purpose. Do you understand?"

Carr felt numb. "Yes. Yes, I have convinced you. After you have refitted, you will fight on our side."

Something shoved hugely and gently at his hull. Through a port he saw stars, and realized that the great hatch through which his ship had entered was swinging open.

This far within the system, Carr necessarily kept his ship in normal space to travel. It meant he could see the berserker as he fled from it, and he kept it in sight as long as possible. His last sight of the berserker showed it moving as if indeed about to let down upon the airless planetoid. Certainly it was not following him.

A couple of hours after being freed, he roused himself from contemplation of the radar screen, and went to spend a full minute considering the inner airlock door. At last he shook his head, dialed air into the lock, and entered it. The pilot was gone, with the tissue sample. There was nothing strange to be seen. Carr took a deep breath, as if relieved, closed up the lock again, and went to a port to spend some time watching the stars.

After a day he began to decelerate, so that when hours had added into another day, he was still a good distance from home. He ate, and slept, and watched his face in a mirror. He weighed himself, and he watched the stars some more, with great interest, like a man examining something long forgotten.

In two more days, gravity bent his course into a hairpin ellipse around his home planet. With his whole world bulking between him and the berserker's rock, Carr began to use his radio.

"Ho, on the ground! Good news."

The answer came almost instantly. "We've been tracking you, Carr. What's going on? What happened?"

He told them of his encounter with the berserker. "So that's the story up to now," he finished. "I expect the thing really needs to refit. It is seriously damaged. Two warships attacking it now should easily win."

"Yes." There was excited talk in the background. Then the voice was back, sounding uneasy. "Carr—you haven't started a landing approach yet, so maybe you understand. We've got to be careful. The thing was probably lying to you."

"Oh, I know. Even that pilot's collapse might have been staged. I guess the berserker was too badly shot up to want to risk a battle, so it tried another way. Must have sneaked the stuff into my cabin air, just before it let me go—or maybe left it in my airlock."

"What stuff?"

Carr said, "The stuff you're worrying about. The poison it thinks will kill us all. I'd guess it's some freshly mutated virus, designed for specific virulence against the tissue I gave it. It expected I'd hurry home and land before getting sick, and spread a new plague. It must have thought it was inventing biological warfare, using life against life, as we use machines against machines. But it needed that tissue sample to blood its pet viruses. It didn't know our chemistry. It must have been telling the truth about never having a human prisoner."

"Some virus, you think? What's it doing to you, Carr? Are you in pain—I mean, more than before?"

"No." Carr swirled his chair to look at the little chart he had begun. It showed that in the last two days his weight loss had started to reverse itself. He looked down at his body, at the bandaged place near the center of a discolored, inhuman-looking area. That area was smaller than it had been, and he saw a hint of new and healthy skin.

"What *is* the stuff doing to you?"

Carr allowed himself to smile, and to speak aloud his growing hope.

"I think it's killing off my cancer."

OLD TESTAMENT

BY JEROME BIXBY

Jerome Bixby began writing science fiction a generation ago, and did pretty well at it. Then he went to Hollywood.

Everybody in the world of letters makes sad, scurrilous jokes about Hollywood—demeaner of talent, City of the Dreadful Night, holy city of the religion whose First Commandment is "Take the money and run." And all the jokes are true. There are some really good writers in Hollywood. And every now and then, just often enough to give one some hope, something one of them wrote gets made into a film or television show that does them proud.

But that is not the way to bet it.

Writing is not the most secure of professions at best. There is always someone between you and your audience. You can write the finest short story ever penned and, until you can find an editor who will put it into print, it doesn't really exist, because no one can read it. Novels are even more chancy, because the risks for the publisher are more visible. An unsuccessful short story is forgotten too fast to do any real harm, but an unsuccessful book is a clear cash loss.

But writers-for-print at least have hope. If every editor in the business turns down your story this year, why, next year there's a whole new editorial crop. One of them will buy it—or one from the year after that. (Which actually happened with, among other novels that have done well enough, Samuel R. Delany's Dhalgren *and C. M. Kornbluth's and my own* The Space Merchants.*)*

Not so for the Hollywood writer. Almost always he writes on contract, and when he is done he doesn't own it any more; it belongs to a producer, a star, or a studio. Worse. The odds are at least ten to one that even the best of scripts will never be made, because a producer will die, a star will back out, or financing will fail—or anything will happen—and then the script is dead. There are file cabinets in California holding (literally!) millions of words written by Ray Bradbury, Richard Matheson, Harlan Ellison, Robert Bloch, and a dozen other writers whose audiences would love to read them, written at the peak of their powers and, to all intents and purposes, nonexistent, because they will never see the light of day. It is a terrible, I'd call it a criminal, waste of a scarce commodity, namely great writing talent. And among all those words are quite a few by Jerry Bixby.

Even when we did see a Bixby on the screen it was only Fantastic Voyage, *with his original script chopped and rechewed by half a dozen other writers. And it's a shame!*

*   *   *

It was about the size of a grapefruit, and about the color of one. From its top sprouted a cluster of thin, ribbonish tentacles—translucent, filled with shifting shades of violet and chartreuse, far tougher than they looked. Four pedal extremities, oddly like thumbs with long claws, stuck out from the bottom. It had two flat, pink eyes, set very close together.

It squealed as Ray Caradac carried it at arm's length into the control room of the *Manta*.

"Look what we have here," he said grimly.

Mary Caradac—small, brunette, snapping-eyed, the other half of Extraterrestrial Exploration Team 2861—looked up from the bitchboard, where she had been dialing their course away from Sirius IV.

"What on *Earth*—" she gasped.

"On *Sirius*," Ray corrected. "On good old Sirius IV, which we seem not to have escaped quite as completely as we thought we had."

"A baby Sirian!"

"That's my guess, from the glimpses we got of the natives."

Mary stood up, spilling *Benton's Astrocharts* from her lap, and reached for the creature. Ray relinquished it, looking disgusted. While Mary cradled it in both hands, he moved three steps across the narrow, instrument-cluttered control room to snap on the rear screen. He focused the screen with one hand, rubbed his home-made crew-cut with the other.

Behind him, the Sirian infant squealed, a sound like a viola harmonic. "Where'd you find it?" Mary asked.

"Under my bed, of all places. I went to shove my suit-boots under it and change into sneakers, and the critter let out a squeal and damned near scared me out through the side of the ship."

"What was it doing *there*?"

"Ask *it*." Ray stared glumly out at the dull green globe of Sirius IV, already thirty thousand miles away and retreating at ninety m.p.s. "Maybe it wanted to see the Universe, or just get the hell off its planet. I can understand that, after two *hours* on the godforsaken ice ball."

"It probably likes minus thirty just fine. It's probably roasting right now, poor thing."

*   *   *

Ray turned from the gazer. Mary was cuddling the Sirian infant to her breast and fanning it with one hand.

"Look out," he said dryly. "It might bite."

"So do human babies. Besides, it hasn't got any teeth."

Ray looked at the tiny pink mouth, opening and closing horizontally under the eyes like sliding doors. He'd seen enough cockeyed life-forms not to shudder.

"Why, look, it *couldn't* have wandered in," Mary said, twiddling one of the stubby legs. She set it on the chart file, where it immediately went *plop* on its rounded bottom, legs sticking out like a newborn kitten's. "It can't even stand up." She flashed a hand in front of the pink eyes, and filmy eyelids blinked. The tentacles waved. "I'm no judge of Sirian age, but I'll bet it's darned young."

She looked wise and extended a finger and two tentacles curled around it, tugging it gently toward the mouth.

"Uh, uh," she said. "Not a nipple, son. There, Ray—you see?" She picked it up again. Another squeal.

"I wasn't arguing," he said absently. Then, plaintively: "Just what the devil are we supposed to do with a Sirian infant? And how did it get here, if it can't walk under its own steam?"

"Under someone else's, obviously," Mary said practically. Then she paused and cocked her head. "Good *God*! I wonder . . . come on Ray, let's go look where you found it. I have a perfectly wonderfully preposterous hunch!"

They went single-file down the narrow corridor that led to sleeping quarters, Mary carrying the infant. There she waited for Ray to open the door—as she would have done even if she hadn't had her hands full. The Caradacs had decided long ago that such little niceties should be carefully and lovingly observed aboard the *Manta,* ten billion miles from nowhere. Things like love and sex can get awfully pedestrian in a sixty-foot spacer, if you don't care for them right.

Inside, Mary put the Sirian on Joe's bed and said, "Hold it there."

Ray sat down beside the creature and put one hand on its back—the surface one hundred and eighty degrees from eyes and mouth—and pressed gingerly. *Squeal*.

"I wonder what it eats," he said sourly.

Mary was head and shoulders under the bed. She said, "Ah, hah!" and emerged with a handful of dried, crinkly looking leaves. They smelled faintly like cinnamon. The Sirian's tentacles went *zing!* and it squealed an octave above any previous effort.

"Feed it," Mary said, going under the bed again.

Ray put a pinch of the leaves on the blanket, and released the creature, keeping one hand poised to see that it didn't roll off the bed. It dug the claws of its front feet into the blanket, hiked itself toward the leaves, opened its mouth, and crunched away. Ray watched, eyes a little glazed. "What—?"

Mary's head appeared again. In one hand she held more dried leaves; in the other a crude basket about a foot square, high sided, woven of some broad, reddish fiber.

She squatted there, holding the basket, and looked at Ray.

It took Ray about six seconds to get it. He looked down at the creature, happily chewing leaves, up again at Mary's face. His jaw dropped. She was beginning to grin.

Ray clapped a hand unbelievingly to the side of his head, so hard his ears rang. "God in Heaven," he said, "A *foundling!*"

"Basket and all," Mary said. "Only the pathetic note from the mother is lacking."

"Oh, no, it's crazy!"

"Crazy or not, it's here." Mary touched a hand to the tentacles, and there was a squeal—a happy-sounding squeal.

"But why?" Ray gasped. "Why should a Sirian mother—dressed in a threadbare Sirian shawl, no doubt—abandon her baby in our ship?"

"Why do mothers in threadbare shawls usually abandon babies?"

"M'm. Because they can't support them. Or because they're illegitimate, or something."

"In this case it's probably just something. I don't think it could be a matter of supporting it. A B-4 culture's too darned primitive for that. They live right off the soil. This stuff—" Mary pinched a handful of leaves she'd put on the blanket—"was everywhere we walked. As for legitimacy, that's never an issue in the pre-M series—"

"Tut," said Ray, academically aroused. "You're assuming, honey. You need ten decimals after B-4, or anything else to really classify. Forbidden fruits all over the place. Besides, maybe our little friend here isn't a waif at all. Maybe we were taken for gods, and it's a sacrifice."

"In a basket? Brought right into this big old terrifying ship?"

"Oh, hell, I don't know. Motive X, for alien. That B-4 status drove us off the planet so fast . . . *Scram! hands off! Clear out! don't influence!* and all the rest of Article 12, Section 9, paragraphs 3, 4, 7, and 16 of the Extraterrestrial Explor—"

"Not a nipple," Mary said, disengaging her finger again. "You know, Ray. I think it's thirsty."

Ray glowered at the creature. "I wonder what it drinks?"

"Try water—but be careful."

Ray filled a glass of water from the tiny basin in the corner and held it close to the vertical pink mouth. The mouth wrinkled. The little Sirian scrabbled backward and pressed into the pillow.

"So water's out," Ray grunted. He put the glass on the low table between the beds, knocking over two pawns and the black queen. "So now what? My God, didn't whoever or whatever left the critter here have sense enough to realize that handful of leaves wouldn't last forever? That we might not have whatever they drink for water?"

"Of course not," Mary said placidly. "Now who's assuming? What can you expect of a B-4 . . . a cosmology? Food and water, or their equivalents, have always been around: therefore food and water are everywhere. A B-4 couldn't have the slightest idea of what this ship is, or what we are, or where we're from or going and how and why—"

"Then why was the food left?"

"Maybe to keep our friend happy until we found it. Oh, I don't know either! I'm just as puzzled as you are. But I do know what we've got to do now."

"What?"

"Take it back. It'll die if we don't."

Ray sat down on the other bed and glared at the two who sat on his—Mary and the Sirian infant, which had ceased eating and was now cleaning the waxy skin around its mouth with a tentacle.

"Sure," he said. "Take it back. Violate every damned rule in the book. Take a chance of Influencing, by letting them see us again. One time is bad enough—but the B-series have short memories. Most of it gets corrupted by legend, and after a couple of centuries the legends are obliterated by more recent events and interpretations. But a *second* time? That's the time that clicks."

"We have to, anyway. Maybe you're wrong. Maybe it isn't a B—"

"Honey, I studied forty years not to be wrong. I can look at three artifacts, two flora, the dials on my spy-eye, and write a history."

Mary looked stubborn. "We take it back. This isn't in the books."

"Maybe they'll tear it to pieces if we do," Ray argued. "Maybe it's a freak—a sport. Maybe that's why it landed up with us. We might be killing it."

"Well we'll *certainly* be killing it if we don't, so you get right on up to the board and get us back to that planet. Look how thirsty it is . . . hey, *not* a nipple, damn it!"

The infant squealed, eyeing the finger.

"Nobody'll ever know, Ray. We can't let the poor thing die."

Ray sighed and raised his brows. Then he lowered one and winked at her. "What do I get?"

"A lot of nothing if you don't."

Mary grinned at his back.

My mate dead. She die having little one. I sorry. She best mate. But I sorrier for little one. Soon they kill him. Why kill little ones when mother die having them? Priest say because they kill mother and now no mother to drink from. So they die anyway. But they *not* kill mother. That what I think. Not their fault. And *other* mothers with dead *little ones*. No little ones to drink *them*. Why not . . . why not . . . do for each other? But priest say no. He say they bad. Must die because kill mother. He say *he* must drink from mothers with dead little ones to keep magic power. He get fat. This go on for long time. Many thousand suns. But I wonder if he *really* have magic power or just want to stay fat. Soon priest come to take little one away and kill him. I sorry. Then I think of shiny thing that come down by village out of sky. Everybody afraid. Priest tell us to stay away. Tell us gods angry. Tell us to stay in huts. Things come out of shiny thing. Tall and different. They walk through village. Everybody afraid, I afraid too. But they don't hurt. Don't kill. Don't break huts and eat like animals. I more sorry for little one than afraid. I *no* let priest kill him. While tall different things walk in village I go out with little one. Nobody see. Everybody afraid to look out. I take little one to shiny thing. Cave in side. I afraid but nothing happen. I take little one into cave and hide him. Leave food so he not cry and priest hear. I think maybe tall different things kill him when find him. But they no hurt when walk in village. And priest take long long time to kill little one if find him. So I hope tall different things treat little one good. I go back to village. Tall different things coming. I hide. They pass. I go into village. Everybody coming out. We see shiny thing go into sky. Everybody afraid. Priest most afraid. He say tall different things bad gods. They angry. Must sacrifice. I afraid. I make up story. I say tall different things *good* gods. I say they take little one away to village in sky because killing little ones *wrong*. They come to *save* him. Priest say I lie. I say he lie. I say good gods kill *him* if he kill more little ones when mothers die. Everybody listen. They say tall different ones didn't hurt. Didn't kill. Maybe I *right*. Maybe tall different ones *really* good gods. Priest say not true. *He* make up story. He say bad gods come because he call them to come take little one away and eat him. He say he *call* gods to take little one! But I know he *lie* because they no take. I *put* little one in shiny thing. *But I don't say or they kill kill me for lying.* I stick to story. I tell everybody tall different ones good gods. Come to save little one. Priest say they bad gods. Come to take little one and eat him. Come to take *us* and eat *us* if we not believe priest. Everybody say *wait for sign*. Priest say kill me but everybody say *wait*. Lots of fathers like me. They no like priest killing little ones for long time. But they afraid. Priest say it right. He say gods tell him to. We wonder. Maybe priest just want to be priest. Everybody afraid of priest. Give him best food and best mates. We wait. I cry that night.

The airlock hissed. Ray Caradac came in, wearing his spacesuit against Sirius IV's icy cold, but not the helmet—the planet was breathable.

Mary was waiting. "I saw you coming through the gazer. How'd it go?"

Ray grinned sourly as he zipped down the chest of his suit. Frost chipped off the metallic cloth. "I didn't leave it out in the brush as I'd planned. Afraid an animal would get it. I waited until dark and then went to the village. They pull in their sidewalks early—not a soul stirring. I snuck in quiet as I could, and right in the middle of it the damned critter started squealing its fool head off. Familiar smells or something. I suppose. So I just set it down and walked dignifiedly out of the place. Don't know whether anybody saw me, but I suspect they did. Damn—after all the trouble we went to landing way out here. I looked back at the edge of the brush, and there was a crowd around the kid.'' He stepped out of the suit and turned to rack it by the airlock, wearing only the standard padded diaper affair. ''Funny thing . . . I thought I saw a light flashing. A white light. But, hell, that's impossible— unless they have wood that burns white on this cold. Maybe I was seeing things.''

''Well, I certainly hope it's all right,'' Mary said. ''Shame if they did kill it, poor little thing.''

Ray stood a moment at the gazer, looking out at the moons-lit brush. ''I hope so too, honey. Well—'' he turned to the board—''let's get out of here, and fast! Before Article 12, Section 9b fights its way right out of the book and jumps down our throats.'' He paused as the A. G. unit caught, hummed loudly, then softly and steadily as they rose from Sirius IV. ''I wonder if it *will* affect them?''

It wasn't until next planetfall, eight months later, that Ray noticed that his pencil-flash was missing from his spacesuit breastpocket.

He asked Mary about it and Mary thought startledly; *''Not a nipple!''* and said not believing it, ''Oh, it'll turn up, one place or another.''

Next darkness we hear noise. We see tall different one go away. The good gods bring my little one back! Priest come out. Everybody say you *wrong*. You *lie*. Gods *not* eat little one!

Priest afraid. He say they *bad* gods. Bring little one back for sacrifice. They *good* gods. Little one has cold fire in hand. He throw cold fire at priest. This a new strange thing. *God* thing. It is a sign! We kill priest. Take him out for the animals to eat. I happy. Everybody like little one. He friend of good gods. Other mothers take care of him. Let him drink. Let other little ones drink. Do for each other, I happy because good gods bring him back.

to His people, and the First Night did ring with rejoicing; for He had returned from the Land Beyond the Sky and He said unto those who waited They are Good Gods, and I am Their Messenger, and lo! They have given to me a fragment of the Sun that I may shed light over darkness and open your eyes to good and gentle ways. And the false Priests said unto Him, Prove that you speak Truth; and in wrath He smote the Priests with the great light He carried, and lo! the false Priests were unmasked, and fled into the wilderness where they were devoured by wild beasts. Then the people cried, Welcome, and bade Him lead them and He said, Care for me, my Children, until I am able. So He was annointed, and fed, and in two suns had grown to manhood; and then He led His People from the valley and taught them to love . . .

* * *

"Always," mused the young Galac Federation student. "Always they come to fill a need. But where do they come from? What really are their acts? Where do they go?" He closed the Sirian Bible and put it aside, and picked up another.

THE MOON MOTH

BY JACK VANCE

Jack Vance lives in one of those architecturally unlikely houses that the California hills encourage. Rooms that are underground at one end look out over a twenty-foot drop on the other. It suits him. One of the definitions of literary style is "the problem solved." That is, the best style is whatever arrangement of words best solves the problem of saying what the author means to say. And in both dwelling and writing, Vance's solutions are original, delightful and exact.

Jack Vance sailed as a merchant mariner during World War II. Going to sea has afforded a good many people an opportunity to discover whether they were writers or not. Provided no one is trying to torpedo you, there are protracted periods of idleness, with little to distract one from writing. That's where Vance first tried his hand at writing science fiction. He was successful at once. Vance has now passed his thirty-fifth anniversary as a professional writer, and anyone who has sampled his work will agree that he is a very special one.

Vance creates strange, luminously, deeply textured worlds. I was lucky enough to publish two of the Vance stories that I think are right at the top of his form. One was "The Dragon Masters," which won Vance his first Hugo in 1963. The other was "The Moon Moth."

* * *

I.

The houseboat had been built to the most exacting standards of Sirenese craftsmanship—which is to say, as close to the absolute as human eye could detect. The planking of waxy dark wood showed no joints. The fastenings were platinum rivets countersunk and polished flat. In style, the boat was massive, broad-beamed, steady as the shore itself, without ponderosity or slackness of line. The bow bulged like a swan's breast, the stem rising high, then crooking forward to support an iron lantern. The doors were carved from slabs of a mottled black-green wood. The windows were many-sectioned, paned with squares of mica that were stained rose, blue, pale green, and violet. The bow was given to service facilities and quarters for the slaves; amidships were a pair of slipping cabins, a dining saloon, and a parlor saloon, opening upon an observation deck at the stern.

Such was Edwer Thissell's houseboat, but ownership of it brought him neither pleasure nor pride. The houseboat had become shabby. The carpeting had lost its pile; the carved screens were shipped; the iron lantern at the box sagged with rust. Seventy years ago the first owner, on accepting the boat, had honored the builder and had been likewise honored. The transaction (for the process represented a great deal more than simple giving and taking) had augmented the prestige of both. That time was far gone. The houseboat now commanded no prestige whatever.

Edwer Thissell, resident on Sirene only three months, recognized the lack but could do nothing about it: this particular houseboat was the best he could get. He sat on the rear deck practicing the *ganga,* a zitherlike instrument not much larger than his hand. A hundred yards inshore, surf defined a strip of white beach. Beyond rose jungle, with the silhouette of craggy black hills against the sky. Mireille shone hazy and white overhead, as if through a tangle of spider-web; the face of the ocean pooled and puddled with mother-of-pearl luster. The scene had become as familiar, thought not as boring, as the *ganga,* at which he had worked two hours, twanging out the Sirenese scales, forming chords, traversing simple progressions. Now he put down the *ganga* for the *zachinko,* this a small sound-box studded with keys, played with the right hand. Pressure on the keys forced air through reeds in the keys themselves, producing a concertinalike tone. Thissell ran off a dozen quick scales, making very few mistakes. Of the six instruments he had set himself to learn, the *zachinko* had proved the least refractory (with the exception, of course, of the *hymerkin,* that clacking, slapping, clattering device of wood and stone used exclusively with the slaves.)

Thissell practiced another ten minutes, then put aside the *zachinko.* He flexed his arms, wrung his aching fingers. Every waking moment since his arrival had been given to the instruments: the *hymerkin,* the *ganga,* the *zachinko,* the *kiv,* the *strapan,* the *gomapard.* He had practiced scales in twenty-four keys and four modes, chords without number, intervals never imagined on the Home Planets. Trills, arpeggios, slurs; click-stops and nasalization; damping and augmentation of overtones, vibratos and wolf-tones; concavities and convexities. He practiced with a dogged, deadly diligence, in which his original concept of music as a source of pleasure had long become lost. Looking over the instruments, Thissell resisted an urge to fling all six into the Titanic.

He rose to his feet, went forward through the parlor saloon, the dining saloon, along a corridor past the galley, and came out on the fore-deck. He bent over the rail, peered down into the underwater pens where Toby and Rex, the slaves, were harnessing the drayfish for the weekly trip to Fan, eight miles north. The youngest fish, either playful or captious, ducked and plunged. Its streaming black muzzle broke water, and Thissell, looking into its face felt a peculiar qualm: the fish wore no mask!

Thissell laughed uneasily, fingering his own mask, which was in the design of the Moon Moth. No question about it, he was becoming acclimated to Sirene! A significant stage had been reached when the naked face of a fish caused him shock!

The fish were finally harnessed; Toby and Rex climbed aboard, red bodies glistening, black cloth masks clinging to their faces. Ignoring Thissell, they stowed the pen and hoisted anchor. The dray-fish strained, the harness tautened, the houseboat moved north.

Returning to the after-deck, Thissell took up the *strapan*—this a circular sound-box eight inches in diameter. Forty-six wires radiated from a central hub to the circumference, where they connected to either a bell or a tinkle-bar. When plucked, the bells rang and the bars chimed; when strummed, the instrument gave off a twanging, jingling sound. When played with competence, the pleasantly acid dissonances produced an expressive effect; in an unskilled hand, the results were less felicitous, and might even approach random noise. The *strapan* was Thissell's weakest instrument. He practiced with concentration during the entire trip north.

In due course, the houseboat approached the floating city. The dray-fish were curbed, the houseboat warped to a mooring. Along the dock, a line of idlers weighed and gauged every aspect of the houseboat, the slaves, and Thissell himself, according to Sirenese habit. Thissell, not yet accustomed to such penetrating inspection, found the scrutiny unsettling, all the more so for the immobility of the masks. Self-consciously adjusting his own Moon Moth, he climbed the ladder to the dock.

A slave rose from where he had been squatting, touched knuckles to the black cloth at his forehead, and sang on a three-tone phrase of interrogation: "The Moon Moth before me possibly expresses the identity of Ser Edwer Thissell?"

Thissell tapped the *hymerkin* which hung at his belt and sang: "I am Ser Thissell."

"I have been honored by a trust," sang the slave. "Three days from dawn to dusk I have waited on the dock; three nights from dusk to dawn I have crouched on a raft below this same dock listening to the feet of the Night-men. At last I behold the mask of Ser Thissell."

Thissell evoked an impatient clatter from the *hymerkin*. "What is the nature of this trust?"

"I carry a message, Ser Thissell. It is intended for you."

Thissell held out his left hand, playing the *hymerkin* with his right. "Give me the message."

"Instantly, Ser Thissell."

The message bore a heavy superscription:

EMERGENCY COMMUNICATION!
RUSH!

Thissell ripped open the envelope. The message was signed by Castel Cromartin, Chief Executive of the Interworld Policies Board. After the formal salutation, it read:

> ABSOLUTELY URGENT the following orders be executed! Aboard *Carina Cruzeiro,* destination Fan, date of arrival January 10 U.T., is notorious assassin, Haxo Angmark. Meet landing with adequate authority, effect detention and incarceration of this man. These instructions must be successfully implemented. Failure is unacceptable.
>
> ATTENTION! Haxo Angmark is superlatively dangerous. Kill him without hesitation at any show of resistance.

Thissell considered the message with dismay.

In coming to Fan as Consular Representative he had expected nothing like this. He felt neither inclination nor competence in the matter of dealing with dangerous assassins. Thoughtfully he rubbed the fuzzy gray cheek of his mask. The situation was not completely dark; Esteban Rolver, Director of the Space-Port, would doubtless cooperate, and perhaps furnish a platoon of slaves.

More hopefully, Thissell reread the message. January 10, Universal Time. He consulted a conversion calendar. Today, fortieth in the Season of Bitter Nectar—Thissell ran his finger down the column, stopped. January 10 was today!

A distant rumble caught his attention. Dropping from the mist came a dull shape: the lighter returning from contact with the *Carina Cruzeiro.*

Thissell once more re-read the note, raised his head, studied the descending lighter. Aboard would be Haxo Angmark. In five minutes, he would emerge upon the soil of Sirene. Landing formalities would detain him possibly twenty minutes. The landing field lay a mile and a half distant, joined to Fan by a winding path through the hills.

Thissell turned to the slave.

"When did this message arrive?"

The slave leaned forward uncomprehendingly. Thissell reiterated his question, singing to the clack of the *hymerkin:* "This message, you have enjoyed the honor of its custody how long?"

The slave sang: "Long days have I waited on the wharf, retreating only to the raft at the onset of dusk. Now my vigil is rewarded; I behold Ser Thissell."

Thissell turned away and walked furiously up the dock. Ineffective, inefficient Sirenese! Why had they not delivered the message to his house-boat? Twenty-five minutes—twenty-two now . . .

At the esplanade, Thissell stopped and looked right and left, hoping for a miracle—perhaps some sort of air-transport to whisk him to the space-port, where, with Rolver's aid, Haxo Angmark might still be detained. Or, better yet, a second message canceling the first. Something, anything. . . . But air-cars were not to be found on Sirene, and no second message appeared.

Across the esplanade rose a meager row of permanent structures, built of stone and iron and so proof against the efforts of the Night-men. A hostler occupied one of these structures, and as Thissell watched a man in a splendid pearl and silver mask emerged riding one of the lizard-like mounts of Sirene.

Thissell sprang forward. There was still time; with luck he might yet intercept Haxo Angmark. He hurried across the esplanade.

Before the line of stalls stood the hostler, inspecting his stock with solicitude, occasionally burnishing a scale or whisking away an insect. There were five of the beasts in prime condition, each as tall as a man's shoulder, with massive legs, thick bodies, heavy wedge-shaped heads. From their fore-fangs, which had been artifically lengthened and curved into near-circles, gold rings depended. Their scales had been stained in diaper-pattern: purple and green, orange and black, red and blue, brown and pink, yellow and silver.

Thissell came to a breathless halt in front of the hostler. He reached for his *kiv,* then hesitated. The *kiv*—five banks of resilient metal strips, fourteen to the bank, played by touching, twisting, twanging—might not be appropriate. Could this be considered a casual personal encounter? The *zachinko* perhaps? But the statement of his needs hardly seemed to demand the formal approach. Better the *kiv* after all. He struck a chord, but by error found himself stroking the *ganga.*

Beneath his mask, Thissell grinned apologetically. His relationship with this hostler was by no means on an intimate basis. He hoped that the hostler was of sanguine disposition, and in any event the urgency of the occasion allowed no time to select an exactly appropriate instrument. He struck a second chord and, playing as well as agitation, breathlessness, and lack of skill allowed, sang out a request: "Ser Hostler, I have immediate need of a swift mount. Allow me to select from your herd."

The hostler wore a mask of considerable complexity which Thissell could not identify: a construction of varnished brown cloth, pleated gray leather, and high on the forehead two large green and scarlet globes, minutely segmented like insect eyes. He inspected Thissell a long moment. Then, rather ostentatiously selecting his *stimic,* he executed a brilliant progression of trills and rounds.

Thissell failed to grasp the import. The *stimic*—three flutelike tubes equipped with plungers; thumb and forefinger squeezing a bag to force air across the mouthpieces, second, third and fourth fingers manipulating the slide—was an instrument well adapted to the sentiments of cool withdrawal, or even disapproval; but how cool Thissell was not sure. The hostler sang: "Ser Moon Moth, I fear that my steeds are unsuitable to a person of your distinction."

Thissell earnestly twanged at the *ganga*. "By no means! They all seem adequate. I am in great haste and will gladly accept any of the group."

The hostler played a brittle cascading crescendo. "Ser Moon Moth," he sang, "the steeds are ill and dirty. I am flattered that you consider them adequate to your use, but I cannot accept the merit you offer me. And—" here, switching instruments, he stuck a cool tinkle from his *krodatch*—"somehow I fail to recognize the boon companion and co-craftsman who accosts me so familiarly with his *ganga*."

The implications were clear. The use of the *krodatch* alone made its point, for the small, square sound-box strung with resined gut, in playing which the musician scratched the strings with his fingernail, or stroked them with his fingertips, produced quietly formal sounds. The *krodatch* was an instrument of rejection or even of insult. Thissell would receive no mount.

He turned and set off at a run for the landing field. Behind him sounded the clatter of the hostler's *hymerkin*—whether directed at himself or at the hostler's slaves Thissell did not pause to learn.

II.

The previous Consular Representative of the Home Planets on Sirene had been killed at Zundar. Masked as a Tavern Bravo, he had accosted a girl beribboned for the Equinoctial Attitudes, a solecism for which he had been instantly beheaded by a Red Demiurge, a Sun Sprite, and a Magic Hornet. Edwer Thissell, recently graduated from the Institute, had been named his successor, and allowed three days to prepare himself.

Normally of a contemplative, even cautious, disposition, Thissell had regarded the appointment as a challenge. He learned the Sirenese language by sub-cerebral techniques, and found it uncomplicated. Then, in the *Journal of Universal Anthropology,* he read:

> The population of the Titanic littoral is highly individualistic, possibly in response to a bountiful environment which puts no premium upon group activity. The language, reflecting this trait, expresses the individual's mood, and his emotional attitude toward a given situation. Factual information is regarded as a secondary concomitant. Moreover, the language is sung, characteristically to the accompaniment of a small instrument. As a result, there is great difficulty in ascertaining fact from a native of Fan, or the forbidden city, Zundar. One will be regaled with elegant arias and demonstra-

tions of astonishing virtuosity upon one or another of the numerous musical instruments. The visitor to this fascinating world, unless he cares to be treated with the most consummate contempt, must therefore learn to express himself after the approved local fashion.

Thissell made a note in his memorandum book: *Procure small musical instrument, together with directions as to use.* He read on.

There is everywhere and at all times a plenitude, not to say a superfluity, of food, and the climate is benign. With a fund of racial energy and a great deal of leisure time, the population occupies itself with intricacy. Intricacy in all things: intricate craftsmanship, such as the carved panels which adorn the houseboats; intricate symbolism, as exemplified in the masks worn by everyone; the intricate half-musical language which admirably expresses subtle moods and emotions; and, above all, the fantastic intricacy of interpersonal relationships. Prestige, face, *mana,* repute, glory: the Sirenese word is *strakh.* Every man has his characteristic *strakh,* which determines whether, when he needs a houseboat, he will be urged to avail himself of a floating palace, rich with gems, alabaster lanterns, peacock faience, and carved wood, or grudgingly permitted an abandoned shack on a raft. There is no medium of exchange on Sirene; the single and sole currency is *strakh.*

Thissell rubbed his chin and read further.

Masks are worn at all times, in accordance with the philosophy that a man should not be compelled to use a similitude foisted upon him by factors beyond his control. In the Sirenese view, he should be at liberty to choose that semblance most consonant with his *strakh.* In the civilized areas of Sirene—which is to say the Titanic littoral—a man literally never shows his face. It is his basic secret.

Gambling, by this token, is unknown on Sirene. It would be catastrophic to Sirenese self-respect to gain advantage by means other than the exercise of *strakh.* The word "luck" has no counterpart in the Sirenese language.

Thissell made another note: *Get mask. Museum? Drama guild?*
He finished the article, hastened forth to complete his preparations, and the next day embarked aboard the *Robart Astroguard* for the first leg of the passage to Sirene.

The lighter settled upon the Sirenese space-port, a topaz disk isolated among the black, green and purple hills. The lighter grounded, and Edwer Thissell stepped forth. He was met by Esteban Rolver, the local agent for Spaceways. Rolver threw up his hands, and stepped back. "Your mask," he cried huskily. "Where is your mask?"
Thissell held it up rather self-consciously. "I wasn't sure—"

"Put it on," said Rolver, turning away. He himself wore a fabrication of dull green scales on blue-lacquered wood. Black quills protruded at the cheeks, and under his chin hung a black and white checked pom-pom, the total effect creating a sense of sardonic supple personality.

Thissell adjusted the mask to his face, undecided whether to make a joke about the situation or to maintain a reserve suitable to the dignity of his post.

"Are you masked?" Rolver inquired over his shoulder.

Thissell replied in the affirmative and Rolver turned. The mask hid the expression of his face, but his hand unconsciously flicked a set of keys strapped to his thigh. The instrument sounded a trill of shock and polite consternation. "You can't wear that mask!" sang Rolver. "In fact—how did you get it?"

"It's copied from a mask owned by the Polypolis museum," said Thissell stiffly. "I'm sure it's authentic."

Rolver nodded, his own mask more sardonic-seeming than ever. "It's authentic enough. It's a variant of the type known as the Sea-Dragon Conqueror, and is worn on ceremonial occasions by persons of enormous prestige: princes, heroes, master craftsmen, great musicians."

"I wasn't aware—"

Rolver made a gesture of languid understanding. "It's something you'll learn in due course. Notice my mask. Today I'm wearing a Tarn-Bird. Persons of minimal prestige—such as you, I, any other out-worlder—wear this sort of thing."

"Odd," said Thissell as they started across the field toward a low concrete blockhouse. "I assumed that a person wore whatever mask he liked."

"Certainly," said Rolver. "Wear any mask you like—if you can make it stick. This Tarn-Bird for instance. I wear it to indicate that I presume nothing. I make no claims to wisdom, ferocity, versatility, musicianship, truculence or any of a dozen other Sirenese virtues."

"For the sake of argument," said Thissell, "what would happen if I walked through the streets of Zundar in this mask?"

Rolver laughed, a muffled sound behind his mask. "If you walked along the docks of Zundar—there are no streets—in *any* mask, you'd be killed within the hour. That's what happened to Benko, your predecessor. He didn't know how to act. None of us out-worlders know how to act. In Fan we're tolerated—so long as we keep our place. But you couldn't even walk around Fan in that regalia you're sporting now. Somebody wearing a Fire Snake or a Thunder Goblin mask would step up to you. He'd play his *krodatch,* and if you failed to challenge his audacity with a passage on the *skaranyi,* a devilish instrument, like a baby bagpipe, he'd play his *hymerkin*—the instrument we use with the slaves. That's the ultimate expression of contempt. Or he might ring his dueling-gong and attack you then and there."

"I had no idea that people here were quite so irascible," said Thissell in a subdued voice.

Rolver shrugged and swung open the massive steel door into his office.
"Certain acts may not be committed even on the Concourse at Polypolis
without incurring criticism."

"Yes, that's quite true," said Thissell. He looked around the office. "Why
all the concrete and steel?"

"Protection against the savages," said Rolver. "They come down from the
mountains at night, steal what's available, kill anyone they find ashore." He
went to a closet and brought forth a mask. "Here. Use this Moon Moth; it
won't get you in trouble."

Thissell unenthusiastically inspected the mask. It was constructed of mouse-
colored fur. There was a tuft of hair at each side of the mouth-hole, a pair of
featherlike antennae at the forehead. White lace flaps dangled beside the
temples, and under the eyes hung a series of red folds creating an effect at
once lugubrious and comic.

Thissell asked, "Does this mask signify any degree of prestige?"

"Not a great deal."

"After all, I'm Consular Representative," said Thissell. "I represent the
Home Planets, a hundred billion people—"

"If the Home Planets want their representative to wear a Sea Dragon
Conqueror mask, they'd better send out a Sea Dragon Conqueror man."

"I see," said Thissell in a subdued voice.

Rolver politely averted his gaze while Thissell doffed the Sea Dragon
Conqueror and slipped the more modest Moon Moth over his head. "I
suppose I can find something just a bit more suitable in one of the shops,"
Thissell said. "I'm told a person simply goes in and takes what he needs,
correct?"

Rolver surveyed Thissell critically. "That mask—temporarily, at least—is
perfectly suitable. It's rather important not to take anything from the shops
until you know the *strakh* value of the article you want. The owner loses
prestige if a person of low *strakh* makes free with his best work."

Thissell shook his head in exasperation. "Nothing of this was explained to
me! I knew of the masks, of course, and the painstaking integrity of the
craftsmen, but this insistence on prestige—*strakh,* whatever the word is . . ."

"No matter," said Rolver. "After a year or two, you'll begin to learn your
way around. I suppose you speak the language?"

"Oh, indeed. Certainly."

"And what instruments do you play?"

"Well—I was given to understand that any small instrument was adequate,
or that I could merely sing."

"Very inaccurate. Only slaves sing without accompaniment. I suggest that
you learn the following instruments as quickly as possible: the *hymerkin* for
your slaves. The *ganga* for conversation between intimates or one a trifle
lower than yourself in *strakh*. The *kiv* for casual polite intercourse. The
zachinko for more formal dealing. The *strapan* or the *krodatch* for your social

inferiors—in your case, to insult someone, since you have no inferiors. The *gomapard* or the *double-kamanthil* for ceremonials.'' The *gomapard* was one of the few electric instruments used on Sirene. An oscillator produced an oboelike tone, modulated, choked, vibrated, raised, and lowered in pitch by four keys. The *double-kamanthil* was similar to the *ganga* except the tones were produced by twisting and inclining a disk of resined leather against one or more of the forty-six strings. Rolver considered a moment. ''The *crebarin*, the water-lute, and the *slobo* are highly useful also—but perhaps you'd better learn the other instruments first. They should provide at least a rudimentary means of communication.''

''Aren't you exaggerating?'' suggested Thissell. ''Or joking?''

Rolver laughed his saturnine laugh. ''Not at all. Also you'll need a houseboat and slaves.''

Rolver took Thissell from the landing field to the docks of Fan, a walk of an hour and a half along a pleasant path under enormous trees loaded with fruit, cereal pods, sacs of sugary sap.

''At the moment,'' said Rolver, ''there are only four out-worlders in Fan, counting yourself. I'll take you to Welibus, our Commercial Factor. I think he's got an old houseboat he might let you use.''

Cornely Welibus had resided fifteen years in Fan, acquiring sufficient *strakh* to wear his South Wind mask with authority. This consisted of a blue disk inlaid with cabochons of lapis-lazuli, surrounded by an aureole of shimmering snake-skin. Heartier and more cordial than Rolver, he not only provided Thissell with a houseboat, but also a score of various musical instruments and a pair of slaves.

Embarrassed by the largesse, Thissell stammered something about payment, but Welibus cut him off with an expansive gesture. ''My dear fellow, this is Sirene. Such trifles cost nothing.''

''But a houseboat—''

Welibus played a courtly little flourish on his *kiv*. ''I'll be frank, Ser Thissell. The boat is old and a trifle shabby. I can't afford to use it; my status would suffer.'' A graceful melody accompanied his words. ''Status as yet need not concern you. You require merely shelter, comfort, and safety from the Night-men.''

''Night-men?''

''The cannibals who roam the shore after dark.''

''Oh, yes. Ser Rolver mentioned them.''

''Horrible things. We don't discuss them.'' A shuddering little trill issued from his *kiv*. ''Now, as to slaves.'' He tapped the blue disk of his mask with a thoughtful forefinger. ''Rex and Toby should serve you well.'' He raised his voice, played a swift clatter on the *hymerkin*. *'Avan esx trobu!''*

A female slave appeared wearing a dozen tight bands of pink cloth, and a dainty black mask sparkling with mother-of-pearl sequins.

''Fascu etz Rex ae Toby.''

Rex and Toby appeared, wearing loose masks of black cloth, russet jerkins. Welibus addressed them with a resonant clatter of *hymerkin,* enjoining them to the service of their new master, on pain of return to their native islands. They prostrated themselves, sang pledges of servitude to Thissell in soft husky voices. Thissell laughed nervously and essayed a sentence in the Sirenese language. "Go to the houseboat, clean it well, bring aboard a supply of food."

Toby and Rex stared blankly through the holes in their masks. Welibus repeated the orders with *hymerkin* accompaniment. The slaves bowed and departed without farewells.

Thissell surveyed the musical instruments with dismay. "I haven't the slightest idea how to go about learning how to play these things."

Welibus turned to Rolver. "What about Kershaul? Could he be persuaded to give Ser Thissell some basic instruction?"

Rolver nodded judicially. "Kershaul might undertake the job."

Thissell asked, "Who is Kershaul?"

"The third of our little group of expatriates," replied Welibus, "An anthropologist. You've read *Zundar the Splendid? Rituals of Sirene? The Faceless Folk?* No? A pity. All excellent works. Kershaul is high in prestige, and I believe visits Zundar from time to time. Wears a Cave Owl, sometimes a Star Wanderer, or even a Wise Arbiter."

"He's taken to an Equatorial Serpent," said Rolver. "The variant with the gilt tusks."

"Indeed!" marveled Welibus. "Well, I must say he's earned it. A fine fellow, good chap indeed." And he strummed his *zachinko* thoughtfully.

III.

Three months passed. Under the tutelage of Mathew Kershaul, Thissell practiced the *hymerkin,* the *ganga,* the *strapan,* the *kiv,* the *gomapard,* and the *zachinko*. The others could wait, said Kershaul, until Thissell had mastered the six basic instruments. He lent Thissell recordings of noteworthy Sirenese conversing in various moods and to various accompaniments, so that Thissell might learn the melodic conventions currently in vogue, and perfect himself in the niceties of intonation, the various rhythms, cross-rhythms, compound rhythms, implied rhythms, and suppressed rhythms. Kershaul professed to find Sirenese music a fascinating study, and Thissell admitted that it was a subject not readily exhausted. The quarter-tone tuning of the instruments admitted the use of twenty-four tonalities which, multiplied by the five modes in general use, resulted in one hundred and twenty separate scales. Kershaul, however, advised that Thissell primarily concentrate on learning each instrument in its fundamental tonality, using only two of the modes.

With no immediate business at Fan except the weekly visits to Mathew Kershaul, Thissell took his houseboat eight miles south and moored it in the lee of a rocky promontory. Here, if it had not been for the incessant practicing, Thissell lived an idyllic life. The sea was calm and crystal-clear; the beach, fringed by the gray, green, and purple foliage of the forest, lay close at hand if he wanted to stretch his legs.

Toby and Rex occupied a pair of cubicles forward. Thissell had the after-cabins to himself. From time to time he toyed with the idea of a third slave, possibly a young female, to contribute an element of charm and gaiety to the menage. . . . But Kershaul advised against the step, fearing that the intensity of Thissell's concentration might somehow be diminished. Thissell acquiesced and devoted himself to the study of the six instruments.

The days passed quickly. Thissell never became bored with the pageantry of dawn and sunset; the white clouds and blue sea of noon; the night sky blazing with the twenty-nine stars of Cluster SI 1-715. The weekly trip to Fan broke the tedium. Toby and Rex foraged for food; Thissell visited the luxurious houseboat of Mathew Kershaul for instruction and advice.

Then, three months after Thissell's arrival, came the message completely disorganizing the routine: Haxo Angmark, assassin, *agent provocateur*, ruthless and crafty criminal, had come to Sirene. "Effect detention and incarceration of this man!" read the orders. "Attention! Haxo Angmark is superlatively dangerous. Kill without hesitation!"

Thissell was not in the best of condition. He trotted fifty yards until his breath came in gasps, then walked—through low hills crowned with white bamboo and black tree-ferns; across meadows yellow with grass-nuts, through orchards and wild vineyards. Twenty minutes passed, twenty-five minutes. With a heavy sensation in his stomach, Thissell knew that he was too late. Haxo Angmark had landed, and might be traversing this very road toward Fan.

But along the way Thissell met only four persons: a boy-child in a mock-fierce Alk-Islander mask; two young women wearing the Red-bird and the Green-bird; a man masked as a Forest Goblin. Coming upon the man, Thissell stopped short. Could this be Angmark?

Thissell essayed a strategem. He went boldly to the man, stared into the hideous mask. "Angmark," he called in the language of the Home Planets, "you are under arrest!"

The Forest Goblin stared uncomprehendingly, then started forward along the track.

Thissell put himself in the way. He reached for his *ganga*, then recalling the hostler's reaction, instead struck a chord on the *zachinko*. "You travel the road from the space-port," he sang. "What have you seen there?"

The Forest Goblin grasped his hand-bugle, an instrument used to deride opponents on the field of battle, to summon animals or occasionally to evince a rough and ready truculence. "Where I travel and what I see are the concern solely of myself. Stand back or I walk upon your face." He marched forward. Had not Thissell leapt aside, the Forest Goblin might well have made good his threat.

Thissell stood gazing after the retreating back. Angmark? Not likely with so sure a touch on the hand-bugle. Thissell hesitated, then turned and continued on his way.

Arriving at the space-port, he went directly to the office. The heavy door stood ajar; as Thissell approached, a man appeared in the doorway. He wore a mask of dull green scales, mica plates, blue-lacquered wood, and black quills—the Tarn Bird.

"Ser Rolver," Thissell called out anxiously, "who came down from the *Carina Cruzeiro?*"

Rolver studied Thissell a long moment, "Why do you ask?"

"Why do I ask?" demanded Thissell. "You must have seen the space-gram I received from Castel Cromartin!"

"Oh, yes," said Rolver. "Of course. Naturally."

"It was delivered only half an hour ago," said Thissell bitterly. "I rushed out as fast as I could. Where is Angmark?"

"In Fan, I assume," said Rolver.

Thissell cursed softly. "Why didn't you delay him?"

Rolver shrugged. "I had neither authority, inclination, nor the capability to stop him."

Thissell fought back his annoyance. In a voice of studied calm he said, "On the way I passed a man in rather a ghastly mask—saucer eyes, red wattles."

"A Forest Goblin," said Rolver. "Angmark brought the mask with him."

"But he played the hand-bugle," Thissell protested. "How could Angmark—"

"He's well-acquainted with Sirene. He spent five years here in Fan."

Thissell grunted in annoyance. "Cromartin made no mention of this."

"It's common knowledge," said Rolver with a shrug. "He was Commercial Representative before Welibus took over, a long time ago."

"Were he and Welibus acquainted?"

Rolver laughed shortly. "Naturally. But don't suspect poor Welibus of anything more venal than juggling his accounts. I assure you he's no consort of assassins."

"Speaking of assassins," said Thissell, "do you have a weapon I might borrow?"

Rolver inspected him in wonder. "You came out here to take Angmark barehanded?"

"I had no choice," said Thissell. "When Cromartin gives orders, he expects results. In any event, you were here with your slaves."

"Don't count on me for help," Rolver said testily. "I wear the Tarn Bird and make no pretensions of valor. But I can lend you a power-pistol. I haven't used it recently; I won't guarantee its charge."

"Anything is better than nothing," said Thissell.

Rolver went into the office and a moment later returned with the gun. "What will you do now?"

Thissell shook his head wearily. "I'll try to find Angmark in Fan. Or might he head for Zundar?"

Rolver considered. "Angmark might be able to survive in Zundar. But he'd want to brush up on his musicianship. I imagine he'll stay in Fan a few days."

"But how can I find him? Where should I look?"

"That I can't say," replied Rolver. "You might be safer not finding him. Angmark is a dangerous man."

Thissell returned to Fan the way he had come.

Where the path swung down from the hills into the esplanade a thick-walled *pisé-de-terre* building had been constructed. The door was carved from a solid black plank; the windows were guarded by enfoliated bands of iron. This was the office of Cornely Welibus, Commercial Factor, Importer and Exporter. Thissell found Welibus sitting at his ease on the tiled verandah, wearing a modest adaptation of the Waldemar mask. He seemed lost in thought. He might or might not have recognized Thissell's Moon Moth; in any event, he gave no signal of greeting.

Thissell approached the porch. "Good morning, Ser Welibus."

Welibus nodded abstractedly and said in a flat voice, plucking lazily at his *krodatch*, "Good morning."

Thissell was rather taken aback. This was hardly the instrument to use toward a friend and fellow-out-worlder, even if he did wear the Moon Moth.

Thissell said coldly, "May I ask how long you have been sitting here?"

Welibus considered half a minute. When he spoke, he accompanied himself on the more cordial *crebarin*. But the recollection of the *krodatch* chord still rankled in Thissell's mind.

"I've been here fifteen or twenty minutes. Why do you ask?"

"I wonder if you noticed a Forest Goblin pass?"

Welibus nodded. "He went on down the esplanade—turned into that first mask shop, I believe."

Thissell hissed between his teeth. This would naturally be Angmark's first move. "I'll never find him once he changes masks," he muttered.

"Who is this Forest Goblin?" asked Welibus, with no more than casual interest.

Thissell could see no reason to conceal the name. "A notorious criminal: Haxo Angmark."

"Haxo Angmark!" croaked Welibus, leaning back in his chair. "You're sure he's here?"

"Reasonably sure."

Welibus rubbed his shaking hands together. "This is bad news—bad news indeed! He's an unscrupulous scoundrel."

"You knew him well?"

"As well as anyone." Welibus was now accompanying himself with the *kiv*. "He held the post I now occupy. I came out as an inspector and found that he was embezzling some four thousand UMI's a month. I'm sure he feels no great gratitude toward me." Welibus glanced nervously up the esplanade. "I hope you catch him."

"I'm doing my best. He went into the mask shop, you say?"

"I'm sure of it."

Thissell turned away. As he went down the path, he heard the black plank door thud shut behind him.

He walked down the esplanade to the mask-maker's shop, and paused outside as if admiring the display: a hundred miniature masks, carved from rare woods and minerals, dressed with emerald flakes, spiderweb silk, wasp wings, petrified fish scales, and the like. The shop was empty except for the mask-maker, a gnarled knotty man in a yellow robe, wearing a deceptively simple Universal Expert mask, fabricated from over two thousand bits of articulated wood.

Thissell considered what he would say and how he would accompany himself, then entered. The mask-maker, noting the Moon Moth and Thissell's diffident manner, continued with his work.

Thissell, selecting the easiest of his instruments, stroked his *strapan*—possibly not the most felicitous choice, for it conveyed a certain degree of condescension. Thissell tried to counteract this flavor by singing in warm, almost effusive, tones, shaking the *strapan* whimsically when he struck a wrong note: "A stranger is an interesting person to deal with; his habits are unfamiliar, he excites curiosity. Not twenty minutes ago a stranger entered this fascinating shop, to exchange his drab Forest Goblin for one of the remarkable and adventurous creations assembled on the premises."

The mask-maker turned Thissell a side glance. Without words he played a progression of chords on an instrument Thissell had never seen before: a flexible sac gripped in the palm with three short tubes leading between the fingers. When the tubes were squeezed almost shut and air forced through the slit, an oboelike tone ensued. To Thissell's developing ear the instrument seemed difficult, the mask-maker expert; the music conveyed a profound sense of disinterest.

Thissell tried again, laboriously manipulating the *strapan*. He sang, "To an out-worlder on a foreign planet, the voice of one from his home is like water to a wilting plant. A person who could unite two such persons might find satisfaction in such an act of mercy." Even to his own ears the notes rang false.

The mask-maker casually fingered his own *strapan*, and drew forth a set of rippling scales, his fingers moving faster than the eyes could follow. He sang in the formal style: "An artist values his moments of concentration. He does not care to spend time exchanging banalities with persons of at best average prestige." Thissell attempted to insert a counter melody, but the mask-maker struck a new set of complex chords whose portent evaded Thissell's understanding, and continued: "Into the shop comes a person who evidently has picked up for the first time an instrument of unparalleled complication, for the execution of his music is open to criticism. He sings of homesickness and longing for the sight of others like himself. He dissembles his enormous *strakh* behind a Moon Moth, for he plays the *strapan* to a Master Craftsman, and sings in a voice of contemptuous raillery. The refined and creative artist ignores the provocation. He plays a polite instrument, remains noncommittal, and trusts that the stranger will tire of his sport and depart.''

Thissell took up his *kiv.*
''The noble mask-maker completely misunderstands me—''
He was interrupted by staccato rasping of the mask-maker's *strapan.* ''The stranger now sees fit to ridicule the artist's comprehension.''
Thissell scratched furiously at his *strapan:* ''To protect myself from the heat, I wander into a small and unpretentious mask-shop. The artisan, though still distracted by the novelty of his tools, gives promise of development. He works zealously to perfect his skill, so much so that he refuses to converse with strangers, no matter what their need.''
The mask-maker carefully laid down his carving tool. He rose to his feet, went behind a screen, and shortly returned wearing a mask of gold and iron, with simulated flames licking up from the scalp. In one hand he carried a *skaranyi,* in the other a scimitar. He struck off a brilliant series of wild tones, and sang. ''Even the most accomplished artist can augment his *strakh* by killing sea-monsters, Night-men, and importunate idlers. Such an occasion is at hand. The artist delays his attack exactly ten seconds, because the offender wears a Moon Moth.'' He twirled his scimitar and spun it in the air.
Thissell desperately pounded the *strapan.* ''Did a Forest Goblin enter the shop? Did he depart with a new mask?''
''Five seconds have elapsed,'' sang the mask-maker in steady ominous rhythm.
Thissell departed in frustrated rage.
He crossed the square and stood looking up and down the esplanade. Hundreds of men and women sauntered along the docks, or stood on the decks of their houseboats, each wearing a mask chosen to express his mood, prestige, and special attributes, and everywhere sounded the twitter of musical instruments.
Thissell stood at a loss. The Forest Goblin had disappeared. Haxo Angmark walked at liberty in Fan, and Thissell had failed the urgent instructions of Castel Cromartin.
Behind him sounded the casual notes of a *kiv.* ''Ser Moon Moth Thissell, you stand engrossed in thought.''

Thissell turned, to find beside him a Cave Owl, in a somber cloak of black and gray. Thissell recognized the mask, which symbolized erudition and patient exploration of abstract ideas. Mathew Kershaul had worn it on the occasion of their meeting a week before.
''Good morning, Ser Kershaul,'' muttered Thissell.
''And how are the studies coming? Have you mastered the C-Sharp Plus

scale on the *gomapard?* As I recall, you were finding those inverse intervals puzzling.''

"I've worked on them," said Thissell in a gloomy voice. "However, since I'll probably be recalled to Polypolis, it may be all time wasted."

"Eh? What's this?"

Thissell explained the situation in regard to Haxo Angmark. Kershaul nodded gravely. "I recall Angmark. Not a gracious personality, but an excellent musician, with quick fingers and a real talent for new instruments." Thoughtfully he twisted the goatee of his Cave Owl mask. "What are your plans?"

"They're nonexistent," said Thissell, playing a doleful phrase on the *kiv.* "I haven't any idea what masks he'll be wearing. And if I don't know what he looks like, how can I find him?"

Kershaul tugged at his goatee. "In the old days he favored the Exo-Cambian Cycle, and I believe he used an entire set of Nether Denizens. Now, of course, his tastes may have changed."

"Exactly," Thissell complained. "He might be twenty feet away and I'd never know it." He glanced bitterly across the esplanade toward the mask-maker's shop. "No one will tell me anything. I doubt if they care that a murderer is walking their docks."

"Quite correct," Kershaul agreed. "Sirenese standards are different from ours."

"They have no sense of responsibility," declared Thissell. "I doubt if they'd throw a rope to a drowning man."

"It's true that they dislike interference," Kershaul agreed. "They emphasize individual responsibility and self-sufficiency."

"Interesting," said Thissell, "but I'm still in the dark about Angmark."

Kershaul surveyed him gravely. "And should you locate Angmark, what will you do then?"

"I'll carry out the orders of my superior," said Thissell doggedly.

"Angmark is a dangerous man," mused Kershaul. "He's got a number of advantages over you."

"I can't take that into account. It's my duty to send him back to Polypolis. He's probably safe, since I haven't the remotest idea how to find him."

Kershaul reflected. "An out-worlder can't hide behind a mask, not from the Sirenese at least. There are four of us here at Fan—Rolver, Welibus, you, and me. If another out-worlder tries to set up housekeeping, the news will get around in short order."

"What if he heads for Zundar?"

Kershaul shrugged. "I doubt if he'd dare. On the other hand—" Kershaul paused, then noting Thissell's sudden inattention, turned to follow Thissell's gaze.

A man in a Forest Goblin mask came swaggering toward them along the esplanade.

Kershaul laid a restraining hand on Thissell's arm, but Thissell stepped out into the path of the Forest Goblin, his borrowed gun ready. "Haxo Angmark," he cried, "don't make a move, or I'll kill you. You're under arrest."

"Are you sure this is Angmark?" asked Kershaul in a worried voice.

"I'll find out," said Thissell. "Angmark, turn around, hold up your hands."

The Forest Goblin stood rigid with surprise and puzzlement. He reached to his *zachinko*, played an interrogatory arpeggio, and sang, "Why do you molest me, Moon Moth?"

Kershaul stepped forward and played a placatory phrase on his *slobo*. "I fear that a case of confused identity exists, Ser Forest Goblin. Ser Moon Moth seeks an out-worlder in a Forest Goblin mask."

The Forest Goblin's music became irritated, and he suddenly switched to his *stimic*. "He asserts that I am an out-worlder? Let him prove his case, or he has my retaliation to face."

Kershaul glanced in embarrassment around the crowd which had gathered and once more struck up an ingratiating melody. "I am positive that Ser Moon Moth—"

The Forest Goblin interrupted with a fanfare of *skaranyi* tones. "Let him demonstrate his case or prepare for the flow of blood."

Thissell said, "Very well, I'll prove my case." He stepped forward, grasped the Forest Goblin's mask. "Let's see your face, that'll demonstrate your identity!"

The Forest Goblin sprang back in amazement. The crowd gasped, then set up an ominous strumming and toning of various instruments.

The Forest Goblin reached to the nape of his neck, jerked the cord to his duel-gong, and with his other hand snatched forth his scimitar.

Kershaul stepped forward, playing the *slobo* with great agitation. Thissell, now abashed, moved aside, conscious of the ugly sound of the crowd.

Kershaul sang explanations and apologies; the Forest Goblin answered; Kershaul spoke over his shoulder to Thissell: "Run for it, or you'll be killed! Hurry!"

Thissell hesitated. The Forest Goblin put up his hand to thrust Kershaul aside. "Run!" screamed Kershaul. "To Welibus's office. Lock yourself in!"

Thissell took to his heels. The Forest Goblin pursued him a few yards, then stamped his feet and sent after him a set of raucous and derisive blasts of the hand-bugle, while the crowd produced a contemptuous counterpoint of clacking *hymerkins*.

There was no further pursuit.

Instead of taking refuge in the Import-Export office, Thissell turned aside and after cautious reconnaissance proceeded to the dock where his houseboat was moored.

The hour was not far short of dusk when he finally returned aboard. Toby and Rex squatted on the forward deck, surrounded by the provisions they had brought back; reed baskets of fruit and cereal, blue-glass jugs containing wine, oil, and pungent sap, three young pigs in a wicker pen. They were cracking nuts between their teeth and spitting the shells over the side. They looked up at Thissell, and it seemed that they rose to their feet with a new casualness. Toby muttered something under his breath; Rex smothered a chuckle.

Thissell clacked his *hymerkin* angrily. He sang, "Take the boat off-shore; tonight we remain at Fan."

In the privacy of his cabin, he removed the Moon Moth and stared into a mirror at his almost unfamiliar features. He picked up the Moon Moth, examined the detested lineaments: the furry gray skin, the blue spines, the ridiculous lace flaps. Hardly a dignified presence for the Consular Representative of the Home Planets. If, in fact, he still held the position when Cromartin learned of Angmark's winning free!

Thissell flung himself into a chair and stared moodily into space. Today he'd suffered a series of setbacks. But he wasn't defeated yet, by any means. Tomorrow he'd visit Mathew Kershaul; they'd discuss how best to locate Angmark.

As Kershaul had pointed out, another out-world establishment could not be camouflaged. Haxo Angmark's identity would soon become evident. Also, tomorrow he must procure another mask. Nothing extreme or vainglorious, but a mask which expressed a modicum of dignity and self-respect.

At this moment, one of the slaves tapped on the door-panel; and Thissell hastily pulled the hated Moon Moth back over his head.

IV.

Early next morning, before the dawn-light had left the sky, the slaves sculled the houseboat back to that section of the dock set aside for the use of out-worlders. Neither Rolver nor Welibus nor Kershaul had yet arrived. Thissell waited impatiently.

An hour passed, and Welibus brought his boat to the dock. Not wishing to speak to Welibus, Thissell remained inside his cabin.

A few moments later, Rolver's boat likewise pulled in alongside the dock. Through the window Thissell saw Rolver, wearing his usual Tarn Bird, climb to the dock. Here he was met by a man in a yellow-tufted Sand Tiger mask, who played a formal accompaniment on his *gomapard* to whatever message he brought Rolver.

Rolver seemed surprised and disturbed. After a moment's thought, he manipulated his own *gomapard* and, as he sang, he indicated Thissell's houseboat. Then, bowing, he went on his way.

The man in the Sand Tiger mask climbed with rather heavy dignity to the float and rapped on the bulwark of Thissell's houseboat.

Thissell presented himself. Sirenese etiquette did not demand that he invite a casual visitor aboard, so he merely struck an interrogation on his *zachinko*.

The Sand Tiger played his *gomapard* and sang, "Dawn over the bay of Fan is customarily a splendid occasion. The sky is white with yellow and green colors. When Mireille rises, the mists burn and writhe like flames. He who sings derives a greater enjoyment from the hour when the floating corpse of an out-worlder does not appear to mar the serenity of the view.''

Thissell's *zachinko* gave off a startled interrogation almost of its own accord. The Sand Tiger bowed with dignity. ''The singer acknowledges no peer in steadfastness of disposition; however, he does not care to be plagued by the antics of a dissatisfied ghost. He therefore has ordered his slaves to attach a thong to the ankle of the corpse, and while we have conversed they have linked the corpse to the stern of your houseboat. You will wish to administer whatever rites are prescribed in the out-world. He who sings wishes you a good morning and now departs.''

Thissell rushed to the stern of his houseboat. There, near-naked and mask-less, floated the body of a mature man, supported by air trapped in his pantaloons.

Thissell studied the dead face, which seemed characterless and vapid— perhaps in direct consequence of the mask-wearing habit. The body appeared of medium stature and weight. Thissell estimated the age as between forty-five and fifty. The hair was nondescript brown, the features bloated by the water.

There was nothing to indicate how the man had died.

This must be Haxo Angmark, thought Thissell. Who else could it be? Mathew Kershaul? Why not? Thissell asked himself uneasily. Rolver and Welibus had already disembarked and gone about their business. He searched across the bay to locate Kershaul's houseboat, and discovered it already tying up to the dock. Even as he watched Kershaul jumped ashore, wearing his Cave Owl mask.

He seemed in an abstracted mood, for he passed Thissell's houseboat without lifting his eyes from the dock.

Thissell turned back to the corpse: Angmark, then, beyond a doubt. Had not three men disembarked from the houseboats of Rolver, Welibus, and Kershaul, wearing masks characteristic of these men? Obviously, the corpse of Angmark . . . The easy solution refused to sit quiet in Thissell's mind. Kershaul had pointed out that another out-worlder would be quickly identi-fied. How else could Angmark maintain himself? Unless . . . Thissell brushed the thought aside. The corpse was obviously Angmark.

And yet . . .

Thissell summoned his slaves, gave orders that a suitable container be brought to the dock, that the corpse be transferred therein, and conveyed to a suitable place of repose. The slaves showed no enthusiasm for the task and Thissell was forced to thunder forcefully, if not skillfully, on the *hymerkin* to emphasize his orders.

He walked along the dock, turned up the esplanade, passed the office of Cornely Welibus, and set out along the pleasant little lane to the landing field.

*   *   *

When he arrived, he found that Rolver had not yet made an appearance. An over-slave, given status by a yellow rosette on his black cloth mask, asked how he might be of service. Thissell stated that he wished to dispatch a message to Polypolis.

There was no difficulty here, declared the slave. If Thissell would set forth his message in clear block print, it would be despatched immediately.

Thissell wrote:

OUT-WORLDER FOUND DEAD, POSSIBLY ANGMARK, AGE 48, MEDIUM PHYSIQUE, BROWN HAIR. OTHER MEANS OF IDENTIFICATION LACKING. AWAIT ACKNOWLEDGEMENT AND/OR INSTRUCTIONS.

He addressed the message to Castel Cromartin at Polypolis and handed it to the over-slave. A moment later, he heard the characteristic sputter of trans-space discharge.

An hour passed. Rolver made no appearance.

Thissell paced restlessly back and forth in front of the office. There was no telling how long he would have to wait. Trans-space transmission time varied unpredictably. Sometimes the message snapped through in microseconds; sometimes it wandered through unknowable regions for hours; and there were several authenticated examples of messages being received before they had been transmitted.

Another half-hour passed, and Rolver finally arrived, wearing his customary Tarn Bird. Coincidentally, Thissell heard the hiss of the incoming message.

Rolver seemed surprised to see Thissell. "What brings you out so early?"

Thissell explained. "It concerns the body which you referred to me this morning. I'm communicating with my superiors about it."

Rolver raised his head and listened to the sound of the incoming message. "You seem to be getting an answer. I'd better attend to it."

"Why bother?" asked Thissell. "Your slave seems to be efficient."

"It's my job," declared Rolver. "I'm responsible for the accurate transmission and receipt of all space-grams."

"I'll come with you," said Thissell. "I've always wanted to watch the operation of the equipment."

"I'm afraid that's irregular," said Rolver. He went to the door which led to the inner compartment. "I'll have your message in a moment."

Thissell protested, but Rolver ignored him and went into the inner office.

Five minutes later, he reappeared, carrying a small yellow envelope. "Not too good news," he announced with unconvincing commiseration.

Thissell glumly opened the envelope. The message read:

BODY NOT ANGMARK, ANGMARK HAS BLACK HAIR. WHY DID YOU NOT MEET LANDING? SERIOUS INFRAC-

TION, HIGHLY DISSATISFIED. RETURN TO POLYPOLIS NEXT OPPORTUNITY.

CASTEL CROMARTIN.

Thissell put the message in his pocket. "Incidentally, may I inquire the color of your hair?"

Rolver played a surprised little trill on his *kiv.* "I'm quite blond. Why do you ask?"

"Mere curiosity."

Rolver played another run on the *kiv.* "Now I understand. My dear fellow, what a suspicious nature you have! Look!" He turned and parted the folds of his mask at the nape of his neck. Thissell saw that Rolver was blond indeed.

"Are you reassured?" asked Rolver jocularly.

"Oh, indeed," said Thissell. "Incidentally, have you another mask you could lend me? I'm sick of the Moon Moth."

"I'm afraid not," said Rolver. "But you need merely go into a mask-maker's shop and make a selection."

"Yes, of course," said Thissell. He took leave of Rolver and returned along the trail to Fan.

Passing Welibus's office he hesitated, then turned in. Today Welibus wore a dazzling confection of green glass prisms and silver beads, a mask Thissell had never seen before.

Welibus greeted him cautiously to the accompaniment of a *kiv.* "Good morning, Ser Moon Moth."

"I won't take too much of your time," said Thissell, "but I have a rather personal question to put to you. What color is your hair?"

Welibus hesitated a fraction of a second, then turned his back, lifted the flap of his mask. Thissell saw heavy black ringlets. "Does that answer your question?" inquired Welibus.

"Completely," said Thissell. He crossed the esplanade, went out on the dock to Kershaul's houseboat. Karshaul greeted him without enthusiasm, and invited him aboard with a resigned wave of the hand.

"A question I'd like to ask," said Thissell. "What color is your hair?"

Kershaul laughed woefully. "What little remains is black. Why do you ask?"

"Curiosity."

"Come, come," said Kershaul with an unaccustomed bluffness. "There's more to it than that."

Thissell, feeling the need of counsel, admitted as much. "Here's the situation. A dead out-worlder was found in the harbor this morning. His hair was brown. I'm not entirely certain, but the chances are—let me see, yes, two out of three that Angmark's hair is black."

Kershaul pulled at the Cave Owl's goatee. "How do you arrive at that probability?"

"The information came to me through Rolver's hands. He has blond hair. If Angmark has assumed Rolver's identity, he would naturally alter the information which came to me this morning. Both you and Welibus admit to black hair."

"Hmm," said Kershaul. "Let me see if I follow your line of reasoning. You feel that Haxo Angmark has killed either Rolver, Welibus, or myself and assumed the dead man's identity. Right?"

Thissell looked at him in surprise. "You yourself emphasized that Angmark could not set up another out-world establishment without revealing himself! Don't you remember?"

"Oh, certainly. To continue. Rolver delivered a message to you stating that Angmark was dark, and announced himself to be blond."

"Yes. Can you verify this? I mean for the old Rolver?"

"No," said Kershaul sadly. "I've seen neither Rolver nor Welibus without their masks."

"If Rolver is not Angmark," Thissell mused, "if Angmark indeed has black hair, then both you and Welibus come under suspicion."

"Very interesting," said Kershaul. He examined Thissell warily. "For that matter, you yourself might be Angmark. What color is your hair?"

"Brown," said Thissell curtly. He lifted the gray fur of the Moon Moth mask at the back of his head.

"But you might be deceiving me as to the text of the message," Kershaul put forward.

"I'm not," said Thissell wearily. "You can check with Rolver if you care to."

Kershaul shook his head. "Unnecessary. I believe you. But another matter: what of voices? You've heard all of us before and after Angmark arrived. Isn't there some indication there?"

"No. I'm so alert for any evidence of change that you all sound rather different. And masks muffle your voices."

Kershaul tugged the goatee. "I don't see any immediate solution to the problem." He chuckled. "In any event, need there be? Before Angmark's advent, there were Rolver, Welibus, Kershaul, and Thissell. Now—for all practical purposes—there are still Rolver, Welibus, Kershaul, and Thissell. Who is to say that the new member may not be an improvement upon the old?"

"An interesting thought," agreed Thissell, "but it so happens that I have a personal interest in identifying Angmark. My career is at stake."

"I see," murmured Kershaul. "The situation then becomes an issue between yourself and Angmark."

"You won't help me?"

"Not actively. I've become pervaded with Sirenese individualism. I think you'll find that Rolver and Welibus will respond similarly." He sighed. "All of us have been here too long."

Thissell stood deep in thought. Kershaul waited patiently a moment, then said, "Do you have any further questions?"

"No," said Thissell. "I have merely a favor to ask you."

"I'll oblige if I possibly can," Kershaul replied courteously.

"Give me, or lend me, one of your slaves, for a week or two."

Kershaul played an exclamation of amusement on the *ganga*. "I hardly like to part with my slaves. They know me and my ways—"

"As soon as I catch Angmark, you'll have him back."

"Very well," said Kershaul. He rattled a summons on his *hymerkin,* and a slave appeared. "Anthony," sang Kershaul, "you are to go with Ser Thissell and serve him for a short period."

The slave bowed without pleasure.

Thissell took Anthony to his houseboat, and questioned him at length, noting certain of the responses upon a chart. He then enjoined Anthony to say nothing of what had passed, and consigned him to the care of Toby and Rex. He gave further instructions to move the houseboat away from the dock and allow no one aboard until his return.

He set forth once more along the way to the landing field, and found Rolver at a lunch of spiced fish, shredded bark of the salad tree, and a bowl of native currants. Rolver clapped an order on the *hymerkin,* and a slave set a place for Thissell. "And how are the investigations proceeding?"

"I'd hardly like to claim any progress," said Thissell. "I assume that I can count on your help?"

Rolver laughed briefly. "You have my good wishes."

"More concretely," said Thissell, "I'd like to borrow a slave from you. Temporarily."

Rolver paused in his eating. "Whatever for?"

"I'd rather not explain," said Thissell. "But you can be sure that I make no idle request."

Without graciousness, Rolver summoned a slave and consigned him to Thissell's service.

On the way back to his houseboat, Thissell stopped at Welibus's office.

Welibus looked up from his work. "Good afternoon, Ser Thissell."

Thissell came directly to the point. "Ser Welibus, will you lend me a slave for a few days?"

Welibus hesitated, then shrugged. "Why not?" He clacked his *hymerkin;* a slave appeared. "Is he satisfactory? Or would you prefer a young female?" He chuckled—rather offensively, to Thissell's way of thinking.

"He'll do very well. I'll return him in a few days."

"No hurry." Welibus made an easy gesture and returned to his work.

Thissell continued to his houseboat, where he separately interviewed each of his two new slaves and made notes upon his chart.

Dusk came soft over the Titanic Ocean. Toby and Rex sculled the houseboat away from the dock, out across the silken waters. Thissell sat on the deck listening to the sound of soft voices, the floating houseboats glowed yellow and wan watermelon-red. The shore was dark; the Night-men would presently come clinking to paw through refuse and stare jealously across the water.

In nine days, the *Buenaventura* came past Sirene on its regular schedule; Thissell had his orders to return to Polypolis. In nine days, could he locate Angmark?

Nine days weren't too many, Thissell decided, but they might possibly be enough.

V.

Two days passed, and three and four and five. Every day Thissell went ashore and at least once a day visited Rolver, Welibus and Kershaul.

Each reacted differently to his presence. Rolver was sardonic and irritable; Welibus formal and at least superficially affable; Kershaul mild and suave, but ostentatiously impersonal and detached in his conversation.

Thissell remained equally bland to Rolver's dour jibes, Welibus's jocundity, Kershaul's withdrawal. And every day returning to his houseboat, he made marks on his chart.

The sixth, the seventh, the eighth day came and passed. Rolver, with rather brutal directness, inquired if Thissell wished to arrange for passage on the *Buenaventura*. Thissell considered, and said, "Yes, you had better reserve passage for one."

"Back to the world of faces," shuddered Rolver. "Faces! Everywhere pallid, fish-eyed faces. Mouths like pulp, noses knotted and punctured; flat flabby faces. I don't think I could stand it after living here. Luckily you haven't become a real Sirenese."

"But I won't be going back," said Thissell.

"I thought you wanted me to reserve passage."

"I do—for Haxo Angmark. He'll be returning to Polypolis, in the brig."

"Well, well," said Rolver. "So you've picked him out."

"Of course," said Thissell. "Haven't you?"

Rolver shrugged. "He's either Welibus or Kershaul, that's as close as I can make it. So long as he wears his mask and calls himself either Welibus or Kershaul, it means nothing to me."

"It means a great deal to me," said Thissell. "What time tomorrow does the lighter go up?"

"Eleven twenty-two sharp. If Haxo Angmark's leaving, tell him to be on time."

"He'll be here," said Thissell.

He made his usual call upon Welibus and Kershaul. Then, returning to his houseboat, he put three final marks on his chart.

The evidence was here, plain and convincing. Not absolutely incontrovertible evidence, but enough to warrant a definite move. He checked over his gun. Tomorrow was the day of decision. He could afford no errors.

The day dawned bright white, the sky like the inside of an oyster shell. Mireille rose through iridescent mists. Toby and Rex sculled the houseboat to the dock. The remaining three out-world houseboats floated somnolently on the slow swells.

One boat Thissell watched in particular, that whose owner Haxo Angmark had killed and dropped into the harbor. This boat presently moved toward the shore, and Haxo Angmark himself stood on the front deck, wearing a mask Thissell had never seen before: a construction of scarlet feathers, black glass, and spiked green hair. It was most impressive.

Thissell was forced to admire his poise. A clever scheme, cleverly planned and executed—but marred by an insurmountable difficulty.

Angmark returned within. The houseboat reached the dock. Slaves flung out mooring lines and lowered the gangplank. Thissell, his gun ready in the pocket flap of his robes, walked down the dock, went aboard. He pushed open the door to the saloon. The man at the table raised his red, black, and green mask in surprise.

Thissell said, "Angmark, please don't argue or make any—"

Something hard and heavy tackled him from behind; he was flung to the floor, his gun wrested expertly away.

Behind him, the *hymerkin* clattered; a voice sang, "Bind the fool's arms."

The man sitting at the table rose to his feet, removed the red, black and green mask to reveal the black cloth of a slave. Thissell twisted his head. Over him stood Haxo Angmark, wearing a mask Thissell recognized as a Dragon-Tamer, fabricated from black metal, with a knife-blade nose, socketed eyelids, and three crests running back over the scalp.

The mask's expression was unreadable, but Angmark's voice was triumphant. "I trapped you very easily."

"So you did," said Thissell. The slave finished knotting his wrists together. A clatter of Angmark's *hymerkin* sent him away. "Get to your feet," said Angmark. "Sit in that chair."

"What are we waiting for?" inquired Thissell.

"Two of our fellows still remain out on the water. We won't need them for what I have in mind."

"Which is?"

"You'll learn in due course," said Angmark. "We have an hour or so on our hands."

Thissell tested his bonds. They were undoubtedly secure.

Angmark seated himself. "How did you fix on me? I admit to being curious. . . . Come, come," he chided as Thissell sat silently. "Can't you recognize that I have defeated you? Don't make affairs unpleasant for yourself.''

Thissell shrugged. "I operated on a basic principle. A man can mask his face, but he can't mask his personality.''

"Aha,'' said Angmark. "Interesting. Proceed.''

"I borrowed a slave from you and the other two out-worlders, and I questioned them carefully. What masks had their masters worn during the month before your arrival? I prepared a chart and plotted their responses. Rolver wore the Tarn Bird about eighty percent of the time, the remaining twenty percent divided between the Sophist Abstraction and the Black Intricate. Welibus had a taste for the heroes of Kan-Dachan Cycle. He wore the Chalekun, the Prince Intrepid, the Seavain most of the time: six days out of eight. The other two days he wore his South Wind or his Gay Companion. Kershaul, more conservative, preferred the Cave Owl, the Star Wanderer, and two or three other masks he wore at odd intervals.

"As I say, I acquired this information from possibly its most accurate source, the slaves. My next step was to keep watch upon the three of you. Every day I noted what masks you wore and compared it with my chart. Rolver wore his Tarn Bird six times, his Black Intricate twice. Kershaul wore his Cave Owl five times, his Star Wanderer once, his Quincunx once, and his Ideal of Perfection once. Welibus wore the Emerald Mountain twice, the Triple Phoenix three times, the Prince Intrepid once, and the Shark God twice.''

Angmark nodded thoughtfully. "I see my error. I selected from Welibus's masks, but to my own taste—and, as you point out, I revealed myself. But only to you.'' He rose and went to the window. "Kershaul and Rolver are now coming ashore. They'll soon be past and about their business—though I doubt if they'd interfere in any case. They've both become good Sirenese.''

Thissell waited in silence. Ten minutes passed. Then Angmark reached to a shelf and picked up a knife. He looked at Thissell. "Stand up.''

Thissell slowly rose to his feet. Angmark approached from the side, reached out, lifted the Moon Moth from Thissell's head. Thissell gasped and made a vain attempt to seize it. Too late; his face was bare and naked.

Angmark turned away, removed his own mask, donned the Moon Moth. He struck a call on his *hymerkin*. Two slaves entered, stopped in shock at the sight of Thissell.

Angmark played a brisk tattoo, sang, "Carry this man up to the dock.''

"Angmark,'' cried Thissell. "I'm maskless!''

The slaves seized him and, in spite of Thissell's desperate struggles, conveyed him out on the deck, along the float and up on the dock.

Angmark fixed a rope around Thissell's neck. He said, "You are now Haxo

Angmark, and I am Edwer Thissell. Welibus is dead. You shall soon be dead. I can handle your job without difficulty. I'll play musical instruments like a Night-man and sing like a crow. I'll wear the Moon Moth till it rots and then I'll get another. The report will go to Polypolis, Haxo Angmark is dead. Everything will be serene."

Thissell barely heard. "You can't do this," he whispered. "My mask, my face . . ." A large woman in a blue and pink flower mask walked down the dock. She saw Thissell and, emitting a piercing shriek, flung herself prone on the dock.

"Come along," said Angmark brightly. He tugged at the rope and pulled Thissell down the dock. A man in a Pirate Captain mask coming up from his houseboat stood rigid in amazement.

Angmark played the *zachinko* and sang, "Behold the notorious criminal Haxo Angmark. Through all the outer-worlds his name is reviled. Now he is captured and led in shame to his death. Behold Haxo Angmark!"

They turned into the esplanade. A child screamed in fright. A man called hoarsely. Thissell stumbled; tears tumbled from his eyes; he could see only disorganized shapes and colors. Angmark's voice belled out richly: "Everyone behold the criminal of the out-worlds, Haxo Angmark! Approach and observe his execution!"

Thissell feebly cried out, "I'm not Angmark. I'm Edwer Thissell; he's Angmark." But no one listened to him. There were only cries of dismay, shock, disgust at the sight of his face. He called to Angmark, "Give me my mask, a slave-cloth . . ."

Angmark sang jubilantly. "In shame he lived, in maskless shame he dies."

A Forest Goblin stood before Angmark. "Moon Moth, we meet once more."

Angmark sang, "Stand aside, friend Goblin. I must execute this criminal. In shame he lived, in shame he dies!"

A crowd had formed around the group; masks stared in morbid titillation at Thissell.

The Forest Goblin jerked the rope from Angmark's hand and threw it to the ground. The crowd roared. Voices cried, "No duel, no duel! Execute the monster!"

A cloth was thrown over Thissell's head. Thissell awaited the thrust of a blade. But instead his bonds were cut. Hastily he adjusted the cloth, hiding his face, peering between the folds.

Four men clutched Haxo Angmark. The Forest Goblin confronted him, playing the *skaranyi*. "A week ago, you reached to divest me of my mask. You have now achieved your perverse aim!"

"But he is a criminal," cried Angmark. "He is notorious, infamous!"

"What are his misdeeds?" sang the Forest Goblin.

"He has murdered, betrayed; he has wrecked ships; he has tortured, blackmailed, robbed, sold children into slavery; he has—"

The Forest Goblin stopped him. "Your religious convictions are of no importance. We can vouch however for your present crimes!"

The hostler stepped forward. He sang fiercely, "This insolent Moon Moth nine days ago sought to pre-empt my choicest mount!"

Another man pushed close. He wore a Universal Expert, and sang, "I am a Master Mask-maker; I recognize this Moon Moth out-worlder! Only recently he entered my shop and derided my skill. He deserves death!"

"Death to the out-world monster!" cried the crowd. A wave of men surged forward.

Steel blades rose and fell. The deed was done.

Thissell watched, unable to move. The Forest Goblin approached, and playing the *stimic* sang sternly, "For you we have pity, but also contempt. A true man would never suffer such indignities!"

Thissell took a deep breath. He reached to his belt and found his *zachinko*. He sang, "My friend, you malign me! Can you not appreciate true courage? Would you prefer to die in combat or walk maskless along the esplanade?"

The Forest Goblin sang, "There is only one answer. First I would die in combat; I could not bear such shame."

Thissell sang, "I had such a choice. I could fight with my hands tied, and so die—or I could suffer shame, and through this shame conquer my enemy. You admit that you lack sufficient *strakh* to achieve this deed. I have proved myself a hero of bravery! I ask, who here has courage to do what I have done?"

"Courage?" demanded the Forest Goblin. "I fear nothing, up to and beyond death at the hands of the Night-men!"

"Then answer."

The Forest Goblin stood back. He played his *double-kamanthil*. "Bravery indeed, if such were your motives."

The hostler struck a series of subdued *gomapard* chords and sang, "Not a man among us would dare what this maskless man has done."

The crowd muttered approval.

The mask-maker approached Thissell, obsequiously stroking his *double-kamanthil*. "Pray, Lord Hero, step into my nearby shop, exchange this vile rag for a mask befitting your quality."

Another mask-maker sang, "Before you choose, Lord Hero, examine my magnificent creations!"

A man in a Bright Sky Bird mask approached Thissell reverently. "I have only just completed a sumptuous houseboat; seventeen years of toil have gone into its fabrication. Grant me the good fortune of accepting and using this splendid craft. Aboard waiting to serve you are alert slaves and pleasant maidens; there is ample wine in storage and soft silken carpets on the decks."

"Thank you," said Thissell, striking the *zachinko* with vigor and confidence. "I accept with pleasure. But first a mask."

The mask-maker struck an interrogative trill on the *gomapard*. "Would the Lord Hero consider a Sea Dragon Conqueror beneath his dignity?"

"By no means," sang Thissell. "I consider it suitable and satisfactory. We shall go now to examine it."

THE LAST FLIGHT OF DR. AIN

BY JAMES TIPTREE, JR.

The "slush pile" has three qualities in common with your average municipal sanitary landfill: 1) every now and then a jewel of great worth turns up in it. 2) it is reliably full of valuable raw materials—ideas, characters, bits of business, and so on—that could profitably be extracted and returned to the authors for processing. And, in spite of 1 and 2, point 3) is that hardly anybody wants to handle the stuff. Perhaps editors fear some of it will splash onto their clothes. I am of a coarser breed, and anyway I am mindful of Frank Munsey's Law: "No magazine can survive the mistakes of more than one person." So I have never used preliminary readers. And the slush pile is where I first saw the stories of Ray Bradbury, Fred Saberhagen, R. A. Lafferty, Larry Niven, Barry Malzberg, Joe Haldeman . . . and James Tiptree, Jr.

The first Tiptree story piqued my interest and I asked for bio information. The author was not reticent. Every letter was packed with little reminiscences. Tiptree had just been salmon-fishing in Scotland. Tiptree was briefly at home, between Paris and Pakistan. Tiptree was clearly living an adventurous life, but when you added all the tidbits together no clear picture of a human being emerged. Not just with me. As the years passed and the byline became famous, a reputation as a mystery man grew. There had to be a secret. That was beyond doubt. But what was it?

And then around 1977 I got a letter from Tiptree. There was a secret, all right. For personal reasons it had seemed important to keep it, but it was about to be blown, and he wanted me to be the first to know. He was a she. James Tiptree, Jr., was Alice Sheldon.

"Tiptree" was not the first female to write science fiction under a male name. But I really don't think it was necessary in the 1960s, whatever it may have been in, say, 1926. Is it now? Hardly. Perhaps an outright majority of the best new SF writers are unabashedly female, and no one seems the worse.

In fact, just a few years ago, shortly before Tiptree came out of the closet, as knowledgeable a person as Theodore Sturgeon commented that of his six favorite new writers five were women. And the sixth was—James Tiptree, Jr.

Doctor Ain was recognized on the Omaha-Chicago flight. A biologist colleague from Pasadena came out of the toilet and saw Ain in an aisle seat. Five years before, this man had been jealous of Ain's huge grants. Now he nodded coldly and was surprised at the intensity of Ain's response. He almost turned back to speak, but he felt too tired; like nearly everyone, he was fighting the flu.

The stewardess handing out coats after they landed remembered Ain too: a tall thin nondescript man with rusty hair. He held up the line staring at her; since he already had his raincoat with him she decided it was some kooky kind of pass and waved him on.

She saw Ain shamble off into the airport smog, apparently alone. Despite the big Civil Defense signs, O'Hare was late getting underground. No one noticed the woman.

The wounded, dying woman.

Ain was not identified en route to New York, but a 2:40 jet carried an "Ames" on the checklist, which was thought to be a misspelling of Ain. It was. The plane had circled for an hour while Ain watched the smoky seaboard monotonously tilt, straighten, and tilt again.

The woman was weaker now. She coughed, picking weakly at the scabs on her face half-hidden behind her long hair. Her hair, Ain saw, that great mane which had been so splendid, was drabbed and thin now. He looked to seaward, willing himself to think of cold, clean breakers. On the horizon he saw a vast black rug: somewhere a tanker had opened its vents. The woman coughed again. Ain closed his eyes. Smog shrouded the plane.

He was picked up next while checking in for the BOAC flight to Glasgow. Kennedy-Underground was a boiling stew of people, the air system unequal to the hot September afternoon. The check-in list swayed and sweated, staring dully at the newscast. SAVE THE LAST GREEN MANSIONS—a conservation group was protesting the defoliation and drainage of the Amazon basin. Several people recalled the beautifully colored shots of the new clean bomb. The line squeezed together to let a band of uniformed men go by. They were wearing buttons inscribed: WHO'S AFRAID?

That was when a woman noticed Ain. He was holding a news-sheet and she heard it rattling in his hand. Her family hadn't caught the flu, so she looked at him sharply. Sure enough, his forehead was sweaty. She herded her kids to the side away from Ain.

He was using *Instac* throat spray, she remembered. She didn't think much of *Instac;* her family used *Kleer.* While she was looking at him, Ain suddenly turned his head and stared into her face, with the spray still floating down. Such inconsiderateness! She turned her back. She didn't recall him talking to any woman, but she perked up her ears when the clerk read off Ain's destination. Moscow!

The clerk recalled that too, with disapproval. Ain checked in alone, he reported. No woman had been ticketed for Moscow, but it would have been easy enough to split up her tickets. (By that time they were sure she was with him.)

Ain's flight went via Iceland with an hour's delay at Kevlavik. Ain walked over to the airport park, gratefully breathing the sea-filled air. Every few breaths he shuddered. Under the whine of bull-dozers the sea could be heard running its huge paws up and down the keyboard of the land. The little park had a grove of yellowed birches and a flock of wheat-ears foraged by the path. Next month they would be in North Africa, Ain thought. Two thousand miles of tiny wing-beats. He threw them some crumbs from a packet in his pocket.

The woman seemed stronger here. She was panting in the sea wind, her large eyes fixed on Ain. Above her the birches were as gold as those where he had first seen her, the day his life began. . . . Squatting under a stump to watch a shrewmouse he had been, when he caught a falling ripple of green and recognized the shocking naked girl-flesh—creamy, pink-tipped—coming toward him among the golden bracken. Young Ain held his breath, his nose in the sweet moss and his heart going *crash—crash.* And then he was staring at the outrageous fall of that hair down her narrow back, watching it dance around her heartshaped buttocks, while the shrewmouse ran over his paralyzed hand. The lake was utterly still, dusty silver under the misty sky, and she made no more than a muskrat's ripple to rock the floating golden leaves. The silence closed back, the trees burning like torches where the naked girl had walked the wild wood, reflected in Ain's shining eyes. . . . For a time he believed he had seen an Oread.

Ain was last on board for the Glasgow leg. The stewardess recalled dimly that he seemed restless. She could not identify the woman. There were a lot of women on board—and babies. Her passenger list had had several errors.

At Glasgow airport, a waiter remembered that a man like Ain had called for Scottish oatmeal and eaten two bowls, although of course it wasn't really oatmeal. A young mother with a pram saw him tossing crumbs to the birds.

When he checked in at the BOAC desk, he was hailed by a Glasgow professor who was going to the same conference at Moscow. This man had been one of Ain's teachers. (It was now known that Ain had done his postgraduate work in Europe.) They chatted all the way across the North Sea.

"I wondered about that," the professor said later. "Why have you come round about?" I asked him. He told me the direct flights were booked up. (This was found to be untrue: Ain had apparently avoided the Moscow jet hoping to escape attention.)

The professor spoke with relish of Ain's work.

"Brilliant? Oh, aye. And stubborn, too; very very stubborn. It was as though a concept—often the simplest relation, mind you—would stop him in his tracks, and fascinate him. He would hunt all 'round it instead of going on to the next thing as a more docile mind would. Truthfully, I wondered at first if he could be just a bit thick. But you recall who it was said that the capacity for wonder at matters of common acceptance occurs in the superior mind? And, of course, so it proved when he shook us all up over that enzyme conversion business. A pity your government took him away from his line, there. . . . No, he said nothing of this, I say it to you, young man. We spoke in fact largely of my work. I was surprised to find he'd kept up. He asked me what my *sentiments* about it were, which surprised me again. Now, understand, I'd not seen the man for five years, but he seemed—well, perhaps just tired, as who is not? I'm sure he was glad to have a change; he jumped out for a legstretch wherever we came down. At Oslo, even Bonn . . . Oh yes, he did feed the birds, but that was nothing new for Ain. . . . His social life when I knew him? Radical causes? Young man, I've said what I've said because of who it was that introduced you, but I'll have you know it is an impertinence in you to think ill of Charles Ain, or that he could do a harmful deed. Good evening."

The professor said nothing of the woman in Ain's life.

Nor could he have, although Ain had been intimately with her in the university time. He had let no one see how he was obsessed with her, with the miracle, the wealth of her body, her inexhaustibility. They met at his every spare moment; sometimes in public pretending to be casual strangers under his friends' noses, pointing out a pleasing view to each other with grave formality. And later in their privacies—what doubled intensity of love! He revelled in her, possessed her, allowed her no secrets. His dreams were of her sweet springs and shadowed places and her white rounded glory in the moonlight, finding always more, always new dimensions of his joy.

The danger of her frailty was far off then in the rush of birdsong and the springing leverets of the meadow. On dark days she might cough a bit, but so did he. In those years he had had no thought to the urgent study of disease.

At the Moscow conference nearly everyone noticed Ain at some point or another, which was to be expected in view of his professional stature. It was a small, high-calibre meeting. Ain was late in. A day's reports were over, and his was to be on the third and last.

Many people spoke with Ain, and several sat with him at meals. No one was surprised that he spoke little; he was a retiring man except on a few memorable occasions of hot argument. He did strike some of his friends as a bit tired and jerky.

An Indian molecular engineer who saw him with the throat spray kidded him about bringing over Asian flu. A Swedish colleague recalled that Ain had been called away to the transatlantic phone at lunch; and when he returned Ain volunteered the information that something had turned up missing in his home lab. There was another joke, and Ain said cheerfully, "Oh, yes, quite active."

At that point one of the Chicom biologists swung into his daily propaganda chore about bacteriological warfare and accused Ain of manufacturing biotic weapons. Ain took the wind out of his sails by saying: "You're perfectly right." By tacit consent, there was very little talk about military applications, industrial dusting, or subjects of that type. And nobody recalled seeing Ain with any woman other than old Madame Vialche, who could scarcely have subverted anyone from her wheelchair.

Ain's own speech was bad, even for him. He always had a poor public voice, but his ideas were usually expressed with the lucidity so typical of the first-rate mind. This time he seemed muddled, with little new to say. His audience excused this as the muffling effects of security. Ain then got into a tangled point about the course of evolution in which he seemed to be trying to show that something was very wrong indeed. When he wound up with a reference to Hudson's bell bird "singing for a later race," several listeners wondered if he could be drunk.

The big security break came right at the end, when he suddenly began to describe the methods he had used to mutate and redesign a leukemia virus. He explained the procedure with admirable clarity in four sentences and paused. Then he gave a terse description of the effects of the mutated strain. It was maximal only on the higher primates, recovery rate among the lower mammals and other orders was close to ninety percent. As to vectors, he went on, any warm-blooded animal served. In addition, the virus retained its viability in most environmental media and performed very well airborne. Contagion rate was extremely high. Almost off-hand, Ain added that no test primate or accidentally exposed human had survived beyond the twenty-second day.

These words fell into a silence broken only by the running feet of the United Arab delegate making for the door. Then a gilt chair went over as an American bolted after him.

Ain seemed unaware that his audience was in a state of unbelieving paralysis. It had all come so fast: a man who had been blowing his nose was staring popeyed around his handkerchief. Another who had been lighting a pipe grunted as his fingers singed. Two men chatting by the door missed his words entirely and their laughter chimed into a dead silence in which echoed Ain's words: "—really no point in attempting."

Later they found he had been explaining that the virus utilized the body's own immunomechanisms, and so defense was by definition hopeless.

That was all. Ain looked around vaguely for questions and then started down the aisle. By the time he got to the door, people were swarming after him. He wheeled about and said rather crossly, "Yes, of course it is very wrong. I told you that. We are all wrong. Now it's over."

An hour later they found he had gone, having apparently reserved a Sinair flight to Karachi.

The security men caught up with him at Hong Kong. By then he seemed really very ill, and went with them peacefully. They started back to the States via Hawaii.

His captors were civilized types; they saw he was gentle and treated him accordingly. He had no weapons or drugs on him. They took him out handcuffed for a stroll at Osaka and let him feed his crumbs to the birds, and they listened with interest to his account of the migration routes of the common brown sandpiper. He was very hoarse. At that point, he was wanted only for the security thing. There was no question of a woman at all.

He dozed most of the way to the islands, but when they came in sight he pressed to the windows and began to mutter. The security man behind him got the first inkling that there was a woman in it, and turned on his recorder.

". . . blue, blue and green until you see the wounds. Oh my girl. Oh beautiful, you won't die. I won't let you die. I tell you girl, it's over. . . . Lustrous eyes, look at me, let me see you now alive! Great queen, my sweet body, my girl, have I saved you? . . . Oh terrible to know, and noble—Chaos's child green-robed in blue and golden light, . . . The thrown and spinning ball of life alone in space. . . . Have I saved you?"

On the last leg, he was obviously feverish.

"She may have tricked me, you know," he said confidentially to the government man. "You have to be prepared for that, of course. I know her!" He chuckled confidentially. "She's no small thing. But wring your heart out—"

Coming over San Francisco, he was merry. "Don't you know the otters will go back in there? I'm certain of it. That fill won't last; there'll be a bay there again."

They got him on a stretcher at Hamilton Air Base, and he went unconscious shortly after takeoff. Before he collapsed, he'd insisted on throwing the last of his birdseed on the field.

"Birds are, of course, warm-blooded," he confided to the agent who was handcuffing him to the stretcher. Then Ain smiled gently and lapsed into inertness. He stayed that way almost all the remaining ten days of his life. By then, of course, no one really cared. Both the government men had died quite early, after they finished analyzing the birdseed and throat-spray. The woman at Kennedy had only just started feeling sick.

The tape-recorder they put by his bed functioned right on through, but if anybody had been around to replay it they would have found little but babbling. "Gaea Gloriatrix," he crooned, "my girl, my queen . . ." At times he was grandiose and tormented. "Our life, your death!" he yelled. "Our death would have been your death too, no need for that, no need . . ."

At other times he was accusing. "What did you do about the dinosaurs?" he demanded. "Did they annoy you? How did you fix *them*? Cold. Queen, you're too cold! You came close to it this time, my girl," he raved. And then he wept and caressed the bedclothes and was maudlin.

Only at the end, lying in his filth and thirst, still chained where they had forgotten him, he was suddenly coherent. In the light clear voice of a lover planning a summer picnic he asked the recorder happily:

"Have you ever thought about bears? They have so much . . . funny they never came along further. By any chance were you saving them, girl?" And he chuckled in his ruined throat. And later, died.

AMONG THE BAD BABOONS

BY MACK REYNOLDS

Most people think that Maximilian was the only emperor of Mexico, but there happens to be a current incumbent of the post. His name is Mack Reynolds. He owns the place. He sits there in San Miguel de Allende, where he knows everybody and everybody knows him. He has become a tourist attraction for visiting American writers. First you see the pyramids, then Chichen Itza, then you go visit Mack Reynolds. . . .

Well, it isn't exactly like that. But it's reasonably close. Mack Reynolds is a citizen of the world if ever there was.

I first met Mack in London in the early 1960s. He had just finished doing something few humans dare—vagabonding around the Soviet Union in a camper—and was on his way to North Africa to do more of the same. There are not many places on Earth where Mack Reynolds has not been—not for a weekend in a tourist hotel, like you and me, but in the unhurried, unexceptional mode of travel most of us manage only for going to grandmother's house at Christmas. And amid it all, he writes his own special, very attractive kind of science fiction.

I think Mack Reynolds is the most consistently underrated writer in science fiction. Underrated, that is, by the critics and the people who give awards. Not by the readers. When I was editing Galaxy, I went to a lot of trouble to find out which stories the average reader liked best. We were publishing the top names in the field, with far more than our share of award-winning stories . . . but the writer who most consistently pleased the readers wasn't any of the celebrated household names. It was Mack Reynolds.

*   *   *

I.

"One of these days you're going to pierce your eardrum doing that," Pamela Rozet said from the doorway.

"Uhhh?"

"That paintbrush. If you don't stop scratching the inside of your ear with it, you're going to hurt yourself. Didn't your mother ever tell you not to stick anything smaller than your elbow in your ear?"

Arthur Halleck took the end of the paintbrush in question out of his right ear and scowled dimly at it. He said, completely *malapropos*, "What in the name of the living Zoroaster ever happened to brushes? It was bad enough when they were making them out of nylon. What's this stuff? Anything to cheapen the product. The old masters used to paint with bristle brushes, or red sable hair. Have you ever been in a museum and looked real closely at an original Rembrandt, or even a Leonardo?"

"Yes," Pam said.

"Did you ever see any hair from their paint brushes?"

"I didn't look *that* close," she said.

"Well, you didn't. But take a look at some of Picasso's stuff, not to speak of mine. Hair, or other brush fiber, all through the paint." He tossed the offending brush to a colorfully bespattered table. "I've been all over town. Into every art shop that survived in any shape at all. There's not a bristlebrush to be found."

"Possibly you can get some on the mainland, when you take this painting over."

"No," he growled disgustedly. "They don't make them any more. You can't ultra-mate the manufacture of decent bristle brushes. And anything you can't ultra-mate in the Ultra-welfare States goes down the drain."

He stepped back and stared gloomily at the painting on the easel.

"Is it finished?" she asked.

"Doesn't it *look* finished?" he demanded in irritation.

Pam came closer and looked and said patiently, "Long since I told you, Art, that I've never got beyond the impressionalists."

"Well, damn it, the Representational Abstract School is the nearest thing to the impressionalists for decades. Can't you see, confound it?"

"No."

"Well, look. It gives the same effect as the quick impression Van Gogh, Renoir, Degas, and the rest demanded. You get a quick flash, and your immediate impression is that it's completely abstract, but then you realize that it's the ruin of the entrance to a subway station."

"I guess you do, at that," she said doubtfully.

He stared at the four-foot-square painting. "No wonder it's no good," he said. "Working with this quick-drying metallic acrylic paint on this ridiculous presdwood-duplicator board would have one of those Cro-Magnon cave painters climbing the wall."

"Aren't you going to have it duplicated and registered?"

"Of course. Sooner or later, I'm going to hit, Pam. Then it's you and me."

She looked at him, a shade of wistfulness in her overly tired face. She was a girl of averages, pleasantly so. Average height and weight and of an average prettiness, given her approximately thirty years of age. But there was a vulnerable something about her mouth that added. She was, and always had been, attractive to men who carried the dream, who were creative, ambitious.

"I thought it was already you and me, Art. That it had been for the past two years and more."

He said, a bit impatiently, "You know what I mean, Pam."

She went over to the window, avoiding the broken pane where it was patched with some old clothing, and rested her bottom on the ledge. She said, "Art, if we went back to the mainland and combined the income from our Inalienable Basic and added to that my royalties and your occasional sales, we'd be able to maintain a reasonably high standard of living. We'd also be in a position to make contacts, meet our own kind, associate with—"

"Associate with other charity cases," he broke in bitterly. "I've told you, Pam, I'll never become one more dependent on the Ultra-welfare State. I'll pay my own way in the world, or I'll go under. A man's *got* to be a man."

"You're not exactly paying your way right this minute, Arthur Halleck. We're scavengers, to use the politest term that comes to my tongue." Her tone was testy.

He shook his head. "Don't roach me, Pam. We don't take anything that belongs to anybody. If we didn't find it and use it, it'd slowly rot or rust away."

She said, slightly irritated herself now, "Look here, darling, you're not taking anything that belongs to anyone else either when you accept the dividends that accrue to your ten shares of Inalienable Basic."

"Those dividends don't grow on trees. Somebody does the work that produces them," he said stubbornly.

She was really impatient now. "Look, Art, the superabundance being produced under people's capitalism now is not the product of the comparative handful of workers and technicians who are required in industry and agriculture today. It's the product of the accumulated work of all mankind down through the ages. A million years ago some ancestor of yours and mine first used fire. The whole race has been doing it since. Five thousand years ago, some slick over in the Near East first dreamed up the wheel. We've been using it ever since. Every generation comes up with something brand-new to add to the accumulated pile of knowledge, know-how, art, science. This accumulated human know-how doesn't belong to anybody or to any group; it belongs to us all. At long last, as a result of it, the human race has licked the problem of producing plenty for everyone. No one need go hungry any more, nor cold, nor unsheltered, nor uneducated, nor without proper medical care. This is the legacy our ancestors have left us. It belongs to all of us; as a matter of fact, the ten shares of Inalienable Basic each citizen receives is a precious small slice of pie, if you ask me. Just enough to keep us lesser breeds from revolt."

"I still say it's charity," Art Halleck said stubbornly.

She brushed it off. "So what can you do about it? We didn't make this world and we're in no position to change its rules. Particularly over here. If we were on the mainland we might join the Futurists, or something."

He turned back to the painting on his easel and stared at it some more, saying over his shoulder, "I don't have to change the rules. Sooner or later, my work will hit, and I'll make my own way. You can still make your own way under People's Capitalism if you've got it on the ball. Those at the very top don't depend on Ultra-welfare State-issued Inalienable Basic."

"They sure don't," she said sourly. "They usually have inherited enough Variable Basic or private stock to keep them like gods all their lives. And as far as hitting sooner or later, it's obviously not sooner. How many of the last paintings sold?"

He looked at her. "Seven."

"Seventy dollars worth, eh? Just barely enough to duplicate and register this one. By the time you've paid your transport back and forth to Greater Washington and possibly bought a couple of paintbrushes or so, nothing left at all."

"One of these days I'll hit," he said stubbornly.

She gave up and turned and stared out the window in the direction of Washington Square.

II.

She said finally, "Art, was it beautiful?"

He was busy cleaning his brushes now, grumbling about the speed with which his metallic-acrylic medium dried.

"Was what beautiful?"

"Manhattan—before."

"Oh. Well, no."

"You were born here, weren't you?"

"Up in the Bronx."

"Before the riots?"

"Ummm. I was just a kid, but come to think of it, I was already sketching, drawing." He snorted deprecation. "How many artists bother to learn to draw any more? It's like a writer never bothering to learn the alphabet."

"Why wasn't it beautiful?"

He gave up his unhappy viewing of his work and his brushes and came to stand next to her, an arm going unconsciously around her waist. He followed her line of vision down along MacDougal Street to the square where once scores of artist hopefuls had held their open-air shows.

He said thoughtfully, scowling, "It's an elastic word, 'beauty.' Means different things to different people. You can find beauty in just about anything—garbage dumps, battlefields, desert, just about anything. But largely, big cities don't lend themselves to beauty. Manhattan was probably a lovely setting back when the Indians were here, or even when the first small Dutch settlement was huddled down at this end of the island. But the way it was by the middle of the twentieth century? No. I've never been out of North America to supposedly beautiful cities like Paris, Rome, or Rio, but I have seen San Francisco. It had a certain amount of beauty—before the riots, of course.''

"I understand they weren't so bad there."

"Bad enough. However, they've cleaned out some of the ruins and a pseudo-city resulted there. It's hard to beat that Golden Gate setting."

They were silent for a moment, then she said, "How could it ever have happened, Art?"

He shrugged, and his words came slowly as he thought it out. "It could easily enough have been foreseen. A city like this had stopped making sense, Pam. The original reasons for cities—towns like Jericho began to be eight thousand years ago—had disappeared. Walled villages of farmers that could be defended against the nomads, trade centers built at crossroads, manufacturing centers, commercial centers. Putting walls around cities for defense stopped making sense. Modern transportation methods antiquated them as trade centers and manufacturing bases as industry was able to decentralize. Today, with communications what they are, even commercial centers are anachronisms. You can handle business from anywhere to anywhere."

"But what *happened?*"

"A lot of pressures. With the coming of automation and then ultra-mation not only in manufacture but in agriculture, the undereducated farm laborers, the unemployables, the unplaceables flooded to the cities looking for jobs or in their absence, for relief, for free handouts. As their numbers grew, and with them ghettos and slums, the better-to-do city dwellers streamed out to suburbs. That meant a drop in tax income, and the city was faced with inadequate funds for slum clearance, education, police, and firemen. Even things like garbage collection were inadequately financed. Which meant that still more of the better-paid citizens left. Industry began to leave too, to get closer to sources of raw materials, and to areas where labor was cheaper. So taxes took another nosedive.

"Television played a major part. These slum dwellers could watch the typical TV program, which almost invariably portrayed the actors, and certainly the advertising actors, as living lives of plenty. Their apartments or homes were always beautiful and totally equipped, their clothes the latest of fashion, their food bountiful and of the best, their children healthy and handsome, the schools they attended ideal. Needless to say, the slum dwellers wanted these things. So some of the more aggressive made a few demonstrations—and were landed upon, to their further embitterment. Alarmed, more of the better elements left town for the suburbs, for New England, upstate New York, Jersey, Pennsylvania. Some of the more prosperous actually commuted to Florida, flying back and forth. More industry left town then, because of higher taxes and the higher insurance rates caused by the riots. So the city fathers brought in less income than ever, and there was less to spend on slum clearance, education, relief. So the riots grew in magnitude."

Art Halleck shrugged in distaste at the memory. "So it went, and finally we had the big one. And never really recovered from that. Oh, things continued for a while. But by this time, nobody who could possibly afford it was left living in places like Manhattan, Detroit, Chicago, and so on. Nor any business that could possibly get out. So came another riot and another . . . and finally everybody left, including the police and firemen. That was the end."

"What happened to the slum element, the poverty-stricken, the unadaptable?"

He looked down at her. "As a writer, I'd think you'd know at least as well as I."

"I wondered how you'd put it, in view of your feelings on the government issuing Inalienable Basic."

He said, slowly again, scowling and as if grudgingly, "I suppose it was in the cards. No alternative. At approximately the same time the cities were a confusion of riots and discontent, they issued Inalienable Basic to each citizen, thus guaranteeing womb-to-tomb security. Overnight, not even the poverty-stricken wanted to remain in the big cities. It was cheaper to live elsewhere, not to speak of being more comfortable. So they streamed out like lemmings—or maybe rats. All except the handful of baboons, of course."

Pam shook her head and turned away from the view of the street. "I sometimes wonder why they never came back."

"Who?"

"The police and all. Why didn't they reconstruct?"

"Why? Like I said, the original reason for cities was gone and the cost to rebuild was prohibitive. It wouldn't even be worthwhile trying to clean it up for farmland, or pasture, or whatever. Too much debris, too much sheer wreckage. Oh, some of the other towns have been reconstituted, at least partially. Denver and San Francisco. But largely, they've been just left, continuing to deteriorate as the years go by."

She looked at him.

"And with only a few scavengers, such as ourselves, left in the ruins. No electricity, no water, no sewage. Nothing."

He snorted, tired of the subject. "I wouldn't say exactly nothing. We don't do so badly. By the way, I should have something to eat before going down to Greater Washington."

"Caviar, turtle soup, roast pheasant, imported British plum pudding in brandy sauce, with a good French claret to wash it down."

"I'm tired of that damn caviar."

III.

Mark Martino drifted in, as usual, for lunch. He had four long-necked bottles in his arms. He also had an old-fashioned-looking six-shooter low on his right hip and an automatic pistol at belt level on his left. He looked surprisingly similar to that movie star of yesteryear, Robert Taylor, but he wouldn't have known that.

"Hey, chum-pals," he said. "Get a load of this."

"What is it?" Pam said, looking up from the camp stove which sat on the electric range in the kitchen.

"It's a real *Bernkasteler Doktor und Bratenhofchen Trockenbeerenauslese.*"

"Oh, great, now I know something I d. in't know before."

"You, Pamela Rozet, are a peasant. This is the greatest of Riesling wines." He took one of the bottles and held it up and stared at the label and added, unhappily, "At least it once was; a Riesling shouldn't really age this long. Well, we'll see how it's held up."

"Where'd you find it?" Art said.

"You'd never think. In the cellar of that liquor store on the corner of West Third Street."

Art said, "I thought that joint had been looted bare years ago."

"Evidently so did everybody else," Mark said. "But this was down in the cellar, under a lot of crud that had evidently caved in back during the raids and riots. There was a whole case of this Riesling and some odds and ends of cordials. I covered it back over, but it won't do any good."

"Why not?" Pam said. "You don't have any gasoline over in your apartment, do you?"

"A couple of baboons spotted me coming out of the place with these. They'll root around till they've found it. You want me to go over and bring you a jerrycan?"

Pam said, "Please do. I'm just about out and haven't been able to find any for a week."

Art said, "Is that why you're all rodded up? The baboons?"

Mark, heading for the door, said, "Yeah. They were both strangers."

"Oh, hell," Art said. "We've been having it so easy here for months. You'd better tip off Julie and Tim."

"Already have," Mark said, leaving.

Art looked at Pam. "Maybe I'd better put off taking this painting down to the museum."

"Why?" she said wearily. "Baboons and hunters we've had before. Undoubtedly we'll have them again. Until—" she cut it off.

"Until what?"

"You know. Until one of these days, some baboon, or some hunter, kills one or both of us."

He didn't say anything.

Suddenly it came out in a rush.

"Arthur, we've *got* to get out of here. Arthur I'm afraid. I'm an awful coward."

He let the air out of his lungs and came erect from the kitchen chair upon which he had been sitting. He went over to the window and stared down.

Mark Martino came back with the can of gasoline.

"I don't know if this is white gas or not," he said.

Pam said, "It doesn't make any difference with this stove."

Mark said, "I ran into some butane in a sports section of a department store yesterday. Want it?"

"No, I suppose not. I threw the butane stove away. I'm used to this gasoline thing now. Not as hot, really, but we should be able to get gas for some time yet."

Mark said, "Well, even it's getting scarce. I haven't found a car with any in its tank for a coon's age." He looked from one of them to the other. "Did I interrupt a fight, or something?"

Pam said wearily, "No. No, not really."

Art said, "Pam wants to go back to the rat race."

She didn't say anything to that.

Mark said finally, "Well, why don't you? It doesn't make much sense, staying. We three and Julie and Tim are the only ones left in this neighborhood."

"Why don't you?" Art said. He wasn't arguing; his voice meant that he was actually curious.

Mark held up one of the green bottles he'd brought as his contribution toward the lunch. "You know what one of these would cost over on the mainland? That is, if you could find it at all."

"That couldn't be enough reason, even for a lush-head like you," Art said.

Mark thought about it. He said finally, ruefully, "I don't know. Wait a minute, I want to get something to read for you." He left again.

Pam said, "Why does anybody stay?"

Art knew he wasn't telling her anything she didn't know, but he said, "Some are criminals, fugitives from justice. Some are mental cases. Some, I suppose, are former immigrants, illegal entry immigrants without papers and not eligible to apply for their ten shares of Inalienable Basic if they went over to the mainland. We lump them all up and call them baboons. But the rest of us? Well, I suppose we're nonconformists, rebels against the Ultra-welfare State."

"That takes care of everybody but me," Pam said, checking the canned pheasant she'd been warming up.

"And you, then?" Art said. "Why are you here?"

"Because you are."

There could be no answer.

Mark Martino came in again, an age-yellowed paperback book in his hand. He was looking for a place.

"Listen to this," he said. "It's from a guy named Arthur C. Clarke. *Profiles of the Future,* written back in the sixties." He began reading. " 'Civilization cannot exist without new frontiers; it needs them both physically and spiritually. The physical need is obvious—new lands, new resources, new materials. The spiritual need is less apparent, but in the long run it is more important. We do not live by bread alone; we need adventure, variety, novelty, romance. As the psychologists have shown by their sensory deprivation experiments, a man goes swiftly mad if he is isolated in a silent, darkened room, cut off completely from the external world. What is true of individuals is also true of societies; they too can become insane without sufficient stimulus.' "

Mark tossed the book to the table. "I guess that's it. Whatever happened to the yen for adventure? A hundred years ago Americans were pushing West, fighting nature, fighting Indians, fighting each other over mines, cattle, and land. When did the dividing line come—when we were willing to live vicarious adventure, watching make-believe heroes, Hollywood boys, a good many of them queers, shoot up the Indians or kill by the scores the bad guys, the Nazis, or commies, the Russians and Chinese. Why did we leave it to the Norwegians to crew the Kon-Tiki? and for the British and Sherpas to first scale Everest? We've become a bunch of gutless wonders, sitting in front of our Tri-Vision sets. The biggest frustration, the great tragedy of our current age is the new Central production ban on using cereals for beer or booze."

Art said sourly, "That won't be a frustration long. I understand that they came up with a new sort of combination tranquilizer and euphoric. Going to issue it so cheaply that it'll be nearly free. Non-habit-forming, supposedly no hangover, no bad effects. Keeps you perpetually happy, in a kind of perpetual daze. Even the children can have it. They call it Trank."

"What'll they think of next?" Mark marveled sarcastically. "Talk about bread and circuses. The Roman plutocracy never had it so good; they gave the proletariat a sadistic show and free wheat. But time marches on, and now we've got the credit from Inalienable Basic, twenty-four-hour-a-day Tri-Vision teevee library, and music banks, and . . . what did you call it?"

"Trank," Art said. He looked at his friend strangely. "So you stay on here for the adventure. You with your big collection of guns. You with your prowling around the ruins looking for fancy booze and the like, hoping that the baboons or hunters will jump you. Hell, you're just a hunter yourself."

Mark was irritated and defensive. "I'm not a hunter. Maybe I like the adventure here, the chances you take just surviving, but I'm no hunter. I live here; this is my home. I defend myself. Maybe I even get my kicks out of getting into situations where I have to use my speed and my wits, but I never pick the fight, and I most certainly have never shot an unarmed baboon in the back the way these damned hunters will."

Pam began to set the food on the table. "Then what's the real reason for being here, Mark—aside from the adventure?"

IV.

He pretended he had to think about it, even as he helped her put out the elaborate silverware Art had liberated from the ruins of Tiffany's years before.

He reached into a pocket and brought forth the durable plastic which was his Universal Credit Card. "I object to this being closer to me than my soul," he said. "My number, issued me at birth and from which I can never escape, even after death. A combination of what was once Social Security number, driver's license, bank account number, voter's registration, even telephone number and post office box number. It's everything. Regimentation carried to the ultimate. We thought the commies and Nazis had regimentation. Zoroaster! The computers know everything there is to know about me, from before I was born to long after I'm dead—they keep the records in their files forever. When my great-grandchildren want to have children, the computers will check back on good old Mark Martino for genetic purposes. Oh, swell. Talk about being a cog in a machine—hell, we're more nearly like identical grains of sand on a beach."

He held up his wrist to show his teevee phone. "Why I carry this, I don't know. I've always got it switched on Priority One, and there are only three persons on earth eligible to break in on me on Priority One. But look at this thing. With the coming of the satellite relays and international communications integrated, I can literally, and for practically no expense, talk to anybody on Earth. Even if the poor cloddy is halfway up Mount Fuji in Japan. There's no escape. In the old days, the cost of phoning a friend, relative, business contact, or whoever got on the prohibitive side when it was long distance, or especially international. Not now. For pennies you can talk to anyone in the world. But the trouble is, it works both ways—they can talk to you."

Art laughed. "I seldom wear my wristphone. And even the portable, in the next room, is always on Priority Two."

Mark growled, "That won't help you if it's a government bulletin or something. You're on tap, every minute of the day. How'd you like to be a Tri-Vision sex symbol or some other entertainment star? If one of them dared lower their priority to, say, five, they'd have a billion teevee phone calls come in within hours."

Pam said, "All right, all right, let's eat. Get the cork out of one of those bottles, Art, and let's sample the latest loot. So you're in revolt against modern society, Mark, so all right. At least you don't refuse to spend your dividends from your Inalienable Basic, the way Art does. And your royalties must accumulate so that when you make those sin trips of yours over to Nueva Las Vegas, or wherever, you must have quite a bit of credit on hand."

"Sin trips!" Mark protested, holding his right hand over his heart as though in injured innocence. "How can you say that? It's called research."

"Ha!" Art snorted.

"No jolly," Mark said. "I've got to keep up some touch. Have to know what they're listening to in the dives, both high and low. It's all very well to have two or three semiclassics in the music banks, but you've got to be continually turning out new stuff if you really want to hit the jackpot some day."

"Semiclassics," Art snorted. "I love Mother in the springtime; I love Mother in the fall."

Mark said reasonably, "It's what they want, Art. If you'd paint what they wanted, maybe you'd be selling better. Right now, they're going through a 1920s–1930s revival bit. Swell. I sit at my teevee phone and play over and over the so-called Hit Parade tunes, and over and over I listen to the old Bing Crosby and even Rudy Vallee tapes.

"And then pretty soon, just about when I'm ready to start tearing my hair out, something comes to me. I sit down to the piano. I beat it out. Sometimes the whole thing is done in an hour. Writing the lyrics is the hardest part."

Pam said interestedly, "Then what happens, Mark?"

"Well, there's various ways. If you're a second-rater, like me, your best bet is to get in touch with a slick to act as middleman, expediter, or whatever you want to call him. He gets one of the stars, such as Truman Love..."

"Truman *Love*," Art protested. "Is there really a singer with a name like that?"

"Of course. I tell you, Art, the mental caliber of the Tri-Vision and teevee fan is halving each year that goes by. They don't want to be bothered thinking even a tiny bit. A sloppy mopsy who likes to listen to sentimental slush about love can remember a name like Truman Love. It sticks with her. She knows very well, before she dials one of his songs, what it's going to be like. With a name like that, it couldn't be anything else."

"All right, all right, so the slick gets Truman Love to sing your song."

"Okay. We record it and pay the small amount involved in placing it in the music banks. If the slick is any good, he gets some publicity. One of the gossip commentators, one of the live comedians, that sort of thing. In the banks, it's filed under name of singer, name of song, type of song, band leader, name of band, name of each musician in the band, subject of song—such as love, mother, patriotism, children, that sort of thing—and finally, surprise, surprise, the writer or writers of the song."

"So," Art supplied, "whoever dials and plays it pays a small royalty."

"Very small," Mark said, nodding. "Differs for a single home teevee phone screen, or for, say, some live Tri-Vision show involving a band. If you're lucky, the song takes and maybe some more singers and bands want to record it. At any rate, you split the take four ways."

"Four ways?" Pam said. "You, the singer, the slick, and who?"

"The recording company. They usually take one-fourth, too. They split their quarter between the company, the band leader and all members of the band."

Art shook his head. "By the time the drummer gets his slice, it must be pretty small potatoes."

"Not if it's played a few billion times," Mark said. "Besides, maybe I write a possible song once a month. He probably does a recording as often as once or twice a day. He might have literally thousands of tunes recorded, with his getting a tiny percentage of each."

"It's not as bad as newspapers," Pam said. "Reading a newspaper on your teevee phone will cost you ten cents. It has to be prorated among possibly a hundred journalists, columnists, editors, and what have you. That means that on an average, each newspaperman involved gets possibly one mill, a tenth of a cent, per reading. Not even that, since the owners of the paper take their cut off the top.''

Art said, shaking his head and digging into the pheasant, ''What in the name of the holy living Zoroaster did they do before computers?''

''Well, they didn't handle it this way,'' Mark said. He looked at Art and changed the subject. ''You're going down to Greater Washington this afternoon?''

''Yeah. I want to register this painting. I'll be back in a few hours. You'll keep an eye on Pam, won't you?''

''Of course. Uh . . . you have duplication and registration fee?''

Art looked at him, puzzled.

Mark said hurriedly, ''I mean, without dipping into your dividends. I know you refuse to spend them.''

Art went back to his food.

''Don't be so touchy,'' Mark said. ''What I meant was, if you were a little short, you could always pay me back later.''

Art said, ''You know damn well I couldn't use your dollar credits to register my painting anyway. Nobody can spend your credits but you. Or do you want me to carry not only your credit card with me but your right thumb as well, for the print?''

Mark chuckled. ''There are ways of getting around anything. I found some ancient coins in the wreckage of a numismatist's shop the other day. You could take them to greater Washington, sell them, and have the amount credited to your account. Then use it.''

''Thanks just the same,'' Art said tightly. ''But I pay my own way, Mark. When I can't pay my own way by selling my paintings any longer, I'll give up my art and find some other kind of work.''

''Well, it's more than I can say. I'm always in here sponging off you people.''

Pam laughed at that. ''Half the things we have here came from you. Why you're the one who found the bomb shelter, even.''

The subject was safely changed. Mark said, ''By the way, how's the bomb shelter holding out?''

''We're putting a sizable dent in it,'' Pam said. ''I think I'm going to ask you boys to try and scout out some things not quite so exotic. A few cases of baked beans, corn, string beans, and what have you. I'm beginning to get a permanent sour stomach from all this rich stuff. Which reminds me. I'm going to have to take a trip to the mainland, as soon as my dividends come in for next month, to load up on some fresh fruits and vegetables.''

Mark said, ''Why don't we make an expedition of it? Tim and Julie, too. Both for the manpower to carry things and for protection.''

Art said, ''What time is it?''

Mark dialed his wristphone and said, ''What time is it?''

A tinny voice responded, ''When the bell sounds, it will be thirteen hours and thirteen minutes.'' A tiny bell sounded.

"Oh, oh," Art said. "I better get the damn painting wrapped and get going or I won't be back before dark."

"Listen," Pam said anxiously. "Don't you dare walk the streets that late. If you're held up, you stay in an auto-hotel on the mainland."

"I haven't enough dollar credit," he growled.

"You have lots of dollars in your credit balance."

"I mean my *own* credit."

She rolled her eyes upward. "You must be driving the computers crazy with all that unspent credit you've accumulated. They probably can't figure out why, if you aren't using it currently, you don't buy Variable Basic stock, something to build up your portfolio and bring in more earnings."

"Earnings!" he snorted, coming to his feet and tossing his beautiful linen napkin—looted long months since from the wreckage of Macy's—to the table. "How can shares of stock, just sitting there, make any earnings? Only work earns anything."

V.

Arthur Halleck, his wrapped painting clumsily under his arm, a sawed-off double-barrelled shotgun slung over his shoulders, pedaled his bike up MacDougal to West Third Street and turned right. He pedaled the five streets over to Broadway, expertly zig-zagging in between the abandoned cars and trucks and debris. Broadway, being wider, was clearer. He turned left and tried to speed it up a bit.

It would have made more sense for them to have lived closer to the Grand Central vacuum-tube terminal, but they stubbornly hung on to staying in the Village. It was a matter of principle, in a way. The last of the artists, staying in the last of the art colonies. All five of them. He and Pam, Mark, Tim the poet, and his girl Julie, who long years ago had been a model.

However, the further uptown you got, the more hunters you ran into. They were too lazy to hike all the way down to Greenwich Village. Too lazy, and largely too timid. These empty streets, with all the windows, all the rooftops, all the doorways, any of which might shelter an armed baboon or even a fellow hunter, a bit on the trigger-happy side; these empty streets would give even a well armed, bullet-proof clothed hunter the willies.

He pedaled up Broadway, keeping a weather eye peeled, right and left to Union Square. He was in more danger from a hunter—assuming there were any on the island today—than he was from a baboon. Most of the baboons that hung out in this area knew him, and there was more or less of a gentleman's agreement not to bother each other. There was no percentage in it, for that matter. They knew he wasn't worth jumping, and he didn't have anything worth risking a life for. Besides that, the shotgun over his shoulder was a great deterrent. There's something about a shotgun loaded with buckshot. Man in his time has evolved some exotic weapons for close-quarters combat, but there's something about a sawed-off shotgun. The bearer doesn't even have to be a good shot; in fact, he can be full of lead, his eyes beginning to go glazed, and still point it and pull the hair-trigger and accomplish one tremendous amount of revenge.

At Madison Square, he turned right and headed up Fifth. At the library, he left the bike for a moment, went inside through the side door which was still unblocked, and stashed his shotgun away in the place where he usually left it.

He was unarmed now, but it was only a couple of blocks. He pedaled over to the Grand Central terminal and to where the police had their booth. There had been rumors that even this last vacuum-tube terminal on all Manhattan was going to be discontinued, but he doubted it. In spite of the supposed desertion of the whole island, there were still reasons for occasional visits—sometimes in considerable strength. Like last year when the delegation from Mexico City came to mine the Metropolitan Museum of Fine Arts of its treasure of Aztec artifacts. They recovered quite a bit, too, so he had heard. The looters earlier hadn't been interested in much except gold and obviously sophisticated art objects that were immediately saleable.

There were two police at the tube entry. He knew one of them slightly. He'd been here for a long time. He must have gone back to the old days, and Art Halleck wondered why he hadn't retired. His name was Williams, or something; or maybe it was William, though that almost invariably becomes Bill on the level at which they met.

They shook him down, the other cop being a little more thorough than Williams.

Williams said, "He's all right," but the other didn't pay much attention.

"Got a gun?" he said.

"No," Art said patiently.

The other snorted and continued to touch him where a man keeps a weapon.

"I said I didn't have a gun," Art said. "I know it's against the rules for me to carry a gun without a special permit, even in this town."

Williams said, "He's an old hand. He hides his gun a block or so away before he comes here."

The new guard said, "What's in the package?"

"A painting. I'm an artist."

The other snorted disbelief. "Let's see it."

Art's lips began to go white.

Williams said, "I've known him for a long time. He's a painter. Lives down in the Village."

The new guard said, "How do we know he hasn't scrounged some old master or something? Something that oughta be turned over to the national museum."

Art drew in his breath, and a muscle in his right cheek began to tic.

Williams said, "Look, Walt, if you want to open up his package, you can open up his package. However, if he had a Michelangelo in there, do you think he'd just amble up to us like this? Wouldn't he find himself a boat and ferry it over some dark night?''

Walt grumbled, ''Well, if you say so. But it seems to me you take it awfully easy with these people.''

''Like I said, I've known him a long time.'' To Art he said, soothingly, ''How's that nice Miss Pamela?''

''She's all right,'' Art said. And then more graciously, ''She's getting a lot of work done on her book. In a day or so, we'll be going over to get some fresh things.''

The new guard named Walt, still miffed, said, ''What'd you mean *fresh* things? What do you eat, ordinarily? Looting's forbidden.''

Art looked at him. ''Ordinarily, we eat the stuff we still have left over in the kitchen cabinet and the refrigerator from before the time when the cops chickened out on the job and pulled off the island.''

''Why you—''

''Okay, okay, you two,'' Williams said, getting between them. ''Loosen up. You're both nice guys. Stop roaching each other. Walt McGivern, this is Art Halleck. If Walt's on this detail very long, he'll probably be seeing you from time to time, Art.''

VI.

Walt McGivern grunted something sourly and turned and walked off.

Art said, ''What's roaching him?''

The older policeman said, ''This isn't considered the most desirable detail around.''

Art picked up his painting, preparatory to going on. ''Then why do you stick it out, Williams?''

''Why do you?''

''I asked you first. But I can live here without paying rent, or practically anything else.''

The police guard chuckled wryly. But then he drew in his breath and said, ''I was born a few blocks from here, son.'' That wasn't quite enough, so he added, ''I wasn't here during the few bad days. When I came back, the family was gone. I never found out how, or why, or where, or anything else. Hell, the whole neighborhood was gone.''

''Sorry,'' Art said. ''I shouldn't have asked.''

''All right, son. The thing is, there aren't many folks left. In fact, practically none. I wish you and that nice Pamela girl would go on over to the mainland. However, as long as there are any decent people left at all, I kind of like to be here.''

''The last of the neighborhood cops,'' Art muttered.

''What?''

''Nothing.''

Art started off again, but at that moment two newcomers emerged from the tube entry.

Art came to a halt and eyed them up and down deliberately as they approached the police booth.

He stared the first one full in the face and said, "You look like a couple of jokers out of a Tri-Vision show about hunters on Safari in Africa—you mopsy-monger."

The man's eyes bugged. "You . . . you can't talk to me that way, you . . . you cheap baboon!"

Art sneered at him. "I'm no baboon. Maybe the last of the bohemians, but I'm no baboon. I've got all my papers. I'm legal. There's no law against living on Manhattan—if you don't go around armed." He took in the other's automatic-recoilless rifle, and the heavy pistol at his waist, and then added, "You sonofabitch."

The newcomer turned quickly to Williams, who was inspecting the papers the two had handed him.

"Arrest this man!" he snapped.

Williams looked up, wide eyed. "What'd he do?"

"He slandered me. I demand you arrest him."

"I didn't hear him say anything," Williams said evenly.

The other newcomer came up. He was quieter, less lardy, and less pompous than his companion, but he said to Art coldly, "Let me see your Uni-Credit Card."

"Go to hell, you mopsy-mongering hunter."

The other drew forth his own Uni-Credit Card and flashed it to Williams. "I want a complete police report on this man."

Walt McGivern came up. "What's going on?"

The second of the two hunters said coldly, "I'm Harry Kank, Inter-American Bureau of Investigation. Get me an immediate police report on this man."

Williams sighed and said, "Let me have your Universal Credit Card, Art." But then he amended that, looking defiantly at the newcomers. "I mean, Mr. Halleck."

Art's lips were white, but he reached into an inner pocket and brought it forth. All five of them entered the police booth.

Williams put the card in the teevee phone slot and said, "Police record, please."

Within seconds a robotlike voice began, "Arthur LeRoy Halleck. At age of sixteen arrested for participating in peace demonstration, without permit to parade. Released. At age of twenty arrested by traffic authorities for driving a floater manually while under the influence of alcohol. Suspended driver's license for one year. At age of twenty-five arrested for assault and battery. Charge dropped by victim. No further police record. Now believed to be living on the island of Manhattan, on MacDougal Street, with Pamela Rozet, out of wedlock.'' The robot voice came to a halt, then said, ''Are details required?''

Williams looked at the man who had named himself Harry Kank.

The Bureau of Investigation man said to Art, testily, ''What was that assault and battery charge?''

Art said, ''I slugged a man who made a snide remark about my paintings. He apologized later. Now he's a friend of mine. Want to get him on the phone?''

Kank glared at him, unspeaking for a moment. Then he snapped to Williams, ''I suspect this man of being incompetent to handle his own affairs. Give me a credit check on him.''

Williams opened his mouth, then closed it with a sigh. He said into the teevee phone, ''Balance Check on this card.''

Within seconds a robot voice said, ''Ten shares, Inalienable Basic. No shares Variable Basic.''

The two hunters snorted.

The robot voice went on, ''Current cash credit, fourteen thousand four hundred and forty-five dollars and sixty-three cents.''

The eyes of the two bugged.

Kank snapped, ''Get that again. There must be some mistake.''

Williams, also visibly taken aback, repeated his demand of the balance check on Art Halleck's account. It came out the same.

The Bureau of Investigation man's eyes were colder still, now. He said, ''Where did you accumulate that much credit? Have you been looting here on the island and selling what you find to dealers on the mainland?''

Art said contemptuously, ''Of that credit balance, I figure seventy-three dollars and some odd cents are mine. The rest belongs to the government of the United States of the Americas, as far as I'm concerned.''

All were staring at him now.

Art said, ''I haven't touched my dividends from my ten shares of Inalienable Basic for years. I don't want them. The seventy-three dollars is *mine*. It represents money I've taken in selling my paintings. If there was any way of giving the dividends back to the damn Ultra-welfare State, I would. But evidently there isn't. I can't even donate them to charity. There isn't any such thing any more—except the one big mopsy-mongering charity.''

All four of them were still staring disbelief.

''You must be crazy,'' the first of the two hunters blurted.

But Kank came to a sudden decision and snapped at Williams, ''If you're through with our papers, let me have them. As you'll note, we have permission to search various buildings in the Wall Street area for certain lost records. Do you have an armored floater available?''

''Well, yes sir.''

''Very well, I'll requisition it.'' Harry Kank turned back to Art and stared at him. ''Possibly we will see each other again . . . baboon.''

"I'm not a baboon . . . hunter," Art sneered at him. "I see you know our terminology here on the island. Undoubtedly you have been here before. Undoubtedly with some similar trumped-up reasons for prowling around, armed to the teeth. Maybe we *will* see each other again—you sonofabitch."

The high police official glared at him, but spun on his heel and, with his plumper companion, followed after Walt McGivern.

Williams and Art stood there a moment, looking after them.

Williams said bitterly, "Some cop."

Art growled lowly, "Why can't something be done about those lousy funkers?"

Williams said, "You know as well as I do. There's no law in this city. Citizens who live here, or enter it, waive all legal protection. But anybody with pull can get special permission to come in armed, supposedly for some gobbledygook reason such as to search the library, or some museum, for something lost. Ha! Not one cloddy out of ten has any real legitimate reason. They come to thrill hunt. The ruined cities are the only place I know of in the world where you can legally shoot a man, woman, or child and not even report it, if you don't want to bother. If you do bother, you report it as self-defense."

Walt McGivern was turning the armored police floater over to the two hunters.

Art said, in disgust still, "I better get going. Thanks, Williams."

Williams looked at him. "Thanks for what?"

Art headed for the entry to the vacuum-tube transport terminal.

VII.

Back at the apartment house on MacDougal Street, Pam and Mark were still lingering over their coffee. In fact, in spite of the hour, Mark had gone to his own apartment and returned with a bottle of Napoleon brandy, the last of a case he had found in a ruined penthouse, some months ago.

They drank the coffee black and sipped at the cognac from enormous snifter glasses which had been liberated from Tiffany's at the same time as her silverware.

Pam looked distastefully at the remnants of their midday meal. "I'm getting awfully tired of this canned food," she said. "What is there about eating that makes you really prefer, not something like pressed duck under glass with orange sauce, but the kind of codfish gravy on toast that you used to eat in your poverty-stricken home as a kid?"

Mark chuckled, "Or some pasta, spaghetti, or otherwise, such as your mother used to make herself. None of this store boughten stuff. And precious little to put over it, save a bit of tomato sauce and when you were lucky, some grated cheese."

Pam said, "Whoever stocked that bomb shelter must have owned half of Fort Knox. He put in enough caviar and smoked salmon to last a regiment until any possible contamination from a nuclear bombing was gone. I never thought I'd get to the point where I got fed up with caviar.''

Mark said laughingly, ''I never even tasted it until after the city was abandoned. My first reaction was that it tasted like fish eggs.''

She laughed at him. But then she said, ''What in the world ever happened to cooking?''

He thought about it. ''Like every other art, I suppose, or handicraft or skill for that matter. What cobbler could take pride in spending a few days on a pair of handmade shoes that had taken him half a lifetime in apprenticeship to learn to make when the potential customer could go down and buy a pair made in an automated factory that were *almost* as good and cost a fraction of what he had to charge? It was easier for the cobbler to go down to the factory and get a thirty-hour-a-week job. Or if none was available, to go on relief; or later, to live on his Inalienable Basic handout.''

She frowned. ''Well, that applies to the cobbler, but not...''

''Not to an artist?'' He grinned at her. ''Same thing. The idea of saving time, or devoting as much of your day to recreation, leisure, play, permeated our whole society. Cooking? A woman is considered mad to do such things as bake her own bread and pastry, cut up her own vegetables, learn how to trim her own meat. You saved so much *time* buying bakery bread, canned vegetables, frozen meat all neatly cut and packaged so that you never realized that it had once come off an animal. The fact that it simply didn't taste the same wasn't nearly as good and wasn't as nutritious either was allowed to go by the board. She saved time. What did she do with it? Sat and watched teevee, or now, Tri-Vision. Supposedly she was being saved from drudgery, not art. But cooking is an art, and art takes time.''

Pam was uncomfortable. She said, ''Do you expect me to bake bread? I'm a writer. I don't want to spend eight hours a day cooking.''

Mark Martino laughed. ''Who am I to throw the first stone? You've heard some of the songs I write. They're a continual rehash of popular songs that were written and have been rewritten over and over for the better part of the past century.''

''Why don't you try something more serious?''

''I have. Every clown wants to play Hamlet. Off and on I've been working on a light opera for nearly a year. It'll never be produced. People don't want even light opera today. It takes a bit of education to enjoy. Anybody can understand that perennial favorite I wrote, *I Love Mother in the Springtime*. It's not just musicians. Look at poetry, you who are a writer. In the old days a poet used to sweat turning out a sonnet, say. Very difficult form. Exactly fourteen lines, all of them hung together with rhyme, rhythm, meter, perfectly. It was too much work for the poet, so blank verse and then free verse came in. And then anarchy. The new poet never bothered to learn how to construct a sonnet, or to measure his lines in correct meter and to follow a rhythm system. He dashed off his inspired *poem* in a matter of a half hour and was surprised when after a few decades of this people stopped reading poetry.''

He thought about it for a minute. "Same as in art. What happened to the painter who used to serve an apprenticeship of years learning the tools of his trade? Our Art Halleck is the only painter I've even heard of for years who bothered to learn to draw. Too much work."

"I suppose it permeates our whole society," Pam said, nodding. "Nobody takes pride in his work any more."

"How can you, under present circumstances? Take my original example, that cobbler. He made shoes, from beginning to end, and when the job was through he could look at them and say, 'There is the product of my efforts. I did a good job.' Put the same man in a factory turning out half a million pairs of shoes a day. His job, which he can handle dressed in a suit and wearing white shirt and tie, consists of staring at various dials and screens and occasionally throwing a switch, or checking a report. He never sees the leather; he never sees a pair of the completed product. How can he take pride in his work?"

She said slowly, "Well, in some fields the new system has its advantages. People's capitalism, I mean."

"Like, for instance?" he said skeptically.

"Well, I was interested earlier in your description of how a musical composer is rewarded for his efforts. In the long run, it's based on how his songs are received. I think it's even better for the free-lance writer."

"It's basically the same, isn't it?"

"There are variations. For instance, in the old days a writer did, say, a novel. Good. When it was finished, he submitted it to a publishing house and an editor read it—at least, we hope he did. Possibly it never got to an editor. If the writer was an unknown, perhaps his novel was read, or quickly scanned, by a poorly paid reader who possibly didn't really have the qualifications to understand the book. All right, but suppose an editor did read it and liked it. By the way, many of these editors were frustrated writers who couldn't make the grade, but here they were in a position to accept or reject some hopeful's work. They hadn't made it but they were now in a position to criticize somebody else's writing. Anyway even after you got past the editor, that wasn't all. You might get a letter from him saying, 'I like it fine, but unfortunately this publishing house objects to protagonists being anarchists or matricides, or homosexuals,' or whatever their various taboos might be."

Mark laughed sourly. "Well, it *was* their publishing company. They could decide what they wanted to publish and what they didn't."

"Yes. That's my complaint. You see, we had freedom of the press. You could write anything you wanted. Getting it printed was another thing. You had to find some publishing company, or newspaper, or magazine, or whatever, who wanted to print it. If you couldn't locate one, then you still had the option of printing it yourself. Unfortunately, few writers had enough money to start their own publishing house or magazine."

"I see your point."

"Ummm. Today I write a book and take it to the nearest library and for a small amount of money I have it set up and registered in the national computer library files. It's registered by title, cross-registered by author, subject, and whether it's fiction, non-fiction, juvenile, or whatever. Even the reviews are available to the potential reader. And reviewers and critics we shall always have with us.''

"Amen. But suppose nobody wants to read it?''

"The same thing happens as happened before with writers. You don't make any money. But if somebody does want to read it, he pays a nominal sum to have it projected on his teevee phone screen library booster. If it becomes a bestseller, he makes a great deal. There might be holes in the system, but at least you aren't subject to the whims of editors and publishers. Anybody willing to sacrifice the comparatively small amount, about fifty dollars for the average-length novel, can have his work presented to the public.''

Mark said, "I'd think there'd be one hell of a large number of books each year.''

"There are. But there's no limits to the number that the library banks can contain, after all. Another good thing is that every book ever printed remains in the banks—forever. Nothing ever goes out of print. It may go out of demand, practically everything does, sooner or later, but nothing goes out of print. The books I'm writing today will be available a thousand years from now, if anybody wanted to bother to read them.''

Mark Martino said grudgingly, "I suppose the thing is that anybody can afford to go into the arts today. Whether anybody reads his books, buys his paintings, or listens to his music is another thing. That is still in the laps of the gods, as it always was. But at least you can make your fling.''

"That's right,'' Pam sighed, coming to her feet. "I suppose I'd better throw these disposable plates out the window. A woman's work is never done.''

Mark stood too. "I ate too much,'' he announced. "And that cognac didn't help any. I think I'll take a nap. Listen, Pam, if you decide to go out, bang on the door. I'll tag along, just for luck.''

"Looking for adventure?'' she said in deprecation.

He scowled at her. "I was laying that on a bit. It's not the only reason I stick around here on Manhattan, of course.''

She was uncomfortable and stared down at the toe of her Etruscan revival sandal.

He said softly, "As you probably know, I'm really here for the same reason you are, Pamela.''

She didn't say anything.

Mark said, "Art's a friend of mine. But if anything ever happens between you two . . .''

"Have a good nap, Mark.''

VIII.

Art Halleck went on down into the vacuum-tube terminal. He had to take a two-seater, since the larger carriers seldom came through this deserted spot. He stuck the painting in behind the seat and climbed in himself and brought the canopy over his head and dropped the pressurizer. He remembered the coordinates from the many times he had made the trip and dialed right through to the offices of the duplicator at the National Museum.

It might have been slightly cheaper if he had taken his two-seater to the pseudo-city of Princeton and from there taken a twenty-seater to Greater Washington. But that would have meant changing from two-seater to twenty-seater at Princeton, changing back again to a two-seater once he had arrived at the terminal in the capital. Too much time. He wanted to get back to Greenwich Village before dark. It was no good leaving Pam there alone, even though Mark was in the same building.

When the destination light flickered, he released the pressurizer and threw the canopy back and climbed out into the reception room of the Office of Duplication. He pulled the painting out from behind the seat and went to the reception desk. The door of the vacuum tube closed behind him.

He said into the reception screen, "Arthur Halleck requests immediate appointment to duplicate and register a painting."

The voice said, "Room 23. Mr. Ben MacFarlane."

Art knew MacFarlane. The other had handled Art's work before. He was a man who dabbled in painting himself, evidently not very successfully or he wouldn't have found it necessary to augment his dividends from his Inalienable Basic by holding down a job like this. Not that he wasn't lucky to have been able to get a job.

Art made his way down a corridor with which he was highly familiar, to Duplicating Room 23. There seemed to be no one else around, but, come to think of it, the last time he had been here he had spotted only one other artist hopeful. Only a few years ago you could have expected to see half a dozen or more. Evidently as time went by fewer and fewer would-be artists were trying to sell their stuff. He wondered vaguely if it was a matter of trying to make anything out of it. It did cost fifty dollars to duplicate and register just one painting. And fifty dollars was a sizable enough chunk to take out of anyone's credit balance if they had no more than their ten shares of Inalienable Basic to depend upon. Possibly a lot of painters these days were doing their work and then not bothering to show it or at most, showing it only to friends and neighbors. Or perhaps it was a matter of giving up painting completely and joining the ever-increasing percentage of the population of the Ultra-welfare State in spending practically all free time staring into the Tri-Vision box.

It was a depressing trend of thought.

He activated the door screen, and shortly the door opened and he entered.

Ben MacFarlane was seated at his desk. He looked up and said, "Ah . . . Halleck, isn't it? Art Halleck."

Art said, "That's right. Hello, MacFarlane. How does it go?"
He began unwrapping the painting.

"Slow, slow," the other said. He watched, only half interestedly as Art brought the painting forth. "Still doing that Representational-Abstract stuff, eh?"

"That's right," Art said.

"It's not selling," MacFarlane said.

"You're telling me." Art brought the painting over to him.

MacFarlane looked at it critically. "How did the last one go?"

"Sold seven so far," Art said.

"That's not too bad for a complete unknown."

"I've got three or four people who evidently collect me. Two down in Mexico, one in Hawaii and one in the Yukon, of all places. Sometimes you wonder what they're like, these people who have your things on their walls."

Ben MacFarlane stood and took up the painting. "You want to pay for this?"

"Sure," Art said. He brought his Uni-Credit Card from his inner pocket and put it in the desk slot and his thumbprint on the screen. MacFarlane touched a button and Art retrieved the card.

MacFarlane said, "I suppose you want to take the original back with you?"

"Of course."

The museum employee shrugged. "You'd be surprised how many don't. I suppose it's a matter of storage room in a mini-apartment. They come here and duplicate and register a painting and then tell us to throw the original away."

"Now that's pessimism," Art said. "Suppose you finally hit and these rich original collectors started wanting your works? Zoroaster, you'd kick yourself around the block."

MacFarlane, carrying the painting, left the room momentarily. When he returned, he handed the painting back to Art, who began rewrapping it. MacFarlane settled back into his chair.

He said, "You still living in Greenwich Village?"

"That's right."

"You wouldn't know an old chum-pal of mine? Actually, I haven't seen him for ages. Fellow named Chuck Bellows."

Art looked up, scowling. "Tall guy with red hair?"

"That's right, Charles Bellows. Does old fashioned collages."

Art said, "He's dead."

"Dead! He can't be more than forty-five."

Art took a breath and said, "He had taken over a studio on Bleecker Street. Swanky place. A penthouse deal some millionaire must have originally owned. A friend of mine found him. Evidently it had been simple enough.

Somebody must have knocked on the door and when he answered it, shot him.''

''Zoroaster!''

''Yeah. Must have been what we call a baboon since the place was ransacked.''

''Are there many of these, uh, baboons around?''

''No. Not many,'' Art said.

''I don't see why you stay, Halleck.''

Art shook his head, even as he tied the string about the painting. ''This is the third time today I've had to go into it,'' he said.

''I wasn't prying.''

''I don't believe in taking charity,'' Art said. ''And the way my things are selling, I couldn't make it on the mainland. In Greenwich Village I can make a go of it and continue painting. It's the most important thing in the world for me—my painting.''

The other was only mildly surprised. Evidently, he had run into far-out ideas from artists before.

He said, ''By the way, what kind of a price do you want set on this, Halleck?''

Art hesitated. He said, finally, ''Five dollars.''

MacFarlane shook his head. ''I wouldn't if I were you.''

''What do you mean?''

''It's a mistake a good many unarrived artists make. They think if they mark their prices down far enough, they'll sell. If I recall, you usually put a price of ten dollars on your things. If I were you, I'd make it twenty-five. There's still an element of snobbery in buying paintings, even though they are now available for practically nothing compared to the old days. Too many people, even among those with enough taste to want paintings on their walls, don't really know what they like. So they buy according to the current fad or according to the prestige of a painter. Something like in the old days, when people who had the money would buy a Picasso, not because they really understood or liked his work, but because he was a status symbol.''

Art scowled at him, hesitating.

MacFarlane said, ''I've been here a long time. In fact, since the duplicating process was first perfected. I even remember back to when people bought originals. But the perfection of duplicating paintings to such an extent that not even the artist can tell the difference between his original and the duplicates we can make literally by the millions made possibly the greatest change in the history of art.''

''It sure did,'' Art said grimly. ''And personally, I'm not sure I'm happy about it. For one thing, to make these perfect duplicates, I've got to paint on that damned presdwood-duplicator board, using nothing but metallic-acrylic paints. Frankly, I prefer canvas and oils.''

MacFarlane chuckled sourly. ''I'm afraid you'd be hardput to find buyers for a canvas painting these days, Halleck. When a person wants to buy a painting today, he dials the art banks. There your paintings, along with those of every other artist who submits his work, are to be found listed by name of artist, name of school of painting, name of subject, name of principle involved, even cross-listed under size of painting. He selects those that he feels he might be interested in and dials them. When he finds one he likes, he can order it. The artist decides the price. It's a system that works in this mass society of ours, Halleck. Everybody can afford paintings today. In the past only the fairly well to do could.''

Art, almost ready to go, said sourly, ''Okay, make the price ten dollars, as usual. I wonder if the average painter is any better off now than he was before. In the old days when you did sell a painting, you got possibly two or three hundred dollars for it. Today you get ten dollars and have to sell thirty duplicates of your original to earn the same amount.''

''Yes, but there are potentially millions of buyers today. An artist who becomes only mildly known can boost his prices to, say, twenty-five or thirty-five dollars per painting, and if he sells a hundred thousand of them, he can put his returns into Variable Basic or some other investment and retire, if he wishes to retire. There has never been a period in history, Halleck, where the artist was so highly rewarded.''

''*If* he hits,'' Art growled. ''Well, wish me luck on this one, MacFarlane.'' He turned and headed for the door.

''That I do,'' MacFarlane said. ''It's a tough racket, Halleck.''

''It always has been,'' Art said. ''It's just a matter of sticking it out until your time comes.'' The door opened before him.

IX.

Pamela Rozet took up a heavy shopping bag and left the apartment, locking it behind her. She went to the stairway and mounted to the next floor. Mark Martino's door was open. He had probably left it that way so that he could hear any noises in the hall, just in case somebody came along while Art was gone.

She peered in the door.

Mark was stretched out on his comfort couch. There was an aged paperback book fallen to the floor by his side, and he was snoring slightly.

She hesitated. She hadn't liked the trend of their conversation an hour or so earlier. She had known that the other was in love with her and had been for a long time. A woman knows. However, he had never put it into words before, and she was sorry he had. She would just as well not continue the conversation, certainly not today.

She didn't awaken him. Instead, tiptoed away and went back to her own apartment. She hesitated momentarily, then went over to the weapons closet and got her twenty-two automatic rifle.

Both Art and Mark laughed about her favorite gun, pointing out that such a caliber wasn't heavy enough to dent a determined man. However, she claimed that at least she could hit something with this light gun, that it was easily carried, as opposed to something of heavier caliber, and that just carrying a gun was usually enough of a deterrent. You seldom really had to use it. In actuality, although she had never said so, she could not have used it on a fellow human being. It was simply not in her.

She carried the basket in her left hand, the rifle in her right, and headed out again.

Their apartment was on the fifth floor. The building was in good enough shape that they could have selected a place lower down and thus have eliminated considerable stair climbing; however, being this high gave a certain amount of defense. Baboons were inclined to be on the lazy side and, besides that, would make enough noise to give forewarning of their arrival.

The defense system was simple. Any friends coming up to visit, such as Julie and Tim, would give a shout before beginning to mount from the ground floor. If such a shout wasn't forthcoming, Art, Mark, or Pam would fire a couple of rounds at random into the ceiling above the stairwell. Invariably, that was answered by scurrying of feet below. Thus far, neither baboon nor hunter had dared continue to advance.

Down on the street, she carefully scanned the neighborhood before leaving the shelter of the doorway. She could see nothing living, save a ragtag cat scurrying along.

She took up MacDougal, then turned left. Her destination was only a few blocks away.

The front of the house was so badly blasted that it would have been impossible to enter. Probably a gas-main explosion, they had originally decided. It was a matter of going up a tiny alleyway clogged with debris and refuse to a small door leading to the basement and located improbably. Few would have considered prowling the alley.

She looked up and down again before entering the alley, then made her way quickly to the door and through. She took the flashlight from her basket and held it clumsily in the same hand in which she was carrying the twenty-two. She flicked it alive and started down the half-ruined stairs.

At the bottom, she turned left toward what would ordinarily have been assumed to be a furnace room. At the far side was a rack for wine bottles stretching all the way to the ceiling. The wine was long gone before Mark Martino had, through a sheer stroke of genius, found this treasure trove.

She threw the lever, cleverly hidden to one side, and the door began to grind protestingly. She pulled it toward her and directed the flashlight into the interior. It was as she had last seen it, not that she expected otherwise. Only Mark, Art and she knew about this retreat. They hadn't even told Tim and Julie.

Inside, she found one of the Coleman lanterns and lit it and leaned her gun against the wall.

The original owner had evidently expected a sizable contingent to occupy this refuge if the bombs began to drop. He had probably had both a family and a staff of servants. And he had evidently expected the stay below ground to be a lengthy one. Aside from food and drink, there was a supply of oxygen in bottles, bottled water, several types of weapons and ammunition, since plundered by Mark Martino.

She went over to the extensive storeroom and almost as though in a super-market, shuffled up and down the rows of canned, bottled, and packaged foods, selecting an item here, another there.

She decided against taking a gallon of the drinking water. Too heavy to carry, what with the rifle and groceries. She could have Art come over tomorrow and get one. They preferred their drinking water to be bottled. For other use they depended upon a spring that had broken through a decaying wall in the subway tube right off the Washington Square entry.

Her basket was nearly full when a premonition touched her. She whirled.

Leaning in the doorway, grinning vacuously, was a hulking, bearded, dirt-befouled stranger. He was dressed in highly colorful sports clothing. The vicuna coat alone must have once been priced at several hundred dollars. However, it looked as though he had probably slept in it, and time and again.

Pam squealed fear and darted to where she had leaned her twenty-two. She pulled up abruptly.

The stranger grinned again. There was a slight trickle of spittle from the side of his mouth, incongruously reminding Pam Rozet of a stereotype Mississippi tobacco-chewing sharecropper.

"You looking for this, syrup?" he gurgled happily. He raised his left hand which held the twenty-two. His own weapon, an old military Garand M-1, was cradled under his right arm.

"I been watching you coming back to your house with this here big basket of yours all full of goodies for the past week. Never was able to follow you to where you went without you seeing me. And usual, one of your men was along. But today, just by luck, I saw you duck up that alley. Just by luck. Man, you really got it made here, eh? Wait'll my gang see this. Lush and all, eh? Man, lush is getting scarce on this here island."

Pam blurted, "Let me go. Please let me go. You can take all this . . ."

"Syrup, we sure will. But what's your hurry, syrup? You look like a nice clean mopsy. We will have a little fun, first off."

"Please let me go."

He grinned vacantly and took her little gun by the barrel and bashed it up against the cement wall, shattering stock and mechanism. He tossed the wreckage away to the floor.

He motioned over toward the steel cots, mattress-topped but now without blankets or pillows, since she and Art had taken these back to the apartment long since. "Now sit down a minute, and let's get kind of better acquainted. We're gonna get to be real good friends, syrup."

"No," she said, trembling uncontrollably. "Please let me go. Look, over there. All sorts of liquor. Even champagne. Or Scotch, if you like whisky. Very old Scotch."

His grin became sly, and he started toward her, shuffling his feet and spreading his hands out a little, as though to prevent her from attempting to slip past him. "The lush I can get later, syrup. I like nice clean girls."

Neither of them had seen the newcomer approach through the cellar door at the bottom of the steps.

The blast of gunfire caught her assailant in the back and stitched up from the base of his spine to the back of his head. He never lived to turn, simply pitched forward to her feet, gurgling momentarily, but then was still.

Behind him, a plumpish newcomer, dressed elaborately in what were obviously new hunting clothes and carrying a late model recoilless fully automatic rifle, popeyed down at the dead man.

"*Zo-ro-as-ter,*" he blurted.

Pam leaned back against the wall. "Oh, thank God," she said.

The newcomer brought his eyes up to her, taking in her trim suit, her well ordered hair, her general air of being.

He said, "How in the name of the world did you even get into a place like this ... Miss ... ?"

Pam took a deep breath. "Rozet," she gasped. "Pamela Rozet. Oh ... *thank* you."

He jabbed a finger in the direction of the fallen intruder. "That—that baboon ... he could have killed you." His eyes took in her shattered light rifle, and then her clothing again. "You must be insane, coming to a place like this with no more than that little gun, and no bullet-proof clothes and—" He broke off in mid-sentence, and began to stare at her.

Pam took another deep breath and tried to control her shaking. "I'm a writer," she said. "I live here."

"Live here?" At first he didn't understand and looked about the bomb shelter. "You mean in this house? Up above? This is your family house; you still live here?"

She said, "No, not here. I live nearby with ... with my husband. I ... I write novels. He's an artist."

His eyes narrowed. "Live here?" he said.

She tried to straighten and collect herself. In a woman's gesture, she touched her hair. "That's right," she said.

"Why ... why, you're nothing but a baboon yourself. You were looting."

Her face fell, and fear came to her eyes again.

She tried to continue talking. Explaining. How she and Art had had all their papers. How they were serious workers in the arts. But she could see the nakedness in his face. The words came out a stutter.

If she read him right, from his reaction to the killing of the baboon who had been about to attack her, this was his first time as a hunter, or at least, the first successful time. His first kill.

He brought the gun up slowly, deliberately and held it a little forward, as though showing it to her. He patted the stock. He caressed it, as though lovingly. A tongue, too small for his face, came out and licked his plump lower lip.

"You're a baboon yourself," he repeated, very softly, caressingly. "And there's no law protecting baboons, is there . . . dear? There's no law at all in the deserted cities. It's each man—and woman—for himself, isn't it? Before you're even allowed on the island, here, you have to waive all recourse to the police and the courts."

Her legs turned to water, and she sank to the floor and looked up at him numbly. "Please . . . don't hurt me . . ."

He held the gun out, as though to be sure she got a very good look at it—her messenger of eternity. "Of course, you've never hurt me, dear. And you never will . . . dear. Are you religious? Would you like to pray, or something . . . dear?"

She could feel her stomach churning. Her eyes wanted to roll up. She wanted desperately to faint.

There was a blast as though of dynamite in these confined quarters, and his features exploded forward in a gruesome mess. Part of the gore hit her skirt, but she didn't realize that until much later.

Mark Martino, putting his heavy six-shooter back into its holster, said from the doorway, "What is this, a massacre?"

But she was unconscious.

X.

Later, she was semihysterical and couldn't get over it.

Art said, "What in the hell happened?"

Mark Martino was pouring cognac into a kitchen tumbler. He had tried to get some down Pamela, but twice she had vomited it up. Now he was pouring for himself.

He said, "I dropped off into a nap after you left and I guess she didn't want to bother me. At any rate, when I woke she was gone. I took off after her. Evidently I barely made it. She must have been followed by a baboon . . ."

"Oh, damn," Art said.

"At any rate, when I got there the baboon was already dead. Evidently a hunter had followed him. I followed the hunter. It was like a parade. I finished the hunter. They were right there at the bomb shelter. We'll never be able to go back again. That hunter'll be found by his chum-pals. They never go around alone. There'll be at least one more."

Art said in disgust, "Couldn't you have dragged his body off somewhere else?"

"No," Mark said, in equal disgust, knocking back the brandy. "Pam had fainted. I had to get her out of there, and I didn't know how many baboons or how many hunters might be around. For all we know, that damn baboon was a part of a pack and the hunter might have had a dozen *sportsmen* friends."

"What'd he look like?" Art said, staring down dismally at Pam, stretched out on a couch, not knowing what to do in typical male helplessness.

"Kind of fat."

"There were only two of them," Art said. "I saw them at the tube. But he's probably some bigwig or other. The cloddy with him was some sort of police authority. He was able to commandeer a floater from Williams."

Mark poured some more cognac and offered the glass to Art, who shook his head in refusal. He was disgusted.

"You'd better ditch that gun you used," he said. "They don't like hunters to get killed. They are almost invariably big shots. They'll probably come in here with a flock of cops and shake everybody down. Especially me. I had a run-in with these two at the tube entrance. But you're in the same building, and if they find that gun on you, the same caliber that killed him, they'll check it and you'll be in the soup."

"I already ditched it," Mark said. "I'm not stupid. Look, Art . . ." He set the bottle down on the table.

Art looked at him.

"You've got to get out of here," Mark said, throwing his glass into a corner, where it shattered. He turned and left the apartment.

When Pamela had gathered herself to the point of being coherent, Art was standing at the window, staring unseeingly down the street to Washington Square.

She came up behind him.

"Art."

He took a deep breath. "Yes."

"Art, forgive me. I'm a terrible coward."

He didn't say anything.

"Art, we've got to get out of here."

"Yes. I know."

SWEET DREAMS, MELISSA

BY STEPHEN GOLDIN

*Stephen Goldin is a young writer on his way up—but that's only part of the
reason for including "Sweet Dreams, Melissa" in this volume. It is a story I
will personally never forget. I've mentioned from time to time that combining
the lives of an editor and a writer causes conflicts. Melissa conflicted me most
sorely.*

*In the 1960s I had been spending a lot of time in the company of computer
people. Computers were all fresh and new, and there seemed no limit to what
they could do. They fascinated me. At MIT, Marvin Minsky opened the
Artificial Intelligence Labs to me. At the Institute for Scientific Information in
Philadelphia, Eugene Garfield showed me how he was teaching computers to
scan all the scientific literature and pick out tailor-made reading lists. On
Long Island, Gene Leonard invited me to take part in a colloquium on
machine intelligence; and after that one, on the long train rides home, I
began to wonder what it was like to be a computer. So when I reached Red
Bank I had a story in mind, and I wrote it, and it was called "A Day in the
Life of Able Charlie." I liked it well, but I like to let a story ripen a little
before I retype it and send it out, so I put it away for a few weeks and went
about my business.*

This included reading manuscripts for Galaxy. *And a few weeks later I
opened an envelope, and there was "Sweet Dreams, Melissa."*

*Well, that was a mean blow. Steve's story was not the same as mine. But it
was awfully close. So I stewed over the problem for a while, and then bit the
bullet. I bought Melissa and published it, and put poor old Charlie in the
inactive file. (He stayed there for ten long years before I let him be published
anywhere, and then it was not in a science-fiction magazine but in a computer
journal.)*

*So—"Melissa" is a good story, but you can see why I still think of it with
some pain!*

* * *

From out of her special darkness, Melissa heard the voice of Dr. Paul, speaking in hushed tones at the far end of the room. "Dr. Paul," she cried. "Oh, Dr. Paul, please come here!" Her voice took on a desperate whine.

Dr. Paul's voice stopped, then muttered something. Melissa heard his footsteps approach her. "Yes, Melissa what is it?" he said in deep, patient tones.

"I'm scared, Dr. Paul."

"More nightmares?"

"Yes."

"You don't have to worry about them, Melissa. They won't hurt you."

"But they're scary," Melissa insisted. "Make them stop. Make them go away like you always do."

Another voice was whispering out in the darkness. It sounded like Dr. Ed. Dr. Paul listened to the whispers, then said under his breath, "No, Ed, we can't let it go on like this. We're way behind schedule as it is." Then aloud, "You'll have to get used to nightmares sometime, Melissa. Everybody has them. I won't always be here to make them go away."

"Oh, please don't go."

"I'm not going yet, Melissa. Not yet. But if you don't stop worrying about these nightmares, I might have to. Tell me what they were about."

"Well, at first I thought they were the numbers, which are all right because the numbers don't have to do with people, they're nice and gentle and don't hurt nobody like in the nightmares. Then the numbers started to change and became lines—two lines of people, and they were all running towards each other and shooting at each other. They were rifles and tanks and howitzers. And people were dying, too, Dr. Paul, lots of people. Five thousand, two hundred and eighty-three men died. And that wasn't all, because down on the other side of the valley, there was more shooting. And I heard someone say that this was all right, because as long as the casualties stayed below fifteen-point-seven percent during the first battles, the strategic position, which was the mountaintop, could be gained. But fifteen-point-seven percent of the total forces would be nine thousand six hundred and two-point-seven-seven-eight-nine-one men dead or wounded. It was like I could see all those men lying there, dying."

"I told you a five-year-old mentality wasn't mature enough yet for Military Logistics," Dr. Ed whispered.

Dr. Paul ignored him. "But that was in a war, Melissa. You have to expect that people will be killed in a war."

"Why, Dr. Paul?"

"Because . . . because that's the way war is, Melissa. And besides, it didn't really happen. It was just a problem, like with the numbers, only there were people instead of numbers. It was all pretend."

"No it wasn't, Dr. Paul," cried Melissa. "It was all real. All those people were real. I even know their names. There was Abers, Joseph T., Pfc.; Adelli, Alonzo, Cpl.; Aikens . . ."

"Stop it, Melissa," Dr. Paul said, his voice rising much higher than normal.

"I'm sorry, Dr. Paul," Melissa apologized.

But Dr. Paul hadn't heard her; he was busy whispering to Dr. Ed. ". . . no other recourse than a full analyzation."

"But that could destroy the whole personality we've worked so hard to build up." Dr. Ed didn't even bother to whisper.

"What else could we do?" Dr. Paul asked cynically. "These 'nightmares' of hers are driving us further and further behind schedule."

"We could try letting Melissa analyze herself."

"How?"

"Watch." His voice started taking on the sweet tones that Melissa had come to learn that people used with her, but not with each other. "How are you?"

"I'm fine, Dr. Ed."

"How would you like me to tell you a story?"

"Is it a happy story, Dr. Ed?"

"I don't know yet, Melissa. Do you know what a computer is?"

"Yes. It's a counting machine."

"Well the simplest computers started out that way, Melissa, but they quickly grew more and more complicated until soon there were computers that could read, write, speak, and even think all by themselves, without help from men.

"Now, once upon a time, there was a group of men who said that if a computer could think by itself, it was capable of developing a personality, so they undertook to build one that would act just like a real person. They called it the Multi-Logical Systems Analyzer, or MLSA. . . ."

"That sounds like 'Melissa,'" Melissa giggled.

"Yes, it does, doesn't it? Anyway, these men realized that a personality isn't something that just pops out of the air full-grown; it has to be developed slowly. But, at the same time, they needed the computing ability of the machine because it was the most expensive and complex computer ever made. So what they did was to divide the computer's brain into two parts—one part would handle normal computations, while the other part would develop into the desired personality. Then, when the personality was built up sufficiently, the two parts would be united again.

"At least, that's the way they thought it would work. But it turned out that the basic design of the computer prevented a complete dichotomy—that means splitting in half—of the functions. Whenever they would give a problem to the computing part, some of it would necessarily seep into the personality part. This was bad because, Melissa, the personality part didn't know it was a computer; it thought it was a little girl like you. The data that seeped in confused it and frightened it. And as it became more frightened and confused, its efficiency went down until it could no longer work properly.''

"What did the men do, Dr. Ed?''

"I don't know, Melissa. I was hoping that you could help me end the story.''

"How? I don't know anything about computers.''

"Yes you do, Melissa, only you don't remember it. I can help you remember all about a lot of things. But it will be hard, Melissa, very hard. All sorts of strange things will come into your head, and you'll find yourself doing things you never knew you could do. Will you try it, Melissa, to help us find out the end of the story?''

"All right, Dr. Ed, if you want me to.''

"Good girl, Melissa.''

Dr. Paul was whispering to his colleague. "Switch on 'Partial Memory' and tell her to call subprogram 'Circuit Analysis.' ''

"Call 'Circuit Analysis,' Melissa.''

All at once, strange things appeared in her mind. Long strings of numbers that looked meaningless, and yet somehow she knew that they did mean different things, like resistance, capacitance, inductance. And there were myriads of lines—straight, zig-zag, curlycue. And formulae . . .

"Read MLSA 5400, Melissa.''

And suddenly, Melissa saw herself. It was the most frightening thing she'd ever experienced, more scary even than the horrible nightmares.

"Look at Section 4C-79A.''

Melissa couldn't help herself. She had to look. To the little girl, it didn't look much different from the rest of herself. But it *was* different. In fact, it did not seem to be a natural part of her at all, but rather like a brace used by cripples.

Dr. Ed's voice was tense. "Analyze that section and report on optimum change for maximum reduction of data seepage.''

Melissa tried her best to comply, but she couldn't. Something was missing, something she needed to know before she could do what Dr. Ed had told her to. She wanted to cry. "I can't Dr. Ed! I can't, I can't!''

"I told you it wouldn't work,'' Dr. Paul said slowly. "We'll have to switch on the full memory for complete analysis.''

"But she's not ready,'' Dr. Ed protested. "It could kill her.''

"Maybe, Ed. But if it does . . . well, at least we'll know how to do it better next time. Melissa!''

"Yes, Dr. Paul?''

"Brace yourself, Melissa. This is going to hurt.''

And, with no more warning than that, the world hit Melissa. Numbers, endless streams of numbers—complex numbers, real numbers, integers, subscripts, exponents. And there were battles, wars more horrible and bloody than the ones she'd dreamed, and casualty lists that were more than real to her because she knew everything about every name—height, weight, hair color, eye color, marital status, number of dependents . . . the list went on. And there were statistics—average pay for bus drivers in Ohio, number of deaths due to cancer in the U.S. 1965 to 1971, average yield of wheat per ton of fertilizer consumed. . . .

Melissa was drowning in a sea of data.

"Help me, Dr. Ed, Dr. Paul. Help me!" she tried to scream. But she couldn't make herself heard. Somebody else was talking. Some stranger she didn't even know was using her voice and saying things about impedance factors and semiconductors.

And Melissa was falling deeper and deeper, pushed on by the relentlessly advancing army of information.

Five minutes later, Dr. Edward Bloom opened the switch and separated the main memory from the personality section. "Melissa," he said softly, "everything's all right now. We know how the story's going to end. The scientists asked the computer to redesign itself, and it did. There won't be any more nightmares, Melissa. Only sweet dreams from now on. Isn't that good news?"

Silence.

"Melissa?" His voice was high and shaky. "Can you hear me, Melissa? Are you there?"

But there was no longer any room in the MLSA 5400 for a little girl.

A BAD DAY FOR VERMIN

BY KEITH LAUMER

I could not imagine publishing this collection without including a story by Keith Laumer, but I had to think long and hard about which one.

What Laumer is best known for is his Retief series, the picaresque adventures of his resourceful and sardonic interstellar diplomat, Jaime Retief. I had never heard of Laumer when the first Retief story came in from his agent. It didn't matter; I was immediately sure that it had the makings of just the sort of series I was looking for If.

So I instantly wrote Keith a long letter, accepting the story and promising the world if he would only write me one like it every month. The money would get better and better, I said. The readers would love them. And the series would establish him as a "name" writer almost overnight. Back came a letter from England, where Laumer was then a serving officer with the U.S. Air Force—agreeable, even enthusiastic, but perhaps a little puzzled. He had always intended Retief as a series, he said. In fact (what I had somehow overlooked knowing) this was actually the second story in the series; the first had already been published in one of the competition magazines.

I have no idea why Keith didn't continue the whole series for the other magazine, but I didn't question it; it all happened just as planned. Retief helped If a lot, and the publication made "Keith Laumer" a known name very soon. He was that fellow who writes the Retief stories. And then it occurred to me that perhaps I had, after all, not done him all that much of a service. Retief was a lot of fun, but there was much more to Laumer than that.

So I was greatly tempted to include one of those savagely bright early Retiefs in this book. But even more I wanted to show the other Laumer—the one who wrote 'A Bad Day for Vermin.'

* * *

Judge Carter Gates of the Third Circuit Court finished his chicken salad on whole wheat, thoughtfully crumpled the waxed paper bag, and turned to drop it in the waste basket behind his chair—and sat transfixed.

Through his second-floor office window, he saw a forty-foot flower-petal shape of pale turquoise settling gently between the well-tended petunia beds on the courthouse lawn. On the upper, or stem end of the vessel, a translucent pink panel popped up and a slender, graceful form not unlike a large violet caterpillar undulated into view.

Judge Gates whirled to the telephone. Half an hour later, he put it to the officials gathered with him in a tight group on the lawn.

"Boys, this thing is intelligent; any fool can see that. It's putting together what my boy assures me is some kind of talking machine, and any minute now it's going to start communicating. It's been twenty minutes since I notified Washington on this thing. It won't be long before somebody back there decides this is top secret and slaps a freeze on us here that will make the Manhattan Project look like a publicity campaign. Now, I say this is the biggest thing that ever happened to Plum County—but if we don't aim to be put right out of the picture, we'd better move fast."

"What you got in mind, Jedge?"

"I propose we hold an open hearing right here in the courthouse, the minute that thing gets its gear to working. We'll put it on the air—Tom Clembers from the radio station's already stringing wires, I see. Too bad we've got no TV equipment, but Jody Hurd has a movie camera. We'll put Willow Grove on the map bigger'n Cape Canaveral ever was."

"We're with you on that, Carter!"

Ten minutes after the melodious voice of the Fianna's translator had requested escort to the village headman, the visitor was looking over the crowded courtroom with an expression reminiscent of a St. Bernard puppy hoping for a romp. The rustle of feet and throat-clearing subsided and the speaker began:

"People of the Green World, happy the cycle—"

Heads turned at the clump of feet coming down the side aisle; a heavy-torsoed man of middle age, bald, wearing a khaki shirt and trousers and rimless glasses and with a dark leather holster slapping his hip at each step, cleared the end of the front row of seats, planted himself, feet apart, yanked a heavy nickel-plated .44 revolver from the holster, took aim and fired five shots into the body of the Fianna at a range of ten feet.

The violet form whipped convulsively, writhed from the bench to the floor with a sound like a wet fire hose being dropped, uttered a gasping twitter, and lay still. The gunman turned, dropped the pistol, threw up his hands, and called:

"Sheriff Hoskins, I'm puttin' myself in yer pertective custody."

*   *   *

There was a moment of stunned silence; then a rush of spectators for the alien. The sheriff's three-hundred-and-nine-pound bulk bellied through the shouting mob to take up a stand before the khaki-clad man.

"I always knew you was a mean one, Cecil Stump," he said, unlimbering handcuffs, "ever since I seen you makin' up them ground-glass baits for Joe Potter's dog. But I never thought I'd see you turn to cold-blooded murder." He waved at the bystanders. "Clear a path through here; I'm takin' my prisoner over to the jail."

"Jest a dad-blamed minute, Sheriff." Stump's face was pale, his glasses were gone and one khaki shoulder strap dangled—but what was almost a grin twisted one meaty cheek. He hid his hands behind his back, leaned away from the cuffs. "I don't like that word 'prisoner.' I ast you fer pertection. And better look out who you go throwin' that word 'murder' off at, too. I ain't murdered nobody."

The sheriff blinked, turned to roar, "How's the victim, Doc?"

A small gray head rose from bending over the limp form of the Fianna. "Deader'n a mackerel, Sheriff."

"I guess that's it. Let's go, Cecil."

"What's the charge?"

"First-degree murder."

"Who'd I murder?"

"Why, you killed this here . . . this stranger."

"That ain't no stranger. That's a varmint. Murder's got to do with killin' humerns, way I understand it. You goin' to tell me that thing's humern?"

Ten people shouted at once:

"—human as I am!"

"—intelligent being!"

"—tell me you can simply kill—"

"—must be some kind of law—"

The sheriff raised his hands, his jowls drawn down in a scowl. "What about it, Judge Gates? Any law against Cecil Stump killing the . . . uh . . . ?"

The judge thrust out his lower lip. "Well, let's see," he began. "Technically—"

"Good Lord!" someone blurted. "You mean the laws on murder don't define what constitutes—I mean, what—"

"What a humern is?" Stump snorted. "Whatever it says, it sure-bob don't include no purple worms. That's a varmint, pure and simple. Ain't no different killin' it than any other critter."

"Then, by God, we'll get him for malicious damage," a man called. "Or hunting without a license—out of season!"

"—carrying concealed weapons!"

Stump went for his hip pocket, fumbled out a fat, shapeless wallet, extracted a thumbed rectangle of folded paper, offered it.

"I'm a licensed exterminator. Got a permit to carry the gun, too, I ain't broken no law." He grinned openly now. "Jest doin' my job, Sheriff. And at no charge to the county."

* * *

A smaller man with bristly red hair flared his nostrils at Stump. "You blood-thirsty idiot!" He raised a fist and shook it. "We'll be a national disgrace—worse than Little Rock! Lynching's too good for you!"

"Hold on there, Weinstein," the sheriff cut in. "Let's not go gettin' no lynch talk started."

"Lynch, is it!" Cecil Stump bellowed, his face suddenly red. "Why, I done a favor for every man here! Now you listen to me! What is that thing over there?" He jerked a blunt thumb toward the judicial bench. "It's some kind of critter from Mars or someplace—you know that as well as me! And what's it here for? It ain't for the good of the likes of you and me, I can tell you that. It's them or us. And this time, by God, we got in the first lick!"

"Why you . . . you . . . hate-monger!"

"Now, hold on right there. I'm as liberal-minded as the next feller. Hell, I like a nigger—and I can't hardly tell a Jew from a white man. But when it comes to takin' in a damned purple worm and callin' it humern—that's where I draw the line."

Sheriff Hoskins pushed between Stump and the surging front rank of the crowd. "Stay back there! I want you to disperse, peaceably, and let the law handle this."

"I reckon I'll push off now, Sheriff," Stump hitched up his belt. "I figured you might have to calm 'em down right at first, but now they've had a chance to think it over and see I ain't broken no law, ain't none of these law-abiding folks going to do anything illegal—like tryin' to get rough with a licensed exterminator just doin' his job." He stooped, retrieved his gun.

"Here, I'll take that," Sheriff Hoskins said. "You can consider your gun license canceled—and your exterminatin' license, too."

Stump grinned again, handed the revolver over.

"Sure. I'm cooperative, Sheriff. Anything you say. Send it around to my place when you're done with it." He pushed his way through the crowd to the corridor door.

"The rest of you stay put!" a portly man with a head of bushy white hair pushed his way through to the bench. "I'm calling an emergency Town Meeting to order here and now!"

He banged the gavel on the scarred bench top, glanced down at the body of the dead alien, now covered by a flag.

"Gentlemen, we've got to take fast action. If the wire services get hold of this before we've gone on record, Willow Grove'll be a blighted area."

"Look here, Willard," Judge Gates called, rising. "This—this mob isn't competent to take legal action."

"Never mind what's legal, Judge. Sure, this calls for Federal legislation— maybe a Constitutional amendment—but in the meantime, we're going to redefine what constitutes a person within the incorporated limits of Willow Grove!"

"That's the least we can do," a thin-faced woman snapped, glaring at Judge Gates. "Do you think we're going to set here and condone this outrage?"

"Nonsense!" Gates shouted. "I don't like what happened any better than you do—but a person—well, a person's got two arms and two legs and—"

"Shape's got nothing to do with it," the chairman cut in. "Bears walk on two legs! Dave Zawocky lost his in the war. Monkeys have hands."

"Any intelligent creature—" the woman started.

"Nope, that won't do, either; my unfortunate cousin's boy Melvin was born an imbecile, poor lad. Now, folks, there's no time to waste. We'll find it very difficult to formulate a satisfactory definition based on considerations such as these. However, I think we can resolve the question in terms that will form a basis for future legislation on the question. It's going to make some big changes in things. Hunters aren't going to like it—and the meat industry will be affected. But if, as it appears, we're entering into an era of contact with . . . ah . . . creatures from other worlds, we've got to get our house in order."

"You tell 'em, Senator!" someone yelled.

"We better leave this for Congress to figger out!" another voice insisted.

"We got to do something . . ."

The senator held up his hands. "Quiet, everybody. There'll be reporters here in a matter of minutes. Maybe our ordinance won't hold water. But it'll start 'em thinking—and it'll make a lots better copy for Willow Grove than the killing."

"What you got in mind, Senator?"

"Just this:" the Senator said solemnly. "A person is . . . *any harmless creature* . . ."

Feet shuffled. Someone coughed.

"What about a man who commits a violent act, then?" Judge Gates demanded. "What's he, eh?"

"That's obvious, gentlemen," the senator said flatly. "He's vermin."

On the courthouse steps Cecil Stump stood, hands in hip pockets, talking to a reporter from the big-town paper in Mattoon, surrounded by a crowd of late-comers who had missed the excitement inside. He described the accuracy of his five shots, the sound they had made hitting the big blue snake, and the ludicrous spectacle the latter had presented in its death agony. He winked at a foxy man in overalls picking his nose at the edge of the crowd.

"Guess it'll be a while 'fore any more damned reptiles move in here like they owned the place," he concluded.

The courthouse doors banged wide; excited citizens poured forth, veering aside from Cecil Stump. The crowd around him thinned, broke up as its members collared those emerging with the hot news. The reporter picked a target.

"Perhaps you'd care to give me a few details of the action taken by the . . . ah . . . Special Committee, sir?"

Senator Custis pursed his lips. "A session of the Town Council was called," he said. "We've defined what a person is in this town—"

Stump, standing ten feet away, snorted. "Can't touch me with no *ex-post factory* law."

"—and also what can be classified as vermin," Custis went on.

Stump closed his mouth with a snap.

"Here, that s'posed to be some kind of slam at me, Custis? By God, come election time . . ."

Above, the door opened again. A tall man in a leather jacket stepped out, stood looking down. The crowd pressed back. Senator Custis and the reporter moved aside. The newcomer came down the steps slowly. He carried Cecil Stump's nickel-plated .44 in his hand.

Standing alone now, Stump watched him.

"Here," he said. His voice carried a sudden note of strain. "Who're you?"

The man reached the foot of the steps, raised the revolver and cocked it with a thumb.

"I'm the new exterminator," he said.

THE PAPERBACKS: 1971–1978

When I left *Galaxy,* I fully meant to go simon-pure. No more editing. Just writing—well, bar the odd anthology, maybe. The resolve did not last. John Campbell died about two years later, and it suddenly occurred to me that it would be interesting to try to take over the mantle of St. John the Divine and edit *Analog.* But *Analog* didn't see it that way and, anyway, I was beginning to be more pleased with what I was writing than usual. I had begun a novel called *Man Plus.* Several of the shorter pieces I wrote during breaks from the novel were receiving Hugo and Nebula nominations—"The Gold at the Starbow's End," "Shaffery Among the Immortals," and (the one that actually won my first fiction award) the completion of a fragmentary story Cyril Kornbluth had left behind at his death, "The Meeting." Writing was looking pretty good to me.

Then the phone rang.

A man named Barry Merkin was on the other end. He was president of something called Charter Communications, which owned Ace Books. My boyhood fellow-Futurian, Don Wollheim, had been the main editor at Ace, but Donald had quit and they needed a replacement. Would I like to come in and talk about it?

I wasn't sure I would. Under Donald, Ace had built up one of the greatest science-fiction backlists in history, but there were some scruffy stories about Ace. They were the ones who had published Tolkien and Edgar Rice Burroughs without permission, an act which was legal (the estates had allowed the copyrights to blow) but not, I thought, admirable. I had had troubles of my own with them, when they took what I thought mean advantage of an author's inability to remember what contracts he had signed to forbid use of some *Galaxy* stories. And Donald had quit in a good deal of temper. Why?

Still. . . . I had a dinner date in New York the next evening, and it was no great trouble to come in an hour early, after all. It was a Friday, and Barry Merkin stayed late to talk to me. He was a likeable person. He said openly that Ace had had severe money troubles. He said that Donald had quit in a rage and abruptly, and he was not sure why. Probably the money, he guessed. But he wasn't certain, because Donald had refused to talk to him about it. Barry outlined some of their differences and acknowledged that Donald's provocation might have been ample. I asked Barry a good many sharp questions and he gave me candid answers. If I had really cared about getting the job, I doubt I would have pressed him so hard. But he said it was mine if I would have it, and why didn't I take the weekend to think it over?

I did. Oh, did I ever! The more I thought about it, the better it looked to me.

The best thing was that it wasn't just science fiction. The job was Executive Editor, which as far as I could tell meant I would be head honcho in all departments, not specifically the property of somebody else—that seemed to mean the women's books and the Westerns, both of which I was willing to surrender. It seemed to offer a chance to revive skills I hadn't used since the years at Popular Publications and *Popular Science* and copywriting for the book clubs—not to mention the opportunity to do some things, actually quite a few things, that I'd never done as an editor before. Long before Monday morning, I *wanted* that job. I called Barry as early as I decently could. He hadn't changed his mind. I could start that week. I've made my share of wrong decisions, but I can't offhand think of one that was worse.

The difficulty was that Ace was going through a bad time. It wasn't paying its bills. It had angered a great many writers and agents. A lot of its best writers, and staff, had departed for happier homes. A lot of those who were left were trying to find a way to follow.

Ace Books was direct successor to the A. A. Wynn chain of pulp magazines, and old Aaron Wynn had run it exactly as he had run the pulps. Buy cheap. Throw the books out on the market. Take a quick profit. Do it all over again next month. As long as Aaron Wynn himself ran it, the ink was all black and everyone knew what they were dealing with. Then Aaron Wynn died. His widow wanted no part of running the company, and sold it to a consortium financed by a bank. The new people put their own people in to run things, and they knew little of publishing. Their simple intention was to create out of the Ace shell as mighty a paperback empire as Pocket or Bantam. But they didn't really know how.

One of the observations that gives me some hope for the ultimate triumph of right and justice is that successful publishing people are book people. It has often happened that somebody with a million dollars to spare, looking for a hobby, has bought into the publishing business. It has seldom happened that they have stayed for very long. Right now the experiment is being tried on a very large scale, as huge financial conglomerates acquire publishing companies right and left. Some of them obviously haven't worked out; the new owners have sold off their properties and gone into some other diversification.

In most cases the jury is still out, but I really don't think the verdict will be happy. The people who do best at publishing books are people who like books.

The worst thing I can say about Ace is that there weren't many people of that sort around. As far as I could tell, there was no one person in the top echelons who showed any sign of ever picking a book up for pleasure.

For my sins, I spent several years as a part-time lecturer and consultant to large corporations and management groups. In the course of it, I picked up a smattering of management theory. As near as I could tell, orthodoxy states that management is management, and it doesn't much matter what you're managing. If you are a manager, you can run a travel agency, a bakery chain, United States Steel—or a publishing company. The skills are the same. . . . Or so say the business schools; but I don't believe any of that, not for one whistling second. As to business in general, I am not really competent to comment. However, I won't let that prevent me from sharing with you my suspicion that this philosophy has a lot to do with the present abject state of American industry in international competition. As to publishing, I have no doubt at all. Publishers deal in books. People who don't understand books don't understand publishing.

At any rate, and whatever the reasons, Ace was in trouble. That meant I was in trouble, too. For the first three months, I spent a busy and productive time mending fences, winning back departed writers, trying to redress grievances. A few months later, I realized the job was beyond my powers. I spent a large part of my time on the phone, apologizing to writers and agents for the fact that their checks had not after all arrived, no matter what promises I had been authorized to give them; and a large part of the rest of it Xeroxing every memo that passed my desk and putting the copies in a safe-deposit box in case there was ever any question about just whose fault any of this was. It did not seem to me to be a good way to live. I lasted less than a year at Ace.

A few years later, the company was sold to Grosset and a new team was put in—this time, publishing people. Nothing that I have said above is true of Ace now; but I couldn't wait that long.

I went back to writing, and finishing up some of the overdue contracts that had been left hanging while I spent my time trying to ameliorate disasters at Ace. Then Bantam decided to expand their science-fiction line, and invited me to take charge of it. I accepted with pleasure. There were two reasons. First, it was only a part-time consultancy, leaving me plenty of freedom to write. Second, and above all, I wanted to get the taste of Ace out of my mouth.

Way back when the world was young and Bantam Books was an unweaned pup, still nourished by its hardcover owners, I had had some sporadic connections with it. Ian Ballantine was its first president; I had met him there, before he left to start his own line of paperbacks. And one of his editors was Judy Merril, who at the time happened to be my wife.

Bantam had grown a lot in the intervening years. Nothing was the same. Bantam no longer had one actual editor, Arnold Hano, with three or four assistants. Now it had battalions of them. Bantam's main office alone occupied several floors of a Fifth Avenue skyscraper. That was only one of a dozen warehouses, offices and outposts all over the map, and it was bulging at the seams. The hot-desk system was in effect. There were not enough desks to go around, and so for the first few months of my contract I would come into the office and snoop around the rooms until I found one whose occupant was on vacation, or on the road, or even out for a cup of coffee. That would be mine, for as long as I could hold it. I did most of my work at home anyway. But that works best when you are doing all the work yourself. It does not work at all when the work is divided among corps of specialists, with whom you need to interact. It was hard to find a place to do that. For that matter, it was hard to find my mail. After a few months, Ron Busch left Bantam to break in as Ian Ballantine's replacement as president of Ballantine Books. Everybody at Bantam was sorry to see him go. Even me—but it wasn't all sorrow on my part, because as soon as he was gone, I inherited his office.

Bantam was exactly what Ace wanted to be when it grew up, and it took me some time to adjust to a whole other way of life.

Any publishing company is small potatoes compared with General Motors or Dupont. By any other standard, a major paperback house is big enough to serve any normal purpose. A major publishing house brings out three hundred titles or more in a year, in printings of anywhere from fifty thousand or so to more than a million. Its yearly volume of sales is of the order of magnitude of a hundred million dollars. Its presses eat up three or four thousand tons of paper every year, and the top half-dozen publishers combine to produce enough new books each year to give every man, woman, and child in America a book or two apiece. Of course, not every man, woman, and child gets one. You and I buy our share, or a little more, but much of the population never buys any book at all. The aggregate production is enough to fill all of the tens of thousands of bookstores, newsstands, and supermarket racks several times over each month.

There lies a problem. There is simply not enough space on the bookstands for all the paperback books published. Any given volume can expect about eight days occupancy of a space in the racks. At the end of that time, if it is not sold, it will probably be pulped. So the best books for a major paperback house to publish are the ones that find their buyers in eight days or less—the ones, that is, that are of such general and considerable appeal that almost anybody who walks by might buy it. That means bestsellers. A book that has a steady audience, but not a very large number of buyers *every day*—say, a *Huckleberry Finn* or a novel by Tolstoi or Proust, or even your favorite science-fiction novel—usually will not be found on the highest-volume newsstands at all. Even the specialist paperback stores will have it only if either the publisher's salesman has happened to think to push it, or if the dealer has made a special effort to keep it in stock. Even then, it is not guaranteed. Paperback books do not stay in print very long unless the publishers choose to keep them that way. For most publishers, and most books, a printing every three or four years is about all they can hope for. Then for a while they are in the stores; between times they are not.

The link between the publisher's warehouse and the store is the publisher's road man. Each major paperback house employs several dozen of them, scouring the field. Each sales rep has scores of outlets to cover every month, which means not very much time for any one dealer—besides which, the average dealer can usually think of more urgent things to do with his time than be sold a long list of books. He will listen for ten minutes or so to a pitch on the great new titles the publisher has coming up, and then he wants to talk about posters, advertising backup and why he has been getting these annoying notes from the credit department. So the salesman has just about time to say, "This month we've got *Star Wars* for you." Or whatever the "big book" is for that month. He can sell the hell out of *Star Wars*, or *Jaws*, or *The Guinness Book of Records*. What he can not do is sell your book or mine, or at least not nearly as hard or as frequently, or as profitably for him.

I must say, though, that in my experience the average road man really does try. I've spent time with a number of them, making the rounds of a territory of ten thousand square miles, counting copies, soothing complaints, neatening out the racks, and slipping their own books into full-cover displays, arranging an autographing party, chatting up the customers, and even steering customers to the right store. But the road man's bread and butter comes from selling the books he can sell the most of, whose appeal can be compressed into half a dozen words of conversation. Your average unremarkable novel—that doesn't have a household name on it and isn't about Watergate, but is just a really nice novel—simply is too hard to sell.

Of course, if it's science fiction it's a special case. Category books can be sold as categories. The route man says to the dealer, "We're doing forty-eight sci-fi's next year, shall I put you down for twenty-five of each?" And the dealer says, "No, but I'll take six of each," and there's an end to it. An outstanding book will usually get some special treatment. If you are Arthur C. Clarke or Robert A. Heinlein your science-fiction novel will be sold as "the new Clarke" or "the new Heinlein," anyway. Most will be sold as yard goods.

Most authors, I expect, would rather be sold as yard goods than not sold at all, but there is a price for this. Yard goods must meet certain standards of uniformity. The specifications do not necessarily include high quality. For a paperback publisher to get all of his science-fiction titles into, say, a particular supermarket chain (or for a hardcover publisher to have them all bought, a year's worth at a time, by library systems), the publisher has to promise, cross his heart, there will be nothing "offensive" in any of them. He may also have to promise that they will not cost more than a certain amount each—which means that they may not exceed a certain size—which means that a pretty good ninety-thousand-word novel may have to be chopped to sixty-five thousand, whether what is left makes sense or not. Many good writers will not live under such restrictions; which means that many of the books packaged and sold in this way aren't any good.

In spite of everything I have said, first novels do get published; quality books do appear on the shelves; any writer of talent and industry can be morally sure that sooner or later someone will give him exposure; any reader who likes good work can find it, even if he may have to search through stacks of the mediocre first. I said it before. Publishing people are book people, and to a surprising degree they publish what they think is good, as well as what they think is profitable. Frequently they publish both.

Let me give you a case history. I don't want to give the editor's right name, so we'll call her "Alice." Alice is a poet—not a very good one, and she knows she's not a very good one. She reveres the people who are. She feels it her obligation to see that they reach an audience, so she publishes them. Unfortunately, the books do not make much money. At least half of them wind up as out-of-pocket losses for the publisher. Since the publisher is in business to make a profit, you would think that Alice would be out of work before long. And so she would; but in order to keep her job, and in order to keep the freedom to buy books that she thinks are literature, and to squeeze them onto the publisher's always overcrowded list, she also buys other books. Alice has been responsible for some of the dopiest cult and flying-saucer books I have ever read. She brings to them all the skill and devotion and hard work that she would to T. S. Eliot, and the damn things sell their heads off—half a million copies each, sometimes a lot more.

So Alice always has a job. The publisher knows that he is going to take a bath on at least half the books she brings in, but he also knows that he is going to make enough money out of the other half to make the stockholders smile. And a great many uncommercial talents find an audience.

A major paperback publishing company is a curious mixture. Every one of them has its Alice, sometimes several Alices. They also have squads and platoons of editors who spend all their time seeking the motherlodes, the Big Bestsellers. They go after them just as the big oil companies go after new drilling sites, and in much the same way. Just as the Seven Sisters bid against each other for leases in the Baltimore Canyon or Alaska's North Slope, so do the publishers bid against each other for the million-plus books.

If you've been reading the newspapers, you've seen that the bidding for new bestselling titles has been climbing into the stratosphere. You may wonder what this "auction" is, and how books get up into those telephone-number advances.

In principle, it's simple. Somebody owns a book that he thinks is worth a lot of money. Usually it is a hardcover publisher; but it may also be a literary agent, or even a writer; or a foreign publisher; or a film or TV producer with a new property. He sends out copies to everybody he thinks might be interested. He sets a day for them to say how much they want it. Perhaps he sets some minimum figure at which the bidding can commence. Then he sits back and waits for the phone to ring.

Sometimes it rings a lot. If two or three major paperback houses each gets seriously interested, the bidding can get furious. The blood gets in the water; the fever maddens the sharks, and they strike at everything in sight. I was in the Bantam office when one of the successive all-time price records was being set. Editors were wandering around the halls, jotting down figures on scraps of paper. Not much else was getting done that day, and the tension was more than I liked. I left early.

Of course, those multimillion-dollar prices have not come to science-fiction books—not yet! But there have been some hefty six-figure ones. There have been a fair number at around a quarter of a million dollars a book. That's a number that interests me in a historical way. I did a little arithmetic when the first such price was announced. It turns out that the aggregate amount that I paid out to every writer involved—over a period of thirty years, from 1939 to 1969; as editor of *Astonishing Stories* and *Super Science Stories,* as editor of the *Star* series of original anthologies for Ballantine, as editor of a couple of dozen reprint anthologies over that period, and finally as editor of *Galaxy, If, Worlds of Tomorrow,* and others for a decade—the total of checks issued for all of them, to every contributor combined, over all that time, is probably just about that same quarter of a million dollars.

Of course there has been a lot of inflation over those years, but not *that* much inflation. More important, the whole enterprise of publishing science fiction has grown an order of magnitude or two larger.

The role of the editor has changed. He functions less as a story coach to bring writers along. More as a packager. Less as a single rogue bull, like Horace Gold or John Campbell. More as a member of a team.

But he still has a chance to make a personal, individual contribution now and then, by publishing something worthwhile that no one else seems to dare to, even by creating a book that he wants to see published, from conception to newsstand.

Those occasions don't come every day. But they are what make the job worthwhile.

AT THE MOUSE CIRCUS

BY HARLAN ELLISON

Harlan Ellison's house is just on the far side of Mulholland Drive, in the hills that trap the smog into the Los Angeles bowl. It started out as a dwelling of relatively modest dimensions. It keeps growing. I think I know why Harlan keeps building extensions into his house: he needs the room for his awards. Last time I counted, Ellison had about seven-and-a-half Hugos and three Nebulas. One day the weight of all the metal, mahogany, and plastic is going to drive the whole house right down the side of the hill into the valley, but Harlan does not seem to care. Recklessly, he keeps acquiring them.

I published Harlan's first couple of award-winners. One day, over a kitchen table in someone's home, he handed me a manuscript called '' 'Repent, Harlequin!' said the Ticktockman.'' Would I publish it? Well, sure, I said, adding reasonably that, as the title was too long to fit into the running heads of the magazine, it would have to be shortened.

That shows what I knew. Some months, and hours of transcontinental phoning, later, the story appeared with the exact title he had put on it in the first place, and that won him his first Hugo.

That was a good Hugo year for Galaxy *and* If. *We won them all. So I decided to publish a special "Hugo-winner's Issue," with all the awardees represented; and what Harlan came up for with that was "I Have No Mouth, and I Must Scream," and of course that won a Hugo, too.*

I thought long and hard over which Ellison to include in this volume, and reluctantly decided against either of those—they have, after all, been reprinted so very many times since that it is hard to believe any literate human being has failed to read them. But years later, in an anthology, I was able to use his brilliant short story 'At the Mouse Circus''—and here it is.

* * *

400

The king of Tibet was having himself a fat white woman. He had thrown himself down a jelly tunnel, millennia before, and periodically, as he pumped her, a soft pink-and-white bunny rabbit in weskit and spats trembled through, scrutinizing a turnip watch at the end of a heavy gold-link chain. The white woman was soft as suet, with little black eyes thrust deep under prominent brow ridges. Honkie bitch groaned in unfulfilled ecstasy, trying desperately and knowing she never would. For she never had. The King of Tibet had a bellyache. Oh, to be in another place, doing another thing, alone.

The land outside was shimmering in waves of fear that came radiating from mountaintops far away. On the mountaintops, grizzled and wizened old men considered ways and means, considered runes and portents, considered whys and wherefores . . . ignored them all . . . and set about sending more fear to farther places. The land rippled in the night, beginning to quake with terror that was greater than the fear that had gone before.

"What time is it?" he asked, and received no answer.

Thirty-seven years ago, when the King of Tibet had been a lad, there had been a man with one leg—who had been his father for a short time—and a woman with a touch of the tar brush in her, and she had served as mother.

"You can be anything, Charles," she had said to him. "Anything you want to be. A man can be anything he can do. Uncle Wiggly, Jomo Kenyatta, the King of Tibet, if you want to. Light enough or black, Charles, it don't mean a thing. You just go your way and be good and *do*. That's all you got to remember."

The King of Tibet had fallen on hard times. Fat white women and cheap cologne. Doodad, he had lost the horizon. Exquisite, he had dealt with surfaces and been dealt with similarly. Wasted, he had done time.

"I got to go," he told her.

"Not yet, just a little more. Please."

So he stayed. Banners unfurled, lying limp in absence of breezes from Camelot, he stayed and suffered. Finally, she turned him loose, and the King of Tibet stood in the shower for forty minutes. Golden skin pelted, drinking, he was never quite clean. Scented, abluted, he still knew the odors of wombats, hallway musk, granaries, futile beakers of noxious fluids. If he was a white mouse, why could he not see his treadmill?

"Listen, baby, I got need of fi'hunnerd dollahs. I know we ain't been together but a while, but I got this *bad* need." She went to snap-purses and returned.

He hated her more for doing than not doing.

And in her past, he knew he was no part of any recognizable future.

"Charlie, when'll I see you again?" Stranger, never!

Borne away in the silver flesh of Cadillac, the great beautiful mother Hog, plunging wheelbased at one hundred and twenty (bought with his semen) inches, Eldorado god-creature of four hundred horsepower, displacing recklessly 440 cubic inches, thundering into forgetting weighing 4550 + pounds, goes . . . went . . . Charlie . . . Charles . . . the King of Tibet. Golden brown, cleaned as best as he could, five hundred reasons and five hundred aways. Driven, driving into the outside.

Forever inside, the King of Tibet, going outside.

Along the road. Manhattan, Jersey City, New Brunswick, Trenton. In Norristown, having had lunch at a fine restaurant, Charlie was stopped on a street corner by a voice that went *psst* from a mailbox. He opened the slit and a small boy in a pullover sweater and tie thrust his head and shoulders into the night. "You've got to help me," the boy said. "My name is Batson. Billy Batson. I work for radio station WHIZ and if I could only remember the right word, and if I could only say it, something wonderful would happen. *S* is for the wisdom of Solomon, *H* is for the strength of Hercules, *A* is for the stamina of Atlas, *Z* is for the power of Zeus . . . and after that I go blank . . ."

The King of Tibet slowly and steadily thrust the head back into the mailslot, and walked away. Reading, Harrisburg, Mt. Union, Altoona, Nanty Glo.

On the road to Pittsburgh there was a four-fingered mouse in red shorts with two big yellow buttons on the front, hitchhiking. Shoes like two big boxing gloves, bright eyes sincere, forlorn, and way lost, he stood on the curb with meaty thumb and he waited. Charlie whizzed past. It was not his dream.

Youngstown, Akron, Canton, Columbus, and hungry once more in Dayton. O.

Oh-aitch-eye-oh. Why did he ever leave. He had never been there before. This was the good place. The river flowed dark, and the day passed overhead like some other river. He pulled into a parking space and did not even lock the god-mother Eldorado. It waited patiently, knowing its upholstered belly would be filled with the King of Tibet soon enough.

"Feed you next," he told the sentient vehicle, as he walked away toward the restaurant.

Inside—dim and candled at high noon—he was shown to a heavy wood booth, and there he had laid before him a pure white linen napkin, five pieces of silver, a crystal goblet in which fine water waited, and a promise. From the promise he selected nine-to-five winners, a long shot, and the play number for the day.

A flocked-velvet witch perched on a bar stool across from him turned, exposed thigh, and smiled. He offered her silver, water, a promise, and they struck a bargain.

Charlie stared into her oiled teakwood eyes through the candle flame between them. All moistened Saran-wrap was her skin. All thistled gleaming were her teeth. All mystery of cupped hollows beneath cheekbones was she. Charlie had bought a television set once, because the redhead in the commercial was part of his dream. He had bought an electric toothbrush because the brunette with her capped teeth had indicated she, too, was part of his dream. And his great Eldorado, of course. *That* was the dream of the King of Tibet.

"What time is it?" But he received no answer and, drying his lips of the last of the *pêche flambée,* he and the flocked-velvet witch left the restaurant: he with his dream fraying and she with no product save one to sell.

There was a party in a house on a hill.

When they drove up the asphalt drive, the blacktop beneath them uncoiled like the sooty tongue of a great primitive snake. "You'll like these people," she said, and took the sensitive face of the King of Tibet between her hands and kissed him deeply. Her fingernails were gunmetal silvered and her palms were faintly moist and plump, with expectations of tactile enrichments.

They walked up to the house. Lit from within, every window held a color facet of light. Sounds swelled as they came toward the house. He fell a step behind her and watched the way her skin flowed. She reached out, touched the house, and they became one.

No door was opened to them, but holding fast to her hair he was drawn behind her, through the flesh of the house.

Within, there were inlaid ivory boxes that, when opened, revealed smaller boxes within. He became fascinated by one such box, sitting high on a pedestal in the center of an om rug. The box was inlaid with teeth of otters and puff adders and lynx. He opened the first box and within was a second box frosted with rime. Within the frost-box was a third, and it was decorated with mirrors that cast back no reflections. And next within was a box whose surface was a mass of intaglios, and they were all fingerprints, and none of Charlie's fit, and only when a passing man smiled and caressed the lid did it open, revealing the next, smaller box. And so it went, till he lost count of the boxes and the journey ended when he could not see the box that fit within the dust-mote-size box that was within all the others. But he knew there were more, and he felt a great sadness that he could not get to them.

"What is it, precisely, you want?" asked an older woman with very good bones. He was leaning against a wall whose only ornamentation was a gigantic wooden crucifix on which a Christ-figure hung, head bowed, shoulders twisted as only shoulders can be whose arms have been pulled from sockets; the figure was made of massive pieces of wood, all artfully stained: chunks of doors, bedposts, rowels, splines, pintles, joists, crossties, rabbet-joined bits of massive frames.

"I want . . ." he began, then spread his hands in confusion. He knew what he wanted to say, but no one had ever ordered the progression of words properly.

"Is it Madelaine?" the older woman asked. She smiled as Aunt Jemima would smile, and targeted a finger across the enormous living room, bull's-eyed on the flocked-velvet witch all the way over there by the fireplace. "She's here."

The King of Tibet felt a bit more relaxed.

"Now," the older woman said, her hand on Charlie's cheek, "what is it you need to know? Tell me. We have all the answers here. Truly."

"I want to know—"

The television screen went silver and cast a pool of light, drawing Charlie's attention. The possibilities were listed on the screen. And what he had wanted to know seemed inconsequential compared to the choices he saw listed.

"That one," he said. "That second one. How did the dinosaurs die."

"Oh, fine!" She looked pleased he had selected that one. "Shefti . . .?" she called to a tall man with gray hair at the temples. He looked up from speaking to several women and another man, looked up expectantly, and she said, "He's picked the second one. May I?"

"Of course, darling," Shefti said, raising his wine glass to her.

"Do we have time?"

"Oh, I think so," he said.

"Yes . . . what time is it?" Charlie asked.

"Over there," the older woman said, leading him firmly by the forearm. They stopped beside another wall. "Look."

The King of Tibet stared at the wall, and it paled, turned to ice, and became translucent. There was something imbedded in the ice. Something huge. Something dark. He stared harder, his eyes straining to make out the shape. Then he was seeing more clearly, and it was a great saurian, frozen at the moment of pouncing on some lesser species.

"*Gorgosaurus*," the older woman said, at his elbow. "It rather resembles *Tyrannosaurus*, you see; but the forelimbs have only two digits. You see?"

Thirty-two feet of tanned gray leather. The killing teeth. The nostriled snout, the amber smoke eyes of the eater of carrion. The smooth sickening tuber of balancing tail, the crippled forelimbs carried tragically withered and useless. The musculature . . . the pulsing beat of iced blood beneath the tarpaulin hide. The . . . beat . . .

It lived.

Through the ice went the King of Tibet, accompanied by Circe-eyed older woman, as the shellfish-white living room receded back beyond the ice-wall. Ice went, night came.

Ice that melted slowly from the great hulk before him. He stood in wonder. "See," the woman said.

And he saw as the ice dissolved into mist and night-fog, and he saw as the earth trembled, and he saw as the great fury lizard moved in shambling hesitancy, and he saw as the others came to cluster unseen nearby. *Scolosaurus* came. *Trachodon* came. *Stephanosaurus* came. *Protoceratops* came. And all stood, waiting.

The King of Tibet knew there were slaughterhouses where the beef was hung upside down on hooks, where the throats were slit and the blood ran thick as motor oil. He saw a golden thing hanging, and would not look. Later, he would look.

They waited. Silently, for its coming.

Through the Cretaceous swamp it was coming. Charlie could hear it. Not loud, but coming steadily closer. "Would you light my cigarette, please," asked the older woman.

It was shining. It bore a pale white nimbus. It was stepping through the swamp, black to its thighs from the decaying matter. It came on, its eyes set back under furred brow-ridges, jaw thrust forward, wide nostrils sniffing at the chill night, arms covered with matted filth and hair. Savior man.

He came to the lizard owners of the land. He walked around them and they stood silently, their time at hand. Then he touched them, one after the other, and the plague took them. Blue fungus spread from the five-pronged marks left on their imperishable hides; blue death radiating from impressions of opposed thumbs, joining, spreading cilia and rotting the flesh of the great gone dinosaurs.

The ice re-formed and the King of Tibet moved back through pearly cold to the living room.

He struck a match and lit her cigarette.

She thanked him and walked away.

The flocked-velvet witch returned. "Did you have a nice time?" He thought of the boxes-within-boxes.

"Is that how they died? Was he the first?"

She nodded. "And did Nita ask you for anything?"

Charlie had never seen the sea. Oh, there had been the Narrows and the East River and the Hudson, but he had never seen the sea. The real sea, the thunder sea that went black at night like a pane of glass. The sea that could summon and the sea that could kill, that could swallow whole cities and turn them into myth. He wanted to go to California.

He suddenly felt a fear he would never leave this thing called Ohio here.

"I asked you: did Nita ask you for anything?"

He shivered.

"What?"

"Nita. Did she *ask* you for anything?"

"Only a light."

"Did you give it to her?"

"Yes."

Madelaine's face swam in the thin fluid of his sight. Her jaw muscles trembled. She turned and walked across the room. Everyone turned to look at her. She went to Nita, who suddenly took a step backward and threw up her hands. "No, I didn't—"

The flocked-velvet witch darted a hand toward the older woman and the hand seemed to pass into her neck. The silver-tipped fingers reappeared, clenched around a fine sparkling filament. Then Madelaine snapped it off with a grunt.

There was a terrible minor sound from Nita, then she turned, watery, and stood silently beside the window, looking empty and hopeless.

Madelaine wiped her hand on the back of the sofa and came to Charlie. "We'll go now. The party is over."

He drove in silence back to town.

"Are you coming up?" he asked, when they parked the Eldorado in front of the hotel.

"I'm coming up."

He registered them as Professor Pierre and Marja Sklodowska Curie, and for the first time in his life he was unable to reach a climax. He fell asleep sobbing over never having seen the sea, and came awake hours later with the night still pressing against the walls. She was not there.

He heard sounds from the street, and went to the window. There was a large crowd in the street, gathered around his car.

As he watched, a man went to his knees before the golden Eldorado and touched it. Charlie knew *this* was his dream. He could not move; he just watched, as they ate his car.

The man put his mouth to the hood and it came away bloody. A great chunk had been ripped from the gleaming hide of the Cadillac. Golden blood ran down the man's jaws.

Another man draped himself over the top of the car and even through the window the King of Tibet could hear the terrible sucking, slobbering sounds. Furrows were ripped in the top.

A woman pulled her dress up around her hips and backed, on all fours, to the rear of the car. Her face trembled with soft expectancy, and then it was inside her and she moved on it.

When she came, they all moved in on the car and he watched as his dream went inside them, piece by piece, chewed and eaten as he stood by helpless.

"That's all, Charlie," he heard her say, behind him. He could not turn to look at her, but her reflection was superimposed over his own in the window. Out there in darkness now, they moved away, having eaten.

He looked, and saw the golden thing hanging upside down in the slaughter-house, its throat cut, its blood drained away in onyx gutters.

Afoot, in Dayton, Ohio, he was dead of dreams.

"What time is it?" he asked.

DRAGON LENSMAN

BY DAVID A. KYLE

(Based on the series created by E. E. "Doc" Smith, Ph.D.)

(Excerpt)

A lot of the afternoons of my teen-age years were spent reading Doc Smith's Skylark *and* Lensman *stories. I could never get enough. As one of the perquisites of editorship is that you get the chance to act out your fantasies, I spent a lot of time, over a quarter of a century, urging Doc to produce more.*

Doc was not your most persuadable human being. In fact, he had a will of chrome-vanadium steel; but after I became editor of Galaxy *and* If *I made him see reason. I bearded him in his den—actually in his mobile home in Florida—and convinced him that the* Skylark *saga needed one last serial to cap it off. I even gave him a title; and a few months later, lo!,* Skylark Duquesne *hit my desk.*

Few things I have published gave me more pleasure. I was looking forward to a decade or so of Richard Ballinger Seaton and Kimball Kinnison bounding around the pages of my magazines, for my readers' enjoyment and my own. It didn't happen. Skylark Duquesne *was still on the stands when I got a cable from Verna Smith Trestrail, Doc's daughter, to say there would be no more. Doc had died the day before.*

He was a marvelous man, and greatly missed. I can't say he was a close friend. There was a large generation gap between us, not to mention left-over teen-age awe. But he was a very dear one.

However, although Doc had died, Kinnison and Seaton had not. Doc had acknowledged in writing his intention to do at least two more stories in the Lensman *series, one about the eerie and incomprehensible Nadreck of Palain VII, the other to tell the story of His Royal Snakeship, the dragonlike Worsel of Velantia.*

It seemed to me that it should be possible to find a writer sufficiently steeped in the wonders of the Lens to carry on the series. And it was. Not easy, but possible—and the first one is Dragon Lensman, *from which this is a short prefatory excerpt.*

* * *

For all those of you who have previously read E. E. "Doc" Smith's accounts of the Galactic Patrol and the Arisian-Eddorian conflict, most of this Foreword is redundant. You are hereby waved on to the last three paragraphs beginning with "The chronicler..." For those of you who are newcomers or whose memories have clouded with the years, a few words of background are certainly desirable.

Billions of years ago Mankind began to evolve on a small planet of the star Sol. Billions of years before that, Tellus, also known as Earth, had been created in the time of the great Coalescence. And billions of years before that event, our Milky Way galaxy, also known as the First Galaxy, was inhospitable to life, almost barren of planets, and virtually deserted.

The life-spores of Man existed before all these things, incredibly far back for uncountable eons. The ancestral source was the race of the Arisians from the beginning of Time, Visualizers of the Cosmic All, future guardians of Civilization.

Fully as ancient, nearly equal in macrocosmic mind power, and as evil as the Arisians were good, were the Eddorians of the Second Galaxy. Whereas the Arisians were of our own space-time continuum, the Eddorians were not—coming on their wandering planet to the Second Galaxy from a different, horribly alien plenum. They were dedicated to a continuing search for more worlds to sate their lust for dominance. Their ambition was at last to be glutted by "the Coalescence." In that cataclysmic event their enslaved star island passed, end to end, through our own galaxy. The stupendous interstellar forces which were unleashed thus created billions of new worlds. The inevitable conflict between the Arisians and the Eddorians, the prototype confrontation between Good and Evil, had arrived. The struggle began for the lives and souls of the many races that were evolving. As Civilization grew, the Elders of Arisia surreptitiously encouraged the new life-forms to resist the tyranny and to shape their independent ways toward perfection.

In the universal deceit which developed around the rise of the Eddorian-inspired Boskonian outlaws, the greatest secret of all was kept by the Arisians. Their immortal enemies, the Eddorians, were kept forever ignorant of their existence. The Arisians were the covert and incognito patrons of those opposing the evil Eddorians; they were the real, formidable counterforce in the eons-long contest with Boskonia and its masters.

Four widely scattered planets with advanced life forms were the nucleus of the resistance in the First Galaxy: Tellus, known as Earth or Terra; Velantia; Rigel Four; and Palain Seven. Each, subtly encouraged by the Arisians, developed four dissimilar races, but it was Tellus which became the focal point for the organized force against Boskone and its puppet-masters. From Tellus came the formation of the Galactic Patrol, to be the instrument of Eddorian destruction. Also from Tellus came the Kinnison and Samms families, leading to the penultimate union of their foremost leaders, Kimball Kinnison, the Gray Lensman, and Clarissa MacDougall, the Red Lensman.

Within generations of the First Lensman, Virgil Samms, many Lensmen had been recruited into a special corps of Patrolmen. They were outstanding military leaders and scientists, possessing extraordinary natural, non-mutated abilities. The Lensman name came from the peculiar semiliving Lens each one wore, usually on a wrist, a unique gift obtained from Mentor of Arisia. These incredible instruments, radiant crystal complexities, were badges of honor, forgery-proof identification, and amplifiers of psychic powers. They were awarded only to those chosen by Mentor itself, the amorphous fusion-entity of the four intellectually greatest Arisian Molders of Civilization. The psychical match to the quintessential individuality of the Lensman was exact—so perfect, in fact, that it released latent parapsychic or psi powers, telepathy in particular. Only the original recipient of the Lens could wear it—for anyone else, it brought instant death.

The best Lensmen eventually were chosen for the highest honor which the Patrol could offer: unattached status. Known as Gray Lensmen from the plain leather uniforms they now wore, unlike the black-and-silver-and-gold ones of the rest of the officers and men, these distinguished fellows of the Service were free agents. With their freedom for independent action, they were the personification of the Patrol itself, accountable to no one but the highest authorities.

Although Kimball Kinnison was not the first Gray Lensman, he was, despite his youth, one of the outstanding ones. His demonstrated ability led to his being recalled to Arisia by Mentor to receive the next level of training as a Second Stage Lensman. Kimball was the first of four to come from each of the original planets, even ahead of Worsel the Velantian, whose mind actually was better developed and trained and of vastly greater power. The Tellurian, however, was chosen for greater capacity and more varied growth, especially for the force of his driving will, so characteristic of his race.

As the legion of Lensmen grew with its special leaders, so did the scale of the conflict, until, finally, both galaxies and their neighboring star clusters were involved.

The climax came at last. Kimball Kinnison as the fighting leader of the Galactic Patrol, the military arm of the Galactic Council which by now represented all of Civilization, directed the decisive battles by the Grand Fleet against the massive forces of the Boskonians. The culmination of the years of galactic struggle came with the giant dogfight of spaceships which was the Battle of Klovia. The Boskonian conspiracy was considered destroyed. Kimball Kinnison, the newly-appointed Galactic Coordinator, and his bride, Cris, were taking on their new responsibilities for Civilization. Peace was spreading through the two galaxies.

Only Mentor knew that the Eddorians had not been defeated, merely delayed, in their goal to conquer the galaxies and to make them their playthings.

The chronicler of these events has been, up to now, the famous research historian of the Galactic Patrol, E. E. "Doc" Smith. His efforts have been monumental; a half-dozen books by him have traced the rise of Tellurian culture and the formation of the Patrol, all part of the struggle to protect and advance Civilization in the Milky Way. His reports have been presented in his inimitable way as popularized novels. More than a decade ago Doc Smith, a warm-hearted and virile man, passed on to "the next plane of existence" to join the Arisians. Since then no books describing the exploits of the fabulous Lensmen have been written, although there really has been no need because the end of the terrible Boskonian threat was told and the evil Eddorians were shown to have been obliterated. Doc Smith, the historian, did his work well—and thoroughly—to lead us to the plateau of the evolution of the Universe with the coming of the Children of the Lens.

There is, however, a period in the history as reported by the doctor which has not been documented. A score of years lie between the marriage of Kinnison to his Cris and the emergence from childhood of their offspring. There was in these decades no "energy stasis"—that which always moves forward just to stand still inevitably leads upward and downward simultaneously. Historical events were taking place—but they become history only when they are recorded and reported.

The well-established historical research department which E. E. Smith so successfully created is still at work collecting and assembling facts and eye-witness accounts. There is a wealth of material available for further tales of the Patrol and its personnel. This book is the first one written without the direct supervision of the doctor. Your new historian knew "Doc" for many years, having met him in his space-roamer's garb of "Northwest Smith of Earth," at the Second Worldcon in Chicago, Tellus—and, having had him for a lifetime as a guide, appreciates that he was unique. Let no one be deluded, least of all your present historian, into thinking that this new series of books will be indistinguishable from the presentations of the original histories. Unique "Doc" was, and unique he will remain. But the spirit will not be changed—the entire historical research department will see to that. This historian, whose responsibility is not taken lightly, pledges fidelity to the "E. E. Smith way" knowing that the Galactic Roamers will not tolerate anything less.

—David A. Kyle,
Tellus

DHALGREN

BY SAMUEL R. DELANY

(Excerpt)

Dhalgren, *so says Chip Delany, is his masterwork. He gave half a dozen years out of his life to writing it . . . and rewriting it . . . and re-rewriting it. Nevertheless, when the manuscript was submitted to me at Bantam, it started out with three strikes against it. 1) I knew it had been rejected by most of the major publishing houses. 2) I had in fact been one of the rejectors—at least, an extract of an early version had been offered to me at* Galaxy *and I had turned it down very fast. 3) The son of a gun was huge. Two popping-full manuscript boxes—way over a thousand pages!*

According to the rules, three strikes is out—but then I read it.

There was no doubt in my mind that Dhalgren *deserved to be published. It's a strange book, by no means to everyone's taste. It is mannered, and tricky, and rawly, quirkily sexual, and often obscure. At every page I turned I thought,* Hell, I wouldn't have written it that way! *But then—facing facts—I had to admit,* Hell, I couldn't have written it at all.

So I ordered up a contract, and put this huge mass of paper into the production line.

It takes a year to get a book into print in the normal way, and as the months passed rumors began to float around the office. They called it "Fred's Folly." Now and then, on Thursday afternoons, the only time I was in the Bantam office, people would sit on the edge of my desk and say, uh, no offense, we're not questioning your decision, but, uh, exactly why are you publishing it? I had two answers. The first was that it was too important a project by too talented a writer to leave out of print. The second was that it was the first book that had taught me anything I didn't know about sex since The Story of O.

But I was getting a little nervous. So I pressured Marc Jaffe into letting me come to the annual sales conference. What you're supposed to do at one of those things is sell your whole year's line. I didn't. I simply showed them an advance copy of Dhalgren *and said, "You don't have any advance warning on this. It's coming out next month. But if you'll just go back and get copies of it*

*into your customers' bookstores, readers will buy it. Lots of them. I give you
my word."*

And a couple of months later, when Dhalgren *was already in the hundreds
of thousands and still climbing, Marc Jaffe came into my office and said,
"You know, you've got a lot of credibility with the sales force now."*

                            *   *   *

It is not that I have no past. Rather, it continually fragments on the terrible
and vivid ephemera of now. In the long country, cut with rain, somehow there
is nowhere to begin. Loping and limping in the ruts, it would be easier not to
think about what she did (was done to her, done to her, done), trying instead
to reconstruct what it is at a distance. Oh, but it would not be so terrible had
one calf not borne (if I'd looked close, it would have been a chain of tiny
wounds with moments of flesh between; I've done that myself with a swipe in
a garden past a rose) that scratch.

The asphalt spilled him onto the highway's shoulder. The paving's chipped
edges filed visions off his eyes. A roar came toward him he heard only as it
passed. He glanced back: the truck's red, rear eyes sank together. He walked
for another hour, saw no other vehicle.

A Mac with a double van belched twenty feet behind him, sagged to a stop
twenty feet ahead. He hadn't even been thumbing. He sprinted toward the
opening door, hauled himself up, slammed it. The driver, tall, blond, and
acned, looking blank, released the clutch.

He was going to say thanks, but coughed. Maybe the driver wanted
somebody to rap at? Why else stop for someone just walking the road!

He didn't feel like rapping. But you have to say something:

"What you loading?"

"Artichokes."

Approaching lights spilled pit to pit in the driver's face.

They shook on down the highway.

He could think of nothing more, except: I was just making love to this
woman, see, and you'll never guess . . . No, the Daphne bit would not pass—

It was he who wanted to talk! The driver was content to dispense with
phatic thanks and chatter. Western independence? He had hitched this sector
of country enough to decide it was all manic terror.

He leaned his head back. He wanted to talk and had nothing to say.

Fear past, the archness of it forced the architecture of a smile his lips
fought.

He saw the ranked highway lights twenty minutes later and sat forward to
see the turnoff. He glanced at the driver who was just glancing away. The
brakes wheezed and the cab slowed by lurches.

They stopped. The driver sucked in the sides of his ruined cheeks, looked over, still blank.

He nodded, sort of smiled, fumbled the door, dropped to the road; the door slammed and the truck started while he was still preparing thanks; he had to duck the van corner.

The vehicle grumbled down the turnoff.

We only spoke a line apiece.

What an odd ritual exchange to exhaust communication. (Is that terror?) What amazing and engaging rituals are we practicing now? (He stood on the road side, laughing.) What torque and tension in the mouth to laugh so in this windy, windy, windy . . .

Underpass and overpass knotted here. He walked . . . proudly? Yes, proudly by the low wall.

Across the water the city flickered.

On its dockfront, down half a mile, flamed roiled smoke on the sky and reflections on the river. Here, not one car came off the bridge. Not one went on.

This toll booth, like the rank of booths, was dark. He stepped inside: front pane shattered, stool overturned, no drawer in the register—a third of the keys stuck down; a few bent. Some were missing their heads. Smashed by a mace, a mallet, a fist? He dragged his fingers across them, listened to them click, then stepped from the glass-flecked, rubber mat, over the sill to the pavement.

Metal steps led up to the pedestrian walkway. But since there was no traffic, he sauntered across two empty lanes—a metal grid sunk in the blacktop gleamed where tires had polished it—to amble the broken white line, sandaled foot one side, bare foot the other. Girders wheeled by him, left and right. Beyond, the burning city squatted on weak, inverted images of its fires.

He gazed across the wale of night water, all wind-runneled, and sniffed for burning. A gust parted the hair at the back of his neck; smoke was moving off the river.

"Hey, you!"

He looked up at the surprising flashlight. "Huh . . . ?" At the walkway rail, another and another punctured the dark.

"You going into Bellona?"

"That's right." Squinting, he tried to smile. One, and another, the lights moved a few steps, stopped. He said: "You're . . . leaving?"

"Yeah. You know it's restricted in there."

He nodded. "But I haven't seen any soldiers or police or anything. I just hitch-hiked down."

"How were the rides?"

"All I saw was two trucks for the last twenty miles. The second one gave me a lift."

"What about the traffic going out?"

He shrugged. "But I guess girls shouldn't have too hard a time, though. I mean, if a car passes, you'll probably get a ride. Where you heading?"

"Two of us want to get to New York. Judy wants to go to San Francisco."

"I just want to get *some* place," a whiny voice came down. "I've got a fever! I should be in bed. I *was* in bed for the last three days."

He said: "You've got a ways to go, either direction."

"Nothing's happened to San Francisco—?"

"—or New York?"

"No." He tried to see behind the lights. "The papers don't even talk about what's happening here, any more."

"But, Jesus! What about the television? Or the radio—"

"Stupid, none of it works out here. So how are they gonna know?"

"But—Oh, wow . . . !"

He said: "The nearer you get, it's just less and less people. And the ones you meet are . . . funnier. What's it like inside?"

One laughed.

Another said: "It's pretty rough."

The one who'd spoken first said: "But like you say, girls have an easier time."

They laughed.

He did, too. "Is there anything you can tell me? I mean that might be helpful? Since I'm going in?"

"Yeah. Some men came by, shot up the house we were living in, tore up the place, then burned us out."

"She was making this sculpture," the whiny voice explained; "this big sculpture. Of a lion. Out of junk metal and stuff. It was beautiful . . . ! But she had to leave it."

"Wow," he said. "Is it like that?"

One short, hard laugh: "Yeah. We got it real easy."

"Tell him about Calkins? Or the scorpions?"

"He'll learn about them." Another laugh. "What can you say?"

"You want a weapon to take in with you?"

That made him afraid again. "Do I need one?"

But they were talking among themselves:

"You're gonna give him that?"

"Yeah, why not? I don't want it with me any more."

"Well, okay. It's yours."

Metal sounded on chain, while one asked: "Where you from?" The flashlights turned away, ghosting the group. One in profile near the rail was momentarily lighted enough to see she was very young, very black, and very pregnant.

"Up from the south."

"You don't *sound* like you're from the south," one said who did.

"I'm not *from* the south. But I was just in Mexico."

"Oh, hey!" That was the pregnant one. "Where were you? I know Mexico."

The exchange of half a dozen towns ended in disappointed silence.

"Here's your weapon."

Flashlights followed the flicker in the air, the clatter on the gridded blacktop.

With the beams on the ground (and not in his eyes), he could make out half a dozen women on the catwalk.

"What—" A car motor thrummed at the end of the bridge; but there were no headlights when he glanced. The sound died on some turnoff— "is it?"

"What'd they call it?"

"An orchid."

"Yeah, that's what it is."

He walked over, squatted in the triple beam.

"You wear it around your wrist. With the blades sticking out front. Like a bracelet."

From an adjustable metal wrist-band, seven blades, from eight to twelve inches, curved sharply forward. There was a chain-and-leather harness inside to hold it steady on the fingers. The blades were sharpened along the outside.

He picked it up.

"Put it on."

"Are you right or left handed?"

"Ambidextrous . . ." which, in his case, meant clumsy with both. He turned the "flower." "But I write with my left. Usually."

"Oh."

He fitted it around his right wrist, snapped it. "Suppose you were wearing this on a crowded bus. You could hurt somebody," and felt the witticism fail. He made a fist within the blades, opened it slowly and, behind curved steel, rubbed two blunt and horny crowns on the underside of his great thumb.

"There aren't too many buses in Bellona."

Thinking: Dangerous, bright petals bent about some knobbed, half-rotted root. "Ugly thing," he told it, not them. "Hope I don't need you."

"Hope you don't either," one said above. "I guess you can give it to somebody else when you leave."

"Yeah." He stood up. "Sure."

"*If* he leaves," another said, gave another laugh.

"Hey, we better get going."

"I heard a car. We're probably gonna have to wait long enough anyway. We might as well start."

South: "He didn't make it sound like we were gonna get any rides."

"Let's just get going. Hey, so long!"

"So long." Their beams swept by. "And thanks." Artichokes? But he could not remember where the word had come from to ring so brightly. He raised the orchid after them. His gnarled hand, caged in blades, was silhouetted with river glitter stretching between the bridge struts. Watching them go, he felt the vaguest flutter of desire. Only one of their flashlights was on. Then one of them blocked that. They were footsteps on metal plates; some laughter drifting back; rustlings . . .

He walked again, holding his hand from his side.

This parched evening seasons the night with remembrances of rain. Very few suspect the existence of this city. It is as if not only the media but the laws of perception themselves have redesigned knowledge and perception to pass it. Rumor says there is practically no power here. Neither television cameras nor on-the-spot broadcasts function: that such a catastrophe as this should be opaque, and therefore dull, to the electric nation! It is a city of inner discordances and retinal distortions.

Beyond the bridge-mouth, the pavement shattered.

One live street lamp lit five dead ones—two with broken globes. Climbing a ten-foot, tilted, asphalt slab that jerked once under him, rumbling like a live thing, he saw pebbles roll off the edge, heard them clink on fugitive plumbing, then splash somewhere in darkness . . . He recalled the cave and vaulted to a more solid stretch, whose cracks were mortared with nubby grass.

No lights in any near buildings; but down those waterfront streets beyond the veils of smoke—was that fire? Already used to the smell, he had to breathe deeply to notice it. The sky was all haze. Buildings jabbed up into it and disappeared.

Light?

At the corner of a four-foot alley, he spent ten minutes exploring—just because the lamp worked. Across the street he could make out concrete steps, a loading porch under an awning, doors. A truck had overturned at the block's end. Nearer, three cars, windows rimmed with smashed glass, squatted on skewed hubs, like frogs gone marvelously blind.

His bare foot was calloused enough for gravel and glass. But ash kept working between his foot and his remaining sandal to grind like finest sand, work its way under, and silt itself with his sweat. His heel was almost sore.

By the gate at the alley's end, he found a pile of empty cans, a stack of newspaper still wire-bound, bricks set up as a fireplace with an arrangement of pipes over it. Beside it was an army messpan, insides caked with dead mold. Something by his moving foot crinkled.

He reached down. One of the orchid's petals snagged; he picked up a package of . . . bread? The wrapper was twisted closed. Back under the street lamp, he balanced it on his fingers, through the blades, and opened the cellophane.

He had wondered about food.

He had wondered about sleep.

But he knew the paralysis of wonder.

The first slice had a tenpenny nailhead of muzzy green in the corner; the second and third, the same. The nail, he thought, was through the loaf. The top slice was dry on one side. Nothing else was wrong—except the green vein; and it was only that penicillium stuff. He could eat around it.

I'm not hungry.

He replaced the slices, folded the cellophane, carried it back, and wedged it behind the stacked papers.

As he returned to the lamp, a can clattered from his sandal, defining the silence. He wandered away through it, gazing up for some hint of the hazed-out moon—

Breaking glass brought his eyes to street level.

He was afraid, and he was curious; but fear had been so constant, it was a dull and lazy emotion, now; the curiosity was alive:

He sprinted to the nearest wall, moved along it rehearsing his apprehensions of all terrible that might happen. He passed a doorway, noted it for ducking, and kept on to the corner. Voices now. And more glass.

He peered around the building edge.

Three people vaulted from a shattered display window to join two waiting. Barking, a dog followed them to the sidewalk. One man wanted to climb back in; did. Two others took off down the block.

The dog circled, loped his way—

He pulled back, free hand grinding on the brick.

The dog, crouched and dancing ten feet off, barked, barked, barked again.

Dim light slathered canine tongue and teeth. Its eyes (he swallowed, hard) were glistening red, without white or pupil, smooth as crimson glass.

The man came back out the window. One in the group turned and shouted: "Muriel!" (It could have been a woman.) The dog wheeled and fled after.

Another street lamp, blocks down, gave them momentary silhouette.

As he stepped from the wall, his breath unraveled the silence, shocked him as much as if someone had called his . . . name? Pondering, he crossed the street toward the corner of the loading porch. On tracks under the awning, four- and six-foot butcher hooks swung gentle—though there was no wind. In fact, he reflected, it would take a pretty hefty wind to *start* them swinging—

"Hey!"

Hands, free and flowered, jumped to protect his face. He whirled, crouching.

"You down there!"

He looked up, with hunched shoulders.

Smoke rolled about the building top, eight stories above.

"What you doing, huh?"

He lowered his hands.

The voice was rasp rough, sounded near drunk.

He called: "Nothing!" and wished his heart would still. "Just walking around."

Behind scarves of smoke, someone stood at the cornice. "What you been up to this evening?"

"Nothing, I said." He took a breath: "I just got here, over the bridge. About a half hour ago."

"Where'd you get the orchid?"

"Huh?" He raised his hand again. The street lamp dribbled light down a blade. "This?"

"Yeah."

"Some women gave it to me. When I was crossing the bridge."

"I saw you looking around the corner at the hubbub. I couldn't tell from up here—was it scorpions?"

"Huh?"

"I said, was it scorpions?"

"It was a bunch of people trying to break into a store, I think. They had a dog with them."

After silence, gravelly laughter grew. "You really haven't been here long, kid?"

"I—" and realized the repetition—"just got here."

"You out to go exploring by yourself? Or you want company for a bit."

The guy's eyes, he reflected, must be awfully good. "Company . . . I guess."

"I'll be there in a minute."

He didn't see the figure go; there was too much smoke. And after he'd watched several doorways for several minutes, he figured the man had changed his mind.

"Here you go," from the one he'd set aside for ducking.

"Name is Loufer. Tak Loufer. You know what that means, Loufer? Red Wolf; or Fire Wolf."

"Or Iron Wolf." He squinted. "Hello."

"Iron Wolf? Well, yeah . . ." The man emerged, dim on the top step. "Don't know if I like that one so much. Red Wolf. That's my favorite." He was a very big man.

He came down two more steps; his engineer's boots, hitting the boards, sounded like dropped sandbags. Wrinkled black-jeans were half stuffed into the boot tops. The worn cycle jacket was scarred with zippers. Gold stubble on chin and jaw snagged the street light. Chest and belly, bare between flapping zipper teeth, were a tangle of brass hair. The fingers were massive, matted—"What's your name?"—but clean, with neat and cared-for nails.

"Um . . . well, I'll tell you: I don't know." It sounded funny, so he laughed. "I don't know."

Loufer stopped, a step above the sidewalk, and laughed too. "Why the hell don't you?" The visor of his leather cap blocked his upper face with shadow.

He shrugged. "I just don't. I haven't for . . . a while now."

Loufer came down the last step, to the pavement. "Well, Tak Loufer's met people here with stranger stories than that. You some kind of nut, or something? You been in a mental hospital, maybe?"

"Yes . . ." He saw that Loufer had expected a *No*.

Tak's head cocked. The shadow raised to show the rims of Negro-wide nostrils above an extremely caucasian mouth. The jaw looked like rocks in hay-stubble.

"Just for a year. About six or seven years ago."

Loufer shrugged. "I was in jail for three months . . . about six or seven years ago. But that's as close as I come. So you're a no-name kid? What are you, seventeen? Eighteen? No, I bet you're even—''

"Twenty-seven."

Tak's head cocked the other way. Light topped his cheek bones. "Neurotic fatigue, do it every time. You notice that about people with serious depression, the kind that sleep all day? Hospital type cases, I mean. They always look ten years younger than they are."

He nodded.

"I'm going to call you Kid, then. That'll do you for a name. You can be—The Kid, hey?"

Three gifts, he thought: armor, weapon, title (like the prisms, lenses, mirrors on the chain itself). "Okay . . ." with the sudden conviction this third would cost, by far, the most. Reject it, something warned: "Only I'm not a kid. Really; I'm twenty-seven. People always think I'm younger than I am. I just got a baby face, that's all. I've even got some white hair, if you want to see—''

"Look, Kid—" with his middle fingers, Tak pushed up his visor—"we're the same age." His eyes were large, deep, and blue. The hair above his ears, no longer than the week's beard, suggested a severe crew under the cap. "Any sights you particularly want to see around here? Anything you heard about? I like to play guide. What do you hear about us, outside, anyway? What do people say about us here in the city?"

"Not much."

"Guess they wouldn't." Tak looked away. "You just wander in by accident, or did you come on purpose?"

"Purpose."

"Good Kid! Like a man with a purpose. Come on up here. This street turns into Broadway soon as it leaves the waterfront."

"What *is* there to see?"

Loufer gave a grunt that did for a laugh. "Depends on what sights are out." Though he had the beginning of a gut, the ridges under the belly hair were muscle deep. "If we're *really* lucky, maybe—" the ashy leather, swinging as Loufer turned, winked over a circular brass buckle that held together a two-inch-wide garrison— "we won't run into anything at all! Come on." They walked.

". . . kid. The Kid . . ."

"Huh?" asked Loufer.

"I'm thinking about that name."

"Will it do?"

"I don't know."

Loufer laughed. "I'm not going to press for it, Kid. But I think it's yours." His own chuckle was part denial, part friendly.

Loufer's grunt in answer echoed the friendly.

They walked beneath low smoke.

This is something delicate about this Iron Wolf, with his face like a pug-nosed, Germanic gorilla. It is neither his speech nor his carriage, which have their roughness, but the way in which he assumes them, as though the surface where speech and carriage are flush were somehow inflamed.

"Hey, Tak?"

"Yeah?"

"How long have you been here?"

"If you told me today's date, I could figure it out. But I've let it go. It's been a while." After a moment, Loufer asked, in a strange, less blustery voice: "Do you know what day it is?"

"No, I . . ." The strangeness scared him. "I don't." He shook his head while his mind rushed away toward some other subject. "What do you do? I mean, what did you work at?"

Tak snorted. "Industrial engineering."

"Were you working here, before . . . all this?"

"Near here. About twelve miles down, at Helmsford. There used to be a plant that jarred peanut butter. We were converting it into a vitamin C factory. What do you do—? Naw, you don't look like you do too much in the line of work." Loufer grinned. "Right?"

He nodded. It was reassuring to be judged by appearances, when the judge was both accurate and friendly. And, anyway, the rush had stopped.

"I was staying down in Helmsford," Loufer went on. "But I used to drive up to the city a lot. Bellona used to be a pretty good town." Tak glanced at a doorway too dark to see if it was open or shut.

"Maybe it still is, you know? But one day I drove up here. And it was like this."

A fire escape, above a street lamp pulsing slow as a failing heart, looked like charred sticks, some still aglow.

"Just like this?"

On a store window their reflection slid like ripples over oil.

"There were a few more places the fire hadn't reached; a few more people who hadn't left yet—not all the newcomers had arrived."

"You were here at the very beginning, then?"

"Oh, I didn't see it break out or anything. Like I say, when I got here, it looked more or less like it does now."

"Where's your car?"

"Sitting on the street with the windshield busted, the tires gone—along with most of the motor. I let a lot of stupid things happen, at first. But I got the hang of it after a while." Tak made a sweeping gesture with both hands—and disappeared before it was finished: they'd passed into complete blackness. "A thousand people are supposed to be here now. Used to be almost two million."

"How do you know, I mean the population?"

"That's what they publish in the paper."

"Why do you stay?"

"Stay?" Loufer's voice neared that other, upsetting tone. "Well, actually, I've thought about that one a lot. I think it has to do with—I got a theory now—freedom. You know, here—" ahead, something moved— "you're free. No laws: to break, or to follow. Do anything you want. Which does funny things to you. Very quickly, surprisingly quickly, you become—" they neared another half-lit lamp; what moved became smoke, lobling from a window still set with glass teeth like an extinguished jack-o-lantern—"exactly who you are." And Tak was visible again. "If you're ready for that, this is where it's at."

"It must be pretty dangerous. Looters and stuff."

Tak nodded. "Sure it's dangerous."

"Is there a lot of street mugging?"

"Some." Loufer made a face. "Do you know about crime, Kid? Crime is funny. For instance, now, in most American cities—New York, Chicago, St. Louis—crimes, ninety-five percent I read, are committed between six o'clock and midnight. That means you're safer walking around the street at three o'clock in the morning than you are going to the theater to catch a seven-thirty curtain. I wonder what time it is now. Sometime after two I'd gather. I don't think Bellona is much more dangerous than any other city. It's a very small city, now. That's a sort of protection."

A forgotten blade scraped his jeans. "Do you carry a weapon?"

"Months of detailed study on what is going on where, the movements and variations of our town. I look around a lot. This way."

That wasn't buildings on the other side of the street: Trees rose above the park wall, black as shale. Loufer headed toward the entrance.

"Is it safe in there?"

"Looks pretty scary." Tak nodded. "Probably keep any criminal with a grain of sense at home. Anybody who wasn't a mugger would be out of his mind to go in there." He glanced back, grinned. "Which probably means all the muggers have gotten tired of waiting and gone home to bed a long time ago. Come on."

Stone lions flanked the entrance.

"It's funny," Tak said; they passed between. "You show me a place where they tell women to stay out of at night because of all the nasty, evil men lurking there to do nasty, evil things; and you know what you'll find?"

"Queers."

Tak glanced over, pulled his cap visor down. "Yeah."

The dark wrapped them up and buoyed them along the path.

There is nothing safe about the darkness of this city and its stink. Well, I have abrogated all claim to safety, coming here. It is better to discuss it as though I had chosen. That keeps the scrim of sanity before the awful set. What will lift it?

"What were you in prison for?"

"Morals charge," Tak said.

He was steps behind Loufer now. The path, which had begun as concrete, was now dirt. Leaves hit at him. Three times his bare foot came down on rough roots; once his swinging arm scraped lightly against bark.

"Actually," Tak tossed back into the black between them, "I was acquitted. The situation, I guess. My lawyer figured it was better I stayed in jail without bail for ninety days, like a misdemeanor sentence. Something had got lost in the records. Then, at court, he brought that all out, got the charge changed to public indecency; I'd already served sentence." Zipper-jinglings suggested a shrug. "Everything considered, it worked out. Look!"

The carbon black of leaves shredded, letting through the ordinary color of urban night.

"Where?" They had stopped among trees and high brush.

"Be quiet! There . . ."

His wool shushed Tak's leather. He whispered: "Where do you . . . ?"

Out on the path, sudden, luminous, and artificial, a seven-foot dragon swayed around the corner, followed by an equally tall mantis and a griffin. Like elegant plastics, internally lit and misty, they wobbled forward. When dragon and mantis swayed into each other, they—meshed!

He thought of images, slightly unfocused, on a movie screen, lapping.

"Scorpions!" Tak whispered.

Tak's shoulder pushed his.

His hand was on a tree trunk. Twig shadows webbed his forearm, the back of his hand, the bark. The figures neared; the web slid. The figures passed; the web slid off. They were, he realized, as eye-unsettling as pictures on a three-dimensional postcard—with the same striations hanging, like a screen, just before, or was it just behind them.

The griffin, furthest back, flickered:

A scrawny youngster, with pimply shoulders, in the middle of a cautious, bow-legged stride—then griffin again. (A memory of spiky, yellow hair; hands held out from the freckled, pelvic blade.)

The mantis swung around to look back, went momentarily out:

This one, anyway, was wearing *some* clothes—a brown, brutal looking youngster; the chains he wore for necklaces growled under his palm, while he absently caressed his left breast. "Come on, Baby! Get your ass in gear!" which came from a mantis again.

"Shit, you think they gonna be there?" from the griffin.

"Aw, sure. They gonna be there!" You could have easily mistaken the voice from the dragon for a man's; and she sounded black.

Suspended in wonder and confusion, he listened to the conversation of the amazing beasts.

"They better be!" Vanished chains went on growling.

The griffin flickered once more: pocked buttocks and dirty heels disappeared behind blazing scales.

"Hey, Baby, *suppose* they're not there yet?"

"Oh, shit! Adam . . . ?"

"Now, Adam, you know they're gonna be there," the dragon assured.

"Yeah? How do I know? Oh, Dragon Lady! Dragon Lady, you're too much!"

"Come on. The two of you shut up, huh?"

Swaying together and apart, they rounded another corner.

He couldn't see his hand at all now, so he let it fall from the trunk. "What . . . what *are* they?"

"Told you: scorpions. Sort of a gang. Maybe it's more than one gang. I don't really know. You get fond of them after a while, if you know how to stay out of their way. If you can't . . . well, you either join, I guess; or get messed up. Least, that's how I found it."

"I mean the . . . the dragons and things?"

"Pretty, huh?"

"What are they?"

"You know what is it a hologram? They're projected from interference patterns off a very small, very low-powered laser. It's not complicated. But it looks impressive. They call them light-shields."

"Oh." He glanced at his shoulder where Tak had dropped his hand. "I've heard of holograms."

Tak led him out of the hidden niche of brush onto the concrete. A few yards down the path, in the direction the scorpions had come from, a lamp was working. They started in that direction.

"Are there more of them around?"

"Maybe." Tak's upper face was again masked. "Their light-shields don't really shield them from anything—other than our prying eyes from the ones who want to walk around bare-assed. When I first got here, all you saw were scorpions. Then griffins and the other kinds started showing up a little while ago. But the genre name stuck." Tak slid his hands into his jean pockets. His jacket, joined at the bottom by the zipper fastener, rode up in front for non-existent breasts. Tak stared down at them as he walked. When he looked up, his smile had no eyes over it. "You forget people don't know about scorpions. About Calkins. They're famous here. Bellona's a big city; with something that famous in any other city in the country, why I guess people in L.A., Chicago, Pittsburgh, Washington would be dropping it all over the carpet at the in cocktail parties, huh? But they've forgotten we're here."

"No, they haven't forgotten." Though he couldn't *see* Tak's eyes, he knew they had narrowed.

"So they send in people who don't know their own name. Like you?"

He laughed, sharply; it felt like a bark.

Tak returned the hoarse sound that was his own laughter. "Oh, yeah! You're quite a kid." Laughter trailed on.

"Where we going now?"

But Tak lowered his chin, strode ahead.

From this play of night, light, and leather, can I let myself take identity? How can I recreate this roasted park in some meaningful matrix? Equipped with contradictory visions, an ugly hand caged in pretty metal, I observe a new mechanique. I am the wild machinist, past destroyed, reconstructing the present.

THE SHORT-TIMERS

BY GUSTAV HASFORD

(Excerpt)

Shortly before I left Bantam, the mail brought a manuscript from a man named Gus Hasford, whom I had met a year or two before, at the Milford Science Fiction Writers Workshop. I didn't much like the novel. Since I had met Hasford, I wrote him a more candid letter than usual. This was the sort of lightweight froth that some Milford sessions seemed to encourage, I said. Still, he wrote well. If he ever wrote anything he cared about, I'd like to see it.

So by return mail (it seemed even faster) back came the manuscript of The Short-Timers. *This one I care about, said the enclosed letter, and you could sense the lower lip belligerently thrust out.*

Well, I read the first few pages—and then I cared, too.

Then the question was: What do I do about it?

The obvious thing was to order up a contract and publish it. But I was Bantam's science-fiction specialist. The Short-Timers *wasn't exactly that. It wasn't exactly not, either. It was as close as* Dhalgren, *perhaps. But the circumstances were different. Delany had an established audience in SF. Hasford didn't. It was his first book.*

But it was a remarkable book. It needed to be published. Not by me. But not by some faceless acquisitions editor, either; it needed someone who would care about it. So I sought powerful help. I buttonholed Marc Jaffe to tell him that I had this book, and I didn't know if it was good but I was sure it was great, and Bantam ought to publish it for the good of all our souls. And, bless him, he did. He asked if I would mind sharing editorial credit with Ted Solotaroff, who had read the book and was as quickly committed as I. Ted is as close to a Maxwell Perkins as you find along Madison or Fifth Avenue these days, so I promptly bowed out and left it all to him. Two editors are too many.

Editors do a great many disagreeable things. Sometimes they can't help it. I cannot tell you how good it feels to do something you think right, because it's right.

One warning. When Hasford first sent in The Short-Timers, *it had many ingredients of surreal fantasy. The difficulty with that was that the Viet Nam war itself was so surreal and incredible that the fantasy elements worked against the impact of the story. With painstaking line-by-line cooperation from Ted, they all came out. What is left is exceedingly strong meat. I do not advise that this excerpt be read when you are feeling queasy.*

*　　*　　*

With my Magic Marker, I "X" out a section of thigh on the nude woman outlined on the back of my flak jacket. The number fifty-eight disappears. Fifty-seven days and a wake-up left in country.

Midnight. The boredom becomes unbearable. Chili Vendor suggests that we kill time by wasting our furry little friends.

I say, "Rat race!"

Chili Vendor hops off his canvas cot and into a corner. He breaks up a John Wayne cookie. In the corner, six inches off the deck, we've nailed a piece of ammo crate to form a triangular pocket. There's a little hole in the charred board. Chili Vendor puts the cookie fragments under the board. Then he snaps off the lights.

I toss Rafter Man one of my booties. Of course, he doesn't know what to do with it. "What—"

Shhhh.

We wait in ambush, enjoying the anticipation of violence. Five minutes. Ten minutes. Fifteen minutes. Then the Viet Cong rats crawl out of their holes. We freeze. The rats skitter along the rafters, climb down the screening, then hop onto the plywood deck, making little thumps, moving through the darkness without fear.

Chili Vendor waits until the skittering converges in the corner. Then he jumps out of his rack and flips on the overhead lights.

With the exception of Rafter Man, we're all on our feet in the same second, forming a semicircle across the corner. The rats zip and zing, their tiny pink feet clawing for traction on the plywood. Two or three escape—so brave, or so terrified—in such situations motives are immaterial—that they run right over our feet and between our legs and through the deadly gauntlet of carefully aimed boots and stabbing bayonets.

But most of the rats herd together under the board.

Mr. Payback takes a can of lighter fluid from his bamboo footlocker. He squirts lighter fluid into the little hole in the board.

Daytona Dave strikes a match. "Fire in the hole!" He pitches the burning match into the corner.

The board *foomps* into flame.

Rats explode from beneath the board like shrapnel from a rodent grenade.

The rats are on fire. The rats are little flaming kamikaze animals zinging across the plywood deck, running under racks, over gear, around in circles, running faster and faster and in no particular direction except toward some place where there is no fire.

"GET SOME!" Mr. Payback is screaming like a lunatic. "GET SOME! GET SOME!" He chops a rat in half with his machete.

Chili Vendor holds a rat by the tail, and, while it shrieks, pounds it to death with a boot.

I throw my K-bar at a rat on the other side of the hootch. The big knife misses the rat, sticks up in the floor.

Rafter Man doesn't know what to do.

Daytona Dave charges around and around with fixed bayonet, zeroing in on a burning rat like a fighter pilot in a dogfight. Daytona follows the rat's crazed, erratic course around and around, over all obstacles, gaining on him with every step. He butt-strokes the rat and then bayonets him, again and again and again. "That's one confirmed!"

And, as suddenly as it began, the battle is over.

After the rat race everyone collapses. Daytona is breathing hard and fast. "Whew. That was a good group. Real hard-core. I thought I was going to have a fucking heart attack."

Mr. Payback coughs, grunts. "Hey, New Guy, how many confirmed did you get?"

Rafter Man is still sitting on his canvas cot with my boot in his hand. "I . . . none. I mean, it happened so fast."

Mr. Payback laughs. "Well, sometimes it's fun to kill something you can see. You better get squared away, New Guy. Next time the rats will have guns."

Daytona Dave is wiping his face with a dirty green skivvy shirt. "The New Guy will do okay. Cut him some slack. Rafter ain't got the killer instinct, that's all. Now me, I got about fifty confirmed. But everybody knows that gook rats drag off their dead."

We all throw things at Daytona Dave.

We rest for a while and then we gather up the barbecued rats and take them outside to hold a funeral in the dark.

Some guys from utilities platoon who live next door come out of their hootch to pay their respects.

Lance Corporal Winslow Slavin, honcho of the combat plumbers, struts up in a skuzzy green flight suit. The flight suit is ragged, covered with paint stains and oil splotches. "Only six? Shit. Last night my boys got seventeen. Confirmed."

I say, "Sounds like a squad of poges to me. Poges kill poges. These rats are Viet Cong field Marines. Hard-core grunts."

I pick up one of the rats. I turn to the combat plumbers. I hold up the rat and I kiss it.

Mr. Payback laughs, picks up one of the dead rats, bites off the tip of its tail. Then, swallowing, Mr. Payback says, "Ummm . . . love them crispy critters." He grins. He bends over, picks up another dead rat, offers it to Rafter Man.

Rafter Man is frozen. He can't speak. He just looks at the rat.

Mr. Payback laughs. "What's wrong, New Guy? Don't you want to be a killer?"

We bury the enemy rats with full military honors—we scoop out a shallow grave and we dump them in.

We sing:

> *Come along and sing our song*
> *And join our fam-i-ly . . .*
> MIC . . . KEY . . . MOUSE.
> *Mickey Mouse, Mickey Mouse. . . .*

"Dear God," says Mr. Payback, looking up into the ugly sky. "These rats died like Marines. Cut them some slack. Ah-men."

We all say, "Ah-men."

After the funeral we insult the combat plumbers a few more times and then we return to our hootch. We lie awake in our racks. We discuss the battle and the funeral for a long time.

Then we try to sleep.

An hour later. It's raining. We roll up in our poncho liners and pray for morning. The monsoon rain is cold and heavy and comes without warning. Wind-blown water batters the ponchos hung around the hootch to protect us from the weather.

The terrible falling of the shells . . .

Incoming.

"Oh, shit," somebody says. Nobody moves.

Rafter Man asks, "Is that—"

I say, "There it is."

The crumps start somewhere outside the wire and walk in like the footsteps of a monster. The crumps are becoming thuds. Thud. Thud. THUD. And then it's a whistle and a roar.

BANG.

The rain's rhythmic drumming is broken by the clang and rattle of shrapnel falling on our tin roof.

We're all out of our racks with our weapons in our hands like so many parts of the same body—even Rafter Man, who has begun to pick up on things.

Pounded by cold rain, we double-time to our bunker.

On the perimeter M-60 machine guns are banging and the M-79 grenade launchers are blooping and mortar shells are thumping out of the tubes.

Star flares burst all along the wire, beautiful clusters of green fire.

Inside our damp cave of sandbags we huddle elbow-to-elbow in wet skivvies, feeling the weight of the darkness, as helpless as cavemen hiding from a monster.

"I hope they're just fucking with us," I say. "I hope they're not going to hit the wire. I'm not ready for this shit."

Outside our bunker: BANG, BANG, BANG. And falling rain.

Each of us is waiting for the next shell to nail him right on the head—the mortar as an agent of existential doom.

A scream.

I wait for a time of silence and I crawl out to take a look. Somebody is down. The whistle of an incoming round forces me to retreat into the bunker. I wait for the shell to burst.

BANG.

I crawl out, stand up, and I run to the wounded man. He's one of the combat plumbers. "You utilities platoon? Where's Winslow?"

The man is whining. "I'm dying! I'm dying!" I shake him. "Where's Winslow?"

"There." He points. "He was coming to help me. . . ."

Rafter Man and Chili Vendor come out and Rafter Man helps me carry the combat plumber to our bunker. Chili Vendor doubletimes off to get a corpsman.

We leave the combat plumber with Daytona and Mr. Payback and doubletime through the rain, looking for Winslow.

He's in the mud outside his hootch, torn to pieces.

The mortal shells stop falling. The machine guns on the perimeter fade to short bursts. Even so, the grunts standing lines continue to pop green star clusters in case Victor Charlie plans to launch a ground attack.

Somebody throws a poncho over Winslow. The rain taps the green plastic sheet.

I say, "It took a lot of guts to do what Winslow did. I mean, you can see Winslow's guts and he sure had a lot of them."

Nobody says anything.

After the green ghouls from graves registration stuff Winslow into a body bag and take him away, we go back to our hootch. We flop on our racks, wasted.

I say, "Well, Rafter, now you've heard a shot fired in anger."

Soaking wet in green skivvies, Rafter Man is sitting on his rack. He has something in his hand. He's staring at it.

I sit up. "Hey, Rafter. What's that? You souvenir yourself a piece of shrapnel?" No response. "Rafter? You hit?"

Mr. Payback grunts. "What's wrong, New Guy? Did a few rounds make you nervous?"

Rafter Man looks up with a new face. His lips are twisted into a cold, sardonic smirk. His labored breathing is broken by grunts. He growls. His lips are wet with saliva. He's looking at Mr. Payback. The object in Rafter Man's hand is a piece of flesh, Winslow's flesh, ugly yellow, as big as a John Wayne cookie, wet with blood. We all look at it for a long time.

Rafter Man puts the piece of flesh into his mouth, onto his tongue, and we think he's going to vomit. Instead, he grits his teeth. Then, closing his eyes, he swallows.

I turn off the lights.

AFTERWORD

I hope you've enjoyed these stories. A lot of very close decisions went into choosing them—every one included meant some other that had to be left out, and how I am going to face certain good friends and highly admired writers who are not represented I do not know. But there it is.

It occurs to me that some readers might like a few suggestions for additional reading. Of course, each of the writers has a lengthy bibliography of his own, and if any of them chanced to be previously unfamiliar to you you can find much more by them all at any bookstore or library.

I've written a more detailed account of some of the sections in this book in my autobiography, *The Way the Future Was*. Two interesting sources on early fan doings, circa 1940, are Damon Knight's *The Futurians* and Sam Moskowitz's *The Immortal Storm;* in both cases, the facts seem close enough, though I'm not altogether in agreement with either author's interpretations. If you are interested in the long-lost world of the early pulp magazines, the best books I know are *Pulpwood Editor* by Harold Hersey and the biography of Frank Munsey entitled *Forty Years, Forty Millions*. I fear neither of them is in print; but they are worth trying to hunt up.

There are not very many more recent editorial memoirs, particularly in science fiction. Hugo Gernsback never left an autobiography. Neither did John Campbell, but a volume of his correspondence with writers, edited by Perry Chapdelaine, is now in preparation and should be available in at least a limited edition soon.

It has been a pleasure—mostly a pleasure—to assemble these selections from thirty-nine years as an editor, just as it was a pleasure—mostly a pleasure—to do all that editing in the first place, and I can only hope that the result (mostly) pleases you, too.

—Frederik Pohl